The
SAM GUNN
Omnibus

3

The
SAM GUNN
Omnibus

Featuring every story ever written

about Sam Gunn, and then some

BEN BOVA

A Tom Doherty Associates Book
New York

This is a work of fiction. All of the characters, organizations, and events portrayed in these stories are either products of the author's imagination or are used fictitiously.

THE SAM GUNN OMNIBUS

Copyright © 2007 by Ben Bova

This book is printed on acid-free paper.

A Tor Book
Published by Tom Doherty Associates, LLC
175 Fifth Avenue
New York, NY 10010

www.tor.com

Tor® is a registered trademark of Tom Doherty Associates, LLC.

Library of Congress Cataloging-in-Publication Data

Bova, Ben, 1932–
    The Sam Gunn omnibus / Ben Bova.—1st ed.
        p. cm.
    "A Tom Doherty Associates book."
    ISBN-13: 978-0-765-31617-2
    ISBN-10: 0-765-31617-X
    I. Title.
    PS3552.O84S25 2007
    813'.54—dc22

                                2006033982

First Edition: February 2007

Printed in the United States of America

0 9 8 7 6 5 4 3 2 1

*These tales are dedicated to the entrepreneurs who are
striving to open the space frontier for all humankind—
and make a few bucks in the process.*

CONTENTS

A thing worth having
is a thing worth cheating for.

———————

AUTHOR'S PREFACE

It isn't easy to put all the tales of Sam Gunn together in any sequence that even vaguely resembles chronological order. Sam's various tales are spread all over the solar system (and even beyond) and span a lifetime filled with adventure, romance, and more than a little trickery.

I've done my best. I've sifted through all the stories about Sam Gunn and even added a couple of new ones. It's been tricky, though. In the pages of this book, Sam's life story is told from its beginning to the present moment. Please don't expect exact chronological order or a well-defined sequence of events. Sam is far too clever to be pinned down like an ordinary person.

All I can offer, at this point, is a quotation from a much better writer than I, Mr. Samuel Clemens, aka Mark Twain:

> Persons attempting to find a motive in this narrative will be prosecuted; persons attempting to find a moral in it will be banished; persons attempting to find a plot in it will be shot.

I suggest you merely read the stories and enjoy them. Trying to make order out of the chaotic events of Sam Gunn's life can drive you to drink. That's one of the things that I like about Sam.

BEN BOVA
Naples, Florida
January 2006

The
SAM GUNN
Omnibus

Selene City

THE STORY OF SAM GUNN IS INEXTRICABLY INTERWOVEN with the story of a beautiful, vulnerable, and determined young woman. Knowing Sam, you would expect she was an object of his rabid testosterone-fed sex drive (or, as Shakespeare put it, the bottomless cistern of his lust).

But you'd be wrong.

She likes to be called Jade, although her name is actually Jane. Jane Avril Inconnu. Sometimes new acquaintances mistake that last name for Romanian, although her flame-red hair and dazzling green eyes speak of more northern and flamboyant lands. She will tolerate such misunderstandings—when there is some advantage to being tolerant.

She received her name from the Quebecois surgeon who adopted her as a foundling at the old original Moonbase, back when that precarious settlement was civilization's rugged frontier. There were no pediatricians on the Moon; the surgeon happened to be on duty when the female infant, red-faced and squalling, was discovered in the corridor just outside the base's small hospital. No more than a few days old, the infant had been placed in a plastic shipping container, neatly bundled and warmly blanketed. And abandoned. Who the baby's mother might be remained a mystery, even though Moonbase hardly supported more than two hundred men and women in those days, plus a handful of visitors.

Her adopted mother's name was Jane, the month was April, and *inconnu* is the French word for "unknown." So the orphaned baby girl became Jane Avril Inconnu, raised alone by the surgeon for the first four years of her life.

By the time the surgeon's five-year contract with Moonbase was completed and she was due to return to Montreal, the medical staff—which doted on the little girl—had discovered that Jane Avril suffered from a congenital bone defect, a rare inability to manufacture sufficient amounts of calcium. Neither exercise nor medicine could help. Although she could walk and run and play normally in the gentle gravity of the Moon, on Earth she would be a helpless cripple, confined to a wheelchair or a mechanical exoskeleton, in constant danger of snapping her brittle, fragile bones.

Her adopted mother bravely decided to remain with the child, but then the news came from Montreal that her own mother was gravely ill, dying. Torn between the generations, the woman returned to Earth, promising to return soon, soon. She never did. There were family obligations on Earth, and later a husband who wanted children of his own.

Jane Avril remained at Moonbase, orphaned once again, raised by a succession of medical personnel at the hospital. Some were warm and loving, some were distant and uncaring. A few were actually abusive now and then.

Moonbase grew, over those years, into the city called Selene. The frontier of civilization crept across the battered old face of the Moon and expanded into cislunar space, where great habitats were built in the dark emptiness to house hundreds of thousands of people. Explorers reached out to Mars, and then farther. Entrepreneurs, some wildly reckless, some patient and cunning, began to reap the wealth of space. Fortunes were built on lunar mining, on power satellites to feed the energy hungers of Earth, on prospecting the metals and minerals of the asteroids.

Of all those daring and dashing fortune-seekers, the first, the most adventurous, the best known of them all was Sam Gunn. As she grew into young womanhood, Jane Avril heard endless stories about Sam Gunn and the fortunes he had found in space. Found and lost. For Sam was more impetuous and unpredictable than a solar storm. Long before Jane Avril acquired the nickname Jade, Sam Gunn was already a living legend.

She could not consider herself beautiful, despite the gorgeous red hair and those dazzling green eyes that gave her the sobriquet. She was small, just a shade over one hundred sixty-five centimeters tall. Her figure was slim, elfin, almost childlike. Her face was just a trifle too long and narrow to suit her, although she could smile very prettily when she wanted to. She seldom did.

Being raised as an orphan had built a hard shell of distrust around her. She knew from painful experience that no relationship ever lasted long, and it was foolish to open her heart to anyone.

Yet that heart of hers was a romantic one. Inside her protective crust was a yearning for adventure and love that would not die, no matter how sternly she tried to repress it. She dreamed of tall handsome men, bold heroes with whom she would travel to the ends of the solar system. She wanted with all her heart to get free of the dreary monotony of Selene, with its gray underground corridors and its unending sameness every day, year after year.

She knew that she was forever barred from Earth, even though she could see its blue beautiful glory shining at her in the dark lunar sky. Earth, with all its teeming billions of people and its magnificent cities and oceans of water so deep and blue and raging wild. Selene was a cemetery by comparison. She had to get away, to fly free, anywhere. If she could never set foot on Earth, there were still the great habitats at the Lagrangian points, and the bridge ships plying out toward Mars, the rugged frontier of the Asteroid Belt, and beyond, to the deadly beautiful dangers of the gas giant worlds.

Such were her dreams. The best she could do, though, was to get a job as a truck driver up on the dusty dead lunar surface.

But still she dreamed. And waited for her opportunity.

The Sea of Clouds

THE SPRING-WHEELED TRUCK ROLLED TO A SILENT STOP ON the Mare Nubium. The fine dust kicked up by its six wheels floated lazily back to the mare's soil. The hatch to the truck cab swung upward, and a space-suited figure climbed slowly down to the lunar surface, clumped a dozen ponderously careful steps, then turned back toward the truck.

"Yeah, this is the spot. The transponder's beeping away, all right."

At first Jade had been excited by her work as a truck driver. Even inside a space suit, being out on the wide-open surface of the Moon, beneath the solemn eyes of the unblinking stars, was almost like being able to run wild and free in comparison to the dreariness of Selene's underground corridors. But now she had been at the job for nearly a year. The excitement had worn away, eroded as inevitably as the meteor-pitted rocks of the Sea of Clouds.

And always in that dead-black sky there hung the glowing jewel of Earth, tantalizing, beautiful, forever out of her reach.

She and the hoist operator (male and married) clambered down from the cab, bulbous and awkward-looking in their bulky space suits. Jade turned a full three hundred sixty degrees, scanning the scene through the gold-tinted visor of her suit's bubble helmet. There was nothing to be seen except the monotonous gray plain, pockmarked by craters like an ancient, savage battlefield that had been petrified into solid stone long eons ago.

"Merde, you can't even see the ringwall from here!" she exclaimed.

"That's what he wanted," came the voice of their supervisor through her helmet earphones. "To be out in the open, without a sign of civilization in sight. He picked this spot himself, you know."

"Helluva place to want to be buried," said the hoist operator.

"That's what he specified in his will. Come on, let's get to work. I want to get back to Selene City before the sun goes down."

It was a local joke: the three space-suited workers had more than two hundred hours before sunset.

Grunting even in the gentle lunar gravity, they slid the gleaming sarcophagus from the back of the truck and placed it softly on the roiled, dusty ground. It was made of stainless steel, delicately inscribed in gold by the solar system's most famous sculptress. At one end, in tastefully small lettering, was a logo: *S. Gunn Enterprises, Unlimited*.

The supervisor carefully paced to the exact spot where the tiny transponder lay blinking, and used a hand laser to draw an exact circle around it. Then he sprayed the stony ground inside the circle with the blue-white flame of a plasma torch. Meanwhile, Jade helped the hoist operator swing the four-meter-high crate down from the truck bed to the ground next to the sarcophagus.

"Ready for the statue?" Jade asked.

The supervisor said nothing as he inspected his own work. The hot plasma had polished the stony ground. Jade and the hoist operator heard him muttering over their helmet earphones as he used the hand laser to check the polished ground's dimensions. Satisfied, he helped them drag the gold-filigreed sarcophagus to its center and slide it into place over the transponder.

"A lot of work to do for a dead man."

"He wasn't just any ordinary man."

"It's still a lot of work. Why in hell couldn't he be recycled like everybody else?" the hoist operator complained.

"He's not in the sarcophagus, dumbskull," snapped the supervisor. "Don't you know any goddamned thing?"

"He's not . . . ?"

Jade had known that the sarcophagus was empty, symbolic. She was surprised that her coworker didn't. Some people pay no attention to anything, she told herself. I'll bet he doesn't know anything at all about Sam Gunn.

"Sam Gunn," said the supervisor, "never did things like everybody else. Not in his whole cussed life. Why should he be like the rest of us in death?"

They chattered back and forth through their suit radios as they uncrated the big package. Once they had removed all the plastic and the bigger-than-life statue stood sparkling in the sunlight, they stepped back and gaped at it.

"It's glass!"

"Christ, I never saw any statue so damned big."

"Must have cost a fortune to get it here. Two fortunes!"

"He had it done at Island One, I heard. Brought the sculptress in from the Belt and paid her enough to keep her at L-4 for two whole years. God knows how many times she tried to cast a statue this big and failed, even in low gee."

"I didn't know you could make a glass statue this big."

"In micro-gee you can. It's hollow. If we were in air, I could ping it with my finger and you'd hear it ring."

"Crystal."

"That's right."

Jade laughed softly.

"What's so funny?" the supervisor asked.

"Who else but Sam Gunn would have the gall to erect a crystal statue to himself and then have it put out in the middle of this godforsaken emptiness, where nobody's ever going to see it? It's a monument to himself, for himself. What ego! What monumental ego."

The supervisor chuckled, too. "Yeah. Sam had an ego, all right. But he was a smart little SOB, too."

"You knew him?" Jade asked.

"Sure. Knew him well enough to tell you that he didn't pick this spot for his tomb just for the sake of his ego. He was smarter than that."

"What was he like?"

"When did you know him?" the hoist operator asked.

"Come on, we've still got work to do. He wants the statue positioned exactly as he stated in his will, with its back toward Selene and the face looking up toward Earth."

"Yeah, okay, but when did you know him, huh?"

"Oh golly, years ago. Decades ago. When the two of us were just young pups. The first time either of us came here, back in—Lord, it's thirty years ago. More."

"Tell us about it. Was he really the rogue that the history disks say he was? Did he really do all the things they say?" Jade found to her surprise that she was eager to know.

"He was a phony!" the hoist operator snapped. "Everybody knows that. A helluva showman, sure, but he never did half the stuff he took credit for. Nobody could have, not in one lifetime."

"He lived a pretty intense life," said the supervisor. "If it hadn't been for that black hole he'd still be running his show from here to Titan."

"A showman. That's what he was."

"What was he like?" Jade asked again.

So, while the two young workers struggled with the huge, fragile crystal statue, the older man sat himself on the lip of the truck's hatch and told them what he knew about the first time Sam Gunn had come to the Moon.

The Supervisor's Tale

THE SKIPPER USED THE TIME-HONORED CLICHE. HE SAID, "Houston, we have a problem here."

There were eight of us, the whole crew of Artemis IV, huddled together in the command module. After six weeks of living on the Moon, the module smelled like a pair of unwashed gym socks. With a woman President, the space agency figured it would be smart to name the second round of lunar exploration after a female: Artemis was Apollo's sister. Get it?

But it had just happened that the computer that made the crew selections for Artemis IV picked all men. Six weeks without even the sight of a woman, and now our blessed-be-to-God return module refused to light up. We were stranded. No way to get back home.

As usual, Capcom in Houston was the soul of tranquility. "Ah, A-IV, we read you and copy that the return module is no-go. The analysis team is checking the telemetry. We will get back to you soonest."

It didn't help that Capcom, that shift, was Sandi Hemmings, the woman we all lusted after. Among the eight of us, we must have spent enough energy dreaming about cornering Sandi in zero gravity to propel each of us right back to Houston. Unfortunately, dreams have a very low specific impulse, and we were still stuck on the Moon, a quarter-million miles from the nearest woman.

Sandi played her Capcom duties strictly by the book, especially since all our transmissions were taped for later review. She kept the traditional Houston poker face, but she managed to say, "Don't worry, boys. We'll figure it out and get you home."

Praise God for small favors.

We had spent hours checking and rechecking the cursed return module. It was engineer's hell: everything checked but nothing worked. The thing just sat there like a lump of dead metal. No electrical power. None. Zero. The control board just stared at us cold and glassy-eyed as a banker listening to your request for an unsecured loan. We had pounded it. We had kicked it. In our desperation we had even gone through the instruction manual, page by page, line by line. Zip. Zilch. The bird was dead.

When Houston got back to us, six hours after the Skipper's call, it was the stony unsmiling image of the mission coordinator glowering at us as if we had deliberately screwed up the return module. He told us:

"We have identified the problem, Artemis IV. The return module's main electrical power supply has malfunctioned."

That was like telling Othello that he was a Moor.

"We're checking out bypasses and other possible fixes," Old Stone Face went on. "Sit tight, we'll get back to you."

The Skipper gave a patient sigh. "Yes, sir."

"We ain't going anyplace," said a whispered voice, just loud enough to be heard. Sam's.

The problem, we finally discovered, was caused by a micrometeoroid, no less. A little grain of sand that just happened to roam through the solar system for four and a half billion years and then decided to crash-dive itself into the main fuel cell of our return module's power supply. It was so tiny that it didn't do any visible damage to the fuel cell; just hurt it enough to let it discharge electrically for most of the six weeks we had been on the Moon. And the two other fuel cells, sensing the discharge through the module's idiot computer, tried to recharge their partner for six weeks. The result: all three of them were dead and gone by the time we needed them.

It was Sam who discovered the pinhole in the fuel cell, the eighteenth time we checked out the power supply. I can remember his exact words, once he realized what had happened:

"Shit!"

Sam was a feisty little guy who would have been too short for astronaut duty if the agency hadn't lowered the height requirements so that women could join the corps. He was a good man, a whiz with a computer and a born tinkerer who liked to rebuild old automobiles and then race them on abandoned freeways whenever he could scrounge up enough old-fashioned petrol to run them. The Terror of Clear Lake, we used to call him. The Texas Highway Patrol had other names for him. So did the agency administrators; they cussed near threw him out of the astronaut corps at least half a dozen times.

But we all liked Sam, back in those days, as we went through training and then blasted off for our first mission on the Moon. He was funny; he kept us laughing. And he did the things and said the things that none of the rest of us had the guts to do or say.

The Skipper loved Sam a little less than the rest of us, especially after six weeks of living in each other's dirty laundry. Sam had a way of *almost* defying any order he received. He reacted very poorly to authority figures. Our Skipper, Lord love him, was as stiff-backed an old-school authority figure as any of them. He was basically a good joe, and I'm cursed if I can remember his real name. But his big problem was that he had memorized the rule book and tried never to deviate from it.

Well, anyway, there we were, stranded on the lunar surface after six weeks of hard work. Our task had been to make a semipermanent underground base out of prefabricated modules that had been, as the agency quaintly phrased it, "landed remotely on the lunar regolith in a series of carefully coordinated unmanned logistics missions." In other words, they had dropped nine different module packages over a fifty-square kilometer area of Mare Nubium and we had to find them all, drag them to the site that Houston had picked for Base Gamma, set them up properly, scoop up enough of the top layers of soil to cover each module and the connecting tunnels to a depth of 0.9144 meters (that's three feet in English), and then link all the wiring, plumbing, heating and air circulation units. Which we had done, adroitly and efficiently, and now that our labors were finished and we were ready to leave—no go. Too bad we hadn't covered the return module with 0.9144 meters of lunar soil; that would have protected the fuel cells from that sharpshooting micrometeoroid.

The Skipper decided it would be bad procedure to let us mope around and brood.

"I want each of you to run a thorough inventory of all your personal supplies: the special foods you've brought with you, your spare clothing, entertainment kits, everything."

"That'll take four minutes," Sam muttered, loud enough for us all to hear him. The eight of us were crammed into the command module again, eight guys squeezed into a space built for three. It was barely high enough to stand in, and the metal walls and ceiling always felt cold to the touch. Sam was pressed in with the guys behind me; I was practically touching noses with the Skipper. The guys in back giggled at Sam's wisecrack. The Skipper scowled.

"Goddammit Gunn, can't you behave seriously for even a minute? We've got a real problem here."

"Yessir," Sam replied. If he hadn't been squeezed in so tightly I'm sure he would have made a snappy salute. "I'm merely attempting to keep morale high, sir."

The Skipper made an unhappy snorting noise, and then told us that we would spend the rest of the shift checking out *all* the supplies that were left: not just our personal stuff, but the mission's supplies of food, the nuclear reactor, the water recycling system, equipment of all sorts, air. . . .

We knew it was busywork, but we had nothing else to do. So we wormed our way out of the command module and crawled through the tunnels toward the other modules that we had laid out and then covered with bulldozed soil. It was a neat little buried base we had set up, for later explorers to use. I got a sort of claustrophobic feeling just then, that this buried base might turn into a mass grave for eight astronauts.

I was dutifully heading back for barracks module A—where four of us had our bunks and personal gear—to check out my supplies, as the Skipper had ordered. Sam snaked up beside me. Those tunnels, back in those days, were prefabricated Earthside to be laid out once we got to the construction site. I think they were designed by midgets. You couldn't stand up in them: they were too low. You had to really crawl along on hands and knees if you were normal size. Sam was able to shuffle through them on bent knees, knuckle-walking like a young chimpanzee. He loved those tunnels.

"Hey, wait up," he hissed to me.

I stopped.

"Whattaya think will get us first, the air giving out or we starve to death?"

He was grinning cheerfully. I said, "I think we're going to poison the air with methane. We'll fart ourselves to death in another couple of days."

Sam's grin widened. "C'mon . . . I'm setting up a pool on the computer. I hadn't thought of air pollution. You wanna make a bet on that?" He started to King-Kong down the shaft to the right, toward the computer and life-support module. If I had had the space I would have shrugged. Instead, I followed him there.

Three of the other guys were in the computer module, huddled around the display screen like Boy Scouts around a campfire.

"Why aren't you checking out the base's supplies, like the Skipper said," I asked them.

"We are, Straight Arrow," replied Mickey Lee, our refugee from Chinatown. He tapped the computer screen. "Why go sorting through all that junk when the computer already has it listed in alphabetical order for us?"

That wasn't what the Skipper wanted and we all knew it. But Mickey was right. Why bother with busywork? We wrote down lists that would make the Skipper happy. By hand. If we had let the computer print out the lists, Skip would have gotten wise right away.

While we scribbled away, copying what was on the screen, we talked over our basic situation.

"Why the hell can't we use the nuke to recharge the fuel cells?" Julio Marx asked. He was our token Puerto Rican Jew, a tribute to the space agency's Equal Opportunity employment policy. Julio was also a cracker-jack structural engineer who had saved my life the day I had started to unfasten my helmet just when one of those blessed prefab tunnels had cracked its airlock seal. But that's another story.

Sam gave Julio a sorrowful stare. "The two systems are incompatible, Jules. Two separate teams of engineers designed them and none of the geniuses in the labs ever thought we might have to run one off the other in an emergency."

Julio cast an unbelieving glance at Sam. So Sam grinned and launched into the phoniest Latino accent you ever heard. "The nuclear theeng, man, it got too many volts for the fuel cells. Like, you plug the nukie to the fuel cells, man, you make a beeg boom an' we all go to dat beeg San Juan in thee sky. You better steek to pluckin' chickens, man, an' leave the eelectreecity alone."

Julio, who towered a good inch and a half over Sam, laughed good-naturedly and answered, "Okay, Shorty, I dig."

"Shorty! Shorty?" Sam's face went red. "All right, that's it. The hell with the betting pool. I'm gonna let you guys die of boredom. Serve you right."

We made a big fuss and soothed his feathers and cajoled him into setting up the pool. With a great show of hurt feelings and reluctant but utterly selfless nobility, Sam pushed Mickey Lee out of the chair in front of the computer terminal and began playing the keyboard like a virtuoso pianist. Within a few minutes the screen was displaying a list of the possible ways for us to die, with Sam's swiftly calculated odds next to each entry. At the touch of a button the screen displayed a graph showing how the odds for each mode of dying changed as time went on.

Suffocation, for example, started off as less than a one percent probability. But within a month the chances began to rise fairly steeply. "The air scrubbers need replacement filters," Sam explained, "and we'll be out of 'em inside of two more weeks."

"They'll have us out of here in two weeks, for Christ's sake," Julio said.

"Or drop fresh supplies for us," said Ron Avery, the taciturn pilot we called Cowboy because of his lean, lanky build and slow western drawl.

"Those are the odds," Sam snapped. "The computer does not lie. Pick your poison and place your bets."

I put fifty bucks down on Air Contamination, not telling the other guys about my earlier conversation with Sam. Julio took Starvation, Mickey settled on Dehydration (Lack of Water) and Cowboy picked Murder—which made me shudder.

"What about you, Sam?" I asked.

"I'll wait till the other guys have a chance," he said.

"You gonna let the Skipper in on this?" asked Julio.

Sam shook his head. "If I tell him . . ."

"I'll tell him," Cowboy volunteered, with a grim smile. "I'll even let him have Murder, if he wants it. I can always switch to Suicide."

"Droll fellow," said Sam.

"Well, hell," Cowboy insisted, "if a feller takes Suicide he can always make sure he wins just by killing himself, can't he now?"

It was one of those rare occasions when Sam had no reply. He simply stared at Cowboy in silence.

Well, you probably read about the mission in your history classes. Houston was supporting three separate operations on the Moon at the same time and they were stretched to the limit down there. Old Stone Face promised us a rescue flight in a week. But they had a problem with the booster when they tried to rush things on the launch pad too much and the blessed launch had to be put back a week, then another week. They sent an unmanned supply craft to us, of course, but the descent stage got gummed up. Our fresh food, air filters and water supply wound up orbiting the Moon fifty miles over our heads.

Sam calculated the odds against all these foul-ups and came to the conclusion that Houston was working overtime to kill us. "Must be some kind of an experiment," he told us. "Maybe they need some martyrs to make people more aware of the space program."

Cowboy immediately asked if that fell under the category of Murder. He was intent on winning the pool, even if it killed him.

We learned afterward that Houston was deep in trouble because of us. The White House was firing people right and left, Congressional committees were gearing up to investigate the fiasco, and the CIA was checking out somebody's crackbrained idea that the Japanese were behind all our troubles. Or maybe Arianespace, the European space company.

Meanwhile, we were stranded on the Mare Nubium with nothing much to do but let our beards grow and hope for sinus troubles that would cut off our ability to sense odors.

Old Stone Face was magnificent, in his unflinching way. He was on the line to us every day, despite the fact that his superiors in Houston and Washington were either being fired directly by the President herself or roasted over the simmering fires of media criticism. There must have been a zillion reporters at Mission Control by the second week of our marooning. We could *feel* the hubbub and tension whenever we talked with Stony.

"The countdown for your rescue flight is proceeding on an accelerated schedule," he told us. It would never occur to him to say, *We're hurrying as fast as we can.* "Liftoff is now scheduled for 0700 hours on the twenty-fifth."

None of us needed to look at a calendar to know that the twenty-fifth was seventeen days away. Sam's betting pool was looking more serious by the hour. Even the Skipper had finally taken the plunge: Suffocation.

If it weren't for Sandi Hemmings we might all have gone crazy. She took over as Capcom during the night shift, when most of the reporters and the agency brass were either asleep or drinking away their troubles. She gave us the courage and desire to pull through, partly by just smiling at us and looking female enough to *make* us want to survive, but mainly by giving us the straight info with no nonsense.

"They're in deep trouble over at Kennedy," she would tell us. "They've had to go on triple shifts and call up boosters that they didn't think they would need until next year. Some Senator in Washington is yelling that we ought to ask the Russians or the Japanese to help us out."

"As if either of them had upper stages that could make it to the Moon without six months worth of modification work," one of our guys grumbled.

"Well," Sandi said with her brightest smile, "you'll all be heroes when you finally get back here. The women will be standing in line to admire you."

"You won't have to stand in line, Sandi," Cowboy answered, in a rare burst of words. "You'll always be number one with us."

The others crowded into the command module added their heartfelt agreement.

Sandi laughed, undaunted by the prospect of having the eight of us grabbing for her. "I hope you shave first," she said.

Remember, she could see us but she couldn't smell us.

A night or two later she spent hours reading to us the suggestions made by the Houston medical team on how to stretch out our dwindling supplies of food, water, and air. They boiled down to one basic rule: lie down and don't exert yourselves. Great advice, especially when you're beginning to really worry that you're not going to make it through this mess. Just what we needed to do, lie back in our bunks and do nothing but think.

I caught a gleam in Sam's eye, though, as Sandi waded through the medics' recommendations. The Skipper asked her to send the whole report through our computer. She did, and he spent the whole next day poring over it. Sam spent the day—well, I couldn't figure out where he'd gotten to. I didn't see him all day long, and Base Gamma really wasn't big enough to hide in, even for somebody as small as Sam.

After going through all the medics' gobbledegook the Skipper ordered us to take tranquilizers. We had a small supply of downers in the base pharmaceutical stores, and Skip divided them equally among us. At the rate of three a day they would last just four days, with four pills left over. About as useful as a cigarette lighter in hell, but the Skipper played it by the book and ordered us to start swallowing the tranquilizers.

"Just the thing for the tension that arises from pre-death syndrome," Sam muttered. Loud enough for Skip to hear, of course.

"The medics say the pills will ease our anxieties and help us to remain as quiet as possible while we wait for the rescue mission," Skip said, glowering in Sam's direction.

He didn't bother to remind us that the rescue mission, according to Sandi's unofficial word, was still twelve days off. We would be out of food in three more days, and the recycled water was starting to taste as if it hadn't been recycled, if you know what I mean. The air was getting foul, too, but that was probably just our imaginations.

Sam appeared blithely unconcerned, even happy. He whistled cheerfully as Skip rationed out the tranquilizers, then gave his pills to me and scuttled off down the tunnel that led toward our barracks module. By the time I got to my bunk Sam was nowhere in sight. His whistling was gone. So was his pressure suit.

I put his pills under his mattress, wondering where he could have gone. Outside? For what? To increase his radiation dose? To get away from the rest of us? That was probably it. Underneath his wiseguy shell Sam was probably just as worried and tense as any of us, and he just didn't want us to know it. He needed some solitude, not chemical tranquility. What better place to find solitude than the airless rocky waste of Mare Nubium?

That's what I thought. That's why I didn't go out after him.

The same thing happened the next "morning" (by which I mean the time immediately after our sleep shift). And the next. The Skipper would

gather us together in the command module, we would each take our ceremonial tranquilizer pill and a sip of increasingly bad water, and then we
would crawl back to our bunks and try to do nothing that would use up
body energy or burn air. All of us except Sam. He faked swallowing his
pill, handed it to me when Skip wasn't watching, and then disappeared
with his pressure suit.

All of us were getting grumpier, surlier. I know I found myself resent-
ing it whenever I had to use the toilet. I kept imagining my urine flowing
straight back into our water tank without reprocessing. I guess I was
starting to go crazy.

But Sam was happy as could be: chipper, joking, laughing it up. He
would disappear each morning for several hours and then show up with a
lopsided grin on his round face, telling jokes and making us all feel a little
better.

Until the day Julio suddenly sat bolt upright on his bunk, the second or
third morning after we had run out of tranquilizers, and yelled:

"Booze!"

Sam had been sitting on the edge of Julio's bunk, telling an outrageous
story of what he planned to do with Sandi once we got back to Houston.

"Booze!" Julio repeated. "I smell booze! I'm cracking up. I must be
loosing my marbles. I smell *booze!*"

For once in his life Sam looked apologetic, almost ashamed.

"You're not cracking up," he said, in as quiet a voice as I've ever heard
Sam use. "I was going to tell you about it tomorrow—the stuff is almost
ready for human consumption."

You never saw three grown men so suddenly attentive.

With a self-deprecating little grin Sam explained, "I've been tinkering
with the propellants and other junk out in the return module. They're not
doing us any good just sitting there. So I tinkered up a small still. Seems
to be working okay. I tasted a couple sips today. It'll take the enamel off
your teeth, but it's not all that bad. By tomorrow . . ."

He never got any further. We did a Keystone Kops routine, rushing for
our pressure suits, jamming ourselves through the airlock and running
out to the inert, idle, cussedly useless return module.

Sam was not kidding us. He had jury-rigged an honest-to-backwoods
still inside the return module, fueling it with propellants from the module's tanks. The basic alcohol also came from the propellant, with water
from the fuel cells and a few other ingredients that Sam had scrounged
from Base Gamma's medical supplies.

We took turns at the still's business end, sticking its little copper tube into the water nipple of our helmets to sample Sam's concoction. It was *terrible*. We loved it.

By the time we had staggered back to our barracks module, laughing and belching, we had made up our minds to let the other three guys in Barracks B share in Sam's juice. But the Skipper was a problem. If we told him about it he'd have Sam up on charges and drummed out of the agency even before the rescue mission reached us. I figured if Old Stone Face found out he'd order the rescue mission to leave Sam behind.

"Have no fear," Sam told us with a giggle. "I myself will reveal my activities to our noble Skipper."

And before we could stop him he had tottered off toward the command module, whistling through the tunnel in a horribly sour off-key way.

An hour went by. Then two. We could hear Skip's voice yelling from the command module, although we couldn't make out the words. None of us had the guts to go down the tunnel and try to help Sam. After a while the tumult and the shouting died. Mickey Lee gave me a questioning glance. Silence. Ominous silence.

"You think Skip's killed him?" Mickey asked.

"More likely Sam's talked the Skipper to death," Julio replied.

Timidly we slunk down the tunnel to the command module. The three other guys were in there with Sam and the Skipper. They were all quaffing Sam's rocket juice and giggling at each other.

We were shocked, but we joined right in. Six days later, when the guys from Base Alpha landed their return module crammed with emergency food and fresh water for us, we invited them to join the party. A week after that, when the rescue mission from Kennedy finally showed up, we had been under the influence for so long that we told them to go away.

I had never realized before then what a lawyer Sam was. He had convinced the Skipper to read the medics' report carefully, especially the part where they recommended using tranquilizers to keep us calm and minimize our energy consumption. Sam had then gotten the Skipper to punch up the medical definition of alcohol's effects on the body, out of Houston's medical files. Sure enough, if you squinted the right way, you could claim that alcohol was a sort of a tranquilizer. That was enough justification for the Skipper, and we just about pickled ourselves in rocket juice until we got rescued.

THE CRYSTAL STATUE glittered under the harsh rays of the unfiltered sun. The supervisor, still sitting on the lip of the truck's hatch, said:

"He looks beautiful. You guys did a good job. Is the epoxy set?"

"Needs another few minutes, just to be sure," said the hoist operator, tapping the toe of his boot against the base that they had poured on the lunar plain.

"What happened when you got back to Houston?" asked Jade. "Didn't they get angry at you for being drunk?"

"Sure," laughed the supervisor. "But what could they do? Sam's booze pulled us through, and we could show that we were merely following the recommendations of the medics. Old Stone Face hushed it all up and we became heroes, just like Sandi told us we'd be—for about a week."

"And Sam?"

"Oh, after a while he left the agency and started his own business: S. Gunn Enterprises, Unlimited. The rest you know about from the history disks. Entrepreneur, showman, scoundrel, trailblazer. It's all true. He was all those things."

"Did he and Sandi ever, uh . . . get together?" the hoist operator asked.

"She was too smart to let him corner her. Sandi used one of the other guys to protect her; married him, finally. Cowboy, if I remember right. They eloped and spent their honeymoon in orbit. Zero gee and all that. Sam pretended to be very upset by it, but by that time he was surrounded by women, all of them taller than he was."

The three of them walked slowly around the gleaming statue.

"Look at the rainbows it makes where the sun hits it," said Jade. "It's marvelous."

"But if he was so smart," the hoist operator said, "why'd he pick this spot way out here for his grave? It's kilometers from Selene City. You can't even see the statue from the City."

"*Imbecile,*" Jade said. "This is the place where Base Gamma was located. Isn't that right?"

"Nope," the supervisor said. "Gamma was all the way over on the other side of Nubium. It's still there. Abandoned, but still there. Even the blasted return module is still sitting there, dumb as ever."

"Then why put the statue here?"

The supervisor chuckled. "Sam was a pretty shrewd guy. In his will he set up a tourist agency that'll guide people to the important sites on the Moon. They'll start at Selene and go along the surface in those big cruisers they've got back at the city. Sam's tomb is going to be a major tourist attraction, and he wanted it to be far enough out on the mare so that people won't be able to see it from Selene; they have to buy tickets and take the bus."

Both the young people laughed tolerantly.

"I guess he was pretty smart, at that," the hoist operator admitted.

"And he had a long memory, too," said the supervisor. "He left this tourist agency to me and the other guys from Artemis IV, in his will. We own it. I figure it'll keep us comfortable for the rest of our lives."

"Why did he do that?"

The supervisor shrugged inside his cumbersome suit. "Why did he build that still? Sam always did what he darned well felt like doing. And no matter what you think of him, he always remembered his friends."

The three of them gave the crystal statue a final admiring glance, then clumped back to the truck and started the hour-long drive to Selene City.

But as she drove across the empty pitted plain, Jade thought of Sam Gunn. She could not escape the feeling that somehow, in some unexplainable way, her future was intimately tied to Sam Gunn's past.

The Hospital and the Bar

JADE'S FIRST MEMORIES WERE NOT OF PEOPLE, BUT OF THE bare-walled rooms and wards of the hospital. The hushed voices. The faintly tangy smell of disinfectant. The hospital had seemed so snug and safe when she had been a child. Even though she had never had a room of her own, and had spent most of her childhood nights sleeping in the main ward, the hospital was the closest thing to a home that Jade had ever had.

She was an adult now, with a job and an apartment of her own. A single room carved deep into the lunar rock, two levels below the hospital, four levels below Selene City's main plaza and the surface. Still, returning to the hospital was like returning to the warmth of home. Almost.

"It would be a really good thing to do," said Dr. Dinant. She was a Belgian, and even though her native language was French, between her Walloon accent and Jade's fragmentary Quebecois, they found it easier to converse in English.

"You mean it would be good for science," Jade replied softly.

"Yes. Of course. For science. And for yourself, as well."

Dr. Dinant was quite young, almost Jade's own age. Yet she reminded Jade of the blurry memory of her adoptive mother. She felt as if she wanted this woman to love her, to take her to her heart as no one ever had since her mother had gone away from her.

But what Dr. Dinant was asking was more than Jade could give.

"All you have to do is donate a few of your egg cells. It's quite a simple procedure. I can do it for you right here in the clinic in just a few minutes."

Dinant's skin was deeply tanned. She must spend hours under the sun lamps, Jade thought. The physician was not a particularly handsome woman: her mousy hair was clipped quite short and her clothes showed that she paid scant attention to her appearance. But she had an air of self-assurance that Jade sorely envied.

"Let me explain it again," Dr. Dinant said gently. Even though the chairs they were sitting in were close enough to touch one another, she kept a distinct separation from the younger woman.

"I understand what you want," Jade said. "You want to make a baby from my eggs so that you can test it for the bone disease I carry in my genes."

"Osteopetrosis," said Dr. Dinant, "is not a disease. . . ."

"It prevents me from living on Earth."

The doctor smiled at her kindly. "We would like to be able to see to it that your children will not be so afflicted."

"You can cure it?"

Dr. Dinant nodded. "We believe so. With gene therapy. We can remove the defective gene from your egg cell and replace it with a healthy one, then fertilize the cell, implant it in a host mother, and bring the fetus to term."

"My—the baby won't have the disease?"

"We believe we can eliminate the condition, yes."

"But not for me," Jade said.

"No, I'm afraid it must be done in the fetal or pre-fetal stage."

"It's too late for me. It was too late when I was born."

"Yes, but your children needn't be so afflicted."

My children? Jade pulled her gaze away from the eager-eyed doctor and glanced around the room. A bare little cell, like all the other offices in the hospital. Like all of Selene City. Buried underground, gray and lifeless, like living in a crypt.

"You must make a decision," insisted the doctor.

"Why? Why now? I'll marry some day. Why shouldn't I have my own children myself?"

An uncomfortable expression crossed Dr. Dinant's face. "Your job, up on the surface. I know they keep the radiation exposure down to acceptable levels, but . . ."

Jade nodded, understanding. She had heard tales about what long-term exposure to the radiation levels up on the surface could do. Even inside the armored space suits the radiation effects built up, over time. That's why they paid a bonus for working up on the surface. She wondered if that was how she had acquired the bone disease in the first place. Was her father a worker on the surface? Her mother?

Osteopetrosis. Marble bones, it was called. Jade remembered pictures of marble statues from ancient Greece and Rome, arms broken off, fingers gone, noses missing. That's what my bones are like; too brittle for Earth's gravity. That's what would happen to me.

Dr. Dinant forced a smile. "I realize that this is a difficult decision for you to make."

"Yes."

"But you must decide, and soon. Otherwise . . ."

Otherwise, Jade told herself, the radiation buildup would end her chances of ever becoming a mother.

"Perhaps you should discuss the matter with your family," the doctor suggested.

"I have no family."

"Your mother—the woman who adopted you, she is still alive, is she not?"

Jade felt a block of ice congealing around her. "I have not spoken to my mother in many years. She doesn't call me and I don't call her."

"Oh." Dr. Dinant looked pained, defeated. "I see."

A long silence stretched between the two women. Finally Dr. Dinant shifted uncomfortably in her chair and said, "You needn't make your decision at just this moment. Go home, think about it. Sleep on it. Call me in a few days."

Slowly, carefully, Jade got to her feet. "Yes. Thank you. I'll call you in a few days."

"Good," said the doctor, without moving from her chair. She seemed relieved to see Jade leave her office.

Jade walked blindly down the corridors of the underground city. Men and women passed her, some nodding or smiling a hello, most staring blankly ahead. Children were still rare in Selene and if she saw any, she paid them no mind. It was too painful. The whole subject tore at her heart, reminding her again of the mother that had abandoned her, of the cold and empty life she was leading.

In those days there were only two bars in Selene City, one frequented by management types and tourists, the other the haunt of the workers. Jade found herself pushing through the crowd at the incongruously named Pelican Bar.

Friends called to her; strangers smiled at the diminutive redhead. But Jade saw and heard them only dimly.

The Pelican's owner tended the bar himself, leaving the robots to handle anyone too much in a hurry for a joke or a story. He was a paunchy middle-aged man, gleamingly bald beneath the overhead fluorescents. He seemed to smile all the time. At least, every time Jade had seen him his face was beaming happily.

"Hey there, Green Eyes! Haven't seen you since your birthday bash."

Her coworkers had surprised her with a party to celebrate her twentieth birthday, several weeks earlier. Jade sat on the last stool in the farthest corner of the bar, as distant from everyone else as she could manage.

"Want your usual?"

She hadn't been to the Pelican—or anywhere else, for that matter—often enough to know what her "usual" might be. But she nodded glumly.

"Comin' right up."

A guy in a tan leather vest and turquoise-cinched bolo tie pulled up the stool next to Jade's, a drink already in his hand. He smiled handsomely at her.

"Hi, Red. Haven't I seen you up at the landing port?"

Jade shook her head. "Not me."

"Must be someplace else. I'm new here, just arrived last week for a year's contract."

Jade said nothing. The newcomer tried a few more ploys, but when they failed to get a response from her he shrugged and moved away.

The bartender returned with a tall frosted glass filled with a dark bubbling liquid and tinkling with real ice cubes.

"Here you go! Genuine Coca-Cola!"

Jade said, "Thanks," as she took the cold sweating glass in her hand.

"You're never gonna win the Miss Popularity contest if you keep givin' guys the cold shoulder, y'know."

"I'm not interested in any contests."

The bartender shrugged. "H'm, yeah, well maybe. But there's somebody over there—" he jabbed a thumb back toward the crowd at the other end of the bar, "—that you oughtta meet."

"Why?"

"You were askin' about Sam Gunn, weren't you? Zach Bonner said you were."

Her supervisor. "Is Zach here?" she asked.

"Naw, too early for him. But this guy here now, he was a buddy of Sam's, back in the early days."

"Really?"

"Yeah. You'll see."

The bartender waddled away, toward the crowd. When he came back, Jade saw that a compactly built gray-haired man was coming down the other side of the bar toward her, holding a pilsner glass half filled with beer in his left hand.

"Jade, meet Felix Sanchez. Felix, this is Jade. I dunno what her last name is 'cause she never told me."

Sanchez was a round-faced Latino with a thick dark mustache. He smiled at Jade and extended his hand. She let him take hers, and for a wild moment she thought he was going to bring it to his lips. But he merely held it for several seconds. His hand felt warm. It engulfed her own.

"Such beautiful eyes," Sanchez said, his voice so low that she had to strain to hear it over the buzz of the crowd. "No wonder you are called Jade."

She felt herself smiling back at him. Sanchez must have been more than fifty years old, she guessed. But he seemed to be in good athletic shape beneath his casual pullover and slacks.

"You knew Sam Gunn?" Jade asked.

"Knew him? I was nearly killed by him!" And Sanchez laughed heartily while the bartender gave up all pretense of working and planted both his elbows on the plastic surface of his bar.

The Long Fall

EVERYBODY BLAMED SAM FOR WHAT HAPPENED—SANCHEZ said—but if you ask me it never would've happened if the skipper hadn't gone a little crazy.

Space station Freedom was a purely government project, ten years behind schedule and a billion bucks or so over budget. Nothing unusual about that. The agency's best team of astronauts and mission specialists were picked to be the first crew. Nothing unusual about that, either.

What was weird was that somehow Sam Gunn was included in that first crew. And John J. Johnson was named commander. See, Sam and Commander Johnson got along like hydrazine and nitric acid—hypergolic. Put them in contact and they explode.

You've got to see the picture. John J. Johnson was a little over six feet tall, lean as a contrail, and the straightest straight-arrow in an agency full of stiff old graybeards. He had the distinguished white hair and the elegant good looks of an airline pilot in a TV commercial.

But inside that handsome head was a brain that had a nasty streak in it. "Jay-Cubed," as we called him, always went by the rule book, even when it hurt. Especially when it hurt, if you ask me.

Until the day we learned that Gloria Lamour was coming to space station Freedom. That changed everything, of course.

Sam, you know, was the opposite of the commander in every way possible. Sam was short and stubby where Johnson was tall and rangy. Hair like rusty Brillo. Funny color eyes; I could never tell if they were blue or green. Sam was gregarious, noisy, crackling with nervous energy; Johnson was calm, reserved, detached. Sam wanted to be everybody's pal; Johnson wanted respect, admiration, but most of all he wanted obedience.

Sam was definitely not handsome. His round face was bright as a penny, and sometimes he sort of looked like Huckleberry Finn or maybe even that old-time child star Mickey Rooney. But handsome he was not. Still, Sam had a way with women. I know this is true because he would tell me about it all the time. Me, and anybody else who would be within earshot. Also, I saw him in action, back at the Cape and during our training sessions in Houston. The little guy could be charming and downright courtly when he wanted to be.

Ninety days on a space station with Sam and Commander Johnson. It was sort of like a shakedown cruise; our job was to make sure all the station's systems were working as they ought to. I knew it wouldn't be easy. The station wasn't big enough to hide in.

There were only six of us on that first mission, but we kept getting in each other's way—and on each other's nerves. It was like a ninety-day jail sentence. We couldn't get out. We had nothing to do but work. There were no women. I think we would've all gone batty if it weren't for Sam. He was our one-man entertainment committee.

He was full of jokes, full of fun. He organized the scavenger hunt that kept us busy every night for two solid weeks trying to find the odd bits of junk that he had hidden away in empty oxygen cylinders, behind sleep cocoons, even floating up on the ceiling of the station's one and only working head. He set up the darts tournament, where the "darts" were really spitballs made of wadded Velcro and the reverse side of the improvised target was a blow-up photo of Commander Johnson.

Sam was a beehive of energy. He kept us laughing. All except the commander, who had never smiled in his life, so far as any of us knew.

And it was all in zero-gee. Or almost. So close it didn't make any real difference. The scientists called it microgravity. We called it weightlessness, zero-gee, whatever. We floated. Everything floated if it wasn't nailed down. Sam loved zero-gee. Johnson always looked like he was about to puke.

Johnson ruled with an aluminum fist. No matter how many tasks mission control loaded on us, Johnson never argued with them. He pushed us to do everything those clowns on the ground could think of, and to do it on time and according to regulations. No shortcuts, no flimflams. Naturally, the more we accomplished the more mission control thought up for us to do. Worse, Johnson *asked* mission control for more tasks. He *volunteered* for more jobs for us to do. We were working, working, working all the time, every day, without a break.

"He's gonna kill us with overwork," grumbled Roger Cranston, our structural specialist.

"The way I figure it," Sam said, "is that Jay-Cubed wants us to do all the tasks that the next crew is supposed to do. That way the agency can cut the next mission and save seventy million bucks or so."

Al Dupres agreed sourly. "He works us to death and then he gets a big kiss on the cheek from Washington." Al was French-Canadian, the agency's token international representative.

Sam started muttering about Captain Bligh and the good ship *Bounty*.

They were right. Johnson was so eager to look good to the agency that he was starting to go a little whacko. Some of it was Sam's fault, of course. But I really think zero-gee affected the flow of blood to his brain. That, and the news about Gloria Lamour, which affected his blood flow elsewhere.

We were six weeks into the mission. Sam had kept his nose pretty clean, stuck to his duties as logistics officer and all the other jobs the skipper thought up for him, kept out of Johnson's silver-fox hair as much as he could.

Oh, he had loosened the screwtop on the commander's coffee squeeze-bulb one morning, so that Johnson splashed the stuff all over the command module. Imagine ten thousand little bubbles of coffee (heavy on the cream) spattering all over, floating and scattering like ten thousand teeny fireflies. Johnson sputtered and cursed and glowered at Sam, his coveralls soaked from collar to crotch.

I nearly choked, trying not to laugh. Sam put on a look of innocence that would have made the angels sigh. He offered to chase down each and every bubble and clean up the mess. Johnson just glowered at him while the bubbles slowly wafted into the air vent above the command console.

Then there was the water bag in the commander's sleep cocoon. And the gremlin in the computer system that printed out random graffiti like: *Resistance to tyranny is obedience to God.* Or: *Where is Fletcher Christian when we really need him?*

Commander Johnson started muttering to himself a lot, and staring at Sam when the little guy's back was to him. It was an evil, red-eyed stare. Sent chills up my spine.

Then I found out about the CERV test.

Crew Emergency Reentry Vehicle, CERV. Lifeboats for the space station. We called them "capsules." Suppose something goes really wrong on the station, like we're hit by a meteor. (More likely, we would've been hit by a piece of man-made junk. There were millions of bits of debris floating around out there in those days.) If the station's so badly damaged we have to abandon ship, we jump into the capsules and ride back down to Earth.

Nobody'd done it, up to then. The lifeboats had been tested with dummies inside them, but not real live human beings. Not yet.

I was on duty at the communications console in the command module that morning when Commander Johnson was on the horn with Houston. All of a sudden my screen breaks up into fuzz and crackles.

"This is a scrambled transmission," the commander said in his monotone, from his station at the command console, three feet to my right. He plugged in a headset and clipped the earphone on. And he *smiled* at me.

I took the hint and made my way to the galley for a squeeze of coffee, more stunned by that smile than curious about his scrambled conversation with mission control. When I got back Johnson was humming tunelessly to himself. The headset was off and he was still smiling. It was a ghastly smile.

Although we put in a lot of overtime hours to finish the tasks our commander so obligingly piled on us, Johnson himself left the command module precisely at seven each evening, ate a solitary meal in the wardroom and then got eight full hours of sleep. His conscience was perfectly at ease, and he apparently had no idea whose face was on the reverse of the darts target.

As soon as he left that evening I pecked out the subroutine I had put into the comm computer and reviewed his scrambled transmission to Houston. He may be the skipper, but I'm the comm officer and *nothing* goes in or out without me seeing it.

The breath gushed out of me when I read the file. No wonder the skipper had smiled.

I called Sam and got him to meet me in the wardroom. The commander had assigned him to getting the toilet in the unoccupied laboratory module to work, so that the scientists who'd eventually be coming up could crap in their own territory. In addition to all his regular duties, of course.

"A CERV test, huh," Sam said when I told him. "We don't have enough to do; he's gonna throw a lifeboat drill at us."

"Worse than that," I said.

"What do you mean?" Sam was hovering a few inches off the floor. He liked to do that; made him feel taller.

Chairs are useless in zero-gee. I had my feet firmly anchored in the foot loops set into the floor around the wardroom table. Otherwise a weightless body would drift all over the place. Except for Sam, who somehow managed to keep himself put.

Leaning closer toward Sam, I whispered, "It won't be just a drill. He's going to pop one of the lifeboats and send it into a real reentry trajectory."

"No shit?"

"No shit. He got permission from Houston this morning for a full balls-out test."

Sam grabbed the edge of the galley table and pulled himself so close to me I could count the pale freckles on his snub of a nose. Sudden understanding lit up those blue-green eyes of his.

"I'll bet I know who's going to be on the lifeboat that gets to take the long fall," he whispered back at me.

I nodded.

"That's why he smiled at me this evening."

"He's been working out every detail in the computer," I said, my voice as low as a guy planning a bank heist, even though we were alone in the wardroom. "He's going to make certain you're in the lab module by yourself so you'll be the only one in the lifeboat there. Then he's going to pop it off."

The thought of riding one of those uncontrolled little capsules through the blazing heat of reentry and then landing God knows where— maybe the middle of the ocean, maybe the middle of the Gobi Desert—it scared the hell out of me. Strangely, Sam grinned.

"You *want* to be the first guy who tries out one of those capsules?" I asked.

"Hell no," he said. "But suppose our noble liege-lord happens to make a small mistake and *he's* the one to take the ride back home?"

I felt my jaw drop open. "How're you going to . . ."

Sam grinned his widest. "Wouldn't it be poetic if we could arrange things so that ol' Cap'n Bligh himself gets to take the fall?"

I stared at him. "You're crazy."

"That's what they said about Orville and Wilbur, pal."

The next week was very intense. Sam didn't say another word to me about it, but I knew he was hacking into the commander's comm link each night and trying to ferret out every last detail of the upcoming lifeboat drill. Commander Johnson played everything close to the vest, though. He never let on, except that he smiled whenever he saw Sam, the sort of smile that a homicidal maniac might give his next victim. I even thought I heard him cackling to himself once or twice.

The other three men in the crew began to sense the tension. Even Sam became kind of quiet, almost.

Then we got word that Gloria Lamour was coming up to the station.

Maybe you don't remember her, because her career was so tragically short. She was the sexiest, slinkiest, most gorgeous hunk of redheaded femininity ever to grace the video screen. A mixture of Rita Hayworth, Marilyn Monroe and Michelle Pfeiffer. With some Katharine Hepburn thrown in for brains and even a flash of Bette Midler's sass.

The skipper called us together into the command module for the news. Just as calmly as if he was announcing a weather report from Tibet he told us:

"There will be a special shuttle mission to the station three days from this morning. We will be visited for an unspecified length of time by a video crew from Hollywood. Gloria Lamour, the video star, will apparently be among them."

It hit us like a shock wave, but Commander Johnson spelled it out just as if we were going to get nothing more than a new supply of aspirin.

"Miss Lamour will be here to photograph the first video drama ever filmed in space," he told us. "She and her crew have received clearance from the highest levels of the White House."

"Three cheers for President Heston," Sam piped.

Commander Johnson started to glare at him, but his expression turned into a wintry smile. A smile that said, *You'll get yours, mister.* None of the rest of us moved from where we stood anchored in our foot restraints.

The commander went on. "The video crew will be using the laboratory module for their taping. They will use the unoccupied scientists' privacy cubicles for their sleeping quarters. There should be practically no interference with your task schedules, although I expect you to extend every courtesy and assistance to our visitors."

The five of us grinned and nodded eagerly.

"It will be necessary to appoint a crew member to act as liaison between the video team and ourselves," said the commander.

Five hands shot up to volunteer so hard that all five of us would have gone careening into the overhead if we hadn't been anchored to the floor by the foot restraints.

"I will take on that extra duty myself," the skipper said, smiling enough now to show his teeth, "so that you can continue with your work without any extra burdens being placed on you."

"Son of a bitch," Sam muttered. If the commander heard him, he ignored it.

Gloria Lamour on space station Freedom! The six of us had been living in this orbital monastery for almost two months. We were practically drooling with anticipation. I found it hard to sleep, and when I did my dreams were so vivid they were embarrassing. The other guys floated through their duties grinning and joking. We started making bets about who would be first to do what. But Sam, normally the cheerful one, turned glum. "Old Jay-Cubed is gonna hover around her like a satellite. He's gonna keep her in the lab module and away from us. He won't let any of us get close enough for an autograph, even."

That took the starch out of us, so to speak.

The big day arrived. The orbiter *Reagan* made rendezvous with the station and docked at our main airlock. The five of us were supposed to be going about our regular tasks. Only the commander's anointed liaison man—himself—went to the airlock to greet our visitors.

Yet somehow all five of us managed to be in the command module, where all three monitor screens on the main console were focused on the airlock.

Commander Johnson stood with his back to the camera, decked out in crisp new sky-blue coveralls, standing as straight as a man can in zero-gee.

"I'll cut off the oxygen to his sleeping cubicle," muttered Larry Minetti, our life-support specialist. "I'll fix the bastard, you watch and see."

We ignored Larry.

"She come through the hatch yet?" Sam called. He was at my regular station, the communications console, instead of up front with us watching the screens.

"What're you doing back there?" I asked him, not taking my eyes off the screens. The hatch's locking wheel was starting to turn.

"Checking into Cap'n Bligh's files, what else?"

"Come on, you're gonna miss it! The hatch is opening."

Sam shot over to us like a stubby missile and stopped his momentum by grabbing Larry and me by the shoulders. He stuck his head between us.

The hatch was swung all the way open by a grinning shuttle astronaut. Two mission specialists—male—pushed a pallet loaded with equipment past the still-erect Commander Johnson. We were all erect too, with anticipation.

A nondescript woman floated through the hatch behind the mission specialists and the pallet. She was in gray coveralls. As short as Sam. Kind of a long, sour face. Not sour, exactly. Sad. Unhappy. Mousy dull brown hair plastered against her skull with a zero-gee net. Definitely not a glamorous video star.

"Must be her assistant," Al Dupres muttered.

"Her director."

"Her dog."

We stared at those screens so hard you'd think that Gloria Lamour would have appeared just out of the energy of our five palpitating, concentrating brain waves.

No such luck. The unbeautiful woman floated right up to Commander Johnson and took his hand in a firm, almost manly grip.

"Hello," she said, in a nasal Bronx accent. "Gloria Lamour is not on this trip, so don't get your hopes up."

I wish I could have seen the commander's face. But, come to think of it, he probably didn't blink an eye. Sam gagged and went over backwards into a zero-gee loop. The rest of us moaned, booed, and hollered obscenities at the screens.

Through it all I clearly heard the commander speak the little speech he had obviously rehearsed for days: "Welcome aboard space station *Freedom,* Miss Lamour. *Mi casa es su casa.*"

Big frigging deal!

What it worked out to was this: The crab apple's name was Arlene Gold. She was a technician for the video company. In fact, she was the entire video crew, all by herself. And her pallet-full of equipment. She was here to shoot background footage. Was Gloria Lamour coming up later? She got very cagey about answering that one.

We got to know her pretty well over the next several days. Commander Johnson lost interest in her immediately, but although he still wouldn't let any of us go into the lab module, she had to come into the wardroom for meals. She was a New Yorker, which she pronounced "Noo Yawkeh." Testy, suspicious, always on guard. Guess I can't blame her, stuck several hundred miles up in orbit with five drooling maniacs and a commander who behaved like a robot.

But god, was she a sourpuss.

Larry approached her. "You handle zero-gee very well. Most of us got sick the first couple of days."

"What'd ya expect," she almost snarled, "screaming and fainting?"

A day or so later Rog Cranston worked up the courage to ask, "Have you done much flying?"

"Whatsit to ya?" she snapped back at him.

It only took a few days of that kind of treatment for us to shun her almost completely. When she came into the wardroom for meals we backed away and gave her the run of the galley's freezers and microwave. We made certain there was an empty table for her.

Except that Sam kept trying to strike up a conversation with her. Kept trying to make her laugh, or even smile, no matter how many times she rebuffed him. He even started doing short jokes for her, playing the buffoon, telling her how much he admired taller women. (She might have been half a centimeter taller than he was on the ground; it was hard to tell in zero-gee.)

Her responses ranged from "Get lost" to "Don't be such a jerk."

I pulled Sam aside after a few evenings of this and asked him when he had turned into a masochist.

Sam gave me a knowing grin. "My old pappy always told me, 'When they hand you a lemon, son, make lemonade.'"

"With *her*?"

"You see any other women up here?"

I didn't answer, but I had to admit that Larry Minetti was starting to look awfully good to me.

"Besides," Sam said, his grin turning sly, "when Gloria Lamour finally gets here, Arlene will be her guardian, won't she?"

I got it. Get close to the sourpuss and she'll let you get close to the sex goddess. There was method in Sam's madness. He seemed to spend all his spare time trying to melt Arlene's heart of steel. I thought he had even lost interest in rigging the skipper's CERV test so that it would be John J. Johnson who got fired off the station, not Sam Gunn.

Sam practically turned himself inside out for Arlene. He became elfin, a pixie, a leprechaun whenever she came to the galley or wardroom.

And it seemed to be working. She let him eat dinner at the same table with her one night.

"After all," I overheard Sam tell her, "we little people have to stick together."

"Don't get ideas," Arlene replied. But her voice had lost some of its sharp edge. She damned near smiled at Sam.

The next morning Johnson called Sam to his command console. "You are relieved of your normal duties for the next few days," the skipper said. "You will report to the lab module and assist Ms. Gold in testing her equipment."

I shot a surprised glance at Larry, who was at his console, next to mine. His eyebrows were rising up to his scalp. Sam just grinned and launched himself toward the hatch. The commander smiled crookedly at his departing back.

"So what's with you two?" I asked him a couple nights later. He had just spent eighteen hours straight in the lab module with Arlene and her video gear.

"What two?"

"You and Arlene."

Sam cocked his head to one side. "With us? Nothing. She needs a lot of help with all that video gear. Damned studio sent her here by herself. They expect her to muscle those lasers and camera rigs around. Hell, even in zero-gee that's a job."

I got the picture. "So when Gloria Lamour finally shows up you'll be practically part of the family."

I expected Sam to leer, or at least grin. Instead he looked kind of puzzled. "I don't know if she's coming up here at all. Arlene's pretty touchy about the subject."

Just how touchy we found out a couple nights later.

Larry and I were in the wardroom replaying Super Bowl XXIV on the computer simulator. I had lost the coin flip and gotten stuck with the Broncos. We had the sound turned way down so we wouldn't annoy the commander, who was staying up late, watching a video drama over in his corner: *Halloween XXXIX*.

Anyway, I had programmed an old Minnesota Vikings defense into the game, and we had sacked Montana four times already in the first quarter. The disgusted look on his face when he climbed up from the fourth burial was so real you'd think we were watching an actual game instead of creating a simulation. The crowd was going wild.

Elway was just starting to get hot, completing three straight passes, when Arlene sailed into the wardroom, looking red in the face, really pissed off. Sam was right behind her, talking his usual blue streak.

"So what'd I say that made you so sore? How could I hurt your feelings talking about the special-effects computer? What'd I do, what'd I say? For chrissakes, you're breaking the Fifth Amendment! The accused has got a right to be told what he did wrong. It's in the Constitution!"

Arlene whirled in midair and gave him a look that would have scorched a rhinoceros. "It's not the Fifth Amendment, stupid."

Sam shrugged so hard he propelled himself toward the ceiling. "So I'm not a lawyer. Sue me!"

Larry and I both reached for the HOLD button on our tabletop keyboard. I got there first. The game stopped with the football in midair and Denver's wide receiver on the ten-yard line behind the Forty-Niners' free safety.

Arlene pushed herself to the galley while Sam hovered up near the ceiling, anchoring himself there by pressing the fingertips of one hand against the overhead panels. Commander Johnson did not stir from his corner, but I thought his eyes flicked from Arlene to Sam and then back to his video screen.

Before Larry and I got a chance to restart our game, Arlene squirted some hot coffee into a squeezebulb and went to the only other table in the wardroom, sailing right past Sam's dangling feet. The commander watched her. As she slipped her feet into the floor restraints he turned off his video screen and straightened up to his full height.

"Ms. Gold . . ." he began to say.

She ignored Johnson and pointed up at Sam with her free hand. "You're hanging around with your tail wagging, waiting for Gloria Lamour to get here."

"Ms. Gold," the commander said, a little louder.

Sam pushed off the ceiling. "Sure. We all are."

"Sure," Arlene mimicked. "We all are." She gave Larry and me a nasty stare.

Sam stopped himself about six inches off the floor. How he did that was always beyond me. Somehow he seemed able to break Newton's First Law, or at least bend it a little to make himself feel taller.

Johnson disengaged himself from his foot restraints and came out from behind his video set. He was staring at Arlene, his own face pinched and narrow-eyed.

"Ms. Gold," he repeated, firmly.

Arlene ignored him. She was too busy yowling at Sam, "You're so goddamned transparent it's pathetic! You think Gloria Lamour would even bother to *glance* at a little snot like you? You think if she came up here she'd let you wipe her ass? Ha!"

"Ms. Gold, I believe you are drunk," said our fearless skipper. The look on his face was weird: disapproval, disgust, disappointment, and a little bit of disbelief.

"You're damned right I'm drunk, *mon capitain*. What th' fuck are you gonna do about it?"

Instead of exploding like a normal skipper would, the commander surprised us all by replying with great dignity, "I will escort you to your quarters."

But he turned his beady-eyed gaze toward Sam.

Sam drifted slowly toward the skipper, bobbing along high enough to be eye-to-eye with Johnson.

"Yes, sir, she has been drinking. Vodka, I believe. I tried to stop her but she wouldn't stop," Sam said.

The commander looked utterly unconvinced.

"I have not touched a drop," Sam added. And he exhaled right into Commander Johnson's face hard enough to push himself backward like a punctured balloon.

Johnson blinked, grimaced, and looked for a moment like he was going to throw up. "I will deal with you later, Mr. Gunn," he muttered. Then he turned to Arlene again and took her by the arm. "This way, Ms. Gold."

She made a little zero-gee curtsy. "Thank you, Commander Johnson. I'm glad that there is at least one gentleman aboard this station." And she shot Sam a killer stare.

"Not at all," said the commander, patting her hand as it rested on his arm. He looked down at her in an almost grandfatherly way. Arlene smiled up at him and allowed Commander Johnson to tow her toward the hatch. Then he made his big mistake.

"And tell me, Ms. Gold," said the skipper, "just when will Gloria Lamour arrive here?"

Arlene's face twisted into something awful. "You too? You too! That's all you bastards are thinking about, isn't it? When's your favorite wet dream going to get here."

The commander sputtered, "Ms. Gold, I assure you . . ."

She pulled free of his arm, sending herself spinning across the wardroom. She grabbed a table and yelled at all of us:

"Lemme tell you something, lover boys. Gloria Lamour ain't comin' up here at all. Never! This is as good as it gets, studs. What you see is what you got!"

The commander had to haul her through the hatch. We could hear her yelling and raving all the way down the connecting passageway to the lab module.

"Where'd she get the booze?" Larry asked.

"Brought it up with her," said Sam. "She's been drinking since five o'clock. Something I said ticked her off."

"Never mind that." I got straight to the real problem. "Is she serious about Gloria Lamour not coming up here?"

Sam nodded glumly.

"Aw shit," moaned Larry.

I felt like somebody had shot Santa Claus.

"There isn't any Gloria Lamour," Sam said, his voice so low that I thought maybe I hadn't heard him right.

"No Gloria Lamour?"

"Whattaya mean?"

Sam steadied himself with a hand on the edge of our table. "Just what I said. There isn't any such person as Gloria Lamour."

"That's her show-business name."

"She's not real!" Sam snapped. "She's a simulation. Computer graphics, just like your damned football game."

"But . . ."

"All the publicity about her . . ."

"All faked. Gloria Lamour is the creation of a Hollywood talent agency and some bright computer kids. It's supposed to be a secret, but Arlene spilled it to me after she'd had a few drinks."

"A simulation?" Larry looked crushed. "Computer graphics can do that? She looked so . . . so *real*."

"She's just a bunch of algorithms, pal." Sam seemed more sober than I had ever seen him. "Arlene's her 'director.' She programs in all her moves."

"The damned bitch," Larry growled. "She could've let us know. Instead of building up our expectations like this."

"It's supposed to be a secret," Sam repeated.

"Yeah, but she should've let us in on it. It's not fair! It's just not fair!"

Sam gave him a quizzical little half-smile. "Imagine how she's been feeling, watching the six of us—even old Jay-Cubed—waiting here with our tongues hanging out and full erections. Not paying any attention to her; just waiting for this dream—this computerized doll. No wonder she got sore."

I shook my head. The whole thing was too weird for me.

Sam was muttering, "I tried to tell her that I liked her, that I was interested in her for her own sake."

"She saw through that," Larry said.

"Yeah . . ." Sam looked toward the hatch. Everything was quiet now. "Funny thing is, I was getting to like her. I really was."

"Her? The Bronx Ball-Breaker?"

"She's not that bad once she lets herself relax a little."

"She sure didn't look relaxed tonight," I said.

Sam agreed with a small nod. "She never got over the idea that I was after Gloria Lamour, not her."

"Well, weren't you?"

"At first, yeah, sure. But . . ."

Larry made a sour face. "But once she told you there wasn't any Gloria Lamour you were willing to settle for her, right?"

I chimed in, "You were ready to make lemonade."

Sam fell silent. Almost. "I don't know," he mumbled. "I don't think so."

The skipper came back into the wardroom, and fixed Sam with a firing-squad stare.

"Lights out, gentlemen. Gunn, you return to your normal duties to-morrow. Ms. Gold will finish her work here by herself and depart in two days."

Sam's only reply was a glum, "Yes, sir."

The next morning when we started our shift in the command module Sam looked terrible. As if he hadn't slept all night. Yet there was a hint of a twinkle in his eye. He kept his face straight, because the skipper was watching him like a hawk. But he gave me a quick wink at precisely ten o'clock.

I know the exact time for two reasons.

First, Commander Johnson punched up the interior camera view of the lab module and muttered, "Ten in the morning and she's not at work yet."

"She must be under the weather, sir," Sam said in a funny kind of stiff, military way of talking. Like he was rehearsing for a role in a war video or trying to get on the skipper's good side. (Assuming he had one.)

"She must be hung over as hell," Al Dupres muttered to me.

"I suppose I should call her on the intercom and wake her up," the commander said. "After all, if she's only got two more days . . ."

"Emergency! Emergency!" called the computer's synthesized female voice. "Prepare to abandon the station. All personnel to Crew Emergency Reentry Vehicles. All personnel to Crew Emergency Reentry Vehicles. Prepare to abandon the station."

Bells and klaxons started going off all over the place. The emergency siren was wailing so loud you could barely hear yourself think. Through it all the computer kept repeating the abandon-ship message. The computer's voice was calm but urgent. The six of us were urgent, but definitely not calm.

"But I postponed the test!" Commander Johnson yelled at his computer screen. It was filled with big block letters in red, spelling out what the synthesizer was saying.

Larry and the others were already diving for the hatch that led to the nearest CERV. They had no idea that this was supposed to be a drill.

I hesitated only a moment. Then I remembered Sam's wink a minute earlier. And the little sonofagun was already flying down the connecting passageway toward the lab module like a red-topped torpedo.

"I postponed the goddamned test!" Johnson still roared at his command console, over the noise of all the warning hoots and wails. Sure he had. But Sam had spent the night rerigging it.

The station had four CERVs, each of them big enough to hold six people. Typical agency overdesign, you might think. But the lifeboats were spotted at four different locations, so no matter where on the station you might be, there was a CERV close enough to save your neck and big enough to take the whole crew with you, if necessary.

They were round unglamorous spheres, sort of like the early Russian manned reentry vehicles. Nothing inside except a lot of padding and safety harnesses. The idea was you belted off the station, propelled by cold gas jets, then the CERV's onboard computer automatically fired a set of retro rockets and started beeping out an emergency signal so the people on the ground could track where you landed.

The sphere was covered with ablative heat shielding. After reentry it popped parachutes to plop you gently on the ocean or the ground, wherever. There was also a final descent rocket to slow your fall down to almost zero.

I caught up with Larry and the other guys inside the CERV and told them to take it easy.

"This is just a drill," I said, laughing.

Rog Cranston's face was dead white. "A drill?" He had already buckled himself into his harness.

"You sure?" Larry asked. He was buckled in, too. So was Al.

"Do you see the skipper in here?" I asked, hovering nonchalantly in the middle of the capsule.

Al said, "Yeah. We're all buttoned up but we haven't been fired off the station."

Just at that moment we felt a jolt like somebody had whanged the capsule with the world's biggest hammer. I went slamming face first into the padded bulkhead, just missing a head-on collision with Larry by about an inch.

"Holy shit!" somebody yelled.

I was plastered flat against the padding, my nose bleeding and my body feeling like it weighed ten tons.

"My ass, a drill!"

It was like going over Niagara Falls in a barrel, only worse. After half a minute that seemed like half a year the g-force let up and we were weightless again. I fumbled with shaking hands into one of the empty harnesses. My nose was stuffed up with blood that couldn't run out in zero-gee and I thought I was going to strangle to death. Then we started feeling heavy again. The whole damned capsule started to shake like we were inside a food processor and blood sprayed from my aching nose like a garden sprinkler.

And through it all I had this crazy notion in my head that I could still hear Commander Johnson's voice wailing, "But I postponed the drill!"

We were shaken, rattled, and frazzled all the way down. The worst part of it, of course, was that the flight was totally beyond our control. We just hung in those harnesses like four sides of beef while the capsule automatically went through reentry and parachuted us into the middle of a soccer field in Brazil. There was a game going on at the time, although we could see nothing because the capsule had neither windows nor exterior TV cameras.

Apparently our final retro rocket blast singed the referee, much to the delight of the crowd.

Sam's CERV had been shot off the station too, we found out later. With the Gold woman aboard. Only the skipper remained aboard the space station, still yelling that he had postponed the test.

Sam's long ride back to Earth must have been even tougher than ours. He wound up in the hospital with a wrenched back and dislocated shoulder. He landed in the Australian outback, no less, but it took the Aussies only a couple of hours to reach him in their rescue VTOLs, once the agency gave them the exact tracking data.

Sure enough, Arlene Gold was in the capsule with him, shaken up a bit but otherwise unhurt.

The agency had no choice but to abort our mission and bring Commander Johnson back home at once. Popping the two CERVs was grounds for six months worth of intense investigation. Three Congressional committees, OSHA and even the EPA eventually got into the act. Thank God for Sam's ingenuity, though. Nobody was able to find anything except an unexplained malfunction of the CERV ejection thrusters.

The agency wound up spending seventeen million dollars redesigning the damned thing.

As soon as we finished our debriefings, I took a few days' leave and hustled over to the hospital outside San Antonio where they were keeping Sam.

I could hear that he was okay before I ever saw him. At the nurses' station half a block away from his room I could hear him yammering. Nurses were scurrying down the hall, some looking frightened, most sort of grinning to themselves.

Sam was flat on his back, his left arm in a cast that stuck straight up toward the ceiling. ". . . and I want a pizza, with extra pepperoni!" he was yelling at a nurse who was leaving the room just as I tried to come in. We bumped in the doorway. She was young, kind of pretty.

"He can't eat solid foods while he's strapped to the board," she said to me. As if I had anything to do with it. The refreshment I was smuggling in for Sam was liquid, hidden under my flight jacket.

Sam took one look at me and said, "I thought your nose was broken."

"Naw, just bloodied a little."

Then he quickly launched into a catalogue of the hospital's faults: bed-pans kept in the freezer, square needles, liquid foods, unsympathetic nurses.

"They keep the young ones buzzing around here all day," he complained, "but when it comes time for my sponge bath they send in Dracula's mother-in-law."

I pulled up the room's only chair. "So how the hell are you?"

"I'll be okay. If this damned hospital doesn't kill me first."

"You rigged the CERVs, didn't you?" I asked, dropping my voice low.

Sam grinned. "How'd our noble skipper like being left all alone up there?"

"The agency had to send a shuttle to pick him up, all by himself."

"The cost accountants must love him."

"The word is he's going to be reassigned to the tracking station at As-cencion Island."

Sam chuckled. "It's not exactly Pitcairn, but it's kind of poetic anyway."

I worked up the nerve to ask him, "What happened?"

"What happened?" he repeated.

"In the CERV. How rugged was the flight? How'd you get hurt? What happened with Arlene?"

Sam's face clouded. "She's back in L.A. Didn't even wait around long enough to see if I would live or die."

"Must've been a punishing flight," I said.

"I wouldn't know," Sam muttered.

"What do you mean?"

Sam blew an exasperated sigh toward the ceiling. "We were screwing all the way down to the ground! How do you think I threw my back out?"

"You and Arlene? The Bronx Ball-Breaker made out with you?"

"Yeah," he said. Then, "No."

I felt kind of stunned, surprised, confused.

"You know the helmets we use in flight simulations?" Sam asked. "The kind that flash computer graphic visuals on your visor so you're seeing the situation the computer is cooking up?"

I must have nodded.

Staring at the ceiling, he continued, "Arlene brought two of them into the lifeboat with us. And her Gloria Lamour disks."

"You were seeing Gloria Lamour . . . ?"

"It was like being with Gloria Lamour," Sam said, his voice almost shaking, kind of hollow. "Just like being with her. I could touch her. I could even taste her."

"No shit?"

"It was like nothing else in the world, man. She was fantastic. And it was all in zero-gee. Most of it, anyway. The landing was rough. That's when I popped my damned shoulder."

"God almighty, Sam. She must have fallen for you after all. For her to do that for you . . ."

His face went sour. "Yeah, she fell for me so hard she took the first flight from Sydney to L.A. I'll never hear from her again."

"But—jeez, if she gave you Gloria Lamour . . ."

"Yeah. Sure," he said. I had never seen Sam so bitter. "I just wonder who the hell was programmed in *her* helmet. Who was she making out with while she was fucking me?"

The Pelican Bar

"YOU MEAN *SHE* WAS SIMULATING IT WITH SOMEONE ELSE, too?" Jade asked.

"You betcha."

"Like a VR parlor," said the bartender.

"Those helmets were an early version of the VRs," Sanchez said.

"VR parlor?" Jade asked. "What's that?"

The bartender eyed Sanchez, then when he saw that the man was blushing slightly, he turned back to Jade.

"Virtual reality," he said. "Simulating the full sensory spectrum. You know, visual, audial, tactile . . ."

"Smell and taste, too?"

Sanchez coughed into his beer, sending up a small spray of suds.

The bartender nodded. "Yep, the whole nine yards. For a while back then, some of the wise guys in the video business figured they'd be able to do away with actors altogether. Gloria Lamour was their first experimental test, I guess."

"But the public preferred real people," Sanchez said. "Not that it made much difference in the videos, but with real people they had better gossip."

Jade thought she understood. But, "So what's a VR parlor? And where are they? I've never seen one."

"Over at the joints in Hell Crater," the bartender said. "Guys go there and they can get any woman they want, whole harem full, if they can afford it."

"And it's all simulated?" Jade prompted.

"Yeah." The bartender grinned. "But it's still a helluva lot of fun, eh Felix?"

"I prefer real women."

"Do women go to the VR parlors?" Jade asked. "I mean, do they have programs of men?"

"Every male heartthrob from Hercules to President Pastoza," said the bartender.

Jade grinned. "Gee, maybe I ought to check it out."

"A nice young lady such as yourself should not go to Hell Crater," Sanchez said firmly.

"Besides, you wouldn't be able to afford it on your salary," the bartender added.

Jade saw that they were slightly embarrassed. She allowed the subject to drop.

Sanchez finished his latest beer and put the pilsner glass on the bar a trifle unsteadily. One of the robot bartenders trundled to it and replaced it with a filled glass, as it had been doing all during his narrative.

"Poor old Sam prob'ly thought that Bronx Ball-Breaker was falling for him, didn't he?" the bartender asked, watching the robot roll smoothly toward the knot of customers further down the bar.

Sanchez seemed happy to return to Sam's story. "I suppose he did, at first. Funny thing is, I think he was actually starting to fall for her. At least a little. Maybe more sympathy than anything else, but Sam was a very empathetic guy, you know."

"Did he ever see her again?" Jade asked.

"No, not her. He tried to call her a few times but she never responded. Not a peep."

"Poor Sam."

"Oh, don't feel so bad about him. Sam had plenty of other fish to fry. He was never down for long. Not Sam."

The bartender gave a hand signal to the nearer of the two robots and it quickly brought a fresh Coke for Jade and a thimble-sized glass of amber-colored liqueur for the bartender himself.

He raised his glass and said with utter seriousness, "To Sam Gunn, the best sonofabitch in the whole goddamned solar system."

Jade felt a little foolish repeating the words, but she did it, as did Sanchez, and then sipped at her new drink.

"Y'know," Sanchez said, after smacking his lips over the beer, "nobody gives a damn about Sam any more. Here he is, dead and gone, and just about everybody's forgotten him."

"Damn shame," the bartender agreed.

"I wouldn't have my business if it wasn't for Sam," Sanchez said. "He set me up when I needed the money to get started. Nobody else would even look at me! The banks—hah!"

"I was helping my Daddy at his bar down in Florida when I first met Sam," said the bartender. "He's the one who first gave me the idea of opening a joint up here. It was still called Moonbase when I started this place. He had to argue a blue streak to get the base administrators to okay a saloon."

Jade, her own troubles pushed to the back of her mind, told them, "You two guys—and Zach, my boss—you're the first I've ever heard say a decent word about Sam. Everything I ever heard from the time I was a kid has been . . . well, not very flattering."

"That's because the stories about him have mostly been spread by the guys who tangled with him," said the bartender.

"The big corporations," Sanchez agreed.

"And the government."

"They hated Sam's guts. All those guys with suits and ties."

"Why?" asked Jade.

The bartender made a sound halfway between a grunt and a snort. "Why? Because Sam was always fighting against them. He was the little guy, trying to get ahead, always bucking the big boys."

Sanchez smiled again. "Don't get the idea that he was some kind of Robin Hood," he said, glancing at the bartender, then fixing his gaze once again on Jade's lustrous green eyes.

The bartender guffawed. "Robin Hood? Sam? Hell no! All he wanted to do was to get rich."

"Which he did. Many times."

"And threw it all away, just as often."

"*And* helped a lot of little guys like us, along the way."

The bartender wiped at his eyes. "Hey, Felix, you remember the time . . ."

Jade did not think it was possible to get drunk on Coca-Cola, so the exhilarated feeling she was experiencing an hour or so later must have been from the two men's tales of Sam Gunn.

"Why doesn't somebody do a biography of him?" she blurted. "I mean, the networks would love it, wouldn't they?"

Both men stopped the reminiscences in mid-sentence. The bartender looked surprised. Sanchez inexplicably turned glum.

"The networks? Pah!" Sanchez spat.

"They'd never do it," said the bartender, turning sad.

"Why not?"

"Two reasons. One: the big corporations run the networks and they still hate Sam, even though he's dead. They won't want to see him glorified. And two: guys like us will tell you stories about Sam, but do you think we'd trust some smart-ass reporter from one of the networks?"

"Oh," said Jade. "I see—I guess."

The men resumed their tales of their younger days. Jade half-listened as she sipped her Coke, thinking to herself, But they're talking to me about Sam. Why couldn't I get other people who knew him to talk to me?

The Audition

IT TOOK JADE THREE MONTHS TO GET HERSELF HIRED AS AN
assistant video editor for the Selene office of the Solar News Network. She
took crash courses in Video Editing and News Writing from the electronic university, working long into the nights in front of her interactive
computer screen, catching a few winks of sleep, and then going to the
garage to put in her hours on the surface driving a truck.

At first Zach Bonner, her supervisor, scowled angrily at her baggy eyes
and slowed reflexes.

"Tell your boyfriend to let you get more sleep, little girl," he growled at
her. "Otherwise you're going to make a mistake out there and kill
yourself—maybe kill me, too."

Shocked with surprise, Jade blurted the truth. "I don't have a
boyfriend, Zach. I'm studying."

Bonner had three daughters of his own. As swiftly as he could, he
transferred Jade to a maintenance job indoors. She gratefully accepted.

"Just remember," he said gruffly, "what you're doing now is holding
other guys' lives in your hands. Don't mess up."

Jade did her work carefully, both day and night, until her certificates of
course completion arrived in her e-mail. Then she tackled the three network news offices at Selene. Minolta/Bell, the largest, turned her down
cold; they had no job openings at the moment, they said, and they only
hired people with experience. BBC accepted her application with a polite
version of the classic, "Don't call us; we'll call you."

Solar News, the smallest of the three and the youngest, was an all-news
network. They paid much less than Jade was making as a truck driver. But
they had an opening for an assistant video editor. Jade took the job without thinking twice about it.

Zach Bonner shook his head warily when she told him she was quitting. "You sure you want to do this?"

"Yes," Jade said. "I'm sure."

He gave a sigh that was almost an exasperated snort. "Okay, kid. If things don't work out for you, come on back here and I'll see what I can do for you."

She had more than half expected him to say that, but his words still warmed her. She stood up on tiptoes and pecked a kiss on his cheek. He sputtered with mixed embarrassment and happiness.

Dr. Dinant was pleased that Jade was moving to a job belowground. "I still would like to do the procedure on you," she said, "before I finish my tour here and return home."

Jade put her off, hoping she would return to Earth and forget about her. Just as her adoptive mother had.

She started her new job, surprised that there were only six people in the entire Selene office of Solar News. Two of them were reporters, one male and one female, who went to the same hairdressing salon and actually appeared on screen now and then, when the network executives permitted such glory. Otherwise, their stories were "reported" by anchorpersons in Orlando who had never been to the Moon.

It took her nearly a year to work up the courage to tell her new boss about her idea of doing a biography of Sam Gunn.

"I've heard of him," said her boss, a middle-aged woman named Monica Bianco. "Some sort of a con man, wasn't he? A robber baron?"

Although Monica affected a veneer of newsroom cynicism, she could not hide her basic good nature from Jade for very long. The two women had much in common in addition to their jobs. Monica had come to Selene to escape pollution allergies that left her gasping helplessly more than half the year on Earth. When Jade confided that she could never go to Earth, her boss broke into tears at the memory of all she had been forced to leave behind. The two of them became true friends after that.

Monica was good-looking despite her years, Jade thought. She admitted to being over forty, and Jade wondered just how far beyond the Big Four-Oh she really was. Not that it mattered much. Especially in Selene, where men still outnumbered women by roughly three to one. Monica was a bit heavier than she ought to be, but her ample bosom and cheerful disposition kept lots of men after her. She confessed to Jade that she had been married twice. "I buried one and dumped the other," she said, without a trace of remorse. "Both bastards. I just seem to pick rotten SOBs for myself."

Jade had nothing to confess beyond the usual teenager's flings. So she told Monica what she knew of Sam Gunn and asked how she might get the decision-makers of Solar News to assign her to do a biography.

"Forget it, honey," advised Monica. "The only ideas they go for are the ones they think up for themselves—or steal from somebody they envy. Besides, they'd never let an inexperienced pup like you tackle an assignment like that."

Jade felt her heart sink. But then Monica added, "Unless . . ."

So several weeks later Jade found herself at dinner with Monica and Jim Gradowsky, the Solar News office chief. They sat at a cozy round table in a quiet corner of the Ristorante de la Luna. Of Selene's five eating establishments, the Ristorante was acknowledged to be the best bargain: lots of good food at modest prices. It was Jumbo Jim Gradowsky's favorite eatery.

Monica wore a black skirt and blouse with a scooped neckline. At Monica's insistence, Jade had spent a week's salary on a glittering green sheath that complemented her eyes. Now that she saw the checkered tablecloths and dripping candles, though, she thought that Monica had overdressed them both.

Gradowsky, who showed up in a wrinkled short-sleeved shirt and baggy slacks, did not seem to notice what they were wearing. He was called Jumbo Jim because of his girth. But never to his face.

"So you can never go Earthside," Gradowsky was saying through a mouthful of *coniglio cacciatore*. His open-collared shirt was already stained and sprinkled with the soup and salad courses.

"It's a bone condition," Jade replied. "Osteopetrosis."

Gradowsky took a tiny roasted rabbit leg in one big hand. Red gravy dripped onto his lap. "Isn't that what little old ladies get? Makes 'em stoop over?"

"That's osteo*porosis*," Jade corrected. "The bones get soft with age. I've got just the opposite problem. My bones are too brittle. They'd snap under a full Earth gravity. They call it Marble Bones."

He shook his head and dabbed at the grease around his mouth with a checkered napkin. "Gee, that's too bad. I could go back Earthside if I wanted to, but the medics say I'd hafta to lose forty-fifty pounds first."

Jade made a sympathetic noise.

"You know, Jim," said Monica, sitting on his other side, "Jade here's got a terrific idea for a special. If you could sell it back in Orlando it'd be quite a feather in your cap."

"Yeah? Really?"

Jade explained her hope to do a biography of Sam Gunn. Gradowsky was obviously cool to the idea, but Monica slid her chair closer to his and insisted that it was the kind of idea that Solar's upper echelons would go for.

"It could mean a boost for you," Monica said, leaning so close to Gradowsky that Jade could see her cleavage from across the table. "A big boost."

The two women went to the ladies' room together as the waiter cleared their table in preparation for dessert. Jade saw that there were greasy paw stains on Monica's skirt.

"You're not throwing yourself at him for me?" Jade asked.

Monica smiled. "Don't worry about it, honey. Jumbo's kind of cute, if you don't mind his table manners."

"Cute?"

"After three bottles of wine."

"Monica, I can't let you . . ."

The older woman smiled sweetly at Jade. "Don't give it another thought, child. Who knows, I might marry the bum and try to civilize him."

Thus it came to pass that Jim Gradowsky sold his idea of doing a biography of Sam Gunn to the top brass of the Solar News Network. He even won the responsibility of picking the reporter to handle the interviews.

Jade faced him alone in his office, a minuscule cubbyhole crammed with a desk, two computer terminals, a battered pseudo-leather couch, and a whole wall full of TV screens.

"Monica says you oughtta get the job of doing the Sam Gunn interviews," Gradowsky said, his eyes narrowing as Jade sat demurely on the couch.

She thought to herself, If he gets up from behind that desk I'll run out of here and to hell with the interviews. Or will I?

Gradowsky stayed in his creaking desk chair. "Well, I'm not sure that somebody with no real experience can handle the assignment. You're awfully young. . . ."

Jade made herself smile at him. "That's just the point. Most of Sam's friends—even his enemies—wouldn't talk to a regular news reporter. But they'll talk to me."

"Why's that?" Gradowsky seemed all business, thank goodness.

"I don't come across as a reporter. I'm a lunar worker, one of the guys."

"Hardly one of the *guys*." Gradowsky smirked.

The phone built into one of the computers chirped. Grunting, he leaned forward and punched a button on its keyboard.

Monica's face took form on a wall screen. "How's it going?" she asked cheerfully.

Gradowsky raised both hands, palms out, as if to show he was un-armed. "Okay so far. We're talkin'."

"Are we set for dinner tonight?"

"Yeah, sure. Where d'you wanna go?"

"I thought I'd cook for you tonight. How about my place at seven-thirty. You bring the wine."

Gradowsky grinned. "Great!"

"See you then."

When he turned back to Jade he was still grinning.

"Okay, listen up, kid. Here's what I'm prepared to do. There's a Russian living over at the retirement center next to Lunagrad. From what my con-tacts tell me, he knew Sam Gunn back in the old days, when Gunn was still a NASA astronaut. But he's never talked to anybody about it."

"Has anyone tried to interview him?" Jade asked.

"Yeah—BBC was after him for years but he always turned them down."

Jade clasped her hands together tightly, surprised to find that her palms were sweating.

"You get the Russkie to talk and the assignment's yours. Fair enough?"

She nodded, almost breathless. "Fair enough," she managed to say.

Diamond Sam

"A THIEF," SAID GRIGORI ALEKSANDROVICH PROKOV. "A thief and a blackmailer."

He said it flatly, without emotion, the way a man might observe that the sky is blue or that grass is green. A fact of life. He said it in excellent English, marred only slightly by the faint trace of a Russian accent.

Jade wrinkled her nose slightly. There was neither blue sky nor green grass here in the Leonov Center for Retired Heroes of the Russian Federation, although there was a distinctly earthy odor to the place.

"Sam Gunn," Prokov muttered. His voice seemed weak, almost quavering. The weakening voice of a dying old man. Then he gave a disdainful snort. "Not even the other capitalists liked him!"

They were sitting on a bench made of native lunar stone near the edge of the surface dome, as far away from the yawning entrance to the underground retirement center as possible. To Jade, that dark entrance looked like the opening of a crypt.

The floor of the dome was bare lunar rock that had been glazed by plasma torches and smoothed to a glassy finish. She wondered how many elderly Heroes of the Russian Federation slipped and broke their necks. Was that their government's ultimate retirement benefit?

The wide curving window in front of the bench looked out on absolute desolation: the barren expanse of the Ocean of Storms, a pockmarked undulating surface without a sign of life as far as the eye could see. Nothing but rocks and bare lunar regolith broiling in the harsh sunlight. The sky remained black, though, and above the strangely close horizon hung the tantalizing blue and white-streaked globe of Earth, a lonely haven of color and life in the stark cold darkness of space.

For the tenth time in the past ten minutes Jade fumbled with the heater control of her electrified jumpsuit. She felt the chill of that merciless vacuum seeping through the tinted glassteel of the big window. She strained her ears for the telltale hiss of an air leak. There were rumors that maintenance at the Leonov Center was far from top-rate.

Prokov seemed impervious to the cold. Or perhaps, rather, he was so accustomed to it that he never noticed it anymore. He was very old, his face sunken in like a rotting Jack-o'-lantern, wrinkled even across his utterly bald pate. The salmon-pink coveralls he wore seemed brand new, as if he had put them on just for this visit from a stranger. Or had the managers of the Center insisted that he wear new clothes whenever a visitor called? Whichever, she saw that the outfit was at least a full size too big for the man. He seemed to be shrinking, withering away before her eyes.

But his eyes glittered at her balefully. "Why do you ask about Sam Gunn? I was given to understand that you were only a student doing a thesis on the history of early space flight."

"That was a bit of a white lie," Jade said, trying to keep the tremble of fear out of her voice. "I—I'm actually trying to do a biography of Sam Gunn."

"That despicable money-grubber," Prokov muttered.

"Would you help me? Please?"

"Why should I?" the old man snapped.

Jade made a little shrug.

"I have never spoken to anyone about Sam Gunn. Not in more than thirty years."

"I know," Jade said.

Frowning, Prokov examined her intently. A little elf, he thought. A child-woman in a pale green jumpsuit. How frightened she looks! Such beautiful red hair. Such entrancing green eyes.

"Ah," he sighed. "If I were a younger man . . ."

Jade smiled kindly at him. "You were a hero then, weren't you? A cosmonaut and a Hero of the Russian Federation."

His eyes glimmered with distant memories.

"Sam Gunn," he repeated. "Thief. Liar. Warmonger. He almost caused World War III, did you know that?"

"No!" said Jade, truly surprised. She checked the recorder in her belt buckle and slid a few centimeters closer to the old man, to make certain that the miniaturized device did not miss any of his words.

There was hardly any other noise in the big, dark, gloomy dome. Far off in the shadows sat a couple of other old people, as still as mummies, as if frozen by time and the indifference that comes from having outlived everyone you loved.

"A nuclear holocaust, that's what your Sam Gunn would have started. If not for *me*," Prokov tapped the folds of cloth that covered his sunken chest, "the whole world might have gone up in radioactive smoke thirty years ago."

"I never knew," said Jade.

Without any further encouragement Prokov began to speak in his whispery trembling voice.

YOU MUST REALIZE that we were then in the grip of what the media journalists now call the Neo-Cold War. When the old Soviet Union broke up, back in the last century, Russia nearly disappeared in chaos and anarchy. But new leaders arose, strong and determined to bring Russia back to its rightful position as one of the world's leading powers. We were proud to be part of that rebirth of Russian strength and courage. *I* was proud to be part of it myself.

I was commander of Mir 5, the largest Russian space station ever. Not like that political compromise, the International Space Station. Mir 5 was Russian, entirely Russian.

My rank was full colonel. My crew had been in space for 638 days and it was my goal to make it two full years—730 days. It would be a new record, fourteen men in orbit for two full years. I would be picked to command the Mars mission if I could get my men to the two-year mark. A big if.

Sam Gunn, as you know, was an American astronaut at that time. Officially he was a crew member of the NASA space station Freedom. Secretly he worked for the CIA, I am certain. No other explanation fits the facts.

You must understand that despite all the comforts that Russian technology could provide, life aboard Mir 5 was—well, spartan. We worked in shifts and slept in hot beds. You know, when one man finished his sleep shift he got out of his zipper bag and a man who had just finished his work shift would get into the bag to sleep. Sixteen hours of work, eight of sleep. Four bunks for twelve crewmen. It was all strictly controlled by ground command.

Naturally, as colonel in command I had my own bunk and my own private cubicle. This was not a deviation from comradely equality; it was necessary and all the crew recognized that fact. My political officer had his own private cubicle as well.

Believe me, after the first eighteen months of living under such stringencies life became very tense inside Mir 5. Fourteen men cooped up inside a set of aluminum cans with nothing but work, no way to relieve their tedium, forced to exercise when there were no other tasks to do—

the tension was becoming dangerously high. Sam must have known that. I was told that the CIA employed thousands of psychologists in those days.

His first visit to our station was made to look like an accident. He waited until I was asleep to call us.

My second-in-command, a thickheaded technician from Omsk named Korolev, shook me awake none too gently.

"Sir!" he said, pummeling my zippered bag. "There's an American asking us for help!"

It was like being the toothpaste in a tube while some big oaf tries to squeeze you out.

"An Ameri—Stop that! I'm awake! Get your hands off me!"

Fortunately, I slept in my coveralls. I simply unzipped the bag and followed Korolev toward the command center. He was a bulky fellow, a wrestler back at home and a decent electronics technician up here. But he had been made second-in-command by seniority only. His brain was not swift enough for such responsibilities.

The station was composed of nine modules—nine aluminum cylinders joined together by airlocks. It was all under zero gravity. The Americans had not even started to build their fancy rotating stations yet.

We floated through the hatch of the command center, where four more of my men were hovering by the communications console. It was cramped and hot; six men in the center were at least two too many.

I immediately heard why they had awakened me.

"Hey, are you guys gonna help me out or let me die?" a sharp-edged voice was rasping on our radio receiver. "I got a dead friggin' OTV here and I'm gonna drift right past you and out into the Van Allen Belt and fry my *cojones* if you don't come and get me."

That was my introduction to Sam Gunn.

Zworkin, my political officer, was already in contact with ground control, reporting on the incident. On my own authority—and citing the reciprocal rescue treaty that had been in effect for many decades—I sent one of our orbital transfer vehicles with two of my best men to rescue the American.

His vehicle's rocket propellant line had ruptured, with the same effect as if your automobile fuel line had split apart. His rocket engine died and he was drifting without propulsion power.

"Goddamn cheap Hong Kong parts." Sam kept up a running monologue all through our rescue flight. "Bad enough we gotta fly birds built by the lowest goddamn bidders, but now they're buying parts from friggin' toy manufacturers! Whole goddamn vehicle works like something put together from a Mattel kit by a brain-damaged chimpanzee. Those mother-humpers in Washington don't give a shit whose neck they put on the mother-humpin' line as long as it ain't theirs."

And so on, through the entire three hours it took for us to send out our transfer vehicle, take him aboard it, and bring him safely to the station.

Once he came through the airlock and actually set foot inside Mir 5 his tone changed. I should say that "set foot" is a euphemism. We were all weightless, and Sam floated into the docking chamber, turned himself a full three-hundred-sixty degrees around, and grinned at us.

All fourteen of us had crowded into the docking chamber to see him. This was the most excitement we had had since Boris Malenovsky's diarrhea, six months earlier.

"Hey!" said Sam. "You guys are as short as me!"

No word of thanks. No formal greetings or offers of international friendship. His first words upon being rescued dealt with our heights.

He was no taller than my own 160 centimeters, although he claimed 165. He pushed himself next to Korolev, the biggest man of our crew, who stood almost 173 centimeters, according to the medical files. Naturally, under zero-gravity conditions Korolev—and all of us—had grown an extra two or three centimeters.

"I'm just about as tall as you are!" Sam exulted.

He flitted from one member of our crew to another comparing heights. It was difficult to make an accurate measurement because he kept bobbing like a floating cork, thanks to the zero gravity. In other words, he cheated. I should have recognized this as the key to his character immediately. Unfortunately, I did not.

Neither did Zworkin, although he later claimed that he knew all along that Sam was a spy.

All in all, Sam was not unpleasant. He was friendly. He was noisy. I remember thinking, in those first few moments he was aboard our station, that it was like having a pet monkey visit us. Amusing. Diverting. He made us laugh, which was something we had not done in many weeks.

Sam's face was almost handsome, but not quite. His lips were a bit too thin and his jaw a little too round. His eyes were bright and glowing like a fanatic's. His hair bristled like a thicket of wires, brownish red. His tongue was never still.

Most of my crew understood English well enough so that Sam had lit-

tle trouble expressing himself to us. Which he did incessantly. Sam kept
up a constant chatter about the shoddy construction of his orbital transfer vehicle, the solid workmanship of our station, the lack of aesthetics in
spacecraft design, the tyranny of ground controllers who forbade alco-
holic beverages aboard space stations, this, that and the other. He even
managed to say a few words that sounded almost like gratitude.

"I guess giving you guys a chance to save my neck makes a nice break
in the routine for you, huh? Not much else exciting going on around here,
is there?"

He talked so much and so fast that it never occurred to any of us, not
even to Zworkin, to ask why he had been flying so near to us. As far as I
knew, there were no Western satellites in orbits this close to our station.
Or there should not have been.

Next to his machine-gun dialogue the thing that impressed my men
most about this American astronaut was his uniform. Like ours, it was
basically a one-piece coverall, quite utilitarian. Like us, he bore a name
patch sewn over his left chest pocket. There the similarities ended.

Sam's coveralls were festooned with all sorts of fancy patches and buttons. Not merely one shoulder patch with his mission insignia. He had
patches and insignia running down both sleeves and across his torso,
front and back, like the tattooed man in the circus. Dragons, comic-book
rocket ships, silhouettes of naked women, buttons that bore pictures of
video stars, strange symbols and slogans that made no sense to me, such
as "Beam me up, Scotty, there's no intelligent life down here" and "King
Kong died for our sins."

Finally I ordered my men back to their duties and told Sam to accompany me to the control center.

Zworkin objected. "It is not wise to allow him to see the control center," he said in Russian.

"Would you prefer," I countered, "that he be allowed to roam through
the laboratories? Or perhaps the laser module?"

Most of my own crew was not allowed to enter the laser module. Only
men with specific military clearance were permitted there. And most of
the laboratories, you see, were testing systems that would one day be the
heart of our Red Shield antimissile system. Even the diamond manufacturing experiment was a Red Shield program, according to my mission
orders.

Zworkin did not reply to my question. He merely stared at me sullenly.
He had a sallow, pinched face that was blemished with acne—unusual for

a man of his age. The crew joked behind his back that he was still a virgin.

"The visitor stays with me, Nikolai Nikolaivich," I told him. "Where I can watch him."

Unfortunately, I had to listen to Sam as well as watch him.

I ordered my communications technician to contact the NASA space station and allow Sam to tell them what had happened. Meanwhile Zworkin reported again to ground control. It was not a simple matter to transfer Sam back to the NASA station. First we had to apprise ground control of the situation, and they had to inform Moscow, where the American embassy and the International Astronautics Commission were duly briefed. Hours dragged by and our work schedule became hopelessly snarled.

I must admit, however, that Sam was a good guest. He handed out trinkets that he fished from the deep pockets of his coveralls. A miniature penknife to one of the men who had rescued him. A pocket computer to the other, programmed to play a dozen different games when it was connected to a display screen. A small flat tin of rock candy. A Russian-English dictionary the size of your thumb.

That dictionary should have alerted my suspicions. But I confess that I was more concerned with getting this noisy intrusion off my station and back where he belonged.

Sam stayed a day. Two days. Teleconferences crackled between Washington and Moscow, Moscow and Geneva, Washington and Geneva, ground control to our station, our station to the NASA station. Meanwhile Sam had made himself at home and even started to learn how to tell jokes in Russian. He was particularly interested in dirty jokes, of course, being the kind of man he was. He began to peel off some of the patches and buttons that adorned his coveralls and hand them out as presents. My crewmen especially lusted after the pictures of beautiful video stars.

He had taken over the galley, where he was teaching my men how to play dice in zero gravity, when I at last received permission to send him back to the American station. Not an instant too soon, I thought.

Still, dear old Mir 5 became suddenly very quiet and dreary once we had packed him off in one of our own reliable transfer craft. We returned to our tedious tasks and the damnable exercise machines. The men growled and sulked at each other. Months of boredom and hard work stretched ahead of us. I could feel the tension pulling at my crew. I felt it myself.

But not for long.

Less than a week later Korolev again rousted me from my zipper bunk. "He's back! The American!"

This time Sam did not pretend to need an emergency rescue. He had flown an orbital transfer vehicle to our station and matched orbit. His OTV was hovering a few hundred meters alongside us.

"Permission to come aboard?" His voice was unmistakable. "Unofficially?"

I glanced at Zworkin, who was of course right beside me in the command center. Strangely, Nikolai Nikolaivich nodded. Nothing is unofficial with him, I knew. Yet he did not object to the American making an "unofficial" visit.

I went to the docking chamber while Sam floated over to us. The airlock of his craft would not fit our docking mechanism, so he went EVA in his pressure suit and jetted across to us using his backpack maneuvering unit.

"I was in the neighborhood so I though I'd drop by for a minute," Sam wisecracked once he got through our airlock and slid up the visor of his helmet.

"Why are you in this area?" Zworkin asked, eyes slitted in his pimpled face.

"To observe your laser tests," replied Sam, grinning. "You guys don't think our intelligence people don't know what you're up to, do you?"

"We are not testing lasers!"

"Not today, I know. Don't worry about it, Ivan, I'm not spying on you, for chrissakes."

"My name is not Ivan!"

"I just came over to thank you guys for saving my ass." Sam turned slightly, his entire body pivoting weightlessly toward me. He reached into the pouches on the legs of his suit. "A couple of small tokens of my gratitude."

He pulled out two small plastic jewel cases and handed them to me. Videodiscs.

"Latest Hollywood releases," Sam explained. "With my thanks."

In a few minutes he was gone. Zworkin insisted on looking at the videos before anyone else could see them. "Probably capitalist propaganda," he grumbled.

I insisted on seeing them with him. I was not going to let him keep them all for himself.

One of the videos was the very popular film, *Rocky XVIII,* in which the geriatric former prizefighter is rejuvenated and gets out of his wheelchair to defeat a nine-foot-tall robot for the heavyweight championship of the solar system.

"Disgusting," spat Zworkin.

"But it will be good to show the crew how low the capitalists sink in their pursuit of money," I said.

He gave me a sour look but did not argue.

The second video was a rock musical that featured decadent music at extreme decibel levels, decadent youths wearing outlandish clothes and weird hairdos, and decadent young women wearing hardly any clothes at all. Their gyrations were especially disturbing, no matter from which point of view you looked at them.

"Definitely not for the crew to see," said Zworkin. None of us ever saw that video again. He kept it. But now and then I heard the music, faintly, from his private cubicle during the shifts when he was supposed to be sleeping. Mysteriously, his acne began to clear up.

Almost two weeks afterward Sam popped up again. Again he asked permission to come aboard, claiming this time he was on a routine inspection mission of a commsat in geosynchronous orbit and had planned his return to the NASA station to take him close to us. He was a remarkable pilot, that much I must admit.

"Got a couple more videos for you," he added, almost as an afterthought.

Zworkin immediately okayed his visit. The rest of my crew, who had cheered the rejuvenated Rocky in his proletarian struggle against the stainless-steel symbol of western imperialism (as we saw it), welcomed him aboard.

Sam stayed for a couple of hours. We fed him a meal of borscht, soysteak and ice cream. With plenty of hot tea.

"That's the best ice cream I've ever had!" Sam told me as we made our weightless way from the galley back to the docking chamber, where he had left his pressure suit.

"We get fresh supplies every week," I said. "Our only luxury."

"I never knew you guys had such great ice cream." He was really marveling over it.

"Moscow is famous for its ice cream," I replied.

With a shake of his head that made his whole body sway slightly, Sam admitted, "Boy, we got nothing like that back at the NASA station."

"Would you like to bring some back to your station?" I asked. Innocent fool that I am, I did not realize that he had maneuvered me into making the offer.

"Gee, yeah," he said, like a little boy.

I had one of the men pack him a container of ice cream while he struggled into his pressure suit. Zworkin was off screening the two new videos Sam had brought, so I did not bother him with the political question of offering a gift in return for Sam's gift.

As he put his helmet over his head, Sam said to me in a low voice, "Each of those videos is a double feature."

"A what?"

Leaning close to me, so that the technician in charge of the docking airlock could not hear, he whispered, "Play the disks at half speed and you'll see another whole video. But *you* look at them yourself first. Don't let that sourball of a political officer see it or he'll confiscate them both."

I felt puzzled, and my face must have shown it. Sam merely grinned, patted me on the shoulder and said, "Thanks for the ice cream."

Then he left.

It took a bit of ingenuity to figure out how to play the disks at half speed. It took even more cleverness to arrange to look at them in private, without Zworkin or any of the other crew members hanging over my shoulders. But I did it.

The "second feature" on each of the tapes was pornographic filth. Disgusting sexual acrobatics featuring beautiful women with large breasts and apparently insatiable appetites. I watched the degrading spectacles several times, despite stern warnings from my conscience. If I had been cursed with acne these videos would undoubtedly have solved the problem overnight. Especially the one with the trapeze.

For the first time since I had been a teenager buying contraband blue jeans I faced a moral dilemma. Should I tell Zworkin about these secret pornographic films? He had seen only the normal, "regular" features on each tape: an ancient John Wayne western and a brand-new comedy about a computer that takes over Wall Street.

In my own defense I say only that I was thinking of the good of my crew when I made my decision. The men had been in orbit for nearly 650 days with almost two full months to go before we could return to our loved ones. The pornographic films might help them to bear their loneliness and perform better at their tasks, I reasoned.

But only if Zworkin did not know about them.

I decided to chance it. One by one I let the crew in on the little secret.

Morale improved six hundred percent. Performance and productivity rose equally. The men smiled and laughed a lot more. I told myself it was just as much because they were pulling one over on the puritanical Zworkin as because they were watching the buxom Oral Roberta and her insatiable girlfriend Electric (AC/DC) Edna.

Sam returned twice more, swapping videos for ice cream. He was our friend. He apparently had an inexhaustible supply of videos, each of them a "double feature." While Zworkin spent the next several weeks happily watching the regular features on each disk and perspiring every time he saw a girl in a bikini, the rest of watched the erotic adventures of airline stewardesses, movie starlets, models, housewife-hookers, and other assorted and sordid specimens of female depravity.

The days flew by with each man counting the hours until Sam showed up with another few videos. We stopped eating ice cream so that we would have plenty to give him in return.

Then Sam sprang his trap on us. On me.

"Listen," he said as he was suiting up in the docking chamber, preparing to leave, "next time, how about sticking a couple of those diamonds you're making into the ice cream."

I flinched with surprise and automatically looked over my shoulder at the technician standing by to operate the airlock. He was busy admiring the four new videocassettes Sam had brought, wondering what was in them as he studied their labels.

"What are you talking about?" I meant to say it out loud but it came out as a whispered croak.

Sam flashed a cocky grin at me. "Come on, everybody knows you guys are making gem-quality diamonds out of methane gas in your zero-gee facility. Pump a little extra methane in and make me a couple to sell Earthside. I'll split the profits with you fifty-fifty."

"Impossible," I snapped. Softly.

His smile became shrewd. "Look, Greg old pal, I'm not asking for any military secrets. Just a couple of stones I can peddle back on Earth. We can both make a nice wad of money."

"The diamonds we manufacture are not of gemstone quality," I lied.

"Let my friends on Forty-seventh Street decide what quality they are," Sam whispered.

"No."

He puffed out a sad sigh. "This has nothing to do with politics, Greg. It's business. Capitalism."

I shook my head hard enough to sway my entire body.

Sam seemed to accept defeat. "Okay. It's a shame, though. Hell, even your leaders in the Kremlin are making money selling their biographies to western publishers. Capitalism is swooping in on you."

I said nothing.

He pulled the helmet over his head, fastened the neck seal. But before sliding down his visor he asked, quite casually, "What happens if Zworkin finds out what's on the videos you guys have been watching?"

My face went red. I could feel the heat flaming my cheeks.

"Just a couple of little diamonds, pal. A couple of carats. That's not so much to ask for, is it?"

He went through the airlock and jetted back to his own craft. I would have gladly throttled him at that moment.

Now I had a *real* dilemma on my hands. Give in to Sam's blackmail or face Zworkin and the authorities back on the ground. It would not only be me who would be in trouble, but my entire crew. They did not deserve to suffer because of my bad decisions, but they would. We would all spend the rest of our lives shoveling cow manure in Siberia or running mining machines on the Moon.

I had been corrupted and I knew it. Oh, I had the best of motives, the loftiest of intentions. But how would they appear next to the fact that I had allowed my crew to watch disgusting pornographic films provided by a capitalist agent of the CIA? Corruption, pure and simple. I would be lucky to be sentenced to Siberia.

I gave in to Sam's demands. I told myself it was for the sake of my crew, but it was to save my own neck, and to save my dear family from disgrace. I had the technicians make three extra small diamonds and embedded them in the ice cream when Sam made his next visit.

That was the exact week, naturally, when the Russian Federation and the western powers were meeting in Geneva to decide on deployment of space weapons. Our own Red Shield system and the American Star Wars system were well into the testing phase. We had conducted a good many of the tests ourselves aboard Mir 5. Now the question was, should each side begin to deploy its own system or should we hammer out some method of working cooperatively?

Sam returned a few days later. I did not want to see him, but was afraid not to. He seemed happy and cheerful, as usual, and carried no less than six new videos with him. I spoke to him very briefly, very coldly. He seemed not to be bothered at all. He laughed and joked. And passed me a note on a tiny scrap of paper as he handed me the new videos.

I read the note in the privacy of my cubicle, after he left. "Good stuff. Worth a small fortune. How many can you provide each week?"

I was accustomed to the weightlessness of zero gravity, but at that instant I felt as if I were falling into a deep, dark pit, falling and falling down into an utterly black well that had no bottom.

To make matters worse, after a few days of progress the conference at Geneva seemed to hit a snag for some unfathomable reason. The negotiations stopped dead and the diplomats began to snarl at each other in the old Cold War fashion. The world was shocked. We received orders to accelerate our tests of the Red Shield laser that had been installed in the laboratory module at the aft end of our station.

We watched the TV news broadcasts from every part of the world (without letting Zworkin or ground control know about it, of course.) Everyone was frightened at the sudden intransigence in Geneva.

Zworkin summed up our fears. "The imperialists want an excuse to strike us with their nuclear missiles before our Red Shield defense is deployed."

I had to admit that he was probably right. What scared me was the thought that *we* might strike at *them* before their Star Wars defense was deployed. Either way it meant the same thing: nuclear holocaust.

Even thickheaded Korolev seemed worried. "Will we go to war?" he kept asking. "Will we go to war?" No one knew.

Needless to say, it was clear that if we did go to war Mir 5 would be a sitting duck for Yankee antisatellite weapons. As everyone knew, the war on the ground would begin with strikes against space stations and satellites.

To make matters even worse, in the midst of our laser test preparations Sam sent a radio message that he was on his way and would rendezvous with our station in three hours. He said he had "something special" for us.

The crisis in Geneva meant nothing to him, it seemed. He was coming for "business as usual." Zworkin had been right all along about him. Sam was a spy. I was certain of it now.

A vision formed in my mind. I would personally direct the test of the Red Shield laser. Its high-energy beam would happen to strike the incoming American spacecraft. Sam Gunn would be fried like a scrawny chicken in a hot oven. A regrettable accident. Yes. It would solve my problem.

Except—it would create such a furor on Earth that the conference in

Geneva would break up altogether. It could be the spark that would lead to war, nuclear war.

Yet—Sam had no business flying a Yankee spacecraft so close to a Soviet station. Both the U.S. and the Russian Federation had clearly proclaimed that the regions around their stations were sovereign territory, not to be violated by the other side's craft. Sam's visits to Mir 5 were strictly illegal, secret, clandestine, except for his first "emergency" visit. If we fried him we would be within out legal rights.

On the other hand—could the entire crew remain silent about Sam's many visits? Would Zworkin stay silent or would he denounce me once we had returned to Mother Russia?

On the *other* hand—what difference would any of that make if we triggered nuclear war?

That is why I found myself sweating in the laser laboratory, a few hours after Sam's call. He knew that we were going to test the laser, he had to know. That was why he was cheerfully heading our way at this precise point in time.

The laboratory was chilly. The three technicians operating the giant laser wore bulky sweaters over their coveralls and gloves with the fingers cut so they could manipulate their sensitive equipment properly.

This section of the station was a complete module in itself; it could be detached and de-orbited, if necessary, and a new section put in its place. The huge laser filled the laboratory almost completely. If we had not been in zero gravity it would have been impossible for the technicians to climb into the nooks and crannies necessary to service all the hardware.

One wide optical-quality window gave me a view of the black depths of space. But no window could withstand the incredible intensity of the laser's high-power beam. The beam was instead directed through a polished copper pipe to the outside of the station's hull, which is why the laboratory was always so cold. It was impossible to keep the module decently warm; the heat leaked out through the laser beam channel. On the outer end of that channel was the aiming mirror (also highly polished copper) that directed the beam toward its target—hypothetical or actual.

One day we would have mirrors and a laser output window of pure diamond, once we had learned how to fabricate large sheets of the stuff in zero gravity. That day had not yet come. It seemed that ground control was more interested in growing gem-quality diamonds than large sheets.

I had calculated Sam's approach trajectory back at the control center and pecked the numbers into my hand computer. Now, as the technicians labored and grumbled over their big laser I fed those coordinates into the laser aiming system. As far as the technicians knew, they were firing their multimegawatt beam into empty space, as usual. Only I knew that when they fired the laser its beam would destroy the approaching Yankee spacecraft and kill Sam Gunn.

The moments ticked by as I sweated coldly, miserable with apprehension and—yes, I admit it freely—with guilt. I had set the target for the laser's aiming mirror. The big slab of polished copper hanging outside the station's hull was already tracking Sam's trajectory, turning ever so slightly each second. The relays directing its motion clicked inside the laboratory like the clicks of a quartz clock, like the tapping of a Chinese water torture.

Then I heard the sighing sound that happens when an airtight hatch between two modules of the station is opened. Turning, I saw the hatch swinging open, its heavy hinges groaning slightly. Zworkin pushed through and floated over the bulky master control console to my side.

"You show an unusual interest in this test," he said softly.

My insides blazed as if I had stuck my hand into the power outlet. "There is the crisis in Geneva," I replied. "Ground control wants this test to proceed flawlessly."

"Will it?"

I did not trust myself to say anything more. I merely nodded.

Zworkin watched the muttering technicians for a few endless moments, then asked, "Do you find it odd that the American is approaching us *exactly* at the time our test is scheduled?"

I nodded once again, keeping my eyes fixed on the empty point in space where I imagined the beam and Sam's spacecraft would meet.

"I received an interesting message from Moscow, less than an hour ago," Zworkin said. I dared not look into his face, but his voice sounded tense, brittle. "The rumor is that the Geneva conference has struck a reef made of pure diamond."

"What?" That spun me around. He was not gloating. In fact he looked just as worried as I felt. No, not even worried. Frightened. The tone of voice that I had assumed was sarcasm was actually the tight dry voice of fear.

"This is unconfirmed rumor, mind you," Zworkin said, "but what they are saying is that the NATO intelligence service has learned we are manufacturing pure diamond crystals in zero gravity, diamond crystals that can be made large enough to be used as mirrors and windows for extremely high-power lasers. They are concerned that we have moved far ahead of them in this key area of technology."

Just at that instant Sam's cocky voice chirped over the station's intercom speakers. "Hey there friends and neighbors, here's your Hollywood delivery service comin' atcha."

The laser mirror clicked again. And again. One of the technicians floated back to the console at my side and pressed the three big red rocker switches that turn on the electrical power, one after the other. The action made his body rise up to the low ceiling of the laboratory each time. He rose and descended slowly, up and down, like a bubble trapped in a sealed glass.

A low whine came from the massive power generators. Even though they were off in a separate module of the station I felt their vibration.

In my mind's eye I could see a thin yellow line that represented Sam's trajectory approaching us. And a heavier red line, the fierce beam of our laser, reaching out to meet it.

"Got something more than videos, this trip," Sam was chattering. "Managed to lay my hands on some really neat electronic toys, interactive games. You'll love 'em. Got the latest sports videos, too, and a bucketful of real-beef hamburgers. All you do is pop 'em in your microwave. Brought mustard and ketchup too. Better'n that soy stuff you guys been eating. . . ."

He was talking his usual blue streak. I was glad that the communications technicians knew to scrub his transmissions from the tapes that ground control monitored. Dealing with Zworkin was bad enough.

Through his inane gabbling I could hear the mirror relays clicking like the rifles of a firing squad being cocked, one by one. Sam approached us blithely unaware of what awaited him. I pictured his spacecraft being hit by the laser beam, exploding, Sam and his videos and hamburgers all transformed instantly into an expanding red-hot ball of bloody vapor.

I reached over and pounded the master switch on the console. Just like the technician I bounded toward the ceiling. The power generators wound down and went silent.

Zworkin stared up at me openmouthed as I cracked my head painfully and floated down toward him again.

I could not kill Sam. I could not murder him in cold blood, no matter what the consequences might be.

"What are you doing?" Zworkin demanded.

Putting out a hand to grasp the console and steady myself, I said, "We should not run this test while the Yankee spy is close enough to watch."

He eyed me shrewdly, then called to the two dumbfounded technicians. "Out! Both of you! Until your commander calls for you again."

Shrugging and exchanging confused looks, the two young men left the laboratory module. Zworkin pushed the hatch shut behind them, leaning against it as he gave me a long quizzical stare.

"Grigori Aleksandrovich," he said at last, "we must do something about this American. If ground control ever finds out about him—if *Moscow* ever finds out . . ."

"What was it you said about the diamond crystals?" I asked. "Do you think the imperialists know about our experiments here?"

"Of course they know! And this Yankee spy is at the heart of the matter."

"What should we do?"

Zworkin rubbed his chin but said nothing. I could not helping thinking, absurdly, that his acne had almost totally disappeared.

So we allowed Sam aboard the station once again and I brought him immediately to my private cubicle.

"Cripes!" he chirped. "I've seen bigger coffins. Is this the best that the workers' paradise can do for you?"

"No propaganda now," I whispered sternly. "And no more blackmail. You will not return to this station again and you will not get any more diamonds from me."

"And no more ice cream?" He seemed entirely unconcerned with the seriousness of the situation.

"No more anything!" I said, straining to make it as strong as I could while still whispering. "Your visits here are finished. Over and done with."

Sam made a rueful grin and wormed his right hand into the hip pocket of his coveralls. "Read this," he said, handing me a slip of paper.

It had two numbers on it, both of them in six digits.

"The first is your private bank account number at the Bank of Zurich, in Switzerland."

"Russian citizens are not allowed to . . ."

"The second number," Sam went on, "is the amount of money deposited in your account, in Swiss francs."

"I told you, I am not—" I stopped and looked at the second number again. I was not certain of the exchange ratio between Swiss francs and rubles, but six digits are six digits.

Sam laughed softly. "Listen. My friends in New York have friends in

Switzerland. That's how I set up the account for you. It's your half of the profit from those little stones you gave me."

"I don't believe it. You are attempting to bribe me."

His look became pitying. "Greg, old pal, three-quarters of your Kremlin leaders have accounts in Switzerland. Don't you realize that the big conference in Geneva is stalled over—"

"Over your report to the CIA that we are manufacturing diamonds here in this station!" I hissed. "You are a spy, admit it!"

He spread his hands in the universal gesture of confession. "Okay, so I've passed some info over to the IDA."

"Don't you mean CIA?"

Sam blinked with surprise. "CIA? Why in hell would I want to talk to those spooks? I'm dealing with the IDA."

"Intelligence Defense Agency," I surmised.

With an annoyed shake of his head, "Naw—the International Diamond Association. The diamond cartel. You know, DeBeers and those guys."

I was too stunned with surprise to say anything.

"The cartel knew you were doing zero-gravity experiments up here, but they thought it was for diamond film and optical quality diamond to use on your high-power lasers. Once my friends in New York saw that you were also making gem-quality stones, they sent word hotfooting to Amsterdam."

"The international diamond cartel . . ."

"That's right, pal," said Sam. "They don't want to see diamonds manufactured in space kicking the bottom out of their market."

"But the crisis in Geneva," I mumbled.

Sam laughed. "The argument in Geneva is between the diamond cartel and your own government. It's got nothing to do with Star Wars or Red Shield. They've forgotten all about that. Now they're talking about *money*!"

I could not believe what he was saying. "Our leaders would never stoop—"

Sam silenced me with a guffaw. "Your leaders are haggling with the cartel like a gang of housewives at a warehouse sale. Your president is talking with the cartel's leaders right now over a private two-way fiber-optic link."

"How do you know this?"

He reached into the big pocket on the thigh of his suit. "Special video recording. I brought it just for you." With a sly smile he added, "Can't trust those guys in Amsterdam, you know."

It was difficult to catch my breath. My head was swimming.

"Listen to me, Greg. Your leaders are going to join the diamond cartel; they're just haggling over the price."

"Impossible!"

"Hard to believe that good socialists would help the evil capitalists rig world prices for diamonds? But that's what's going on right now, so help me. And once they've settled on their terms, the conference in Geneva will get back to dealing with the easy questions, like nuclear war."

"You're lying. I can't believe that you are telling me the truth,"

He shrugged good-naturedly. "Look at the video. Watch what happens in Geneva. Then, once things settle down, you and I can start doing business again."

I must have shaken my head without consciously realizing it.

"Don't want to leave all those profits to the cartel, do you? We can make a fair-sized piece of change—as long as we stay small enough so the cartel won't notice us. That's still a lot of money, pal."

"Never," I said. And I meant it. To do what he asked would mean working against my own nation, my own people, my own government. If the secret police ever found out!

I personally ushered Sam back to the docking compartment and off the station. And never allowed him back on Mir 5 again, no matter how he pleaded and wheedled over the radio.

After several weeks he finally realized that I would not deal with him, that when Grigori Aleksandrovich Prokov says "never" that is exactly what I mean.

"Okay friends," his radio voice said, the last time he tried to contact us. "Guess I'll just have to find some other way to make my first million. So long, Greg. Enjoy the workers' paradise, pal."

THE OLD MAN'S tone had grown distinctly wistful. He stopped, made a deep wheezing sigh, and ran a liver-spotted hand over his wrinkled pate.

Jade had forgotten the chill of the big lunar dome. Leaning slightly closer to Prokov, she asked:

"And that was the last you saw or heard of Sam Gunn?"

"Yes," said the Russian. "And good riddance, too."

"What happened after that?"

Prokov's aged face twisted unhappily. "What happened? Everything went exactly as he said it would. The conference in Geneva started up again, and East and West reached a new understanding. My crew achieved its mission goal; we spent two full years in Mir 5 and then went home. The Russian Federation became a partner in the international diamond cartel."

"And you went to Mars," Jade prompted.

Prokov's wrinkled face became bitter. "No. I was not picked to command the Mars expedition. Zworkin never denounced me, never admitted his own involvement with Sam, but his report was damning enough to knock me out of the Mars mission. The closest I got to Mars was a weather observation station in Antarctica!"

"Wasn't your president at that time the one who—"

"The one who retired to Switzerland after he stepped down from leading the nation? Yes. He is living there still like a bloated plutocrat."

"And you never dealt with Sam Gunn again?"

"Never! I told him never and that is exactly what I meant. Never."

"Just that brief contact with him was enough to wreck your career."

Prokov nodded stonily.

"Yet," Jade mused, "in a way it was *you* who got Russia into partnership with the diamond cartel. That must have been worth hundreds of millions each year to your government."

The old man's only reply was a bitter, "Pah!"

"What happened to your Swiss bank account? The one Sam started for you?"

Prokov waved a hand in a gesture that swept the lunar dome and asked, "How do you think I can afford to live here?"

Jade felt herself frown with puzzlement. "I thought the Leonov Center was free. . . ."

"Yes, of course it is. A retirement center for Heroes of the Russian Federation. Absolutely free! Unless you want some real beef in your Stroganoff. That costs extra. Or an electric blanket for your bed. Or chocolates—chocolates from Switzerland are the best of all, did you know that?"

"You mean that your Swiss bank account . . ."

"It is an annuity," said Prokov. "Not much money, but a nice little annuity to pay for some of the extra frills. The money sits there in the bank and every month the faithful Swiss gnomes send me the interest by e-mail. Compared to the other Heroes living here I am a well-to-do man. I can even buy vodka for them now and then."

Jade suppressed a smile. "So Sam's bank deposit is helping you even after all these years."

Slowly the old man nodded. "Yes, he is helping me even after his death." His voice sank lower. "And I never thanked him. Never. Never spoke a kind word to him."

"He was a difficult man to deal with," said Jade. "A very difficult personality."

"A thief," Prokov replied. But his voice was so soft it sounded almost like a blessing. "A blackmailer. A scoundrel."

There were tears in his weary eyes. "I knew him for only a few months. He frightened me half to death and nearly caused nuclear war. He disrupted my crew and ruined my chance to lead the Mars expedition. He tricked me and used me shamefully. . . ."

Jade made a sympathetic noise.

"Yet even after all these years the memory of him makes me smile. He made life exciting, vibrant. How I wish he were here. How I miss him!"

Decisions, Decisions

"HEY, THAT'S NOT BAD," SAID JIM GRADOWSKY AS HE turned off the recorder. He grinned across his desk at Jade. "You did a good job, kid."

She was sitting on the front inch and a half of her boss's couch. "It's only a voice disk," she said apologetically. "I couldn't get any video."

Gradowsky leaned back and put his slippered feet on the desktop. "That's okay. We'll do a simulation. There's enough footage on Sam Gunn for the computer graphics program to paint him with no sweat. The viewers'll never know the difference. And we can recreate what Prokov must've looked like from his current photo; I assume he'll have no objection to having his portrait done in 3-D."

"He might," Jade said in a small voice.

Shrugging, her boss answered, "Then we'll fake it. We'll have to fake the other people anyway, so what the hell. Public's accustomed to it. We put a disclaimer in small print at the end of the credits."

So that's how they do the historical documentaries, Jade said to herself, suddenly realizing how the networks showed such intimate details of people long dead.

"Okay, kid, you got the assignment," Gradowsky said grandly. "There must be dozens of people here in Selene and over at Lunagrad that knew Sam. Track 'em down and get 'em to talk to you."

She jumped to her feet eagerly. "I've already heard about a couple of mining engineers who're over at the base in Copernicus. And there's a hotel executive at the casino in Hell Crater, a woman who—"

"Yeah, yeah. Great. Go find 'em," said Gradowsky, suddenly impatient. "I'll put an expense allowance in your credit account."

"Thanks!" Jade felt tremendously excited. She was going to be a real reporter. She had won her spurs.

As she reached the door of Gradowsky's office, though, he called to her. "Don't let the expense account go to your head. And I want a copy of every bill routed to me, understand?"

"Yes. Of course."

The weeks rolled by. Jade found that the real trick of interviewing people was to get them started talking. Once they began to talk the only problem was how much storage space her microrecorder carried. Of course, many of her intended subjects refused to talk at all. Almost all of them were suspicious of Jade, at first. She learned how to work around their suspicions, how to show them that she was not an ordinary network newshound, how to make them understand that she *liked* Sam Gunn and wanted this biography to be a monument to his memory. Still, half the people she tried to see refused to be interviewed at all.

Jade tried to plan her travels logically, efficiently, to make the best use of the network's expense money. But an interview in Copernicus led to a tip about a retired accountant living in Star City, all the way over on the Farside. The exotic woman who claimed that Sam had jilted her at the altar knew about a tour guide who lived by the Tranquility Base shrine, where the Apollo 11 lander sat carefully preserved under its glassteel meteor dome. And on, and on.

Jade traveled mostly by tour bus, trundling across the pockmarked lunar plains at a reduced fare, packed in with visitors from Earth. For the first time she saw her home world as strangers see it: barren yet starkly beautiful, new and rugged and wild. When they talked of their own homes on Earth they mostly complained about the weather, or the taxes, or the crowds of people at the spaceport. Jade looked through the bus's big tinted windows at the lovely blue sphere hanging above the horizon and wondered if she would find Earth crowded and dirty and humdrum if she lived there.

Once she took a passenger rocket for the jaunt from Selene to Aristarchus, crossing Mare Nubium and the wide Sea of Storms in less than half an hour. She felt her insides drop away for the few minutes the rocket soared in free fall at the top of its ballistic trajectory. The retros fired and she felt weight returning before her stomach became unmanageable.

She piled up more voice disks, more stories about Sam Gunn. Some were obviously fabrications, outright lies. Others seemed outrageous exaggerations of what might have originally been true events.

"You've got to get some corroboration for this stuff," Gradowsky told her time and again. "Even when your pigeons are talking about people who're now dead, their families could come out of nowhere and sue the ass off us."

Corroboration was rare. No two people seemed to remember Sam Gunn in exactly the same way. A single incident might be retold by six different people in six different ways. Jade had to settle for audio testaments, where her interviewee swore on disk that the information he or she had given was true, to the best of his or her recollection.

Clark Griffith IV, for example, had plenty to say about Sam, and he had no qualms about telling his story—as he saw it.

Statement of Clark Griffith IV

(Recorded at Lunar Retirement Center, Copernicus)

THAT'S RIGHT, I'VE KNOWN SAM GUNN LONGER THAN ANY-body still living. Except maybe for Jill Meyers.

How long? I knew the little sonofabitch when he was a NASA astronaut, back in the days when we were first setting up a permanent base here on the Moon, over at Alphonsus.

I was his boss, believe it or not. It was like trying to train a cat—Sam always went his own way, fractured the rules left and right and somehow managed to come out smelling like a rose. Most of the time. He stepped into the doggie-doo now and then, but usually he was too fast on his feet for it to matter. By the time we'd catch up to him he was off somewhere else, raising more hell and giving us more trouble back in Washington.

Another thing about Sam. He's not that much younger than I am, yet he was off flitting around the goddamned solar system like some kid on pills. How did he do that? And from what I hear he was still chasing women from here to Pluto when he fell into that black hole. At his age! Well, maybe it's because he spent so much of his life in low-gravity environments. Keeps you young, so I hear. That's why I retired here to the Moon, but it doesn't seem to be helping me much.

Digressing? I'm digressing? I was talking about Sam. That's what you want, isn't it?

No, I don't believed he's dead. Never believed he fell into that mini–black hole out there past Pluto, either. It's all a fraud. A load of bullcrap. Pure Sam Gunn, another one of his tricky little gambits.

He'll be back, you can bet on it. Mini–black hole my greatgrandmother! It's a scam, the whole thing; don't think otherwise.

When did I first meet Sam? God, let me think. It was back . . . never mind. Let me tell you about Sam's last days with NASA. I got to fire the little pain-in-the-butt. Bounced him right out of the agency, good and proper. Happiest day of my life.

Tourist Sam

WHY DID NASA FIRE SAM GUNN? IT'D BE BETTER TO ASK why we didn't fire the little SOB. out of a cannon and get rid of him once and for all. Would've been a service to the human race.

I'm no detective, but I smelled a rat when Sam put in a formal request for a three-month leave of absence. I just stared at my desktop screen. Sam Gunn, going through regular channels? Something was fishy. I mean, Sam *never* did things according to regulations. Give him a road map with a route on the interstates plotted out by AAA and he'd go down every dirt road and crooked alley he could find, just to drive my blood pressure up to the bursting point.

Trouble was, the sawed-off little runt was a damned good astronaut. About as good as they came, as a flyer and ingenious troubleshooter. Like the time he saved the lunar mission by jury-rigging a still and getting all the stranded astronauts plastered so they'd be unconscious most of the time and use up less oxygen.

That was typical of Sam Gunn. A hero who left the rules and regulations in a shambles every time.

He had just come off his most notorious stunt of all, getting the first skipper of space station Freedom to punch the abandon ship alarm and riding back down to Earth in an emergency escape capsule with some young woman from a movie studio. He had to be hospitalized after they landed; he claimed it was from stress during reentry, but everybody at the Cape was wondering who was reentering what.

Anyway, there was his formal request for a three-month leave of absence, all filled out just as neat and precise as I would have done it myself. He was certainly entitled to the leave. But I knew Sam. Something underhanded was going on.

I called him into my office and asked him point-blank what he was doing. A waste of time.

"I need a rest," he said. Then he added, "Sir."

Sam's face was as round and plain as a penny, and his wiry hair was kind of coppery color, come to think of it. Little snub of a nose with a scattering of freckles. His teeth had enough spaces between them so that he reminded me of a Jack-o'-lantern when he grinned.

He wasn't grinning as he sat in front of my desk. He was all perfectly polite earnestness, dressed in a *tie* and a real suit, like an honest-to-Pete straight-arrow citizen. His eyes gave him away, though: they were as crafty as ever, glittering with visions that he wanted to keep secret from me.

"Going anyplace special?" I asked, trying to make it sound nonchalant.

Sam nonchalanted me right back. "No, not really. I just need to get away from it all for a while."

Yeah, sure. Like Genghis Khan just wanted to take a little pony ride.

I had no choice except to approve his request. But I had no intention of letting the sneaky little sumbitch pull one over on me. Sam was up to something; I knew it, and the glitter in his eyes told me that he knew I knew it.

As I said, I'm no detective. So I hired one. Well, she really wasn't a detective. My niece, Ramona Perkins, was an agent with the Drug Enforcement Agency—a damned stupid name, if you ask me. Makes it sound like the government is *forcing* people to do drugs.

Well, anyway, Ramona wasn't too thrilled with the idea of trailing a furloughed astronaut for a few weeks.

"Yes, Uncle Griff, I have three weeks of vacation time coming, but I was going to wait until December and go to Alaska."

That was Ramona, as impractical as they come. She was pretty, in a youngish, girl-next-door way. Nice sandy-blonde hair that she always kept pinned up; made her look even younger than she was. And there was no doubt about her courage. Anybody who makes a career out of posing as an innocent kid and infiltrating drug gangs has more guts than brains, if you ask me.

She had just gone through a pretty rough divorce. No children, thank Pete, but her ex-husband made a big to-do about their house and cars. Seemed to me he cared more about their damned stereo and satellite TV setup than he did about my niece.

I made myself smile at her image in my phone screen. "Suppose I could get you three months of detached duty, assigned to my office. Then you wouldn't use up any of your vacation time."

"I don't know. . . ." She sort of scrunched up her perky face. I figured she was trying to bury herself in her work and forget about her ex.

"It'd do you good to get away from everything for a while," I said.

Ramona's cornflower-blue eyes went curious. "What's so important about this one astronaut that you'd go to all this trouble?"

What could I tell her? That Sam Gunn had been driving me nuts for years and I was certain he was up to no good? That I was afraid Sam would pull some stunt that would reflect dishonorably on the space agency? That if and when he got himself in trouble the agency management would inevitably dump the blame on me, since I was in charge of his division.

I wasn't going to have Sam botch up my record, dammit! I was too close to retirement to let him ruin me. And don't think the little SOB wasn't trying to do me dirt. He'd slit my throat and laugh about it, if I let him.

But to my sweet young niece, I merely said, "Ramona, this is a matter of considerable importance. I wouldn't be asking your help if it weren't. I really can't tell you any more than that."

Her image in my phone screen grew serious. "Does it involve narcotics, then?"

I took a deep breath and nodded. "That's a possibility." It was a lie, of course; Sam was as straight as they come about drugs. Wasn't even much of a drinker. His major vice was women.

"All right," she said, completely businesslike. "If you can arrange the reassignment, I'll trail your astronaut for you."

"That's my girl!" I said, really happy with her. She'd always been my favorite niece. At that point in time it never occurred to me that sending her after Sam might put her in more danger than the entire Colombian cartel could throw at her.

The three weeks passed. No report from her. I began to worry. Called her supervisor at DEA and he assured me she'd been phoning him once a week, just to tell him she was okay. I complained that she should've been phoning me, so a few days later I got an e-mail message:

EVERYTHING IS FINE BUT THIS IS
GOING TO TAKE LONGER THAN WE THOUGHT.

It took just about the whole three damned months. It wasn't until then that Ramona popped into my office, sunburnt and weary-looking, and told me what Sam had been up to. This is what she told me:

I KNOW THIS investigation took a lot longer than you thought it would, Uncle Griff. It was a lot more complicated than either one of us thought it'd be. *Nothing* that Sam Gunn does is simple!

To begin with, by the time I started after him, Sam had already gone to Panama to set up the world's first space tourist line.

That's right, Uncle Griff. A tourist company. In Panama.

He called his organization Space Adventure Tours and registered it as a corporation in Panama. All perfectly legal, but it started alarm bells ringing in my head right from the start. I knew that Panama was a major drug-transshipment area, and a tourist company could be a perfect front for narcotics smuggling.

By the time I arrived in Colón, on the Caribbean side of the Panama Canal, Sam had established himself in a set of offices he rented on the top floor of one of the three-storey stucco commercial buildings just off the international airport.

As I said, my first thought was that he was running a smuggling operation, probably narcotics, and his wild-sounding company name was only a front. I spent a week watching his office, seeing who was coming and going. Nobody but Sam himself and a couple of young Panamanian office workers. Now and then an elderly guy in casual vacation clothes or a silver-haired couple. Once in a while a blue-haired matronly type would show up. Seldom the same people twice. No sleazebags in five-hundred-dollar suits. No Uzi-toting enforcer maniacs.

I dropped in at the office myself to look the place over. It seemed normal enough. An anteroom with a couple of tacky couches and armchairs, divided by a chest-high counter. Water stains on the ceiling tiles. On the other side of the counter sat the two young locals, a male and a female, both working at desktop computers. Beyond them was a single door prominently marked S. GUNN, PRESIDENT AND CEO.

Most smuggling operators don't put their own names on doors.

The young woman glanced up from her display screen and saw me standing at the counter. Immediately she came out from behind her desk, smiling brightly, and asked in local-accented English, "Can I help you?"

I put on my best Dorothy-from-Kansas look and said, "What kind of tours do you offer?"

"An adventure in space," she said, still smiling.

"In space?"

"Yes. Like the astronauts."

"For tourists?"

"Si—Yes. Our company is the very first in the world to offer a space flight adventure."

"In space?" I repeated.

She nodded and said, "Perhaps Mr. Gunn himself should explain it to you."

"Oh, no, I wouldn't want to bother him."

"No bother," she said sweetly. "He enjoys speaking to the customers."

She must have pressed a buzzer, because the s. GUNN door popped open and out walked Sam, smiling like a used-car salesman.

The first thing about him to strike me was how short he was. I mean, I'm barely five-five in my flats and Sam was a good two inches shorter than I. He seemed solidly built, though, beneath the colorful flowered short-sleeve shirt and sky-blue slacks he was wearing. Good shoulders, a little thick in the midsection.

His face was, well . . . *cute*. I thought I saw boyish enthusiasm and charm in his eyes. He certainly didn't look like your typical drug lord.

"I'm Sam Gunn," he said to me, sticking his hand out over the counter. "At your service."

I got the impression he had to stand on tiptoe to get his arm over the counter.

"Ramona Perkins," I said taking his hand in mine. He had a firm, friendly grip. With my free hand I activated the microchip recorder in my shoulder bag.

"You're interested in a space adventure?" Sam asked, opening the little gate at the end of the counter and ushering me through.

"I really don't know," I said, as if I were taking the first step on the Yellow Brick Road. "It all seems so new and different."

"Come into my office and let me explain it to you."

Sam's office was much more posh than the outer room. He had a big modernistic desk, all polished walnut and chrome, and two chairs in front of it that looked like reclinable astronauts' seats. I learned soon enough that they were reclinable, and Sam liked to recline in them with female companions.

No windows, but the walls were lined with photographs of astronauts hovering in space, with the big blue curving Earth as a backdrop. Behind Sam's desk, on a wide walnut bookcase, there were dozens of photos of Sam in astronaut uniform, in a space suit, even one with him in scuba gear with his arm around a gorgeous video starlet in the skimpiest bikini I've ever seen.

He sat me in one of the cushioned, contoured recliners and went around behind his desk. I realized there was a platform back there, because when Sam sat down he was almost taller than he had been standing up in front of the desk.

"Ms. Perkins . . . may I call you Ramona?"

"Sure," I said, in a valley-girl accent.

"That's a beautiful name."

"Thank you."

"Ramona, until now the thrill of flying in space has been reserved to a handful of professional astronauts like myself—"

"Haven't some politicians and video stars gone into orbit?" I asked, with wide-eyed innocence.

"Yes indeed they certainly have. A few mega-millionaires, too," Sam answered. "And if *they've* flown in space there's no good reason why *you* shouldn't have the experience, too. You, and anyone else who wants the adventure of a lifetime!"

"How much does it cost?" I asked.

Sam hiked his rust-red eyebrows at me. And launched into a nonstop spiel about the beauties and glories and excitement of space travel. He wasn't really eloquent; that wasn't Sam's style. But he was persistent and energetic. He talked so fast and so long that it seemed as if he didn't take a breath for half an hour. I remember thinking that he could probably go out for an EVA space walk without oxygen if he put his mind to it.

For the better part of an hour Sam worked up and down the subject.

"And why shouldn't ordinary people, people just like you, be allowed to share in the excitement of space flight? The once-in-a-lifetime adventure of them all! Why do government agencies and big, powerful corporations refuse to allow ordinary men and women the chance to fly in space?"

I batted my baby blues at him and asked, in a breathless whisper, "Why?"

Sam heaved a big sigh. "I'll tell you why. They're all big bureaucracies, run by petty-minded bureaucrats who don't care about the little guy. Big corporations like Rockledge could be running tourists into orbit right now, but their bean-counting bureaucrats won't let that happen for fear that some tourist might get a little nauseous in zero gravity and sue the corporation when he comes back to Earth."

"Maybe they're afraid of an accident," I said, still trying to sound naive. "I mean, people have been killed in rocket launches, haven't they?"

"Not in years," Sam countered, waggling a hand in the air. "Besides, the launch system we're gonna use is supersafe. And gentle. We take off like an airplane and land like an airplane. No problems."

"But what about space sickness?" I asked.

"Likewise, no problem. We've developed special equipment that eliminates space sickness just about completely. In fact, you feel just as comfortable as you would in your own living room for just about the entire flight."

"Really?"

"Really," he said, with a *trust-me* nod of his head.

"Wouldn't you be better off operating in the States?" I probed. "I mean, like, I just ran across your office kind of by accident while I was checking on my flight back home."

Sam scowled at me. "The U.S. government is wrapped up with bureaucrats and—worse—lawyers. You can't do *anything* new there anymore. If I tried to start a space tourist company in the States I'd have sixteen zillion bozos from NASA, OSHA, the Department of Transportation, the Commerce Department, the State Department, the National Institutes of Health and St. Francis of Assisi knows who else coming down on my head. I'd be filling out forms and talking to lawyers until I was old and gray!"

"It's easier to get started in Panama, then."

"Much easier."

I sat there, gazing at Sam, pretending to think it all over.

Then I asked again, "How much does it cost?"

Sam looked at his wristwatch and said, "Hey! It's just about time for our first space cruiser to land! Let's go out and see it come in!"

I felt a little like the first time I went out to buy a car on my own, without Daddy or any of my big brothers with me. But I let Sam take me by the hand to his own car—a leased fire-engine-red BMW convertible—and drive me out to an immense empty hangar with a newly painted SPACE ADVENTURE TOURS sign painted across its curved roof.

"Used to be a blimp hangar," Sam said over the rushing wind as we drove up to the hangar. "U.S. Navy used 'em for antisubmarine patrol. It was falling apart from neglect. I got it for a song."

The DEA had considered asking the Navy to use blimps to patrol the sea-lanes that drug smugglers used, I remembered.

"You're going into space in a blimp?" I asked as we braked to a gravel-spitting stop.

"No no no," Sam said, jumping out of the convertible and running

over to my side to help me out. "Blimps wouldn't work. We're using . . .
well, look! Here it comes now!"

I turned to look where he was pointing and saw a huge, lumbering
Boeing 747 coming down slowly, with ponderous grace, at the far end of
the long concrete runway. And attached to its back was an old space shuttle orbiter.

"That's one of the old shuttles!" I cried, surprised.

"Right," said Sam. "That's what we ride into space in."

"Gosh." I was truly impressed.

The immense piggyback pair taxied right up to us, the 747's four jet
engines howling so loud I clapped my hands over my ears. Then it cut
power and *loomed* over us, with the shuttle orbiter riding high atop it. It
was certainly impressive.

"NASA sold off its shuttle fleet, so I got a group of investors together
and bought one of 'em," Sam said, rather proudly, I noticed. "Bought the
piggyback plane to go with it, too."

While the ground crew attached a little tractor to the 747's nose wheel
and towed it slowly into the old blimp hangar, Sam explained that he and
his technical staff had worked out a new launch system: the 747 carried
the orbiter up to more than fifty thousand feet, and then the orbiter disconnected and lit up its main engines to go off into space.

"The 747 does the job that the old solid rocket boosters used to do
when NASA launched shuttles from Cape Canaveral," Sam explained to
me. "Our system is cheaper and safer."

The word *cheaper* reminded me. "How much does a tour cost?" I asked
still again, determined this time to get an answer.

We had walked into the hangar by now. Technicians were setting up
ladders and platforms up and down the length of the plane. The huge
shadowy hangar echoed with the clang of metal equipment and the clat-
ter of their voices, yelling back and forth in Spanish.

"Want to go aboard?" Sam asked, with a sly grin.

I sure did, but I answered, "Not until you tell me how much a flight
costs."

"Ten thousand dollars," he said, without flicking an eyelash.

"Ten thou. . . ." I thought I recalled that the shuttle cost ten thousand
dollars *a pound* when NASA was operating it. Even the new Clipperships,
which were entirely reusable, cost several hundred dollars per pound.

"You can put it on your credit card," Sam suggested.

"Ten thousand dollars?" I repeated. "For a flight into orbit?"

He nodded solemnly. "You experience two orbits and then we land back here. The whole flight will last a little more than four hours."

"How can you do it so cheap?" I blurted.

Sam spread his arms. "I'm not a big, bloated government agency. I keep a very low overhead. I don't have ten zillion lawyers looking over my shoulder. My insurance costs are much lower here in Panama than they'd be in the States. And . . ." He hesitated.

"And?" I prompted.

With a grin that was almost bashful, Sam told me, "I want to do good for the people who'll never be able to afford space flight otherwise. I don't give a damn if I make a fortune or not: I just want to help ordinary people like you to experience the thrill and the wonder of flying in space."

I almost believed him.

In fact, right then and there I really *wanted* to believe Sam Gunn. Even though I had a pretty good notion that he was laying it on with a trowel.

I told Sam that even though ten thousand was a bargain for orbital flight it was an awfully steep price for me to pay. He agreed and invited me to dinner. I expected him to keep up the pressure on me to buy a ticket, but Sam actually had other things in mind. One thing, at least.

He was charming. He was funny. He kept me laughing all through the dinner we had at a little shack on the waterfront that served the best fish in onion sauce I've ever tasted. He told me the story of his life, several times, and each time was completely different. I couldn't help but like him. More than like him.

Sam drove me back to my hotel and rode up the creaking elevator with me to my floor. I intended to say good-night at the door to my room but somehow it didn't work out that way. I never said good-night to him at all. What I said, much later, was good morning.

Now, Uncle Griff, don't go getting so red in the face! It was the first time I'd let anybody get close to me since the divorce. Sam made me feel attractive, wanted. I needed that. It was like . . . well, like I'd run away from the human race. Sam brought me back, made me alive again. He was thoughtful and gentle and somehow at the same time terrifically energetic. He was great fun.

And besides, by the time we were having breakfast together in the hotel's dining room he offered to let me fly on his space cruiser for free.

"Oh no, Sam, I couldn't do that. I'll pay my own way," I said.

He protested faintly, but I had no intention of letting him think I was in his debt. Going to bed with Sam once was fun. Letting him think I *owed* him was not.

So I phoned Washington and told my boss to expect a ten-grand charge to come through—which you, Uncle Griff, will be billed for. Then I got into a taxi and drove out to the offices of Space Adventure Tours and plunked down my credit card.

Sam took me to lunch.

But not to dinner. He explained over lunch that he had a business conference that evening.

"This space-tour business is brand new, you gotta understand," he told me, "and that means I have to spend most of my time wining and dining possible customers."

"Like me," I said.

He laughed, but it was bitter. "No, honey, not like you. Old folks, mostly. Little old widows trying to find something interesting to do with what's left of their lives. Retired CEOs who want to think that they're still on the cutting edge of things. They're the ones with the money, and I've got to talk forty of 'em out of some of it."

"Forty?"

"That's our orbiter's passenger capacity. Forty is our magic number. For the next forty days and forty nights I'm gonna be chasing little old ladies and retired old farts. I'd rather be with you, but I've gotta sell those seats."

I looked rueful and told him I understood. After he left me back at my hotel, I realized with something of a shock that I really was rueful. I missed Sam!

So I trailed him, telling myself that it was stupid to get emotionally involved with the guy I'm supposed to be investigating. Sam's business conference turned out to be a dinner and show at one of Colón's seamier night clubs. I didn't go in, but the club's garish neon sign, *The Black Hole*, was enough for me to figure out what kind of a place it was. Sam went in with two elderly gentlemen from the States. To me they looked like middle-class retired businessmen on a spree without their wives.

Sure enough, they were two more customers, I found out later.

Sam was busy most evenings, doing his sales pitch to potential customers over dinners and night-club shows. He squired blue-haired widows and played tour guide for honeymooning couples. He romanced three middle-aged woman on vacation from their husbands, juggling things so well that the first time they saw one another was at the one-day training seminar in Sam's rented hangar.

It didn't quite take forty days and forty nights, but Sam gave each of his potential customers the full blaze of his personal attention. As far as I know, each and every one of them signed on the dotted line.

And then he had time for me again.

I had extended my stay in Colón, waiting for the flight that Sam promised. Once he had signed up a full load of paying customers, he brought us all out to the hangar for what he called an "orientation."

So there we were, forty tourists standing on the concrete floor of the hangar with the big piggyback airplane cum orbiter looming in front of us like a freshly painted aluminum mountain. Sam stood on a rusty, rickety metal platform scrounged from the maintenance equipment.

"Congratulations," he said to us, his voice booming through the echo chamber of a hangar. "You are the very first space tourists in the history of the world."

Sam didn't need a megaphone. His voice carried through to our last row with no problem at all. He started off by telling us how great our flight was going to be, pumping up our expectations. Then he went on to what he said were the two most important factors.

"Safety and comfort," he told us. "We've worked very hard to make absolutely certain that you are perfectly safe and comfortable throughout your space adventure."

Sam explained that for safety's sake we were all going to have to wear a full space suit for the whole four-hour flight. Helmet and all.

"So you can come in your most comfortable clothes," he said, grinning at us. "Shorts, T-shirts, whatever you feel happiest in. We'll all put on our space suits right here in the hangar before we board the orbiter."

He explained, rather delicately, that each suit was equipped with a waste disposal system, a sort of high-tech version of the pilot's old relief tube, which worked just as well for women as it did for men, he claimed.

"Since our flight will be no more than four hours long, we won't need the FCS—fecal containment system—that NASA's brainiest scientists have developed for astronauts to use." And Sam held up a pair of large-sized diapers.

Everybody laughed.

"Now I'm sure you've heard a great deal about space sickness," Sam went on, once the laughter died away. "I want to assure you that you won't be bothered by the effects of zero gravity on this flight. Your space suits include a special anti-sickness system that will protect you from the nausea and giddiness that usually hits first-time astronauts."

"What kind of a system is it?" asked one of the elderly men. He looked like a retired engineer to me: shirt pocket bristling with ballpoint pens.

Sam gave him a sly grin. "Mr. Artumian, I'm afraid I can't give you any details about that. It's a new system, and it's proprietary information. Space Adventure Tours has developed this equipment, and as soon as the major corporations learn how well it works they're going to want to buy, lease, or steal it from us."

Another laugh, a little thinner than before.

"But how do we know it'll work?" Artumian insisted.

Very seriously, Sam replied, "It's been thoroughly tested, I assure you."

"But we're the first customers you're trying it on."

Sam's grin returned. "You're the first customers we've had!"

Before Artumian could turn this briefing into a dialogue, I spoke up. "Could you tell us what we'll feel when we're in zero gravity? Give us an idea of what to expect?"

Sam beamed at me. "Certainly, Ms. Perkins. When we first reach orbit and attain zero-gee, you'll feel a moment or two of free fall. You know, that stomach-dropping sensation you get when an elevator starts going down. But it'll only last a couple of seconds, max. Then our proprietary anti-disequilibrium system kicks in and you'll feel perfectly normal."

Artumian muttered "Ah-hah!" when Sam used the term anti-disequilibrium system. As if that meant something to his engineer's brain.

"Throughout the flight," Sam went on, "you may feel a moment now and then of free fall, kind of like floating. But our equipment will quickly get your body's sensory systems back to normal."

"Sensory systems," Artumian muttered knowingly.

Sam and two people in flight attendants' uniforms showed us through the orbiter's passenger cabin. The attendants were both really attractive: a curvaceous little blonde with a megawatt smile and a handsome brute of a Latino guy with real bedroomy eyes.

We had to climb a pretty shaky metal ladder to get up there because the orbiter was still perched on top of the 747. The plane and the orbiter were gleaming with a fresh coat of white paint and big blue SPACE ADVENTURE TOURS running along their sides. But the ladder was flaking with rust.

It made me wonder just what kind of shoestring Sam was operating on: this big airplane with a NASA surplus space shuttle orbiter perched atop it, and we all had to clamber up this rusty, clattery ladder. Some of Sam's customers were pretty slow and feeble; old, you know. I heard plenty of wheezing going up that ladder.

The orbiter's cabin, though, was really very nice. Like a first-class section aboard an airliner, except that the seats were even bigger and more plush. Two seats on either side of the one central aisle. I saw windows at each row, but they were covered over.

"The windows are protected by individual opaque heat shields," Sam explained. "They'll slide back once we're in orbit so you can see the glories and beauties of Earth and space."

There were no toilets in the cabin, and no galley. The passengers would remain strapped into their seats at all times, Sam told us. "That's for your own safety and comfort," he assured us.

"You mean we won't get to float around in zero gravity like they do in the videos?" asked one of the elderly women.

"'Fraid not," Sam answered cheerfully. "Frankly, if you tried that, you'd most likely get so sick you'd want to upchuck. Even our very sophisticated anti-disequilibrium equipment has its limitations."

I wasn't close enough to hear him, but I saw Artumian's lips mouth the word, "Limitations."

That evening all forty of us, plus Sam, had a festive dinner together on the rooftop of the local Hyatt Hotel. It was a splendid night, clear and filled with stars. A crescent moon rose and glittered on the Caribbean for us.

Sam flitted from table to table all through the dinner; I doubt that he got to swallow more than a few bites of food. But he ended the evening at my table and drove me to my hotel himself, while all the other customers rode to their hotels in a rattletrap gear-grinding, soot-puffing big yellow school bus that Sam had rented.

"Tomorrow's the big day," Sam said happily as we drove through the dark streets. "Space Adventure's first flight."

My romantic interest in Sam took a back seat to my professional curiosity.

"Sam," I asked over the rush of the night wind, "how can you make a profit if you're only charging ten thousand per passenger? This flight must cost a lot more than four hundred thousand dollars."

"Profit isn't everything, my blue-eyed space beauty," he said, keeping his eyes on his driving.

"But if it costs more to fly than you make from ticket sales you'll go out of business pretty quickly, won't you?"

He shot a glance at me. "My pricing schedule is pretty flexible. You got the bargain rate. Others are paying more; a lot more."

"Really?"

"Uh-huh. That's another reason I'm operating here in Panama. Let the fat cats open their wallets wider than ordinary folks. If I tried that in the States I'd have a ton of lawyers hitting me with discrimination suits."

I thought about that as we pulled up in front of my hotel.

"Then how much will you make from this flight?" I asked, noticing that Sam kept the motor running.

"Gross? About a million-two."

"Is that enough to cover your costs?"

Sam grinned at me. "I won't go bankrupt. It's like the old story of the tailor who claims that he sells his clothing at prices *below* his own costs. 'On each and every individual sale we lose money,' he tells a customer. 'But on the volume we make a modest profit.'"

I didn't see anything funny in it. It didn't make sense.

Suddenly Sam shook me out of my musing. He grabbed me by the shoulders, kissed me on the lips, and then announced, "I'd love to go up to your room and make mad, passionate love to you, Ramona, but I've got an awful lot to do between now and takeoff tomorrow morning. See you at the hangar!"

He leaned past me and opened my door. Kind of befuddled, I got out of the car and waved good-bye to him as he roared off in a cloud of exhaust smoke.

Alone in my room, I started to wonder if our one night of passion had merely been Sam's way of closing the sale.

The next day, Space Adventure Tours' first flight was just about everything Sam had promised.

All forty of us gathered at the hangar bright and early. It took nearly two hours to get each of us safely sealed up inside a space suit. Some of the older tourists were almost too arthritic to get their creaky arms and legs into the suits, but somehow—with Sam and his two flight attendants pushing and pulling—they all managed.

Instead of that rickety ladder, Sam drove a cherry picker across the hangar floor and lifted us in our space suits, two by two like Noah's passengers, up to the hatch of the orbiter. The male attendant went up first and was there at the hatch to help us step inside the passenger cabin and clomp down the aisle to our assigned seats.

Sam and I were the last couple hoisted up. With the visor of my suit helmet open, I could smell the faint odor of bananas in the cherry picker's cab. It made me wonder where Sam had gotten the machine, and how soon he had to return it.

After we were all strapped in, Sam came striding down the cabin, crackling with energy and enthusiasm. He stood up at the hatch to the flight deck and grinned ear to ear at us.

"You folks are about to make history. I'm proud of you," he said. Then he opened the hatch and stepped into the cockpit.

Three things struck me, as I sat strapped into my seat, encased in my space suit. One: Sam didn't have to duck his head to get through that low hatch. Two: he wasn't wearing a space suit. Three: he was probably going to pilot the orbiter himself.

Was there a copilot already in the cockpit with him? Surely Sam didn't intend to fly the orbiter into space entirely by himself. And why wasn't he wearing a space suit, when he insisted that all the rest of us did?

No time for puzzling over it all. The flight attendants came down the aisle, checking to see that we were all firmly strapped in. They were in space suits, just as we passengers were. I felt motion: the 747 beneath us was being towed out of the hangar. The windows were sealed shut, so we couldn't see what was happening outside.

Then we heard the jet engines start up; actually we felt their vibrations more than heard their sound. Our cabin was very well insulated.

"Please pull down the visors on your helmets," the blonde flight attendant singsonged. "We will be taking off momentarily."

I confess I got a lump in my throat as I felt the engines whine up to full thrust, pressing me back in my seat. With our helmet visors down I couldn't see the face of the elderly woman sitting beside me, but we automatically clasped our gloved hands together, like mother and daughter. My heart was racing.

I wished we could see out the windows! As it was, I had to depend on my sense of balance, sort of flying by the seat of my pants, while the 747 raced down the runway, rotated its nose wheel off the concrete, and then rose majestically into the air—with us on top of her. Ridiculously, I remembered a line from an old poem: *With a sleighful of toys and St. Nicholas, too.*

"We're in the air," came Sam's cheerful voice over our helmet earphones. "In half an hour we'll separate from our carrier plane and light up our main rocket engines."

We sat in anticipatory silence. I don't know about the others—it was impossible to see their faces or tell what was going through their minds— but I twitched every time the ship jounced or swayed.

"Separation in two minutes," Sam's voice warned us.

I gripped my seat's armrests. Couldn't see my hands through the thick space suit gloves, but I could feel how white my knuckles were.

"You're going to hear a banging noise," Sam warned us. "Don't be alarmed; it's just the explosive bolts separating the struts that're clamping us to the carrier plane."

Explosive bolts. All of a sudden I didn't like that word *explosive*.

The bang scared me even though I knew it was coming. It was a really loud, sharp noise. But the cabin didn't seem to shake or shudder at all, thank goodness.

Almost immediately we felt more thrust pushing us back into our seats again.

"Main rocket engines have ignited on schedule," Sam said evenly. "Next stop, LEO!"

I knew that he meant Low Earth Orbit, but I wondered how many of the tourists were wondering who this person Leo might be.

The male flight attendant's voice cut in on my earphones. "As we enter Earth orbit you will experience a few moments of free fall before our anti-disequilibrium equipment balances out your inner sensory systems. Don't let those few moments of a falling sensation worry you; they'll be over almost before you realize it."

I nodded to myself inside my helmet. Zero-gee. My mouth suddenly felt dry.

And then I was falling! Dropping into nothingness. My stomach floated up into my throat. I heard moans and gasps from my fellow tourists.

And just like that it was over. A normal feeling of weight returned and my stomach settled back to where it belonged. Sam's equipment really worked!

"We are now in low Earth orbit," Sam's voice said, low, almost reverent. "I'm going to open the viewport shutters now."

Since I had paid the lowest price for my ride, I had an aisle seat. I leaned forward in my seat harness and twisted my shoulders sideways as far as I could so that I could peer through my helmet visor and look through the window.

The Earth floated below us, huge and curving and so brightly blue it almost hurt my eyes. I could see swirls of beautiful white clouds and the sun gleaming off the ocean and swatches of green ground and little brown wrinkles that must have been mountains and out near the curving sweep of the horizon a broad open swath of reddish tan that stretched as far as I could see.

"That's the coast of Africa coming up. You can see the Sahara a little to our north," Sam said.

The cabin was filled with gasps and moans again, but this time they were joyous, awestruck. I didn't care how much the ticket price was; I would have paid my own way to see this.

I could see the horn of Africa and the great rift valley where the first protohumans made their camps. Sinbad's Arabian Sea glittered like an ocean of jewels before my eyes.

Completely around the world we went, not in eighty days but a little over ninety minutes. The Arabian peninsula was easy to spot, not a wisp of a cloud anywhere near it. India was half blotted out by monsoon storms, but we swung over the Himalayas and across China. It was night on that side of the world, but the Japanese islands were outlined by the lights of their cities and highways.

"Mt. Everest's down there under the clouds," Sam told us. "Doesn't look so tall from up here."

Japan, Alaska, and then down over the heartland of America. It was an unusually clear day in the midwest; we could see the Mississippi snaking through the nation's middle like a coiling blood vessel.

Twice we coasted completely around the world. It was glorious, fascinating, an endless vision of delights. When Sam asked us how we were enjoying the flight the cabin echoed with cheers. I didn't want the flight to end. I could have stayed hunched over in that cumbersome space suit and stared out that little window for the rest of my days. Gladly.

But at last Sam's sad voice told us, "I'm sorry, folks, but that's it. Time to head back to the barn."

I could feel the disappointment that filled the cabin.

As the window shutters slowly slid shut Sam announced casually, "Now comes the tricky part. Reentry and rendezvous with the carrier plane."

Rendezvous with the carrier plane? He hadn't mentioned that before. I heard several attendant call buttons chiming. Some of the other tourists were alarmed by Sam's news, too.

In a few minutes he came back on the intercom. In my earphones I heard Sam explain, "Our flight plan is to rendezvous with the carrier plane and reconnect with her so she can bring us back to the airport under the power of her jet engines. That's much safer than trying to land this orbiter by herself.

"However," he went on, "if we miss rendezvous we'll land the orbiter just the way we did it for NASA, no sweat. I've put this ninety-nine ton glider down on runways at Kennedy and Edwards, no reason why I can't land her back at Colón just as light as a feather."

A ninety-nine ton feather, I thought, can't be all that easy to land. But reconnecting to the carrier plane? I'd never heard of that even being tried before.

Yet Sam did it, smooth as pie. We hardly felt a jolt or rattle. Sam kept up a running commentary for us, since our window shutters had been closed tight for reentry into the atmosphere. There were a few tense moments, but only a few.

"Done!" Sam announced. "We're now connected again to the carrier plane. We'll be landing at Colón in twenty-seven minutes."

And that was it. I felt the thud and bounce of the 747's wheels hitting the concrete runway, and then we taxied back to the hangar. Once we stopped and the engines whined down, the flight attendants opened the hatch and we went down to the ground in the same banana-smelling cherry picker.

The plane had stopped outside the hangar. There were a couple of photographers at the base of the cherry picker taking each couple's picture as they stood on terra firma once again, grinning out from their space suit helmets. The first tourists in space.

Sam popped out of the cockpit and personally escorted me to the hatch and went down the cherry picker with me and my seat companion. He posed for the photographer between us, his arms on our shoulders, standing on tiptoe.

The thirty-nine other tourists went their separate ways that afternoon, clutching their photographs and smiling with their memories of space flight the way a new saint smiles at the revelation of heaven. They were converts, sure enough. They would go back home and tell everyone they knew about their space adventure. They were going to be Sam's best sales force.

I had a decision to make. I had started out investigating Sam for you, Uncle Griff, with the probability that his so-called tourist operation was a front for narcotics smuggling. But it sure didn't look that way to me.

Besides, I really liked the little guy. He was a combination of Huckleberry Finn and Long John Silver, with a bit of Chuck Yeager thrown in.

Yet I had come on to Sam as a wide-eyed tourist. If I hung around Colón, sooner or later he'd realize that I hadn't told him the exact truth about myself. I discovered, to my own surprise—shock, really—that I didn't want to hurt Sam's feelings. Worse, I didn't want him to know that I had been spying on him. I didn't want Sam Gunn to hate me.

So I had to leave. Unless Sam *asked* me to stay.

Like a fool, I decided to get him to ask me.

He invited me to dinner that evening. "A farewell dinner," he called it. I spent the afternoon shopping for the slinkiest, sexiest black lace drop-dead dress I could find. Then I had my hair done: I usually wore it pinned up or in a ponytail, part of my sweet-sixteen pose. Now I had it sweeping down to my bare shoulders, soft and alluring.

I hoped.

Sam's eyes bugged out a bit when he saw me. That was good.

"My god, Ramona, you're . . ." He fished around for a compliment. ". . . you're *beautiful*!"

"Thank you," I said, and swept past him to settle myself in his convertible, showing plenty of thigh in the process.

Don't growl, Uncle Griff. I was emotionally involved with Sam. I know I shouldn't have been, but at the time there wasn't much I could do about it.

Sam was bouncing with enthusiasm about his first flight, of course.

"It worked!" he shouted, exultant, as he screeched the convertible out of my hotel's driveway. "Everything worked like a mother-loving charm! Nothing went wrong. Not one thing! Not a transistor or a data bit out of place. Perfect! One thousand batting average. Murphy's Law sleeps with the fishes."

He was so excited about the successful flight that he really wasn't paying much attention to me. And the breeze as we drove through the twilight was pulling my carefully done coiffure apart.

Sam took me to a quiet little restaurant out in a suburban shopping mall, of all places. The food was wonderful, but our conversation—over candlelight and wine—continued to deal with business instead of romance.

"If we start the flights at seven in the morning instead of nine, we can get in an afternoon flight, too," Sam was musing, grinning like an elf on amphetamines. "Double our income."

"Will your customers be able to get up that early?" I heard myself asking, intrigued by his visions of success despite myself. "Some of them are pretty old and creaky."

Sam waved a hand in the air. "We'll schedule the oldest ones for afternoon flights. Take the spryer ones in the morning. Maybe give 'em a slight break in the price for getting up so early."

I wanted Sam to pay attention to me, but his head was filled with plans for the future of Space Adventure Tours. Feeling a little downhearted, I decided that if I couldn't beat him I might as well join him.

"It was a great flight," I assured him. Not that he needed it; I did. "I'd love to go again, if only I could afford it."

Either Sam didn't hear me or he paid me no attention.

"I was worried something would go wrong," he rattled on. "You know, something always gets away from you on a mission as tricky as this one. But it all worked fine. Better than fine. Terrific!"

It took a while before Sam drew enough of a breath for me to jump into his monologue. But at last I said:

"Sam, I've been thinking. Your anti-disequilibrium system—"

"What about it?" he snapped, suddenly looking wary.

"It worked so well. . . ."

His expression eased. His elfin grin returned. "Sure it did."

"Why don't you license it to NASA or some of the corporations that are building space stations in orbit? It could be a steady source of income for you."

"No," he said. Flat and final.

"Why not? You could make good money from it—"

"And let Masterson or one of the other big corporations compete with Space Adventure Tours? They'd drive us out of business in two months."

"How could they do that?" I really was naive, I guess.

Sam explained patiently, "If I let them get their foot in the door they'll just price tours so far below cost that I'll either lose all my customers or go bankrupt trying to compete with 'em."

"Oh."

"Besides," he added, his eyes avoiding mine, "if they ever got their hands on my system they'd just duplicate it and stop paying me."

"But you've patented the system, haven't you?"

His eyes became really evasive. "Not yet. Patents take time."

Suddenly our celebration dinner had turned glum. The mood had been broken, the charm lost, the enchantment gone. Maybe we were both tired from the excitement of the day and our adrenaline rush had petered out. Whatever the reason, we finished dinner and Sam drove me back to my hotel.

"I guess you're going back to the States," he said, once he'd stopped the convertible at the hotel's front entrance.

"I guess," I said.

"It's been fun knowing you, Ramona. You've been a good-luck charm for me."

I sighed. "Wish I didn't have to leave."

"Me too."

"Maybe I could find a job here," I hinted.

Sam didn't reply. He could have said he'd find a position for me in his company, but it's probably better that he didn't, the way things worked out.

The hotel doorman came grudgingly up to the car and opened my door with a murmured, *"Buenas noches."*

I went up to my room, feeling miserable. I couldn't sleep. I tossed in the bed, wide awake, unhappy, trying to sort out my feelings and take some control of them. Didn't do me one bit of good. After hours of lying there in the same bed Sam and I had made love in, I tried pacing the floor.

Finally, in desperation, I went back to bed and turned on the TV. Most of the channels were in Spanish, of course, but I flicked through to find some English-speaking movie or something else that would hypnotize me to sleep.

And ran across the weather channel.

I almost missed it, surfing through the channels the way I was. But I heard the commentator say something about a hurricane as I surfed through. It took a couple of seconds for the words to make an impression on my conscious mind.

Then I clicked back to the weather. Sure enough, there was a monster hurricane roaring through the Caribbean. It was too far north to threaten Panama, but it was heading toward Cuba and maybe eventually Florida.

When we orbited over the region, not much more than twelve hours ago, the Caribbean had been clear as crystal. I remember staring out at Cuba; I could even see the little tail of the keys extending out from Florida's southern tip. No hurricane in sight.

I punched up my pillows and sat up in bed, watching the weather. The American midwest was cut in half by a cold front that spread early-season snow in Minnesota and rain southward all the way to Louisiana. The whole Mississippi valley was covered with clouds.

But the Mississippi was clearly visible for its entire length when we'd been up in orbit that morning.

Could the weather change that fast?

I fell asleep with the weather channel bleating at me. And dreamed weird, convoluted dreams about Sam and hurricanes and watching television.

The next morning I packed and left Colón, but only flew as far as Panamá city, on the Pacific side of the canal. I was determined to find out how Sam had tricked me. Deceived all forty of us. But I was taking no chances on bumping into Sam in Colón.

Within a week Sam was doing a roaring business in space tours. He hadn't gotten to the point where he was flying two trips per day, but a telephone call to his company revealed that Space Adventure Tours was completely booked for the next four months. The smiling young woman who took my call cheerfully informed me that she could take a reservation for early in February, if I liked.

I declined. Then I phoned my boss at the DEA in Washington, to get him to find me an Air Force pilot.

"Someone who's never been anywhere near NASA," I told my boss. I didn't want to run the risk of getting a pilot who might have been even a chance acquaintance of Sam's. "And make sure he's male," I added. Sam was just too heart-meltingly charming when he wanted to be. I would take no chances.

What they sent me was Hector Dominguez, a swarthy, broad-shouldered, almost totally silent young pilot fresh from the Air Force Academy. I met him in the lobby of my hotel, the once-elegant old Ritz. It was easy to spot him: he wasn't in uniform, but he might as well have been, with a starched white shirt, knife-edged creases on his dark blue slacks, and a military buzz cut. He'd *never* make it as an undercover agent.

I needed him for flying, thank goodness, not spying. I introduced myself and led him to the hotel's restaurant, where I explained what I wanted over lunch. He nodded in the right places and mumbled an occasional, "Yes, ma'am." His longest conversational offering was, "Please pass the bread, ma'am."

He made me feel like I was ninety! But he apparently knew his stuff, and the next morning when I drove out to the airport he was standing beside a swept-wing jet trainer, in his flier's sky-blue coveralls, waiting for me.

He helped me into a pair of coveralls, very gingerly. I got the impression that he was afraid I'd complain of sexual harassment if he actually touched me. Once I had to lean on his shoulder, when I was worming into the parachute harness I had to put on; I thought he'd break the Olympic record for long jump, the way he flinched away from me.

The ground crew helped me clamber up into the cockpit, connected my radio and oxygen lines, buckled my seat harness and showed me how to fasten the oxygen mask to my plastic helmet. Then they got out of the way and the clear bubble of the plane's canopy clamped down over Hector and me.

Once we were buttoned up in the plane's narrow cockpit, me up front and him behind me, he changed completely.

"We'll be following their 747," Hector's voice crackled in my helmet earphones, "up to its maximum altitude of fifty thousand feet."

"That's where the orbiter is supposed to separate from it," I said, needlessly.

"Right. We'll stay within visual contact of the 747 until the orbiter returns."

If it ever actually leaves the 747, I thought.

Hector was a smooth pilot. He got the little jet trainer off the runway and arrowed us up across the Panama Canal. In less than fifteen minutes we spotted the lumbering 747 and piggybacking orbiter, with their bright blue SPACE ADVENTURE TOURS stenciled across their white fuselages.

For more than three hours we followed them. The orbiter never separated from the 747. The two flew serenely across the Caribbean, locked together like Siamese twins. Far below us, on the fringe of the northern horizon, I could see bands of swirling gray-white clouds: the edge of the hurricane.

Sam's 747-and-orbiter only went as high as thirty thousand feet, then leveled out.

"He's out of the main traffic routes," Hector informed me. "Nobody around for a hundred miles, except us."

"They can't see us, can they?"

"Not unless they have rear-looking radar."

Hector kept us behind and slightly below Sam's hybrid aircraft. Then I saw the 747's nose pull up; they started climbing. Hector stayed right on station behind them, as if we were connected by an invisible chain.

Sam's craft climbed more steeply, then nosed over into a shallow dive. We did the same, and I felt my stomach drop away for a heart-stopping few moments before a feeling of weight returned.

In my earphones I heard Hector chuckling. "That's how he gave you a feeling of zero-gee," he said. "It's the old Vomit Comet trick. They use it at Houston to give astronauts-in-training a feeling for zero gravity."

"What do you mean?" I asked.

"You fly a parabolic arc: up at the top of the arc you get a few seconds of pretty near zero gravity."

"That's when we felt weightless!" I realized.

"Yeah. And when they leveled off you thought his anti-space-sickness equipment was working. All he did was start flying straight and level again."

Magic tricks are simple when you learn how they're done.

"What did you say about a vomit something or other?"

Hector laughed again. It was a very pleasant, warm sound. "At Houston, they call the training plane the Vomit Comet. That's because they fly a couple dozen parabolic arcs each flight. You go from regular gravity to zero-gee and back again every few minutes. Makes your stomach go crazy."

So Sam's entire space adventure was a total shuck. A sham. A hoax. I had felt disappointed when I'd first suspected Sam. Now that I had the evidence, I felt even worse: bitter, sad, miserable.

I know, Uncle Griff! You told me he was no good. But—well, I still felt awful.

That evening I just couldn't bear the thought of eating alone, so I invited Hector to have dinner with me. He was staying at the Ritz, too, so we went to the hotel's shabby old restaurant. It must have once been a splendid place, but it was tacky and run-down and not even half filled. The waiters were all ancient, and even though the food was really good, the meal left me even more depressed than I had been before.

To make it all worse, Hector reverted to his monosyllabic introversion once we left the airport.

Is it me? I wondered. Is he naturally shy around women? Is he gay? That would've been a shame, I thought. He was really handsome, in a dark, smoldering sort of way. Gorgeous big midnight eyes. And I imagined that his hair would grow out curly if he ever allowed it to. His voice was low and dreamy, too—when he chose to say a word or two.

I tried to make conversation with him, but it was like pulling teeth. It took the whole dinner to find out that he was from New Mexico, he wasn't married, and he intended to make a career of the Air Force.

"I like to fly." That was his longest sentence of the evening.

I went to bed wanting to cry. I dreamed about Sam; I dreamed that I was a hired assassin and I had to kill him.

Hector and I trailed Sam's plane again the next day, but this time I brought a video camera and photographed his entire flight sequence. Evidence.

A job is a job, and no matter how much I hated doing it, I was here to get the goods on Sam Gunn. So he wasn't smuggling drugs. What he was doing was still wrong: bilking people of their hard-earned money on phony promises to fly them into space. Scamming little old widows and retired couples living on pensions. Swindling honeymoon couples.

And let's face it, he swindled me, too. In more ways than one.

That afternoon I had Hector fly me over to Colón and, together, we went to the offices of Space Adventure Tours.

Sam seemed truly delighted to see us. He ushered us into his elegant office with a huge grin on his apple-pie face, shook hands with Hector, bussed me on the cheek, and climbed the ramp behind his walnut and chrome desk and sat down in his high-backed leather swivel chair. Hector and I sat on the two recliners.

"Are you two a thing?" Sam asked, archly.

"A thing?" I asked back.

"Romantically."

"No!" I was surprised to hear Hector blurt the word out just as forcefully as I did. Stereophonic denial.

"Oh." Sam looked slightly disappointed, but only for a moment. "I thought maybe you wanted to take a honeymoon flight in space."

"Sam, you never go higher than thirty-five thousand feet and I have a video to prove it."

He blinked at me. It was the first time I'd ever seen Sam Gunn go silent.

"Your whole scheme is a fake, Sam. A fraud. You're stealing your customers' money. That's theft. Grand larceny, I'm sure."

The sadness I had felt was giving way to anger: smoldering burning rage at this man who had seemed so wonderful but was really such a scoundrel, such a rat, such a lying, sneaking, thieving bastard. I had trusted Sam! And he had been nothing but deceitful.

Sam leaned back in his luxurious desk chair and puckered his lips thoughtfully.

"You're going to jail, Sam. For a long time."

"May I point out, oh righteous, wrathful one, that you're assuming the laws of Panama are the same as the laws of the good old US of A."

"They have laws against fraud and bunko," I shot back hotly, "even in Panama."

"Do you think I've defrauded my customers, Ramona?"

"You certainly have!"

Very calmly, Sam asked, "Did you enjoy your flight?"

"What's that got to do with it?"

"Did you enjoy it?" Sam insisted.

"At the time, yes, I did. But then I found out—"

"You found out that you didn't actually go into orbit. You found out that we just fly our customers around and make them *feel* as if they're in space."

"Your whole operation is a fake!"

He made an equivocal gesture with his hands. "We don't take you into orbit, that's true. The scenes you see through the spacecraft's windows are videos from real space flights, though. You're seeing what you'd see if you actually did go into space."

"You're telling your customers that you take them into space!" I nearly screamed. "That's a lie!"

Sam opened a desk drawer and pulled out a slick, multicolor sales brochure. He slid it across the desk toward me.

"Show me where it says we take our customers into orbit."

I glanced at the brochure's cover. It showed a picture of an elderly couple smiling so wide their dentures were in danger of falling out. Behind them was a backdrop of the Earth as seen from orbit.

"Nowhere in our promotional literature or video presentations do we promise to take our customers into space," Sam said evenly.

"But—"

"The contracts our customers sign say that Space Adventure Tours will give them an *experience* of space flight. Which is what we do. We give our customers a simulation: a carefully designed simulation so that they can have the *experience* of their lives."

"You tell them you're taking them into space!"

"Do not."

"You do too! You told *me* you'd fly me into orbit!"

Sam shook his head sadly. "That may be what you heard. What you wanted to hear. But I have never told any of my customers that Space Adventure Tours would actually, physically, transport them into orbit."

"You did! You did!"

"No I didn't. If you'd recorded our conversations, you'd find that I never told you—or anybody else—that I'd fly you into space."

I looked at Hector. He sat like a graven idol: silent and unmoving.

"When we were in the orbiter," I remembered, "you made all this talk about separating from the 747 and going into orbit."

"That was part of the simulation," Sam said. "Once you're on board the orbiter, it's all an act. It's all part of the experience. Like an amusement park ride."

Exasperated, I said, "Sam, your customers are going home and telling their friends and relatives that they've really flown in space. They're sending new customers to you, people who expect to go into orbit for real!"

With a shrug, Sam answered, "Ramona, honey, I'm not responsible for what people think, or say, or do. If they wanna believe they've really been in space, that's their fantasy, their happiness. Who am I to deny them?"

I was beyond fury. My insides felt bitter cold. "All right," I said icily. "Suppose I go back to the States and let the news media know what you're doing? How long do you think customers will keep coming?"

Sam's brows knit slightly. "Gimme two more months," he said.

"Two more months?"

"Let me operate like this for two more months, and then I'll close down voluntarily."

"You're asking me to allow you to defraud the public for another two months?"

His eyes narrowed. "You know, you're talking like a lawyer. Or maybe a cop."

"What and who I am has nothing to do with this," I snapped.

"A cop," Sam said, with a heavy sigh.

Out of nowhere, Hector spoke up. "Why do you want two months?"

I whirled on the poor guy. "So he can steal as much money as he can from the poor unsuspecting slobs he calls his customers, why else?"

"Yeah," Hector said, in that smoky low voice of his, "okay, maybe so. But why two months?"

Before I could think of an answer, Sam popped in. "Because in two months I'll have proved my point."

"What point?"

"That there's a viable market for tourists in space. That people'll spend a good-sized hunk of change just for the chance to ride into orbit."

"Which you don't really do," I reminded him.

"That doesn't matter," Sam said. "The point I'm making is that there really is a market for space tourism. People have been talking about space tourism for years; I'm doing something about it."

"You're stealing," I said. "Swindling."

"Okay, so I'm faking it. Nevertheless, people are plunking down their money for a space adventure."

"So what?" I sneered.

Hunching forward, leaning his forearms on the gleaming desktop, Sam said, "So with three whole months of this operation behind me, I can go back to the States and raise enough capital to lease a Clippership that'll *really* take tourists into orbit."

I stared at him.

Hector got the point before I did. "You mean the financial people won't believe there's a market for space tourism now, but they will after you've operated this fake business for three months?"

"Right," Sam answered. "Those Wall Street types don't open up their wallets until you've got solid numbers to show 'em."

"What about venture capitalists?" Hector asked. "They back new, untried ideas all the time."

Sam made a sour face. "Sure they do. I went to some of 'em. First thing they did was ask me why the big boys like Rockledge and Global Technologies aren't doing it. Then they go to the 'experts' in the field and ask their opinion of the idea. And who're the experts?"

"Rockledge and Global," I guessed.

Shaking his head, Sam said, "Even worse. They went to NASA. To Clark Griffith IV, my own boss, for crap's sake! By the time he got done scaring the cojones off them, they wouldn't even answer my e-mail."

"NASA shot you down?"

"They didn't know it was me. They talked to a team that the venture capitalists put together."

I asked, "But shouldn't NASA be in favor of space tourism? I mean, they're the space agency, after all."

"Some people in NASA are in favor of it, sure," Sam said. "But the higher you go in the agency the more conservative they get. Up at the top they have nightmares of a spacecraft full of tourists blowing up, like the old *Challenger*. That'd set back everything we do in space by ten years, at least."

"So when the venture capitalists asked . . ."

"The agency bigwigs threw enough cold water on the idea to freeze the Amazon River," Sam growled.

"And that's when you started Space Adventure Tours," I said.

"Right. Set the whole company up while I was still working at the Cape. Then I took a three-month leave to personally run the operation. I've got two months left to go."

Silence. I sat there, not knowing what to say next. Hector looked thoughtful, or maybe puzzled is a better description of the expression on his face. Sam leaned back in his high chair, staring at me like a little boy who's been caught with his hand in the cookie jar, but is hoping to get a cookie out of it instead of a spanking.

I was in a turmoil of conflicting emotions. I really liked Sam, even though he had quite literally screwed me. But I couldn't let him continue to swindle people; that was wrong any way you looked at it, legally or morally.

On the other hand, Sam wasn't really hurting anybody. Was he? Did any of his customers empty their retirement accounts to take his phony ride? Would any of those retired couples spend their declining years in poverty because Sam bilked them out of their life savings?

I shook my head, trying to settle my spinning thoughts into some rational order. Sam was breaking all kinds of laws, and he'd have to stop. Right now.

"All right," I said, my mind finally made up. "I'm not going to report this back to your superiors at NASA."

Sam's face lit up.

"And I'm not going to blow the whistle on you or bring in the authorities," I continued.

Sam grinned from ear to ear.

"On one condition," I said firmly.

His rusty eyebrows hiked up. "One condition?"

"You've got to shut this operation down, Sam. Either shut down voluntarily, or I'll be forced to inform the authorities here in Panama and the news media in the States."

He nodded solemnly. "Fair enough. In two months I'll close up shop."

"Not in two months," I snapped. "Now. Today. You go out of business *now* and refund whatever monies you've collected for future flights."

I expected Sam to argue. I expected him to rant and holler at me. Or at least plead and wheedle. He did neither. For long, long moments he simply sat there staring at me, saying nothing, his face looking as if I'd just put a bullet through his heart.

I steeled myself and stared right back at him. Hector stirred uneasily in his chair beside me, sensing that there was more going on than we had expressed in words, but saying nothing.

At last Sam heaved an enormous sigh and said, in a tiny little exhausted voice, "Okay, if that's what you want. I'm in no position to fight back."

I should have known right there and then that he was lying through his crooked teeth.

Hector flew me back to Panamá City and we repaired to our separate hotel rooms. I felt totally drained, really out of it, as if I'd spent the day fighting dragons or climbing cliffs by my fingernails.

Then things started to get weird.

I had just flopped on my hotel room bed, not even bothering to take off my clothes, when the phone rang. My boss from DEA headquarters in Washington.

"You're going to have a visitor," he told me, looking nettled in the tiny phone screen. "Her name will be Jones. Listen to what she has to tell you and act accordingly."

"A visitor?" I mumbled, feeling thickheaded, confused. "Who? Why?"

My boss doesn't nettle easily, but he sure looked ticked off. "She'll explain it all to you. And this is the last goddamned time I let you or any other of my people go off on detached duty to help some other agency!"

With that, he cut off the connection. I was looking at a blank phone screen, wondering what on earth was going on.

The phone buzzed again. This time it was Hector.

"I just got a phone call from my group commander at Eglin," he said. "Some really weird shit has hit the fan, Ramona. I'm under orders to stay here in Panama with you until we meet with some woman named Jones."

"I got the same orders from my boss," I told him.

Hector's darkly handsome face went into brooding mode. "I don't like the sound of this," he muttered.

"Neither do I," I confessed.

We didn't have long to wait. Ms. Jones arrived bright and early the following morning. In fact, Hector and I were having breakfast together in the hotel's nearly empty dining room, trying to guess what was going on, when she sauntered in.

She didn't hesitate a moment, just walked right up to our table and sat down, as if she'd been studying photographs of us for the past week or two.

"Adrienne Jones," she said, opening her black leather shoulder bag and pulling out a leather-encased laminated ID card. It said she was with the U.S. Department of State.

She didn't look like a diplomat. Adrienne Jones—if that was really her name—was a tall, sleek, leggy African-American whose skin was the color of polished ebony. She had a fashion model's figure and face: high cheekbones, almond eyes, and a tousled, careless hairdo that must have cost a fortune. Her clothes were expensive, too.

Hector stared at her, too stunned to speak. I felt dismal and threadbare beside her in my shapeless slacks and blouse, with a belly bag strapped around my middle.

I hated her immediately.

"If you're really with the State Department." I said as she snapped her ID closed and put it back in her capacious shoulder bag, "then I'm from Disney World."

She smiled at me the way a snake does. "That's the one in Florida, isn't it?"

Hector found his voice. "CIA, right? You've got to be with the CIA."

Jones ignored his guess. "You both have been informed that you are to cooperate with me, correct?"

"I was told to listen to what you have to say," I said.

"Me too," said Hector.

"Very well, then. Here's what I have to say: Leave Sam Gunn alone. Let him continue to operate. Do not interfere with him in any way."

What kind of strings had Sam pulled? He had come across to me as the little guy struggling against the big boys, but here was the State Department or the CIA—or *some* federal agency—ordering me to keep my hands off.

"Why?" I asked.

"You don't have to know," said Jones. "Just leave Sam be. No interference with his operation."

Hector scratched his head and glanced at me. He was an Air Force officer, I realized, and had to follow orders. His career depended on it. Me, I had a career, too. But I wasn't going to let this fashion model stranger order me around, no matter what my boss said.

"Okay," I told her, "I've listened to what you have to say. That doesn't mean I'm going to do what you're asking me to do."

Jones smiled again, venomously. "I'm not asking you. I'm telling you."

"You can tell me whatever you like. I'm not going to go along with it unless I know the whys and wherefores."

Her smile faded into grimness. "Look, Ms. Perkins, your superior at DEA has been briefed and he agreed to cooperate. He's told you to cooperate, and that's what you'd better do, if you know what's good for you."

"You briefed him? Then brief me."

She snorted through her finely chiseled nostrils. "All I can tell you is that this is a high-priority matter, and it has the backing of the highest levels of authority."

"Highest levels?" I asked. "Like the White House?"

She didn't answer.

"The Oval Office? The President himself?"

Jones remained as silent and still as the Sphinx.

I heard myself say, "Not good enough, Ms. Jones. Anybody can claim they're working on orders from the White House. I've heard even fancier stories, in my line of work. What's going on?"

She merely shook her head, just the slightest of motions but clearly a negative.

"Okay then." I got up from my chair. "I'm catching the next flight to Miami and going straight to the news media. They'll be really interested to hear that the CIA is backing a fraudulent tourist operation in Panama."

"I wouldn't try that if I were you," Jones said.

Hector stood up beside me. "You threaten her, you've got to go through me."

I gaped at him. "You don't have to protect me. I can take care of myself."

"I'm in this, too," he insisted. "We're partners."

Jones threw her head back and laughed. "What you two are," she said, "is a couple of babes in the woods. And if you don't start behaving yourselves, you're going to end up as babes in a swamp, feeding alligators."

I unzipped my belly bag and pulled out my cellphone. "CNN, Atlanta, USA," I said to the phone system's computer. "News desk."

"Put it down," Jones said.

I kept the phone pressed against my ear, listening to the computer chatter as the system made the connection.

"Put it down," she repeated. Her voice was flat, calm, yet menacing. I realized that her black leather shoulder bag was big enough to hold a small arsenal.

"News," I heard a tired voice answer.

Jones said, "We can cut a deal, if you're reasonable."

"News desk," the voice repeated, a little irked.

I put the phone down and clicked it off. "What kind of a deal?"

Jones gestured with both her hands; she had long, graceful fingers, I noticed. I sat down, then Hector took his seat beside me.

"God spare me the righteous amateurs," Jones muttered. "You two have no idea of what you're messing with."

"Then tell us," I said.

"I can't tell you," she replied. "But if you want to, you can come back to Colón with me and watch it happen."

I didn't know what to say.

Jones misinterpreted my silence as reluctance, so she went on, "You give me your word you won't go blowing off to the media or anybody else and you can come with me and see what this is all about. After it's over you can go back home, safe and sound. Deal?"

I'd seen enough drug deals to know that she was showing us only the tip of the iceberg. But I was curious, and—to tell the absolute truth—I was wondering how Sam got himself mixed up with the CIA and whether he was in danger or not.

So I glanced at Hector, who remained silent, suspicious. But he looked at me and his expression said that he'd back whatever move I made. So I said, "Deal."

We couldn't squeeze a third body into Hector's training jet, and Jones didn't trust us out of her sight, so we flew back to Colón again in her plane: a twin-engined executive jet. I was beginning to feel like a Ping-Pong ball, bouncing from Colón to Panamá city and back again.

Hector was impressed with the plane's luxurious interior. "Like a movie," he said, awed. Instead of sitting beside me, he asked to go up into the cockpit. Jones gave him a friendly smile and said okay. I didn't see him again until we landed.

An unmarked Mercedes four-door sedan was waiting for us at the runway ramp, the kind of luxury car the drug dealers call a "cocaine Ford." Two men in dark suits bustled Hector and me into the rear seat. Jones sat up front with the driver. The other man followed us in another unmarked Mercedes. I felt distinctly nervous.

But all we did is drive across the airport to Sam's converted blimp hangar.

"Mr. Gunn is doing a special flight this afternoon," Jones told us cryptically, half turned in her seat to face us. "Once it's finished, you two can go back to the States—*if* you promise not to blow the whistle on Space Adventure Tours."

"And if we don't promise?" I asked. Instead of strong and forceful, my voice came out as a little girl's squeak, which made me disgusted with myself.

Jones didn't answer; she merely reverted to her cobra-type smile.

We pulled up outside the hangar. Inside, I could see the big 747 with the orbiter clamped atop it. Technicians were swarming all over it.

"Sam had his regular flight this morning," I muttered to Hector. "Now they're getting the plane ready for another flight."

Hector nodded. "Looks like."

We sat and watched, while our Mercedes's engine purred away so the car's air conditioning could stay on. Sam came out of an office up on the catwalk above the hangar floor, with two slick-looking lawyerly types flanking him. He was grinning and gabbing away a mile a minute, happy as a kid in a candy store. Or so it seemed from this distance.

Jones opened her door. "You stay here," she said—as much to the driver as to us, I thought. "Don't leave this car."

So we sat in the car with the afternoon sun beating down on us and the air conditioner laboring to keep the interior cool. Our driver was old enough to be gray at the temples; solidly built, and I guessed that he was carrying a nine-millimeter automatic in a shoulder holster under his dark suit jacket. He looked perfectly comfortable and prepared to sit and watch over us for hours and hours.

I was bursting to find out what was going on. There were more technicians clambering over the ladders and scaffolds surrounding the piggyback planes than I had ever seen in Sam's employ. Most of them must be Jones's people, I thought. Something very special is being cooked up here.

Then a fleet of limousines drove into view, coming slowly across the concrete rampway until they stopped in front of the hangar. Eleven limos, I counted. One of them had stiff little flags attached to its front fenders: blue with some kind of shield or seal in the middle, surrounded by six five-pointed white stars.

Dozens of men jumped out of the limos, about half of them in olive-green army fatigues. They didn't look like Americans. Each soldier carried a wicked-looking assault rifle with a curved magazine. The rest of the men wore business suits that bulged beneath their armpits and the kind of dark sunglasses that just screamed "bodyguard."

They spread out, poking their noses—and rifle muzzles—into every corner of the hangar. A couple of the suits came up to our car, where the glamorous Ms. Jones greeted them with a big toothy smile. I couldn't make out what she was saying to them, but it sounded like she was speaking in Spanish.

Sam came bubbling over, practically drooling once he feasted his eyes on Jones. He didn't notice us inside the car, behind the heavily tinted windows.

At last, the leader of the suits turned to the team of soldiers surround-

ing the beflagged limo and gave a curt nod. They opened the rear door
and out stepped a little girl, with big dark eyes and long hair that just had
to be naturally curly. She couldn't have been more than ten years old. She
smiled at the soldiers, as if she knew them by name. She was very nicely
dressed in a one-piece jumpsuit of butter yellow.

She turned back and said something to someone who was still inside
the limo. She reached her hand in to whoever it was. A tall, lean man of
about fifty came out of the limo and stretched to his full height. He was
wearing army fatigues and smoking an immense cigar.

My jaw fell open. "That's the president of Cuba!" I gasped. "The man
who took over when Castro died."

"No," Hector corrected me. "He's the man who took over after the
bloodbath in Havana when Castro died."

"That must be his daughter."

"What're they doing here?" Hector wondered.

"Taking one of Sam's phony rides into space," I said. "I wonder if they
know it's a phony?"

Hector turned to face me. "Maybe it's not."

"Not what?"

"Not a phony," he said grimly. "Maybe they're going to have an accident up there. On purpose."

It hit me like a shot of pure heroin. "They're going to assassinate the
president of Cuba!"

"And make it look like an accident."

"Oh my god!"

The driver turned slightly to tell us, "Don't get any crazy ideas—"

He never got any further. I jammed my thumbs into his carotids and
held on. In a few seconds he was unconscious.

"Where'd you learn that?" Hector asked, his tone somewhere between
amazement and admiration.

"South Philadelphia," I answered as I yanked the nine-millimeter from
the driver's holster. "Come on."

Hector grasped my shoulder. "You're not going to get far in a shoot-out."

He was right, dammit. I had to think fast. Outside, I could see Jones
leading the president of Cuba and his daughter toward the plane. Half the
Cuban security force walked a respectful distance behind them, the other
half was deployed on either side of them.

"Most of those ground crew personnel must be security guys from the

States," Hector pointed out. "Must be enough firepower out there to start World War III."

My eye lit on Sam. He was still standing in the sunshine of the ramp, outside the hangar, hardly more than ten meters from our car.

"Come on," I said, leaning past the unconscious driver to pop the door lock.

I stuffed the pistol in my belly bag, keeping the bag unzipped so I could grab the gun quickly if I needed to.

Sam turned as we approached him. He looked surprised, then delighted.

"Ramona!" he said with a big grin. "I thought you two had gone back to the States."

"Not yet," I said grimly. "We're taking this flight with you."

For an instant Sam looked puzzled, but then he said, "Great. Come on, you can ride in the 747 with me."

"You're not going aboard the orbiter?"

"Not this flight," Sam said easily.

Of course not, I thought. On this flight the orbiter's really going to be released from the 747. Instead of going into space, as Sam promised, it was going to crash into the Caribbean. With the president of Cuba aboard. And his ten-year-old daughter.

"Sam, how could you do this?" I asked as we walked into the hangar.

"Listen, I was just as surprised as you would be when the State Department asked me to do it."

"With his little daughter, too."

We reached the ladder. "It was his daughter's idea," Sam said. "She wanted to take the space ride. Poppa's only doing this to please his little girl—and for the international publicity, of course."

With Sam leading the way we climbed up the ladder into the 747. Its interior was strictly utilitarian: no fancy decor. Most of the cavernous passenger cabin was empty. There were only seats up in the first-class section, below the cockpit. Sam, Hector and I went up the spiral stairs and entered the cockpit, where a young woman in a pilot's uniform was already sitting in the right-hand seat.

"Can you fly this plane?" I asked Hector.

He stared at the control panels; the gauges and buttons and keypads seemed to stretch for miles. Looking out the windshield, I saw we were already so high up we might as well have been on oxygen.

"I've got a multiengine license," Hector muttered.

"But can you fly *this* plane?" I insisted.

He nodded tightly. "I can fly anything."

Sam put on a quizzical look. "Why should he have to fly? I'm going to pilot this mission myself and I've got a qualified copilot here."

I pulled the pistol from my belly bag and pointed it at the copilot. "Get out," I said. "Hector, you take her place."

She stared at me, wide-eyed, frozen.

"Vamos," Sam said, in the most un-Spanish accent I'd ever heard. The woman slipped out of the copilot's chair.

"What's this all about?" Sam asked, more intrigued than scared. "Why the toy cannon?"

I pointed the gun at him. "Sam, you're going to fly this plane just the way you would for any of your tourist flights. No more and no less."

He gave me one of his lopsided grins. "Sure. What else?"

There were two jump seats behind the pilots' chairs. I took one and Sam's erstwhile copilot the other. I kept the pistol in my hand as we rolled out of the hangar, lit up the engines, and taxied to the runway.

"What do you think is going on here," Sam asked, "that makes you need a gun?"

"You know perfectly well what's going on," I said.

"Yeah," he answered ruefully. "But I don't know what *you* know."

"Who's in the orbiter's cockpit?" I asked.

"Some guy the State Department insisted on. They wanted their own people up there with *El Presidente* and his daughter."

"Do they have parachutes?"

"Parachutes? What for?"

"They're all going down with the president and his daughter?"

"Whither he goest," Sam replied.

We took off smoothly and headed out over the Caribbean. Is this part of the Bermuda Triangle? I asked myself. Will this fatal accident be chalked up as another mystical happening, or the work of aliens from outer space?

"How could you let them use you like this, Sam?" I blurted.

He glanced over his shoulder at me, saw how miserable I felt, and quickly turned back to the plane's controls.

"Ramona, honey, when people that high up in the federal government want to make you jump, you really don't have all that much of a choice."

"You could have said no."

"And miss the chance of a lifetime! No way!"

So despite all his blather about hating bureaucracies and wanting to help ordinary people, the little guy, against the big shots of government and industry, Sam sold out when they put the pressure on him. He probably didn't have much of a choice, at that. Do what they tell you or you're out of business. Maybe they threatened his life. I'd heard stories about the CIA and how they worked both sides of the street. They'd even been involved in the drug traffic, according to rumors around headquarters.

We flew in dismal silence across a sparkling clear sea. At least, I grew silent. Sam spent the time acquainting Hector with the plane's controls and particular handling characteristics.

"Gotta remember we've got a ninety-nine-ton brick on our backs," he chattered cheerfully, as if he didn't have a care in the world.

Hector nodded and listened, listened and nodded. Sam jabbered away, one pilot to another, oblivious to everything else except flying.

Me, I was starting to worry about what was going to happen when we returned to Colón with the orbiter still intact and the Cuban president very much alive. Jones and her people would probably put the best face they could on it, like that's what they had intended all along: a goodwill flight to help cement friendly relations between Cuba and the U.S. But I knew that if the CIA didn't get me, some fanatical old anti-Castro nutcake in Miami would come after me.

And Hector, too, I realized. I'd put his life in danger, when all he wanted was to protect me.

I felt really miserable about that. The poor guy was in as much danger as I was, even though none of this was his fault.

I studied his face as he sat in the copilot's chair next to Sam. Hector didn't look worried. Or frightened. Or even tense. He was happy as a clam, behind the controls of this monstrous plane, five miles over the deep blue sea.

"Now comes the tricky part," Sam was telling him, leaning over toward Hector slightly so he could hear him better.

Sitting on the jump seat behind Sam, I tightened my grip on the pistol. "You're not going to separate the orbiter," I said firmly.

Without even glancing back at me, Sam broke into cackling laughter. "Couldn't even if I wanted to, oh masked rider of the plains. The bird's welded on. You'd need a load of primacord to blast 'er loose."

"What about the explosive bolts?" I asked.

Sam cackled again. "That's part of the simulation, kiddo. There aren't any."

I saw that Hector was grinning, as if he knew something that I didn't.

"Then how do you intend to separate the orbiter?" I demanded.

"I don't," Sam replied.

"Then how . . ." The question died in my throat. I had been a fool. A stupendous fool. This wasn't an assassination plot; Sam was taking the president of Cuba—and his ten-year-old daughter—for a space flight experience, just as he'd taken several hundred other tourists.

I could feel my face burning. Hector, his smile gentle and sweet, turned toward me and said softly, "Maybe you should unload the gun, huh? Just to be on the safe side."

I clicked on the safety, then popped the magazine out of the pistol's grip.

I sat in silence for the rest of the flight. There was nothing for me to say. I had been an idiot, jumping to conclusions and suspecting Sam of being a partner in a heinous crime. I felt *awful*.

After the regular routine over the Caribbean, Sam turned us back to Colón, and we landed at the airport without incident. Sam taxied the plane to his hangar, where a throng of news reporters and photographers were waiting.

With his daughter clinging to his side, the president of Cuba gave a long and smiling speech in Spanish to the news people. Sam squirmed out of his pilot's chair and rushed down to the hangar floor so he could stand beside the Cuban president and bask in the glow of publicity. Naturally, he grabbed the woman who was supposed to be his copilot and took her along with him.

I stayed in the cockpit with Hector, watching the whole thing. I could see Ms. Jones hovering around the edge of the crowd, together with her people; even she was smiling.

El Presidente put his arm around Sam's shoulders and spoke glowingly. It was still in Spanish, but the tone was very warm, very friendly. Cuban-American relations soared almost as high as the president thought he'd flown. Sam signed his autograph for the president's daughter. She was almost as tall as he, I noticed.

Cameras clicked and whirred, vidcams buzzed away, reporters shouted questions in English and Spanish. It was a field day—for everybody but me.

Hector shook his head and gave me a rueful grin. "I guess we were a little wrong about all this," he said, almost in a whisper.

"It's my fault," I said. "I got you into this."

"Don't look so sad. Everything came out okay. Sam's a hero."

All I wanted to do was to stay in that cockpit and hide forever.

At last *El Presidente* and his daughter made their way back to their limousine. The fleet of limos departed and the crowd of media people broke up. Even the American State Department people started to leave. That's what they were, I reluctantly admitted to myself. Jones and her people really were from the State Department, not the CIA.

Finally Sam came strolling the length of the 747's cabin and climbed up the spiral staircase to the cockpit, whistling horribly off-key every step of the way.

He popped his head through the hatch, grinning like a Jack-o'-lantern. "You want me to send some pizzas up here or are you gonna come out and have dinner with me?"

Hector took me by the hand, gently, and got to his feet. He had to bend over slightly in the low-ceilinged cockpit, a problem that Sam didn't have to worry about.

"We're coming out," he said. I let him lead me, like a docile little lamb.

We went straight to Sam's favorite restaurant, the waterfront shack that served such good fish. Jones was already there, sipping at a deadly-looking rum concoction and smiling happily.

"I ought to be angry with you two," she said, once we sat at the little round table with her.

"It's my fault," I said immediately. "I'm the one to blame."

Hector started to say something, but Jones shushed him with a gesture of her long, graceful hand. "No harm, no foul. The flight went *beautifully*, and I'm not going to screw up my report by even mentioning your names."

Sam was aglow. He ordered drinks for all of us, and as the waiter left our table, he looked over at the bar.

"Lookit that!" Sam said, pointing to the TV over the joint's fake-bamboo bar.

We saw the president of Cuba smiling toothily, his daughter on one side of him and Sam Gunn on the other.

"Worldwide publicity!" Sam crowed. "I'm a made man!"

Hector shook his head. "If anybody ever finds out that your orbiter never left the 747, Sam, the publicity won't be so good."

For Hector, that was a marathon speech.

Sam grinned at him. "Now who's going to tell on me? The Department of State?"

Jones shook her head. "Not us."

"NASA?" Sam asked rhetorically. "You think some rocket expert in NASA's gonna stand up and declare that you can't remate the orbiter with its carrier plane once it's been separated?"

Before any of us could reply, Sam answered his own question. "In a pig's eye! The word's going through the agency now, from top to bottom: no comment on Space Adventure Tours. Zip. Nada. Zilch. The lid is on and it's on tight."

"What about you two?" Jones asked, arching a perfect brow.

Hector glanced at me, then shrugged. "I'm in the Air Force. If I'm ordered to keep quiet, I'll keep quiet."

"And you, Ms. Perkins?" Jones asked me.

I focused on Sam. "You promised to end this bogus business, Sam."

"Yeah, that's right, I did."

"Did you tell the president of Cuba that all he got was a simulation?" I asked.

Sam screwed up his face and admitted, "Not exactly."

"What happens to Cuban-American relations when he finds out?"

Jones's smile had evaporated. "Which brings us back to the vital question: are you going to try to blow the whistle?"

I didn't like the sound of that *try to*.

"No, she's not," Sam said. "Ramona's a good American citizen and this is a matter of international relations now."

The gall of the man! He had elevated his scam into an integral part of the State Department's efforts to end the generations-old split between Cuba and the U.S. I wondered who in Washington had been crazy enough to hang our foreign policy on Sam Gunn's trickery and deceit. Probably the same kind of deskbound lunkheads who had once dickered with the Mafia to assassinate Castro with a poisoned cigar.

"I want to hear what you have to say, Ms. Perkins," Jones said, her voice low but hard as steel.

What could I say? What did I *want* to say? I really didn't know.

But I heard my own voice tell them, "Sam promised to close down Space Adventure Tours in two more months. I think that would be a good idea."

Sam nodded slowly. "Sure. By that time I oughtta be able to raise enough capital to buy a Clippership and take tourists into orbit for real."

Jones looked from me to Sam and back again.

Sam added, "Of course, it would help if the State Department ponied up some funding for me."

She snapped her attention to Sam. "Now wait a minute . . ."

"Not a lot," Sam said. "Ten or twenty million, that's all."

Jones's mouth dropped open. Then she yelped, "That's extortion!"

Sam placed both hands on his flowered shirt in a gesture of aggrieved innocence. "Extortion? Me?"

"AND THAT'S JUST about the whole story, Uncle Griff," Ramona said to me.

I leaned back in my desk chair and stared at her. "That business with the president of Cuba happened two months ago. What kept you down there in Panama until now?"

She blushed. Even beneath her deep suntan I could see her cheeks reddening.

"Uh . . . well, I wanted to stay on Sam's tail and make certain he closed up his operation when he promised he would."

Sam hadn't closed Space Adventure Tours, I knew. He had suspended operations in Panama and returned to the agency. Gone back on duty. He was scheduled for a classified Air Force mission, of all things. I had talked myself blue in the face, trying to get the astronaut office in Houston to replace him with somebody else, but they kept insisting Sam was the best man they had for the mission. Lord knows who he bribed, and with what.

"You didn't have to stay in Panama all that time," I pointed out to my niece. "You could have kept tabs on him from here in Washington."

She blushed even more deeply. "Well, Uncle Griff, to tell the truth . . . it was sort of like a, you know, kind of like a honeymoon."

I snorted. Couldn't help it. The thought of my own little niece shacked up with . . .

"You were *living* with him?" I bellowed.

She just smiled at me. "Yes," she said, dreamily.

I was furious. "You let Sam Gunn—"

"Not Sam!" Ramona said quickly. Then she grinned at me. "You thought I was living with Sam?" She laughed at me.

Before I could ask, she told me, "Hector! We fell in love, Uncle Griff! We're going to get married."

That was different. Sort of. "Oh. Congratulations, I suppose. When?"

"Next year," my niece answered. "When Sam starts *real* flights into orbit, Hector and I are going to spend our official honeymoon in space!"

I wanted to puke.

So that's why we had to fire Sam Gunn. Government regulations specifically state that you can't be running a business of your own while you're on the federal payroll. Besides, the little SOB made a shambles of everything he touched.

It wasn't easy, though. Actually firing somebody from a government job is never easy, and Sam played every delaying trick in the book. Just to see if he could give me apoplexy, I'm sure.

The little conniving sneak was even working out an arrangement to rent a section of a new space station and turn it into an orbiting honeymoon hotel before I finally got all the paperwork I needed to fire his butt out of the agency.

And he didn't leave quietly. Not Sam. Know what his final masterstroke was? He left me a prepaid ticket to ride his goddamned Clippership into orbit and spend a full week in his orbiting hotel.

He knew damned well I'd never give him the satisfaction! Probably the little bastard thought I was too old to enjoy sex. Or maybe he expected me to bust a blood vessel while I'm making love in weightlessness.

But I fooled him. Good and proper. I grew a beard. I got hair implants. The little wiseass never recognized me.

When they opened this retirement center here at Copernicus I was one of the first residents. I thought maybe Sam would come here, sooner or later, if and when he finally retired.

That's what I'm waiting for. I know he's not dead. Sooner or later he's going to show up again, and sooner or later he'll end up here in this low-gravity old folks' home. Retired, with nothing to do. Then I can drive him nuts, for a change.

That's something worth living for!

The Show Must Go On!

"PRETTY SHAKY," GRADOWSKY MUTTERED, AFTER LISTEN-ing to Griffith's narration. "Even with his sworn testament the lawyers aren't going to like this."

Jade slumped in the battered old couch, feeling exhausted from her weeks of travel and tension.

"You don't mean that we can't use *any* of it, do you?"

"That's not my decision, kid," said Gradowsky from behind his desk. "We'll have to let the lawyers listen to what you've got."

She nodded glumly, too tired to argue. Besides, it would do no good to fight Gradowsky on this. His hands were tied. She began to get an inkling of how Sam Gunn had felt about being hemmed in by office procedures and red tape.

"So where do you go from here?" Gradowsky asked her.

Jade pulled herself up straighter in the chair, startled by the question. "You mean we're going on with the project?"

"Sure. Until the lawyers pull the plug on us. Why not? I think what you're getting is great stuff. I just worry about people suing us, that's all."

Jade's weariness seemed to wash away like water-paint under a fire hose.

"Well," she said, "several of the people I talked to said there's a man at space station Alpha who—"

"Alpha? That's in Earth orbit."

"Right."

"We don't have the budget to send you out there," Gradowsky said.

"We don't?"

"Hell, kiddo, you've just about used up the whole expense budget I gave you just traipsing around the different lunar settlements. Do you have any idea of what it costs to fly back Earthside?"

"I wouldn't be going all the way to Earth," Jade answered. "Just to the space station."

"Yeah, I know." Gradowsky seemed embarrassed with the recollection that Jade could not go to Earth even if she wanted to.

"I've covered just about everybody I could find here on the Moon," she said. "But there are plenty of people elsewhere: on Alpha, in the Lagrange habitats, even out in the Belt."

Gradowsky puffed his cheeks and blew out a heavy sigh. "The Asteroid Belt. Christ!"

Jade knew she had to do something, and quickly, or the Sam Gunn project was finished.

"When I first started this job," she said to her boss, "you told me that a good reporter goes where the story is, regardless of how far or how difficult it might be."

He grinned sheepishly at her. "Yeah, I know. But I forgot to tell you the other half of it—*as long as the big brass okays the expenses.*"

Straightening her spine, Jade replied, "We'll have to talk to the big brass, then."

Gradowsky looked surprised for an instant. Then he ran both his hands over his ample belly and said, "Yeah. I guess maybe we will."

Several weeks later, one of the corporation's big brass came to Selene City for the annual "fear of god" meeting that every branch office of Solar News Network received from management.

His full name was Arak al Kashan, although he smilingly insisted on being called Raki. "Raki," he would say, almost self-deprecatingly, "not Rocky." Yet Jade overheard Gradowsky mumble to one of the technicians, "Count your fingers after you shake hands with him."

Raki was tall and tan and trim, dark of hair and eye, old enough to be a network vice president yet young enough to set women's hearts fluttering. The grapevine had it that he was descended from very ancient blood; his aristocratic lineage went all the way back to the earliest Persian emperors. He had the haughtiness to match the claim. Jade heard him with her own ears saying disdainfully, "The unlamented Pahlavi Shahs were nothing more than upstart peasants."

Jade thought he was the handsomest man she had ever seen. Raki dressed in hand-tailored suits of the latest fashion, darkly iridescent lapel-less jackets in shades of blue or charcoal that fit him like a second skin over pale pastel turtlenecks. Tight slacks that emphasized his long legs and bulging groin.

If Raki noticed Jade among the half-dozen employees at the Solar office he gave no outward sign of it. His task, as vice president in charge of human resources, was to have a brief personal chat with each man and woman at the Selene City office, review their job performances, and assure them that headquarters, back in Orlando, had their best interests at heart—even though there were to be no salary increases this year.

"Be careful of him," Monica warned Jade when she saw the look in her young friend's eyes. "He's a lady-killer."

Jade smiled at Monica's antique vocabulary. With the Sam Gunn project stalled, Jade had been assigned to covering financial news. Her current project was a report on the growth in tourism at Selene. Next she would tackle the consortium that was trying to raise capital for building a new mass driver that would double Selene's export capacity. Hardly as thrilling as tracking down Sam Gunn's old lovers and adversaries.

"Jumbo Jim says that Raki could get headquarters to okay my Sam Gunn project," Jade told Monica.

"Honey, I'm warning you. All he'll want to do is get into your bed."

They were sitting in Monica's cubbyhole office, sipping synthetic coffee before starting the day's tasks. Through the window that took up one whole wall they could see the dimly lit editing room where two technicians were bent over their computers, using the graphics program to "re-create" the construction of the new mass driver, from the first ceremonial shovel of excavation to the ultimate finished machine hurling hundreds of tons of cargo into space per hour.

Monica's office was too small for a desk. There were only the two chairs and a computer console built into the back wall. Its keyboard rested on the floor until Monica needed it.

Jade appreciated Monica's warning. "Mother Monica," she called her older friend. But she had other ideas in mind.

Trying not to smile too broadly, she told Monica, "You know, Sam Gunn used to say that he wanted to get laid without getting screwed. Maybe that's what I've got to do."

Monica gave her a long, troubled look.

"I mean," Jade said, "I wouldn't mind having sex with him. It might even be fun. The question is: how do I make sure that he'll okay the project afterward?"

Shaking her head like the weary mother superior of a rowdy convent, Monica said, "My god, you kids have it easy nowadays. When I was your age we had to worry about herpes, and chlamydia—and AIDS. Sex was punishable by death in those days!"

Somewhat surprised, Jade said, "But you managed . . ."

With a huff, Monica replied, "Sure, we managed. But you had to get a guy's blood report first. There were even doctors making fortunes faking medical records!"

"That must have been tough," Jade said.

"Why do you think people got married back then? And then divorced?"

"But Monica, he'll only be here for another three days. I've got to get him to okay the Sam Gunn biography by then!"

Monica's disapproving expression softened. "I know, honey. I understand. It's just that I hate to see you using yourself like this. Meaningless sex might seem like fun at first. . . ."

"Sam always said that there's no such thing as meaningless sex."

"Sam's dead, child. And he left a trail of hurt people behind him. Women, mostly."

Jade had to admit that she was right. "There was one woman I interviewed. She works at Dante's Inferno, over in Hell Crater. She was Sam's fiancee. She claims he left her at the altar and went off to the Asteroid Belt."

"I'll bet. And what kind of work does she do at Dante's?" Monica asked, her eyes narrowing.

ISHTAR'S WAS ACKNOWLEDGED to be the finest restaurant not merely in Selene, but the finest in all the Moon. Carved out of the lunar rock at the end of a long corridor, Ishtar's interior was shaped like a dome, with video screens showing views of the heavens so cunningly devised that it actually looked as though the dome were up on the surface.

The restaurant was small, intimate. Each table was niched into its own semicircular banquette of high, plush lunar pseudo-leather, creating a semicircle of virtually complete privacy. Lovers could snuggle close, although at the prices Ishtar's charged the restaurant's clientele was mostly executives who had access to golden expense accounts. All the waiters were human; there were no robots at all, not even as busboys.

"I've never had champagne before," Jade said, with a slight giggle.

Arak al Kashan leaned back in the plush banquette and steepled his long manicured fingers in front of his chin, admiring her from across their damask-covered table.

"You should have it every evening," Raki said, smiling. "A creature as lovely as you should have oceans of champagne. You should bathe in champagne."

Jade lifted an eyebrow slightly. "I don't think there's that much champagne in Selene."

"Then you can come to France with me. We'll rent a chateau and bathe in champagne every night."

"Oh, I can't come to Earth," Jade said lightly.

"I could see to it that you get a much better position with the network. In France. Or in Florida. We could see each other every day if you came to Florida."

She had already drunk enough champagne to dull the pain of what she had to tell him. "I can never come to Earth, Raki. My bones are too brittle for it."

His mouth dropped open for an instant, but he immediately recovered his composure.

"Then I must come to Selene more often," he said gallantly.

Jade accepted the compliment with a smile and a totally unpremeditated batting of her eyelashes. In the center of the restaurant the head waiter supervised the creation of a spectacularly flaming dish that brought murmurs of approval from the watching diners.

He's a doll! Jade thought to herself. Raki is a handsome, elegant, charming, living doll.

He was also an accomplished lover, as she found later that night, in the suite that the network maintained for visiting executives. Jade felt herself swept away like a cork in a tidal wave under Raki's experienced hands and tongue. She felt as if she would suffocate; she felt as if her heart would burst in her chest. Electric thrills tingled every square centimeter of her skin.

Slowly, ever so slowly, she floated back to reality. As if awakening from a dream, Jade gradually sensed the bed firmly beneath her, the darkness of the room eased only by the luminous digits of the clock on the night table, the animal heat of the man sleeping next to her naked body.

Jade could make out the form of Raki's body, coiled like a panther, his face half buried in his pillow.

She took a long shuddering breath. Now you've done it, she told herself. It's over and done with. It was exciting, but it's finished now. Tomorrow he'll be leaving. Tomorrow he'll go back to Earth and you'll be alone again.

"What's the matter?" Raki's voice was whisper-soft.

Startled that he was awake, she said, "What?"

"You were muttering. I thought you might be talking in your sleep."

Jade almost laughed. "Just talking to myself. Sorry if I woke you."

"It's all right," he said, turning over onto his back.

"You'll be going home tomorrow."

"The day after—oh, yes, it's Tuesday morning now, isn't it? Yes, tomorrow."

"Do you live in Orlando?" Jade asked, her voice as flat and unemotional as she could make it.

He laughed softly. "You want to know if I'm married, don't you?"

"I already know that. I looked up your personnel file."

"You have access to the files?" He sounded surprised.

"No," she said. "But I'm a reporter."

"Ah."

Silence. Jade had watched enough old videos to know that this was the moment the lovers usually lit cigarettes. She wondered what it would taste like, whether she would feel the carcinogens attacking her lungs.

"You know that I am married and have two children," Raki said. "Statistically, it should be one point seven, but we found it difficult to produce only seven-tenths of a child."

Jade did not laugh. "Is it a happy marriage?"

"Yes, I'm afraid it is."

"I'm glad," she lied.

"As a practicing Moslem," Raki said lightly, "I can take four wives, you know. The state of Florida would object, I'm sure, but I doubt that the government of Selene would mind."

"A wife in every port," Jade muttered. "That might get expensive."

"My wife is a practicing psychologist. She makes an excellent living. And you, of course, are employed as a reporter. . . ."

"Don't joke about it!" Jade burst. "It isn't a joking matter."

"No, of course not. I'm sorry."

Silence again.

At length, Raki asked, "What is it you want?"

Jade tried to swallow down the lump in her throat.

Raki turned toward her. "I know I am devilishly handsome and utterly suave and urbane, practically irresistible. But you accepted my invitation to dinner knowing that it would lead here, and you accepted that because you want something from me. What is it?"

Jade blinked back tears.

"It's happened before, you know," Raki said. His voice was still gentle, almost sad. "Women seem so willing to offer their bodies in trade."

"You make it sound dirty."

"Oh no! Not dirty. There's nothing dirty about making love. It's just . . . disappointing."

"Disappointing?"

He sighed like a heartbroken lover. "I had hoped that you liked me for myself, not for what I could do for you. But I knew better, all along. You want something: a raise in salary, a promotion . . . something."

Jade felt her spirits sinking out of sight.

"Well," Raki said, "you might as well tell me what it is."

Confused, Jade stammered, "There . . . there *was* something . . . I thought . . ." She did not know what to say.

Raki whispered, "You can tell me. I'm accustomed to being used."

"It isn't like that!" Jade burst. "Yes, all right, I admit that I wanted something from you—at first. But now, now that I know you . . ."

Raki smiled in the darkness and reached for her young trembling body. Jade flung herself into his arms and they made love until they both fell asleep exhausted.

"AND THEN WHAT happened?" Monica asked as they walked down the busy corridor from the cafeteria toward her office. It was nearly 0800 hours, the start of the business day. The women were dressed in their business clothes: Monica in comfortably loose black slacks and sweat-shirt, Jade in a stylish auburn jumpsuit and glossy thigh-length boots.

"It was morning when we woke up," Jade answered with a small shrug. "I had to dash back to my place to change for work."

With an unhappy shake of her head Monica replied, "And Raki's in Jim's office bragging about how he screwed you all night long."

"No! He wouldn't. . . ."

"Want to bet?"

Jade could not look Monica square in the face. "I've got to get to work," she said. "I'm interviewing that architect at ten sharp."

"Want to bet?" Monica repeated sternly.

"Yes!" Jade snapped, feeling anger surging within her. "I'll bet he's con-ducting ordinary business with Jim."

They had reached the door to Solar News's suite of cubbyhole offices. With a sweeping gesture, Monica ushered Jade through, then led the way past the trio of unoccupied desks to her own office. Gradowsky's office door was closed, Jade saw.

Monica plopped into her chair and picked the keyboard off the floor.

Jade remained standing, her back to the window that looked into the editing room. No one was in there yet.

"Don't you ever tell Jumbo that I've bugged his office," Monica said, frowning slightly as she worked the keyboard.

"Bugged it! Why?"

"I might marry the bum one of these days, but that doesn't mean I altogether trust him." She pulled a pair of wire-thin headsets from the cabinet in the corner of the room and handed one of them to Jade.

Reluctantly Jade slipped the set over her hair. Monica plugged them both in, then held one earphone to her ear, her head cocked like a fat robin looking for a juicy worm.

". . . if I say so myself, I'm a very good teacher." Raki's voice. Unmistakable.

"Well, uh, you know she's just a kid. Got some good ideas, though." Gradowsky sounded uncomfortable, embarrassed.

"Really? I'll bet she's got better ones now." Raki laughed. Jade heard nothing from Jumbo Jim.

After a brief silence Raki asked, "You said she wants to do a biography?"

"Yeah. Of Sam Gunn. I think . . ."

"Sam Gunn! No, that would never wash."

"I dunno, Raki. She's already gotten a lot of really good stuff. Sam's good material. Sex, adventure, excitement."

Raki made a humming noise. Then, "You think so?"

"Yeah, I do."

"No, the executive board would never buy it. Half of them hate Sam's guts, even now, and the other half wouldn't give a damn."

"But if you recommended it," Gradowsky suggested.

"Listen, my friend, I didn't get this far in the network by sticking my neck out."

Jade sensed Jumbo Jim shaking his head. "Then what're you gonna tell her?"

"Me? Nothing?"

"You're not gonna see her again tonight?"

"Of course not. Why should I?"

Monica's face looked like a stone carving of vengeance. Jade felt her own cheeks flaming.

"I thought, well, after you had such a good time last night."

Raki laughed again. It sounded cruel. "The thrill is in the chase, James. Now that I've bagged her, what is there to getting her again? No, tonight

I'll go to Hell Crater and enjoy myself with the professionals. I've had enough of little girls who must be taught everything."

Jade ripped the headset off so hard she thought her ears were coming off with it.

Monica looked as if she would cry. "I'm sorry, honey. But you had to know."

Jade went through her morning as if disembodied, watching this red-headed young woman from an enormous distance as she made her way down the gray tunnels of Selene, conducted a perfunctory interview with a dull whining architect, then ate a solitary lunch in the darkest corner of the Pelican Bar, speaking to no one, not even a robot waiter. She punched up her order on the keyboard built into the wall of her booth.

There is no one you can trust, Jade told herself. Absolutely no one. Not even Monica. She's bugged her fiance's office. Not one single human being in the whole solar system can be trusted. Not a damned one. I'm alone. I've always been alone and I always will be.

A robot brought her lunch tray. She ignored its cheerful programmed banter and it rolled away.

Jade could not eat more than a single mouthful. The food stuck in her throat. The cola tasted flat and sour.

She leaned her head against the back of the booth, eyes filling with tears, alone and lost in a world that had never cared whether she lived or died. It's not fair! she cried silently. It's just not fucking goddamned shitting fair.

Life is never fair. She remembered somebody told her that Sam Gunn had often said that. No, not quite. Sam had put it differently. "Life isn't fair, so the best thing you can do is load the dice in your own favor." That's what Sam had said.

Don't get mad, Jade told herself. Get even.

Grimly she slid out of the booth and headed for the ticket office of Lunar Transport.

"THIS IS GOING to be kind of tough for me to talk about," Jade said.

"Don't give it a second thought, little one," said Yoni, Mistress of Ecstasy. "Monica filled my ears with the whole story while you were on your way here."

Here was the employee's lounge of Dante's Inferno, the biggest casino/hotel/house of pleasure in Hell Crater. It had been Sam Gunn's sardonic idea of humor to turn Hell into a complex of entertainment centers. The crater had been named after an eighteenth-century Jesuit astronomer, Maximilian Hell, who once directed the Vienna Observatory.

Jade had overspent her personal credit account to ride the passenger rocket from Selene, after telling Monica what she was going to do. Mother Monica apparently had gotten on the fiber-optic link with Yoni as soon as Jade hung up.

The lounge was small but quite plush. Yoni sat on a small fabric-covered couch; Jade on a softly cushioned easy chair.

Jade had interviewed the Mistress of Ecstasy weeks earlier. Yoni had been left at the altar by Sam Gunn more than twenty years ago. But although she had every reason to hate Sam, she said, "I guess I still have a soft spot in my heart for the little SOB."

Yoni claimed to be the child of a mystical pleasure cult from deep in the mysterious mountains of Nepal. Actually she had been born in the mining settlement at Aristarchus, of Chinese-American parents from San Francisco. She was tall for an oriental, Jade thought, and her bosom was so extraordinary, even though the rest of her figure was willowy slim, that Jade decided she must have been enhanced by implants. She wore a tight-fitting silk sheath of shining gold with a plunging neckline and skirt slashed to the hip.

She had worn a luxurious auburn wig when Jade had first interviewed her. Now she sat, relaxed, her hair cropped almost as short as a military cut. It was sprinkled with gray. Yoni was still beautiful, although to Jade she seemed awfully elderly for her chosen line of work. Cosmetic surgery had done its best, but there were still lines in her face, veins on the backs of her hands. Her dark almond eyes seemed very knowing, as if they had witnessed every possible kind of human frailty.

"Then you know," Jade choked out the words, "about Raki . . . and me."

Yoni smiled sadly and patted Jade's knee. "You're not the first woman to be roughed up by a man."

"Can you help me?"

Yoni's almond eyes became inscrutable. "In what way? I won't risk damaging this house's reputation just to help you get even with a jerk."

Jade blinked at her. "No, that isn't what I want at all."

"Then what?"

"I want him to approve my doing a biography of Sam Gunn."

It was Yoni's turn to look surprised. "Is that what you're after?"

"Yes."

Yoni leaned back in her couch and crossed her long legs. "Let me get this straight. You want me to make him change his mind about this video biography you want to do."

Jade nodded.

"Why should I help you?"

For a moment Jade had no answer. Then she heard herself say, "For Sam's sake."

"For Sam's sake!" Yoni tilted her head back and laughed heartily. "Why in the name of the seventy-seven devils of Tibet should I care an eyelash about Sam? He's dead and gone and that's that."

Jade said, "I thought you had a soft spot in your heart for him."

"In my heart, little one. Not my head."

"You don't feel any obligation toward Sam?"

"If he were here I'd kick him in the balls. And he'd know why."

"Even though he gave you the controlling interest in Dante's Inferno?"

After her interview with Yoni, Jade had accessed all the records she could find about Dante's. S. Gunn Enterprises, Unlimited, had originally built the place. Yoni had been a licensed prostitute in the European lunar settlement, New Europa, when Sam had briefly fallen in love with her. He had left her at the altar, true enough. He had also left her fifty-five percent of the shares of the newly opened Dante's Inferno. The rest he had sold off to help finance a venture to the Asteroid Belt.

Yoni gazed up at the smooth, faintly glowing ceiling panels, then across the lounge at the computer-graphics images mounted on the walls. They were all of tall, buxom women, blonde, redheaded, gleaming black hair. They wore leather, or daintily feminine lace, or nothing but jewelry. They were all Yoni, Mistress of Ecstasy, in her various computer-simulated embodiments.

Finally she looked back at Jade. "You're right," she admitted. "I owe the little bastard."

"Then you'll help me?"

Without answering, Yoni got to her feet and started for the door. "Come on down to my office. I'll have to look up your john's file."

YONI'S OFFICE LOOKED to Jade like a millionaire's living room. Bigger than any office she had ever seen; bigger than any apartment, for that matter. And there were doors leading to other rooms, as well. Oriental carpets on the floor. Video windows on every wall. The furniture alone must have cost millions to tote up from Earth: Chinese prayer tables of real wood, lacquered and glistening; long low settees covered in striped fabrics; even a hologram fireplace that actually threw off heat.

Jade stood in the middle of the huge room, almost breathless with admiration, while Yoni went straight to a delicately small desk tucked into a corner and tapped on the keyboard cunningly built into its gleaming top.

The silk painting of misty mountains above the desk turned into a small display screen.

"Most johns don't use their real names here," Yoni muttered, mostly to herself, "but we can usually trace their credit accounts, even when they've established a temporary one to cover their identity."

Jade drifted toward the desk, resisting the urge to touch the vases, the real flowers, the ivory figurines resting on an end table.

"You said he calls himself Rocky?"

"Raki." Jade spelled it.

"H'm. Here he is, full name and everything. He's not trying to hide from anybody."

"He's married. . . ."

"Two wives," Yoni said, as the data on the screen scrolled by. "One in Orlando and one in Istanbul. Plus a few girlfriends that he sees regularly, here and there."

Jade let herself drop into the little straight-backed chair beside the desk.

"He doesn't make any secret of it, so there's no way to use this information as leverage on him."

"Does he have . . . girlfriends . . . here on the Moon?"

Yoni gave her a sidelong look. "No, when he's here he comes to us. To me."

Jade felt her face redden.

Yoni smiled knowingly at her. "He's never seen me, little one. Not in the flesh. It's been years since I've done business with anyone flesh-to-flesh."

"Oh?"

"The VR nets," Yoni said, as if that explained everything. When she saw that Jade did not understand she went on, "Most of my customers come here for our simulations. They're quite lifelike, with the virtual reality systems. We just zip them up into a cocoon so the sensory net's in contact with every centimeter of their body, and then we play scenarios for them."

"They don't want sex with real women?" Jade felt stupid asking it.

"Some do, but what men want most is not sex so much as power. For most men, they feel powerful when they're screwing a woman. It makes them feel strong, especially when the woman is doing exactly what they desire. That's why the VR nets are so popular. A john can have any woman he wants, any number of women, for the asking."

"Really?"

Yoni gave her a knowing smile. "We have vids of Cleopatra, Marilyn Monroe, Catherine the Great. One john wants Jacqueline Kennedy Onassis; nobody else, just her. Another has a fixation on Eleanor of Aquitaine. Thinks he's Richard the Lionheart, I guess."

"And it's all preprogrammed simulations?"

"The basic scenario is preprogrammed. We always have a live operator in the loop to make sure everything's going right and to take care of any special needs that come up."

Jade completely missed Yoni's pun. But she caught the unspoken implication.

"You keep disks of each session?"

"No!" Yoni snapped, almost vehemently. Then, more gently, "Do you realize the kinds of corporate and government people we have as clientele here? One hint, even the slightest rumor, that we record their sessions and we would be out of business—or dead."

"Oh. I didn't realize . . ."

Yoni smiled mysteriously. "We don't have to blackmail our guests, or even threaten to. These VR sessions can be very powerful; they have a strong impact on the mind. Almost like a posthypnotic suggestion, really."

"You can influence people?" Jade asked.

"Not directly. But—no one actually understands what long-term effects these VR sessions have on a person's mind. Especially a habitual user. I have commissioned a couple of psychologists to look into it, but so far their results have been too vague for any practical use."

"Could you—influence—Raki?"

With a shrug, Yoni said, "I don't know. He's been here often, that's true. But he's not an addict, like some I could name."

Jade hesitated, feeling embarrassed, then asked, "What kind of sex does he go in for?"

Glancing back at the computer screen, Yoni said, "I don't think you understand, little one. The man doesn't come here for sex. He gets his sexual needs fulfilled from flesh-and-blood creatures like yourself."

"Then what . . . ?"

"For power, little one. Not sexual power. *Corporate* power."

Jade's eyes went wide. She understood. And she knew what had to be done.

ARAK AL KASHAN gazed through his office window at the Orlando
skyline: tower after tower, marching well past the city limits, past the
open acreage of Disney World, and on out to the horizon. There was
power there, majesty and might in the modern sense. Beyond his line of
sight, he knew, construction crews were hard at work turning swampland
and citrus groves into more corporate temples of enduring concrete,
stainless steel and gleaming glass.

He leaned back in his plush leather chair and sighed deeply. The moment had come. His trip to the Moon had been relaxing, diverting. Now
the moment of truth had arrived.

Getting to his feet, Raki squared his shoulders as he inspected his image in the full-length mirror on the door to his private lavatory. The
jacket fit perfectly, he saw. Its camel's-hair tone brought out his tan.
Good.

He snapped his fingers once and the mirror turned opaque. Then he
stepped around the desk and started toward the door and the meeting of
the board of directors of Solar News Network, Inc. This was going to be
the meeting. The one where he took charge of the entire corporation,
where he seized the reins of power from the doddering old hands of the
CEO and won the board's approval as the new chief of Solar News.

The day had come at last.

But before he could take three steps across the precious Persian carpet,
the door opened and a short, disheveled man rushed in.

"You're in trouble, pal. Deep shit, if you don't mind the expression."

"Who the hell are you?" Raki demanded.

"That's not important. You've got a real problem and I'm here to
help you."

Raki took a step backward, then another, and felt his desk against the
back of his legs. The little man seemed terribly agitated, perhaps insane.
His wiry rust-red hair was cropped short, yet it still looked tangled and
dirty. He wore coveralls of faded olive green, stained here and there with
what looked like grease or machine oil.

Raki groped with one hand toward the intercom on his desk, still facing the strange intruder.

"Never mind calling security," the man said. "I'm on your side, pal. I
can help you."

"Help me? I don't need—"

"The hell you don't need help! They're waiting for you upstairs," he cast his eyes toward the ceiling, "with knives sharpened and a vat of boiling oil. All for you."

"What do you mean?"

The man smiled, a lopsided sort of grin in his round, snub-nosed face.

"You think you're gonna waltz right in there and take control of the corporation, huh? You think the CEO's just gonna bend over and let you boot him in the butt?"

"What do you know about it?"

"Plenty, pal," said the little man. "I was never the guy for corporate politics. Had no time for boards of directors and all the crap that goes with a big bureaucracy. But lemme tell you, they're out to get you. They're gonna pin your balls to the conference table, Raki, old pal."

Raki felt his knees giving way. He sank to a half-sitting position on the edge of his desk.

His visitor strutted across the carpet, looked out the window. "Nice view. Not as good as the view from Titan, but what the hell, this is the best you can do in Florida, I guess."

"What did you mean?" Raki asked.

"About the view from Titan?"

"About the board of directors. They're waiting for me upstairs—"

"You bet your busy little ass they're waiting. With assorted cutlery and boiling oil, like I said."

"You're crazy!"

"Mad?" The little man screwed up his face and crossed his eyes. "Hannibal was mad. Caesar was mad. And surely Napoleon was the maddest of them all."

"Talk sense, dammit!"

The man chuckled tolerantly. "Look. You're going up to the board of directors to tell them that the corporation would be better off with you as CEO instead of the old fart that's running the network now. Right?"

"Right," said Raki.

"Well, what's your plan?"

"My plan?"

"Yeah. You need a plan to lay out on the table, a blueprint to show them what changes you're gonna make, how you're gonna do bigger and better things for dear ol' Solar News."

"I . . . I . . ." Raki suddenly realized he did not have a plan. Not an idea in his head. He could feel cold sweat breaking out all over his body.

"C'mon, c'mon," the little man demanded, "the board's waiting. What's your plan?"

"I don't have one!" Raki wailed.

His visitor shook his head. "Just as I thought. No plan."

"What can I do?" Raki was trembling now. He saw his dream of conquest crumbling. They'll fire me! I'll lose everything!

"Not to worry, pal. That's why I'm here. To help you." The little man pulled a computer disk from his grubby coverall pocket. It was smaller than the palm of his hand, even though his hand was tiny.

He handed the disk to Raki. It felt warm and solid in his fingers.

"Show 'em that, pal. It'll knock 'em on their asses."

Before Raki could think of anything to say, he was standing at the foot of the long, long conference table. The entire board of directors was staring at him from their massive chairs. The old CEO and his henchmen sat up near the head of the table, flanking the chairman of the board, a woman upon whom Raki had lavished every possible attention. She was smiling at him, faintly, but the rest of the board looked grim.

"Well," snapped the CEO, "what do you have there in your hand, young man?"

Raki took a deep breath. "I hold here in my hand," he heard his own voice saying, smoothly, without a tremor, "the salvation of Solar News."

A stir went around the conference table.

Holding up the tiny disk, Raki went on, "This is a documented, dramatized biography of one of the solar system's most colorful personalities—the late Sam Gunn."

The board erupted into an uproar.

"Sam Gunn!"

"No!"

"It couldn't be!"

"How did you manage it?"

One of the truly elderly members of the board, frail and pasty-faced, waved his skeletal hands excitedly. "I have it on very good authority that BBC was planning to do a biography of Sam Gunn. You've beaten them to the punch, young man! Bravo."

The chairman turned a stern eye on her CEO. "How come you didn't do this yourself?" she demanded of the cowering executive. "Why did Raki have to do this all on his own?" And she gave Raki a wink full of promise.

The entire board of directors got to their feet and applauded. Walter

Cronkite appeared, in a white linen double-breasted suit, to join the acclamation. The old CEO faded, ghostlike, until he disappeared altogether.

Raki smiled and made a little bow. When he turned, he saw that Yoni was waiting for him, reclining on a bank of satin pillows beside a tinkling fountain in a moonlit garden scented by warm blossoms.

His strange little visitor stepped out from behind an azalea bush, grinning. "Way to go, pal. Give her everything you've got."

JADE KNEW THAT her ploy had failed. Raki had returned to Orlando two weeks ago, and there was no word from him at all. Nothing.

She went through her assignments perfunctorily, interviewing a development tycoon who wanted to build retirement villages on the Moon, a visiting ecologist from Massachusetts who wanted a moratorium declared on all further lunar developments, an astrobiologist who was trying to raise funds for an expedition to the south lunar pole to search for fossilized bacteria: "I *know* there's got to be evidence of life down there someplace; I just know it."

All the help that Yoni had given her, all the support that Monica gave, had been for nothing. Jade saw herself trapped in a cell of lunar stone, blank and unyielding no matter which way she turned.

Gradowsky warned her. "You're sleepwalking, kid. Snap out of it and get me stories I can send to Orlando, not this high-school junk you've been turning in."

Another week went by, and Jade began to wonder if she really wanted to stay on as a reporter. Maybe she could go back to running a truck up on the surface. Or ship out to Mars: they needed construction workers there for the new base the scientists were building.

When Gradowsky called her in to his office she knew he was going to fire her.

Jumbo Jim had a strange, uncomfortable expression on his face as he pushed aside a half-eaten hero sandwich and a mug of some foaming liquid while gesturing Jade to the chair in front of his desk.

Swallowing visibly, Gradowsky said, "Well, you did it."

Jade nodded glumly. Her last assignment had been a real dud: the corporate board of Selene City never gave out any news other than their official media release.

"The word just came in from Orlando. You leave for Alpha tomorrow."

It took Jade a moment to realize what Jumbo Jim was telling her. She felt her breath catch.

"Raki must have fought all the way up to the board of directors," Gradowsky was saying. "It must've been some battle."

Instead of elation, instead of excitement, Jade felt numb, smothered, encased in a block of ice. I've got to make it work, she told herself. I've got to get to every person who knew Sam and make them tell me everything. I owe it to Monica and Yoni. I owe it to Raki.

She looked past Gradowsky's fleshy, flabby face, still mouthing words she did not hear, and realized that Raki had put his career on the line. And so had she.

Space Station Alpha

THEY FACED EACH OTHER SUSPICIOUSLY, FLOATING WEIGHT-lessly in emptiness.

The black man was tall, long-limbed, loose, gangling; on Earth he might have made a pro basketball player. His utilitarian coveralls were standard issue, frayed at the cuffs and so worn that whatever color they had been originally had long since faded into a dull gray. They were clean and pressed to a razor sharpness, though. The insignia patch on his left shoulder said ADMINISTRATION. A strictly nonregulation belt of royal blue, studded with rough lumps of meteoric gold and clamped by a heavy gold buckle, cinched his pencil-thin waist and made him look even taller and leaner.

He eyed the reporter warily. She was young, and the slightly greenish cast to her pretty features told him that she had never been in zero gravity before. Her flame-red hair was shoulder length, he judged, but she had followed the instructions given to groundlings and tied it up in a zero-gee snood. Terrific big emerald eyes, even if they did look kind of scared.

Her coveralls were spanking new white. She filled them nicely enough, a trim, coltish figure that he almost admired. She looked like a forlorn little waif floating weightlessly, obviously fighting down the nausea that was surging through her.

Frederick Mohammed Malone was skeptical to the point of being hostile toward this female interloper. Jade could see the resentment smoldering in the black man's red-rimmed eyes. Malone's face was narrow, almost gaunt, with a trim little Vandyke jutting out from his chin. His forehead was high, receding; his hair was cropped close to the skull. His skin was very black. She guessed Malone's age at somewhere in his early sixties, although she knew that living in zero gravity could make a person look much younger than his or her calendar age.

She tried to restart their stalled conversation. "I understand that you and Sam Gunn were, uh, friends."

"Why're you doing a story on Sam?" Malone asked, his voice low and loaded with distrust.

The two of them were in Malone's "office." Actually it was an observation blister in the central hub of space station Alpha. Oldest and still biggest of the Earth-orbiting commercial stations, Alpha was built on the old wheels-within-wheels scheme. The outermost rim, where most of the staff lived and worked, spun at a rate that gave it almost a full Earth gravity, out-of-bounds for Jade. Two-thirds of the way toward the hub there was a wheel that spun at the Moon's one-sixth g. That was where she was quartered for her visit. The hub itself, of course, was for all practical purposes at zero-gee, weightless.

Malone's aerie consisted of one wall on which were located a semicircular sort of desk and communications center, a bank of display screens that were all blankly gray at the moment, and an airtight hatch that led to the spokes that radiated out to the various wheels. The rest of the chamber was a transparent glassteel bubble from which Malone could watch the station's loading dock—and the overwhelming majesty of the huge, curved, incredibly blue and white–flecked Earth as it slid past endlessly, massive, brilliant, ever-changing, ever-beautiful.

To Jade, though, it seemed as if they were hanging in empty space itself, unprotected by anything at all, and falling, falling, falling toward the ponderous world that filled her peripheral vision. The background rumble of the bearings that bore the massive station's rotation while the hub remained static sounded to her like the insistent bass growl of a giant grinding wheel that was pressing the breath out of her.

She swallowed bile, felt it burn in her throat, and tried to concentrate on the job at hand.

She said to Malone, "I've been assigned to do a biography of Mr. Gunn for the Solar News Network. . . ."

Despite himself, Malone suddenly chuckled. "First time I ever heard him called *Mr.* Gunn."

"Oh?" Jade's microchip recorder, imbedded in her belt buckle, was already on, of course. "What did the people here call him?"

That lean, angular black face took on an almost thoughtful look. "Oh . . . Sam, mostly. 'That tricky bastard,' a good many times." Malone actually laughed. "Plenty times I heard him called a womanizing sonofabitch."

"What did you call him?"

The suspicion came back into Malone's eyes. "He was my friend. I called him Sam."

Silence stretched between them, hanging as weightlessly as their bodies. Jade turned her head slightly and found herself staring at the vast bulk of Earth. Her adoptive mother was down there, somewhere, living her own life without a thought about the daughter she had run away from. And her real mother? Was she on Earth, too, forever separated from the baby she had borne, the baby she had left abandoned, alone, friendless and loveless?

Jade's mind screamed as if she were falling down an elevator shaft. Her stomach churned queasily. She could not tear her eyes away from the world drifting past, so far below them, so compellingly near. She felt herself being drawn toward it, dropping through the emptiness, spinning down the deep swirling vortex. . . .

Malone's long-fingered hand squeezed her shoulder hard enough to hurt. She snapped her attention to his dark, unsmiling face as he grasped her other shoulder and held her firmly in his strong hands.

"You were drifting," he said, almost in a whisper.

"Was I . . . ?"

"It's all right," he said. "Gets everybody, at first. Don't be scared. You're perfectly safe."

His powerful hands steadied her. She fought down the panic surging inside.

"If you got to upchuck, go ahead and do it. Nothing to be ashamed of." His grin returned. "Only, use the bags they gave you, please."

He looked almost handsome when he smiled, she thought. After another moment he released her. She took a deep breath and dabbed at the beads of perspiration on her forehead. The retch bags that the technicians had attached to her belt were a symbol to her now. I won't need them, she insisted to herself. I'm not going to let this get to me. I'm not going to let *them* get to me.

"I . . . didn't think . . . didn't realize that zero gravity would affect me."

"Why not? It gets to everybody, one way or another."

"I'm from Selene," Jade said. "I've lived all my life under lunar gravity."

Malone gazed at her thoughtfully. "Still a big difference between one-sixth g and none at all, I guess."

"Yes." It was still difficult to breathe. "I guess there is."

"Feel better?" he asked.

There was real concern in his eyes. "I think I'll be all right. Thanks."

"*De nada*," he said. "I didn't know you'd never been in weightlessness before."

His attitude had changed, she saw. The sullenness had thawed. He had insisted on conducting the interview in the station's zero-gravity area. He had allowed no alternative. But she was grateful that his shell of distrust seemed to have cracked.

It took several moments before she could say, "I'm not here to do a hatchet job on Mr. Gunn."

Malone made a small shrug. "Doesn't make much difference, one way or th'other. He's dead; nothing you can say will hurt him now."

"But we know so little about him. I suppose he's the most famous enigma in the solar system."

The black man made no response.

"The key question, I suppose . . . the thing our viewers will be most curious about, is why Sam Gunn exiled himself up here. Why did he turn his back on Earth?"

Malone snorted with disdain. "He didn't! Those motherfuckers turned their backs on him."

"What do you mean?"

"It's a long story," Malone said.

"That's all right. I've got as much time as it takes." Even as she said it Jade wished that Malone would volunteer to return back to the lunar-g wheel, where the gravity was normal. But she dared not ask the man to leave his office. Once a subject starts talking, never interrupt! That was the cardinal rule of a successful interview. Jumbo Jim had drilled that into her. Besides, she was determined not to let weightlessness get the better of her.

"Would you believe," Malone was saying, "that it all started with a cold?"

"A cold?"

"Sam came down with a cold in the head. That's how the whole thing began."

"Tell me about it."

Isolation Area

SAM WAS A FEISTY LITTLE BASTARD—MALONE REMINISCED—
full of piss and vinegar. If there was ten different ways in the regulations
to do a job, he'd find an eleventh, maybe a twelfth or a fourteenth, just because he couldn't abide being bound by the regs. A free spirit, I guess
you'd call him.

He'd had his troubles with the brass in Houston *and* Washington. Why
he ever became an astronaut in the first place is beyond me. Maybe he
thought he'd be like a pioneer out on the frontier, on his own, way out in
space. How he made it through training and into flight operations is
something I'll never figure out. I just don't feature Sam sitting still long
enough to get through kindergarten, let alone flight school and astronaut
training.

Anyway, when I first met him he was finished as an astronaut. He had
put in seven years, which he said was a Biblical amount of time, and he
wanted out. And the agency was glad to get rid of him, believe me. But he
had this cold in the head and they wouldn't let him go back Earthside until it cleared up.

"Six billion people down there with colds, the flu, bad sinuses and
postnasal drips and those assholes in Houston won't let me go back until
this goddamned sniffle clears up."

Those were the first words Sam ever said to me. He had been assigned
to my special isolation ward, where I had reigned alone for nearly four
years. Alpha was under construction then. We were in the old Mac-Dac
Shack, a glorified tin can that passed for a space station back in those
primitive days. It didn't spin, it just hung there. Everything inside was
weightless.

My isolation ward was a cramped compartment with four zero-gee
sleep restraints Velcroed to the four walls together with lockers to stow
personal gear. Nobody but me had ever been in it until that morning.
Sam shuffled over to the bed next to mine, towing his travel-bag like a kid
with a sinking balloon.

"Just don't sneeze in my direction, Sniffles," I growled at him.

That stopped Sam for about half a second. He gave me that lopsided grin of his—his face sort of looked like a scuffed-up soccer ball, kind of round, scruffy. Little wart of a nose in the middle of it. Longest hair I ever saw on a man who works in space; hair length was one of the multitudinous points of contention between Sam and the agency. His eyes sparkled. Kind of an odd color, not quite blue, not really green. Sort of in-between.

"Malone, huh?" He read the name-tag clipped over my sleep restraint.

"Frederick Mohammed Malone," I said.

"Jesus Christ, they put me in with an Arab!"

But he stuck out his hand. Sam was really a little guy; his hand was almost the size of a baby's. After a moment's hesitation I swallowed it in mine.

"Sam," he told me, knowing I could see his last name on the tag pinned to his coveralls.

"I'm not even a Muslim," I said. "My father was, though. First one in Arkansas."

"Good for him." Sam disengaged his Velcro shoes from the carpeting and floated over to one of the sleeping bags. His travel-bag hung alongside. He ignored it and sniffed the air. "Goddamned hospitals all smell like somebody's dying. What're you in for? Hangnail or something?"

"Something," I said. "Acquired Immune Deficiency Syndrome."

His eyes went round. "AIDS?"

"It's not contagious. Not unless we make love."

"I'm straight."

"I'm not."

"Terrific. Just what I need, a gay black Arab with AIDS." But he was grinning at me.

I had seen plenty of guys back away from me once they knew I had AIDS. Some of them had a hang-up about gays. Others were scared out of their wits that they'd catch AIDS from me, or from the medical personnel or equipment. I had more than one reason to know how a leper felt, back in those days.

Sam's grin faded into a puzzled frown. "How the hell did the medics put me in here if you've got AIDS? Won't you catch my cold? Isn't that dangerous for you?"

"I'm a guinea pig. . . ."

"You don't look Italian."

"Look," I said, "if you're gonna stay in here, keep off the ethnic jokes, okay? And the puns."

He shrugged.

"The medics think they got my case arrested. New treatment that the gene therapy people have come up with."

"I get it. If you don't catch my cold, you're cured."

"They never use words like 'cured.' But that's the general idea."

"So I'm a guinea pig too."

"No, you are a part of the apparatus for this experiment. A source of infection. A bag of viruses. A host of bacteria. Germ city."

Sam hooked his feet into his sleep restraint's webbing and shot me a dark look. "And this is the guy who doesn't like ethnic jokes."

The Mac-Dac Shack had been one of the first space stations that the agency had put up. It wasn't fancy, but for years it had served as a sort of research laboratory, mainly for medical work. Naturally, with a lot of MDs in it, the Shack sort of turned into a floating hospital in orbit. With all the construction work going on in those days there was a steady stream of injured workmen and technicians.

Then some bright bureaucrat got the idea of using one module of the Shack as an isolation ward where the medics could do research on things like AIDS, ebola, the New Delhi virus, and some of the paralytic afflictions that required either isolation or zero gravity. Or both. The construction crew infirmary was moved over to the yet-unfinished Alpha while the Shack was turned into a pure research facility with various isolation wards for guinea pigs like me.

Sam stayed in my ward for three-four days; I forget the exact time. He was like an energetic little bee, buzzing all over the place, hardly ever still for a minute. In zero-gee, of course, he could literally climb the curved walls of the ward and hover up on the ceiling. He terrified the head nurse in short order by hanging near the ceiling or hiding inside one of the sleeping bags and then launching himself at her like a missile when she showed up with the morning's assortment of needles.

Never once did Sam show the slightest qualm at having his blood sampled alongside mine, although he watched the nurses taking the samples *very* closely. I've seen guys get violent from the fear that they'd get a needle contaminated by my blood and catch what I had. But Sam never even blinked. Me, I never liked needles. Couldn't abide them. Couldn't look when the nurse stuck me; couldn't even look when she stuck somebody else. Sam looked. He told me so.

By the end of the first day Sam noticed something. "All the nurses are women."

"All six of them," I affirmed.

"The doctors are all males?"

"Eight men, four women."

"That leaves two extra women for us."

"For you. I'm on the other side."

"How come all women nurses?" he wondered.

"I think it's because of me. They don't want to throw temptation in my path."

Sam started to frown at me but it turned into that lopsided grin. "They didn't think about *my* path."

He proceeded to cause absolute havoc among the nurses. With the single-minded determination of a sperm cell seeking blindly for an ovum, Sam pursued them all: the fat little redhead, the cadaverous ash-blonde, the really good-looking one, the kid who still had acne—all of them, even the head nurse, who threatened to inject him with enough estrogen to grow boobs on him if he didn't leave her and her crew alone.

Nothing deterred Sam. He would be gone for long hours from the ward, and when he'd come back he would be grinning from ear to ear. As politely as I could I'd ask him how he made out.

"It matters not if you win or lose," he would say. "It's how you play the game. . . . as long as you get laid."

When he finally left the isolation ward it seemed as if we had been friends for years. And it was damned quiet in there without him. I was alone again. I missed him. I realized how many years it had been since I'd had a friend.

I sank into a real depression of self-pity and despair. I had caught Sam's cold, sure enough. I was hacking and sneezing all day and night. One good thing about zero gravity is that you can't have a postnasal drip. One bad thing is that all the fluids accumulate in your sinuses and give you a headache of monumental proportions. The head nurse seemed to take special pleasure in inflicting upon me the indignity of forcing tubes up my nose to drain the sinuses.

The medics were overjoyed. Their guinea pig was doing something interesting. Would I react to the cold like any normal person and get over it in a few days? Or would the infection spread through my body and worsen, turn into pneumonia or maybe kill me? I could see them writing their learned papers in their heads every time they examined me, which was four times a day.

I was really unfit company for anyone, including myself. I went on for months that way, just wallowing in my own misery. Other patients came and went: an African kid with a new strain of polio; an asthmatic who had developed a violent allergy to dust; a couple of burn victims from the Alpha construction crew who had to be suspended in zero-gee. I stayed while they were treated in the other wards and sent home.

Then, without any warning at all, Sam showed up again.

"Hello, Omar, how's the tent-making business?" My middle name had become Omar, as far as he was concerned.

I gaped at him. He was wearing the powder-blue coveralls and shoulder insignia of Rockledge Industries, Inc., which in those days was just starting to grow into the interplanetary conglomerate it has become.

"What the hell you doing back here?" My voice came out a full octave higher than normal, I was so surprised. And glad.

"I work here."

"Say what?"

He ambled over to me in the zero-gee strides we all learn to make: maintain just enough contact with the carpeted flooring to keep from floating off toward the ceiling. As Sam approached my bunk the head nurse pushed through the ward's swinging doors with a trayful of the morning's indignities for me.

"Rockledge Industries just won the contract for running this tin can. The medical staff still belongs to the government, but everybody else will be replaced by Rockledge employees. I'm in charge of the whole place."

Behind him, the head nurse's eyes goggled, her mouth sagged open, and the tray slid from her hand. It just hung there, revolving slowly as she turned a full one-eighty and flew out of the ward without a word. Or maybe she was screaming so high that no human ear could hear it, like a bat.

"You're in charge of this place?" I was laughing at the drama that had been played out behind Sam's back. "No shit?"

Sam seemed happy that I seemed pleased. "I got a five-year contract."

We got to be *really* friends then. Not lovers. Sam was the most heterosexual man I have ever seen. One of the shrinks aboard the station told me Sam had a Casanova complex: he had to take a shot at any and every female creature he saw. I don't know how good his batting average was, but he surely kept busy—and grinning.

"The thrill is in the chase, Omar, not the capture," he said to me many times. Then he would always add, "As long as you get laid."

But Sam could be a true friend, caring, understanding, bringing out the best in a man. Or a woman, for that matter. I saw him help many of the station's female employees, nurses, technicians, scientists, completely aside from his amorous pursuits. He knew when to put his Casanova complex in the back seat. He was a surprisingly efficient administrator and a helluva good leader. Everybody liked him. Even the head nurse grew to grant him a grudging respect, although she certainly didn't want anybody to know it, especially Sam.

Of course, knowing Sam you might expect that he would have trouble with the chain of command. He had gotten himself out of the space agency, and it was hard to tell who was happier about it, him or the agency. You could hear sighs of relief from Houston and Washington all the way up to where we were, the agency was so glad to be rid of the pestering little squirt who never followed regulations.

It didn't take long for Sam to find out that Rockledge Industries, Inc. had its own bureaucracy, its own sets of regulations, and its own frustrations.

"You'd think a multibillion-dollar company would want to make all the profits it can," Sam grumbled to me, about six months after he had returned to the Shack. "Half the facilities on Alpha are empty, right? They overbuilt, right? So I show them how to turn Alpha into a tourist resort and they reject the goddamned idea. 'We are not in the tourism business,' they say. Goddamned assholes."

I found it hard to believe that Rockledge didn't understand what a bonanza they could reap from space tourism. It's not just twenty-twenty hindsight; Sam had me convinced then and there that tourism would be worth a fortune to Alpha. But Rockledge just failed to see it, no matter how hard Sam tried to convince them. Maybe the harder he tried the less they liked the idea. Some outfits are like that. The old Not-Invented-Here syndrome. Or more likely, the old If-Sam's-For-It-I'm-Against-It syndrome.

Sam spent weeks muttering about faceless bureaucrats who sat on their brains, and how much money a zero-gravity honeymoon hotel could make. At least, that's what I thought he was doing.

The big crisis was mostly my fault. Looking back on it, if I could have figured out a different way to handle things, I would have. But you know how it is when your emotions are all churned up; you don't see any alternatives. Truthfully, I still don't see how I could have done anything else except what I did.

They told me I was cured.

Yeah, I know I said they never used words like that, but they changed their tune. After more than five years in the isolation ward of the station, the medics asked me to join them in the conference room. I expected another one of their dreary meetings; they made me attend them at least once a month, said it was important for me to "maintain a positive interaction with the research staff." So I dragged myself down to the conference room.

They were all grinning at me, around the table. Buckets of champagne stood at either end, with more bottles stashed where the slide projector usually hung.

I was cured. The genetic manipulations had finally worked. My body's immune system was back to normal. My case would be in the medical journals; future generations would bless my memory (but not my name: they would protect my anonymity). I could go back home, back to Earth.

Only, I didn't want to go.

"You don't want to go?" Sam's pudgy little face was screwing up into an incredulous expression that mixed equal amounts of surprise, disapproval, and curiosity.

"Back to Earth? No, I don't want to go," I said. "I want to stay here. Or maybe go live on Alpha or one of the new stations they're building."

"But why?" Sam asked.

We were in his office, a tiny cubbyhole that had originally been a storage locker for fresh food. I mean, space in the Shack was *tight*. I thought I could still smell onions or something faintly pungent. Sam had walled the chamber with blue-colored spongy plastic, so naturally it came to be known as the Blue Grotto. There were no chairs in the Grotto, of course; chairs are useless in zero-gee. We just hung in midair. You could nudge your back against the slightly rough wall surfacing and that would hold you in place well enough. There wasn't any room to drift around. Two people were all the chamber could hold comfortably. Sam's computer terminal was built into the wall; there was no furniture in the Grotto, no room for any.

"I got nothing to go back for," I answered, "and a lot of crap waiting for me that I'd just as soon avoid."

"But it's *Earth*," he said. "The world . . ."

So I told him about it. The whole story, end to end.

I had been a soldier, back in that nasty little bitch of a war in Mexico. Nothing glamorous, not even patriotism. I had joined the Army because it was the only way for a kid from my part of Little Rock to get a college education. They paid for my education and right afterward they pinned a lieutenant's gold bars on my shoulders and stuck me inside a heavy tank.

Well, you know how well the tanks did in those Mexican hills. Nothing to shoot at but cactus, and we were great big noisy targets for those smart little missiles they brought in from Korea or wherever.

They knocked out my tank. I was the only one of the crew to survive. I wound up in an Army hospital in Texas where they tried to put my spine back together again. That's where I contracted AIDS, from one of the male nurses who wanted to prove to me that I hadn't lost my virility. He was a very sweet kid, very caring. But I never saw him again once they decided to ship me to the isolation ward up in orbit.

Now it was five years later. I was cured of AIDS, a sort of anonymous hero, but everything else was still the same. Earth would be still the same, except that every friend I had ever known was five years' distance from me. My parents had killed themselves in an automobile wreck when I was in college. I had no sisters or brothers. I had no job prospects. Soldiers coming back five years after the war weren't greeted with parades and confetti, and all the computer stuff I had learned in college was obsolete by now. Not even the Army used that generation of software any more.

And Earth was dirty, crowded, noisy, dangerous—it was also *heavy,* a full one g. I tried a couple days in the one-g wheel over at Alpha and knew that I could never live in Earth's full gravity again. Not voluntarily.

Sam listened to all this in complete silence, the longest I had ever known him to go without opening his mouth. He was totally serious, not even the hint of a smile. I could see that he understood.

"Down there I'll be just another nobody, an ex-soldier with no place to go. I can't handle the gravity, no matter what the physical therapists think they can do for me. I want to stay here, Sam. I want to make something of myself and I can do it here, not back there. The best I can be back there is another veteran on a disability pension. What kind of a job could I get? I can *be* somebody up here, I know I can."

He put his hand on my shoulder. Had to rise up off the floor a ways to do it, but he did it. "You're sure? You're absolutely certain that this is what you want?"

I nodded. "I can't go back, Sam. I just can't."

The faintest hint of a grin twitched at the corners of his mouth. "Okay, pal. How'd you like to go into the hotel business with me?"

You see, Same had already been working for some time on his own ideas about space tourism. If Rockledge wouldn't go for a hotel facility over on Alpha, complete with zero-gee honeymoon suites, then Sam figured he could get somebody else interested in the idea. The people who like to bad-mouth Sam say that he hired me to cover his ass so he could spend his time working on his tourist hotel deal while he was still collecting a salary from Rockledge. That isn't the way it happened at all; it was really the other way around.

Sam hired me as a consultant and paid me out of his own pocket. To this day I don't know where he got the money. I suspect it was from some of the financial people he was always talking to, but you never know, with Sam. He had an inexhaustible fund of rabbits up his sleeves. Whenever I asked him about it he just grinned at me and told me not to ask questions.

I was never an employee of Rockledge Industries. And Sam worked full time for them, eight hours a day, six days a week, and then some. They got their salary's worth out of him. More. But that didn't mean he couldn't spend nights, Sundays, and the odd holiday here and there wooing financiers and lawyers who might come up with the risk capital he needed for his hotel. Sure, sometimes he did his own thing during Rockledge's regular office hours. But he worked plenty of overtime hours for Rockledge, too. They got their money's worth out of Sam.

Of course, once I was no longer a patient whose bills were paid by the government Rockledge sent word up from corporate headquarters that I was to be shipped back Earthside as soon as possible. Sam interpreted that to mean, when he was good and ready. Weeks stretched into months. Sam fought a valiant delaying action, matching every query of theirs with a detailed memorandum and references to obscure government health regulations. It would take Rockledge's lawyers a month to figure out what the hell Sam was talking about and then frame an answering memo.

In the meantime Sam moved me from the old isolation ward into a private room—a coffin-sized cubbyhole—and insisted that I start paying for my rent and food. Since Sam was paying me a monthly consultant's stipend he was collecting my rent and food money out of the money he was giving me himself. It was all done with the Shack's computer system, so no cash changed hands. I had the feeling that there were some mighty weird subroutines running around inside that computer, all of them programmed by Sam.

While all this was going on the Shack was visited by a rather notorious U.S. Senator, one of the most powerful men in the government. He was a wizened, shriveled old man who had been in the Senate almost half a century. I thought little of it; we were getting a constant trickle of VIPs in those days. The bigwigs usually went to Alpha, so much so that we began calling it the Big Wheel's Wheel. Most of them avoided the Shack. I guess

they were scared of getting contaminated from our isolation ward patients. But a few of the VIPs made their way to the Shack now and then.
Sam took personal charge of the Senator and his entourage and showed
him more attention and courtesy than I had ever seen him lavish on a visitor before. Or since, for that matter. Sam, kowtowing to an authority figure? It astounded me at the time, but I laughed it off and forgot all about
it soon enough.

Then, some six months after the Senator's visit, when it looked as if
Sam had run out of time and excuses to keep me in the Shack and I would
have to pack my meager bag and head down the gravity well to spend the
rest of my miserable days in some overcrowded ghetto city, Sam came
prancing weightlessly into my microminiaturized living quarters, waving
a flimsy sheet of paper.

"What's that?" I knew it was a straight line but he wasn't going to tell
me unless I asked.

"A new law." He was smirking, canary feathers all over his chin.

"First time I ever seen you happy about some new regulation."

"Not a regulation," he corrected me. "A *law*. A federal law, duly passed
by the U.S. Congress and just today signed by the President."

I wanted to play it cool but he had me too curious. "So what's it say?
Why's it so important?"

"It says," Sam made a flourish that sent him drifting slowly toward the
ceiling as he read, " 'No person residing aboard a space facility owned by
the United States or a corporation or other legal entity licensed by the
United States may be compelled to leave said facility without due process
of law.' "

My reply was something profound, like, "Huh?"

His scrungy little face beaming, Sam said, "It means that Rockledge
can't force you back Earthside! As long as you can pay the rent, Omar,
they can't evict you."

"You joking?" I couldn't believe it.

"No joke. I helped write this masterpiece, kiddo," he told me. "Remember when old Senator Winnebago was up here, last year?"

The Senator was from Wisconsin but his name was not Winnebago.
He had been a powerful enemy of the space program until his doctors
told him that degenerative arthritis was going to make him a pain-
racked cripple unless he could live in a low-g environment. His visit to
the Shack proved what his doctors had told him: in zero-gee the pains
that hobbled him disappeared and he felt twenty years younger. All of a

sudden he became a big space freak. That's how Sam was able to convince him to sponsor the "pay your own way" law, which provided that neither the government nor a private company operating a space facility could force a resident out as long as he or she was able to pay the going rate for accommodations.

"Hell, they've got laws to protect tenants from eviction in New York and every other city," Sam said. "Why not here?"

I was damned glad of it. Overjoyed, in fact. It meant that I could stay, that I wouldn't be forced to go back Earthside and drag my ass around at my full weight. What I didn't realize at the time, of course, was that Sam would eventually have to use the law for himself. Obviously, *he* had seen ahead far enough to know that he would need such protection sooner or later. Did he get the law written for his own selfish purposes? Sure he did. But it served *my* purpose, too, and Sam knew that when he was bending the Senator's tin ear. That was good enough for me. Still is.

For the better part of another year I served as Sam's leg man—a job I found interesting and amusingly ironic. I shuttled back and forth from the Shack to Alpha, generally to meet bigshot business persons visiting the Big Wheel. When Sam was officially on duty for Rockledge, which was most of the time, he'd send me over to Alpha to meet the visitors, settle them down, and talk about the money that a tourist facility would make. I would just try to keep them happy until Sam could shake loose and come over to meet them himself. Then he would weave a golden web of words, describing how fantastic an orbital tourist facility would be, bobbing weightlessly around the room in his enthusiasm, pulling numbers out of the air to show how indecently huge would be the profit that investors would make.

"And the biggest investors will get their own suites, all for themselves," Sam promised, "complete with every luxury—every service that the well-trained staff can provide." He would wink hard enough to dislocate an eyeball at that point, to make certain the prospective investor knew what he meant.

I met some pretty interesting people that way: Texas millionaires, Wall Street financiers, Hollywood sharks, a couple of bull-necked types I thought might be Mafia but turned out to be in the book and magazine distribution business, even a few very nice middle-aged ladies who were looking for "good causes" in which to invest. Sam did not spare them his "every service that the staff can provide" line, together with the wink. They giggled and blushed.

"It's gonna happen!" Sam kept saying. Each time we met a prospective backer his enthusiasm rose to a new pitch. No matter how many times a prospect eventually turned sour, no matter how often we were disappointed, Sam never lost his faith in the idea or the inevitability of its fruition.

"It's gonna happen, Omar. We're going to create the first tourist hotel in orbit. And you're going to have a share of it, pal. Mark my words."

When we finally got a tentative approval from a consortium of Greek and Italian shipping magnates Sam nearly rocked the old Shack out of orbit. He whooped and hollered and zoomed around the place like a crazy billiard ball. He threw a monumental party for everybody in the Shack, doctors, nurses, patients, technicians, administrative staff, security guards, visitors, even the one consultant who lived there—me. Where he got the caviar and fresh brie and other stuff I still don't know. But it was a party none of us will ever forget. The Shack damned near exploded with merriment. It started Saturday at five PM, the close of the official work week. It ended, officially, Monday at eight AM. There are those who believe, though, that it's still going on over there at the Shack.

Several couples sort of disappeared during the party. The Shack wasn't so big that people could get lost in it, but they just seemed to vanish. Most of them showed up by Monday morning, looking tired and sheepish. Three of the couples eventually got married. One pair of them was stopped by a technician when they tried to go out an airlock while stark naked.

Sam himself engaged in a bit of EVA with one of the nurses, a tiny little elf of fragile beauty and uncommon bravery. She snuggled into a pressure suit with Sam and the two of them made several orbits around the Shack, outside, propelled by nothing more than their own frenetic pulsations and Newton's Third Law of Motion.

Two days after the party the Beryllium Blonde showed up.

Her real name was Jennifer Marlow, and she was as splendidly beautiful as a woman can be. A figure right out of a highschool boy's wettest dreams. A perfect face, with eyes of china blue and thickly glorious hair like a crown of shining gold. She staggered every male who saw her, she stunned even me, and she sent Sam into a complete tailspin.

She was Rockledge Industries's ace troubleshooter. Her official title was Administrative Assistant (Special Projects) to the President. The word we got from Earthside was that she had a mind like a steel trap, and a vagina to match.

The official excuse for her visit was to discuss Sam's letter of resignation with him.

"You stay right beside me," Sam insisted as we drifted down the Shack's central corridor toward the old conference room. "I won't be able to control myself if I'm in there alone with her."

His face was as white as the Moon's. He looked like a man in shock.

"Will you be able to control yourself *with* me in there?" I wondered.

"If I can't, rap me on the head. Knock me out. Give me a Vulcan nerve pinch. Anything! Just don't let me go zonkers over her."

I smiled.

"I'm not kidding, Omar!" Sam insisted. "Why do you think they sent her up here instead of some flunky? They know I'm susceptible. God knows how many scalps she's got nailed to her teepee."

I grabbed his shoulder and dug my Velcroed slippers into the floor carpeting. We skidded to a stop.

"Look," I said. "Maybe you want to avoid meeting with her altogether. I can represent you. I'm not . . . uh, susceptible."

His eyes went so wide I could see white all around the pupils. "Are you nuts? Miss a chance to be in the same room with her? I want to be protected, Omar, but not that much!"

What could I do with him? Sam was torn in half. He knew the Beryllium Blonde was here to talk him out of resigning but he couldn't resist the opportunity of letting her try her wiles on him any more than Odysseus could resist listening to the Sirens.

Like a couple of schoolboys dragging ourselves down to the principal's office, we made our way slowly along the corridor and pushed through the door to the conference room. She was already standing at the head of the table, wearing a chinese red jumpsuit that fit her like skin. I gulped down a lump in my throat at the sight of her. I mean, she was *something*. She smiled a dazzling smile and Sam gave a weak little moan and rose right up off the floor.

He would have launched himself at her like a missile if I hadn't grabbed his belt and yanked him down to the table level. Being in zero-gee, there was no need for chairs around the table. But I sure wished I had one then; I would have tied Sam into it. As it was, I hovered right next to him and kept the full length of the polished imitation wood table between us and the Blonde.

"I think you know why I'm here," she said. Her voice was music.

Sam nodded dumbly, his jaw hanging open. I thought I saw a bit of saliva foaming at the corner of his mouth.

"Why do you want to leave us, Sam? Don't you *like* us any more?"

It took three tries before he could make his voice work. "It's . . . not that. I . . . I . . . I want to go into . . . uh, into business . . . for myself."

"But your employment contract has almost two full years more to run."

"I can't wait two years," he said, in a tiny voice. "This opportunity won't keep. . . ."

"Sam, you're a very valued employee of Rockledge Industries, Incorporated. We want you to stay with us. *I* want you to stay with us."

"I . . . can't."

"But you signed a contract with us, Sam. You gave us your word."

I stuck in my dime's worth. "The contract doesn't prohibit Sam from quitting. He can leave wherever he wants to." At least, that's what the lawyers Sam had hired had told us.

"But he'll lose all his pension benefits and health care provisions."

"He knows that."

She turned those heartbreakingly blue eyes on Sam again. "It will be a big disappointment to us if you leave, Sam. It will be a *personal* disappointment to me."

To his credit, Sam found the strength within himself to hold his ground. "I'm awfully sorry . . . but I've worked very hard to create this opportunity and I can't let it slip past me now."

She nodded once, as if she understood. Then she asked, "This opportunity you're speaking about: does it have anything to do with the prospect of opening a tourist hotel on Space Station Alpha?"

"That's right! But not just a hotel, a complete tourist facility. Sports complex, entertainment center, zero-gravity honeymoon suites . . ." He stopped abruptly and his face turned red. Sam blushed! He actually blushed.

Miss Beryllium smiled her dazzling smile at him. "But Sam dear, that idea is the proprietary intellectual property of Rockledge Industries, Incorporated. Rockledge owns the idea, not you."

For a moment the little conference room was absolutely silent. I could hear nothing except the faint background hiss of the air circulation fans. Sam seemed to have stopped breathing.

Then he squawked, "WHAT?"

With a sad little shake of her gorgeous head, the Blonde replied, "Sam, you developed that idea while an employee of Rockledge Industries. We own it."

"But you turned it down!"

"That makes no difference, Sam. Read your employment contract. It's ours."

"But I made all the contacts. I raised the funding. I worked everything out—on my own time, goddammit! *On my own time!*"

She shook her golden locks again. "No, Sam. You did it while you were a Rockledge employee. It is not your possession. It belongs to us."

Sam leaped out of my grasp and bounded to the ceiling. This time he was ready to make war, not love. "You can't do this to me!"

The Blonde looked completely unruffled by his display. She stood there patiently, a slightly disappointed little pout on her face, while I calmed Sam down and got him back to the table.

"Sam, dear, I know how you must feel," she cooed. "I don't want us to be enemies. We'd be happy to have you take part in the tourist hotel program as a Rockledge employee. There could even be a raise in it for you."

"It's mine, dammit!" Sam screeched. "You can't steal it from me! It's mine!"

She shrugged deliciously. "I suppose our lawyers will have to settle it with your lawyers. In the meantime I'm afraid there's nothing for us to do but to accept your resignation. With reluctance, of course. With my own personal and very sad reluctance."

That much I saw and heard with my own eyes and ears. I had to drag Sam out of the conference room and take him back to his own quarters. She had him whipsawed, telling him that he couldn't claim possession of his own idea and at the same time practically begging him to stay on with Rockledge and run the tourist project for them.

What happened next depends on who you ask. There are as many different versions of the story as there are people who tell it. As near as I can piece it all together, though, it went this way:

The Beryllium Blonde was hoping that Sam's financial partners would go along with Rockledge Industries once they realized that Rockledge had muscled Sam out of the hotel deal. But she probably wasn't as sure of everything as she tried to make Sam think. After all, those backers had made their deal with the little guy; maybe they didn't want to do business with a big multinational corporation. Worse still, she didn't know exactly what kind of a deal Sam had cut with his backers. If Sam had legally binding contracts naming him as their partner they just might scrap the whole project when they learned that Rockledge had cut Sam out. Especially if it looked like a court battle was shaping up.

So she showed up at Sam's door that night. He told me that she was still wearing the same skintight jumpsuit, with nothing underneath it except her own luscious body. She brought a bottle of incredibly rare and expensive cognac with her. "To show there's no hard feelings."

The Blonde's game was to keep Sam with Rockledge and get him to go through with the tourist hotel deal. Apparently, once Rockledge's management got word that Sam had actually closed a deal for creating a tourist facility on Alpha, their greedy little brains told them they might as well take the tourist business for themselves. Alpha was still badly underutilized; a tourist facility suddenly made sense to those jerkoffs.

So instead of shuttling back to Phoenix, as we had thought she would, the Blonde knocked on Sam's door that night. The next morning I saw him floating along the Shack's central corridor. He looked kind of dazed.

"She's staying here for a few more days," Sam mumbled. It was like he was talking to himself instead of to me.

But there was that happy little grin on his face.

Everybody in the Shack started to make bets on how long Sam could hold out. The best odds had him capitulating in three nights. Jokes about Delilah and haircuts became uproariously funny to everybody—except me. My future was tied up with Sam's. If the tourist project collapsed it wouldn't be long before I got shipped back to Earth, I knew.

After three days there were dark circles under Sam's eyes. He looked weary. Dazed. The grin was gone.

After a week had gone by I found Sam snoring in the Blue Grotto. As gently as I could I woke him.

"You getting any food into you?" I asked.

He blinked, gummy-eyed. "Chicken soup. I been taking chicken soup. Had some yesterday. . . . I think it was yesterday. . . ."

By the tenth day more money had changed hands among the bettors than on Wall Street. Sam looked like a case of battle fatigue. His cheeks were hollow, his eyes haunted.

"She's a devil, Omar," he whispered hoarsely. "A devil."

"Then get rid of her, man!" I urged. "Send her packing!"

He smiled wanly, like a man who knew he was addicted. "And quit show business?" he said weakly.

Two weeks to the day after she arrived, the Blonde packed up and left. Her eyes were blazing with anger. I saw her off at the docking port. She looked just as perfectly radiant as the day she had first arrived at the Shack. But what she was radiating now was rage. *Hell hath no fury . . .* I thought. But I was happy to see her go.

Sam slept for two days straight. When he managed to get up and around again he was only a shell of his old self. He had lost ten pounds. His eyes were sunken into his skull. His hands trembled. His chin was stubbled. He looked as if he had been through hell and back. But his crooked little grin had returned.

"What happened?" I asked him.

"She gave up."

"You mean she's going to let you go?"

He gave a deep, soulful, utterly weary sigh. "I guess she finally figured out that she couldn't change my mind and she couldn't kill me—at least not with the method she was using." His grin stretched a little wider.

"We all thought she was wrapping you around her little finger," I said.

"So did she."

"You outsmarted her!"

"I outlasted her," Sam said, his voice low and truly sorrowful. "You know, at one point there, she almost had me convinced that she had fallen in love with me."

"In love with you?"

He shook his head slowly, like a man who had crawled across miles of burning desert toward an oasis that turned out to be a mirage.

"You had me worried, man."

"Why?" His eyes were really bleary.

"Well . . . she's a powerful hunk of woman. Like you said, they sent her up here because you're susceptible."

"Yeah. But once she tried to steal my idea from me I stopped being so susceptible. I kept telling myself, 'She's not a gorgeous hot-blooded sex-pot of a woman. She's a company stooge, an android they sent here to nail you, a bureaucrat with boobs. Great boobs."

"And it worked."

"By a millimeter. Less. She damned near beat me. She damned near did. She should never have mentioned marriage. That woke me up."

What had happened, while Sam was fighting the Battle of the Bunk, was that when Sam's partners-to-be realized that Rockledge was interested in the tourist facility, they became absolutely convinced that they had a gold mine on their hands. They backed Sam to the hilt. *Their* lawyers challenged Rock-ledge's lawyers, and once the paper-shufflers down in Phoenix saw that, they understood that Miss Beryllium's mission to the Shack was doomed. The Blonde left in a huff when Phoenix ordered her to return. I guess she was enjoying her work. Or maybe she thought she had Sam weakening.

"Now lemme get another week's worth of sleep, will you?" Sam asked me. "And, oh yeah, find me about a ton and a half of vitamin E."

So Sam became the manager and part owner of the human race's first extraterrestrial tourist facility. I was his partner and, the way things worked out, a major shareholder in the project. Rockledge got some rent money out of it. Actually, so many people enjoyed their vacations and honeymoons aboard the Big Wheel that a market eventually opened up for low-gravity retirement homes. Sam beat Rockledge on that, too. But that's another story.

MALONE WAS HANGING weightlessly near the curving transparent dome of his chamber, staring out at the distant Moon and cold unblinking stars.

Jade had almost forgotten her fear of weightlessness. The black man's story seemed finished. She blinked and turned her attention to here and now. Drifting slightly closer to him, she turned off the recorder with an audible click, then thought better of it and turned it on again.

"So that's how this hotel came into being," she said.

Malone nodded, turning in midair to face her. "Yep. Sam got it started and then lost interest in it. He had other things on his mind, bigger fish to fry. He went into the advertising business, you know."

"Oh yes, everybody knows about that," she replied. "But what happened to the woman, the Beryllium Blonde? And why didn't Sam ever return to Earth again?"

"Two parts of the same answer," Malone said tiredly. "Miss Beryllium thought she was playing Sam for a fish, using his Casanova complex to literally screw him out of his hotel deal. Once she realized that *he* was playing *her,* fighting a delaying action until his partners got their lawyers into action, she got damned mad. Powerfully mad. By the time it finally became clear back at Phoenix that Sam was going to beat them, she took her revenge."

"What do you mean?"

"Sam wasn't the only one who could riffle through old safety regulations and use them for his own benefit. She found a few early NASA regs, then got some bureaucrats in Washington—from the Office of Safety and Health, I think—to rewrite them so that anybody who'd been living in zero-gee for a year or more had to undertake six months' worth of retraining and exercise before he could return to Earth."

"Six months? That's ridiculous!"

"Is it?" Malone smiled with humor. "That regulation is still on the books, lady. Nobody pays attention to it anymore, but it's still there."

"She did that to spite Sam?"

"And she made sure Rockledge put all its weight behind enforcing it. Made people think twice before signing an employment contract to work up here. Stuck Sam, but good. He wasn't going to spend no six months re-training! He just never bothered going back to Earth again."

"Did he want to go back?"

"Sure he did. He wasn't like me. He *liked* it back there. There were billions of women on Earth! Sam wanted to return but he just could never take six months out of his life to do it."

"That must have hurt him terribly."

"Yeah, I guess. Hard to tell with Sam. He didn't like to bleed where other people could watch."

"And you never went back to Earth."

"No," Malone said. "Thanks to Sam I stayed up here. He made me manager of the hotel, and once Sam bought the rest of this Big Wheel from Rockledge, I became manager of the whole Alpha Station."

"And you've never had the slightest yearning to see Earth again?"

Malone gazed at her solemnly for long moments before answering. "Sure I get the itch. But when I do I go down to the one-g section of the Wheel here. I sit in a wheelchair and try to get around with these crippled legs of mine. The itch goes away then."

"But they have prosthetic legs that you can't tell from the real thing," she said. "Lots of paraplegics . . ."

"Maybe *you* can't tell them from the real thing, but I guarantee you that any paraplegic who uses those legs can tell." Malone shook his head stubbornly. "Naw, once you've spent some time up here in zero-gee you realize that you don't need legs to get around. You can live a good and useful life here instead of being a cripple down there."

"I see," Jade said softly.

"Yeah. Sure you do."

"Sure I do," Jade said softly. "I can never go to Earth, either."

"Never?" Malone sounded skeptical.

"Bone disease. I was born with it."

An uncomfortable silence rose between them. She turned off the recorder in her belt buckle, for good this time.

Finally Malone softened. "Hey, I'm sorry. I shouldn't've been nasty with you. It's just that . . . thinking about Sam again. He was a great guy, you know. And now he's dead and everybody thinks he was just a troublemaking bastard."

"I don't," she said. "A womanizing sonofabitch, like you said. A male chauvinist of the first order. But after listening to you tell it, even at that he doesn't seem so awful."

The black man smiled at her. "Look at the time! No wonder I'm hungry! Can I take you down to the dining room for some supper?"

"The dining room in the lunar-gravity section?"

"Yes, of course."

"Won't you be uncomfortable there? Isn't there a galley in the microgravity section?"

"Sure, but won't you be uncomfortable there?"

She laughed. "I think I can handle it."

"Really?"

"I can try. And maybe you can tell me how Sam got himself into the retirement home business."

"All right. I'll do that."

As she turned she caught sight of the immense beauty of Earth sliding past the observation dome; the Indian Ocean a breathtaking swirl of deep blues and greens, the subcontinent of India decked with purest white clouds. The people who lived there, she thought. All those people. And the two, in particular, who were hiding away from her.

"But . . ." She looked at Malone, then asked in a whisper, "Do you ever miss being home, being on Earth? Don't you feel isolated here, away from . . ."

His booming laughter shocked her. "Isolated? Up here?" Malone pitched himself forward into a weightless somersault, then pirouetted in midair. He pointed toward the ponderous bulk of the planet and said, "*They're* the ones who're isolated. Up here, I'm free!"

Then he offered his arm to her and they floated together toward the gleaming metal hatch, their feet a good eight inches above the chamber's floor.

Still, Jade glanced back over her shoulder at the gleaming expanse of cloud-decked blue. She thought of the two women who lived among the billions down there, the two women who would never see her, whom she could never see. There are many kinds of isolation, Jade thought. Many kinds.

Lagrange Habitat
Jefferson

THE DINING ROOM IN ALPHA'S ZERO-GRAVITY SECTION WAS actually a self-service galley. Malone helped Jade to fill her tray with prepackaged courses, then they fit their slippered feet into loop restraints on the spindly legs of a table, Jade using the highest level of the plastic loops, long-legged Malone the lowest.

Their dinner together was relaxed and pleasant. Malone recommended for dessert what he called "the Skylab bomb": a paper-thin shell of vanilla ice cream filled with strawberries.

"You can only make it this thin in zero-gee," he pointed out.

As they finished their squeezebulbs of coffee, Malone said, "Y'know, there's a guy over in the new habitat at L-5, the one they've named Jefferson. You'd do well to talk to him."

Jade turned on her belt recorder to get the man's name and location.

"Yeah. Spence Johansen," Malone continued. "He knew Sam when they were both astronauts with the old NASA. Then they went into business together."

"What kind of business?" Jade asked.

Malone grinned at her. "Junk collecting."

"IT'S JUST A small increment on the fare," Jade said to Raki's image on the phone screen. She was leaning against the side wall of the cubicle she had rented aboard Alpha, her bags packed, ready to head back to Selene by way of habitat Jefferson.

Raki had a strange smile on his darkly handsome face. "You got the story from this man Malone?" he asked.

"Yes. It's really good, Raki. Very personal stuff. Great human interest. And Malone told me about this Spencer Johansen who's living at Jefferson. I can get there on the transfer ship that's leaving in half an hour."

He shook his head. "What would you do if I said no?"

She grinned at his image. "I'd go there anyway; the difference in fare is so small I'd pay it myself."

He puffed out a sigh. "Do you realize how far out on a limb I am with you? The CEO *hates* Sam Gunn. If Sam were alive today the old man would want to have him murdered."

Jade said nothing. She merely hung there weightlessly, her back plastered to the wall to prevent her from drifting out of range of the phone's camera eye.

"All right," Raki said finally, with a little shrug of acquiescence. "I think it's crazy. I think maybe *I'm* crazy. But go ahead, get everything you can."

"Thanks!" Jade said. "You won't regret it, Raki."

"I already regret it."

"CALL ME SPENCE," he said, dropping his lanky, sweaty frame onto the bench beside her.

In spite of herself, Jade felt her heart skip a couple of beats. She was breathless, but not merely from the exertion of a hard game of low-g tennis.

Spencer Johansen was tall and lean, with the flat midsection and sharp reflexes that come only from constant exercise. His eyes were sky blue, his face handsome in a rugged, clean-cut, honest way. When he smiled, as he was doing now, he looked almost boyish despite his silver-gray hair. He was older than Raki, she knew. Yet he seemed more open; innocent, almost.

His smile was *deadly*. Jade had to remind herself that this man was the subject of an interview, not an object of desire. She was here to get a story out of him, and he was refusing to talk.

Jefferson was the newest of the Lagrange habitats being built at the L-4 and L-5 libration points along the Moon's orbit. A vast tube of asteroidal steel, twenty kilometers long and five wide, its interior was landscaped to look like a pleasant Virginia countryside, with rolling wooded hills and picturesque little villages dotting the greenery here and there. Best of all, from Jade's point of view, was that Jefferson rotated on its long axis only fast enough to give an almost lunar feeling of weight inside. The entire habitat, with its population of seventy-five thousand, was pleasantly low-gee.

"Why Sam?" Johansen asked, still smiling. But those clear blue eyes were wary, guarded.

They were both still puffing from their punishing game. Out on the huge low-gee court, safely behind a shatterproof transparent wall, the next two players were warming up with long slow low-gravity lobs and incredible leaps to hit the ball five meters above the sponge metal surface of the court.

"Solar Network wants to do his biography," Jade replied, surreptitiously pressing the microswitch that activated the recorder built into her belt buckle.

"Solar, huh?" Spencer Johansen huffed.

"Well . . . it's really me," Jade confessed. "I've become fascinated by the man. *I* want to get Solar to do a special on him. I need all the help I can get. I need your story."

Johansen looked down at her. Sitting beside him she looked small, almost childlike, in a loose-fitting sleeveless gym top and shorts of pastel yellow.

"You're not the first woman to be fascinated by ol' Sam," he muttered. His own tennis outfit was nothing more than an ancient T-shirt and faded denim cutoffs.

"Couldn't you tell me *something* about him? Just some personal reminiscences?"

"We made a deal, you and me."

She sighed heavily. "I know. And I lost."

His smile returned. "Yeah, but you played a helluva game. Never played in low-g before?"

"Never," she swore. "There's no room for tennis courts in Selene. And this is my first time to a Lagrange habitat."

He seemed to look at her from a new perspective. The smile widened. "Come on, hit the showers and put on your drinking clothes."

"You'll give me the interview? Even though I lost the game?"

"You're too pretty to say no to. Besides, you played a damned good game. A couple days up here and you'll be beating me."

Vacuum Cleaner

BACK IN THE OLD NASA DAYS SAM GUNN AND I WERE buddies—said Johansen to Jade over a pair of L-5 "libration libations."

They had height limitations for astronauts back then, even for the old shuttle. I just barely made it under the top limit. Little Sam just barely made it past the low end. Everybody used to call us Mutt and Jeff. In fact, Sam himself called me Mutt most of the time.

I never figured out exactly why it was, but I *liked* the little so-and-so. Maybe it's because he was always the underdog, the little guy in trouble with the big boys. Although I've got to admit that most of the time Sam started the trouble himself. I'm no angel; I've raised as much hell as the next guy, I guess. But Sam—he was unique. A real loose cannon. He *never* did things by the book. I think Sam regarded the regulations as a challenge, something to be avoided at all costs. He'd drive everybody nuts. But he'd get the job done, no matter how many mission controllers turned blue.

He quit the agency, of course. Too many rules. I've got to confess that flying for the agency in those days was a lot like working for a bus line. If those desk-jockeys in Washington could've used robots instead of human astronauts they would've jumped at the chance. All they wanted was for us to follow orders and fill out their damned paperwork.

Sam was itching to be his own boss. "There's m-o-n-e-y to be made out there," he'd spell out for me. "Billions and billions," he'd say in his Carl Sagan voice.

He got involved in this and that while I stayed in the agency and tried to make the best of it despite the bureaucrats. Maybe you heard about the tourist deal he got involved in. Later on he actually started a tourist hotel at Alpha. But at this point Alpha hadn't even been started yet; the only facilities in orbit were a couple of Russian jobs and the American station, Freedom. Sam had served on Freedom, part of the very first crew. Ended the mission in a big mess.

Well, meantime, all I really wanted was to be able to fly. That's what I love. And back in those days, if you wanted to fly you either worked for the agency or you tried to get a job overseas. I just couldn't see myself sitting behind a desk or working for the French or the Japs.

Then one fine day Sam calls me up.

"Pack your bags and open a Swiss bank account," he says.

Even over the phone—I didn't have a videophone back then—I could hear how excited he was. I didn't do any packing, but I agreed to meet him for a drink. The Cape was just starting to boom again, what with commercial launches (unmanned, in those days) and the clippers ferrying people to space stations and all that. I had no intentions of moving; I had plenty of flight time staring me in the face even if it was nothing more than bus driving.

Sam was usually the center of attention wherever he went. You know, wisecracking with the waitresses, buying drinks for everybody, buzzing all over the bar like a bee with a rocket where his stinger ought to be. But that afternoon he was just sitting quietly in a corner booth, nursing a flat beer.

Soon as I slid into the booth Sam starts in, *bam,* with no preliminaries. "How'd you like to be a junk collector?"

"Huh?"

Jabbing a thumb toward the ceiling he says, "You know how many pieces of junk are floating around in low orbit? Thousands! Millions!"

He's talking in a kind of a low voice, like he doesn't want anybody to hear him.

I said back to him, "Tell me about it. On my last mission the damned canopy window got starred by a stray piece of crap. If it'd been any bigger . . ."

There truly were thousands of pieces of debris floating in orbit around the Earth back then. All kinds of junk: discarded equipment, flakes of paint, pieces of rocket motors, chunks of crap of all kinds. Legend had it that there was still an old Hasselblad camera that Mike Collins had fumbled away during the Gemini 10 mission floating around out there. And a thermal glove from somebody else.

In fact, if you started counting the really tiny stuff, too small to track by radar, there might actually have been millions of bits of debris in orbit. A cloud of debris, a layer of man-made pollution, right in the area where we were putting space stations in permanent orbits.

Sam hunched across the table, making a shushing gesture with both his hands. "That's just it! Somebody's gonna make a fuckin' fortune cleaning up that orbiting junk, getting rid of it, making those low orbits safe to fly in."

I gave him a sidelong look. Sam was trying to keep his expression serious, but a grin was worming its way out. His face always reminded me of a leprechaun: round, freckled, wiry red hair, the disposition of an imp who never grew up.

"To say nothing," he damn near whispered, "of what they'll pay to remove defunct commsats from geosynchronous orbit."

He didn't really say "geosynchronous orbit," he called it "GEO" like we all do. "LEO" is low Earth orbit. GEO is 22,300 miles up, over the equator. That's where all the communications satellites were. We damned near got into a shooting war with half a dozen equatorial nations in South America and Africa over GEO rights—but that's a different story.

"Who's going to pay you to collect junk?" I asked. Damned if my voice didn't come out as low as his.

Sam looked very pleased with himself. "Our dear old Uncle Sam, at first. Then the fat-cat corporations."

Turns out that Sam had a friend who worked in the Department of Commerce, of all places, up in Washington. I got the impression that the friend was not a female, which surprised me. Seemed that the friend was a Commerce Department bureaucrat, of all things. I just couldn't picture Sam being chummy with a desk-jockey. It seemed strange, not like him at all.

Anyway, Commerce had just signed off on an agreement with the space agency to provide funding for removing junk from orbit. Like all government programs, there was to be a series of experimental missions before anything else happened. What the government calls a "feasibility study." At least two competing contractors would be funded for the feasibility study.

The winner of the competition, Sam told me, would get an exclusive contract to remove debris and other junk from LEO on an ongoing basis.

"They've gotta do something to protect the space station," Sam said.

"Freedom?"

He bobbed his head up and down. "Sooner or later she's gonna get hit by something big enough to cause real damage."

"The station's already been dinged here and there. Little stuff, but some of it causes damage. They've got guys going EVA almost every day for inspection and repair."

"And the corporations who own the commsats are going to be watching this competition very closely," Sam went on, grinning from ear to ear.

I knew that GEO was getting so crowded that the International

Telecommunications Authority had put a moratorium on launching new commsats. The communications companies were only being allowed to replace old satellites that had gone dead. They were howling about how their industry was being stifled.

"Worse than that," Sam added. "The best slots along the GEO are already so damned crowded that the commsat signals are interfering with one another. Indonesia's getting porno movies from the Polynesian satellite!"

That made me laugh out loud. Must have played holy hob with Indonesia's family planning program.

"How much do you think Turner or Toshiba would pay to have dead commsats removed from orbit so new ones can be spotted in the best locations?" Sam asked.

"Zillions," I said.

"At least!"

I thought it over for all of ten seconds. "Why me?" I asked Sam. I mean, we had been buddies but not all that close.

"You wanna fly, don'tcha? Handling an OMV, going after stray pieces of junk, that's going to call for *real* flying!"

An OMV was an orbital maneuvering vehicle: sort of a little sports car built to zip around from the space station to other satellites; never comes back to Earth. Compared to driving the space shuttle, flying an OMV would be like racing at Le Mans.

I managed to keep a grip on my enthusiasm, though. Sam wasn't acting out of altruism, I figured. Not without some other reason to go along with it. I just sat there sipping at my beer and saying nothing.

He couldn't keep quiet for long. "Besides," he finally burst out, "I need somebody with a good reputation to front the organization. If those goons in Washington see my name on top of our proposal they'll send it to the Marianas Trench and deep-six it."

That made sense. Washington was full of bureaucrats who'd love to see Sam mashed into corn fritters. Except, apparently, for his one friend at Commerce.

"Will you let me be president of the company?" I asked.

He nodded. The corners of his mouth tightened, but he nodded.

I let my enthusiasm show a little. I grinned and stuck my hand out over the table. Sam grinned back and we shook hands between the beer bottles.

But I had a problem. I would have to quit the agency. I couldn't be a government employee—even on long-term leave—and work for a private company. Washington's ethics rules were very specific about that. Oh yeah, Sam formed a private company to tackle the job. Very private: he owned it all. He called it VCI. That stood for *Vacuum Cleaners, Inc.* Cute.

I solved my problem with a single night's sleepless tussling. The next morning I resigned from the agency. Hell, if Sam's plan worked I'd be getting more flying time than a dozen shuttle-jockeys. And I'd be doing some real flying, not just driving a big bus.

If things didn't work out with Sam I could always re-up with the agency. They'd take me back, I felt sure, although all my seniority and pension would be gone. What the hell. It was only money. Most of my salary went to my first three wives anyway.

JADE NEARLY DROPPED the tall frosty glass from which she had been sipping.

"Your first three wives?" she gulped.

Johansen inched back in the fabric-covered slingchair. He looked flustered, embarrassed. "Uh, I've been married six times," he said, in a low fumbling voice.

"Six?"

He seemed to be mentally counting. Then he nodded, "Yeah, six. Funny thing, Sam always had the reputation for chasing . . . women. But somehow I always wound up getting married."

Jade's heart fluttered with disappointment. Yet a tiny voice deep within her noted that seven is a lucky number. She felt shocked, confused.

It took an effort of will to pull her eyes away from Johansen and gaze out at the scenery. The patio on which they sat hung out over the curving landscape of the gigantic habitat. Jade saw gentle grassy hills with a lazy stream meandering among them, in the distance a little village that looked like a scene for a Christmas card except there was no snow. Farther still there were farms, kilometers off, like a checkerboard of different shades of green. Her eyes followed the curve of this vast structure, up and up, woods and fields and more villages overhead, all the way around until her gaze settled on Johansen's relaxed, smiling face once again.

"It's quite a sight, isn't it?" he said. "A complete self-sufficient ecology, man-made, inside a twenty-kilometer cylinder."

"Quite a sight," she murmured.

Putting the glass down on the little cocktail table between them, Jade forced herself to return to the subject at hand. "You were talking about leaving the agency to go to work for Sam."

OH, YEAH—JOHANSEN replied, deftly ordering a new round of drinks with a hand signal to their robot waiter.

Sam had two problems to wrestle with: how to raise the money to make VCI more than a bundle of paper, and how to get the government to award us one of the two contracts for the experimental phase of the junk removal program.

Sam raised the money, just barely. He got most of it from a banker in Salt Lake City who had a daughter that needed marrying. And did *that* cause trouble later on! Let me tell you.

But I don't want to get ahead of myself.

We rented a dinky office on the second floor of a shopping mall, over a women's swimwear shop. Sam spent more time downstairs than he did in the office. At least, when the stores were open. Nights he worked with me writing our proposal. He seemed to work better after the sun went down. Me, I worked night and day. Writing a proposal was not easy for me.

Sam went out and hired a wagonload of big-time consultants from academia and industry, guys with fancy degrees and lists of publications longer than a gorilla's arm.

"Gee, Sam, how can we afford all these fancy pedigrees?" I asked him.

He just grinned. "All we need 'em for is to put their names on our letterhead and their resumes in our proposal. That doesn't cost a damned thing. They only get paid when we ask them to consult with us, and we don't have to ask 'em a thing once we win the contract."

That sounded a little shady to me, but Sam insisted our proposal needed some class and I had to agree with him there. Our only real employees were two bright kids who were still students at Texas A&M, and four local technicians who were part-time until we got the government contract. We leased or borrowed every piece of office equipment. Most of the software our Texas kids invented for us or pirated from elsewhere. We really needed that impressive list of consultants.

Those two youngsters from Texas had come up with a great idea for removing debris from orbit. At least, it looked like a great idea to me. On paper. I knew enough engineering to get by, but these kids were really sharp.

"How'd you find them?" I asked Sam.

"They wrote a paper about their idea," he said. "Published it in an aerospace journal. Their professor put his name on it, just like they all do, but I found those two kids who did the real work and put 'em on the payroll."

I was impressed. I had never realized that Sam kept up with the technical journals.

Well, we finished writing the proposal and e-mailed it up to Washington just under the deadline. You know how the government works: you could have the greatest invention since canned soup but they won't look at it if it isn't in their hands by "close-of-business" on the day they specify. Thank god for the Internet. We just barely made it.

Then we waited. For weeks. Months.

I got nervous as hell. Sam was as cool as liquid hydrogen. "Relax, Mutt," he told me a thousand times during those months. "It's in the bag." And he would smile a crooked little smile.

So there I sat, behind a rented desk in a dinky office, while the days ticked by and our money ran out. I was president of a company that was so close to bankruptcy I was starting to think about moonlighting as a spare pilot for Federal Express.

Then we got the letter from Washington. Very official, with a big seal on it and everything.

We were invited to send a representative to a meeting in Washington to defend our proposal against a panel of government experts. The letter said that there were four proposals being considered. The four companies were Rockledge International, Lockwood Industries, Texas Aerospace, and VCI—us.

"Holy Christmas!" I said when I read the letter. "We're never going to get a contract. Look at who the competition is: three of the biggest aerospace corporations in the world!"

Sam made like a Buddha. He folded his hands over his little belly and smiled enigmatically.

"Don't worry about it, Mutt," he said for the thousand-and-first time. "It's in the bag. If there's any real problem, I've got four magic words that will take care of everything."

"What did you say?"

"Four magic words," Sam repeated.

I did not share his confidence. In fact, I thought he had gone a little nutty under the pressure.

I was nervous as a kid on his first solo as I flew to Washington on the appointed day. I had spent every day and night since we'd received that letter cramming every bit of technical and financial data into my thick skull. We had even flown over to College Station for a week, where our two bright Texas A&M youngsters stuffed all their info into me directly.

I was surprised to see that one of Sam's two young geniuses was female. Sort of round and chubby, but she had huge dark soulful Mediterranean eyes that followed Sam wherever he moved like twin radar dishes locked onto a target. I figured that maybe Sam had met her *before* he had read their paper in that journal.

Anyway, there I was, stepping into an office in some big government building in Washington, my head bursting with facts and figures. As offices go, it wasn't much bigger or better furnished than our own little place in Florida. Government-issue desk, table and chairs. Metal bookcases on one side. Faded pastel walls, hard to tell what color they were supposed to be originally. Everything looked kind of shabby.

I was the last one to arrive. Representatives of our three competitors were already sitting side-by-side on one end of the long table that took up most of the room. They sure looked well-off, knowledgeable, slick and powerful. I felt like an intruder, an outsider, well beyond my depth.

But Sam had given me those four magic words of his to use in an emergency, and I whispered them to myself as I took the last chair, at the foot of the table.

Sitting at the head of the table was a guy from the agency I had met once, when he had visited the Cape for the official ceremonies when we opened space station Freedom. That had been years ago, and I hadn't seen him anywhere around the working parts of the agency since then. On his right-hand side sat three more government types: old suits, gray hair or none at all, kind of pasty faces from being behind desks all their lives.

The three industry reps were dressed in much better suits: not flashy, but obviously expensive. Two of them were so young their hair was still all dark. The third, from Rockledge International, was more my own age. His hair was kind of salt-and-pepper; looked like he spent plenty on haircuts, too. And tanning parlors. He was the only one who smiled at me as I sat down and introduced myself. I didn't know it right at that moment, but it was the kind of smile a shark gives.

"We're glad you could make it, Mr. Johansen," said the guy at the head of the table. The others sort of snickered.

"My flight was delayed in Atlanta," I mumbled. In those days, when you flew out of Florida, even if you died and were sent to hell you had to go by way of Atlanta.

He introduced himself as Edgar Zane. Thin hair, thin lips, thin nose, and thin wire-frames on his bifocals. But his face looked round and bloated, too big for his features. Made him look like a cartoon character, almost. From what I could see of his belly behind the table, that was bloated too.

Zane introduced everybody else around the table. The government types were from the Department of Transportation, the Environmental Protection Agency, and the Department of Commerce.

Commerce? Was this bald, sallow-faced, cranky-looking old scarecrow Sam's pigeon in the Commerce Department? He sure didn't give me any reason to think so. He squinted at me like an undertaker taking measurements.

"Before we begin," said the Rockledge guy, Pierre D'Argent, "I'd like to ask Mr. Johansen for a clarification."

Zane peered at him through the top half of his bifocals. "You're here to answer questions, Mr. D'Argent, not ask them."

He beamed a smile toward the head of the table. "Yes, I understand that. But I believe we all have the right to know exactly who we are dealing with here."

He turned his handsome face to me. "VCI is a new firm in this field. I think we'd all like to know a bit more about your company's financial backing and management structure."

I knew right away what he wanted. He wanted me to tell them all that Sam Gunn was the man behind VCI.

I gave him the standard spiel that Sam had drummed into me, like a POW reciting name, rank, and serial number: "VCI is a privately held company. I am the president and Chief Executive Officer. While our staff is small and elite we have an extensive list of consultants who can provide world-class technical, management and financial expertise on every aspect of our program. VCI's principal financial backer is the First Federal Bank of Utah. Our accounting firm is Robb and Steele, of Merritt Island, Florida."

D'Argent smiled at me with all his teeth. "And what role does Mr. Gunn play in VCI?"

"Who?" My voice squeaked a little.

"Sam Gunn," D'Argent said.

I looked up the table. Zane was scowling at me through his wire-frame glasses. He knew Sam, that was for sure.

Never lie to the government, Sam had instructed me, when there's a good chance that they'll catch you at it.

"Mr. Gunn is the founder of VCI," I said.

"His name doesn't appear in your proposal," Zane practically snarled.

"Yes it does, sir," I corrected him. "On page four hundred and sixty-three." That was back in the boilerplate section where we were required to put in a history of the company. Ordinarily nobody read the boilerplate, but now I knew that Zane and his three harpies would go over it with electron microscopes. How Sam managed to produce forty-seven pages of history about a company that wasn't even forty-seven weeks old was beyond me.

Zane gave D'Argent a glance, then asked me, "Is Sam Gunn going to be actively involved in the project—if you should be fortunate enough to win one of the contracts?"

"We have no intention to actively involve him in the day-to-day work," I said. It was pretty close to the truth.

Zane looked as if he didn't believe a word of it. I figured we had been shot down before we even got off the runway. D'Argent gave me another one of his shark smiles, looking pleased with himself.

But the bald scarecrow from Commerce cleared his throat and rasped, "Are we here to discuss the competing proposals or to conduct a witch hunt? Sounds to me like a cult of personality."

Zane huffed through his pinched nose and started the official proceedings.

The one thing we had going for us was our technical approach. I quickly saw that all three of our giant corporate competitors had submitted pretty much the same proposal: the old Nerf ball idea. You know, launch a balloon and blow it up to full size once it's in orbit. The balloon's surface is sort of semi-sticky. As it runs into debris in space it bounces them into orbits that spin down into the atmosphere, where the junk burns up. The idea had been around for decades. It was simple and would probably work—except for sizable chunks of debris, like discarded pieces of rocket stages or hand tools that got away.

It also required a lot of launches, because the Nerf ball itself got slowed down enough after a few orbits to come spiraling back into the atmosphere. The Nerfs could be launched with small unmanned boosters pretty cheaply, or ride piggyback on bigger boosters. They could even be tucked into spare corners of shuttle payload bays and injected into orbit by the shuttle crews.

Our proposal was different. See, the junk hanging around up there picked up an electrical charge after a couple of orbits. From electrons in the solar wind, if I remember correctly. Sam's idea was to set up a big electromagnetic bumper on the front end of space station Freedom and deflect the debris with it, neatly clearing out the orbit that the station was flying through. Kind of like the cowcatcher on the front of an old locomotive, only instead of being made of steel our bumper was an invisible magnetic field that stretched hundreds of meters into space out in front of the station.

"The equipment we need is small enough to fit into a shuttle's student experiment canister," I explained. "The bumper itself is nothing more than an extended magnetic field, generated by a superconducting coil that would be mounted on the forward-facing side of the space station."

"The costs . . ." Zane started to mutter.

"The program will cost less than a continuing series of Nerf ball launches," I said before he could turn to the relevant pages in our proposal. "And the elegant thing is that, since this program's primary aim is to keep Freedom's orbit clear of debris, we will be doing exactly that."

"And nothing else," D'Argent sniped.

I smiled at him for a change. "Once Freedom's orbit has been cleared we could always detach the equipment, mount it in an orbital maneuvering vehicle, and clean out other orbits. The equipment is very portable, yet durable and long-lasting."

We went into some really heavy-duty arguing, right through lunch (a plate of soggy sandwiches and cans of soda brought in to us by a delivery boy who had dirt under every one of his fingernails) and all through the long afternoon.

"I've got to admit," Zane finally said as it started to get dark outside, "that VCI's technical proposal is extremely interesting."

"But can a newly hatched company be expected to carry through?" D'Argent asked. "I mean, after all, they have no track record, no real financial strength. Do you really trust Sam Gunn, of all people, to get the job done?"

I held onto my temper. Partly because Sam had drilled it into me that they'd drop our proposal if they thought I was as flaky as he was. But mostly because I heard Sam's four magic words.

"Small business set-aside."

They were spoken by the cadaver from Commerce. Everything stopped. The room fell so quiet I could hear the going-home traffic from out on the streets below even through the double-paned sealed windows of the office.

"This program has a small business set-aside provision," the Commerce scarecrow said, his voice crackling as if it was coming over a radio link from Mars. "VCI is the only small business firm to submit a proposal. Therefore, if their proposal is technically sound—which we all agree that it is—and financially in line, we have no choice but to award them one of the two contracts."

D'Argent's handsome chin dropped to his expensive rep tie. Zane glared at his crony from Commerce. The others muttered and mumbled to themselves. But there was no way around it. Decades earlier the Congress had set up a system so that little companies could compete against the big guys. Sam had found that old government provision and used it.

Later, when I told Sam how things had gone, he whooped and danced on my desktop. Nothing made him happier than using the government's own red tape to his advantage.

"WAIT A MINUTE," Jade said, putting down the tall cool glass she had been holding for so long that its contents had melted down to ice water.

Johansen, who had hardly touched his own drink, eyed her quizzically.

"Was that old man Sam's contact in the Commerce Department, after all? Had he tipped Sam off about the small business set-aside?"

I THOUGHT THE same thing—Johansen answered—but the guy slipped out of the meeting room like a ghost disappearing into thin air. And when I asked Sam about it, back in Florida, he just got quiet and evasive. There was something going on, but I couldn't figure out what it was. Not until a lot later.

Anyway, about six weeks afterward we got the official notification that we had won one of the two contracts for what the government called "The Orbital Debris Removal Test and Evaluation Program, Phase I." The other contract went to Rockledge.

"We're in!" Sam yelped. "We did it!"

We partied all that weekend. Sam invited everybody from the swimwear shop downstairs, for starters, and pretty soon it seemed like the whole shopping mall was jammed into our little office. Sometime during the weekend our two geniuses from Texas A&M showed up and joined the fun.

The hangover was monumental, but the party was worth it. Then the work began.

I saw trouble right away. The kids from Texas were really brilliant about superconductors and magnetic bumpers, but they were emotionally about on the level of junior high school.

The girl—uh, woman—her name was Melinda Cardenas. It was obvious that she had the hots for Sam. She followed him with those big brown eyes of hers wherever Sam went. She was kind of cute although pretty badly overweight. Could have been a real beauty, I guess, if she could stay away from sweets and junk food. But that's just about all she ate. And every time I looked at her, she was eating.

Her boyfriend—Larry Karsh—ate as much junk food as she did, but never put on an ounce. Some people have metabolisms like that. He never exercised. He just sat all day long at the desktop computer he had brought with him, designing our magnetic bumper and munching on sweet rolls and greaseburgers from the fast-food joint a few doors down the mall from our office. He could lose weight just by breathing, while Melinda gained a pound and a half every time she inhaled.

It took me a while to figure out that Larry was plying Melinda with food so she'd stay too fat for anybody else to be interested in her. They were rooming together, but "like brother and sister," according to Melinda. One look at Larry's pasty unhappy face, sprinkled with acne, told me that the brother-and-sister thing was making him miserable.

"You gotta get her away from me," Sam told me, a little desperation in his voice, one evening down in the bar where we had originally formed VCI.

"Melinda?"

"Who else?"

"I thought you liked her," I said.

"She's just a kid." Sam would not meet my eyes. He concentrated instead on making wet rings on the tabletop with his beer bottle.

"Pretty well-developed kid."

"You gotta get her off me, Mutt." He was almost pleading. "If you don't, Larry's going to pack up and leave."

I finally got the picture. Sam had used his charm to get Melinda to join VCI because he had known that Larry would come wherever she went. But now Larry was getting resentful. If he broke up our design team VCI would be in deep yogurt.

"Just how much charm did you use on her?" I asked.

Sam raised his hands over his head. "I never touched her, so help me. Hell, I never even took her out to dinner without Larry coming with us."

"Did he have acne back in Texas?"

"Yeah. I think they're both virgins." Sam said it as if it were a crime.

I can see now, with twenty-twenty hindsight, that what I should have done was buddy up to Larry, give him a few pointers about personal grooming and manners. The kid was brilliant, sure, but his idea of evening wear was an unwashed T-shirt and a pair of cutoffs. And he was so damned shy that he hid behind his computer just about all the time. He never went anywhere and he never did anything except massage his computer. And eat junk food. He had that dead-fish complexion of a guy in solitary confinement. He was about as much fun as staring at a blank wall.

To tell the truth, I just couldn't see myself buddying up to the kid. So, instead, I made the mistake of trying to get Melinda interested in me, rather than Sam. I invited her out to dinner. That's all it took. I didn't even hold her hand, but the next morning there was a love poem on my desk, signed with a flowery M. And Larry didn't show up in the office.

"Where is he?" Sam snapped the minute he entered the office—around ten-thirty. He headed straight for his desk, which I called "Mount Blanc" because of the mountain of paperwork heaped on top of it. Sam paid practically no attention to any incoming paper. The mountain just grew bigger. How he ever found anything in that pile I never knew, but whenever I couldn't find some form or some piece of important correspondence, Sam would rummage through the mountain and pull out the right piece of paper in half a minute.

Neither Melinda nor I answered Sam's question. I didn't know where the kid was. Melinda was watching me shyly from behind her computer. Then I realized that Larry's desk was bare. He had taken his computer.

"Where the hell is he?" Sam screeched.

It took me about ten seconds to figure out what had happened. Ten seconds, plus reading Melinda's poem. It was pretty awful. Can you imagine a poem that rhymes dinner, winner, and thinner?

"Where the hell is Larry?" Sam asked her directly.

She shrugged from behind her computer screen. "He's very immature," she said, batting her eyelashes at me. Good lord, I realized that she was wearing makeup. Lots of it.

"Of all the gin-joints in all the towns in all the world," Sam growled, scurrying from behind his desk and heading for the door. "Come on, Mutt! I've got to meet Bonnie Jo at the airport and you've got to find that kid before he runs back to Texas!"

"Bonnie Jo?" I called after him. I flicked my phone console to automatic answer and then dashed out after him. Melinda sat where she had been since eight that morning; her only exercise was reaching for a bag of nacho chips.

Bonnie Jo Murtchison was the daughter of our financial backer, the banker who wanted his daughter married.

"She's coming in on the eleven o'clock plane," Sam said over his shoulder as we rattled down the stairs and ran out to his leased Jaguar convertible. I never saw it with the top up, yet somehow it was always under shelter when Florida decided to have a cloudburst. Sam was uncanny that way.

"You'll never make it to the airport by eleven," I said, vaulting over the Jag's door.

Sam gave me a sour look as he slid behind the wheel. "And when's the last time *any* goddamned commercial airliner arrived on schedule?"

He had a point there.

The apartment that Larry and Melinda shared was on the way to the airport. Sam's intention was to drop me off, assuming Larry was still there, and hustle on to the airport.

We spotted him on the driveway of the old frame three-storey house, packing all his belongings into their battered old Volvo station wagon. As far as I could see, Larry's belongings consisted of one duffel bag of clothes and seventeen cartons of computer hardware and documentation books.

He was just getting into the car when we pulled up and blocked the driveway, just like the Highway Patrol.

"Where're you going?" Sam yelped as he bounded out of the Jag. I followed behind, my boots crunching on the driveway's gravel.

The three of us looked like a set of Russian dolls, the kind that fit one inside of the other. Sam stood about shoulder-high to Larry, who stood little more than shoulder-high to me.

"Back to Texas," he said, his voice kind of cracking. "You want Melinda, she's all yours."

"I don't want her!" Sam said. "I want her to stop pestering me, for cryin' out loud."

Larry put down the cardboard carton he was carrying on the tailgate of the Volvo and drew himself up to his full height.

"She's not interested in you anymore, Mr. Gunn. She's gone batty over this guy." He jutted his lower lip at me.

For a ridiculous instant I felt like a gunslinger in a Western, about to be challenged by a callow youth.

"Listen, son," I said as reasonably as I could, "I was just trying to get her mind off Sam."

He kind of sagged, as if he'd been holding himself together for so long that his strength had given out. I thought he might drop to the ground and start crying.

But he didn't. "Sam, you—what's the difference? She doesn't like me anymore. I guess she never really liked me in the first place."

I looked at Sam and he looked at me. Then he got a sort of strange, benign smile on his face, an almost saintly kind of expression I had never seen on Sam before.

He went over to Larry and slid an arm around the kid's skinny shoulders, as much to prop him up as anything else. "Larry," he asked in a quiet, kindly sort of voice, "have you ever heard of a fella named Cyrano de Bergerac?"

"Who?"

"CYRANO?" JADE LOOKED sharply into Johansen's sparkling blue eyes.

"You know the play?" he asked.

"I played Roxane in our high school drama class," she said.

"Oh." Johansen looked slightly uncomfortable. "I think I saw it on video once. Had a lot of sword fighting in it."

She sighed and nodded. "Yes, a lot of sword fighting. And Cyrano coached Christian so that he could win Roxane's heart—even though he loved her himself."

Johansen nodded back at her. "Yep. That's just what Sam did. Or at least, that's what he got me to do."

IT WAS SHEER desperation—Johansen continued. Without Larry we'd never be able to build our hardware on the schedule we had promised in our proposal. Or maybe not at all.

"Don't worry about a thing," Sam told the kid, right there in the driveway. "Mutt and I know everything there is to know about women. With us helping you, she'll fall into your arms in no time flat."

The kid's face reddened. "I get kind of tongue-tied when I t-try to t-talk sw-sw-sweet to her."

Sam stared at the kid. A stuttering lover? It didn't look good.

Then I got the idea of the century. "Why don't you talk to her through your computers?"

Larry got really excited about that. Computers were something he understood and trusted. As long as he didn't have to actually speak to her face-to-face he could say anything we gave him.

"Okay," Sam said, glancing at his wristwatch. "Mutt, you take our lovesick friend here to the library and borrow as many poetry books as they'll let you take out. I gotta get to the airport and meet Bonnie Jo."

Melinda looked surprised when we came back into the office; those big brown eyes of hers flashed wide. But then she stuck her nose into her computer screen and began pecking at the keyboard as fast as her chubby little fingers would go.

It was getting near to noon. I went to my desk and ran off the phone's answering machine. There was only one call, from Sam. Bonnie Jo's plane from Salt Lake City was running late. Delays and congestion in Dallas.

So what else is new? I sat Larry down at his desk and helped him unfold his computer and set it up again. Melinda glanced at us from time to time, but whenever she saw me looking she quickly snapped her eyes back to her own screen.

Larry hadn't said a word to her. While he checked out his machine I thumbed madly through one of the poetry books. God almighty, I hadn't even looked at that stuff since they made me read it in high school English classes. I ran across one that I vaguely remembered.

Without speaking, I showed the page to Larry, then left the book on his desk and went over to my own, next to the window. As nonchalantly as I could I booted up my own machine, waiting to see if the kid actually worked up the nerve to send the poem to Melinda, sitting four and a half feet away from him.

Sure enough, the words began to scroll across the screen: "Come live with me and be my Love . . ."

I don't know what Melinda was working on, but I guess when she saw the message light blink on her machine she automatically set the screen to receive it.

Her eyes went *really* wide. Her mouth dropped open as she read the lines of poetry scrolling onto her screen. To make sure she didn't think they were coming from me, I picked up the telephone and tapped the first button on my automatic dialer. Some guy's bored voice told me that the day's high would be eighty-two, with a seventy-five percent chance of showers in the afternoon.

Melinda looked at me kind of puzzled. I ignored her and looked out my window, where I could watch her reflection without her knowing it. I saw a suspicion on her face slowly dawn into certainty. She turned and looked at Larry, who promptly turned flame-red.

A good beginning, I thought.

Then Sam burst into the office, towing Bonnie Jo Murtchison.

When it came to women Sam was truly democratic. Tall or short, plump or anorexic, Sam made no distinctions based on race, creed, color, or previous condition of servitude. But he did seem to hit on blondes preferentially.

Bonnie Jo Murtchison was blonde, the kind of golden blonde with almost reddish highlights that is one of the triumphs of modern cosmetic chemistry. Her hair was frizzed, shoulder length, but pushed back off her face enough to show two enormous bangle earrings. She had a slight figure, almost boyish. Good legs, long and strong and nicely tanned. A good tennis player, I thought. That was the first thing that popped into my mind when I saw her.

She was wearing a neat little miniskirted sleeveless frock of butter yellow, the kind that costs a week's pay. More jewelry on her wrists and fingers, necklaces dangling down her slim bosom. She clattered and jangled as she came into the office, towering over Sam by a good five-six inches.

The perfect spoiled princess, I thought at once. Rich father, beautiful mother, and no brothers or sisters. What a pain in the butt she's going to be.

I was right, but for all the wrong reasons.

The first thing that really jolted me about Bonnie Jo was her voice. I expected the kind of shrill yapping that you hear from the cuties around the condo swimming pool; you know, the ones who won't go into the water because it'd mess up the hairdo they just spent all morning on.

Bonnie Jo's voice was low and ladylike. Not quite husky, and certainly not soft. Controlled. Strong. She didn't hurt your ears when she talked.

Sam introduced her to Larry, who mumbled and avoided her eyes, and to Melinda, who looked her over like a professional prizefighter assessing a new opponent. Then he brought her across the room to my desk.

"This is our president, Spence Johansen," Sam said. "I call him Mutt."

She reached across the desk to take my hand in a firm grip. Her eyes were gray-green, a color that haunted me so much I looked it up in a book on precious stones at the local library. The color of Brazilian tourmaline: deep, mysterious, powerful grayish green.

"And what would you like me to call you, Mr. Johansen?" she asked in that marvelous voice.

She just sort of naturally drew a smile out of me. "Spence will be fine," I said.

"Good. I'm Bonnie Jo."

I think I fell in love with her right then and there.

"THAT WAS PRETTY quick," Jade sniffed.

Johansen shrugged. "It happens that way, sometimes."

"Really?"

"Haven't you ever fallen in love at first sight?"

She tried to conjure up Raki's image in her mind. The drinks she had been swilling made her head spin slightly.

"Yes, I guess I have, at that," she said at last. That smile of his made her head swim even more.

Johansen looked out across the grassy hills that stretched below them to the edge of the toylike village. Sunlight filtering through the big solar windows slanted long shadows down there.

"It's going to be sunset pretty soon," he said. "I know a fine little restaurant down in Gunnstown, if you're ready for dinner."

"Gunnstown?" she asked.

"That's the name of the village down there." He pointed with an outstretched arm.

"Should I change?"

Grinning, "I like you the way you are."

"My clothes," she said.

He cocked his head slightly. "It's a very nice little continental restaurant. Tablecloths and candles, that sort of thing."

She said, "Meet me at my hotel room in an hour."

When he called for her, precisely one hour later, Johansen was wearing a comfortable pair of soft blue slacks and a slate-gray velour pullover, the closest thing to formal attire on the space habitat. Jade had shopped furiously in Gunnstown's only two boutiques until she found a miniskirted sleeveless frock of butter-yellow.

Once they were sitting across a tiny table, with a softly glowing candle between them, she saw that Johansen was staring at her intently.

Almost uncomfortable, Jade tried to return to the subject of Sam Gunn.

But Johansen said, "Your eyes are beautiful, you know? The prettiest I've ever seen."

Silently Jade retorted, Prettier than Bonnie Jo's? But she dared not say it aloud. Instead, she said:

"Just before you suggested dinner, you were telling me about Bonnie Jo." Jade struggled to keep her voice even. "About falling in love with her."

IT WASN'T A tough thing to do—Johansen replied. I had expected a spoiled rich kid. Her father, the banker, had insisted on having one of his own people join the VCI team as treasurer. Apparently his daughter insisted just as stubbornly that she take the job. So there she was, at the desk we shoehorned into our one little office, two feet away from mine.

She had degrees in economics and finance from BYU, plus an MBA from Wharton. She really knew her business. And she was strictly no-nonsense. Sam wined and dined her, of course, but it didn't go any further than that, far as I could tell. I knew Sam had no real intention of getting married to anybody. I didn't think she did, either. Or if she did, she was willing to wait until VCI started making big bucks.

We were all living practically hand-to-mouth, with every cent we got from the government and from Bonnie Jo's father's bank poured into building the hardware for removing debris from orbit. Bonnie Jo was never hurting for spending money, of course, but she never lorded it over us. The weeks rolled by and we sort of became a real team: you know, working together every day, almost living together, you come to know and respect each other. Or you explode.

Bonnie Jo even started helping Melinda in her personal life. Gave her hints about her clothes. Even went on a diet with her; not that Bonnie Jo needed it, but Melinda actually started to slim down a little. They started going to exercise classes down the way in the shopping mall.

I was giving myself a cram course in romantic poetry and passing it all on to Larry. On Valentine's Day he wanted to give Melinda a big heart-shaped box of chocolates. I suggested flowers instead. I figured she wouldn't eat flowers, although I wasn't altogether certain.

"And write a note on the card they put in with the flowers," I insisted.

He gulped. "Sh-should I s-s-s-sign my n-n-name?"

"Damned right."

Larry turned pale. But I marched him to the florist section of the supermarket and we picked out a dozen posies for her. I towed him to the counter where they had a little box full of blank cards. I handed him my government-issue ballpoint pen, guaranteed to write under water or in zero gravity.

He looked at me, panic-stricken. "Wh-what'll I say?"

I thought for a second. " 'To the woman who has captured my heart,' " I told him.

He scribbled on the little card. His handwriting was awful.

"Sign it."

He stared at me.

"Better yet," I said. "Just put your initial. Just an 'L.' "

He did that. We snuck the bouquet into the office while Melinda and Bonnie Jo were out at their exercise class. Larry laid the flowers on her desk with a trembling hand.

Well, the last time I had watched a scene like what followed was in an old video called "Love Is a Many-Splendored Thing." Melinda sort of went into shock when she saw the flowers on her desk, but only for a moment. She read the card, then spun around toward Larry—who looked white as a sheet, scared—and launched herself at him. Knocked him right off his desk chair.

Sam gave them the rest of the day off. It was Friday, so they had the whole weekend to themselves.

A few minutes after the lovers left the office, Sam frowned at his computer screen.

"I gotta check out the superconducting coils down at the Cape," he said. "Those suckers in Massachusetts finally delivered them. Arrived this morning."

Two weeks late. Not good, but within the tolerable limits we had set in our schedule. The manufacturer in Massachusetts had called a couple months earlier and said that delivery would be three months late, due to a big order they had to rush for Rockledge International.

Sam had screamed so loud and long into the phone that I thought every fiber-optic cable between Florida and Massachusetts would have melted. The connection actually broke down three times before he finished convincing our manufacturing subcontractor that: (a) their contract with us had heavy penalty clauses for late delivery; (b) since this order from Rockledge had come in *after* our order we clearly had priority; and (c) this was obviously an attempt by Rockledge to sabotage us.

"Tell your goddamned lawyers to stock up on NoDoz," Sam yelled into the phone. "I'm going to sue you sneaking, thieving bastards sixteen ways from Sunday! You'll go down the tubes, buddy. Bankrupt. Broke. Dead in the water. Kaput! You just watch!"

He slammed the phone down hard enough to make the papers on my desk bounce.

"But Sam," I had pleaded, "if you tie them up or shut them down *we'll* go out of business with them. We need that superconducting coil. And the backup."

A sly grin eased across his face. "Don'tcha think I know that? I'm just putting the fear of lawyers into them. Now," he reached for the phone again, "to put the fear of God almighty into them."

I didn't eavesdrop on purpose, but our desks were jammed so close together that I couldn't help hearing him ask for Albert Clement. At the Department of Commerce.

Sam's tone changed enormously. He was stiffly formal with Clement, almost respectful, explaining the situation and his suspicion that Rockledge was trying to club us to death with their money. I wondered if this guy Clement was the same Commerce Department undertaker who had been at the evaluation hearing in D.C.

Well, it all got straightened out. The next day I got a very apologetic phone call from the director of contracts at the Massachusetts firm, some guy with an Armenian name. Terrible misunderstanding. Of course they wouldn't let this enormous order from Rockledge get in the way of delivering what they had promised to us. On schedule, absolutely. Maybe a week or so late, nothing more than that. Guaranteed. On his mother's grave.

I said nice things back to him, like, "Uh-huh. That's fine. I'm glad to hear it." Sam was watching me, grinning from ear to ear.

The guy's voice dropped a note lower, as if he was afraid he'd be overheard. "It's so much pleasanter dealing with you than that Mr. Gunn," he said. "He's so excitable!"

"Well, I'm the president of the firm," I said back to him, while Sam held both hands over his mouth to stifle his guffaws. "Whenever a problem arises, feel free to call me."

He thanked me three dozen times.

I no sooner had put the phone down than it rang again. Pierre D'Argent, calling from Rockledge headquarters in Pennsylvania.

In a smarmy, oily voice he professed shock and surprise that *anyone* would think that Rockledge was trying to sabotage a smaller competitor. I motioned for Sam to pick up his phone and listen in.

"We would never stoop to anything like that," he assured me. "There's no need for anyone to get hysterical."

"Well," I said, "it seemed strange to us that Rockledge placed such a large order with the outfit that's making our teeny little coils, and then tried to muscle them into shunting our work aside."

"We never did that," D'Argent replied, like a saint accused of rifling the poor-box. "It's all a misunderstanding."

Sam said sweetly into his phone, "We've subpoenaed their records, oh silver-tongued devil."

"What? Who is that? Gunn, is that you?"

"See you in Leavenworth, Pee-air."

D'Argent hung up so hard I thought a gun had gone off in my ear. Sam fell off his chair laughing and rolled on the floor, holding his middle and kicking his feet in the air. We had not subpoenaed anybody for anything, but it cost Rockledge a week's worth of extremely expensive legal staff work to find that out.

Anyway, that had happened months earlier, and now the superconducting coils had finally arrived at the Cape and Sam had to buzz over there to inspect them. Leaving Bonnie Jo and me alone in the office. Friday afternoon. The weekend looming.

I did my level best to avoid her. She was staying at the Marriott hotel in Titusville, so I steered clear of the whole town. Kept to myself in my little rattrap of a one-room apartment. Worked on my laptop all day Saturday, ate a microwaved dinner, watched TV. Then worked some more. Did not phone her, although I thought about it now and then. Maybe once every other minute.

Sunday it rained hard. I started to feel like a convict in prison. By noontime I had convinced myself that there was work to do in the office; anything to get out of my room. It was pouring so thick I got soaked running from my parking space to the covered stairs that led up to our office. First thing I did there was phone Sam's hotel down at the Cape. Checked out. Then I phoned his apartment. Not there.

I slid into my desk chair, squishing wet. Okay. He's back from the Cape. He's with Bonnie Jo. Good. I guess.

But I guessed wrong, because Bonnie Jo came into the office, brighter than sunshine in a bright yellow slicker and plastic rain hat.

"Oh," she said. "I didn't know you'd be here."

"Where's Sam?" I asked her.

She peeled off the hat and slicker. "I thought he'd be here. Probably he stayed at the Cape for the weekend."

"Yeah. He's got a lot of old buddies at the Cape."

"And girlfriends?"

"Uh, no. Not really." I was never much good at shading the truth.

Bonnie Jo sat at her desk and picked up the phone. "Highway Patrol," she said to the dialing assistance computer program.

She saw my eyebrows hike up.

"On a stormy day like this, maybe he drove off the road."

The Highway Patrol had no accidents to report between where we were and the Cape. I puffed out a little sigh of relief. Bonnie Jo put the phone down with a bit of a dark frown on her pretty face.

"You worry about Sam that much?" I asked her.

"My job is to protect my daddy's investment," she said. "And my own."

Well, one thing led to another and before I knew it we were having dinner together in the Japanese restaurant down at the end of the mall. I had to teach Bonnie Jo how to use chopsticks. She caught on real fast. Quick learner.

"Are you two engaged, or what?" I heard myself ask her.

She smiled, kind of sad, almost. "It depends on who you ask. My father considers us engaged, although Sam has never actually popped the question to me."

"And what do you think?"

Her eyes went distant. "Sam is going to be a very rich man someday. He has the energy and drive and willingness to swim against the tide, and that will make him a multimillionaire eventually. If somebody doesn't strangle him first."

"So that makes him a good marriage prospect."

Her unhappy little smile came back. "Sam will make a terrible husband. He's a womanizer who doesn't give a thought to anybody but himself. He's lots of fun to be with, but he'd be hell to be married to."

"Then why . . . ?"

"I already told you. To protect my daddy's investment."

"You'd *marry* him? For that?"

"Why not? He'll have his flings, I'll have mine. As long as I can present my daddy with a grandson, everyone will be satisfied."

"But . . . love. What about love?"

Her smile turned bitter. "You mean like Melinda and Larry? That's for the peasants. In my family marriage is a business proposition."

I dropped the chunk of sushi in my chopsticks right into my lap.

Bonnie Jo leaned across the little table. "You're really a very romantic guy, aren't you, Spence? Have I shocked you?"

"Uh, no, not . . . well, I guess I never met a woman with your outlook on life."

"Never dated an MBA before?" Her eyes sparkled with amusement now. She was teasing me.

"Can't say that I have."

She leaned closer. "Sam's out at the Cape chasing cocktail waitresses and barmaids. Maybe I ought to go to a bar and see what I can pick up."

"Maybe you ought to go home before you pick up something that'll increase your father's health insurance premiums," I said, suddenly feeling sore at her.

She gave me a long look. "Maybe I should, at that."

And that was our dinner together. I never touched her. I never told Sam about it. But the next morning when he showed up at the office looking like every blue Monday morning in the history of the world—bleary-eyed, pasty-faced, muttering about vitamin E—I knew I couldn't hang around there with Bonnie Jo so close.

Melinda and Larry arrived hand in hand. I swear his stuttering had cleared up almost entirely in just that one weekend. Bonnie Jo came in around ten, took a silent look at Sam, and went to her desk as cool as liquid nitrogen. Sam was inhaling coffee and orange juice in roughly equal quantities.

"Sam," I said, my voice so loud that it startled me, "since I'm president of this outfit, I've just made an executive decision."

He looked over toward me with bloodshot eyes.

"I'm going over to the Cape," I announced.

"I was just there," he croaked.

"I mean to stay. Hardware's starting to arrive. We need somebody to direct the assembly technicians, somebody there on the scene all the time, not just once a week. Somebody with the power to make decisions."

"The techs know what they're doing better than you do, Mutt," argued Sam. "If they run into any problems they've got phones, e-mail, faxes—they can even use the agency's video link if they have to."

"It'll be better if I'm on the scene," I insisted, trying not to look at Bonnie Jo. "We can settle questions before they become problems."

Sam shook his head stubbornly. "We haven't budgeted for you to be living in a hotel at the Cape. You know how tight everything is."

"The budget can be stretched," Bonnie Jo said. "I think Spence is right. His being on the Cape could save us a lot of problems."

Sam's head swiveled from her to me and back to her again. He looked puzzled, not suspicious. Finally he shrugged good-naturedly and said, "Okay, as long as it won't bust the bank."

So I moved to the Cape. During the weeks I was there supervising the assembly and checkout of our equipment I actually did save a couple of minor glitches from growing into real headaches. Larry drove over once a week to check the hardware against his design; then he'd drive back to Melinda again that evening. I knew I could justify the expenses legitimately, if to came to that. Most important, though, was that I had put some miles between myself and Bonnie Jo. And she must have realized how attracted I was to her, because she convinced Sam I should get away.

A couple of my old agency buddies snuck me some time on the OMV simulator, so I spent my evenings and spare weekends brushing up on my flying. Our official program didn't call for any use of orbital maneuvering vehicles. What we had proposed was to set up our magnetic bumper on the forward end of space station Freedom and see how well it deflected junk out of the station's orbital path. Called for some EVA work, but we wouldn't need to fly OMVs.

But Sam had warned me to be prepared for flying an OMV, back when we first started writing the proposal.

"Whattaya think we oughtta do," he had asked me, "if we scoop up something valuable?"

"Valuable?" I had asked.

"Like that glove Ed White lost. Or the famous Hasselblad camera from back in the Gemini days."

I stared at him. "Sam, those things reentered and burned up years ago."

"Yeah, yeah, I know." He flapped an annoyed hand in the air. "But suppose—just suppose, now—that we scoop up something like that."

We had been sitting in our favorite booth in our favorite bar. Sam liked Corona in those days; slices of lime were littered across his side of the table, with little plastic spears stuck in their sides. They looked like tiny green harpooned whales. Me, I liked beer with more flavor to it: Bass Ale was my favorite.

Anyway, I thought his question was silly.

"In the first place," I said, "the magnetic field won't scoop up objects; it'll deflect them away from the path of the station. Most of them will be bounced into orbits that'll spiral into the atmosphere. They'll reenter and burn up."

"But suppose we got to something really *valuable*," Sam insisted. "Like a spacer section from the Brazilian booster. Or a piece of that European upper stage that blew up. Analysts would pay good money to get their hands on junk like that."

"Analysts?"

"In Washington," Sam said. "Or Paris, for that matter. Hell, even our buddy D'Argent would like to be able to present his Rockledge lab boys with chunks of the competition's hardware."

I had never thought of that.

"Then there's the museums," Sam went on, kind of dreamy, the way he always gets when he's thinking big. "How much would the Smithsonian pay for the *Eagle*?"

"The Apollo 11 lunar module?"

"Its lower section is still up there, sitting on the Sea of Tranquility."

"But that's the Moon, Sam. A quarter-million miles away from where we'll be!"

He gave me his sly grin. "Brush up on your flying, Mutt. There are interesting times ahead. Ve-r-r-y interesting."

I could see taking an OMV from the space station and flitting out to retrieve some hunk of debris that looked important or maybe valuable. So I spent as many of my hours at the Cape as possible in the OMV simulator. It helped to keep me busy; helped me to not think about Bonnie Jo.

At first I thought it was an accident when I bumped into Pierre D'Argent in the Shuttle Lounge. It was mid-afternoon, too soon for the after-work crowd. The lounge was cool and so dark that you could break your neck tripping over cocktail tables before your eyes adjusted from the summer glare outside.

I actually did bump into D'Argent. He was sitting with his back to the aisle between tables, wearing an expensive dark suit that blended into the shadows so well I just didn't see him.

I started to apologize, then my eyes finally adjusted to the dimness and I saw who he was.

"Mr. Johansen!" He professed surprise and asked me to join him.

So I sat at his little table. With my back to the wall. Just the two of us, although there were a few regulars up at the bar watching a baseball game from Japan.

I ordered a Bass. D'Argent already had a tall frosted glass of something in front of him, decorated with enough fruit slices to start a plantation. And a little paper umbrella.

"Your friend Gunn sent our legal department into quite a spin," he said, smiling with his teeth.

"Sam's a very emotional guy," I said as the waitress brought my ale. She was a cute little thing, in a low-cut black outfit with a teeny-tiny skirt.

"Yes, he is indeed." D'Argent let out a sigh. "I'm afraid Mr. Gunn has no clear idea of where his own best interests lie."

I took a sip of ale instead of trying to answer.

"Now you, Mr. Johansen," he went on, "you look like someone who understands where your best interests lie."

All I could think of to say was, "Really?"

"Really." D'Argent leaned back in his chair, looking like a cool million on the hoof: elegant from his slicked-back salt-and-pepper hair to the tips of his Gucci suede loafers.

"I must confess that I thought your technical proposal was little short of daring. Much better than the job my own technical people did. They were far too conservative. Far too."

Was he pumping me for information? I mumbled something noncommittal and let him go on talking.

"In fact," he said, smiling at me over his fruit salad, "I think your technical approach is brilliant. Breathtaking."

The smile was very slick. He was insurance-salesman handsome. Trim gray mustache neatly clipped; expensive silk suit, dark gray. I couldn't tell the color of his eyes, the lighting in the lounge was too dim, but I expect they were gray too.

I shrugged off his compliment. But he persisted. "A magnetic deflector system actually mounted on the space station. Very daring. Very original."

"It was Sam's idea," I said, trying to needle him.

It didn't faze him a bit. "It was actually the idea of Professor Luke Steckler, of Texas A&M. Our people saw his paper in the technical literature, but they didn't have the guts to use the idea. You did."

"Sam did."

He hiked his eyebrows a bit. They were gray, too. "You're much too modest, Spence. You don't mind if I call you Spence, do you?"

I did mind. I suddenly felt like I was in the grip of a very slick used-car salesman. But I shook my head and hid behind my mug of ale.

D'Argent said, "Spence, I know that my technical people at Rockledge would love to have you join their team. They need some daring, someone willing to take chances."

I guess my eyebrows went up, too.

Leaning forward over the tiny table, D'Argent added in a whisper, "And we'll pay you twice what Gunn is paying."

I blinked. Twice.

The lounge was slowly filling up with "happy hour" customers: mostly engineers from the base and sales people trying to sell them stuff. They all talked low, almost in whispers. At least, until they got a couple of drinks into them. Then the noise volume went up and some of the wilder ones even would laugh now and then. But while I was sitting there trying to digest D'Argent's offer without spitting beer in his face, I could still hear the soft-rock music coming through the ceiling speakers, something old and sad by the Carpenters.

"I would like you to talk with a few of my technical people, Spence. Would you be willing to do that?"

Twice my VCI salary. And that was just for openers. It was obvious he'd be willing to go higher. Maybe a lot higher. I'd been living on Happy Hour hors d'oeuvres and junk food. I was four months behind on the rent for my seedy dump of an apartment—which was sitting empty, because of Bonnie Jo.

But I shook my head. "I'm happy with VCI." *Happy* wasn't exactly the right word, but I couldn't leave Sam in the lurch. On the other hand, this might be the best way to make a break with Bonnie Jo.

Turning slightly in his chair, D'Argent sort of nodded toward a trio of guys in suits sitting a few tables away from us.

"I've taken the liberty of asking a few of my technical people to come here to meet you. Would you be willing to talk with them, Spence? Just for a few minutes."

Son of a bitch! It was no accident that we bumped into each other. It was a planned ambush.

"I think, with your help, we can adapt the magnetic bumper concept easily enough," he was saying, silky-smooth. "We'd even pay you a sizable bonus for joining Rockledge: say, a year's salary."

They wanted to steal Sam's idea and squeeze him out of the picture. And they thought I'd help them do it. For money.

I got to my feet. "Mr. D'Argent, Rockledge doesn't have enough money in its whole damned corporate treasury to buy me away from VCI."

D'Argent shrugged, very European-like, and made a disappointed sigh. "Very well, although your future would be much more secure with Rockledge than with a con-man such as Mr. Gunn."

Through gritted teeth I said, "I'll take my chances with Sam." And I stalked out of the lounge, leaving him sitting there.

"THAT WAS A pretty noble thing to do," Jade said.

They were more than halfway through their dinners. She had ordered trout from the habitat's aquaculture tanks. Johansen was eating braised rabbit. Jade had to remind herself that rabbit was bred for meat here in the space habitat, just as it was on Selene. But she had never eaten rabbit at home and she could not bring herself to order it here.

"Nothing noble about it," he said easily. "It made me feel kind of slimy just to be sitting at the same table with D'Argent. Working with the . . . gentleman, well, I just couldn't do it."

"Even though you were trying to get away from Bonnie Jo."

He shook his head slightly, as if disappointed with himself. "That was the really tough part. I wanted to get away from her and I wanted to be with her, both at the same time."

"So what did you do?"

He grinned. "I got away. I went up to space station Freedom."

SAM HAD SERVED aboard Freedom when he'd been in the agency—Johansen explained. He was definitely persona non grata there, as far as the bureaucrats in Washington and the Cape were concerned, even though all the working stiffs—the astronauts and mission specialists—they all asked me how he was and when he would be coming up. Especially a couple of the women astronauts.

Living aboard Freedom was sort of like living in a bad hotel, without gravity. The quarters were cramped, there was precious little privacy, the hot water was only lukewarm, and the food was as bland as only a government agency can make it. I spent ten-twelve hours a day inside a space suit, strapped into an MMU—a manned maneuvering unit—assembling our equipment on a special boom outside the station.

The agency insisted that the magnetic field could not be turned on until every experiment being run inside the lab module was completed. Despite all our calculations and simulations (including a week's worth of dry run on the station mock-up in Huntsville) the agency brass was worried that our magnetic field might screw up some delicate experiment the scientists were doing. It occurred to me that they didn't seem worried about screwing up the station's own instrumentation or life-support systems. That would just have threatened the lives of astronauts and mission specialists, not important people like university scientists sitting safe on their campuses.

Anyway, after eleven days of living in that zero-gee tin can I got the go-ahead from mission control to turn on the magnetic field. Maybe the fact that one of the big solar panels got dinged with a stray chunk of junk hurried their decision. The panel damage cut the station's electrical power by a couple of kilowatts.

Rockledge had already launched two of their Nerf balls, one on a shuttle mission and the other from one of their own little commercial boosters. They were put into orbits opposite in direction to the flow of all the junk floating around, sort of like setting them to swim upstream.

Right away they started having troubles. The first Nerf ball expanded only partway. Instead of knocking debris out of orbit it became a piece of junk itself, useless and beyond anybody's control. The second one performed okay, although the instrumentation aboard it showed that it was getting sliced up by some of the bigger pieces of junk. Rather than being nudged out of orbit when they hit the sticky balloon, they just rammed right through it and came out the other end. Maybe they got slowed enough to start spiraling in toward reentry. But it wouldn't take more than a couple of weeks before the Nerf ball was ripped to shreds—and became still yet another piece of orbiting junk.

"They're part of the problem," I said to Sam over the station's videophone link, "instead of being part of the solution."

Sam's round face grinned like a Jack-o'-lantern. "So that's why D'Argent's looking like a stockbroker on Black Tuesday."

"He's got a lot to be worried about," I said.

Sam cackled happily. Then, lowering his voice, he said, "A friend of mine at the tracking center says the old original Vanguard satellite is going to reenter in a couple weeks."

"The one they launched in '58?"

"Yep. It's only a couple of pounds. They called it the Grapefruit back then."

I looked over my shoulder at Freedom's crew members working at their stations. I was in the command module, standing in front of the videophone screen with my stockinged feet anchored in floor loops to keep me from floating around the place weightlessly. The crew—two men and a woman—were paying attention to their jobs, not to me. But still . . .

"Sam," I said in a near-whisper, "you want me to try to retrieve it?"

"Do you have any idea of what the Smithsonian will pay for it?" he whispered back. "Or the *Japanese*?"

I felt like a fighter pilot being asked to take on a risky mission. "Shoot me the orbital data. I'll see what I can do."

It took a lot of good-natured wheedling and sweet-talking before Freedom's commander allowed me to use one of the station's OMVs. There was a provision for it in our contract, of course, but the station commander had the right to make the decision as to whether VCI might actually use one of the little flitters. She was a strong-willed professional astronaut; I'd known her for years and we'd even dated now and then. She made me promise her the Moon, just about. But at last she agreed.

The orbital maneuvering vehicles were sort of in-between the MMUs that you could strap onto your back and the orbital transfer vehicles that were big enough for a couple of guys to go all the way to GEO. The OMVs were stripped-down little platforms with an unpressurized cockpit, a pair of extensible arms with grippers on their ends, and a rocket motor hanging out the rear end.

I snatched the old Vanguard grapefruit without much trouble, saving it from a fiery death after it had spent more than half a century in space. It was just about the size and shape of a grapefruit, with a metal skin that had been blackened by years of exposure to high-energy radiation. Its solar cells had gone dead decades ago.

Anyway, Sam was so jubilant that he arranged to come up to Freedom in person to take the satellite back to Earth. Under his instructions I had not brought the grapefruit inside the station; instead I stored it in one of the racks built into the station's exterior framework. Sam was bringing up a special sealed vacuum container to bring the satellite back to the ground without letting it get contaminated by air.

Sam was coming up on one of the regular shuttle resupply flights. Since there wasn't any room for more personnel aboard the station he would only stay long enough to take the Vanguard satellite and bring it back to Earth with him.

That was the plan, anyway.

Well, the news that a private company had recaptured the old satellite hit the media like a Washington scandal. Sam was suddenly hot news, proclaiming the right of salvage in space while all sorts of lawyers from government agencies and university campuses argued that the satellite by rights belonged to the government. The idea of *selling* it to the Smithsonian or some other museum seemed to outrage them.

I saw Sam on the evening TV news the night before he came up to the station. Instead of playing the little guy being picked on by the big bullies, Sam went on the attack:

"That grapefruit's been floating around up there as dead as a doornail since before I was born," he said to the blonde who was interviewing him. "My people located it, my people went out and grabbed it. Not the government. Not some college professor who never even heard of the Vanguard 1958b until last week. My people. VCI. Part of S. Gunn Enterprises, Unlimited."

The interviewer objected, "But you used government facilities . . ."

"We are *leasing* government facilities, lady. We pay for their use."

"But that satellite was paid for by the American taxpayer."

"It was nothing but useless junk. It went unclaimed for decades. The law of salvage says whoever gets it, owns it."

"But the law of salvage is from maritime law. No one has extended the law of salvage into space."

"They have now!" Sam grinned wickedly into the camera.

It didn't help, of course, when some Japanese billionaire offered thirty million yen for the satellite.

Next thing you know, the shuttle resupply flight has no less than five guests aboard. They had to bump an astronomer who was coming up to start a series of observations and a medical doctor who was scheduled to replace the medic who'd been serving aboard the station for ninety days.

Five guests: Sam; Ed Zane from the space agency; Albert Clement from the Department of Commerce; Pierre D'Argent of Rock-by-damn-ledge.

And Bonnie Jo Murtchison.

Sam was coming up to claim the satellite, of course. Zane and Clement were there at the request of the White House to investigate this matter of space salvage before Sam could peddle the satellite to anyone—especially the Japs. I wasn't quite sure what the hell D'Argent was doing there, but I knew he'd be up to no good. And Bonnie Jo?

"I'm here to protect my investment." She smiled when I asked her why she'd come.

"How did you get them to allow you . . . ?"

We were alone in the shuttle's mid-deck compartment, where she and Sam and the other visitors would be sleeping until the shuttle undocked from the station and returned to Earth—with the satellite, although who would have ownership of the little grapefruit remained to be seen.

Bonnie Jo was wearing a light blue agency-issue flight suit that hugged her curves so well it looked like it was tailor-made for her. She showed no signs of space adaptation syndrome, no hint that she was ill at ease in zero-gee. Looked to me as if she enjoyed being weightless.

"How did I talk them into letting me come up here with Sam? Simple. I am now VCI's legal counsel."

She sure was beautiful. She had cropped her hair real short, almost a crew cut. Still she looked terrific. I heard myself ask her, as if from a great distance away, "You're a lawyer, too?"

"I have a law degree from the University of Utah. Didn't I tell you?" The whole situation seemed to amuse her.

When a government employee gets an order from the White House, even if it's from some third assistant to a janitor, he jumps as high as is necessary. In the case of Zane and Clement, they had been told to settle this matter about the Vanguard satellite, and they had jumped right up to space station Freedom. Clement looked mildly upset at being in zero gravity. I think what bothered him more than anything else was that he had to wear coveralls instead of his usual chalky gray three-piece suit. Darned if he didn't find a gray flight suit, though.

Zane was really sick. The minute the shuttle went into weightlessness, Sam gleefully told me, Zane had started upchucking. The station doctor took him in tow and stuck a wad of antinausea slow release medication pads on his neck. Still, it would take a day or more before he was well enough to convene the hearing he'd been sent to conduct.

Although the visitors were supposed to stay aboard the shuttle, Sam showed up in the station's command module and even wheedled permission to wriggle into a space suit and go EVA to inspect our hardware. It was working just the way we had designed it, deflecting the bits of junk and debris that floated close enough to the station to feel the influence of our magnetic bumper.

"I must confess that I didn't think it would work so well."

I turned from my console in the command module and saw Pierre D'Argent standing behind me. "Standing" is the wrong word, almost, because you don't really stand straight in zero-gee; your body bends into a sort of question-mark kind of semi-crouch, as if you were floating in very salty water. Unless you consciously force them down, your arms tend to drift up to chest height and hang there.

It made me uneasy to have D'Argent hanging (literally) around me. My console instruments showed that the bumper system was working within its nominal limits. I could patch the station's radar display onto my screen to see what was coming toward us, if anything. Otherwise there were only graphs to display and gauges to read. Our equipment was mounted outside and I didn't have a window. The magnetic field itself was invisible, of course.

"The debris actually gains an electrical charge while it orbits the Earth," he murmured, stroking his gray mustache as he spoke.

I said nothing.

"I wouldn't have thought the charge would be strong enough to be useful," he went on, almost as if he was talking to himself. "But then your magnetic field is very powerful, isn't it, so you can work with relatively low charge values."

I nodded.

"We're going to have to retrieve our Nerf balls," he said with a sad little sigh. "The corporation will have to pay the expense of sending a team up to physically retrieve them and bring them back to Earth for study. We won't be launching any more of them until we find out where we went wrong with these."

"The basic idea is wrong," I said. "You should have gone magnetic in the first place."

"Yes," D'Argent agreed. "Yes, I see that now."

When I told Sam about our little conversation he got agitated.

"That sneaky sonofabitch is gonna try to steal it out from under us!"

"He can't do that," I said.

"And rain makes applesauce."

It all came to a head two days later, when Zane finally got well enough to convene his meeting.

It took place in the shuttle's mid-deck compartment, the six of us crammed in among the zippered sleeping bags and rows of equipment trays. Bonnie Jo anchored herself next to the only window, the little round one set into the hatch. D'Argent managed to get beside her, which made me kind of sore. I plastered my back against the airlock hatch at the rear of the compartment; that gave me enough traction to keep from floating around.

Sam, being Sam, hovered up by the ceiling, one arm wrapped casually on a rung of the ladder that led up to the cockpit. Zane and Clement strapped themselves against the rows of equipment trays that made up the front wall of the compartment.

Zane still looked unwell, even more bloated in the face than usual, and queasy green. His coveralls showed off his pear-like shape. Clement seemed no different than he'd been in Washington; it was as if his surroundings made no impact on him at all. Even in a flight suit he was a thin, gray old man and nothing more.

Yet he avoided looking at Sam. And I noticed that Sam avoided looking at him. Like two conspirators who didn't want the rest of us to know that they were working secretly together.

"This is a preliminary hearing," Zane began, his voice a little shaky. "Its

purpose is to make recommendations, not decisions. I will report the results of this meeting directly to the Vice President, in his capacity as
chairman of the Space Council."

Vice President Benford had been a scientist before going into politics.
I doubted that he would look on Sam's free-enterprise salvage job with
enthusiasm.

"Before we begin . . ." There was D'Argent with his finger raised in the
air again.

"What's he doing here, anyway?" Sam snapped. "What's Rockledge got
to do with this hearing?"

Zane had to turn his head and look up to face Sam. The effort made
him pale slightly. I saw a bunch of faint rings against the skin of his neck,
back behind his ear, where medication patches had been. Looked like he'd
been embraced by a vampire octopus.

"Rockledge is one of the two contractors currently engaged in the orbital debris removal feasibility program," Zane said carefully, as if he was
trying hard not to throw up.

Sam frowned down at Zane, then at D'Argent.

Bonnie Jo said, "VCI has no objection to Rockledge's representation at
this hearing."

"We don't?" Sam snapped.

She smiled up at him. "No, we don't."

Sam muttered something that I couldn't really hear, but I could imagine what he was saying to himself.

D'Argent resumed, "I realize that this hearing has been called to exam-
ine the question of space salvage. I merely want to point out that there is a
larger question involved here, also."

"A larger question?" Zane dutifully gave his straight line.

"Yes. The question of who should operate the debris removal system
once the feasibility program is completed."

"Who should operate . . ." Sam turned burning red.

"After all," D'Argent went on smoothly, "the debris removal system
should be used for the benefit of its sponsor—the government of the
United States. It should *not* be used as a front for shady fly-by-night
schemes to enrich private individuals."

Sam gave a strangled cry and launched himself at D'Argent like a
guided missile. I unhooked my feet from the floor loops just in time to get
a shoulder into Sam's ribs and bounce him away from D'Argent. Otherwise
I think he would have torn the guy limb from limb right then and there.

Bonnie Jo yelled, "Sam, don't!" Clement seemed to faint. My shoulder felt as if something had broken in there.

And Zane threw up over all of us.

That broke up the meeting pretty effectively.

It took Bonnie Jo and me several hours to calm Sam down. He was absolutely livid. We carried him kicking and screaming out of the shuttle and into the station's wardroom, by the galley. The station physician, the guy who had to stay aboard longer than the usual ninety days because of Sam and the others commandeering the shuttle seats, came in and threatened to give him a shot of horse tranquilizer.

What really sobered Sam up was Bonnie Jo. "You damned idiot! You're just proving to those government men that you shouldn't be allowed to operate anything more sophisticated than a baby's rattle!"

He blinked at her. I had backed him up against the wall of the wardroom and was holding him by his shoulders to stop him from thrashing around. The station's doctor was sort of hovering off to one side with a huge hypodermic syringe in his hand and an expectant smile on his face. Bonnie Jo was standing squarely in front of Sam, her eyes snapping like pistols.

"I screwed up, huh?" Sam said, sheepishly.

"You certainly showed Zane and Clement how mature you are," said Bonnie Jo.

"But that sonofabitch is trying to steal the whole operation right out from under us!"

"And you're helping him."

I waved the medic away. He seemed disappointed that he wouldn't have to stick a needle into Sam's anatomy. We drifted over to the table. There was only one of them in the cramped little wardroom, rising like a flat-topped toadstool from a single slim pedestal. It was chest-high; nobody used chairs in zero-gee: you stuck your feet in the floor loops and let your arms drift to their natural level.

Sam hung onto the table, letting his feet dangle a few inches off the floor. He looked miserable and contrite.

Before I could say anything, the skipper poked her brunette head into the wardroom.

"Can I see you a minute, Spence?" she asked. From the look on her face I guessed it was business, and urgent.

I pushed over to her. She motioned me through the hatch and we both headed for the command module, like a pair of swimmers coasting side by side.

"Got a problem," she said. "Mission control just got the word from the tracking center that Rockledge's damned Nerf ball is on a collision course with us."

I got that sudden lurch in the gut that comes when your engine quits or you hear a hiss in your space suit.

"How the hell could it be on a collision course?" I didn't want to believe it.

She pulled herself through the hatch and swam up to her command station. Pointing to the trio of display screens mounted below the station's only observation window, she said, "Here's the data; see for yourself."

I still couldn't believe it, even though the numbers made it abundantly clear that in less than one hour the shredded remains of one of the Nerf balls was going to come barreling into the station at a closing velocity of more than ten miles per second.

"It could tear a solar panel off," the commander said tightly. "It could even puncture these modules if it hits dead center."

"How the hell . . ."

"It banged into the spent final stage of the Ariane 4 that was launched last week. Got enough energy from the collision to push it up into an orbit that will intersect with ours in . . ." She glanced at the digital clock on her panel. ". . . fifty-three minutes."

"The magnetic field won't deflect it," I said. "It hasn't been in space long enough to build up a static electrical charge on its skin."

"Then we'll have to abandon the station. Good thing the shuttle's still docked to us."

She moved her hand toward the communications keyboard. I grabbed it away.

"Give me five minutes. Maybe there's something we can do."

I called Sam to the command module. Bonnie Jo was right behind him. Swiftly I outlined the problem. He called Larry, back in Florida, who immediately agreed that the magnetic bumper would have no effect on the Nerf ball. He didn't look terribly upset; to him this was a theoretical problem. I could see Melinda standing behind him, smiling into the screen like a chubby Mona Lisa.

"There's no way we could deflect it?" Sam asked, a little desperation in his voice.

"Not unless you could charge it up," Larry said.

"Charge it?"

"Spray it with an electron beam," he said. "That'd give it enough of a surface charge for the magnetic field to deflect it."

Sam cut the connection. Forty-two minutes and counting.

"We have several electron beam guns aboard," the skipper said. "In the lab module."

"But they're not powerful enough to charge the damned Nerf ball until it gets so close it'll hit us anyway," Sam muttered.

"We could go out on one of the OMVs," I heard myself suggest.

"Yeah!" Sam brightened. "Go out and push it out of the way."

I had to shake my head. "No, Sam. That won't work. The Nerf ball is coming toward us; it's in an opposite orbit. The OMV doesn't have enough delta-v to go out there, turn around and match orbit with it, and then nudge it into a lower orbit."

"You'd have to ram the OMV into it," the commander said. "Like a kamikaze."

"No thanks," Sam said. "I'm brave but I'm not suicidal." He started gnawing his fingernails.

I said, "But we could go out on an OMV and give it a good squirt with an electron gun as we passed it. Charge it up enough for the magnetic bumper to do the job."

"You think so?"

"Forty minutes left," Bonnie Jo said. Not a quaver in her voice. Not a half-tone higher than usual. Not a hint of fear.

The commander shook her head. "The OMVs aren't pressurized. You don't have enough time for pre-breathe."

See, to run one of the OMVs you had to be suited up. Since the suits were pressurized only to a third of the normal air pressure that the station used, you had to pre-breathe oxygen for about an hour before sealing yourself inside the suit. Otherwise nitrogen bubbles would collect in your blood and you'd get the bends, just like a deep-sea diver.

"Fuck the pre-breathe," Sam snapped. "We're gonna save this goddamned station from Rockledge's runaway Nerf ball."

"I can't let you do that, Sam," the skipper said. Her hand went out to the comm keyboard again.

Sam leveled a stubby finger at her. "You let us give it a shot or I'll tell everybody back at the Cape what *really* happened when we were supposed to be testing the lunar rover simulator."

Her face flushed dark red.

"Listen," Sam said jovially. "You get everybody into the shuttle and pull away from the station. Mutt and I will go out in the OMV. If we can deflect the Nerf ball and save the station you'll be a hero. If not, the station gets shredded and you can give the bill to Rockledge International."

I hadn't thought of that. Who would be responsible for the destruction of this twenty-billion-dollar government installation? Who carried damage insurance on the space station?

"And the two of you will die of the bends," she said. "No, I won't allow it. I'm in charge here and . . ."

"Stick us in an airlock when we get back," Sam cajoled. "Run up the pressure. That's what they do for deep-sea divers, isn't it? You've got a medic aboard, use the jerk for something more than ramming needles into people's asses!"

"I can't, Sam!"

He looked at her coyly. "I've got videodisks from the lunar simulator, you know."

Thirty-five minutes.

The skipper gave in, of course. Sam's way was the only hope she had of saving the station. Besides, whatever they had done in the lunar simulator was something she definitely did not want broadcast. So ten minutes later Sam and I are buttoning ourselves into space suits while the skipper and one of her crew are floating an electron gun down the connecting tunnel to the airlock where the OMVs were docked. Everybody else was already jamming themselves into the shuttle mid-deck and cockpit. It must have looked like a fraternity party in there, except that I'll bet everybody was scared into constipation.

Everybody except Bonnie Jo. She seemed to have ice water in her veins. Cool and calm under fire.

I shook my head to get rid of my thoughts about her as I pulled on the space suit helmet. Sam was already buttoned up. My ears popped when I switched on the suit's oxygen system, but otherwise there were no bad effects.

The orbital maneuvering vehicle had a closed cockpit, but it wasn't pressurized. I lugged the electron gun and its power pack inside. "Lugged" isn't the right word, exactly. The apparatus was weightless, just like everything else. But it was bulky and awkward to handle.

Sam did the piloting. I set up the electron gun and ran through its checks. Every indicator light was green, although the best voltage I could crank out of it was a bit below max. That worried me. We'd need all the juice we could get when we whizzed past the Nerf ball.

We launched off the station with a little lurch and headed toward our fleeting rendezvous with the runaway. Through my visor I saw the station dwindle behind us, two football fields long, looking sort of like a square double-ended paddle, the kind they use on kayaks, with a cluster of little cylinders huddled in its middle. Those were the habitat and lab modules. They looked small and fragile and terribly, terribly vulnerable.

For the first time in my life I paid no attention to the big beautiful curving mass of the Earth glowing huge and gorgeous below us. I had no time for sightseeing, even when the sights were the most spectacular that any human being had ever seen.

The shuttle was pulling away in the opposite direction, getting the hell out of the line of fire. Suddenly we were all alone out there, just Sam and me inside this contraption of struts and spherical tanks that we called an OMV.

"Just like a World War I airplane movie," Sam said to me over the suit radio. "I'll make a pass as close to the Nerf ball as I can get. You spray it with the gun."

I nodded inside my helmet.

"Five minutes," Sam said, tapping a gloved finger on the radar display. In the false-color image of the screen the Nerf ball looked like a tumbling mass of long thin filaments, barely hanging together. Something in my brain clicked; I remembered an old antimissile system called Homing Overlay that looked kind of like an umbrella that had lost its fabric. When it hit a missile nose cone it shattered the thing with the pure kinetic energy of the impact. That's what the tatters of the aluminized plastic Nerf ball would do to the thin skin of the space station, if we let it hit. I could picture those great big solar panels exploding, throwing off jagged pieces that would slice up the lab and habitat modules like shards of glass going through paper walls.

"Three minutes."

I swung the cockpit hatch open and pushed the business end of the electron gun outside with my boots.

"How long will the power pack run?" I asked. "The longer we fire this thing the more chance we'll have of actually charging up the ball."

Sam must have shrugged inside his suit. "Might as well start now, Mutt. Build up a cloud that the sucker has to fly through. Won't do us a bit of good to have power still remaining once we've passed the god-damned spitball."

That made sense. I clicked the right switches and turned the power dial up to max. In the vacuum I couldn't hear whether it was humming or not, although I thought I felt a kind of vibration through my boots. All the dials said it was working, but that was scant comfort.

"One minute," Sam said. I knew he was flying our OMV as close to the Nerf ball as humanly possible. Sam was as good as they came at piloting. Better than me; not by much, but better. He'd get us close enough to kiss that little sucker, I knew.

We were passing over an ocean, which one I don't know to this day. Big wide deep blue below us, far as the eye could see, bright and glowing with long parades of teeny white clouds marching across it.

I saw something dark hurtling toward us, like a black octopus waving all its arms, like a silent banshee coming to grab us.

"There it . . . was," Sam said.

The damned thing thrashed past us like a hypersonic bat out of hell. I looked down at the electron gun's gauges. Everything read zero. We had used up all the energy in the power pack.

"Well, either it works or it doesn't," Sam said. All of a sudden he sounded tired.

I nodded inside my helmet. I felt it too: exhausted, totally drained. Just like the electron gun; we had given it everything we had. Now we had nothing left. We had done everything we could do. Now it was up to the laws of physics.

"We'll be back at the station in an hour," Sam said. "We'll know then."

We knew before then. Our helmet earphones erupted a few minutes later with cheers and yells, even some whistles. By the time we had completed our orbit and saw the station again, the shuttle was already redocked. Freedom looked very pretty hanging up there against the black sky. Gleaming in the sunlight. Unscathed.

So all we had to worry about was the bends.

"WAS IT VERY painful?" Jade asked.

Johansen gave her a small shrug. "Kind of like passing kidney stones for sixteen or seventeen hours. From every pore of your body."

She shuddered.

"We came out of it okay," he said. "But I wouldn't want to go through it again."

"You saved the station. You became heroes."

WE SAVED THE station—Johansen agreed—but we didn't become heroes. The government didn't want to acknowledge that there had been
any danger to Freedom, and Rockledge sure as hell didn't want the public
to know that their Nerf ball had almost wrecked the station.

Everybody involved had to sign a secrecy agreement. That was Ed
Zane's idea. To give the guy credit, though, it was also his idea to force
Rockledge to pay a cool ten million bucks for the cost of saving the station from their runaway Nerf ball. Rockledge ponied up without even
asking their lawyers, and Zane saw to it that the money was split among
the people who had been endangered—which included himself, of
course.

Each of us walked away with about five hundred thousand dollars, although it wasn't tax-free. The government called it a hazardous duty
bonus. It was a bribe, to keep us from leaking the story to the media.

Everybody agreed to keep quiet—except Sam, of course.

The medics took us out of the airlock, once we stopped screaming
from the pain, and hustled us down to a government hospital on Guam.
Landed the blessed shuttle right there on the island, on the three-mile-
long strip they had built as an emergency landing field for the shuttle.
They had to fly a 747 over to Guam to carry the orbiter back to Edwards
Space Base. I think they got Rockledge to pay for that, too.

Anyway, they put Sam and me in a semiprivate room. For observation
and tests, they said. I figured they wouldn't let either one of us out until
Sam signed the secrecy agreement.

"Five hundred thousand bucks, Sam," I needled him from my bed. "I
could pay a lot of my bills with that."

He turned toward me, frowning. "There's more than money involved
here, Mutt. A lot more."

I shrugged and took a nap. I wouldn't sign their secrecy agreement unless Sam did, of course. So there was nothing for me to do but wait.

Zane visited us. Sam yelled at him about kidnapping and civil rights.
Zane scuttled out of the room. A couple of other government types visited
us. Sam yelled even louder, especially when he heard that one of them was
from the Justice Department in Washington.

I was starting to get worried. Maybe Sam was carrying things too far.
They could keep us on ice forever in a place like Guam. They wouldn't let
us call anybody; we were being held incommunicado. I wondered what
Bonnie Jo was doing, whether she was worried about us. About me.

And just like that, she showed up. Like sunshine breaking through the clouds she breezed into our hospital room the third day we were there, dressed in a terrific pair of sand-colored slacks and a bright orange blouse. And a briefcase.

She waltzed up between the beds and gave us each a peck on the cheek.

"Sorry I couldn't get here sooner," she said. "The agency wouldn't answer any questions about you until my Uncle Ralph issued a writ."

"Your Uncle Ralph?" Sam and I asked in unison.

"Justice Burdette," she said, sounding a little surprised that we didn't recognize the name. "The Supreme Court. In Washington."

"Oh," said Sam. "*That* Uncle Ralph."

Bonnie Jo pulled up a chair between our beds, angling it to face Sam more than me. She placed her slim briefcase neatly on the tiled floor at her feet.

"Sam, I want you to sign the secrecy agreement," she said.

"Nope."

"Don't be stubborn, Sam. You know it wouldn't be in the best interests of VCI to leak this story to the media."

"Why not? We saved the friggin' space station, didn't we?"

"Sam—you have proved the feasibility of the magnetic bumper concept. In a few months the agency will give out a contract to run the facility. If you don't sign the secrecy agreement they won't give the contract to VCI. That's all there is to it."

"That's illegal!" Sam shot upright in his bed. "You know that! We'll sue the bastards! Call the news networks! Call . . ."

She reached out and put a finger on his lips, silencing him and making me feel rotten.

"Sam, the more fuss you make the less likely it is that the government will award you the contract. They can sit there with their annual budgets and wait until you go broke paying lawyers. Then where will you be?"

He grumbled under his breath.

Bonnie Jo took her finger away. "Besides, that's not really what you want, is it? You want to operate the debris removal system, don't you? You want to sell the Vanguard satellite to the Smithsonian, don't you?"

He kind of nodded, like a kid being led to the right answer by a kindly teacher.

"And after that?"

"Remove defunct commsats from GEO. Retrieve the Eagle from Tranquility Base and sell it to the highest bidder."

Bonnie Jo gave him a pleased smile. "All right, then," she said, picking up the briefcase. She placed it on her lap, opened it, and pulled out a sheaf of papers. "You have some signing to do."

"What about me?" I asked, kind of sore that she had ignored me.

Bonnie Jo peeled the top sheet from the pile and held it up in the air by one corner. "This one's for Sam. It's the secrecy agreement. There's one for you, too, Spence. All the others have to be signed by the president of VCI."

"Over my dead body," Sam growled.

"Don't tempt me," Bonnie Jo answered sweetly. "Read them first. All of them. Engage brain before putting mouth in gear."

Sam glared at her. I tried not to laugh and wound up sputtering. Sam looked at me and then he grinned, too, kind of self-consciously.

"Okay, okay," he said. "I'll read."

He put the secrecy agreement on the bed to one side of him and started going through the others. As he finished each document, he handed it to me so I could read it, too.

The first was a sole-source contract from the agency to run the debris removal system for space station Freedom for five years. Not much of a profit margin, but government contracts never give a high percentage of profit. What they do is give you a steady income to keep your overhead paid. On the money from this contract Larry and Melinda could get married and take a honeymoon in Tasmania, if they wanted to.

The second document made my eyes go wide. I could actually feel them dilating, like camera lenses. It was a contract from Rockledge International for VCI to remove six of their defunct commsats from geosynchronous orbit. I paged through to the money numbers. More zeroes than I had seen since the last time I had read about the national debt!

When I looked up, Bonnie Jo was grinning smugly at me. "That's D'Argent's peace offering. You don't blab about the Nerf ball incident and you can have the job of removing their dead commsats."

"What about retrieving the Nerf balls before they reenter the atmosphere?" I asked. "I'd think that Rockledge would want to get their hands on them, see why they failed."

"Yeah," Sam said. "I want a separate contract from Rockledge to retrieve their Nerf balls and . . ."

"Keep reading," Bonnie Jo said. "It's in the pile there."

She had done it all. VCI would be the exclusive contractor for garbage removal not only for the government, but for Rockledge as well. With that kind of a lead, we'd be so far ahead of any possible competitors that nobody would even bother to try to get into the business against us.

I signed all the contracts. With a great show of reluctance, Sam signed the secrecy agreement. Then I signed mine.

"You're marvelous," I said to Bonnie Jo, handing her back all the documents. "To do all this . . ."

"I'm just protecting my daddy's investment," she said coolly. There was no smile on her face. She was totally serious. "And my own."

I couldn't look into those gray-green eyes of hers. I turned away.

Somebody knocked at the door. Just a soft little tap, kind of weak, timid.

"Now what?" Sam snapped. "Come on in," he yelled, exasperated. "Might as well bring the Mormon Tabernacle Choir with you."

The door opened about halfway and Albert Clement slipped in, thin and gray as ever, back in his usual charcoal three-piece undertaker's suit.

"I'm sorry if I'm intruding," he said, softly, apologetically.

Sam's frown melted. "You're not intruding."

Clement sort of hovered near the door, as if he didn't dare come any further into the room.

"I wanted to make certain that you were all right," he said.

"You came all this way?" Sam asked. His voice had gone tiny, almost hollow.

Clement made a little shrug. "I had a few weeks' annual leave coming to me."

"So you came out to Guam."

"I wanted to . . . that was a very courageous thing you did, son. I'm proud of you."

I thought I saw tears in the corners of Sam's eyes. "Thanks, Dad. I—" He swallowed hard. "I'm glad you came to see me."

"DAD?" JADE WAS startled. "That withered old man was Sam's father?"

"He sure was," Johansen replied. "He and Sam's mother had divorced when Sam was just a baby, from what Sam told me later on. Sam was raised by his stepfather, took his name. Didn't even know who his real father was until just before he started up VCI."

Jade felt her own heart constricting in her chest. Who is my father? My mother? Where are they? Why did they abandon me?

"Hey, are you okay?" Johansen had a hand on her shoulder.

"What? Oh, yes. I'm fine . . . just . . . fine."

"You looked like you were a million miles away," he said.

"I'm all right. Sorry."

He leaned back away from her, but his eyes still looked worried.

"So it was his father who fed him the inside information from the Department of Commerce," Jade said, trying to recover her composure.

"Right. That's how Sam learned that the program had a small business set-aside," Johansen explained. "Which was public knowledge, by the way. Clement didn't do anything wrong."

"But he certainly didn't want anyone to know about their relationship, either, did he?"

Johansen nodded. "I guess not. You know, I never saw Sam so—I guess *subdued* is the right word. He and Clement spent a solid week together. Once the hospital people let us get up and walk around, they even went deep-sea fishing together."

"I'll have to check him out," Jade said, mostly to herself.

"Clement died a few years later. He retired from the Commerce Department and applied for residency in the first of the L-4 habitats, the old Island One. Thought the low gravity would help his heart condition, but he died in his sleep before the habitat was finished building. Sam gave him a nice funeral. Quiet and tasteful. Not what you'd expect from Sam at all."

"And his mother? Is she still alive?"

Johansen shook his head. "He would never talk about his mother. Not a word. Maybe he discussed her with Clement, but I just don't know."

Jade sat back in her chair, silent for a long moment while the candlelight flickered across her face. She had not seen her adopted mother, not even spoken with her by videophone, in more than ten years. The link between them was completely broken.

"So that's how Sam made his first fortune. With Vacuum Cleaners, Incorporated," she said at last.

"VCI," Johansen corrected. "Yeah, he made a fortune all right. Then he squandered it all on that bridge-ship deal a couple years later. By then he was completely out of VCI, though. I stayed on as president until Rockledge eventually bought us out."

"Rockledge?"

"Right. The big corporations always win in the end. Oh, I got a nice hunk of change out of it. Very nice. Set me up for life. Allowed me to buy a slice of this habitat and become a major shareholder."

"Did Sam ever marry Bonnie Jo?"

Johansen grimaced.

THAT GOT DECIDED while we were still on Guam—Johansen replied.

Bonnie Jo hung around, just like Clement did. Sam seemed to spend more time with his father than with her, so I wound up walking the hospital grounds with her, taking her out to dinner, that kind of stuff.

Finally, one night over dinner, she told me she and Clement would be leaving the next day.

I said something profound, like, "Oh."

"When will you and Sam be allowed to leave the hospital?" she asked. We were in the best restaurant in the capital city, Agana. It was sort of a dump; the big tourist boom hadn't started yet in Guam. That didn't happen until a few years later, when Sam opened up the orbital hotel and built the launch complex there.

Anyway, I shrugged for an answer. I hadn't even bothered to ask the medics about when we'd be let go. The week had been very restful, after all the pressures we had been through. And as long as Bonnie Jo was there I really didn't care when they sent us packing.

"Well," she said, "Albert and I go out on the morning flight tomorrow." There was a kind of strange expression on her face, as if she was searching for something and not finding it.

"I guess you'll marry Sam once we get back to the States," I said.

She moved her eyes away from mine and didn't answer. I felt as low as one of those worms that lives on the bottom of the ocean.

"Well . . . congratulations," I said.

In a voice so low I could barely hear her, Bonnie Jo said, "I don't want to marry Sam."

I felt my jaw muscles tighten. "But you still want to protect your father's investment, don't you? And your own."

Her eyes locked onto mine. "I could do that by marrying the president of VCI, couldn't I?"

I know how it feels to have your space suit ripped open. All the air whooshed out of me.

"Spence, you big handsome lunk, *you're* my investment," she said. "Didn't you know that?"

"Me?"

"Yes, you."

I nearly knocked the table over kissing her. I never felt so happy in all my life.

"WHICH NUMBER WIFE was she?" Jade was surprised at the acid in her voice.

Johansen pushed his chair slightly back from the restaurant table. "Number four," he said, somewhat reluctantly.

"And it didn't work out?"

"Wasn't her fault," he said. "Not really. I spent more time in orbit than at home. She met this kid who was an assistant vice president at her father's bank. They had a lot more in common. . . ."

Johansen's voice trailed off. The candle between them was guttering low. The table was littered with the crumbs of dessert, emptied coffee cups. The restaurant was deserted except for one other couple and the stumpy little robot waiters standing impassively by each table.

Jade had one more question to ask. "I know that nobody ever retrieved the Apollo 11 lunar module. What happened to Sam's plan?"

Johansen made a tight grin. "The little guy was nobody's fool. Once the world court decided that the right of salvage was pretty much the same in space as it is at sea, we went to the Moon and laid claim to all the hardware the Apollo astronauts had left behind, at all six landing sites."

"But it's all still there," Jade said. "I've been to Tranquility Base. And Gamma and all the others . . ."

"That's right." Johansen's smile broadened, genuinely pleased. "Sam's original thought was to auction the stuff off to the highest bidder. The Japanese were hot for it. So was the Smithsonian, of course. And some group of high-tech investors from Texas."

"So who bought them?"

"Nobody," Johansen said. "Because Sam got the bright idea of offering it for free to Selene. I think it was still called Moonbase then. Anyway, the people there loved him for it. Thanks to Sam, Selene legally owns all the Apollo hardware resting on the Moon. Those landing sites are big tourist attractions for them."

"That was generous."

"Sure was. And, of course, Sam could get just about anything he wanted from Selene for years afterward."

"I see," said Jade.

Johansen signaled for the bill. The robot trundled over, digits lighting up on the screen set into its torso. Johansen tapped out his okay on the robot's keyboard and let the photocell take an impression of his thumbprint. Jade turned off her recorder.

Johansen moved gracefully around the little table and held her chair while she stood up, feeling strangely unhappy that this interview was at an end.

As they strolled slowly down the footpath that led to the hotel where she was staying, Johansen suggested, "How'd you like to go hang gliding tomorrow morning? In this low gravity there's no danger at all."

Jade was surprised at how much she wanted to say yes.

"I can't," she heard herself say. "I'm leaving tomorrow morning."

"Oh," said Johansen, sounding disappointed.

They walked along the footpath in the man-made twilight toward the little cluster of low buildings that was Gunnstown, where her hotel was situated. Johansen pointed out the lights of other towns overhead. In the darkness they could not see that the habitat's interior curved up and over them.

"They're like stars," Jade said, gazing up at the lights.

"Some people even see constellations in them," he told her. "See, there's a cat—over there. And the mouse, down further . . ."

She leaned closer to him as he pointed out the man-made constellations.

"Do you think you'll ever marry again?" she asked in a whisper.

"Not until I'm certain it will last," he answered immediately. "I've had enough hit-and-runs in my life. I want somebody I can settle down with and live happily ever after."

Happily ever after, Jade said to herself. Does anyone ever do that? She pulled away from Johansen slightly, thinking of Raki and what she owed him, what she owed herself.

I'm leaving tomorrow. Good. I'll leave and go out and interview more of Sam's friends and enemies. I'll leave and never see this man again. It's better that way. Six wives! Who can trust a man who's had six wives?

She felt almost glad that she was leaving habitat *Jefferson* in the morning.

Almost glad.

Selene City

WHEN JADE GOT BACK TO HER OFFICE THE NEXT MORNING
there was a message waiting for her. From Spence!

Her heart thumping, she hit the playback tab on her desktop keyboard. Spence's handsome face appeared on her screen, crinkling a smile at her.

"Hi, Jade. Guess who I ran into right after I saw you off? Larry Karsh. You know, the VCI engineer I told you about. He's on his way to Selene and he says he has an audio disk that Sam himself recorded. About the time when he opened his honeymoon hotel in Earth orbit. Thought you'd want to listen to it."

Jade nodded eagerly at Spence's image.

"Okay, that's it. Thought you ought to know about it. Larry's on his way to Selene. Maybe you can get him to let you hear the disk. 'Bye."

And his image winked out.

Not a word about me, she thought as she stared at the blank screen. Not a word about us. He's just doing a favor for a friend. Nothing more.

She felt crushed, terribly let down. For long moments she simply sat at her desk trying to fight back the disappointment that threatened to engulf her.

He doesn't care about me. Not the way I want him to. Not the way I care about him.

Suddenly she felt the shock of realizing that she truly did care about Spence. Am I in love with him? she asked herself. She had no answer.

At last she shook her head, as if trying to clear the cobwebs of emotion that were entangling her. You're a news reporter, she told herself sternly. Spence has given you a lead on a hot story. Sam's own voice!

Without even asking Jumbo Jim, she checked the incoming flight arrivals, then made her way to Selene's spaceport.

Armstrong Spaceport

"YEAH, I WORKED FOR SAM FOR SEVERAL YEARS BACK IN the old days," said Larry Karsh.

He was a lean, lanky, long-limbed man with the kind of baby face that would keep him looking youthful into his seventies, Jade thought. She had just barely arrived at the spaceport in time to meet him as he disembarked from the shuttle from habitat *Jefferson*.

"I'm on my way to the construction base on Mercury," he'd told her. "Yamagata Corporation's building a set of solar power satellites there, y'know."

Jade maneuvered him to the tiny bar set between terminal gates and offered him a drink on Solar News's expense. He smiled gratefully and asked for orange juice. Selene's citrus groves were famous off-Earth. Jade had South Pole water.

"Y'know, in a way, Sam was a big factor in my marriage," Karsh said as he sipped his drink. "But my wife and I could never forgive him for kidnapping our baby. That ended it between Sam and me, for good."

"Kidnapped your baby?" Jade asked, shocked.

"Oh, T.J.'s none the worse for the experience. He was still in diapers when it happened. Now he's heading up the Ecological Protection Service on Mars, making sure that the tourists don't do any harm to the Martian environment so the scientists can keep on studying the life forms in the rocks. He's a bright young man, my son is.

"Y'know, the power we generate from those sunsats in Mercury orbit will be beamed to the Mars stations. We'll be providing electrical power for most of the inner solar system, how about that? And we'll still have plenty left over to power the sailships out to Alpha Centauri and Lalande 21185."

Jade made approving noises, then asked, "But about Sam . . . ?"

"Sam? I kinda miss him, sure. But don't let my wife hear that! She'd just as soon boil Sam in molten sulfur, even after all these years."

"I can understand that, I guess."

"Well sure, Sam felt pretty bad about what happened. Or so he said. He even sent me a long letter explaining his side of it. Not a written letter,

Sam never liked to commit very much to writing. It's an audio disk, from his diary."

"Sam kept a diary?"

"He sure did. Like a running log of everything he did. No, I haven't the faintest idea of where he stored it. Probably carried it with him wherever he went, knowing Sam. Editing it every day, most likely, changing it to suit his mood or the needs of the moment, y'know.

"The only part of the diary I've got is the bit he sent me, which deals about the time he kidnapped my son."

Her insides trembling with anticipation, Jade murmured, "You wouldn't have it with you, by any chance?"

"Yeah, sure, I've got it here in my stuff someplace. Always carry it with me. Figured it might be a valuable historical document some day. Wanna hear it?"

It took all Jade's energy to keep from grabbing Karsh's carry-bag off his shoulder and tearing through it.

Nursery Sam

TRYING TO HIDE HER EXCITEMENT, JADE SLIPPED THE thumb-sized disk that Larry Karsh handed her into her digital player and wormed it into her ear.

I WAS TRYING to get away from the Senator who wanted to marry me. (Sam's voice was a sharp-edged tenor; Jade pictured his freckled, snub-nosed face as she listened.)

So I'm sitting in the Clipper—riding tourist fare—waiting for the engines to light off and fly us to my zero-gee hotel, when who traipses into the cabin but Jack Spratt and his wife.

With a baby.

I scrunched *way* down in my seat. I didn't want them to see me. I had enough troubles without a pissed-off former employee staring daggers at me for the whole ride up to orbit.

His name wasn't really Jack Spratt, of course. It was Larry Karsh, and he had been a pretty key player in my old company, VCI. But that goddamnable Pierre D'Argent, the silver-haired slimeball, had hired him away from me, and Larry wouldn't have gone to work at Rockledge if he hadn't been sore at me for some reason. Damned if I knew what.

Okay, maybe I shouldn't have called them the Spratts. But you know, Larry was so skinny he hardly cast a shadow and Melinda was—well, the kindest word is *zaftig*, I guess. She could just look at a potato chip and gain two kilos. Larry could clean out a whole shopping mall's worth of junk food and never put on an ounce. So with him such a classic ectomorph and Melinda so billowy despite every diet in the world, it just seemed natural to call them Jack Spratt and his wife.

I guess it irritated Larry.

Well, I didn't like the idea of bringing a baby up to my zero-gee hotel. Business was lousy enough up there without some mewling, puking ball of dirty diapers getting in everybody's way. Heaven—that was my name for the hotel—was supposed to be for honeymooners. Oh, I'd take tourists of any sort, but I always thought of Heaven as primarily a honeymoon hotel. You know, sex in free fall; weightless lovemaking.

For the life of me, I couldn't figure out why people didn't flock to Heaven. I thought I had a terrific motto for the hotel: "If you like water beds, you'll love zero-gee."

Okay, okay, so most people got sick their first day or so in weightlessness. It's a little like seasickness: you feel kind of nauseated, like you're coming down with the flu. You feel like you're falling all the time; you want to upchuck and just generally die. Of course, after a while it all goes away and you're floating around in zero-gee and you start to feel terrific. Scientists have even written reports about what they call "microgravity euphoria." It's wonderful!

But first you've got to get over the miseries. And I knew damned well that Rockledge was working on a cure for space sickness, right there in the same space station as my Hotel Heaven. But even if they found the cure, who do you think would be the *last* person in the solar system that Pierre D'Argent would sell it to?

That's right. Sam Gunn, Esq. Me.

Me, I love weightlessness. God knows I've spent enough time in zero-gee. The idea for the honeymoon hotel came out of plenty of practical experience, believe me. In fact, the Senator who wanted to marry me had been one of my first datum points in my research on zero-gee sex, years ago. She had been a fellow astronaut, back in the days when we both worked for the old NASA.

But it only takes a few newlyweds tossing their cookies when free-fall first hits them to sour the whole damned travel industry on the idea of honeymooning in Heaven. As one travel agent from North Carolina told me, sweetly, "Even if you don't get sick yourself, who wants to spend a vacation listening to other people puking?"

I tried beefing up the acoustical insulation in the suites, but Heaven got the reputation of being like an ocean liner that's always in rough seas. And to this day I'm still convinced that D'Argent used Rockledge's high-powered public relations machine to badmouth Heaven. D'Argent hated my guts, and the feeling was mutual.

And now Jack Spratt and his wife were bringing a baby up to Heaven. Perfect.

They sat two rows in front of me: Larry Karsh, Melinda, and a squirming dribbling baby that couldn't have been more than nine or ten months old. Larry had filled out a little in the couple of years since I had last seen him, but he still looked like an emaciated scarecrow. Melinda had slimmed down a trace. Maybe. They still looked like Jack Spratt and his wife. And baby.

I could feel my face wrinkling into the grandfather of all frowns. A baby aboard a space station? That's crazy! It's sabotage! Yet, try as I might, I couldn't think of any company rules or government regulations that prohibited people from bringing babies to Heaven. It just never occurred to me that anybody would. Well, I'll fix *that*, I told myself. What the hell kind of a honeymoon hotel has a baby running around in it? Upchucking is bad enough; we don't need dirty diapers and a squalling brat in orbit. They're going to ruin the whole idea of Heaven.

The Clipper took off normally; we pulled about three gs for a minute or so. The cabin was less than half full; plenty of empty seats staring at me like the Ghost of Bankruptcy To Come. I scrunched deeper in my seat so Jack Spratt and his wife wouldn't see me. But I was listening for the yowling that I knew was on its way.

Sure enough, as soon as the engines cut off and we felt weightless, the baby started screaming. The handful of paying passengers all turned toward the kid, and Larry unbuckled himself and drifted out of his seat.

"Hey, T.J., don't holler," he said, in the kind of voice that only an embarrassed father can put out. While he talked, he and Melinda unbuckled the brat from his car seat.

The baby kicked himself free of the last strap and floated up into his father's arms. His yowling stopped. He gurgled. I knew what was coming next: his breakfast.

But instead the kid laughed and waved his chubby little arms. Larry barely touched him, just sort of guided him the way you'd tap a helium-filled balloon.

"See?" he cooed. "It's fun, isn't it?"

The baby laughed. The passengers smiled tolerantly. Me, I was stunned that Jack Spratt had learned how to coo.

Then he spotted me, slumped down so far in my seat I was practically on the floor. And it's not easy to slump in zero-gee; you really have to work at it.

"Sam!" he blurted, surprised. "I didn't know you were on this flight." And Melinda turned around in her chair and gave me a strained smile.

"I didn't know you had a baby," I said, trying not to growl in front of the paying customers.

Larry floated down the aisle to my row, looking so proud of his accomplishment you'd think nobody had ever fathered a son before. "Timothy James Karsh, meet Sam Gunn. Sam, this is T.J."

He glided T.J. in my direction, the baby giggling and flailing both his arms and legs. For just the flash of a second I thought of how much fun it would be to play volleyball with the kid, but instead I just sort of held him like he was a Ming vase or something. I didn't know what the hell to do with a baby!

But the baby knew. He looked me straight in the eye and spurted out a king-sized juicy raspberry, spraying me all over my face. Everybody roared with laughter.

I shoved the kid back to Larry, thinking that baseball might be more fun than volleyball.

In the fifty-eight minutes it took us to go from engine cutoff to docking with the space station, T.J. did about eleven thousand somersaults, seventy-three dozen midair pirouettes, and God knows how many raspberries. Everybody enjoyed the show, at first. The women especially gushed and gabbled and talked baby talk to the kid. They reached out to hold him, but little T.J. didn't want to be held. He was having a great time floating around the tourist cabin and enjoying weightlessness.

I had feared, in those first few moments, that seeing this little bundle of dribble floating through the cabin would make some of the passengers queasy. I was just starting to tell myself I was wrong when I heard the first retching heave from behind me. It finally caught up with them; the baby's antics had taken their minds off that falling sensation you get when zero-gee first hits you. But now the law of averages took its toll.

One woman. That's all it took. One of those gargling groans and inside of two minutes almost everybody in the cabin is grabbing for their whoopie bags and making miserable noises. I turned up the air vent over my seat to max, but the stench couldn't be avoided. Even Melinda started to look a little green, although Larry was as unaffected as I was and little T.J. thought all the noise was hysterically funny. He threw out raspberries at everybody.

When we finally got docked we needed the station's full medical crew and a fumigation squad to clean out the cabin. Three couples flatly refused to come aboard Heaven; green as guacamole, they cancelled their vacations on the spot, demanded their money back, and rode in misery back to Earth. The other eight couples were all honeymooners. They wouldn't cancel, but they looked pretty damned unhappy.

I went straight from the dock to my cubbyhole of an office in the hotel.

"There's gotta be a way to get rid of that baby," I muttered as I slid my slippered feet into their restraint loops. I tend to talk to myself when I'm upset.

My office was a marvel of zero-gee ergonomic engineering: compact as a fighter plane's cockpit, cozy as squirrel's nest, with everything I needed at my fingertips, whether it was up over my head or wherever. I scrolled through three hours worth of rules and regulations, insurance, safety, travel rights, even family law. Nothing there that would prevent parents from bringing babies onto a space station.

I was staring bleary-eyed at old maritime law statutes on my display screen, hoping that as owner of the hotel I had the same rights as the captain of a ship and could make unwanted passengers walk the plank. No such luck. Then the phone light blinked. I punched the key and growled, "What?"

A familiar voice said coyly, "Senator Meyers would like the pleasure of your company."

"Jill? Is that you?" I cleared my display screen and punched up the phone image. Sure enough, it was Sen. Jill Meyers (R-NH).

Everybody said that Jill looked enough like me to be my sister. If so, what we did back in our youthful NASA days would have to be called incest. Jill had a pert round face, bright as a new penny, with a scattering of freckles across her button of a nose. Okay, so I look kind of like that, too. But her hair is a mousy brown and straight as a plumbline, while mine is on the russet side and curls so tight you can break a comb on it.

Let me get one thing absolutely clear. I am taller than she. Jill is not quite five-foot three, whereas I am five-five, no matter what my detractors claim.

"Where are you?" I asked.

"Roughly fifty meters away from you," she said, grinning.

"Here? In Heaven?" That was not the best news in the world for me. I had come up to my zero-gee hotel to get away from Jill.

See, I had been sort of courting her down in Washington because she's a ranking member of the Senate Commerce Committee and I needed a favor or two from her. She was perfectly happy to do me the favor or two, but she made it clear she was looking for a husband. Jill had been widowed maybe ten years earlier. I had never been married and had no intention of starting now. I like women way too much to marry one of them.

"Yes, I'm here in Heaven," Jill said, with a big grin. "Came up on the same flight you did."

"But I didn't see you."

"Senators ride first class, Sam."

I made a frown. "At the taxpayers' expense."

"In this case, it was at the expense of Rockledge International Corporation. Feel better?"

No, I didn't feel better. Not at all. "Rockledge? How come?"

"I've been invited to inspect their research facilities here at their space station," Jill said. "Pierre D'Argent himself is escorting me."

I growled.

Maybe I should tell you that the Rockledge space station was built of three concentric wheels. The outermost wheel spun around at a rate that gave it the feeling of regular Earth gravity: one g. The second wheel, closer to the hub, was at roughly one-third g: the gravity level of Mars. The innermost wheel was at one-sixth g, same as the Moon. And the hub, of course, was just about zero gravity. The scientists call it microgravity but it's so close to zero-gee that for all intents and purposes you're weightless at the hub.

I had rented half the hub from Rockledge for my Hotel Heaven. Zero-gee for lovers. Okay, so it's not exactly zero-gee, so what? I had built thirty lovely little mini-suites around the rim of the hub and still had enough room left over to set up a padded gym where you could play anything from volleyball to blind man's bluff in weightlessness.

Once I realized that most tourists got sick their first day or so in orbit, I tried to rent space down at the outermost wheel, so my customers could stay at normal Earth gravity and visit the zero-gee section when they wanted to play—or try weightless sex. No dice. D'Argent wouldn't rent any of it to me. He claimed Rockledge was using the rest of the station—all of it—for their research labs and their staff. Which was bullcrap.

I did manage to get them to rent me a small section in the innermost wheel, where everything was one-sixth g. I set up my restaurant there, so my customers could at least have their meals in some comfort. Called it the Lunar Eclipse. Best damned restaurant off Earth. Also the only one, at that time. Lots of spilled drinks and wine, though. Pouring liquids in low gravity takes some training. We had to work hard to teach our waiters and waitresses how to do it. I personally supervised the waitress training. It was one of the few bright spots in this black hole that was engulfing me.

"How about lunch?" Jill asked me, with a bright happy smile.

"Yeah," I said, feeling trapped. "How about it?"

"What a charming invitation," said Jill. "I'll see you at the restaurant in fifteen minutes."

Now here's the deal. The first big industrial boom in orbit was just starting to take off. Major corporations like Rockledge were beginning to realize that they could make profits from manufacturing in orbit.

They had problems with workers getting space sick, of course, but they weren't as badly affected as I was with Heaven. There's a big difference between losing the first two days of a week-long vacation because you're nauseated and losing the first two days of a ninety-day work contract. Still, Rockledge was searching for a cure. Right there on the same space station as my Hotel Heaven.

Anyway, I figured that the next step in space industrialization would be to start digging up the raw materials for the orbital factories from the Moon and the asteroids. A helluva lot cheaper than hauling them up from Earth, once you get a critical mass of mining equipment in place. The way I saw it, once we could start mining the Moon and some of the near-approach asteroids, the boom in orbital manufacturing would really take off. I'd make zillions!

And I was right, of course, although it didn't exactly develop the way I thought it would.

I wanted to get there first. Start mining the Moon, grab an asteroid or two. Mega-fortunes awaited the person who could strike those bonanzas.

But the goddamned honeymoon hotel was bleeding me to death. Unless and until somebody came up with a cure for space sickness, Heaven was going to be a financial bottomless pit. I was losing a bundle trying to keep the hotel open, and the day D'Argent became Rockledge's Chief of Space Operations, he doubled my rent, sweetheart that he is.

But I knew something that D'Argent didn't want me to know. Rockledge was working on a cure for space sickness. Right here aboard the space station! If I could get my hands on that, my troubles would be over. Pretty much.

It occurred to me, as I headed for the Lunar Eclipse, that maybe Jill could do me still another favor. Maybe her being here on the station might work out okay, after all.

I pushed along the tube that went down to the inner ring. You had to be careful, heading from the hub towards the various rings, because you were effectively going downhill. Flatlanders coming up for the first time could flatten themselves but good if they let themselves drop all the way down to the outermost wheel. The Coriolis force from the station's spin would bang them against the tube's circular wall as they dropped downward. The farther they dropped, the bigger the bangs. You could break bones.

That's why Rockledge's engineers had designed ladder rungs and safety hatches in the tubes that connected the hub to the wheels, so you had something to grab on to and stop your fall. I had even thought about padding the walls, but D'Argent nixed my idea: too expensive, he claimed. He'd rather see somebody fracture a leg and sue me.

I was almost at the lunar level. In fact, I was pulling open the hatch when I hear a yell. I look up and a bundle of screaming baby comes tumbling past me like a miniature bowling ball with arms and legs.

"Catch him! Stop him!"

I look around and here comes Larry Karsh, flailing around like a skinny spider on LSD, trying to catch up with his kid.

"Sam! Help!"

If I had thought about it for half a microsecond I would've let the kid bounce off the tube walls until he splattered himself on the next set of hatches. And Larry after him.

But, no—instinct took over and I shot through the hatch and launched myself after the baby like a torpedo on a rescue mission. S. Gunn, intrepid hero.

It was a long fall to the next set of hatches. I could see the kid tumbling around like a twenty-pound meteoroid, bare-ass naked, hitting the wall and skidding along it for a moment, then flinging out into midair again. His size worked for him: a little guy like he was didn't hit the wall so hard—at first. But each bump down the tube was going to be harder, I knew. If I didn't catch him real fast, he'd get hurt. Bad.

There was nobody else in the damned tube, nobody there to grab him or break his fall or even slow him down a little.

I started using the ladder rungs to propel myself faster, grabbing the rungs with my fingertips and pushing off them, one after another, faster and faster. Like the Lone Ranger chasing a runaway horse. Damned Coriolis force was getting to me, though, making me kind of dizzy.

As I got closer and closer, I saw that little T.J. wasn't screaming with fear. He was screeching with delight, happy as a little cannonball, kicking his arms and legs and tumbling head over bare ass, laughing hard as he could.

Next time he hits the wall he won't be laughing anymore, I thought. Then I wondered if I could reach him before he slammed into the hatch at the bottom of this level of the tube. At the speed I was going I'd come down right on top of him, and the kid wouldn't be much of a cushion.

Well, I caught up with him before either of us reached the next hatch, tucked him under one arm like he was a wriggling football, and started trying to slow my fall with the other hand. It wasn't going to work, I saw, so I flipped myself around so I was coming down feet-first and kept grabbing at rungs with my free hand, getting dizzier and dizzier. Felt like my shoulder was going to come off, and my hand got banged up pretty good, but at least we slowed down some.

The baby was crying and struggling to get loose. He'd been having fun, dropping like an accelerating stone. He didn't like being saved. I heard Larry yelling and looked up; he was clambering down the ladder, all skinny arms and legs, jabbering like a demented monkey.

I hit the hatch feet-first like I'd been dropped out of an airplane. I mean, I did my share of parachute jumps back when I was in astronaut training, but this time I hit a hell of a lot harder. Like my shinbones were shattering and my knees were trying to ram themselves up into my ribcage. I saw every star in the Milky Way, and the wind was knocked out of me for a moment.

So I was sprawled on my back, kind of dazed, with the kid yelling to get loose from me, when Larry comes climbing down the ladder, puffing like *he'd* been trying to save the kid, and takes the yowling little brat in his arms.

"Gee, thanks, Sam," he says. "I was changing his diaper when he got loose from me. Sorry about the mess."

That's when I realized that the ungrateful little so-and-so had peed all down the front of my shirt.

So I was late for my lunch date with Senator Meyers. My hand was banged up and swollen, my legs ached, my knees felt like they were going to explode, and the only other shirt I had brought with me was all wrinkled from being jammed into my travel bag. But at least it was dry. Even so, I got to the restaurant before she did. Jill was one of those women who has a deathly fear of arriving anywhere first.

I was so late, though, that she was only half a minute behind me. I hadn't even started for a table yet; I was still in the restaurant's teeny little foyer, talking with my buddy Omar.

"Am I terribly late?" Jill asked.

I turned at the sound of her voice and, I've got to admit, Jill looked terrific. I mean, she was as plain as vanilla, with hardly any figure at all, but she still looked bright and attractive and, well, I guess the right word is *radiant*. She was wearing a one-piece zipsuit, almost like the coveralls that we used to wear back on the NASA shuttle. But now her suit was made of some kind of shiny stuff and decorated with color accents and jewels. Like Polonius said: rich, not gaudy.

Her hair was a darker shade than I remembered it from the old days, and impeccably coiffed. She was dyeing it, I figured. And getting it done a lot better than she did when she'd been a working astronaut.

"You look like a million dollars," I said as she stepped through the hatch into the restaurant's foyer.

She grinned that freckle-faced grin of hers and said, "It costs almost that much to look like this."

"It's worth it," I said.

Omar, my buddy from years back, was serving as the maitre d' that afternoon. He was the general manager of the hotel, but everybody was pulling double or triple duty, trying to keep the place afloat. He loomed over us, painfully gaunt and tall as a basketball star, his black pate shaved bald, a dense goatee covering his chin. In the easy lunar gravity Omar could walk normally with nothing more than the lightest of braces on his atrophied legs. Omar had more to lose than I did if the hotel went bust. He'd have to go back to Earth and be a cripple.

As he showed us to our table, all dignity and seriousness, Jill cracked, "You're getting gray, Sam."

"Cosmic rays," I snapped back at her. "Not age. I've been in space so much that primary cosmic rays have discolored my pigmentation."

Jill nodded as if she knew better but didn't want to argue about it. The restaurant was almost completely empty. It was the only place aboard the station to eat, unless you were a Rockledge employee and could use their cafeteria, yet still it was a sea of empty tables. I mean, there wasn't any other place for the tourists to eat—it was lunch hour for those who came up from the States—but the Eclipse had that forlorn look. Three tables occupied, seventeen bare. Twelve human waiters standing around with nothing to do but run up my salary costs.

As Omar sat us at the finest table in the Eclipse (why not?) Jill said, "You ought to get some new clothes, Sam. You're frayed at the cuffs, for goodness' sake."

I refrained from telling her about T.J.'s urinary gift. But I gave her the rest of the story about my thrilling rescue, which nobody had witnessed except the butterfingered Jack Spratt.

"My goodness, Sam, you saved that baby's life," Jill said, positively glowing at me.

"I should've let him go and seen how high he'd bounce when he hit the hatch."

"Sam!"

"In the interest of science," I said.

"Don't be mean."

"He's supposed to be a bouncing baby boy, isn't he?"

She did not laugh.

"Dammit, Jill, they shouldn't have brought a kid up here," I burst. "It's not right. There ought to be a regulation someplace to prevent idiots from bringing their lousy brats to my hotel!"

Jill was not helpful at all. "Sam," she told me, her expression severe, "we made age discrimination illegal half a century ago."

"This isn't age discrimination," I protested. "That baby isn't a voting citizen."

"He's still a human being who has rights. And so do his parents."

I am not a gloomy guy, but it felt like a big rain cloud had settled over my head. Little T.J. was not the only one pissing on me.

But I had work to do. As long as Jill was here, I tried to make the best of it. I started spinning glorious tales of the coming bonanza in space manufacturing, once we could mine raw materials from the Moon or asteroids.

I never mentioned our weightless escapades, but she knew that I held that trump card. Imagine the fuss the media would make if they discovered that the conservative Senator from New Hampshire had once been a wild woman in orbit. With the notorious Sam Gunn, of all people!

"What is it you want, Sam?" Jill asked me. That's one of the things I liked best about her. No bull-hickey. She came straight to the point.

So I did, too. "I'm trying to raise capital for a new venture."

Before I could go any farther, she fixed me with a leery eye. "Another new venture? When are you going to stop dashing around after the pot of gold at the end of the rainbow, Sam?"

I gave her a grin. "When I get my hands on the gold."

"Is that what you're after, money? Is that all that you're interested in?"

"Oh no," I said honestly. "What I'm really interested in is the things money can buy."

She frowned; it was part annoyance, part disappointment, I guess. Easy for her. She was born well-off, married even better, and now was a wealthy widowed United States Senator. Me, I was an orphan at birth, raised by strangers. I've always had to claw and scrabble and kick and bite my way to wherever I had to go. There was nobody around to help me. Only me, all five foot three—excuse me, five foot five inches of me. All by myself. You're damned right money means a lot to me. Most of all, it means respect. Like that old ballplayer said, the home-run hitters drive the Cadillacs. I also noticed, very early in life, that they also get the best-looking women.

"Okay," I backpedaled. "So money can't buy happiness. But neither can poverty. I want to get filthy rich. Is there anything wrong with that?"

Despite her New England upbringing, a faint smile teased at the corners of Jill's mouth. "No, I suppose not," she said softly.

So I went into the details about my hopes for lunar mining and asteroid prospecting. Jill listened quietly; attentively, I thought, until I finished my pitch.

She toyed with her wine glass as she said, "Mining the Moon. Capturing asteroids. All that's a long way off, Sam."

"It's a lot closer than most people realize," I replied, in my best-behaved, serious man of business attitude. Then I added, "It's not as far in the future as our own space shuttle missions are in the past."

Jill sighed, then grinned maliciously. "You always were a little bastard, weren't you?"

I grinned back at her. "What's the accident of my birth got to do with it?"

She put the wine glass down and hunched closer to me. "Just what are you after, Sam, specifically?" I think she was enjoying the challenge of dealing with me.

I answered, "I want to make sure that the big guys like Rockledge and Yamagata don't slit my throat."

"How can I help you do that?"

"You're on the Commerce Committee and the Foreign Relations Committee, right? I need to be able to assure my investors that the Senate won't let my teeny little company be squashed flat by the big guys."

"Your investors? Like who?"

I refused to be rattled by her question. "I'll find investors," I said firmly, "once you level the playing field for me."

Leaning back in her chair, she said slowly, "You want me to use my in-fluence as a United States Senator to warn Rockledge and the others not to muscle you."

I nodded.

Jill thought about it for a few silent moments, then she asked, "And what's in it for me?"

Good old straight-from-the-shoulder Jill. "Why," I said, "you get the sat-isfaction of helping an old friend to succeed in a daring new venture that will bring the United States back to the forefront of space industrialization."

She gave me a look that told me that wasn't the answer she had wanted to hear. But before I could say anything more, she muttered, "That might win six or seven votes in New Hampshire, I guess."

"Sure," I said. "You'll be a big hero with your constituents, helping the little guy against the big, bad corporations."

"Cut the serenade, Sam," she snapped. "You've got something else go-ing on in that twisted little brain of yours; I can tell. What is it?"

She was still grinning as she said it, so I admitted, "Well, there's a ru-mor that Rockledge is developing an antinausea remedy that'll stop space sickness. It could mean a lot for my hotel."

"I hear your zero-gee sex palace is on its way to bankruptcy."

"Not if Rockledge will sell me a cure for the weightless whoopies."

"You think they'd try to keep it from you?"

"Do vultures eat meat?"

She laughed and started in on her plate of soyburger.

After lunch I took Jill down to her mini-suite in the hub and asked how she liked her accommodations.

"Well," she said, drawing the word out, "it's better than the old shuttle mid-deck, I suppose."

"You suppose?" I was shocked. "Each one of Heaven's rooms is a luxu-rious, self-contained mini-suite." I quoted from our publicity brochure.

Jill said nothing until I found her door and opened it for her with a flourish.

"Kind of small, don't you think?" she said.

"Nobody's complained about the size," I replied. Then I showed her the controls that operated the minibar, the built-in sauna, the massage equipment, and the screen that covered the observation port.

"A real love nest," Jill said.

"That's the idea."

I opened the observation port's screen and we saw the Earth hanging out there, huge and blue and sparkling. Then it slid past as the station re-volved and we were looking at diamond-hard stars set against the velvet black of space. It was gorgeous, absolutely breathtaking.

And then we heard somebody vomiting in the next compartment. The hotel's less than one-quarter full and my crackbrained staff books two zero-gee compartments next to one another!

But Jill just laughed. "This hotel isn't going to prosper until somebody comes up with a cure for space sickness."

"That's what Rockledge is doing," I grumbled. "Right aboard this station."

"You're sure?"

"I'm sure."

Jill pursed her lips. Then, "Let me ask D'Argent about that. Unoffi-cially, of course. But maybe I can find out something for you."

My eyes must have widened. "You'd do that for me?"

Jill touched my cheek with cool fingertips. "Of course I would, Sam. You have no idea of the things I'd do for you, if you'd only let me."

That sounded dangerous to me. So I bid her a hasty adieu and pushed through her doorway, heading for my cubbyhole of an office. Jill just gave me a sphinx-like inscrutable smile as I floated out of her compartment.

When I got back to my office there was more depressing news on my computer screen. A contingent of Rockledge board members and junior executives were scheduled for a tour of the station and its facilities. They would be staying for a week and had booked space in my hotel—at the discount prices Rockledge commanded as my landlord. Those prices, ne-gotiated before I had ever opened Heaven, were lower than the rent D'Ar-gent was now charging me. If I filled the hotel with Rockledge people I could go bankrupt even faster than I already was.

And they were all bringing their wives. And children! Larry, Melinda, and their bouncing baby boy were just the first wave of the invasion of the weightless brats. I began to think about suicide. Or murder.

I can't describe the horrors of that week. By actual count there were only twenty-two kids. The oldest was fifteen and the youngest was little T.J., ten months or so. But it seemed like there were hundreds of them, thousands. Everywhere I turned there were brats getting in my way, pok-ing around the observation center, getting themselves stuck in hatches, playing tag along the tubes that connected the station's hub with its vari-ous wheels, yelling, screaming, tumbling, fighting, throwing food around, and just generally making my life miserable.

Not only my life. Even the honeymooners started checking out early, with howls of protest at the invasion of the underage monsters and dire threats about lawsuits.

"You'll pay for ruining our honeymoon," was the kindest farewell statement any of them made.

The brats took over the zero-gee gym. It looked like one of those old martial arts films in there, only in weightlessness. They were swarming all over the padded gym, kicking, thrashing, screaming, arms and legs everyplace, howls and yelps and laughing and crying. One five-year-old girl, in particular, had a shriek that could cleave limestone.

I tried to get the three teenagers among them to serve as guardians—guards, really—for the younger tots. I offered them damned good money to look after the brats. The two girls agreed with no trouble. The one boy—fourteen, sullen, face full of zits—refused. He was the son of one of the board members. "My mother didn't bring me up here to be a babysitter," he growled.

As far as I could see, the only thing the pizza-faced jerk did was hang around the hub weightlessly and sulk.

I couldn't blame the honeymooners for leaving. Who wants to fight your way through a screaming horde of little monsters to get to your zero-gee love nest? It was hopeless. I could see D'Argent smiling that oily smile of his; he knew I was going down in flames and he was enjoying every minute of it.

And right in the middle of it were Larry and Melinda and their bouncing baby boy—who really did bounce around a lot off the padded walls of the gym. T.J. loved it in there, especially with all the other kids to keep him company. The two teenaged girls made him their living doll. And T.J. seemed to look out with his ten-month-old eyes at the whole noisy, noisome gang of kids as if they were his personal play-toys, a swirling, riotous, colorful mobile made up of twenty-two raucous, runny-nosed, rotten kids.

Make that twenty-one kids and one fourteen-year-old moper.

I found that Larry and Melinda started feeding the baby in the gym. "It's easier than doing it in the restaurant or in our own quarters," Melinda said, as T.J. gummed away at some pulpy baby goop. "Practically no mess at all."

I could see what she meant. They just hovered in midair with the baby. Three-fourths of what they aimed at the brat's mouth wound up in his ear or smeared over his face or spit into the air. Being weightless, most of the stuff just broke into droplets or crumbs and drifted along in the air currents until they stuck on one of the intake ventilator screens. At the end of the meal Larry would break out a hand vacuum and clean off the screens while Melinda cleaned the baby with premoistened towels. Not bad, I had to admit. Didn't have to mop the floor or clean any furniture.

The other kids liked to eat in zero-gee, too. Made their food fights more interesting. It was okay with me; anything that kept them out of the restaurant or the other areas where adult human beings lived and worked was a score for our side, far as I was concerned. But zero-gee sex was a thing of the past as long as they held the station's gym in their grubby little paws. My honeymoon hotel had turned into an orbital camp for tots.

"You were right, Sam," Jill told me over dinner the third or fourth night of Hell Week.

The restaurant was almost empty. Nearly every one of Rockledge's junior executives took their meals in their rooms. Too cheap for the restaurant, they used the fast-food dispensers and the cafeteria in the Rockledge research facility.

At least the Eclipse was quiet. No kids. I had thought about trying to make a rule that nobody under twenty-one was allowed into the Lunar Eclipse, but Omar, my long-suffering hotel manager, had convinced me that it would just cause a ruckus with the parents. They were happy as Torquemada in a synagogue to be in the restaurant without their little darlings. But if I said they weren't allowed to bring their kids to the Eclipse they'd get pissed off and *demand* their rights.

So the restaurant was nice and quiet and civilized with all the kids up in the gym dashing around and playing zero-gee games.

"I was right about what?" I asked. I must have looked as miserable as I felt. My mind was echoing with the screeches of all those brats yowling at the top of their lungs and the somber prediction of my accountant that the hotel would sink beneath the financial waves in another two weeks. All day long I had been receiving cancellation notices from travel agencies. The word was going around at the speed of light.

Jill nudged her chair a little closer to mine. "Rockledge really is working on a preventative for space sickness. Pierre D'Argent showed me the laboratory studies they've done so far. It looks as if they've got it."

No sooner had she mentioned D'Argent's name than the silver-haired sonofabitch showed up at the restaurant's door, leading a contingent of six senior Rockledge board members and their trophy wives. The men all looked like grumpy old farts, white-haired or bald; the women were heavy with jewelry. I wondered which one of them owned that fourteen-year-old sourpuss.

"What lovely women," Jill said.

I made no response.

"Don't you think they're beautiful, Sam?"

I grunted. "Who cares."

Jill gave me a funny expression. I didn't realize it at the time, but her expression was a mixture of surprise and admiration. She thought I had finally matured to the point where I didn't salivate like one of Pavlov's dogs every time I saw a good-looking woman. What Jill didn't realize was that I was too down in the dumps to be interested in a bevy of expensively dressed advertisements for cosmetic surgery who were already married. I never chased married women. Never. That's a point of honor with me. It also saves you a lot of threats, fights, lawsuits and attempts on your life.

Jill returned to her original subject. "Didn't you hear me, Sam? Rockledge is going to market a skin patch that prevents space sickness."

"Yeah," I said gloomily. "The day after this hotel closes, that's when they'll put it on the market."

I was watching D'Argent and his troupe as they sat at the biggest table in the restaurant. Laughing softly among themselves, happy, relaxed, their biggest worry was how to evade the taxes that were due on their enormous profits. The more they ate and drank, at their discount prices, the deeper into the red they pushed me.

Jill shook me by my wrist and made me look at her. She had a kind of pixie grin on her face. Almost evil. "Suppose I could get D'Argent to use your hotel customers as a field trial for their new drug?"

"Suppose you could get the Pope to pee off the roof of the Vatican."

"Wouldn't that help you?" she insisted.

I had to admit that it might.

"Then that's what I'll do," Jill said, as firmly as a U.S. Senator announcing she was running for reelection.

I had no romantic interest in Jill, and for the life of me I couldn't figure out why she was interested in me. What did it matter? I was in such a funk over those brats infesting my hotel that I wouldn't have noticed if Helen of Troy had been sitting naked in my bed with her arms out to me. Well, maybe.

What was going through my mind was an endless vicious circle. The hotel is failing. When the hotel goes down the tubes it'll drag my company, VCI, down with it. VCI was technically in the black, making steady

money selling magnetic bumpers that protected space facilities from orbiting debris. But legally, VCI owned Hotel Heaven and the hotel's accu-
mulated debts would force VCI into bankruptcy. I would be broke.
Nobody would lend me a cent. There went my dreams for mining the
Moon and making myself the tycoon of the asteroids. I'd have to find a
job someplace.

Unless—there was only one way I could see out of the black pit that
was staring at me. I had to swallow hard several times before I could work
up the nerve to even put out a feeler. But it was either that or bankruptcy,
the end of all my dreams. So the next morning I gritted my teeth (having
swallowed hard several times) and took the first little step on the road to
humiliation.

"Hi, Larry old pal, how's it going?" The words almost stuck in my
throat, but I had to get started somehow.

Oh, that's right, I haven't told you about Larry and Melinda and the
Gunn Shield. Here's the story.

I had first started VCI, years earlier, to build magnetic bumpers for
space stations, to protect them against the orbiting junk whizzing around
up there. Larry designed them for me. They're called Gunn Shields, of
course. Without them, a space station would get dinged constantly from
the crap zipping around in orbit. Even a chip of paint hits with the impact
of a high-power bullet, and there's a helluva lot more than paint chips flying around in the low orbits.

The Russians finally had to abandon their original Mir space station
because it was starting to look like a target in a shooting gallery. And the
more stations and factories people built in orbit, the more debris they
created and the more they needed Gunn Shields. A nice, steady, growing
market. Not spectacular, not enough to bring in the kind of cash flow I
needed, but dependable.

Back in those days Melinda had a crush on me. Just a kid's crush, that's
all it was, but Larry loved her madly and hated me for it. She was kind of
pretty underneath her avoirdupois, but not my type.

That surprises you? You heard that Sam Gunn chases all types of
women, didn't you. No discrimination at all. Well, that's about as true as
all the rest of the bull manure they spread about me.

Melinda was not my type. But she had this thing about me and Larry
had his heart set on her. So I hired Melinda to come to work for me at
VCI, and then kind of offhand asked Larry if he'd like to come along too.
Larry was the guy I needed, the one I had to have if VCI was going to be a

success. He was the semi-genius who thought up the idea for magnetic bumpers in the first place. Poor fish rose to the bait without even stopping to think. They both moved to Florida and together we put VCI into business.

So while Larry was designing the original bumper, I was touting Melinda off me and onto Larry. Cyrano de Gunn, that's me. Made her fall in love with him. Voila. Once we tested the original bumper and it worked, I got it patented and Larry got Melinda to marry him. Everybody was happy, I thought. Wrong!

For some unfathomable reason, Larry got pissed at me and went off to work for D'Argent, the sneaky sleazoid, over at Rockledge. And when he quit VCI, Melinda did, too.

Oh, yeah, we almost got into a shooting war over the rights to the geocentric orbit. But that's another story. Larry only played a minor role in that one.

Anyway, I had spent a sleepless night tussling over my problems and couldn't see a way out. Except to sell the goddamned hotel to Rockledge. And the rights to the Gunn Shield, too. Dump it all for cash. D'Argent had tried before to sneak the magnetic bumper design away from me. He had tried bribery and even theft. Hell, he had hired Larry with the idea of getting the kid to figure out a way to break my patent. I knew that, even if Larry himself didn't.

So now I toadied up to Larry, in the middle of the mayhem of the station's gym. The kids had taken it over completely. Larry and I were the only adults among the yowling, zooming, screeching, barfing little darlings. Even the two teenaged girls who were supposed to be watching the kids were busy playing free-fall tag and screaming at the top of their considerable voices.

Larry gave me a guarded look. He was feeding T.J., who was happily spraying most of his food into weightless droplets that hovered around him like tiny spheres of multicolored glop before drifting slowly toward the nearest ventilator grid.

"Where's Melinda?" I asked, trying to radiate good cheer and sincerity while dodging the goo that the baby was spewing out.

"She's down in the second wheel, doing aerobics," he said. He spooned a bit of puke-colored paste out of a jar and stuck it in front of T.J.'s face. The baby siphoned it off with a big slurping noise and even managed to get some of it past his two visible teeth and into his mouth.

Gradually, with every ounce of self-control and patient misdirection I could muster, I edged the topic of conversation to the Gunn Shields. All the time we were both dodging flying kids and the various missiles they were throwing at each other, as well as T.J.'s pretty constant spray of food particles. And I had to shout to make myself heard over the noise the brats were making.

I only hoped that none of them figured out the combinations for the electronic locks on the zero-gee mini-suites. I could just see the little SOBs breaking into the minibars and throwing bottles all over the place or scalding themselves in the saunas. Come to think of it, boiling a couple of them might have been fun.

But I had work to do.

The more I talked to Larry about the magnetic shields, though, the more he seemed to drift away from me. I mean, literally move away. He kept floating backward through the big, padded zero-gee compartment and I kept pushing toward him. We slowly crossed the entire gym, with all those kids whooping and zooming around us. Finally I had him pinned against one of the padded walls, T.J. floating upside-down above him and the jar of baby food hovering between us. It was only then that I realized Larry was getting red in the face.

"What's the matter?" I asked, earnestly. "Are you getting sick?"

"Dammit, Sam, they shouldn't be called Gunn Shields!" Larry burst out. "I designed the bumpers, not you! They ought to be called Karsh Shields!"

I was stunned. I had never even thought of that. And he certainly had never mentioned it to me before.

"You mean, all this time you've been sore at me over a public relations title?"

"It means a lot to me," he said, as surly as that teenaged grump.

"Is that why you left me for Rockledge?"

Larry nodded petulantly.

It was my big chance. Maybe my only chance. I let my head droop as if I had suddenly discovered religion and was ashamed of my past life.

"Gee, Larry," I said, just loudly enough to be heard over the screams of the kids, "I never realized how much it meant to you."

"Well, it's my invention but you took out the patent and you took all the credit, too."

I noticed that he had not spoken a word about money. Not a syllable. Larry was pure of heart, bless his unblemished soul.

I looked him in the eye with the most contrite expression I could manage. It was hard to keep from giggling; this was going to be like plucking apples off a blind man's fruit stand.

"If that's the way you feel about it, kid," I said, trying to keep up the hangdog expression, "then we'll change the name. Look—I—I'll even license Rockledge to manufacture and sell the shields. That's right! Let Rockledge take it over completely! Then you can call them Karsh Shields with no trouble at all!"

His eyes goggled. "You'd do that for me, Sam?"

I slid an arm around his shoulder. "Sure I would. I never wanted to hurt you, Larry. If only you had told me sooner . . ." I let my voice fade away. Then I nodded, as if I had been struggling inside myself. "I'll sell Rockledge the hotel, too."

"No!" Larry gasped. "Not your hotel."

"I know D'Argent wants it." That wasn't exactly the truth. But I had a strong suspicion the silver-haired bastard would be happy to take the hotel away from me—as long as he thought it would break my heart to part with it.

Larry's face turned red again, but this time he looked embarrassed, not angry. "Sam . . ." He hesitated, then went on, "Look, Sam, I'm not supposed to tell you this, but the company's been working on a cure for space sickness."

I blinked at him, trying to generate a tear or two. "Really?"

"If it works, it should help to make your hotel a success."

"If it works," I said, with a big sigh.

The way I had it figured, Rockledge would pay a nice royalty for the license to manufacture and sell the magnetic bumpers. Not as much as VCI was making in profits from the shields, but the Rockledge royalties would go to me, personally, as the patent-holder. Not to VCI. The damned hotel's debts wouldn't touch the royalties. VCI would go down the tubes, but what the hell, that's business. I'd be moving on to lunar mining and asteroid hunting. ET Resources, Inc. That's what I would call my new company.

Let Larry call them Karsh Shields, I didn't give a fart's worth about that. Let D'Argent do everything he could to make the world forget I had anything to do with them, as long as he sent me the royalty checks on time. What I really wanted, what I desperately needed, was the money to start moving on ET Resources, Inc.

"Maybe I can talk D'Argent into letting you use their new drug," Larry suggested. "You know, try it out on your hotel customers."

I brightened up a little. "Gee," I said, "that would be nice. If only I could keep my hotel." I sighed again, heavier, heavy enough to nudge me slightly away from Larry and the baby. "It would break my heart to part with Heaven."

Larry gaped at me while T.J. stuck a sticky finger in his father's ear.

"It would make both of us happy," I went on. "I could keep the hotel and Rockledge could take over the magnetic bumpers and call them Karsh Shields."

That really turned him on. "I'll go find D'Argent right now!" Larry said, all enthusiasm. "Would you mind looking after T.J. for a couple of minutes?"

And he was off like a shot before I could say a word, out across the mayhem of all those brats flinging themselves around the gym. Just before he disappeared through the main hatch he yelled back at me, "Oh, yeah, T.J.'s going to need a change. You know how to change a diaper, don't you?"

He ducked through the hatch before I could answer. The kids swarmed all through the place and little T.J. stared after his disappearing father.

I was kind of stunned. I wasn't a babysitter! But there I was, hanging in midair with twenty crazed kids zipping all around me and a ten-month-old baby hanging a couple of feet before my eyes, his chin and cheeks smeared with baby food and this weird expression on his face.

"Well," I said to myself, "what the hell do I do now?"

T.J. broke into a bawling cry. He wanted his father, not this stranger. I didn't know what to do. I tried talking to him, tried holding him, even tried making faces at him. He didn't understand a word I said, of course; when I tried to hold him he squirmed and shrieked so loud even the other kids stopped their games to stare at me accusingly. And when I made a few faces at him he just screamed even louder.

Then I smelled something. His diaper.

One of the teenaged girls gave me a nasty look and said firmly, "I'm going to call his mother!"

"Never mind," I said. "I'll bring the kid to her myself."

I nudged squalling T.J. weightlessly toward the hatch and started the two of us down the connector tube toward the second-level wheel, where the Rockledge gym was. It had been a stroke of genius (mine) to put their exercise facility in the wheel that rotated at about one-third gee, the gravity you'd feel on Mars. You can lift three times the weight you'd be able to handle on Earth and feel like you've accomplished something without straining yourself. But do you think D'Argent or any of his Rockledge minions would give me credit for the idea? When hell freezes over—maybe.

T.J. stopped yowling once I got his flailing little body through the hatch and into the tube. This was a different enough place for his curiosity to override the idea that his father had abandoned him, and whatever discomfort his loaded diaper might be causing him. He was fascinated with the blinking lights on the hatch control panel. I opened and shut the damned hatch half a dozen times, just to quiet him down. Then I showed him the color-coded guide lines on the tube's walls, and the glowing light strips. He pointed and smiled. Kind of a goofy smile, with just two teeth to show. But it was better than crying.

By the time we reached the second wheel we were almost pals. I let him smear his greasy little hands over the hatch control panel; like I said, he liked to watch the lights blink, and there wasn't much damage he could do to the panel except make it sticky. I even held his hand and let him touch the keypads that operated the hatch. He laughed when it started to swing open. After we went through he pointed at the control panel on the other side and made it clear he wanted to play with that one, too.

There was enough of a feeling of gravity down at this level for me to walk on the floor, with T.J. crawling along beside me. I tried to pick him up and carry him, despite his smell, but he was too independent for that. He wanted to be on his own.

Kind of reminded me of me.

Melinda was sweaty and puffing and not an ounce lighter than she had been when she entered the exercise room. T.J. spotted her in the middle of all the straining, groaning women doing their aerobics to the latest top-forty pop tunes. He let out a squeal and all the women stopped their workout to surround the kid with cooing gushing baby talk. Melinda was queen of them all, the mother of the center of their attention. You'd think the brat had produced ice cream.

I beat a hasty retreat, happy to be rid of the kid. Although, I've got to admit, little T.J. was kind of fun to be with. When he wasn't crying. And if you held your breath.

True to his naive word, Larry arranged a meeting between D'Argent and me that very afternoon. I was invited to the section of the station where Rockledge had its lab, up in the lunar wheel, alongside my restaurant.

You might have thought we were trying to penetrate a top-secret military base. Between the Lunar Eclipse and the hatch to the Rockledge Laboratory was a corridor no more than ten meters long. Rockledge had packed six uniformed security guards, an X-ray scanner, three video cameras and a set of chemical sniffers into those ten meters. If we didn't have a regulation against animals they would have probably had a few Dobermans in there, too.

"What're you guys doing in here?" I asked D'Argent, once they had let me through the security screen and ushered me into the compartment he was using as an office. "You've got more security out there than a rock star visiting the Emperor of Japan."

D'Argent never wore coveralls or fatigues like the rest of us. He was in a spiffy silk suit, pearl gray with pencil-thin darker stripes, just like he wore Earthside. He gave me one of his oily little smiles. "We need all that security, Sam," he said, "to keep people like you from stealing our ideas."

I sat at the spindly little chair in front of his desk and gave him a sour look. "The day you have an idea worth stealing, the Moon will turn into green cheese."

He glared at me. Larry, sitting at the side of D'Argent's desk, tried to cool things off. "We're here to discuss a business deal, not exchange insults."

I looked at him with new respect. Larry wasn't a kid anymore. He was starting to turn into a businessman. "Okay," I said. "You're right. I'm here to offer a trade."

D'Argent stroked his pencil-thin mustache with a manicured finger. "A trade?"

Nodding, I said, "I'll license Rockledge to manufacture and market the magnetic bumpers. You let me buy your space sickness cure."

D'Argent reached for the carafe on his desk. Stalling for time, I thought. He poured himself a glass of water, never offering any to Larry or me. In the soft lunar gravity of the inner wheel, the water poured at a gentler angle than it would on Earth. D'Argent managed to get most of the water into his glass; only a few drops messed up his desk.

He pretended not to notice it. "What makes you think we've developed a cure for space sickness?" And he gave Larry a cold eye.

"Senator Meyers told me," I said calmly. D'Argent looked surprised. "Jill and I are old friends. Didn't you know?"

"You and Senator Meyers?" I could read the expression on his face. A new factor had entered his calculations.

We went around and around for hours. D'Argent was playing it crafty. He wanted the magnetic bumper business, that was clear to see. And Larry was positively avid to call them Karsh Shields. I pretended that I wanted the space sickness cure to save my hotel, while all the time I was trying to maneuver D'Argent into buying Heaven and taking it off my hands.

But he was smarter than that. He knew that he didn't have to buy the hotel; it was going to sink of its own weight. In another two weeks I'd be in bankruptcy court.

So he blandly kept insisting, "The space-sickness cure isn't ready for public use, Sam. It's still in the experimental stage."

I could see from the embarrassed red of Larry's face that it was a gigantic lie.

"Well then," I suggested, "let me use it on my hotel customers as a field trial. I'll get them to sign waivers, take you off the hook, legally."

But D'Argent just made helpless fluttering gestures and talked about the Food and Drug Administration, this law, that regulation, scientific studies, legal red tape, and enough bullcrap to cover Iowa six feet deep.

He was stalling, waiting for my hotel to collapse so he could swoop in, grab Heaven away from me, and get the magnetic bumper business at a bargain.

But while he talked in circles, I started to think. What if I could get my hands on his space-sickness cure and try it out on a few of my customers? What if I steal the damned cure right out from under D'Argent's snooty nose and then get a tame chemist or two to reproduce whatever combination of drugs they've got in their cure? That would put me in a better bargaining position, at least. And it would drive the smooth-talking sonofabitch crazy!

So I decided to steal it.

It was no big deal. D'Argent and his Rockledge security types were too Earthbound in their attitudes. They thought that by guarding the corridor access to the laboratory area they had the lab adequately protected. But there were four emergency airlocks strung along that wheel of the station. Two of them opened onto the restaurant; the other two opened directly into the Rockledge research laboratory.

All I had to do was wait until night, get into a space suit, and go EVA to one of those airlocks. I'd be inside the lab within minutes and the guards out in the corridor would never know it.

Then I had a truly wicked idea. A diversion that would guarantee that the Rockledge security troops would be busy doing something else instead of guarding the access to their lab.

The meeting with D'Argent ran out of steam with neither one of us making any real effort to meet the other halfway. Halfway? Hell, neither D'Argent nor I budged an inch. Larry looked miserably unhappy when we finally decided to call it quits. He saw his Karsh Shield immortality sliding away from him.

I went straight from D'Argent's office to the station's gym. Nothing had changed there, except that T.J. was gone. The place still looked like a perpetual-motion demonstration, kids flapping and yelling everywhere. All except that surly teenaged boy.

I glided over to him.

"Hi!" I said brightly.

He mumbled something.

"You don't seem to be having a good time," I said.

"So what?" he said sourly.

I made a shrug. "Seems a shame to be up here and not enjoying it."

"What's to enjoy?" he grumbled. "My mother says I have to stay here with all these brats and not get in anybody's way."

"Gee, that's a shame," I said. "There's a lot of really neat stuff to see. You want a tour of the place?"

For the first time his face brightened slightly. "You mean, like the command center and all?"

"Sure. Why not?"

"They threw me out of there when I tried to look in, a couple days ago."

"Don't worry about it," I assured him. "I'll get you in with no trouble."

Sliding an arm across his skinny shoulders as we headed for the command center, I asked him, "What's your name, anyway, son?"

"Pete," he said.

"Stick with me, Pete, and you'll see stuff that hardly any of the adults ever see."

So I took him on a tour of the station. I spent the whole damned afternoon with Pete, taking him all over the station. I showed him everything from the command center to my private office. While we were in the command center I booted up the station security program and found that Rockledge didn't even have intruder alarms or motion sensors inside their lab area. Breaking in through the airlock was going to be easy.

It would have been nifty if I could've used Pete as an excuse to waltz through the Rockledge lab, just to get a look at the layout, but it was off-limits, of course. Besides, Pete grandly informed me that he had already seen them. "Just a bunch of little compartments with all kinds of weird glass stuff in them," he said.

He wasn't such a bad kid, it turned out. Just neglected by his parents, who had dragged him up here, shown off Daddy's place of work, and then dumped him with the other brats. Like any reasonable youth, he wanted to be an astronaut. When he learned that I had been one, he started to look up to me, at least a little bit. Well, actually he was a teeny bit taller than I, but you know what I mean.

We had a great time in one of the escape pods. I sat Pete at the little control panel and he played astronaut for more than an hour. It only took a teeny bit of persuasion to get him to agree to what I wanted him to do. He even liked the idea. "It'll be like being a real astronaut, won't it?" he enthused.

"Sure it will," I told him.

While he was playing astronaut in the escape pod I ducked out to my office and made two phone calls. I invited Jill to an early dinner at the Eclipse. She accepted right away, asking only why I wanted to eat at five o'clock.

"I'll be babysitting later," I said.

Her face on my display screen looked positively shocked. "Babysitting? You?"

"There are more things in Heaven and Earth, Horatio, than are dreamed of in your philosophy." That was all I could think of to say. And at that, it was probably too much.

Then I tracked down Melinda by phone and invited her and Larry to have dinner, on me, in the Eclipse at eight o'clock.

She was back in the damned exercise room, walking on one of the treadmills. "Dinner?" she puffed. "I'd love to, Sam, but by eight T.J.'s usually in bed for the night."

"Oh, that's all right," I said as casually as I could manage. "I'll take care of him."

"You?" Her eyes went round.

"Sure. We're old pals now. I'll babysit while you and Larry have a decent meal for a change. Why should D'Argent and the old farts on his board of directors be the only ones to enjoy good food?"

"I don't know. . . ." She wavered.

"The best cooking in the solar system," I tempted her. "My chef is *cordon bleu*." Which was almost true. He had worked in Paris one summer. As a busboy.

"I'll have to check with Larry," she said.

"Sure. Do that."

I noticed that she turned up the speed on her treadmill. Like I said, taking apples off a blind man's fruit stand.

So I had a nice, relaxed dinner with Jill early that evening. Then I escorted her back to her mini-suite in the zero-gee section. Some of the kids were still in the gym area, whizzing around and screaming at each other.

"You're not going to get much sleep until they get put away," I said to Jill.

She gave me a crooked grin as she opened the door to her suite. "I wasn't planning to sleep—not yet."

I didn't like the sly look in her eye. "Uh, I promised Larry and Melinda I'd watch their baby. . . ."

"When do you have to be there?" Jill asked, gliding through the doorway and into her zero-gee love nest.

I glided in after her, naturally, and she maneuvered around and shut the door, cutting off the noise of the kids playing outside.

I can recognize a trap when I see one, even when the bait is tempting. "Jill—uh, I've got to go. Now."

"Oh, Sam." She threw her arms around my neck and kissed me passionately. I've got to admit that while I was kissing her back a part of my brain was calculating how much time I had left before I had to show up at Larry and Melinda's door. Which was just on the opposite side of the wailing banshees in the gym.

Reluctantly I disengaged from Jill and said, "I don't have the time. Honest." My voice sounded odd, like some embarrassed acne-faced teenager's squeak.

Jill smiled glumly and said, "A promise is a promise, I suppose."

"Yeah," I answered weakly. And I didn't want to make any promises to a United States Senator that I didn't intend to keep.

So I left Jill there in her suite, looking sad and disappointed, and zipped through the gym area, heading straight for the Karshes' suite.

Larry and Melinda were waiting for me. He was wearing an actual suit, dark blue, and a tie that kept floating loose from his shirt front. Melinda had a dress full of flounces that billowed in zero-gee like a waterfall of lace. Jack Spratt and the Missus. They'd look better in the restaurant's lunar gravity.

Melinda floated me into the bedroom of their suite, where T.J. was zippered into a sleep cocoon. They had stuffed it with pillows because it was way too big for him. The kid was sound asleep with a thumb in his mouth. I've got to admit, he looked like a little angel.

"He won't wake up for at least four hours," she assured me. "We'll be back by then." Still, she gave me the whole orientation demonstration: bottle, milk, diapers, ass wipes, the whole ugly business.

I kept a smile on my face and shooed them out to their dinner. Then I went back into T.J.'s room.

"Okay, kid," I whispered. "It's you and me now."

I fidgeted around their suite for more than an hour, waiting for Larry and Melinda to get through most of their meal, thinking that I might swing back to Jill's suite and—no, no; there lay madness. Finally I went into the baby's room and gently, gently picked up T.J., blankets and all, and headed for the escape pod where I had stashed Pete.

The baby stirred and half woke up when I lifted him, but I shushed and rocked him. He kind of opened one eye, looked at me, and made a little smile. Then he curled himself into my arms and went back to sleep. Like I said, we were old pals by now.

I've got to admit that I felt a slight pang of conscience when I thought about how Larry and especially Melinda would feel when they came back from dinner and found their darling baby missing. I'd be missing, too, of course, and probably at first they'd be more miffed than scared. They'd phone around, trying to find me, figuring I had their kid with me, wherever I was. But after fifteen minutes, half an hour at most, they would panic and call for the security guards.

I grinned to myself at that. While the goons were searching the station I'd be in a space suit, breaking into the Rockledge lab from the outside. The one place nobody would bother looking for me because it was already so heavily guarded. Hah!

Okay, so Larry and Melinda would have a rough hour or two. They'd forget it when I returned their kid to them and they saw he was none the worse for wear. And if Larry wanted to call the bumpers Karsh Shields he owed me some kind of payment, didn't he?

Pete was in the escape pod waiting for me. I had told him only that he could play astronaut in the pod for a couple of hours, as long as he watched the baby. I had some work to do but I'd be back when I was finished. The kid was as happy as an accordion player in a Wisconsin polka bar. Little T.J. was snoozing away, the picture of infant innocence.

"I'll take good care of him, Mr. Gunn," Pete assured me. He had come a long way from the surliness he had shown earlier. He was even grinning at the thought of playing inside the pod for hours.

I'm not a complete idiot, though. I carefully disconnected the pod's controls. Pete could bang on the keyboard and yank at the T-yokes on the control panel till his arms went numb; nothing would happen—except in his imagination. I disconnected the communications link, too, so he wouldn't be able to hear the commotion that was due to come up. Wouldn't be able to call to anybody, either.

"Okay, captain," I said to Pete. "You're in charge until I return."

"Aye, aye, sir!" And he snapped me a lopsided salute. The grin on his face told me that he knew what we were doing was not strictly kosher, and he loved it.

I carefully sealed the pod's hatch, then closed the connecting airlock hatch and sealed it. I hustled down the corridor to the emergency airlock and my personal space suit, which I had stashed there. It was going to be a race to get into a suit and out the airlock before any of the security types poked their noses in this section of the corridor. I had disabled the surveillance cameras earlier in the afternoon and duly reported the system malfunction in the station's log. By the time they got them fixed I'd be long gone.

As if on cue, the intercom loudspeakers in the corridor started blaring, "SAM GUNN, PLEASE REPORT TO SECURITY AT ONCE. SAM GUNN, PLEASE REPORT TO SECURITY AT ONCE."

They had found T.J. was missing and had called security. The panic was on.

You know, the more you hurry the slower things seem to go. Felt like an hour before I had the suit sealed up, the helmet screwed on, and was opening the emergency airlock.

But once I popped outside, I got that rush I always get when I'm back in space, on my own. My suit was old and smelled kind of ripe, but it felt homey inside it. And there was the big curving ball of Earth, huge and blue and sparkling in the sunlight. I just hung there for a minute or so and watched the sunset. It happens fast from orbit, but the array of colors are dazzling.

Now we were in shadow, on the night side. All the better to sneak around in. The controls to my maneuvering pack were on the equipment belt of my suit. I worked them as easily and unconsciously as a pianist playing scales and jetted over to the laboratory airlock on the innermost wheel.

I kept my suit radio tuned to the station's intercom frequency. Plenty of jabbering going on. They were looking for me and T.J. Starting a compartment-to-compartment search. There would be plenty more disgruntled customers before this night was through, but most of them were

Rockledge people staying at my hotel at a ruinous discount, so what the hell did I care?

I got to the lab's emergency airlock with no trouble. The light was dim, and I didn't want to use my helmet lamp. No sense advertising that I was out here. Over my shoulder the lights of nightside cities and highways twinkled and glittered like a connect-the-dots map of North America.

I was just starting to work the airlock's control panel when the station shuddered. At first I thought I had hiccupped or something, but almost immediately I realized that the airlock hatch had shaken, shivered. Which meant that the whole damned station must have vibrated, quivered for some reason.

Which meant trouble. The station was big, massive. It wouldn't rattle unless it had been hit by something dangerous, or somebody had set off an explosion inside it, or—

I spun around and my eyes damn near popped out of my head. An escape pod had just fired off! Somebody had set off the explosive separation bolts and detached it from the station. It was floating away like a slow-motion cannonball.

And I knew exactly which pod it was. Pete must have figured out how to override my disconnect and booted up the pod's mother-loving systems. Now he was riding off into the sunrise, on an orbit of his own, with T.J. aboard. Son of a motherless she-dog!

I jetted after the goddamned pod. I didn't stop to think about it, I just went out after it. Everything else dropped out of my mind. All I could think of was that little T.J. and Pete were in there and they stood a better than even chance of getting themselves killed if somebody didn't get to them before they sailed out beyond reach. And it was all my fault.

If I had been really smart, I would have just reported the loose pod over my suit radio and gone about my business of burglarizing the Rockledge lab. The security people would have fired up another pod to go out and rescue the kids, everybody in the station would be plastered to the view ports or display screens to watch the scene, and I could pilfer away inside the lab without being disturbed.

But I'm not that smart. I went chasing after the damned pod. It was only after I had been barreling toward it for a few minutes that I realized I had damned well better reach it because I didn't have enough juice in my jet pack to get me back to the station again.

Pete must be scared purple, I thought, floating off into his own orbit. He apparently hadn't figured out how to reconnect the radio, because I heard nothing from the pod when I tapped into its assigned frequency. Maybe he was yelling himself hoarse into the microphone, but he was getting no response. Poor kid must have been crapping his pants by now.

Fortunately, he hadn't lit off the pod's main thruster. That would've zoomed him out so far and so fast that I wouldn't have had a prayer of reaching him. He had just fired the explosive disconnect bolts, which blew the pod away from the station. If he fired the main thruster without knowing how to use the pod's maneuvering jets, he'd either blast the damned cannonball down into the atmosphere so steeply that he'd burn up like a meteor, or he'd rocket himself out into a huge looping orbit that would take days or even weeks to complete.

As it was, he was drifting in an independent orbit, getting farther from the station every second. And I was jamming along after him, hard as I could.

I knew I had to save enough of my fuel to slow myself down enough to latch onto the pod. Otherwise I'd go sailing out past them like some idiotic jerk and spend the rest of my numbered hours establishing my own personal orbit in empty space. I wondered if anybody would bother to come out and pick up my body, once they knew what had happened to me.

Okay, I was on-course. The pod was growing bigger, fast, looming in front of me. I turned myself around and gave a long squirt of my maneuvering jet to slow me down. Spun around again and saw the pod coming up to smack me square in the visor. I was still coming on too fast! Christ, was my flying rusty.

I had to jink over sideways a bit, or splatter myself against the pod. As the jets slid me over, I yanked out the tether from my equipment belt and whipped it against the curving hull of the pod as I zoomed by. Its magnetized head slid along the hull until it caught on a handhold. The tether stretched a bit, like a bungee cord, and then held.

As I pulled myself hand over hand to the pod, I glanced back at the station. It was so far away now it looked like a kid's toy hanging against the stars.

Grunting, puffing, totally out of shape for this kind of exercise, I finally got to the pod's airlock and lifted open its outer hatch. I was pouring sweat from every square inch of my skin. Got the hatch shut again, activated the pump, and as soon as the telltale light turned green I popped the inner hatch with one hand and slid my visor up with the other.

There sat Pete at the controls, ecstatic as a Hungarian picking pockets. And little T.J. was snoozing happily in the arms of Senator Jill Meyers.

"Hello, Sam," she said sweetly to me. "What kept you?"

It was then that I realized I had been nothing but the tool of a superior brain.

Jill had reconnected the pod's systems and blown the explosive bolts. She had known exactly what I was doing because she had stuck a microminiaturized video homing beacon on the back of my shirt when she had clutched me so passionately there in the doorway of her suite.

"It's standard equipment for a U.S. Senator," she quipped, once she had plucked it off my shirt.

For once in my life I was absolutely speechless.

"When you told me you were babysitting—*voluntarily*—I started to smell a rodent," Jill said as she almost absently showed Pete how to maneuver the pod back to the station. "I knew you were up to something," she said to me.

I just hung there in midair, all my hopes and plans in a shambles.

"I've got to be invisible now," Jill said as we neared the station. She glided over to the equipment locker built into the pod's curving bulkhead and slid its hatch open. "It'll be a snug fit," she said, eying it closely. "Glad I didn't have dessert tonight."

"Wait a minute!" I burst. "What's going on? How did you—I mean, why—what's going on?" I felt like a chimpanzee thrown into a chess tournament.

As she squeezed herself into the equipment locker, Jill said, "It's simple, Sam. You were walking with the baby when Pete here accidentally set off the pod."

Pete turned in his pilot's chair and grinned at me.

"And then you got into your suit, with little T.J., and rescued Pierre D'Argent's only son. You're going to be a hero."

"Pete is D'Argent's son?" I must have hit high C.

"In return for your bravery in this thrilling rescue, D'Argent will let you have the space-sickness cure. So everything works out fine."

Like I said, I was just the tool of a superior brain.

"Now," said Jill, "you'd better help Pete to make rendezvous with the station and re-berth this pod." And with that she blew me a kiss, then slid the hatch of the equipment locker shut.

It didn't work out exactly as Jill had it figured. I mean, D'Argent was furious, at first, that I'd let his kid into one of the pods and then left him alone. But his wife was enormously grateful, and Pete played his role to a T. He lied with a straight face to his own father and everybody else. I figured that one day, when D'Argent realized how his son had bamboozled him, he'd be truly proud of the lad. Probably send him to law school.

In the meantime, D'Argent did indeed let me have the space-sickness cure. Grudgingly. "Only for a limited period of testing," he growled. Mrs. D'Argent had prodded him into it, in return for my heroic rescue of their only son. She got a considerable amount of help from Jill—who sneaked off the pod after all the commotion had died down.

Larry and Melinda didn't know whether they should be sore at me or not. They had been scared stiff when T.J. turned up missing, and then enormously relieved when I handed them their little bundle of joy, safe and sound, gurgling happily. I knew Larry had forgiven me when he reminded me, almost sheepishly, about changing the name of the magnetic bumpers to Karsh Shields.

So we all got what we wanted. Or part of it, at least.

The space-sickness cure helped Heaven a lot. The hotel staggered into the black, not because honeymooners took a sudden fancy to it, but because the word started to spread that it was an ideal spot for children! It still cost more than your average luxury vacation, but wealthy families started coming up to Heaven. My zero-gee sex palace eventually became a weightless nursery. And—many years later—a retirement home. But that's another story.

I licensed the *Karsh* Shields to Rockledge. A promise is a promise, and the money was good because Rockledge had the manufacturing capacity to make three times as many of the shields as I could. And, once the hotel started showing a profit, I let D'Argent buy it from me. He's the one who turned it into a nursery. I was long gone by then.

With Jill's help I raised enough capital to start a shoestring operation in lunar mining. It was touch-and-go for a while, but the boom in space manufacturing that I had prophesied actually did come about and I got filthy rich.

Of course, I more or less had to marry Jill. I owed her that, she had been so helpful. Why she wanted to marry me was a mystery to me, but she was damned determined to do it.

Of course, I was just as damned determined not to get married. So I—but that's another story.

Selene City

JIM GRADOWSKY GUFFAWED AND LEANED BACK IN HIS swivel chair so far that Jade feared he would topple over.

"That's terrific, kid! Great story." Wiping his eyes, he smiled at Jade as he asked, "What's next?"

Jade had dreaded this moment. "I don't really know," she replied. "I've run out of people to interview."

Gradowsky's happy face turned to gloom. "Come on, Jade, there must be half a zillion people who've known Sam over all those years."

"They're all back on Earth," she said, her voice low.

"Oh. And you can't go to Earth, is that it?"

"That's it, Jim."

He took in a deep breath and reached into his desk drawer for a cookie. "You'll have to do it by videophone, then."

Nodding, grateful that her boss understood, she said, "There's this one woman I've got a lead on, in Ecuador. She's the daughter of their former president and the wife of their current president."

"Go get her!"

"It won't be easy," Jade said. "She says she's busy with their space tower project and—"

Gradowsky puffed out an exasperated sigh. "Jade, honey, if it was easy *anybody* could do it. You get to her. One way or another."

Jade nodded. "I'll try."

"We all try, kid. You've got to succeed."

Statement of Juanita Carlotta Maria Rivera y Queveda

(Recorded at Mt. Esperanza, Ecuador)

"I HAVE NO TIME TO SPEAK TO YOU ABOUT SAM GUNN. THAT phase of my life ended long ago. Believe me, directing the construction of the first space elevator on the Earth keeps me quite busy, thank you."

Even in the small screen in Jade's office the space elevator was impressive: a massive tower that rose from the mountaintop and disappeared into the clouds high above.

Juanita Rivera y Queveda looked impressive, too. Her face was round, the skin golden brown, her hair thick and midnight dark. Jade couldn't see much of her outfit, but it seemed to be more like a general's braid-heavy uniform than the simple coveralls of an engineer.

"Look at it!" she said, gesturing toward the elevator off in the hazy distance. "Even in its half-finished condition, is it not magnificent? A tower to the heavens, an elevator that rises from this mountaintop all the way up to the geosynchronous orbit, nearly forty thousand kilometers high! Ah, these are wonderful times to be alive."

Jade started to ask a question, then realized it would take nearly three seconds before the woman's answer could cover the round-trip distance between Earth and the Moon.

"As you undoubtedly know," the Ecuadorian went on, "my husband is the former president of Ecuador, as was my father. But I have never been involved in politics, except for that brief time when Sam Gunn intruded into my life. In fact the first time I heard of the idea of a space elevator, it was Sam who told me about it. He called it a 'skyhook.' I thought it was foolishness then, but now I know better.

"What can I tell you that you do not already know? Sam was a whirlwind, a force of nature. He was constantly in motion, always tumbling and jumbling everything and everyone around him. It was like living in a perpetual hurricane, being near Sam.

"I understand that he died out in deep space somewhere. Too bad. I am not interested in him, whether he is dead or alive. My interest is in this space elevator, which you in the media call the Skyhook Project. When it is finished, people will be able to ride from our site in my native Ecuador all the way up to the geostationary orbit for pennies! Merely the price of electricity to operate the elevator, plus a modest profit for our company.

"Yes, it is costing billions to build the elevator, but we have had no trouble in finding investors.

"Of course, if Sam were here among us he would be one of our biggest investors, certainly. But what chaos he would cause! We are much better off without him.

"Oh, I suppose I really do hope he is not dead. I miss him, to tell the truth. But I'm glad he is not here! This project is too important to have him involved in it."

The woman stopped speaking. Her eyes seemed to focus dreamily on something in the past.

Jade took the opportunity. "Couldn't you tell me just a little about Sam? Your impression of him? How he affected your life?"

Juanita Rivera y Queverda smiled, a little sadly, Jade thought.

"Very well," she said softly. "I will take a brief break and have a *café con leche* while I will speak of the time I worked for Sam Gunn. And the revolution. But only one cup! Then I must get back to my work."

Sam's War

I KNOW IT IS INCREDIBLE TO BELIEVE THAT SAM GUNN, OF all people, saved civilization-as-we-know-it. But the chauvinistic little gringo did. Although he never got the credit for it.

Yet he was lucky, at that. After all, I was supposed to murder him.

Not that I am a professional assassin, you understand. The daughter of *El Presidente* is no common thug. I followed a higher calling: national honor, patriotism, love of my people and my father. Especially, love of my father.

Ecuador was, and still is, a democracy. My beloved father was, but sadly is no longer, its *Presidente*. Above all else, you must realize that Ecuador was, and always had been, among the poorest nations of the Earth.

Ah, but we owned something of inestimable value. Or at least, we owned a part of it. Or at the very least, we claimed ownership of a part of it.

The Equator. It runs across our noble country. Our nation's very name is equatorial. An imaginary line, you say. Not entirely imaginary. For above the Equator, some thirty-five thousand kilometers above it, lies the only region of space where satellites may be placed in stationary orbits. The space people call it the *geostationary orbit*, or GEO.

A satellite in GEO rotates around the Earth in precisely the same twenty-three hours, fifty-six minutes and few odd seconds that the Earth itself takes to turn one revolution. Thus a satellite in GEO will appear to hover over one spot above the Equator. Communications satellites are placed in GEO so that antennas on the ground can lock onto them easily. They do not wander around the sky, as satellites at lower or higher altitudes do.

It was my father's genius to understand the value of the Equator. It was also his sad destiny to have Sam Gunn as his nemesis.

"The gringos and the Europeans get rich with their satellites," my father told the other eleven delegations to the meeting.

"And the Japanese, too," said the representative from Zaire.

"Exactly so."

As host to this meeting of the Twelve Equatorial Nations, my father stood at the head of the long polished conference table and gave the opening speech. He was a majestic figure in the captain-general's uniform of sky-blue that he had chosen to wear. With the lifts in his gleaming boots he looked almost tall. The uniform tunic's shoulders were broad and sturdy, the medals gleaming on its breast looked impressive even though they were decorations he had awarded himself. He had long been darkening his hair, but now it was thinning noticeably. He had brought in specialists from North America, from Europe and even China; there was nothing they could do except recommend an operation to replace his disappearing hair. My father was brave in many ways, but the thought of personal pain made him hesitate.

So he stood before the other delegates with a receding hairline. I thought his high forehead made him look more handsome, more intellectual. Yet he longed for the full leonine mane of his younger days.

My father had spent the better part of two years working, pleading, cajoling to bring these Twelve together. They had come reluctantly, grudgingly, I thought. But they had come. There was much to gain if we could capture the geostationary orbit for ourselves.

I served my father as his personal secretary, so I sat against the wall to one side of his imposing figure, together with the other secretaries and aides and bodyguards. The delegates were of all hues and sizes: the massive Ugandan so dark his skin seemed almost to shine; the Brazilian dapper and dainty in his white silk suit; the silver-haired representative from Kiribati dressed in the colorful robes of his Pacific atolls. One could say that these Twelve truly represented the entire human race in all its variety, except for the fact that they were all male. I was the only woman present. Not even one of the other aides was a woman.

Although Ecuador was a poor nation, my father had spared no expense for this conference. The table was sumptuously set with decanters of wine and stronger spirits, trays of Caspian caviar and Argentine beef. The people may be poor, my father often said, but the *Presidente* must rise above their shortcomings. After all, what are taxes for? The miserable revolutionaries in the mountains vowed to put an end to my father's displays of wealth, and the sour-faced journalists in the cities coined slogans against him, but the people accepted their *Presidente* as they always have accepted the forces of nature over which they have no control.

My father thundered on, his powerful voice making the wines vibrate in their crystal decanters. "The corporations of the northern hemisphere use *our* territory and give us nothing for it. Imperialism! That's what it is, nothing but naked imperialism!"

The representatives applauded his words. They were stirred, I could see. They all agreed with my father, each and every one of them. The rich and powerful corporations had taken something that we wanted for ourselves.

But the Indonesian, slim and dark, with the big soulful eyes of a frightened child, waited until the applause ended and then asked softly, "But what can we do about it? We have tried appeals to the United Nations and they have done nothing for us."

"We have a legal right to the equatorial orbit," insisted the Kenyan, preaching to the choir. "Our territorial rights are being violated."

The Brazilian shook his head. "Territorial rights end at the edge of the atmosphere." The Brazilians had their own space operations running, although they claimed they were not making any profits from it. Rumor had it that key members of their government were siphoning the money into their own pockets.

"They most certainly do not!" my father snapped. "Territorial rights extend to infinity."

Two-thirds of the men around the table were lawyers and they immediately fell to arguing. I knew the legal situation as well as any of them. Historically, a nation's territorial rights extended from its boundaries out to infinity. But such legal rights became a shambles once satellites began orbiting the Earth.

The Russians started it all back in 1957 with their original Sputnik, which sailed over virtually every nation on Earth without obtaining prior permission from any of them. No one could shoot down that first satellite, so it established the de facto precedent. But now things were different; antisatellite weapons existed. True, the big nations refused to sell them to their smaller neighbors. But such weapons were built by corporations, and there were ways to get what one wanted from the corporations—for money.

My father's strong voice cut through the babble of argument. "To hell with the legalities!"

That stunned them all into silence.

"When a nation's vital interests are being usurped by foreigners, when a nation's legal rights are being trampled under the heels of imperialists, when a nation's wealth is being stolen from its people and their chosen leaders— then that nation must fight back with any and every means at its disposal."

The Indonesian paled. "You are speaking of war."

"Exactly so!"

"War?" echoed the Ugandan, dropping the finger sandwich he had been nibbling.

"We have no other course," my father insisted.

"But . . . war?" squeaked the slim and timid representative from the Maldives. "Against the United States? Europe? Japan?"

My father smiled grimly. "No. Not against any nation. We must make war against the corporations that are operating in space."

The Brazilian ran a fingertip across his pencil-thin moustache. "It should be possible to destroy a few satellites with ASATs." He was showing that he knew not only the political and military situation, but the technical jargon as well.

"Fire off a single antisatellite weapon and the U.N. Peacekeepers will swoop down on you like avenging angels," warned the delegate from Gabon.

"The same U.N. that refuses to consider our request for justice," my father grumbled.

The Colombian representative smiled knowingly. "There are many ways to make war," he said. "Space facilities are extremely fragile. A few well-placed bombs, they can be very small, actually. A few very public assassinations. It can all be blamed on the Muslims or the ecologists."

"Or the feminists," snapped the Indonesian, himself a Muslim and a devoted ecologist. Everyone else in the room laughed.

"Exactly so," said my father. "We pick one corporation and bend it to our will. Then the others will follow."

Thus we went to war against Sam Gunn.

My father was no fool. Making war—even the limited kind of terrorist's war—against one of the giant multinational corporations would have been dangerous, even suicidal. After all, a corporation such as Rockledge International had an operating budget larger than the Gross National Product of most of the Twelve Nations. Their corporate security forces outgunned most of our armies.

But Sam Gunn's corporation, VCI, was small and vulnerable. It looked like a good place to start.

So our meeting ended with unanimous agreement. The Twelve Equatorial Nations issued the Declaration of Quito, proclaiming that the space over the Equator was our sovereign territory, and we intended to defend it against foreign invaders just as we would defend the sacred soil of our homelands.

The Declaration was received with nearly hysterical fervor all through Latin America. In Ecuador, even the revolutionaries and the news media reluctantly praised my father for his boldness. North of the Rio Grande, however, it was ignored by the media, the government, and the people. Europe and Japan received it with similar iciness.

My far-seeing father had expected nothing more. A week after the meeting of the Twelve he told me over dinner, "The gringos choose to ignore us. Like ostriches, they believe that if they pay us no attention we will go away."

"What will be your next move, Papa?" I asked.

He smiled a fatherly smile at me. "Not my move, Juanita, my beautiful one. The next move will be yours."

I was stunned. Flattered. And a bit frightened.

My father had chosen me for the crucial task of infiltrating VCI. I had been educated at UCLA and held a degree in computer programming, despite my father's grumbling that a daughter should study more feminine subjects, such as nutrition (by which he meant cooking). I also had a burning fervor to help my people. Now I received a rapid course in espionage and sabotage from no less than the director of our secret police himself.

"You must be very careful," my father told me, once my training was concluded.

"I will be, Papa," I said. I had joined him for breakfast on the veranda of the summer palace, up in the foothills where the air was clean and deliciously cool.

He looked deep into my eyes, and his own eyes misted over. "To send my only child to war is not an easy thing, you know." He was being slightly inaccurate. I was his only legitimate child, and it was obvious that he had been planning to use me this way for some time.

"Yet," he went on, "I must think and act as *El Presidente,* rather than as a loving father."

"I understand, Papa."

"You will be a heroine for your people. A new Mata Hari."

The original Mata Hari had been a slut and so poor at espionage that she was caught and executed. I realized that my father did not know that. He was a politician, not a student of history.

Turning his head to look out over the balcony to the terraced hillsides where the peons were hard at work on the coca fields, he murmured, "There is much money to be made in space."

There was much money being made from the coca, I knew. But since the cocaine trade was still illegal the money that came from it could not be put into the national treasury. My father had to keep it for himself and his family, despite his heartfelt desire to help the destitute peons who were forced to labor from sunrise to sunset.

The rebels in the hills claimed that my father was corrupt. They were radical ecologists, I was told, who wanted to stop the lumbering and mining and coca cultivation that provided our poor nation's pitiful income. My father saw our seizure of the equatorial orbit as a means of making more money for our country, money that he desperately needed to buy off the rebels—and the next election.

He dabbed at his eyes with his damask napkin, then rose from the breakfast table. I got up too. The servants began clearing the dishes away as we walked side by side from the veranda into the big old house, heading for the door and the limousine waiting for me.

"Be a good soldier, my child," he said to me once we had reached the front door. The butler was waiting there with my packed travel bag. "Be brave. Be fearless."

"I will do my best, Papa."

"I know you will." He gripped me in a full embrace, unashamed of the tears that streamed from his eyes or the fact that he was so much shorter than I that I had to bend almost double to allow him to kiss my cheeks.

My own eyes were misty, as well. Finally he let go of me and I went quickly down the steps to the waiting limousine. While the butler put my bag into the trunk, I turned back to my father, came to attention, and snapped a military salute to him. He returned my salute, then turned away, unable to watch me step into the limo and start the long ride to the airport.

Thus I went to war.

I HAD BEEN surprised, at first, that Sam Gunn's company had hired me on nothing more than the strength of the faked university credentials of the fictitious person that my father's secret police had created for me. Of course, I knew enough computer programming to pass—I hoped. And of even more course, it would never do for the VCI people to know that I was the daughter of the man who had issued the Declaration of Quito. Even if they ignored our Declaration, I reasoned, they could not possibly be ignorant of it.

VCI was a surprisingly small operation. I reported to their headquarters in Orlando, a modest office building quite near the vast Disney World complex. There were only a couple of dozen employees there, including the company's president, a lanky silver-haired former astronaut named Spencer Johansen.

"Call me Spence," he said when I met him, my first day at VCI. I had just sat down at my own desk in my own office—actually nothing more than a cubbyhole formed by movable plastic partitions that were only shoulder high.

Johansen strolled in, smiling affably, and sat casually on the corner of my bare desk. He offered his hand and I took it in a firm grip.

You must understand that, by any reasonable standard, I was quite an attractive young lady. My hair is the honey blonde of my Castilian ancestry. My figure is generous. I have been told that my eyes are as deep and sparkling as a starry midnight sky. (The young lieutenant who told me that was quickly transferred to a remote post high in the Andes to fight the rebels.) I am rather tall for a woman in my country, although many North American women are as tall as I, and even taller. Nonetheless, I was not that much shorter than Spence, whom I judged to be at least one hundred and ninety centimeters in height.

"Welcome aboard," he said. His smile was dazzling.

"Thank you," I answered in English. "I am happy to be here." I had worked hard to perfect the Los Angelino accent that my fictitious persona called for.

His eyes were as blue as a Scandinavian summer sky. Despite his smile, however, I got the impression that he was probing me, searching for my true motives.

"We had planned to start you off on some of the more routine stuff, but we've got a bit of an emergency cooking and we're kinda shorthanded—as usual."

Before I could reply he went on, "Can you handle a VR-17 simulator? Reprogram it?"

I nodded cautiously, wondering if this was a true emergency or some kind of a test.

"Okay," Spence said. "Come on down to the simulations center." He headed for the opening in the partitions that was the doorway to my cubicle. There was no door to it.

I followed him, stride for stride, as he hurried along the corridor. He was wearing a soft blue open-necked, short-sleeved shirt and denim jeans. I wore a simple modest blouse of salmon pink and comfortable russet slacks. He glanced at me and grinned. "You play tennis?"

"A little." I had won every tournament I had ever entered; the daughter of *El Presidente* had to win, but I thought it would be best to be modest with him.

"Thought so."

"Oh?"

"You're not puffing," he said. "Not many of these desk-jockeys can keep up with me."

"I am curious," I said as we entered the simulations center. It was nothing more than a large windowless room, empty except for the big mainframe computer standing in its center and the desks with terminals atop them set up in a ring around the mainframe. The four corners of the room were bare but for a single cheap plastic chair in each corner.

A man was sitting in one of those chairs, with a virtual realty helmet covering his face and data gloves on both his hands, which twitched in the empty air, manipulating controls that existed only in the VR programming.

"Curious about what?" Spence asked as he showed me to one of the computer terminals.

I slid into the little wheeled chair. "You are the president of this company, right?"

"Yep."

"But I had the impression that the company belonged to someone named Sam Gunn."

Before Spence could answer, the man in the VR helmet began swearing horribly at the top of his voice. He called down the wrath of God on everyone connected with the machinery he was supposed to be operating, on the person or persons who had programmed the VR simulation, on Isaac Newton and Albert Einstein and all the mathematicians in the world. All the while his hands gesticulated wildly, as if he were desperately trying to ward off a host of devils.

Strangely, Spence grinned at the interruption. Then he turned back to me and said, loud enough to be heard over the continuing tirade of abuse, "I'm the president of VCI, but Sam Gunn is the founder and owns more stock than anybody else. He doesn't like to sell shares to anyone who isn't an employee."

"I can become a stockholder?"

"We have a very generous stock option plan," Spence replied, almost yelling to be heard over the continuing screaming. "Didn't you watch your employee orientation video?"

In truth, I had not. It had never occurred to me that employees might become partial owners of the company. A very clever gringo, this Sam Gunn. He undoubtedly keeps the majority of shares in his own hands and doles out a pittance to his employees, thereby gaining their loyalty.

As if he could read my thoughts, Spence said, "Sam's a minority stockholder now. My wife and I own more shares than anybody else except Sam, but no individual owns more than a few percent."

Wife? Spence was married. For some reason I felt a pang of disappointment.

"Sam Gunn must be an unusual man," I said, loud enough to be heard over the rantings from the corner of the room. But the instant I started to speak, the ravings stopped, and my voice shrilled stupidly. I felt my face flame red. Spence's grin widened but he said nothing.

"I would like to meet him some day," I said, more softly, as I turned to the computer terminal.

"You can meet him right now," said Spence. "That's him in the VR rig."

My mouth must have dropped open. I spun the little chair around to see Spence looking off toward the corner. The man there was pulling off his VR helmet, still muttering obscenities.

I stared at Sam Gunn as he got up from the chair and tugged the data gloves off. He was short, much shorter than I. His torso was stocky, solid, although I could see that his belly bulged the faded blue coveralls he wore. His face was round, with a little snub of a nose and a sprinkling of freckles. Hair the color of rusted wire, cut very short, and sprinkled with gray—which he insisted (I soon learned) was due to exposure to cosmic radiation in space, not from age. From this distance, halfway across the room, I could not tell the color of his eyes. But I could easily see that he was angry, blazing furious, in fact.

"Goddammit, Spence," he said, stamping toward us, "if we don't get this simulation fixed and fixed damned soon somebody's gonna lose his ass out there."

Spence put a fatherly hand on my shoulder. "Here's the gal who's going to fix it. Just started with us this morning." My shoulder tingled from his touch.

Sam gave me a stern look. "This kid?"

"Juanita O'Rourke," Spence introduced me. It was my alias, of course.

Sam stared at me. He was about the same height standing as I was sitting. I saw that his eyes were a bluish-green hazel color, flecked with golden highlights.

"From Los Angeles," Spence added. "Computer programming degree from—"

"I don't care where you're from or where you went to school," said Sam Gunn. "I love you."

I had heard that he was a womanizer of the worst sort. Some of his escapades had been included in the dossier my father's secret police had given me to study. The dossier hinted at much more. Strangely, my father never mentioned the danger that Sam Gunn might pose to me. Perhaps he did not know of it. After all, his attention was focused on affairs of state, not affairs of the bedroom.

I got to my feet and put on a modest smile. Partly it was because I towered nearly thirty centimeters over Sam Gunn. The feeling gave me joy.

"You give your heart quickly," I said, adding to myself silently, And very often.

His round, freckled face turned into an elf's delighted countenance. "Will you have dinner with me tonight?"

I hesitated just long enough to let him think I seriously considered his invitation. "Not tonight," I said. "I just arrived here and there's so much to do. . . ."

Spence cleared his throat and said, "You want this simulation checked out, don't you?"

All Sam's anger and frustration had disappeared as quickly as a dry leaf is blown away by a gust of wind. "Okay, Esmeralda—"

"Juanita," I corrected.

Sam shook his head. "To me you're Esmeralda, the beautiful gypsy girl that Quasimodo loves."

"I am not a gypsy."

"But you're beautiful," he said.

"And you will be Quasimodo?"

Sam dropped into a crouch and twisted his head up at a bizarre angle. "I'll be whoever you want me to be, Esmeralda."

He made me laugh.

"The simulation," Spence reminded him.

"Oh. Yeah. That."

Fortunately, the problem was simple enough for me to solve, although it took several days' intense work. VCI's major business was removing old commsats that had ceased to function from the geosynchronous orbit so that new commsats could be placed there. There were only a finite number of slots available in GEO, and they were strictly allocated by the International Telecommunications Authority. VCI crews flew from space stations in low Earth orbit (LEO) to GEO and removed the dead commsats to make room for new ones.

It was a small part of the satellite communications industry, but a key factor. VCI also had contracts to sweep debris out of the lower orbits where the space stations flew. I learned that the company's name originally stood for Vacuum Cleaners, Incorporated. Sam's company cleaned up the vacuum of orbital space.

More recently, Sam had begun sending people up to GEO to repair malfunctioning commsats. It was cheaper to fix them than to replace them—in theory, at least. In practice, the costs of sending astronauts to GEO even for a few hours was almost as much as replacing a malfunctioning satellite.

The virtual reality simulation that Sam was frustrated over was one in which an operator could remain aboard the space station in LEO and remotely direct an unmanned spacecraft to repair a malfunctioning satellite in GEO.

"Bring the dead back to life," as Sam put it.

"It would be much safer for our people if they could stay in the space station rather than fly up to GEO," Spence explained to me. "GEO's in the middle of the outer Van Allen Belt. Astronauts can't stay there very long because of the radiation."

"I see," I said.

"We could save a bundle of money if we could do this job remotely," said Sam eagerly. "Just the drop in our insurance costs could pay for the whole program."

Spence added, "In the long run we could operate right here from the ground. No need to send people to one of the space stations, even."

"That'd save even more money," Sam agreed happily.

"But the simulation keeps glitching," said Spence.

"And until we get it right in the simulator we can't try it in the real world."

Thus the burden of their hopes was placed on my young shoulders. I thought it strange that something so vital would be entrusted to a totally new and untried employee. Was this a trap of some sort? Or a test? Soon enough I learned that it was typical of the way Sam Gunn ran his company. He kept his staff as small as he possibly could, hiring only when there was no other way to get a necessary job done. And make no mistake about it, Sam

Gunn ran VCI. Despite his lofty title, Spence took orders from Sam. Most of the time.

The problem with the simulation was not terribly difficult. If Sam had not been so impatient his own staff personnel or a consultant would eventually have found it. But what Sam wanted was instant results, which meant that I spent virtually twenty-four hours a day working on the problem. Except for the hour or so each day I spent fending off Sam's invitations to dinner, to lunch, to a suite in the zero-gravity honeymoon hotel he wanted to build in orbit.

Within a few days I had the program running so smoothly that Sam was willing to try a test in orbit. And I realized that I could sabotage his operation quite easily. In fact, I planted a bug in the program that I could activate whenever I chose to.

I discussed my accomplishment with my father on the direct phone link from our consulate in Orlando. I drove to the consulate in the dark of night, well past midnight, to make certain that no one from VCI would see me.

I had feared that I would wake my father from his justly-earned sleep. As it turned out, he was in bed, but not asleep. At first he did not activate the phone's video, which puzzled me. When he finally did, I realized that he was not alone in his bed. He tried to hide her, but I could see that a tousle-haired young trollop lay beside him, bundled under the sheets. She peeked out from behind my father's back, showing a bare shoulder, a pair of flashing dark eyes, and piles of raven black hair.

My father was delighted with the progress I had made in little more than a week.

"I can sabotage their mission to repair satellites," I reported to him, trying to ignore his companion. She could not have been much older than I. "And they will never even know that sabotage has occurred."

"Good!" He beamed at me. "Excellent! But do not attack them just yet. Let them run a successful mission or two. Wait until the strategic moment to strike."

"I understand, Papa."

"You are doing well, my child."

I looked past him to the young woman sharing his bed. My mother had been dead for many years and my father was still a man of vigor. Yet I felt angry. I did not tell him that Sam Gunn was attracted to me.

"And you are well, Papa?" My question sounded acidly cynical to my own ears.

Yet my beloved father obviously did not feel my anger. "I am in good health," he reported smilingly. "Although the rebels have surrounded the army base at Zamora."

"What?" I felt a double pang of alarm. The lieutenant who had been infatuated with me was at the Zamora base.

"Not to worry, my daughter. We are reinforcing the base by helicopter and will soon drive the scum back to their caves in the mountains."

Yet I did worry. The rebels seemed to get bolder, stronger, each year. I went back to work, angry with my father yet frightened for him. We needed to wrest control of the equatorial orbit from the gringo corporations, quickly. I began to look for more ways to sabotage VCI. I even let Sam take me out to dinner several times, although each evening ended at the front door of my apartment building with nothing more romantic than a handshake. Sam was not exactly a perfect gentleman: he was a persistent as a goat in mating season. I fended him off, however. My arms were longer than his.

"Esmeralda," he complained one evening, "you're turning my love life into the petrified forest."

We were at the entrance to my apartment building. I thought of it as my castle, its walls and electronic door locks my defense against Sam's assaults.

"I agreed to have dinner with you," I said, "nothing more."

He sighed heavily. "I guess I'm paying you too much."

"Paying me . . ."

With an almost wicked grin he said, "If you were broke and hungry you'd appreciate me more, I betcha."

"What an evil thing to say!"

"Well, look at this apartment building," he went on. "It's a frigging luxury palace! I'm just paying you too much money. You're living too well—"

I had to cut off his line of thought before he realized that my salary could never pay the rent on my apartment. Before he began to ask himself how a poor computer programmer from Los Angeles could afford the clothes and the sports car I had.

"So you want women to be starving and poor," I snapped at him. "Or perhaps you prefer them barefoot and pregnant?"

He shrugged good-naturedly. "Barefoot is okay."

I did not have to pretend to be angry. I could feel the blood heating my cheeks. "Sam, the days of male domination over women were finished long ago," I told him. "Don't you understand that?"

"I'm not interested in domination. All I want is a little cooperation."

"You are a hopeless chauvinist, Sam."

He broke into an impish grin. "Not quite hopeless, Esmeralda. I still have some hope."

It was impossible to dislike Sam, even though I tried. But at least I stopped him from asking himself how I could afford my lifestyle on the salary he was paying me.

Yet it was Spence that I felt drawn to. He was quietly competent, always even-tempered, extremely capable. I knew he was married, but somehow I felt that his marriage was not all that happy for him. Perhaps it was because I wanted to believe so. Perhaps it was because he was a kind, fatherly, caring, truly gentle man.

And then I met Spence's wife. Her name was Bonnie Jo. Apparently she had once been engaged to marry Sam Gunn but somehow had married Spence instead. The story I gathered from my fellow workers was that her father had provided the money for Sam to start VCI. Spence had mentioned that he and his wife were both stockholders, which made me wonder if her father was still a financial backer of the company.

But it was not her finances that stunned me. It was her beauty. Bonnie Jo's hair was the color of lustrous gold, her eyes a rich, deep, mysterious grayish green. She was almost as tall as I, her figure slim and athletic, her clothes always impeccably stylish. Compared to her, I felt fat and stupid. Her voice was low, melodious; not the piercing high-pitched shrill of so many gringo women. But her eyes were hard, calculating; her beauty was cold, like an exquisite statue or a fashionably draped mannequin.

It quickly became clear to me that she no longer loved Spence, if she ever had. She was cool to him, sometimes cruelly so, as when she bought herself a sapphire ring for her own birthday and loudly announced that Spence could not have afforded it on the salary Sam gave him.

For his part, Spence buried himself in his work, driving himself deeper and deeper into the technical side of VCI, leaving the administration to Bonnie Jo and the office staff. This brought us together every day. I realized that I was falling in love with this handsome, kind, suffering older man. I also realized that he saw me as nothing more than another employee, young enough almost to be his daughter.

Spence traveled to Space Station Alpha to personally test the program for remotely repairing satellites in GEO. I remained in Orlando, at VCI's mission control center. It was a tiny room, big enough only for three monitoring stations. Windowless, it would have been unbearably stuffy if the air conditioning had not been turned up so high that it became unbearably frigid. The front wall was one huge display screen, which could be broken into smaller displays if we desired.

I sat at the right-hand monitor, almost shivering despite the sweater I wore, ready to give whatever assistance I could to the man who was actually controlling Spence's mission. We both wore earphones clamped over our heads, with pin-sized mikes at our lips. However, the mission controller was supposed to do all the talking; I was told to remain silent. Sam took the third seat, on the left, but it was empty most of the time because Sam hardly sat still for two seconds at a time. He was constantly bouncing out of his chair, pacing behind us, muttering to himself.

"This has gotta work, guys," he mumbled. "The whole future of the company's riding on this mission."

I thought he was being overly dramatic. Only later did I come to realize that he was not.

The big display screen before us showed a telescope view from Alpha of our Orbital Transfer Vehicle as it approached the satellite that needed repair. The OTV was an ugly contraption: clusters of spherical tanks and ungainly metal struts. At its front a pair of mechanical arms poked out stiffly. Ridiculously small rocket nozzles studded the vehicle fore and aft and around its middle; they reminded me of the bulbous eyes of a mutant iguana.

I could feel Sam's breath on my neck as Spence's voice said, "Shifting to onboard camera view."

"Roger, onboard view," said the mission controller, sitting at my elbow.

The screen abruptly showed a close-up view of the malfunctioning satellite. It seemed huge as it hung serenely against the black backdrop of space.

"Starting rendezvous sequence," Spence's voice said. Calmly, quietly, as unruffled as a man tying his shoelaces.

Sam was just the opposite. "Keep your eyes glued on the readouts," he snapped. "And your finger on the abort button. The *last* thing we want is a collision out there."

He was speaking to the mission controller, I knew, but his words applied to me as well. I had inserted a subroutine into the automatic rendezvous program that would fire an extra burst of thrust at the critical moment. Not only would the OTV be destroyed, but the communications satellite, too. VCI would be sued by the commsat's insurer, at the very least. All I had to do was touch one keypad on the board in front of me. Despite the frigid air-conditioning I began to perspire.

But I kept my hands in my lap. Calmly, methodically, Spence achieved the rendezvous and then directed the OTV's machinery to remove the malfunctioning power conditioner from the commsat and insert the new one. I watched the screen, fascinated, almost hypnotized, as the robot arms did their delicate work, directed by Spence's fingers from more than thirty thousand kilometers' distance.

At last the mission controller said into his microphone, "I copy power conditioning checkout in the green. Move off for communications test."

"Moving off for comm test." The mission plan called for the OTV to back away from the commsat while its owners in Tokyo tested the new power conditioner to make certain it properly fed electrical power to the satellite's forty transponders.

The display screen showed the commsat dwindling away. And then the great glowing blue curve of the Earth swung into view, speckled with dazzling white clouds. I felt my breath gush from me. It was overwhelming.

I heard Spence chuckle in my earphone. "I'll bet that's Juanita."

"Yes," I replied without thinking. I glanced at the mission controller. Instead of frowning at my breaking the mission protocol, he was grinning at me.

"Never seen the view from orbit before, huh?" Spence asked.

"Only photographs in magazines or videos," I said.

"Welcome to the club," said Spence. "It still gets me, every time."

"Let's get back to work, shall we?" Sam said. But his voice was strangely subdued.

The word came from Tokyo that the power conditioner functioned perfectly. A seventy-million-dollar commsat had been saved by replacing one faulty component.

Now it was Sam who gushed out a heartfelt sigh. "Good work, guys. C'mon, I'm gonna buy you all the best dinner in town."

I wanted to stay at my monitoring station and talk with Spence. But I could not. The mission controller cut the link to him even before I could say adios.

For some reason, Sam insisted that Bonnie Jo join us. So he bundled the four of us into his leased Mercedes and drove us to a Moroccan restaurant on the strip just outside Disney World.

"You're gonna love this place," Sam assured us as our turbanned host guided us to a table by the dance floor, a big round engraved brass table, barely a few centimeters off the floor. There were no chairs, only pillows scattered around the table.

"Relax, kick your shoes off," Sam said as he flopped onto one of the big pillows. "The belly dancers start in a few minutes."

The restaurant was small, almost intimate. Although smoking in restaurants had been outlawed for decades, the management filtered a thin gray haze (nontoxic, the menu assured us) through the air-conditioning system. For "atmosphere," the menu said. The food was surprisingly good, roasted goat and couscous and a tangy sauce that reminded me of the best Mexican dishes. But it was clear that Sam had come to see the dancers. And that he had seen them many times before. They all seemed to recognize him and to spend most of their performances close enough to our table for me to smell the heavy perfumes they used.

Our mission controller's name was Gene Redding. He was well into his forties, balding, portly and very competent at his job. As he sat on the pillows gazing up at the dancers gyrating within arm's reach, his face turned redder and redder and his bald pate began to glisten with perspiration. His glasses kept fogging, and he constantly removed them to wipe them clear, squinting at the dancers all the while. From the silly grin on his face it was obvious that he was enjoying the entertainment.

Conversation was impossible while the dancers were on. The reedy music and thumping percussion were too loud, and the men were too engrossed. I saw that Bonnie Jo was just as interested in the dancers as the men were. I must admit that they were fascinating: erotic without being vulgar. God knows what fantasies they stirred in the men's minds.

It was on the drive back to the office that the argument began.

"We turned the corner today," Sam said happily as he drove along Interstate 4. "Now the money's gonna start pouring in."

"And you'll pour it all out again, won't you, Sam?" said Bonnie Jo.

She was sitting in the back seat, with me. Gene was up front with Sam.

"I'm gonna invest it in the company's growth," Sam said lightly.

"You're going to sink it into your idiotic orbital hotel scheme." It sounded to me as if Bonnie Jo was speaking through gritted teeth.

"Idiotic?" Sam snapped. "Whattaya mean, idiotic? People are gonna pay good money for vacations in zero-gee. It's gonna be the honeymoon capital of the world!"

"Sam, if just for once you'd think with your brain instead of your testicles, you'd see what a damned fool scheme this is!"

"Yeah, sure. They laughed at Edison, too."

"We can't piss away our profits on your harebrained schemes, Sam!"

"As long as I'm the biggest stockholder I can."

I noticed that we were going faster as the argument got hotter. Sam was using neither the highway's electronic guidance system nor the car's cruise control; his rising blood pressure made his foot lean harder on the car's accelerator.

Bonnie Jo said, "Not if I can get a bloc to outvote you at the annual meeting."

"You tried that before and it didn't get you very far, did it?"

"Spence will vote on my side this time," she said.

The other cars were blurring past us, streaks of headlights on one side, streaks of red tail lights on the other. I felt like a crew member in a relativistic starship.

"The hell he will," Sam yelled back. "Spence is solidly behind me on this. So's your father."

"My father has already given me his proxy."

Sam was silent for several moments. We sped past a huge double trailer rig like a bullet passing a tortoise.

"So what," he said at last. "Most of the employees'll vote my way. And that includes Spence."

"We'll see," said Bonnie Jo.

"We sure as hell will."

So there were internal strains within VCI's top management. My discovery of this pleased me very much, mainly, I must confess, because I realized that Spence and Bonnie Jo were truly unhappy with one another. I began to think that I might use their differences to destroy VCI—and their marriage.

But Sam had other ideas. So did my father. And also, so did the rebels.

THE FOLLOWING FRIDAY afternoon Sam popped into my cubbyhole of an office, whistling off-key and grinning at the same time. It made him look rather like a lopsided Jack-o'-lantern.

"Got any plans for this weekend?" he asked me as he pulled up the only other chair in my cubicle, turned it backwards, and straddled it.

I certainly did. I was planning to spend the weekend at my desk, studying every scrap of data I could call up on my computer about VCI's finances. I already knew enough about the technical operations of the company. Sam's argument with Bonnie Jo had opened my eyes to the possibilities of ruining the corporation by financial manipulations.

"I will be working all weekend," I said.

"You sure will," said Sam, crossing his arms over the back of the little plastic chair and leaning his chin on them.

His mischievous grin told me that he had something unusual in mind. I merely stared at him, saying nothing, knowing that he was bursting to tell me whatever it was.

Sure enough, Sam could not remain silent for more than two heartbeats. "Ever been in orbit?" he asked. Quickly he added, "Literally, I mean. In space."

I blinked with surprise. "No. Never."

His grin widened. "Okay, then. Pack an overnight bag. You're going up tomorrow morning. I'll have you back here in time to be at your desk first thing Monday morning."

"You're taking me into space?"

"Space Station Alpha," he said. "You'll love it."

"With you?"

He tried to put on a serious expression. "Strictly business, Esmeralda. Strictly business. You'll have a private compartment in the one-g section."

"But why?"

"Company policy. Everybody who works for VCI gets a chance to go into orbit."

"This is the first time anyone's told me about it," I said.

His grin returned. "Well . . . it's a new company policy. I just made it, as a matter of fact."

I realized his intention. "So you merely want to get *me* into space with you."

"It'll be business, I swear," Sam said, trying to look innocent.

"What business?" I asked. All my instincts were ringing alarm bells within me.

"I need a woman's opinion about my plans for the orbital hotel. Can't ask Bonnie Jo, she's dead-set against the idea."

I must have frowned, because he swiftly added, "I'm talking about the way the compartments are done up, the facilities and the decorations and all that. The food service. I need a woman's point of view, honest."

He almost sounded reasonable.

But his grin would not fade away. "Of course, if the mood strikes you and you start to feel romantic I could show you the zero-gee section of the station and we could accomplish feats that could never be done on Earth."

"No!" I snapped. "Never!"

"Aw, come on," Sam pleaded like a little boy. "I'll behave myself, honest. I really do need your opinion. It's business, really it is."

My mind was racing furiously. The more I knew about Sam's operations the easier it would be to trip him up, I reasoned. However, I knew that no matter how much he protested, his lecherous male mind still entertained the hope that he could seduce me, still harbored fantasies of making love with me in zero gravity. I had to admit to myself that I harbored a similar fantasy—except that it was Spence I fantasized about, not Sam.

"Listen," Sam said, interrupting my train of thought. "I know you think I'm a male chauvinist and all that. Okay, maybe I am. But I'm not a rapist. If anything happens between us it'll be because you want it to happen as much as I do."

"I should be perfectly safe, then."

He laughed. "See? You've got nothing to fear."

Still I hesitated. His reputation worried me. Apparently he could be irresistibly charming when he wanted to be.

He heaved a great, disappointed sigh, threw his hands up over his head and said, "All right, all right. You want a chaperone to go with us? You got it. I'll ask Spence to come along, too. How's that?"

I had to exert every iota of self-control I possessed to keep myself from leaping out from behind my desk and shouting Yes! Yes! Very deliberately, I turned my gaze away from Sam's eager eyes and studied the blank wall behind him, pretending to think mightily.

At last I said, "A chaperone is proper. But it should be a woman. A *dueña*."

Sam sighed again, this time from exasperation. "Look, I can't shuttle people up and back to a space station just to keep your Hispanic proprieties. D'you know how much it costs?"

"But you are taking me," I said.

"I need your mother-loving feminine opinion about the hotel accommodations, dammit! And Spence has useful work to do for the company at Alpha. That's it!"

"Very well," I said with as much reluctance as I could feign. "Spence is a married gentleman. He is not as good as a proper *dueña*, but I suppose he can be trusted to act as our chaperone."

Sam jumped to his feet, bowed deeply, and pranced out of my cubicle. Only when I was certain that he could not see me did I allow myself to smile.

Less than a quarter-hour later a young man appeared at my open doorway. He looked like a Latino: somber dark eyes, thick curly black

hair, skin the color of smoked parchment. He was handsome, in a smoldering, sullen way. Sensuous lips.

"Ms. O'Rourke?" he asked.

"Yes."

"I'm supposed to give you an orientation tour. For your ride up to Alpha." His tone was little short of insolent.

"Right now? I'm busy. . . ."

He shrugged disdainfully. "Whenever you're ready, princess. Sam told
me to hang around until you've got an hour of free time."

Princess? I seethed inwardly, but maintained a calm exterior. I would
not give this sneering youth the satisfaction of seeing that he could
anger me.

"I won't be ready until sometime after six," I said.

Again he shrugged. "Then I'll hafta hang around until after six."

"Where will I find you?"

A spark of something glinted in his eyes. Perhaps it was anger. "I'll be
in the simulations lab, back down the main corridor, past—"

"I know where the simulations lab is," I said.

"Okay. See you whenever you get there." He turned and started to
leave.

"Wait!" I called. "What is your name?"

"Ricardo Queveda," he answered over his shoulder. "Extension 434."

It was close to seven-thirty before I finished my day's work and
made my way to the simulations lab. Although quitting time at VCI
was nominally six, there were still plenty of people in the corridors and
offices. Many of Sam's employees worked long hours. Most of them, in
fact.

But the simulations lab seemed deserted. The computer in its center
was dark and silent. The overhead lights were dimmed. I stood in the
doorway frowning with uncertainty. He had said he would be here. How
dare he leave without informing me?

"You ready for your orientation spin?"

The voice behind me startled me. I turned and saw that it was
Queveda. He held a frosted can of cola in one hand.

"Dinner," he said, hoisting the can before my face. "Want some?"

"No thank you. Let's get this over with."

"Okay. It's pretty simple," he said as he ushered me inside the lab. The
ceiling lights brightened automatically. "IAA safety regulations require

anyone flying into orbit for the first time to have an orientation simulation and lecture. The lecture is recorded and you can see it on one of the display screens here or take a copy home with you and view it at your leisure. Which do you prefer?"

"I'll see it here," I said.

He nodded. "Sure. There's another half-hour I'll have to hang around twiddling my thumbs."

His attitude angered me. "Really!" I snapped. "If it's your job to do this, why are you so nasty about it?"

He stared straight into my eyes. "My *job*, señorita, is maintaining these goddamned computers. What I'm doing now is extra."

"Maintaining the computers? But I've never seen you here."

"You haven't noticed," he replied sullenly. "I've been here. I've seen you plenty of times. But you just look right past the hired help, like some goddamned princess or something."

"That's no reason to be angry with me."

"That's not why I'm pissed off."

"And there's no need for such vulgar language!"

"*Dispense Usted perdón, princesa,*" he said, with a horrible accent.

"Where are you from?" I demanded.

"Los Angeles," he said as he guided me to one of the monitoring desks that ringed the computer.

"And what makes you so angry?"

He snorted. "The thought that a refined lady like you would willingly ride into a tryst in space with an Anglo."

"A tryst? Is that what you think I'm doing?"

"What else?"

I wanted to slap his sullen, accusing face. But I decided that I would not dignify his anger with any response whatsoever.

"Let's get this orientation over with," I said, barely controlling my temper. "Then we can both go home."

I watched the recorded lecture. Then he silently led me to one of the simulation areas and helped me don the VR helmet and gloves. I "rode" in virtual reality aboard a Delta Clipper from Cape Canaveral to Space Station Alpha. The simulation did not provide the physical sensations of acceleration or zero gravity: it was strictly a safety review, showing the interior layout of the Clipper's passenger cabin, the escape hatches, and the emergency oxygen system.

At last it was finished and I pulled the helmet off. Queveda was standing beside me; he took the helmet from my hands.

"I am not engaging in a tryst with Sam Gunn," I heard myself mutter as I wormed off the VR gloves.

He gave me a smoldering look. "I'm glad to hear it, even if it's not true."

"I do not tell lies!"

For the first time, he smiled at me. It was only half a smile, really, but it made him look much better. "I'm sure you're telling the truth. But you don't know Sam."

I almost wanted to tell him that I loved Spence, not Sam. But that would have been foolish. Apparently the rumors flew thick and fast through the whole company. Already it was taken for granted that Sam and I would make out in zero-gee. Besides, telling him how I felt about Spence would have made him angry all over again.

So I tried to shift the conversation as we walked along the corridor to the building's front entrance. The halls were mostly deserted now. Even Sam's most dedicated employees eventually went home to their families and friends.

"I am from Los Angeles, too, you know," I said.

"Really? What part?"

Quickly I realized I had put my foot into a quagmire. "Oh, I went to UCLA," I said. "I lived just off the campus."

"Westwood, huh?"

Actually I had lived in a leased condominium in Pacific Palisades, with a magnificent view of the beach and the sunsets over the ocean.

"When I said Los Angeles," he told me as we reached the front door, "I meant the city. The barrio. Downtown."

"Oh." I had heard about the squalor and crime in the downtown area, but had never visited such a slum.

We stepped out into the soft warm breeze of a balmy Florida evening.

"You were born there?" I asked as we walked toward our cars.

It was dark in the parking lot. Suddenly I was glad of his companionship.

"No," he answered. "My parents came to Los Angeles when I was an infant."

"And where were you born?" I asked.

"In Quito."

I felt stunned. Quito!

"That's the capital of Ecuador," he explained, misunderstanding my silence. "My father was a university professor there but he was driven out by the dictator."

"Dictator?" I snapped. "Ecuador is a democracy."

"Democracy hell! It's a dictatorship, run by a little clique of fascist bastards."

I felt myself shaking from head to toe. My throat went dry with suppressed anger.

"Someday I'll go back to Ecuador," Ricardo Queveda said. "Someday there's going to be a reckoning. The people won't stand for this corrupt regime much longer. Revolution is on the way, you'll see."

In the shadows of the parking lot I could not make out the expression on his face or the fire in his eyes. But I could hear it in his voice, his passionate, fervent voice, filled with hatred for my father. And if he knew who I really was, he would hate me, too.

I SLEPT HARDLY at all that night, worrying about my father and the rebels and the seething hatred I had heard in young Ricardo Queveda's voice. When I did manage to close my eyes I was racked by terrifying nightmares in which I was struggling to climb the sheer face of a high cliff with Sam up above me and Spence below. I saw the rope connecting me to Sam begin to fray. I tried to shout but no sound would come from my throat. I tried to scream but I was helpless. The rope snapped and I plunged down into the abyss, past Spence who reached out to save me, but in vain.

I woke screaming, bathed in perspiration, tangled in my bedsheets. And I realized that in the last moment of my nightmare the man who reached toward me was not Spence after all. It was Ricardo.

Dawn was breaking. Time to get up anyway.

I was applying the final dab of mascara when the apartment's intercom chimed. I called out to it and Sam's voice rasped, "Arise Esmeralda. Your knight in shining armor is here to whisk you away to the promised land."

I had seldom heard such a mixture of metaphors.

We drove to the Cape in Spence's reconditioned antique Mustang, gleaming silver, with me crammed into the tiny rear seat and the top down. My careful hairdo was blown to tatters once we hit the highway but I did not care; it was glorious to race in the early morning sunlight.

Despite my VR orientation, I gulped as we strapped ourselves into the contoured chairs of the Delta Clipper. It was a big, conical-shaped craft, sitting in the middle of a concrete blast pad. It reminded me of the ancient round pyramids of Michoacan, in Mexico: massive, tall and enduring. But this "pyramid" was made of lightweight alloys and plastics, not stone. And it was intended to fly into space.

After all my fears, the actual takeoff was almost mild. The roar of the rocket engines was muffled by the cabin's acoustical insulation. The vibration was less than my orientation simulation had led me to believe. Before I fully realized we were off the ground the ship had settled down into a smooth, surging acceleration.

And then the engines shut off and we were coasting in zero gravity. My stomach felt as if it were dropping away to infinity and crawling up my throat, both at the same time. The medicinal patch Sam had given me must have helped, though, because in a few moments my feeling of nausea eased. It did not disappear entirely, but it sank to a level where I could turn to Spence, sitting beside me, and make a weak grin.

"You're doing fine," he said, treating me to that dazzling smile of his. I did not even mind that the loose end of his shoulder belt was floating in the air, bobbing up and down like a flat gray snake.

Sam, of course, unclipped his harness as soon as the engines cut off and floated up to the padded ceiling.

"This is the life!" he announced to the ten other passengers. Then he tucked his knees up under his chin and did a few zero-gee spins and tumbles.

The other passengers were mostly experienced engineers and technicians riding up to Alpha for a stint of work on the space station. One of them, however, must have been new to zero-gee. I could hear him retching into one of the bags that had been thoughtfully placed in our seatbacks. The sound of it made me gag.

"Ignore it," Spence advised me, placing a cool, calm hand on my arm. With his other hand he pointed at the acrobatic Sam. "And ignore him, too. He does this every trip, just to see who he can get to throw up."

Once we docked with Alpha and got down to the main wheel of the station, everyone felt much better. Except Sam. I believe he truly preferred zero-gee to normal gravity.

Alpha station was a set of three nested wheels, each at a different distance from the center to simulate a different level of gravity. The outermost wheel was at one g, normal Earthly gravity. The second was at one-third gee, roughly the same as Mars. The innermost was at the Moon's level of one-sixth gee. The hub of the station was, of course, effectively zero gravity, although some of the more sensitive scientific and industrial experiments were housed in "free flyers" that floated independently of the space station's huge, rotating structure.

Much of the main wheel was unoccupied, I saw. Long stretches of the sloping corridor stood bare and empty as Sam and I walked through them. Nothing but bare structural ribs and dim overhead lights. Not even any windows.

"Plenty room for hotel facilities here," Sam kept muttering.

Spence had disappeared into the area on the second wheel that VCI had leased from Alpha's owner, Rockledge Industries. He had come up to work on the satellite repair facility we had established there, not merely to chaperone me.

"But Sam," I asked as we strolled through the dismally empty corridor, "why would anyone pay the price of a ticket to orbit just to be cooped up in cramped compartments in a space station? It's like being in a small ocean liner, down in steerage class, below the water line."

He smiled as if I had stepped into his web. "Two reasons, Esmeralda. One—the view. You can't imagine what it's like to see the Earth from up here until you've done it for yourself."

"I've seen photos and videos. They're breathtaking, yes, but—"

"But not the real experience," Sam interrupted. "And then there's the second reason." He broke into a lecherous leer. "Making love in zero gravity. It's fantastic, lemme tell you."

I did not respond to that obvious ploy.

"Better yet, lemme show you."

"I think not," I said coolly. But I wondered what it would be like to make love in zero gravity. Not with Sam, of course. With Spence.

Sam's expression turned instantly to wounded innocence. "I mean, lemme show you the zero-gee section of the station."

"Oh."

"Did you think I was propositioning you?"

"Of course."

"How could you? This is a business trip," he protested. "I even brought you a chaperone. My intentions are honorable, cross my heart." Which he did, and then raised his right hand in a Boy Scout's salute.

I trusted Sam as far as I could throw the cathedral of Quito, but I followed him down the long passageway to the hub of the space station. It was a strange, eerie journey. The passageway was nothing more than a long tube studded with ladderlike rungs. With each step we descended the feeling of gravity lessened until it felt as if we were floating, rather than climbing. Sam showed me how to let go of the rungs altogether, except for the faintest touch against them now and then to propel myself up the tube. Soon we were swimming, hardly touching the rungs at all, hurtling faster and faster along the long metal tube.

I realized why the standard uniform for the space station was one-piece coveralls that zippered at the cuffs of the trousers and sleeves. Anything else would have been undignified, perhaps even dangerous.

The tube was only dimly lit, but I could see up ahead a brighter glow coming from an open hatch at the end. We were whipping along by now, streaking past the rungs like a pair of dolphins.

And then we shot into a huge, empty space: a vast hollow sphere with padded walls. Sam zoomed straight across the center and dove headfirst into the curving wall. It gave and he bounced back toward me. I felt as if I had been dropped out of an airplane. I was falling and there was no way I could control myself.

Then Sam grabbed me as we passed each other. His hands gripped my flailing arms and I was surprised at how strong he was. We spun around each other, two astronomical bodies suddenly caught in a mutual orbit. I was breathless, unable to decide whether I should scream or laugh. Slowly we drifted to the wall and nudged against it. Sam flattened his back against the padding, gaining enough traction to bring us both to a stop.

"Fun, huh?"

It took me several moments to catch my breath. Once I did, I realized that Sam was holding me in his arms and his lips were almost touching mine.

I pushed away, gently, and floated toward the middle of the huge enclosure. "Fun, yes," I admitted.

We spent nearly an hour playing games like a pair of school children let loose for recess. We looped and dived and bounced off the padded walls. We played tag and blindman's bluff, although I was certain that Sam cheated and peeked whenever he felt like it.

Finally we hovered in the middle of the empty sphere, sweating, panting, an arm's length from one another.

"Well," Sam said, running a hand over his sweaty brow, "whattaya think? Worth the price of a ticket to orbit?"

"Yes! Well worth it. I believe people will gladly pay to come here for vacations."

"And honeymoons," Sam added, with his impish grin. "You haven't even tried the best part of it yet."

I laughed lightly. There was no sense getting angry at him. "I think I can imagine it well enough."

"Ah, but the experience, that's the thing."

I looked into his devilish hazel eyes and, for the first time, felt sad for Sam Gunn. "Sam," I said as gently as I could, "you must remember that Esmeralda loves the young poet, not Quasimodo."

His eyes widened with surprise for a moment. Then his grin returned. "Hell, you don't have to follow the script *exactly*, do you?"

He was truly incorrigible.

"It must be time for dinner," I said. "We should get back to the galley, shouldn't we?"

So we started up the tube and, as the gravity built up, found ourselves clambering down the rungs of the ladder like a pair of firefighters descending to the street.

"You mean you're in love with somebody else?" Sam's voice echoed along the metal walls of the tube.

He was below me. I could see his face turned up toward me, like a round ragamuffin doll with scruffy red hair. I pondered his question for a few moments.

"I think I am," I answered.

"Somebody younger? Somebody your own age?"

"What difference does it make?"

He fell silent for several moments. At last he said softly, "Well, he better treat you right. If he gives you any trouble you tell me about it, understand?"

I was so surprised at that I nearly missed my step on the next rung. Sam Gunn being fatherly? I found it hard to believe, yet that was what he seemed to be saying.

Spence was already in the galley when we got there.

Sam showed me how to work the food dispensers as he explained, "This glop is barely fit for human consumption. I think Rockledge has some kind of experiment going about how lousy the food has to be before people stop eating it and let themselves starve."

I accepted a prepared tray from the machine and went to the table where Spence was sitting. There were only ten tables in the galley, and most of them were empty.

"Experienced workers bring their own food up with them and microwave it," Sam kept rattling on. "Of course, when I open the hotel I'll have a *cordon bleu* chef up here and the best by-damn food service you ever saw. Cocktail lounge, too, with real waitresses in cute little outfits. None of those idiot robots like they have down at the Cape. . . ."

He chattered and babbled straight through our meager dinner. In truth, the food was not very appetizing. The soy burger was too cool and the iced tea too warm. I am sure it was nutritious, but it was also bland and dull.

Spence could barely get a word in, the way Sam was nattering. I was content to let him do the talking. Suddenly I felt extremely tired, worn out. It had been a demanding day, with the flight from the Cape and Sam's zero-gee acrobatics. I had barely slept the night before and had arisen with the dawn.

I yawned in Sam's face. And immediately felt terribly embarrassed. "Sorry," I apologized. "But I am very tired."

"Or bored," Sam said, without a trace of resentment.

"Tired," I repeated. "Fatigued. I didn't sleep well last night."

"Too much excitement," Sam said.

Spence said nothing.

"I must get some sleep," I said, pushing my chair back.

"Can you find your room all right?" Spence asked.

"I think so."

"I'll walk you to your door," he said, getting to his feet.

Sam remained seated, but he glanced first at me and then at Spence. "I've got a few things to attend to," he said, "soon as I finish this glorious Rockledge repast."

So Spence walked with me along the sloping corridor toward the area where the sleeping compartments were.

"Sam works very long hours, even up here," I said.

Spence chuckled. "He's working on a couple of Rockledge people. Of the female variety."

"Oh?"

"The little guy's always got something going. Although I've got to admit," Spence added, "that he gets a lot of dope about what Rockledge is doing from his—uh, contacts."

"A sort of masculine Mata Hari?" I asked.

Spence laughed outright.

As we neared the door to my compartment I heard myself asking

Spence, "Why don't they have windows in the compartments? It makes them feel so small and confined."

Even as I spoke the words I wondered if I wanted to delay the moment I must say good-night to Spence, or if there was another reason.

"The station's spinning, you know," he replied, completely serious. "If you had a window in your compartment you'd see the stars looping around, and then the Earth would slide past, and maybe the Moon, if it was in the right position. Could make you pretty queasy, everything spinning by like that."

"But Sam said the view was magnificent."

"Oh, it is! Believe me. But that's the view from outside, or down at the observation blister in the hub."

"I see."

"Sam plans to put a video screen in each of his hotel rooms. It'll look like a window that gives you a steady view of the Earth or whatever else you'd like to see."

So after all his talk about seeing "the real thing," Sam was prepared to show his hotel guests little more than video images of the Earth from space. That was just like the gringo capitalist exploiter, I told myself.

Yet I heard myself asking Spence, "Is the view truly magnificent?"

"Sam didn't show you?"

"No."

His face lit up. "Want to see it now? You're not too tired, are you? It'll only take—"

"I'm not too tired," I said eagerly. "I would like very much to see this fabulous view."

All the way along the long tube leading to the station's hub a voice in my mind reprimanded me. You know why you asked him about the windows, it scolded. You *wanted* Spence to take you to the zero-gee section.

We floated into the big padded gym. Spence propelled himself to a particular piece of the padding and peeled it back, revealing a small hatch. He opened it and beckoned me to him. I pushed off the curving wall and swam to him, my heart racing so hard I feared it would break my ribs.

Spence helped me wriggle through the narrow hatch, then followed me into a small, cramped dome. There was barely room enough for the two of us. He swung the hatch shut and we were in total darkness.

"Hang on a minute. . . ." he mumbled.

I heard a click and then the whir of an electric motor. The dome seemed to split apart, opening like a clamshell. And beyond it—

The Earth. A huge brilliant blue curving mass moving slowly, with ponderous grace, below us. The breath gushed out of me.

Spence put his arm around my shoulders and whispered, "Lord, I love the beauty of thy house, and the place where thy glory dwells."

It was—there are no words to do it justice. We huddled together in the transparent observation blister and feasted our eyes on the world swinging past, immense and glorious beyond description. Deep blue seas and swirling purest white clouds, the land brown and green with wrinkles of mountains and glittering lakes scattered here and there. Even the dark night side was spectacular with the lights of cities and highways outlining the continents.

"No matter how many time you've seen it," Spence said, "it still takes your breath away. I could watch it for hours."

"It's incredible," I said.

"We'll have to build more observation blisters for the hotel guests. Stud the whole zero-section with them."

The panorama was ever-changing, one spectacular scene blending imperceptibly into another. We saw the sun come up over the curving horizon, shooting dazzling streamers of red and orange through the thin layer of the atmosphere. I recognized the isthmus of Panama and the curving bird's head of the Yucatan.

"Where is Ecuador?" I asked.

"Too far south for us to see on this swing. Why do you want to see Ecuador?"

In my excitement I had forgotten that I was supposed to be from Los Angeles.

"Ricardo Queveda," I temporized quickly. "He told me was born in Ecuador."

By the time we were watching our second sunrise, nearly two hours later, I had melted into Spence's arms. I turned my face up to his, wanting him to kiss me.

He understood. He felt the same passion that I did.

But he said, very gently, "I'm a married man, Juanita."

"Do you love Bonnie Jo?"

"I used to. Now . . ." He shook his head. In the light from the glowing Earth I could see how troubled and pained he was.

"I love you, Spence," I told him.

He smiled sadly. "Maybe you think you do, but it isn't a smart move. I wouldn't be very good for you, kid."

"I know my own heart," I insisted.

"Don't make it any tougher than it has to be, Juanita. I'm old enough to be your father and I'm married. Not happily, true enough, but that's my fault as much as Bonnie Jo's."

"I could make you happy."

"You shouldn't be getting yourself involved with old married men. Pay some attention to guys your own age, like Ric."

"Queveda? That . . . that would-be revolutionary?"

He looked totally surprised. "Revolutionary? What are you talking about?"

"Nothing," I snapped. "Nothing at all."

The mood was shattered, the spell broken. I had confessed my love to Spence and he had treated me like a lovesick child.

"We'd better leave," I said coldly.

"Yeah," Spence said. "We could both use some sleep."

But I did not sleep. Not at all. I seethed with anger all night. Spence had not only rejected me, he had belittled me. He did not see me as a desirable woman; he thought of me as a child to be lectured, to be palmed off on some young puppy dog whose only passion is to avenge his miserable family's supposed honor.

What a fool I had been! I did not love Spence. I hated him! I spent the whole night telling myself so.

WHEN WE BOARDED the Clipper for the return flight to Florida, Sam was not with us.

"Where is he?" I asked Spence.

"He left a message. Went off to visit a buddy of his in the old Mac Dac Shack."

"The what?"

"One of the smaller stations. It's a medical center now."

"Sam needs medical attention?"

Spence broke into a grin. "Maybe after last night, he does, after all."

I did not find that funny.

Sam did not appear at the office until three days later, and when he did finally show up he was grinning like a cat who had feasted on canaries.

He breezed into the mission control center while I was monitoring our latest repair mission. Ricardo Queveda sat in the left-hand chair, busily removing a set of computer boards that had to be replaced with upgrades.

"I've got everything lined up for the hotel," Sam announced loudly, plopping himself into the chair on my right.

"Congratulations," I said.

"Yep. Finally got Rockledge to agree to a reasonable leasing fee. Got my buddy Omar set to handle the logistics up in orbit. Contractors, a personnel outfit to hire the staff—everything's in place."

He smiled contentedly and leaned back in the little swivel chair. "All I need is the money."

I had to smile at him. "That would seem to me to be a major consideration."

"Nah." Sam waved an arm in the air. "I'll get the board to approve it at the next stockholder's meeting. That's only six weeks away."

He popped to his feet and strode confidently out of the center, whistling in his usual off-key fashion.

"Gringo imperialist," muttered Ricardo Queveda.

"You accept his paychecks," I taunted.

He gave me a dark look. "So do you."

"I don't call him names."

"No. But you don't need his money, do you? You live in a fine condo and drive a fancy sports car. Your clothing costs more than your salary."

"You've been spying on me?"

He laughed bitterly. "No need for spying. You are as obvious as an elephant in a china shop."

"So my family has money," I said. "What of it?"

"You don't come from Los Angeles and you don't need this job, that's what of it. Why are you here?"

I could not answer. My brain froze in the laser beams of his dark eyes.

"Is it because you are Sam's mistress?"

"No!"

He smiled tightly. "But you are in love with Spence, aren't you?"

"No I am not!"

"It's obvious," Ricardo said.

"I *hate* him!"

"Yes," he said. "Anyone can see that."

THE ANNUAL STOCKHOLDERS' meeting took place six weeks later. In that time I had become quite expert at running the mission control board. During my first weeks on the job I merely sat alongside Gene Redding and watched how he handled the job. Within two weeks he was allowing me to take over when he took a break. Within a month we were sharing the duty on long, ten and even twelve-hour shifts.

Sam needed more mission controllers because the volume of work was increasing rapidly. As he had predicted, the money was beginning to pour in to VCI. The ability to repair malfunctioning commsats and to replenish the fuel they used for their attitude-control thrusters suddenly made VCI a major force in the communications satellite industry. Instead of replacing aging commsats the corporations could get VCI to refurbish them, at a fraction of the replacement cost.

Spence worked closely with us, handling most of the remotely controlled missions himself, operating the unmanned OTVs that now ran regular repair-and-refurbishment missions to GEO.

Sam practically danced with joy. "I'll be able to declare a dividend for the stockholders," he told us, "and *still* have a wad of moolah to get the hotel started."

Bonnie Jo frowned at him. "We could give the stockholders a bigger dividend if you'd forget about your orbital sex palace."

Sam laughed. "Are you kidding? My hotel's gonna be the biggest moneymaker you've ever seen in space. I've even got an advertising motto for it: 'If you like water beds, you're gonna *love* zero-gee!'"

Bonnie Jo huffed.

Spence spent more time in the simulator than at home with Bonnie Jo. Sam was frugal when it came to hiring more staff; he might take on a very junior computer programmer from Los Angeles, but astronauts and mission controllers carried much higher price tags, and he refrained from hiring them. We worked extremely long hours, and Sam himself "flew" many of the remote missions; Spence did the rest of them—more than Sam did, by actual count.

It seemed to me that Spence was glad of the excuse to spend so much time away from his wife. Anyone could sense that their marriage was ripping apart. It made me sad to see him so unhappy, and I had to remind myself often that he had treated me like a schoolgirl and I hated him. For her part, Bonnie Jo seemed perfectly content to have Spence spend most of his time on the remote missions. She herself began to fly back to Salt Lake City every weekend.

Naturally, with my duties as the second mission controller and his as principal operator of the remote satellite repairs, we were together quite a bit.

Well, not together in the physical sense, precisely. Spence was in another room, some twenty meters down the hall from my mission control desk. But somehow, when I was not on duty I often found myself walking down that hallway to watch him at work. He sat in an astronaut's contoured couch, his hands covered with metallic gloves that trailed hair-thin fiber-optic cables, the top half of his handsome face covered by the stereo screens that showed him what the OTV's cameras were seeing.

I told myself that I was studying his moves, learning how to sabotage the repair missions. When the time came I would strike without mercy. When I was not hanging by the doorway to the remote manipulator lab, studying him like a avenging angel, I was at my mission control console, actually speaking with Spence, connected electronically to him, closer to him than anyone else in the world. Including his wife. I wanted to be close to him; that made it easier to find a way to sabotage his work, his company, his life.

"You planning to attend the stockholders' meeting?" Spence asked me during a lull in one of the missions.

I was startled that he asked a personal question. "Say again?" I asked, in the professional jargon of a mission controller.

Spence chuckled. "It's okay, Juanita. The OTV's still in coast mode. It'll be another hour before we have to get to work. Loosen up."

"Oh. Yes. Of course."

"You bought some stock, didn't you?"

"A few shares," I said. In actuality I was spending my entire salary on shares of VCI. If there had been a way to buy up all the existing shares I would have done it, using my father's treasury to deliver the company into his hands.

As fate would have it, the annual stockholders' meeting took place on the same day that my father gave his famous speech at the United Nations.

He told me about the speech the night before the meeting. As usual, I had driven to the consulate late at night and called him on the videophone. At least he had the good sense to receive my calls in his office, when he knew I was going to contact him.

My father was glowing with pride. His smile was brilliant, the shoulders of his suit wider than ever. He had even faced the necessity of replacing his thinning hair. Although his new mane of curly brown hair looked as if it had been stolen from a teenaged rock star, it was so wild and thick, it obviously made him feel younger and more vigorous.

"With Brazil in the chair at the Security Council and the Committee of the Twelve Equatorial Nations lining up support among the small nations in the General Assembly, I have high hopes for our cause."

"And your speech?" I asked him. "What will you say?"

His smile became even wider, even more radiant. "You must watch me on television, little one. I want you to be just as surprised as the rest of the world will be."

He would tell me no more. I of course reported in full to him about VCI's continuing success in repairing and refurbishing satellites remotely. And of the growing strains in the company's management.

"You still have the capability of destroying their spacecraft?" he asked me.

"Yes," I replied, thinking of how much damage I could do to Spence.

"Good," said my father. "The time is fast approaching when we will strike."

"Will it be necessary—"

But his attention was suddenly pulled away from me. I heard an aide shouting breathlessly at him, "The rebels have ambushed General Quintana's brigade!"

"Ambushed?" my father snapped, his eyes no longer looking at me. "Where? When?"

"In the mountains of Azuay, south of Cuenca. The general has been captured and his troops are fleeing for their lives!"

My father's face went gray, then red with fury. He turned back to me. "Excuse me, daughter. I have urgent business to attend to."

"Go with God," I mumbled, feeling silly at using such an archaic phrase. But it was all I could think to say.

The rebels were very clever. They must have known that my father was scheduled to fly to New York to deliver his speech to the United Nations. Now he either had to cancel his speech and admit to the world that his nation was in the throes of a serious internal conflict, or go to New York and leave his army leaderless for several days.

I COULD NOT sleep that night. When I arrived at the stockholders' meeting my eyes were red and puffy, my spirits low. How can I help my father? I kept asking myself. What can I do? He had sent me here to help him triumph over Sam Gunn and these other gringos. But he was being threatened at home and I was thousands of kilometers away from him. I felt miserable and stupid and helpless.

Spence noticed my misery.

More than a hundred people were filing into the room in the big hotel where the stockholders' meeting was being held. Employees and their spouses, all ages, all colors. Blacks and Hispanics and Asians, women and men, Sam had brought together every variety of the human species in his company. He hired for competence; VCI was truly a company without prejudice of any kind. Except that it helped if you were female and young and attractive. That was Sam's one obvious weakness.

Out of that throng Spence noticed me. He made his way through the crowd that was milling around the coffee and doughnuts and came to my side.

"What's the matter, Juanita?"

I looked up into his clear blue eyes and saw that he too was sad-faced.

"Family problems," I muttered. "Back home."

He nodded grimly. "Me too."

"Oh?"

Before he could say more, Sam's voice cut through the hubbub of conversations. "Okay, let's get this show on the road. Where's our noble president? Hey, Spence, you silver-haired devil, come on up here and preside, for god's sake, will ya?"

Spence lifted my chin a centimeter and gave me a forced grin. "Time to go to work," he said. Then he turned and almost sprinted up to the front of the room and jumped up onto the makeshift dais.

Sam, Bonnie Jo, and two other men flanked Spence at the long table set up on the dais. The board of directors, I realized. Each of them had a microphone and a name card in front of them. I was fairly certain that the older of the two strangers—Eli G. Murtchison—was Bonnie Jo's father.

There were two mammoth television sets on either side of the dais as well. I wondered if the hotel kept them there all the time, or if they had been brought in for some specific reason.

The rest of us took the folding plastic chairs that the hotel had set along the floor of the meeting room. They were hard and uncomfortable: a stimulus to keep the meeting short, I thought. The meeting began with formalities. Spence asked that the minutes of the last meeting be accepted. Bonnie Jo read her treasurer's report so fast that I could not understand a word of it.

Then Sam, as chairman of the board, began his review of the year's business and plans for the coming year.

I could feel the tension in the air. Even as Sam spoke glowingly to the stockholders about VCI's new capabilities in remote satellite repair, even while they loudly applauded his announcement of a dividend, the room seemed to crackle with electricity.

And all the while I wondered where my father was, what he was doing, what decisions he was making.

A stockholder—Gene Redding, of all people—rose to ask a question. "Uh, Sam, uh, why isn't our dividend bigger, if we're, uh, making such good profits now?"

I turned in my chair to see Gene better. He was standing: portly, bald, looking slightly flustered. I had never before seen him in a suit and tie; he had always worn jeans and sports shirts at the office. But his suit was rumpled and his tie hung loosely from his unbuttoned shirt. It seemed to me that he felt guilty about asking his question. He was on Bonnie Jo's side, I realized.

Sam said tightly, "We have always plowed our profits back into the company, to assure our growth. This year the profits have been big enough to allow a dividend. But we are still plowing some of the profits back into growth."

Gene got red in the face, but he found the strength to ask, "Back into the growth of VCI's existing projects, or, uh, some other program?"

Sam shot a glance along the head table toward Bonnie Jo. Then he grinned at Gene. "You can sit down, Gene. This is gonna take some time, I can see that."

Bonnie Jo said, "Sam wants to put our profits—*your* profits—into building an orbital tourist hotel."

"A honeymoon hotel," Sam corrected.

A few chuckles arose from the stockholders.

"And we don't have to build it," Sam added. "We can lease space aboard Alpha from Rockledge International."

"Didn't you try that once before, when Global Technology first built Space Station Alpha?" asked another stockholder, a woman I did not recognize.

"And it didn't work out?" asked another.

"You went broke on that deal, didn't you?" still another asked. I realized that Bonnie Jo had recruited her troops carefully.

"Yeah, yeah," Sam answered impatiently. "That was years ago. Rockledge has taken over Alpha now and they're looking for customers to lease space."

"Under what terms?" Bonnie Jo asked.

"It's a bargain," said Sam enthusiastically. "A steal!"

I looked at Spence, sitting between Sam and Bonnie Jo. His face was a mask, his usual smile gone, his features frozen as if he wished to betray not even the slightest sign of emotion or partisan bias.

Gene Redding rose to his feet once again. I could see that his hands were trembling, he was so nervous.

"I . . ." he cleared his throat, "I want to make a, uh, a motion."

Spence said grimly, "Go ahead."

"I move . . . that the board of directors . . ." he seemed to be reciting a memorized speech, "refuse to allocate, uh, any monies . . . for any programs . . . not directly associated with VCI's existing lines of business." Gene said the last words in a rush, then immediately sat down.

"Second!" cried Bonnie Jo.

Spence stared at the back wall of the meeting room as he said automatically, "Movement made and seconded. Discussion?"

I had expected Sam to jump up on the table and do a war dance. Or at least to rant and scream and argue until we all dropped from exhaustion. Instead, he glanced at his wristwatch and said:

"Let's postpone the discussion for a bit. There's a speech coming up at the UN that we should all take a look at."

Spence agreed to Sam's suggestion so quickly that I knew the two of them had talked it over beforehand. Bonnie Jo looked surprised, nettled, but her father laid a hand on her arm and she refrained from objecting.

The UN speech was by my father, of course, although no one in the room knew that I was the daughter of Ecuador's *presidente*. I felt a surge of pride when his handsome face appeared on the giant TV screens. If only his new hair had matched his face better! He wore a civilian's business suit of dark blue, with the red sash of his office slanting across his chest. He looked bigger than normal, his chest broader and deeper. I realized he must have been wearing a bulletproof vest. Was he worried that the rebels would try to assassinate him? Or merely wary of New York?

My father's speech was marvelous, although I had to listen to the English translation instead of hearing his dramatic, flowery Spanish. Still, it was dramatic enough. My father explained the legal origins of our claim to the equatorial orbit, the injustice of the rich corporations who refused to share their wealth with the orbit's rightful owners, and the complicity of the United Nations for allowing this terrible situation to persist.

I sat in my hard little folding chair and basked in the glow of my fa-ther's unassailable logic and undeterrable drive.

"Is there no one to help us?" he asked rhetorically, raising his hands in supplication. "Cannot all the apparatus of international law come to the aid of the Twelve nations who have seen their territory invaded and usurped? Will no one support the Declaration of Quito?"

Suddenly his face hardened. His hands balled into fists. "Very well, then! The Twelve Equatorial Nations will defend their sacred territory by themselves, if necessary. I serve notice, on behalf of the Twelve Equatorial Nations, that the equatorial orbit belongs to *us*, and to no other nation, corporation, or entity. We are preparing to send an international team of astronauts to establish permanent residence in the equatorial orbit. Once there, they will dismantle or otherwise destroy the satellites that the in-vaders have placed in our territory."

The audience in the UN chamber gasped. So did we, in the hotel's meeting room. I felt a thrill of hot blood race through me.

"We will defend our territory against the aggressors who have invaded it," my father declared. "If this means war, then so be it. To do anything less would be to bow to the forces of imperialism!"

The people around me stared at one another, stunned into silence.

All except Sam, who yelled, "Jesus H. Christ on a motorcycle!"

As the TV picture winked off, one of the stockholders shouted, "What the hell are we going to do about *that*?"

All sense of order in our meeting room dissolved. Everyone seemed to talk at once. Spence rapped his knuckles on the table but no one paid any attention to him. The argument about Sam's orbital hotel was forgotten. My father had turned our meeting into chaos.

Until Sam jumped up on the table and waved his arms excitedly. "Shut the hell up and listen to me!" he bellowed.

The room silenced. All eyes turned to the pudgy rust-haired elf stand-ing on the head table.

"We're gonna get there before they do," Sam told us. "We're gonna put a person up there in GEO before they can and we're gonna claim the or-bit for ourselves. They wanna play legal games, we can play 'em too. Faster and better!"

Spence objected, "Sam, nobody can stay in GEO for long. It's in the middle of the outer Van Allen belt, for gosh sakes."

"Pull a couple of OTVs together, fill the extra propellant tanks with water. That'll provide enough shielding for a week or so."

"How do you know? We've got to do some calculations, check with the experts—"

"No time for that," Sam snapped. "We're in a race, a land rush, we gotta go *now*. Do the calculations afterward. Right now the vital thing is to get somebody parked up there in GEO before those greedy sonsofbitches get there!"

"But who would be nuts enough to—"

"I'll do it," Sam said, as if he had made up his mind even before Spence asked the question. "Let's get busy!"

That broke up our meeting, of course. Spence officially called for an adjournment until a time to be decided. Everyone raced for their cars and drove pell-mell back to the office. Except for Sam and Spence, who jumped into Spence's convertible Mustang and headed off toward Cape Canaveral.

DESPITE MY FEELINGS of patriotism and love of my father, I felt thrilled. It was tremendously exciting to dash into the mission control center and begin preparations for launching Sam to GEO. Spence went with him as far as Space Station Alpha. Together they hopped up to the station where our OTVs were garaged on the next available Delta Clipper, scarcely thirty-six hours after my father's speech.

Even Bonnie Jo caught the wave of enthusiasm. She came into the control center as Sam and Spence were preparing the two OTVs for Sam's mission. It was night; I was running the board, giving Gene a rest after he had put in twelve hours straight. Bonnie Jo slid into the chair beside me and asked me to connect her with Sam up at Alpha.

"We've been monitoring the Brazilian launch facility," she said, once Sam's round, freckled face appeared on the screen. "They're counting down a manned launch. They claim it's just a scientific research team going up to the Novo Brasil space station. But get this Sam: the Brazilians are also counting down an unmanned launch."

"With what payload?"

"An old storm cellar that the U.S. government auctioned off five years ago."

"A what?"

"A shielded habitat module, like the ones the scientists used on their first Mars missions to protect themselves from solar flare radiation," Bonnie Jo said.

Sam looked tired and grim. "They ain't going to Mars."

"According to the flight plan they filed, they're merely going to the Brazilian space station."

"My ass. They're heading for GEO."

"Can you get there first?" Bonnie Jo asked.

He nodded. "Got the second OTV's tanks filled with water. Rockledge bastards charged us two arms and a leg for it, but the tanks are filled. Spence is out on EVA now, rigging an extra propulsion unit to the tanker."

"Where did you get an extra propulsion unit?"

"Cannibalized from a third OTV."

Bonnie Jo tried not to, but she frowned. "That's three OTVs used for this mission. We only have two left for our regular work."

"There won't be any regular work if we don't get to GEO and establish our claim."

Her frown melted into a tight little smile. "I think I can help you there."

"How?"

"The Brazilians haven't filed an official flight plan with the IAA safety board."

The International Astronautical Administration had legal authority over all flights in space.

"Hell, neither have we," said Sam.

"Yes, but you didn't have that fatheaded Ecuadorian spouting off about sending a team to occupy GEO."

Fatheaded Ecuadorian! I almost slapped her. But I held on to my soaring temper. There was much to be learned from her, and I was a spy, after all.

Sam was muttering, "I don't see what—"

With a smug, self-satisfied smile, Bonnie Jo explained, "I just asked my uncle, the Senator from Utah, to request that our space agency people ask the IAA if they've inspected the Brazilian spacecraft to see if it's properly fitted out for long-term exposure to high radiation levels."

Sam grinned back at her. "You're setting the lawyers on them!"

"The safety experts," corrected Bonnie Jo.

"Son of a bitch. That's great!"

Bonnie Jo's smile shrank. "But you'd better get your butt off the space station and on your way to GEO before the IAA figures out what you're up to."

"We'll be ready to go in two shakes of a sperm cell's tail," Sam replied happily.

If Bonnie Jo was worried about Sam's safety up there in the Van Allen radiation, she gave no indication of it. I must confess that I felt a twinge of relief that it was Sam who was risking himself, not Spence. But still I smoldered at Bonnie Jo's insulting words about my father.

And suddenly I realized that I had to tell Papa about her scheme to delay the Brazilian mission. But how? I was stuck here in the mission control center until eight AM.

I could risk a telephone call, I thought. Later, in the dead of night, when there was little chance of anyone else hanging around.

The hours dragged by slowly. At midnight Queveda and another technician were in the center with me, helping Sam and Spence to check out their jury-rigged OTV prior to launch. By one-thirty they were almost ready to start the countdown.

I found myself holding my breath as I watched Sam and Spence go through the final inspection of the OTV, both of them encased in bulky space suits as they floated around the ungainly spacecraft, checking every strut and tank and electrical connection. Their suits had once been white, I suppose, but long use had turned them both dingy gray. Over his years in space Sam had brightened his with decorative patches and pins, but they too were frayed and faded. I could barely read the patch just above his name stencil. It said, *The meek shall inherit the Earth. The rest of us are going to the stars.*

"Hey Esmeralda," Sam called to me, "why don't you come up here with me? It's gonna be awful lonesome up there all by myself."

"Pay attention to your inspection," I told him.

But Sam was undeterred, of course. "We could practice different positions for my zero-gee hotel."

"Never in a million years," I said.

He grinned and said, "I'll wait."

At last the inspection was finished and we began the final countdown. I cleared my display screen of the TV transmission from Alpha and set up the OTV's interior readouts. For the next half-hour I concentrated every molecule of my attention on the countdown. A man could be killed by the slightest mistake now.

A part of my mind was saying, so what if Sam is killed? That would stop his mission to GEO and give your father the chance he needs to triumph. But I told myself that my father would not condone murder or even a political assassination. He would triumph and keep his hands clean. And mine. It was one thing to tinker with a computer program so that an unmanned spacecraft would be destroyed. I was not a murderer and neither was my father. Or so I told myself.

"Thirty seconds," said Ricardo Queveda, sitting on my left.

Sam had become very quiet. Was he nervous? I wondered. I certainly was. My hands were sweaty as I stared at the readouts on my display screen.

"Fifteen seconds."

Everything seemed right. All systems functioning normally. All the readouts on my screen in the green.

"Separation," the tech announced.

The launch was not dramatic. I cleared my display screen for a moment and switched to a view from one of the space station's outside cameras and saw Sam's ungainly conglomeration move away, without so much as a puff of smoke, and dwindle into the star-filled darkness.

I felt inexpressibly sad. He was my enemy, the sworn foe of my people. I should have hated Sam Gunn. Yet, as he flew off into the unknown dangers of living in the radiation belt for who knew how long, I did not feel hatred for him. Admiration, perhaps. Respect for his courage, certainly.

Suddenly I blew him a kiss. To my shock, I found that I actually *liked* Sam Gunn.

"It's a good thing he couldn't see that," Ricardo growled at me. "He would turn the OTV around and come to carry you off with him."

I leaned back in my chair, my head throbbing from the tension, glad that this Queveda person was there to remind me of my true responsibilities.

"Sam is a rogue," I said loftily. "One can admire a rogue without being captivated by him."

Ricardo snorted his disdain and got up from his chair, leaving me alone in the control center.

I waited until almost dawn before daring to phone my father. The mission was going as planned: Sam was coasting out to GEO, all systems were within nominal parameters, there was nothing for anyone to do. We had not even chatted back and forth since the launch; there was no need to, although I found myself wondering if Sam was so worried about his brash jaunt into the radiation dangers of GEO that he had finally lost the glibness of his tongue.

Somewhere a band of university scientists that Spence had hired as consultants were figuring out how long Sam could remain in GEO safely.

Queveda and the other technicians went home. Other technicians came in and sat on either side of me. After an hour of nothing to do, I told them to take a break, take a nap if they liked. I could monitor the controls by myself. I promised to call them if I needed them.

I phoned my father instead. He was still in New York, where he planned to wait for the success of the Brazilian mission. I woke him, of course, but at least this time he was alone in his bed. Or so it seemed.

"He is already on his way?" My father's sleepy eyes opened wide once I told him about Sam.

"Yes," I said. "And the United States is asking the IAA to make a safety investigation of the Brazilian spacecraft."

He seemed confused by that.

"It will delay the Brazilian mission for days!" I hissed, not daring to raise my voice. "Sam will be in GEO and claim the territory before they even get off the space station."

My father lapsed into a long string of heartfelt curses so foul that even today I blush at the memory.

He raged at me, "And what have you done about it? Nothing!"

"There is nothing I can do, Papa."

"Bah! I am surrounded by traitors and incompetents! My own daughter cannot raise a finger to help me."

"But Papa—"

"Do you realize what this gringo is doing? He is turning our own position against us! He is using my speech as a pretext for taking the equatorial orbit away from us! I will look like a fool! Before the United Nations, before the news media, before the whole world—I will be made to appear like a fool!"

I was shocked and saddened to realize that my father's concern was not for his people or for the injustice of the situation. His first concern was about his own image.

"But Papa," I asked tearfully, "what can we do about it?"

"You must act!" he said. "You said you were prepared to sabotage their spacecraft. Now is the time to do it. Strike! Strike now!"

I stared at his image in horror. My father's face was contorted with fury and hate.

"Kill that gringo bastard!" he snarled at me. "He must never reach the equatorial orbit alive."

THE BUG THAT I had inserted into the mission control program merely allowed me to fire an OTV's thrusters when I chose to. Originally I had thought that I could send an unmanned OTV crashing into a communications satellite; a neat piece of sabotage.

Sam was not planning to park his spacecraft close enough to a commsat for my plan to work, however. He merely wanted to establish himself in GEO long enough to make the territorial claim that my father wanted for the Twelve—and for the UN to recognize that claim.

I could not send him crashing into a satellite, I realized. But what if I used my bug to fire his thrusters as he approached GEO? He would go careening past the orbit, farther out into space. His trajectory would undoubtedly carry him into a wildly looping orbit that would either fling him into deep space forever, or send him hurtling back toward the Earth, to plunge into the atmosphere and burn up like a meteor.

Yes, I told myself, I could kill Sam Gunn with the touch of a finger. I was alone in the mission control center. No one would see me do it. I could then erase the bug in the program and no one would ever know why Sam's thrusters misfired.

But—murder Sam? Only a few hours earlier I had been telling myself that my father was too good a man to stoop to murder. And now—

"They're going to assassinate him."

I whirled in my chair to see Ricardo standing just inside the control center's doorway. His face was grim, his eyes red and sleepless.

"I thought you had gone home," I said.

"Didn't you hear me?" He stalked toward me, angry or frightened or both, I could not tell. "They're going to kill him! Assassinate him!"

"No . . . I can't. . . ." My voice choked in my throat.

"It's all set up," Ricardo said, padding to the chair beside me like a hunting cat. "There's nothing you can do about it."

"I can't kill Sam," I said, nearly breaking into sobs.

"Sam?" Ricardo's brows knit. "I'm not talking about Sam. It's your father. The rebels are going to assassinate him in New York."

"What? How do you know?"

"Because I'm one of them," he snapped. "I've been with them all along. And now I've been assigned to kidnap you."

"Kidnap me?" My voice sounded like a stranger's to me: pitched high with surprise and fear. Yet inwardly I was not afraid. Shocked numb, perhaps, but not frightened.

Ricardo's expression was unfathomable, but he seemed to be in torment. "Kidnap you," he repeated. "Or assassinate you if kidnapping becomes impossible."

"You wouldn't dare!"

He made a bitter, twisted smile. "This is our moment, princess. Your father is in New York, where we have enough people to get past his security team. You are his only living relative—or the only one he admits to. General Quintana is already storming the main army barracks in the capital."

"General Quintana? But he's . . ." The words choked in my mouth as I realized that Quintana was a traitor.

"He will be our next president," Ricardo said, then added, "he thinks."

I could feel my eyes widening.

Still with his twisted smile, Ricardo explained, "Do you think we are fools enough to trust a traitor? Or to put a general in the president's chair?"

"No, I suppose you are not."

Ricardo fell silent for a long moment, then he asked, "Will you allow me to kidnap you? It will be merely for long enough to keep you from warning your father."

"So that you can murder him."

"I didn't want them to do that. I thought we could overthrow him without bloodshed, but the others want to make certain that he won't be able to stop us."

I said nothing. I was desperately trying to think of something to do, some way to escape Ricardo and warn my father.

"After we finish Sam's mission I'll have to take you with me." His expression changed. He seemed almost shy, embarrassed. "I promise you that you will not be harmed in any way. Unless you try to resist, of course."

"Of course," I snapped.

He pointed to my display screen. "It's almost time for you to activate your bug."

"You know about that?"

"Of course I know about it," he said. "I have been watching you very closely since the first day you came here, pretending to be from Los Angeles."

My heart sank. I had not fooled him for a moment. Yet, somehow, I was forced to admire how clever Ricardo had been, even though he was my enemy. Or rather, my father's enemy.

"It will be a shame to kill Sam," he said, with real regret in his voice. "Maybe his trajectory will bring him close enough to one of the space stations so that somebody can rescue him."

"Not much chance of that," I said.

He shrugged. Unhappily, I thought. "It must be done. We can't allow Sam to claim the equatorial orbit."

"So your glorious rebels want the orbit for themselves," I taunted.

"Yes! Why not? It is the one chance that a poor nation such as Ecuador has to gain some of the wealth these corporations are making in space."

"So you will kill Sam as well as my father."

"No," he said grimly. "*You* will kill Sam."

At that instant Spence's voice came through the radio receiver, "Preparing for OIB."

Spence's voice. Not Sam's.

Ric looked surprised. I felt a flame of shock race through me. I whirled my chair back to the console and toggled the radio switch.

"Spence! Where are you?"

"Aboard the OTV, Juanita honey. Sam got a brilliant idea at the last minute and we switched places."

"Where is Sam?"

"He ought to be in New York by now."

"New York?" we both said in unison.

"Yeah. Anyway, I'm five minutes away from OIB. You copy?"

Orbital insertion burn. The final firing of the OTV's thrusters to place the spacecraft in the geosynchronous orbit. The time when my bug would make the thrusters fire much longer than they should and fling the craft into a wild orbit that would undoubtedly kill its pilot.

But the pilot was Spence! I had found it troubling to think of killing Sam, but it was Spence inside that OTV! No matter how angry I was with him, no matter how much I told myself I hated him, I could not knowingly, willingly, send him to his death.

"For what it's worth," Spence reported cheerfully, "the radiation monitors in this ol' tin can show everything's in the green. Radiation's building up outside, but the shielding's protecting me just fine. So far."

I turned from the display screen to Ric. His face looked awful.

"I can't do it," I whispered. "I can't kill him."

He reached out his hand toward my keyboard, then let it drop to his side. "Neither can I."

"OIB in three minutes," Spence's voice called out. "You copy?"

I looked at the mission timeline clock as I flicked the radio switch again. "We copy OIB in two minutes, fifty-six seconds."

Ric sank down onto the chair next to me, his head drooping. "Some revolutionary," he muttered.

"Let me warn my father," I pleaded. "You don't want his blood on your hands."

"No," he said, shaking his head stubbornly. "I can't go that far."

"But Sam will be with him, don't you understand?"

"Sam? Why would—"

"Sam went to New York! That's what Spence told us. The only reason for Sam to go to New York is to see my father. Sam will be in the line of fire when your assassins strike. They'll kill him too!"

Ric looked miserable, but he said in a hoarse croak, "That can't be helped. There's nothing I can do."

"Well, I can," I said, reaching for the telephone.

"Don't!"

"What will you do? Kill me?"

He grabbed my arm. I tried to pull free but he was stronger. I struggled but he held me in his powerful arms and pulled me to him and kissed me. Before I realized what I was doing I was kissing him, wildly, passionately, with all the heat of a jungle beast.

At last Ric pulled loose. He stared into my eyes for a long, timeless moment, then said, "Yes. Call your father. Warn him. I can't be a party to murder. It's one thing to talk about it, plan for it. But I just can't go through with it."

"OIB in one minute," Spence's voice chirped.

"Copy OIB in fifty-nine seconds," I said as I took up the telephone. My eyes were still on Ric. He smiled at me, the sad smile of a man who has given up everything. For me.

"You are not a killer," I said to him. "That is nothing to be ashamed of."

"But the revolution—"

"To hell with the revolution and all politics!" I snapped as I tapped out the number for my father's hotel room.

"We are sorry," said a computer-synthesized voice, "but the number you have called is not in service at this time."

Cold terror gripped my heart.

I called the hotel's main number. It was busy. For half an hour, while Spence's OTV settled into its equatorial orbit and he read off all the radiation monitors inside and outside the spacecraft, the hotel's main switch-board gave nothing but a busy signal.

I was ready to scream when Ric suddenly bolted from the control cen-ter and came back a moment later with a hand-sized portable TV. He turned it to the all-news channel.

". . . hostage situation," said a trench-coated reporter standing in front of a soaring hotel tower. It was drizzling in New York but a huge throng had already gathered out on the streets.

"Is the president of Venezuela still in there?" asked an unseen anchor woman.

"It's the president of Ecuador, Maureen," said the reporter on the street. "And, yes, as far as we know he's still in his suite with the gunmen who broke in about an hour ago."

"Do you know who's in there with him?"

The reporter, bareheaded in the chilly drizzle, squinted into the cam-era. "A couple of members of his staff. The gunmen let all the women in the suite go free about half an hour ago. And there is apparently an Amer-ican businessman in there, too. The hotel security director has identified the American as a Sam Gunn, from Orlando, Florida."

"How could the rebels get past my father's security guards?" I won-dered out loud.

"Bribes," said Ric. He spoke the word as if it were a loathsome thing. "Some men will sell their souls for money."

I told Spence what was happening, of course. He seemed strangely nonchalant.

"Sam's been in fixes like this before. He always talks his way out of 'em."

He was trying to keep my spirits up, I thought. "But these men are killers!" I said. "Assassins."

"If they haven't shot anybody yet, the chances are they won't. Unless the New York cops get trigger-happy."

That was not very encouraging.

"For what it's worth," Spence added, "the radiation monitors inside my cabin are still in the green."

We had not had time to link the radiation monitors to the telemetry system, so there was no readout for them on my console.

"Maybe you could pipe the television news up to me," he suggested. "I've got nothing else to do for a stretch."

I did that. We watched the tiny television screen until Gene Redding and his assistants showed up at eight AM A murky morning was breaking through the clouds in New York. I thought about hiring a jet plane to fly up there, but realized it would do no good. The hostage crisis dragged on, with the hotel surrounded by police and no one entering or leaving the penthouse suite of my father.

All the employees of VCI were watching the TV scene by now. It seemed as if at least half of them were jammed into the mission control center. Gene Redding had taken over as controller; I had moved to the right-hand chair, a headset still clamped over my ear.

"Want to make a bet Sam talks them out of whatever they came for?" Spence asked me.

I shook my head, then realized that he could not see me. "No," I said. "Not even Sam could—"

"Wait a minute!" said the news reporter. Like the rest of us, he had been on the scene all night without relief. "Wait a minute! There seems to be some action up there!"

The camera zoomed up to the rooftop balcony of my father's suite. And there stood Sam, grinning from ear to ear, and my father next to him, also smiling—although he looked drawn and pale, tired to the point of exhaustion. Behind them, three of the rebel gunmen were pulling off their ski masks. They too were laughing.

I rented the fastest jet available at the Orlando airport and flew to New York. With Ric at my side.

By the time we reached my father's hotel suite the police and the crowds and even the news reporters had long since gone. Sam was perched on the edge of one of the big plush chairs in the sitting room, looking almost like a child playing in a grown-up's chair. He was still wearing the faded coveralls that he had put on for the space mission.

My father, elegantly relaxed in a silk maroon dressing gown and white silk ascot, lounged at his ease in the huge sofa placed at a right angle to Sam's chair. The coffee table before them was awash with papers.

My father was smoking a cigarette in a long ivory holder. He was just blowing a cloud of gray smoke up toward the ceiling when Ric and I burst into the room.

"Papa!" I cried.

He leaped to his feet and put the cigarette behind him like a guilty little boy. Sam laughed.

"Papa, are you all right?" I rushed across the room to him. Awkwardly, he balanced the long cigarette holder on the arm of the sofa as I flung my arms around his neck.

"I am unharmed," he announced calmly. "The rebels have gone back to Quito to form the new government."

"New government?"

"General Quintana will head the provisional government," my father explained, "until new elections are held."

"Quintana?" I blurted. "The traitor?"

Ric's face clouded over. "The army will run the government and find excuses not to hold elections. It's an old story."

"What else could I do?" my father asked sadly.

Still seated in the oversized chair, Sam grinned up at us. "You didn't do too badly, Carlos old buddy."

Sam Gunn, on a first-name basis with my father?

Getting to his feet, Sam said to me, "Meet the new co-owner of Orb-Hotel, Inc."

One shock after another. It took hours for me to get it all straight in my head. Gradually, as my father and Sam told me slightly conflicting stories, I began to put the picture together.

Sam had barged into my father's hotel suite just as the rebel assassination team had arrived, guns in hand.

"They had bribed two of my security guards," my father said grimly. "They just walked in through the front door of the suite, wearing those ridiculous ski masks."

Sam added, "They were so focused on your father and the other two guys in his security team that I walked in right behind them and they never even noticed. Some assassins. A trio of college kids with guns."

Once they realized that an American citizen was in the suite the student-assassins became confused. Sam, of course, immediately began bewildering them with a nonstop monologue about how rich they could become if they would merely listen to reason.

"They're all shareholders in my new corporation," Sam told us happily. "Sam Gunn Enterprises, Unlimited. Neat title, isn't it?"

"They refrained from assassinating my father in exchange for shares in a nonexistent corporation?" I asked.

"It'll exist!" Sam insisted. "It's going to be the holding company for all my other enterprises—VCI, OrbHotel, I got lots of other ideas, too, you know."

My father's face turned somber. "They did not settle merely for shares in Sam's company."

"Oh? What else?"

"I had to resign as president of Ecuador and name Quintana as head of the interim government."

"Until elections can be held," Ric added sarcastically.

"Who is this young man?" my father asked.

"I am Ricorio Esteban Horacio Queveda y Diego, son of Professor Queveda, who fled from your secret police the year you became president."

"Ah." My father sagged down onto the sofa and picked up his cigarette holder once again. "Then you want to murder me, too, I suppose."

"Papa, you're murdering yourself with those cigarettes!"

"No lectures today, little one," he said to me. Then he puffed deeply on his cigarette. "I have been through much these past twenty hours."

"Ric did not condone assassinating you," I told my father. "He wanted me to warn you." That was stretching the truth, of course, and I wondered why I said it. Until I took a look at Ric, so serious, so handsome, so brave.

For his part, Ric said, "So you have joined forces with this gringo imperialist."

"Imperialist?" Sam laughed.

"I have invested my private monies in the orbital hotel project, yes," my father admitted.

"Drug money," Ric accused. "Cocaine money squeezed from the sweat of the poor farmers."

"We're going to make those farmers a lot richer," Sam said.

"Yes, of course." Ric looked as if he could murder them both.

"Listen to me, hothead," said Sam, jabbing a stubby finger in Ric's direction. "First of all, I'm no flogging imperialist."

"Then why have you claimed the equatorial orbit for yourself?"

"So that nobody else could claim it. I don't give a crap whether the UN recognizes our claim or not, I'm *giving* all rights to the orbit to the UN itself. That orbit belongs to the people of the world, not any nation or corporation."

"You're giving . . . ?"

"Yeah, sure. Why let the lawyers spend the next twenty years wrangling over the legalities? I claim the orbit, then voluntarily give up the claim to the people of the world, as represented by the United Nations. So there!" And Sam stuck his tongue out at Ric, like a self-satisfied little boy.

Before either of us could reply, Sam went on, "There's big money to be made in space, kids. VCI's just the beginning. OrbHotel's gonna be a winner, and with Carlos bankrolling it, I won't have to fight with VCI's stockholders for the start-up cash."

"And how are you going to make the farmers of Ecuador rich?" Ric asked, still belligerent.

Sam leaned back in the plush chair and clasped his hands behind his head. His grin became enormous.

"By making the government of Ecuador a partner in Sam Gunn Enterprises, Unlimited."

Ric's face went red with anger. "That will make Quintana rich, not the people!"

"Only if you let Quintana stay in office," Sam said smugly.

"A typical gringo trick."

"Wait a minute. Think it out. Suppose I announce that I'm willing to make a *democratically elected* government of Ecuador a partner in my corporation? Won't that help you push Quintana out of power?"

"Yes, of course it would," I said.

Ric was not so enthusiastic. "It might help," he said warily. But then he added, "Even so, how can a partnership in your corporation make millions of poor farmers rich?"

"It won't make them poorer," replied Sam. "It may put only a few sucres into their pockets, but that'll make life a little sweeter for them, won't it?"

Sam had made a bilingual pun! I was impressed, even if Ric was not.

"And we'll be buying all our foodstuffs for OrbHotel from Ecuadorian producers, naturally," Sam went on. "And I'll sell Ecuadorian produce to the other orbital facilities, too. Make a nice profit from it, I betcha. Sure, there's only a few hundred people living in orbit right now but that's gonna grow. There'll be thousands pretty soon, and once the Japanese start building their solar power satellites they're going to need food for a lot of workers."

Without seeming to draw a breath Sam went on, "Then there's the hotel training facility we're gonna build just outside Quito. We'll hire Ecuadorians preferentially, of course. Your father drove a hard bargain, believe me, Esmeralda."

My father smiled wanly.

"And one of these days we could even build a skyhook, an elevator tower up to GEO," Sam continued. "That'd make Ecuador the world's center for space transportation. People won't need rockets; they'll ride the elevator, starting in Ecuador. It'll cost peanuts to get into space that way."

He talked on and on until even Ric was at least halfway convinced that Sam would be good for the people of Ecuador.

It was growing dark before Sam finally said, "Why don't we find a good restaurant and celebrate our new partnership?"

I looked at Ric. He wavered.

So I said, for both of us, "Very well. Dinner tonight. But tomorrow Ric and I leave for Quito. We have much work to do if Quintana is to be prevented from cementing his hold on the government."

Sam smiled at us both. "You'll be going to Quito as representatives of Sam Gunn Enterprises, Unlimited. I don't want this Quintana character to think you're revolutionaries and getting you kids getting into trouble."

"But we are revolutionaries," Ric insisted.

"I know," said Sam. "The best kind of revolutionaries. The kind that're really going to change things."

"Do you think we can?" I asked.

My father, surprisingly, said, "You must. The future depends on you."

"Don't look so gloomy, Carlos, old buddy," Sam said. "You've got to understand the big picture."

"The big picture?"

"Sure. There's money to be made in space. Lots of money."

"I understand that," said my father.

"Yeah, but you gotta understand the rest of it." And Sam looked squarely at Ric as he said, "The money is made in space. But it gets spent here on Earth."

My father brushed thoughtfully at his mustache with a fingertip. "I see."

"So let's spread it around and do some good."

Ric almost smiled. "But I think you will get more of the money than anyone else, won't you?"

Sam gave him a rueful look. "Yeah, that's right. And I'll spend it faster than anybody else, too."

So Ric and I returned to Ecuador. General Quintana reluctantly stepped aside and allowed elections. Democracy returned to Ecuador, although Ric claimed it arrived in our native land for the first time. Quintana retired gracefully, thanks to a huge bribe that Sam and my father provided. My father actually was voted back into the presidency, in an election that was mostly fair and open.

Spence and Bonnie Jo eventually were divorced, but that happened years later. By that time I had married Ric and he was a rising young politician who would one day be president of Ecuador himself. The country was slowly growing richer, thanks to its investment in space industries. Sam's orbital hotel was only the first step in the constantly growing commerce in space.

I never saw Sam again. Not face-to-face. Naturally, we all saw him in the news broadcasts time and again. Just as he said, he spent every penny of the money he made on OrbHotel and went broke.

But that is another story. And, *gracias a dios,* it is a story that does not involve me.

Habitat New Chicago

"SURE, I KNEW SAM—BRIEFLY," RUSSELL CHRISTOPHER SAID as he and Jade stood on the edge of the playground. "This ball field wouldn't be here if it weren't for Sam."

Jade was at Solar News's virtual reality center. Like Christopher, she was wearing a full-sensor VR helmet and gloves. While she was still in the low lunar gravity of Selene, she could see and feel everything that Christopher saw and felt, standing at the playground in the New Chicago habitat, a quarter-million miles from the Moon.

"You said something about Sam being a grandfather?" Jade asked. Then she had to wait for an annoying three seconds for Christopher's reply to reach her.

He was a good-looking man, Jade thought: tall and lean, with an earnest, honest-looking face and clear light blue eyes. He reminded Jade of Spence.

"Grandfathered," Christopher replied at last. "I said Sam was grandfathered, not a grandfather."

"What do you mean?"

Again the interminable three-second delay.

"It's kind of complicated," said Christopher.

I'll never get the story out of him like this, Jade thought. It'll take a week, with this time lag.

"Look," she said, "why don't you just tell me the whole story in your own words. Can you do that?"

"Sure," Christopher answered, after another three seconds.

Grandfather Sam

IT LOOKED EXTREMELY ROCKY FOR THE NEW CHICAGO CUBS that day. Okay, so I stole the line from "Casey at the Bat." But it really was the bottom of the ninth, and the New White Sox were ahead of us, 14-13, there were two out, and little Sam Gunn was coming up to bat.

To everybody except Hornsby and me it was just a pickup game being played on the last unzoned open space in New Chicago. Nobody was playing for anything except fun. Except him and me. And Sam, although I didn't know it then.

We had acquired quite a crowd, considering this was just a sandlot game. Not even sandlot. There wasn't a real infield, nothing but grass and a few odd pieces to mark the bases. Sam's expensive suede jacket was second base, for instance. My old cap was home plate. You didn't need a cap to play baseball in New Chicago, or sunglasses, either. Sunlight comes into the habitat through long windows; it's not a big glaring ball in the sky, except once in a while when a window happens to be facing directly sunward.

New Chicago was—is—an O'Neill-type space habitat. You know, a big cylinder built along the Moon's orbit at the L-5 point, just hanging there like an oversized length of pipe. About the length of Manhattan island and a couple of kilometers in diameter, New Chicago spins along its central axis a lazy once per minute; that's enough to produce an artificial gravity inside that's almost exactly the same as Earth's.

Newcomers get a little disconcerted the first time they come out into the open and look up. Instead of sky, there's more of New Chicago up there. The landscaped ground just curves up along the inside of the cylinder, all the way around. With binoculars you can see people standing upside-down up there, staring at you through their binoculars because you look upside-down to them.

New Chicago is really a lovely place, or it was until the real-estate tycoons got their hooks into it. It was nowhere as big as sprawling Old Chicago had been before the greenhouse floods, of course. It was beautifully landscaped on the inside with hills and woods and small, livable villages scattered here and there with plenty of open green space in between.

It was that green space that had attracted Sam and me and the other applicant—Elrod Hornsby, a lawyer representing a big construction firm from Selene City—to this morning's meeting of the Zoning Board. To developers like Sam and Hornsby, open green space was an open invitation to making money. Convert the green space into something profitable, like an extra condo complex or an amusement center. Why not? New Chicago was originally spec'd to hold fifty thousand families, with plenty of living space for everybody.

But the builders, developers, lawyers, politicians, they all saw that the habitat could actually hold a lot more people. Millions, if they had the same average living space that people once had in Old Chicago. Tens of millions, if they were packed in the way they were in Delhi or Mexico City or Port Nairobi.

Go on, pack 'em in! That's what the developers wanted. They made their money by overbuilding in the space habitats and then moving back Earthside, to some quiet little gated community on a mountaintop where nobody but megamillionaires were allowed in, while the communities they wrecked sank into slums rife with crime and disease.

What do they care?

Like I said, Sam and Hornsby both had their eyes on this open green field. I did too, but for a very different reason.

So there I was, standing on first base, puffing hard from running out a dribbler of a ground ball to shortstop. A real ballplayer would have pegged me out by twenty feet, but the teenager playing short for the White Sox had a scattergun for an arm; when he threw the ball, the crowd behind first base hit the ground. I think maybe even the people watching from overhead through their binoculars might have ducked. That's how I got to first.

Now, Sam wasn't much of a hitter. So far, he'd produced a couple of pop flies to the infield, struck out once (but got to first when he dropped his bat on the catcher's foot and the poor kid, howling and hopping in pain, dropped the ball) and had a pair of bunt singles. Hadn't hit the ball farther than forty feet, except for the pop-ups, which went pretty high, but not very far.

Oh yeah, and Sam had walked a couple of times. After all, he was a small target up there at the plate.

Board member Pete Nostrum was grinning like a clown from the pitcher's mound. It wasn't a mound, really, just a scuffed-up part of the grass field. See, Hornsby and the whole Zoning Board were on the White Sox side of the game, while Sam and I were on the Cubs. Both sides filled in their teams with some of the kids who'd been playing when the Zoning Board meeting adjourned to this open field.

So there was Nostrum on the mound, Bonnie McDougal creeping in toward the plate from her position at third base, anticipating another bunt, and the rest of the Zoning Board scattered through the field.

This was all Sam's idea. The morning had started in the Zoning Board's regular meeting chamber, with Sam, me, and Hornsby all petitioning the Board for a zoning change for this chunk of open ground. Hornsby wanted to build a fancy high-rise condo complex, with towers that went up a hundred flights, almost up to the habitat's centerline, where the spingrav dwindled down to almost nothing.

Sam wanted permission to build what he called an amusement center. And he'd had the gall to start his presentation by referring to Old Chicago.

"I was born and raised in Old Chicago, y'know," Sam said to the assembled savants of Zoning Board. "That's why I want to settle here and add something to the community."

The assembled savants, up there behind their long table, said nothing, although grumpy old Fred Arrant, at the end of the table, looked as if he wanted to puke.

I myself thought the "born in Chicago" line was probably a bit much. Sam Gunn must have been born somewhere, but I was pretty sure it wasn't in Old Chicago.

Sam Gunn was a legend and he knew it. He just sat there between me and Hornsby, the third applicant, with a choirboy's angelic smile on his round hobgoblin's face. He was wearing a faun-tan collarless suede jacket and neatly pressed slacks, with an open-necked shirt of pale lemon. It made my faithful old olive-drab coveralls look positively crummy, by comparison. Hornsby, overweight and completely bald, wore an awful micromesh suit of coral pink; it made him look like a giant newborn rat.

Being a legend carries a great deal of freight with it. Sam was known throughout the settled parts of the solar system as a pioneer, an entrepreneur, a guy with a vision as wide as the skies and a heart to match. He had made who knew how many fortunes and lost every last one of them, usually because he was such a soft touch that he couldn't refuse a friend in need. But he was also known as a loudmouthed, womanizing, scheming wheeler-dealer who wouldn't think twice about bending the law to the snapping point if he thought he could get away with it. He'd left a trail of broken hearts and fuming, furious tycoons, lawyers, corporate bigwigs and government officials all the way out to Saturn and back again.

His friends—who were few but loyal—said that Sam's one big weakness was that he couldn't stand by and let the big guys in business or government push the little guys around. His enemies—who were legion and powerful—howled that Sam was a king-sized pain in the butt.

I had to laugh about the "king-sized." Sam was tiny, an elf, a chunky, fast-talking little guy with bristling red hair and a sprinkling of Huck Finn freckles across his nub of a nose. His eyes were sort of hazel, sometimes they looked blue, sometimes green, sometimes something in-between. Shifty eyes, the kind a gambler or cat burglar might have.

"So naturally," he was saying to the Zoning Board, "I thought that New Chicago would be the ideal place for me to build my amusement center."

The members of the Zoning Board glanced back and forth among themselves.

"Amusement center, Mr. Gunn?" asked the chairperson, Bonnie Mc-Dougal. She was an elegant blonde, tall, cool, very much in possession of herself. No doubt Sam wanted to possess her, too. There was hardly a woman he'd ever met that he didn't try to bed—according to his legend.

"Aren't you the guy who built that orbital whorehouse a few years back?" growled Arrant, who was known as the Zoning Board's bulldog. His first reaction to any request was always a loud, "No!" Then he'd get really negative.

"It was a zero-gravity honeymoon hotel," Sam replied politely. "Perfectly legitimate, sir. Our motto was, 'If you like waterbeds, you'll love zero-gee.'"

"Zero-gee?" McDougal asked, a cool smile on her lips. "Like we have along the centerline here in New Chicago?"

Sam smiled back at her; it looked more like a leer. "Exactly the same. Precisely. You can float around weightlessly up there."

Their eyes met. She turned away first.

"You see," Sam went on in his oh-so-reasonable manner, "I really want to give this community something it needs, something that will be useful."

"Like a gambling casino," Rick Cole said. Cole had a reputation for being the smartest member of the five-person board. He was about my own age: pushing eighty, calendar-wise, but physically as youthful as a thirty-year-old, thanks to rejuvenation therapy. A former lawyer who had renounced the legal profession when he came up to New Chicago and took up a new career in public service. In other words, he'd made his money, and now he wanted respect.

"What's wrong with a gambling casino?" asked Pete Nostrum, sitting next to Cole. "We don't have one yet, do we?"

Cole gave him a look that would shrivel Mount Everest, but it just bounced off Nostrum's silly face.

Nostrum couldn't get respect if he paid for it. God knows he'd tried that route. Nostrum was a mental lightweight who'd won a seat on the Zoning Board by spending enough money to buy a majority of the community council that appointed the Board. He wanted any public office he could find, so he could have a platform to push his one, single-minded passion: holiday bonfires. No matter how many times the safety people nixed the idea, no matter how many times the New Chicago council of directors pushed his nose into the habitat's book of regulations, Nostrum still pushed for bonfires in the big central park to celebrate every holiday from Christmas to Bastille Day to the return of Halley's Comet.

"Surely this board won't permit a gambling casino to be erected in New Chicago!" Hornsby protested in a high, almost girlish voice, raising a chubby hand over his head as he spoke. He was badly overweight, a fact that his coral pink micromesh suit emphasized; he had piggy little eyes set deep in a puffy-cheeked pink face and tight little ears plastered flat against the sides of his head.

"It's not a gambling casino," Sam corrected.

"Mr. Hornsby, you are out of order," said Chairperson McDougal, but so sweetly that Hornsby just sort of grinned foolishly and muttered an apology.

Turning to Sam, she said, "Your application is very vague as to just what this 'amusement center' is to be, Mr. Gunn."

Sam got his feet, all five-four or thereabouts of him, and announced grandly, "Because, oh most gracious of chairpersons, I want to leave it to the good citizens of New Chicago to decide for themselves what kind of entertainments they would like to have."

John Morris, the crafty-eyed board member at the end of the table, steepled his fingers in front of his face as he asked, "And just what do you mean by that, Mr. Gunn?"

Morris had recently been accused of accepting bribes in return for his vote. He'd denied the charge, claiming that the sudden spurts in his bank account had been all pure luck in the stock market.

"I mean, sir," Sam replied, "that I intend to furnish a fifty-storey building in which each floor consists of an open area in which all four walls are covered with hologrammic smart screens. The floors and ceilings, too. The citizens of New Chicago will be able to program their amusement center for whatever kinds of recreation they seek. . . ."

Sam strode out from behind the applicants' table as he talked, his voice rising in fervor as he extolled the wonders of his idea: "Think of it! The finest symphony orchestras of Earth can perform here. The greatest sports teams! Pop singers! Ballet! Great dramas, dance, athletic competitions, virtually anything at all! In the amusement complex."

"We can get all that in our own homes," Arrant groused, "through virtual reality."

"Without having to buy a ticket from you, or anyone else," Cole added.

"Yes, that's true," Sam replied, sweetly reasonable. "But home entertainment doesn't provide the thrill of the crowd, the amplified excitement of being together with thousands of other people, the sheer exhilaration of interacting with other people."

Sam spread his stubby arms as wide as they would go. "Study after study has shown that home entertainment doesn't compare in emotional impact with theater performances. Let me show . . ."

And on he talked, on and on and on. He gave a one-man performance that I've never seen equaled in its sheer bravado, vigor, and élan. The board members sat mesmerized by Sam's leather-lunged presentation. He didn't use slides or videos or VR simulations. He just talked. And talked. Even grouchy old Arrant had stars in his eyes before long. Hell, Sam pretty nearly had me convinced.

Bonnie McDougal brought us all down to earth. "So the essence of your proposal, Mr. Gunn, is to establish a hologrammic facility with full VR capability?"

Sam teetered for a moment like a man who'd just stopped himself from falling over a cliff. "Yes, Madam Chairperson," he said at last. "That's putting it very succinctly."

McDougal smiled brightly at him. "Thank you for your presentation, Mr. Gunn. And it's Miss Chairperson."

Sam's face lit up.

"Now then," McDougal said, glancing at the display screen built into the tabletop before her, "it's your turn, Mr. Hornsby."

Hornsby had slides and videos aplenty. The developers he represented, Woodruff and Dorril, wanted to build a three-hundred-unit condo complex on the ground in question, complete with three swimming pools, tennis courts, and a running track for joggers. There were no structures higher than four storeys in the entire New Chicago habitat, but Hornsby extolled the high-rise approach as being environmentally friendly.

"If you put three hundred condo units into four-storey buildings, it would cover the entire parcel and even spill over into the adjacent properties."

Pete Nostrum found this amusing. Looking down the table to fellow board member Morris, Nostrum said loudly, "Hey, you own property abutting this parcel, don't you Johnny? What's this gonna do to your property's value?"

Morris curled his lip at the laughing Nostrum.

McDougal said softly, "Mr. Hornsby, the issue here is not how we house three hundred additional families. New Chicago is not actively seeking more population."

"But you should, Madam Chairperson," Hornsby said earnestly, sweat trickling down his fat cheeks. "You must! A community must grow or wither! There's no third choice."

McDougal sighed. Cole snapped, "That's flatland thinking, Mr. Hornsby. We're quite content with a stable population here."

"Maybe you are," said Morris, "but I tend to agree with Mr. Hornsby. A little growth would be beneficial."

"A little growth? Three hundred new families?"

"A drop in the bucket."

Arrant spoke up. "A foot in the door, you mean. If we let this outfit build new housing, how can we deny the same opportunity to other builders?"

"I don't see it as a precedent," said Morris.

"Of course you don't. . . ."

"Gentlemen," said McDougal, "Mr. Christopher is waiting to make his proposal."

"Why don't we break for lunch first?" Arrant suggested.

"Let's hear out Mr. Christopher before lunch," McDougal said, pleasant but firm.

I got to my feet, feeling nervous. "Uh . . . this won't take long. What I'd like to do with the parcel is . . . well, leave it alone. In perpetuity."

"Leave it alone?" Morris was shocked.

"Undeveloped?" Arrant asked.

"Forever?" Barney Wilhelm, sitting at the other end of the table, stared at me in disbelief.

"Yessir. . . . uh, sirs. And lady. Leave it alone forever. Zone it as a public playground in perpetuity."

"We have plenty of public parks in New Chicago."

"Lots of green space."

"That's true," I admitted, "but there's no open place where kids can play—"

"What do you mean?" Cole snapped. "There's the Little League baseball field, the Hallas football field—"

"Olympic Stadium," Nostrum jumped in, "the soccer field, tennis courts, four golf courses. And not one of them permits bonfires!"

"I know all that," I said. "But all those fields are for organized sports. You have to be a member of a team. They all have strict rules about who can play on them, and at what time."

"So what do you want?" Wilhelm asked.

"Just a playground. No regulations. Open all the time to any kids who want to have a catch, or play a pickup game, or just run around and have fun."

"No regulations?"

"No set hours of operation?"

"Just anybody could come in and play, whenever they felt like it?"

I nodded. "That's exactly what I'm asking for."

I could tell from their faces that they thought I was crazy. As I sat down, Hornsby smirked at me, looking superior. But Sam looked thoughtful.

He leaned toward me and whispered, "They'd never pick me for a team when I was a kid. I always had to be the batboy."

Bonnie McDougal looked up and down the table at her fellow Zoning Board members and said, "Shall we vote on the three proposals now, gentlemen? That would finish today's agenda and we could take the rest of the day off."

They voted, using the keyboards built into the table before each seat. The tally came up on McDougal's screen, flush with the tabletop.

I knew my proposal didn't have a chance. It was between Sam and Hornsby, and with Sam's reputation, I figured Hornsby's high-rise condo complex was a shoo-in.

I was wrong.

McDougal blinked several times at her screen, then looked up at us and announced, "We have a tie. Two votes for each applicant. We'll have to reconvene after lunch and work this out."

We got up and left the meeting room. I was surprised, but not very hopeful. After all, I only got two votes out of six. I had nothing to offer that would sway the other four. They'd ditch me after lunch, when they got down to the serious wheeling and dealing.

Sam was at my elbow as we walked out into the sunlight. "Sonofabitch," he muttered. "I expected better."

"Did you?" I said, heading for the sandwich joint on the corner of the courthouse square.

Sam kept stride with me, despite my longer legs. "Yeah. I bought Arrant and Cole. I know Hornsby's bought Morris and Wilhelm."

"Bought?" I was aghast. "You mean bribed?"

Sam grinned up at me, a freckled and crafty Huck Finn. "Don't look so shocked, Straight Arrow. Happens all the time."

"But . . . bribery? In New Chicago?"

With a laugh, Sam told me, "You're missing the point. McDougal and Nostrum voted for you. Why? What're they after?"

"Maybe they're honest," I said.

"McDougal, maybe," Sam replied. "Now, if I could figure out a way to turn Nostrum around . . ." Sam snapped his fingers. "Virtual bonfires! That'd get him!"

I strode away from him and had my lunch alone.

It only took five minutes to gobble down a sandwich. The Zoning Board wasn't set to reconvene for another hour and a half. Inevitably, I drifted over to the open lot that we were debating over. A gaggle of teenagers were playing baseball on the threadbare grass. Younger kids were flying kites over in what passed for center field. They were laughing, running, calling back and forth to one another. Having a good time, relaxed, with no regimentation, no pressure to win or set a new record.

"They sure seem to be having fun, don't they?"

It was Sam. He had come up behind me.

I sighed. "They won't, once your amusement center gets built. Or Hornsby's condo complex."

Sam squinted up at the kites. Beyond them I could see the curve of the habitat: the long solar window running the length of the structure, the landscaped hills and winding bicycle paths. What had originally been neat little villages was already growing into sprawling towns. There was still a good deal of green space, but it was dwindling. And you had to belong to an official team to use any of it; you had to show up at a specific time and compete in organized leagues where parents screamed in vicarious belligerence, teaching their kids that winning is more important than playing, outdoing the other guy more important than having fun.

"I used to play a pretty good third base."

We both turned, and there was Bonnie McDougal. She was nearly my height; much taller than Sam. But he grinned up at her, his eyes alight with what I thought was obvious lust.

"Instead of reconvening the meeting," Sam said, "why don't we settle this business with a baseball game!"

McDougal and I both said, "A baseball game?"

"Sure, why not? Isn't it better out here in the sunshine than in that dusty old meeting room?"

"It's not a dusty old room," McDougal protested.

"Sam," I pointed out, "how can we settle a three-way tie with a ball game?"

He looked at me as though I had missed the point entirely. "Because, oh noble sportsman, I've decided to withdraw my application. It's you against Hornsby now."

"Withdraw . . . ?" I turned to McDougal. "Can he do that?"

She nodded at me and smiled at Sam, all at the same time. "He certainly can. But it will call for a new vote of the board."

"Vote, schmote," Sam said. "Let's play ball!"

So that's how we got to the bottom of the ninth, the White Sox ahead of us, 14-13, two out, and Sam coming up to bat.

I was standing on first, trying to get my breathing back to normal after running out my infield hit. Funny how quickly the body falls out of condition. I'd been an athlete all my life, and now I was puffing after digging hard for ninety lousy feet.

All my life. I'd been one of those kids: Little League, high school football, basketball and baseball in college, all the while my father hounding me, pushing me, trying to make me into the star he'd never been. I'd almost made it, too; had a tryout with the real Chicago White Sox, back in Old Chicago, before Lake Michigan drowned ancient old Comiskey Park in the greenhouse floods.

My dad was dead by then, killed in an auto wreck, driving to see me play against Notre Dame. Still I pursued his dream. And I'd almost been good enough to make it. Almost. Instead, after half a lifetime batting around the minor leagues, I finally came up to New Chicago to take up a career counseling kids who were having trouble adjusting to living off-Earth.

Well, anyway, there I was at first base, with Sam coming up to bat. Bonnie McDougal was creeping in from third, expecting another bunt, wearing a tattered old glove she'd borrowed from one of the kids. Nostrum was grinning hugely; he was enjoying himself so much I thought maybe he'd forget about bonfires. The rest of the Zoning Board was waiting for Sam to step up to the plate.

"What're you waiting for?" yelled grouchy old Arrant. He was playing first base for the Sox; didn't have to move much, and the throws he missed were our best offensive weapon, so far.

"Just what are you doing?" Hornsby demanded. He was the catcher for the Sox, looking even more ridiculous than before in a borrowed chest protector that barely covered his big belly and a mask that scrunched his face into a mass of wrinkles.

Sam was standing off to the side of home plate (my old cap), the game's one and only carbon-fiber bat leaning against his hip, tapping away at his pocket computer, oblivious to their complaints.

"Play ball!" McDougal yelled in from third.

"Play ball!" the other White Sox began to holler. Even the crowd started chanting, "Play ball! Play ball!"

I was wondering what the devil Sam was doing with that computer of his. Checking the stock market? Making reservations for his flight back to Selene City? What?

At last he tucked the tiny machine back into his pants pocket and stepped up to the plate, gripping the bat right down at the end, ready to swing for the fences. Except that we didn't have any fences, just a few kids way out in center field flying kites and playing tag.

Nostrum looked down at Hornsby behind the plate. They didn't have any signals. Nostrum couldn't throw anything except a medium-fast straight pitch. No curve, no change-up. I'd walloped two of them for home runs; he'd been lucky to get me to chop a grounder to short here in the bottom of the ninth.

Nostrum kicked his foot high and threw. I lit out for second base. Sam swung mightily and missed by a foot. I didn't even have to slide into second; there was no way Hornsby could get a throw down there ahead of me.

"Hey, that's not fair!" Nostrum yelled. "Stealing bases isn't fair."

"It's part of the game," I said, standing on second, puffing.

"Not this game," Nostrum hollered, stamping around, red in the face.

If Sam was right, Nostrum had been one of my two votes. I didn't want to antagonize him. Still, this game was supposed to decide whether I won the zoning decision or Hornsby did. So I stood on second base (Sam's expensive coat) and folded my arms across my chest.

"We're playing baseball," I said. "Nobody said stealing bases was a no-no."

"Nobody stole a base until now!" Nostrum shouted.

I could see he was getting really sore. Bonnie McDougal trotted over from third base to him. Hornsby came up from home. Even crabby old Arrant creaked over toward the mound from first base.

"Why don't we make a rule that stealing bases is prohibited from now on," McDougal said gently, "but since Mr. Christopher stole second before the rule went into effect, he can stay on second base."

Arrant shrugged. Hornsby nodded. Nostrum glared at me for a moment, but then broke into a sheepish grin.

"Aw, all right," he said.

"Is that all right with you, Mr. Christopher?" McDougal asked me.

I saw Sam, back near home plate, nodding so hard I thought his eyeballs would fall out.

"Okay," I said, still standing on Sam's coat.

Hornsby squeezed his face back into the catcher's mask, but not before saying, "Okay, now can we get this game over with?"

But Sam was playing with his pocket computer again. The crowd began to chant "Play ball!" again, and Sam put the thing away and stepped up to the plate with a sly smile on his face.

Nostrum threw. I stayed on second. Sam swung mightily and missed again.

"Strike two!" Hornsby crowed. One more strike and we were dead.

Sam seemed unconcerned. I realized that both his swings had been terrible uppercuts, as if he was trying to blast the ball out of sight.

"Never mind the home run, Sam!" I yelled to him. "Just make contact with the ball!"

Nostrum cackled at that. He cranked up and threw his hardest. Sam swung, another big uppercut.

And popped the ball up into a monumental infield fly. I took off from second: with two outs, you run like hell no matter where the ball's hit. But while I was heading for third I craned my neck to see where the ball was going.

Up and up, higher and higher. It seemed to hang up there, floating like a little round cloud. As I raced around third I saw Hornsby throw off his mask and stagger toward Nostrum. McDougal was coming in from third base, also staring up into the cloud-free sky. Even Arrant and the wild-armed kid shortstop were converging toward the pitcher.

"Mine!" McDougal called out.

"I got it!"

"All mine!"

I was around third by now. Sam was trotting around first, heading for second base. Suddenly Hornsby and all the others seemed to freeze in their tracks. McDougal threw her arms over her head. Arrant stumbled and fell to his knees. Nostrum yelped so loud I thought someone had put a match to his backside.

The sun, the blazing, dazzling, glorious sun was shining through the habitat window like a zillion-megawatt spotlight. The whole White Sox infield was blinded by the glare. Sam's pop-up was coming down now, just short of second base. The kid in center field made a belated dash in for it, but the ball hit the grass after I had crossed the plate with the tying run.

And Sam was racing madly for third, his little arms pumping, stumpy legs churning, his mouth wide open sucking air, his eyes even wider.

The whole Sox infield was still staggering around, seeing sunspots in their eyes. The center fielder had the ball in his hands, but nobody to throw it to. His face flashed surprise, then consternation. Then he did the only thing he could—he started running toward home.

It was a foot race. The youngster was faster than Sam, but Sam was already around third and roaring home. The kid cut across the infield and dived at Sam just as Sam launched himself into a hook slide while the Sox infield stood around blinking and groping.

It was close, but Sam's left foot neatly hooked my cap and carried it along for several feet while the teenager flopped on his belly so hard that the ball bounced out of his outstretched hand.

We won, 15-14. The crowd went, as they say, wild. There weren't that many of them, but they whooped and yelled and danced little jigs and jags all across the field. I rushed over and picked Sam up off the grass. The leg of his slacks was ripped from the knee down and green with grass stain, but he was grinning like a gap-toothed Jack-o'-lantern.

"We won! We won!" Sam danced up and down.

I went over to the kid center fielder and helped him to his feet. "Great play, kid," I told him. "Terrific hustle."

He grinned, too, a little weakly.

Hours later, Sam and I were having a drink at the patio of Pete's Tavern, just off the courthouse square. We had both cleaned up after the game and the perfunctory Zoning Board meeting—held right there at the open lot—that approved my proposal.

"You must be the luckiest guy in the solar system," I said to him, between sips on my cranberry juice.

Sam was sipping something more potent. He gave me a sly look. "Chance favors the prepared mind, Chris, old pal."

"Sure," I said.

"What do you think I was doing with my faithful pocket whizbang just before I came up to bat?" he asked.

I had forgotten about that. Before I could think of an answer, Sam told me, "I was calculating the precise time when the sun would shine through the habitat window, old Straight Arrow. That's why I was trying to hit a pop-up."

"You deliberately—" I couldn't believe it.

"I had to get you home with the tying run, didn't I? I'm no slugger; I have to use my smarts." Sam tapped his temple.

I didn't believe it. "Sam, nobody can deliberately hit a pop-up. Not deliberately."

He screwed up his face a little. "Yeah, maybe you're right. I figure you've got only one chance in three to get it right."

"One chance in three," I echoed. He had swung and missed twice, I remembered.

"So," Sam finished his drink and put it down on the table in front of him, "you've got your playground, in perpetuity."

"Thanks to you, Sam."

He shrugged. "I guess we're kind of partners, huh?"

"I guess so."

He stuck his hand out across the little table. I took it and we shook hands. But even as we were doing that, Sam was looking past my shoulder. He broke into a big grin and scrambled to his feet.

I turned in my chair. Bonnie McDougal was coming along the walk, looking coolly elegant in a white sheath dress decorated with gold thread.

"You know," she said as she came up to our table, "my fellow Zoning Board members might take our having dinner together as an inappropriate act."

Holding a chair for her, Sam said innocently, "But I have dinner every evening."

"Inappropriate for me, Sam," she said as she sat down.

I was wondering when he'd had the chance to invite her to dinner.

"But the vote's over and done with," Sam said, returning to his chair. "This isn't a payoff. We won the ball game, fair and square."

"You won," Bonnie said, smiling.

Sam grinned hugely and tapped me on the shoulder. "The gold dust twins, Chris and me. Partners."

I grinned back at him. "Partners."

"And the amusement center won't interfere with the playground at all," Sam said.

"Amusement center?" Bonnie and I both asked.

"It'll be way up above the playground," Sam said genially. "It'll start roughly one hundred fifty-two point four meters above the grass and go up to the habitat's centerline. You'll hardly notice the support piers."

"Sup . . . support piers?" I sputtered.

"Roughly one hundred fifty-two point four meters?" Bonnie asked, with a sardonic smile.

"That'll give me almost eighteen hundred and forty-eight meters to build in," Sam said, pulling out his pocket computer.

"Build? Build what?"

"Our entertainment center, partner." His fingers tapping furiously on the computer's tiny keypad, Sam muttered, "Figuring four meters per floor, we can put in—wow! That's enormous!"

"But, Sam, you can't build over the park!"

"Why not? It won't hurt anything. And it'll protect the kids from getting the sun in their eyes." He laughed heartily.

I sank back in my chair.

"You'll get half the earnings, partner. Ought to be able to help a lot of kids with that kind of income."

Bonnie's smile vanished. "Sam, you can't build over the playground. It's—"

"Sure I can," he countered. "There's nothing in your zoning regulations that forbids it."

"There will be tomorrow!" she snapped.

"Yes, but I've already registered my plan with your computer. You can't apply a new regulation to a preexisting plan. I'm grandfathered in."

"Sam, you . . . that's . . . of all . . ." She ran out of words.

I looked him in his shifty eyes. "It won't affect the playground?"

Sam raised his right hand solemnly. "I swear it won't. Honest injun. Hope to die. The support piers will be at the corners of the field. The building will shade the playground, that's all."

Bonnie was still looking daggers at him.

Sam smiled at her. "The top floor of the complex, up near the center-line, will be in microgravity. Not zero-gee, exactly, but so close you'll never tell the difference."

"Never!" she snapped. "You'll never get me up there. Never in a million years."

Sam sighed. "Never?" he asked, in a small, forlorn voice. I swear there was a tear in the comer of his left eye.

"Never in a million years," Bonnie repeated. Less vehemently than a moment before.

"Well," he said softly, "at least we can have this one dinner together."

With a sad little smile, Sam got to his feet again and held Bonnie's chair as she stood.

As they walked away I heard Sam ask, "Have you ever slept on a waterbed?"

"Well, yes," Bonnie replied. "As a matter of fact, that's what I have in my home."

I doubted that it would take Sam a million years.

Solar News Offices, Selene City

"BUT NONE OF THEM WILL SEE ME!" JADE BLURTED. "NOT one of them!"

"Out of six survivors of the mission, not one will talk to you?" Jim Gradowsky demanded.

"Not one," Jade replied glumly.

Jumbo Jim leveled a stern finger at her. "You mean you haven't gotten to any of them, that's what you're really saying."

"I've tried, Jim, I've really tried."

Gradowsky leaned both his heavy forearms on his desktop, nearly flattening a chocolate bar that lay there half unwrapped. Jade, sitting tensely on the cubbyhole office's shabby couch, unconsciously leaned back away from his ponderous form.

"They're all on Earth, aren't they?" he asked, his voice slightly softer.

Jade defended herself. "But I've been hounding them, Jim. I could interview them by videophone, but not one of them will even answer my calls! The best I've gotten is a return call from one of their lawyers telling me to stop annoying them."

"Orlando claims that some private detective agency ran a check on you."

"To see if I'm really a Solar News reporter?"

Gradowsky knitted his brows slightly. "More than that, looks like. They wanted a complete dossier on you: age, date and place of birth, previous employment, the whole nine yards."

"Who was the agency working for?"

"One of the people you're trying to interview."

"Which one?"

"The Margaux woman; the recluse who lives in Maine."

"Why would she . . . ?"

"Who the hell knows? That's why you've got to get to these people, Jade. They're trying to hide something. I can feel it in my bones. There's something big they're hiding down there!"

"But I can't go to Earth, Jim. You know that. Raki knows it, too."

Gradowsky fixed her with an unhappy frown. "How many time have I told you, kid? A reporter has to go to where the story is. You've got to camp on their doorsteps. You've got to *force* them to see you."

"On Earth?"

He shrugged so hard that his wrinkled short-sleeved shirt almost pulled free of his pants.

"On Earth," Jade repeated.

"Raki's under pressure to get this show finished, one way or the other. What you've got so far is fine, but if you could get an interview with one of the survivors of that asteroid jaunt—just one of them—both of you would look like angels to the board of directors."

"I'd have to wear an exoskeleton," Jade said. "Get a powered wheel-chair. A heart-booster pump."

Gradowsky's fleshy face broke into a grin. "That's the stuff! They couldn't turn you down if you showed up like that! They'd have to talk to you. Hell, you might drop dead right on their doorsteps!"

"Yes," Jade muttered. "I might."

"So? What's keeping you?"

"There's one survivor living off-Earth," she said.

"Yeah, you told me. On a bridge ship. That's too far away, kid. It'd cost a fortune to send you there, all the way out to Mars. And we can't wait for the ship to loop back here."

"The ship goes past Mars and on to the Belt."

"I know."

"The sculptress lives on an asteroid out there. The woman who worked with Sam when he got into the advertising business."

Gradowsky shook his head. "We can't let you spend two years tootling around on a bridge ship."

"I could hire a high-boost shuttle. They run back and forth to the bridge ships all the time."

With an exaggerated show of patience, Gradowsky said, "Jade, honey, there are six survivors of Sam's first expedition to the asteroids. Five of them live on Earth. Any other reporter would be there now, chasing them down."

"I can't go to Earth!"

"Then you're off the assignment," Gradowsky said flatly. "I can't help it, but those are the orders from Orlando. Either you get the job done or they'll give the assignment to another reporter."

"Is that what Raki said?"

"It's out of his hands, kid. There's a dozen staff reporters down there salivating for the chance to get in on this. You've opened a big can of worms, Jade. Now they're all hot to grab the story away from you."

Jade felt cold anger clutching at her heart. "So either I go to Earth or I'm off the Sam Gunn bio?"

"That's the choice you have, yeah." Gradowsky tried to look tough, but instead he simply looked upset.

Without another word Jade got up from the chair and made her way from Gradowsky's office to Monica's. There was nowhere else for her to run.

Before Jade could say anything Monica handed her palmcomp to her. "There was a call for you. From Earth. Maine, USA."

"Jean Margaux lives in Maine," Jade said, suddenly breathless with expectation. She sat in Monica's spare chair and tapped the proper keys on the board.

A man's long, hound-sad face appeared on the wall screen. He was sitting behind a huge desk of polished wood, bookcases neatly lined with leather volumes at his back. He wore a suit jacket of somber black and an actual necktie, striped crimson and deep blue.

"This message is for Ms. Jane Avril Inconnu. Would you kindly hold your right thumb up to the screen so that the scanner can check it? Otherwise this message will terminate now."

With a glance at Monica, Jade pressed her right thumb against the palmcomp's tiny screen. When she lifted it, the image of the gravely unsmiling man froze for a few seconds. Then:

"Thank you, Ms. Inconnu. I have the unpleasant task of informing you that Ms. Jean Margaux was killed yesterday in an automobile accident. As her attorney, I have been empowered by the four other partners in the *Argo* expedition who live on Earth to inform you that any further attempts to call, interview, photograph, or contact them in any way, by any employee of the Solar News Network, Inc., will be regarded as a breach of privacy and will result in an appropriate suit against said Solar News Network, Inc. Thank you."

The screen went blank.

Jade felt just as blank, empty, as if her insides had just been pulled out of her, as if she had suddenly stepped out an airlock naked into the numbing vacuum of deep space.

Monica broke the spell. "Well, I'll be a daughter of a bitch! How do you like that?"

Fifteen minutes later Jade was back in Gradowsky's office and Raki's handsome face shone on the display screen built into the office wall.

"Yes, we've been notified too," Raki was saying. He looked annoyed, tight-lipped. Lawyers and threats to sue were taken very seriously in Orlando.

"What the hell are they trying to hide?" Gradowsky asked, his newsman's nose twitching.

"Whatever it is, we'd better stay clear of the four remaining survivors for the time being. I've got the legal staff checking into this, but you know how long it takes them to come up with a recommendation."

"That's 'cause you pay them by the hour," Gradowsky said.

Raki was not amused. "They always give us the most conservative advice. They'll tell us to avoid the risk of a lawsuit, stay away from the remaining four."

Jade was listening with only part of her mind. An inner voice was puzzling over the fact that Jean Margaux had detectives investigate her background, and then she was killed in an auto accident. Was it an accident? Or murder? She remembered hearing somewhere that many people on Earth commit suicide by crashing their cars and making it look like an accident. That way they left their heirs the double indemnity money from their insurance.

Jean Margaux was a very wealthy woman. Jade knew that from her own research into the survivors of Sam Gunn's expedition out to the asteroids. And childless. As far as Jade could learn, she had no heirs.

I'll have to check out the terms of her will, she told herself. Did one of the other four murder her? Not for money, maybe, but because they were afraid she would eventually talk to me?

"That finishes it," Raki was saying, his lips turned down into an unaccustomed frown. "The Sam Gunn bio stops right here and now."

"There's a fifth survivor of the expedition," Jade heard herself say. "And he isn't part of this threatened lawsuit."

Gradowsky immediately replied, "Yeah, but he's all the way to hell out by Mars on a bridge ship."

"They're hiding something," Jade snapped. "Something so important to them that Jean Margaux died to keep it secret."

It took a couple of seconds for Raki to answer from Earth, "It was an accident, Jade."

"Was it? Are we sure of that?"

Neither man replied.

Jade hunched forward in her chair. "The only other survivor of that expedition is on the bridge ship *Golden Gate*. The sculptress who made Sam's statue is living out in the Belt. And the professor who was with Sam when he died is outfitting a deep-space mission at Titan. I could get to all three of them!"

"And not get back for two years," Gradowsky grumbled.

"Okay, so what?" Jade felt eagerness trembling through her. "Raki, you can put the Sam Gunn bio on hold, can't you? Let those lawyers think we've dropped the project. Meantime I'll get out to the *Golden Gate* and see what they're trying to hide. And then go on to the other two. I can do it! I know I can!"

Gradowsky was staring at her. Raki had a faraway look in his eyes.

"We'd have to pay you salary for two years while you're doing nothing," Raki said.

"I'm getting minimum," Jade shot back. "You won't be losing much. Or just pay my travel costs while I'm going back and forth; put me on salary only for the time I'm actually working."

"H'mm."

"We could slip her aboard a high-boost shuttle," Gradowsky said. "Trade her fare for advertising time. Get her out to the *Golden Gate* in a few weeks, maybe for free. Or at a reduced fare, at least."

Raki fingered his handsome mustache. Jade felt her heart stop while he pondered.

Finally he said, "Very well. Travel expenses only unless you're actually working. Jim, see what you can do about getting her to that bridge ship quickly. And not a word about this to anybody!"

"We won't let their lawyers know what we're doing," Gradowsky said, grinning. "Don't worry."

"I'm not worried about their damned lawyers," Raki answered. "I don't want the CEO to know what I've just agreed to!"

Bridge Ship *Golden Gate*

"YES, I WAS ONE OF THE INVESTORS IN THAT MAD EXPEDI-
tion," said Rick Darling. "It was probably the most foolish thing I've ever
done, in a long life of foolishness."

Jade could not quite fathom the expression on Darling's face. He was
immensely fat, the kind of obesity that can only be achieved in a low-
gravity environment. He looked like a layered mountain, rolls upon rolls
of fat bulging beneath his flamingo-pink robe.

In the shadowy half-light of his private quarters, his face looked like a
gibbous moon, bloated cheeks and tiers of chins. He was smiling, but his
eyes were so deeply set in folds of fat that Jade could not tell if his smile
was pleased or pained.

"Sam Gunn." Darling sighed heavily and took a sip from the gem-
encrusted goblet engulfed in his fat, bejeweled hand. "I thought I'd never
hear his name spoken in polite society again. The little bastard."

Jade felt ill at ease, despite the fact that Darling's quarters were at a
comfortable lunar gravity. But of all the people she had interviewed over
the months of her travels, of all the people that Sam Gunn had worked
with, lived with, loved and hated with, Rick Darling gave her a strong
sense of foreboding.

His private quarters were little short of sybaritic, from the pile of
sumptuous pillows on which Darling reclined like an overweight ma-
harajah to the splendid tapestries lining the walls and the richly carved
genuine wood low tables scattered across the room. The tables were the
only furniture she could see. Like her host, Jade sat on a mound of pillows, softly yielding yet comfortably supportive. The scenes embroidered
on the pillows were wildly erotic. The tapestries flaunted every form of
perversion she had ever heard of and several that were totally new to her.

Darling himself wore more rings and bracelets and heavy necklaces of
gold and glittering jewels than she had ever seen on one person, male or
female. She felt distinctly shabby in her jade green slacks and vest, adorned
by nothing more than a faux pearl necklace and matching earrings.

The very air of this latter-day Arabian Nights chamber was sickly sweet with perfume. Or was it more than perfume? It would be simple enough for this smiling pile of flesh to put a narcotic in the air-circulation system. Or an aphrodisiac.

The thought alarmed her.

Sitting up straight, a current of apprehension tingling through her body, she asked in as businesslike a voice as she could summon up:

"You didn't like Sam Gunn?"

"*No one* liked him, dear lady," replied Rick Darling. His voice was a clear sweet tenor, almost angelic. "Sam was not a likable person, believe me."

"Yet you knowingly invested in his venture. Nobody forced you to go out and spend two years of your life in that spacecraft with him."

Darling's smile revealed that he even had diamonds set into his teeth. For the first time she noticed the earrings half hidden beneath his glistening tightly curled hair. The man looked like a jewelry display case.

"No *one* forced me to go, true enough." He sighed again, like a mountain heaving. "But there were circumstances, my dear. Circumstances often force us to do things we really would rather not do."

"Really?"

"Certainly." Darling reached for the splendid gold pitcher on the low table at his side. He raised the pitcher and his eyebrows, which were flecked with sparkling chips of diamond.

"No thanks, I'm fine," said Jade. And I intend to stay that way, she added silently. She had taken one sip of what Darling had claimed to be the finest wine produced off-Earth. She had no intention of taking more.

"Circumstances," Darling went on, as he filled his own cup, "dictate our actions. For example, you yourself are not comfortable here. You are not comfortable with me, are you?"

Jade blinked several times before admitting, "No, I guess I'm not."

Darling nodded, sending ripples through his many chins. "You fought and battled to get to me. You argued and bribed your way past the ship's security people. You literally camped at my door until I finally agreed to see you. Now that you are here, you frown with disapproval at my decor, my lifestyle, myself. Yet you remain, because of circumstances."

She forced a smile. "I thought *I* was interviewing *you*."

He smiled back, glittering diamonds at her. "I live the way I live. I am rich enough to afford whatever it takes to make me happy. And, to a considerable extent, whoever."

"You got rich because of Sam Gunn."

"Yes, that's true. Damn him."

"Why?" She leaned forward, eager for the answer. "I've tried to interview all of the other surviving members of that expedition and none of them would even speak to me. What happened? What did Sam do?"

Darling heaved another titanic sigh. "I have his disks, you know."

"What?"

"I suppose you could call them the ship's log. After all, he *was* the captain of the vessel."

"You have Sam's log of the mission?"

"Yes."

"In his own voice?"

"Yes."

She could not hide her eagerness. "Can . . . can I hear them? Copy them?"

He hesitated a long moment, whether from true indecision or merely to dangle her on the hook of her own impatience, Jade could not tell.

Finally Darling said slowly, "You can listen to them, but not copy them. You must agree to the conditions I insist on before I will allow you to hear the disks."

She tensed. "What conditions?"

He raised a thick, blunt, ringed finger. "Before that, you must also agree to grant me one request after you have heard the disks."

"One request."

"You must agree beforehand. Now."

"Without knowing what the request is?"

He nodded solemnly.

She glanced around at the scenes on the tapestries. Mother of mercy, suppose he wants me to do something like that?

"What are the conditions?"

"You will listen to the disks here in this room. You will strip yourself naked and give all your clothing and your shoulder bag to me before I present you with the disks."

Jade felt a surge of bile rising in her throat.

"I assure you," Darling quickly added, "that the nudity is entirely a security precaution. I do not want the disks copied. I must make certain that you do not have a copying device on you."

She stared hard at him, her thoughts swirling.

"I will leave the room," Darling said. "A robot will take your clothing and bag to me."

"Uh-huh."

"I will insist, however, on making certain that you are entirely—unequipped—by making a visual inspection of you via a video intercom."

Dieu, she thought, he's a voyeur. And immediately she regretted the three kilos she had gained over the past month. In low gravity the body puffs up anyway; I'll look pretty bad. Or maybe he likes flab. He's got plenty of his own.

"Do you agree?" Darling asked, just a hint of anxiousness in his high rich voice.

"To the conditions, yes," she heard herself say, almost surprised. "But I can't agree to grant you whatever request you want afterward. After all . . ."

"I promise you that it will not involve pain or humiliation," Darling said.

Her heart froze inside her. *Sacre coeur,* what does he have in mind?

"Wh—what is it?" she asked timidly.

Darling folded his heavy hands over his immense belly. His arms were barely long enough to make it.

"You have worked very hard to get this far. Now you can listen to Sam Gunn's disks, if you wish to. I will grant your request. If you will grant mine. That is all I intend to tell you."

The log of the mission that made Sam Gunn a billionaire. In his own voice. It had been an epic, pioneering flight, the first true expedition out beyond the orbit of Mars, the first commercial voyage out to the rich bonanza of the Asteroid Belt.

Rick Darling had never returned to Earth after his voyage with Sam Gunn. He lived in isolated splendor aboard the *Golden Gate.* Isolated, but not alone. *Golden Gate* was one of the huge "bridge" spacecraft that plied a long parabolic orbit that looped from the Earth-Moon system out to the Asteroid Belt and back again. Darling was rich enough to set himself up in magnificent style in a private villa aboard the ten-kilometer-long spacecraft. Yet, even in the midst of never less than four thousand human souls, Darling saw almost no one. He preferred to be served by robots.

There were five "bridge" ships sailing the years-long orbit out to the Belt. Way stations on the road to the asteroids. Bridges between the worlds. Their very existence was based on ideas that Sam Gunn had pioneered. Not that anybody gave him credit for it. Or a share of their profits.

But that was a different matter. Jade looked at Darling's fleshy face, tried to peer into those fat-hidden eyes.

"Well?" he demanded.

She took a deep breath. "All right, I'll grant your request, whatever it is," she said, thinking that if it got too nasty she would knee him in the balls and run the hell out of there, naked or not.

EVEN THOUGH THE room was far from cold, she shivered as the robot took the last item of her clothing, flowered bikini panties, into its velvet-padded steel claw of a hand. She felt defenseless, exposed, vulnerable.

"The earrings, please," said the robot with Rick Darling's voice.

The bastard is watching me. She unscrewed the tiny faux pearls and handed them to the patient robot. One of those earrings was an emergency screamer that would bring the *Golden Gate*'s security team crashing in if she activated it. She was truly on her own now.

She stood totally naked before the robot, knowing that Darling was inspecting her through its eyes.

"Turn around please."

She pirouetted slowly, hoping that he would not insist on an internal examination. She heard a brief buzzing sound, barely enough to register on her consciousness.

"Thank you," Darling's voice said from the speaker in the robot's head. "The X-ray scan is finished."

Planting her fists on her hips, she snapped, "X-rays? What's next, neutrinos?"

No reply. Instead the robot reached into a slot in its torso and handed her six miniature disks, each of them roughly the size of a walnut. She took them eagerly into her hands.

"There is a laser player built into the table set against the far wall, beneath the video screen," Darling's voice instructed. "Unfortunately, Sam chose to make an audio log only. There is no video. I assume that you know what he looked like. If you would like, I can project still pictures of Sam and the various others who made the voyage onto the screen. I also have some video footage of our ship, the *Argo*. And blueprints, if you want."

Forgetting her nudity, she answered, "Yes, all the visual images you have. I'd like to see them."

"I will project them in sync with Sam's disks, as closely as I can." Darling's voice sounded pleased, almost amused.

She hurried across the room and sat cross-legged before the low table. What looked at first like inlays and carvings were actually the controls for a laser player. The legs of the table held its speakers. Spreading the six tiny disks on the table top, she saw that they were clearly numbered.

As she inserted the first one into the slot the screen above her lit up with a view of the *Argo*. She smiled at the name. Sam certainly didn't lack for hubris. What was the Yiddish word for it? Chutzpa.

The ship was shaped like a fat tubular wheel, with slender spokes running down to a large hub. She recognized the design instantly: living quarters in the "tire" section, which was spun to give a feeling of gravity; the hub was low-gravity, practically zero-gee at its very center.

Sam's voice startled her.

"Log of the *Argo* expedition to the Asteroid Belt. Date: thirty-one March."

In the recording that Larry Karsh had given her months earlier, Sam's voice had been sharp, insistent, almost irritating. Now, though, he spoke in a calm baritone, a little on the reedy side perhaps, but a much softer and more relaxed voice than she had anticipated. Everyone said Sam's eye color changed with his mood: did the timbre of his voice change, too?

"It feels kinda funny being captain of this ship, commander of this expedition, CEO of this operation. I've always been under other people's thumbs, pretty nearly always, at least. I wonder how I'm going to like being the guy in charge?"

Two Years Before the Mast

THEY'RE ALREADY MAKING WISECRACKS ABOUT THIS voyage—Sam's voice continued. Since we break Earth orbit tomorrow we're officially launching the expedition on April First. Some of the media jerkoffs are already calling us The Ship of Fools.

I had nothing to do with selecting the launch date. The goddamned International Astronautical Authority picked the date, with their usual infinite wisdom. Had to wait two weeks here in orbit because their tracking facilities were completely tied up on the latest Mars expedition. Six scientists and three astronauts going to spend ninety days on the Martian surface—some big-time expedition!

Anyway, the two-week delay gave those nervous nellies down in the banks a chance to send up their so-called experts for *another* check of all the ship's systems. Everything's fine, all systems go, they couldn't find anything wrong. Even though we'll be out for at least two years, they had to admit that the ship and the crew I picked are fully up to the mission.

Wish I could say the same about my partners.

I had to form a limited partnership to get this venture going. Seven limited partners. Very limited. Three men and four women who were willing to put up ten million bucks apiece for the privilege of being the first human beings to ride out to the Asteroid Belt. Without their backing the banks wouldn't have even looked at my deal. I needed their seed money, but now I'm gonna have to put up with them for two years or more.

What the hell! I'm the captain. If any of them gives me a hard time I'll make the sucker walk the plank.

JADE STOPPED THE disk.

"I don't have my notes with me," she said to the empty room. "I want to refresh my memory of who those partners were—besides you."

Darling did not answer, but the picture on the screen above her changed to show a group of eight people, four women and four men, all dressed in snappy flight suits. Sam was front and center, the shortest of

THE SAM GUNN OMNIBUS

357

the men and shorter than two of the women. His round, freckled face gave him the look of an aging leprechaun. Wiry red hair cropped close. Sly grin. The beginnings of wrinkles in the corners of his eyes.

"Which one is you?" Jade called out.

A long moment, then a circle appeared around the face of the man standing farthest to the left.

"My god, you were beautiful!" she blurted.

Rick Darling, at that age, was little less than an Adonis. Handsome face, tanned, full-lipped, framed by dark wavy hair. Broad shoulders, muscular build that showed even through the flight suit. Not a single piece of jewelry on him.

"Yes, I was, wasn't I?" Darling's voice, even through the speakers, sounded unutterably wistful.

She leaned forward and touched the disk player's control button once again.

THE COMPUTER CAN fill in the date—Sam's voice said. He sounded edgy, almost out of breath.

Well, we're off, on schedule. High-energy boost. We'll pass the Mars expedition in a couple of weeks. Too bad we won't get close enough to wave to 'em. Good friend of mine from back in my astronaut days is commanding the flight. She's the first woman to command a Mars mission. Hope that makes her happier than I ever could.

Everything's okay here, all systems in the green. My partners are having a ball. Literally, some of them. I introduced two of the women to zero-gee fun and games last night. They liked it so much that I almost had to call for help. Almost.

WOMEN ARE BLABBERMOUTHS! Now the two that I *didn't* take down to the hub are sore at me. And one of the men, that Darling character, is starting to make hints.

I hired one of the crewmen to help keep the passengers amused. Erik Klein. He's a blond, tanned, beach boy type. Not too bright, but muscular enough to keep the women happy. The other two—my *real* crew—I've got to keep separated from the partners. These seven dwarf-brained numbskulls think they're here for fun and games. I thought they'd entertain each other, pretty much. With Erik and me helping out a little, now and then.

Two years of this. Two years of *this*?

I HAD TO give them a lecture. Imagine it! Me, laying down the rules to somebody else.

But they're going to wreck this mission before we get halfway to where we're going. Hell, they could even wreck the damned ship and kill us all.

Trouble is, they think they're here to be entertained. I guess that's the impression they got, somehow, from the way I described the trip to them, way back when.

Seven partners. Seven movers and shakers from the media, high society, the arts and sciences. Hell, even the astronomer is acting like a freshmen away from home for the first time in his life.

And they're bothering the crew. I don't mind if they screw themselves into catatonia, among themselves. But the crew's gotta run this ship. They've got to be in top physical and mental condition when we start prospecting among the asteroids.

It all seemed so simple, back on Earth. Get seven prominent scatterbrains to put up the seed money for an expedition to the asteroids. Use their credentials to impress the banks enough to put up the real backing. Go out to the asteroids, find a nice chunk of nickel/iron, smelt and refine it on the way back to Earth, then sell it for enough to give everybody a nice profit.

It's the sweetest deal I've ever put together, especially since the seven dwarfs will be getting their shares from the *net* profit we make, while I'll be drawing my own off the top, from the gross.

But, lord! are those seven airheads a shipload of trouble. I may have to shove one of them out an airlock, just to impress the others that I mean business.

Imagine it! *Me* trying to enforce discipline on *them*.

I HATE THIS job.

Listen, this log is going to have to be confidential. I'm going to give the computer a security code word so nobody can break into it and hear what I've got to say.

Let's see . . . computer, this is a command. Code this log under, uh, umm—code word "supercalifragelistic-expialidotious."

[Computer]: Code word accepted.

Okay, good. I hadn't intended to get so paranoid, but I'm stuck here for the next twenty-three months with nobody I can trust. I've got to talk to *somebody* or I'll go nuts. So I'll talk to you, computer.

[Computer]: I contain artificial intelligence programs that can provide limited responses to your inputs.

When I want you to answer me, I'll tell you! Otherwise, keep your voice synthesizer quiet. Understood?

[Computer]: Understood.

Part of the reason for locking up this log is that I'm going to start naming names and I don't want anybody else to know what those names are. Christ knows I've done enough screwing around in my time, but I've always believed a gentleman doesn't kiss and tell. Well, maybe I'm not a gentleman and I certainly ain't talking about just kissing, but I've never gone around embarrassing anybody I was lucky enough to go to bed with.

But I can't talk things out without naming names. It just won't work. Am I making any sense?

[Pause]

Hey, computer, am I making any sense?

[Computer]: Your statements are internally consistent.

Great. How do I call up your psychotherapy program?

[Computer]: Ask for Guidance Counselor.

Jeez, just like in high school. Okay, gimme the Guidance Counselor.

[Computer, same voice]: How may I help you?

Just listen and then tell me what I should do after I finish, okay?

[Computer]: If that's what you really want.

Oh brother!

[Computer]: Is that part of your problem, your brother? I have your biographical dossier in my files, but there is no mention of a brother.

No, no, no! I haven't started yet!

[Computer]: I see.

I'm starting now. Got it?

[Computer]: Go on.

Let's see . . . I think it was Nelson Algren who said that three rules for a happy life are: One, never play cards with any man named 'Doc.' Two: never eat at any place called 'Mom's.' And three: never, never go to bed with a woman whose troubles are worse than your own.

[Computer]: Um-hmm.

I went to bed with Sheena Chang last night. Big mistake.

[Computer]: Sheena Chang, video actress. Proclaimed one of the ten most beautiful women in the world by 21st-Century Fox/United Artists/MGM/Fujitsu Corporation. Latest starring role: Tondaleo, the sultry Eurasian prostitute with a heart of gold, in *Invasion of the Barbarians from Outer Space*. Age: twenty-seven. Height . . .

Yeah, yeah, yeah. That's her. Sultry Eurasian, all right. I was really surprised when her agent told me she had agreed to come on this voyage. I had only called her on a lark; thought it'd be fun to be on a slow boat to China with her.

[Computer]: To China? Navigational data shows we are heading . . .

Just a figure of speech, dammit! Stop interrupting!

Anyway, I never thought she'd give up two years in the middle of her career to come sailing out to the Asteroid Belt with me. But she did. Last night I found out why.

She was all hot breath and sizzle until I got her clothes off her and put her in my bed. We had made it before, in the threesome with Marj Dupray down in the zero-gee section. Sheena had been a wild woman then; Marj wasn't so bad herself, for a skinny fashion designer. They were both tanked up on champagne and whatnot. After all, that was our first night out.

[Computer]: I see.

Well, anyway, last night Sheena and I have a private little supper in my quarters. She's wearing a low-cut dress so slinky she must have sprayed it on. One thing leads to another and finally we're both in the buff and on the bed.

I say to her, "I was really knocked out when you agreed to come on this trip."

That's all it took. The floodgates opened.

[Computer]: Floodgates?

She started crying! At first I thought she had drunk too much wine with dinner, but then I remembered that she had downed a tub of champagne that first night without batting an eye. She just blubbered away and babbled for hours, right there in the bed. Naked. One of the ten most beautiful women in the world.

[Computer]: Why was she crying?

That's what I asked her. And she told me. And told me. And told me! Her career is going down the tubes; her last three videos lost money; her implants are slumping; her husband is suing her for divorce; her boyfriend's left her for a younger starlet; her agent's making bad deals for her; her cat died. . . . Jeez, she just went on and on about how her life was ruined and she was going to kill herself.

[Computer]: Perhaps she should speak to me. I may be able to help her.

Yeah, maybe. Anyway, it turns out that her publicity agent convinced her that taking this voyage would be just the thing to give her career a boost. When she comes back she'll be the first actress to have flown to the Asteroid Belt. They'll make a docudrama out of it. They'll get Michael J. Fox III to play my role. Ta-da, ta-dum, ta-dee—so off she goes on the good ship *Argo*.

[Computer]: Ta-da, ta-dum, ta-dee?

Ignore it. Two days out, Sheena starts thinking that maybe she made a mistake. Two weeks out she's certain of it. Her publicity guy and her agent have connived behind her back to get her out of the way so that the new starlet her boyfriend's shacked up with can take her place. Her career is ruined. Her body's falling apart and she can't sue the plastic surgeons because the publicity would ruin her even more. She'll be out of the limelight for two whole years. By the time she gets back everybody'll have forgotten who the hell she is, and she'll be an old woman by then anyway, past thirty.

[Computer]: According to her dossier she will be only twenty-nine when this mission ends.

So she lied about her age! Anyway, Sheena doesn't want to make love, she wants to kill herself. It took me all goddamned night to calm her down, cheer her up, and convince her that when we get back from the asteroids she'll be rich enough to *buy* 21st-Century, et al.

[Computer]: According to the prospectus filed with the Securities and Exchange Commission—

I know, I know! So I exaggerated a little. She needed cheering up.

By the time I got her to stop talking about killing herself, it was damned near morning. I had to get dressed and go to the bridge for the first-shift systems review. She wriggled back into that slinky dress of hers, still sniffling a little. Then she dropped the bombshell.

[Computer]: Should I activate the damage-control program?

No, stupid. But gimme the logistics program.

[Computer]: Logistics.

Sheena Chang is not to receive any drugs, medications or pharmaceuticals of any kind. Understand? In fact, all requests for medication, stimulants or relaxers from any of the partners is to be reported to me immediately. Understood?

[Computer]: Understood.

Okay. Get the guidance counselor back.

[Computer]: Guidance counselor.

The bombshell Sheena handed me was metaphorical. You understand what metaphorical means?

[Computer]: I have a thorough command of twenty languages, including English.

Wonderful. She told me that one of the partners is an agent for Rockledge International, the multinational megacorporation, the soulless bloodsucking vampires of the corporate world, the gutless sneaking bastards who'd steal your cojones and sell them to the highest bidder if you gave them the chance. I've tangled with them before; they're always trying to grab everything for themselves, the two-bit sonsofbitches.

[Computer]: You disapprove of them.

Only as much as I disapprove of cannibalism, genocide, and selling your mother to a Cairo brothel.

[Computer]: I see.

So there's Sheena sniffling and squeezing her boobs into her dress, and she tells me I've been so nice and kind and patient that she's going to warn me that one of the partners is secretly working for Rockledge.

"Which one?" I asked her.

"I don't know," she says.

"Then how do you know that one of them is on Rockledge's payroll?"

She finally gets her bosom adjusted—believe me, it took all my powers of concentration not to go over to her and give her a hand. Anyway, she says:

"A couple of nights ago, it was kind of late and we were in the lounge having a nightcap or two. . . ."

"We? Who?"

She shrugged. I was still in the buff and immediately came to attention. Sheena paid no attention and I thought she'd probably seen bigger. But not better.

I asked her again, "Who was in the lounge with you?"

"Oh, golly, we had been drinking for a while. And Rick had handed out some really weird candy; he's got a whole trunkful of shit, you know. . . ."

"I know." I was starting to get exasperated with her birdbrain act. "So Darling was there. Who else?"

"Oh, Marjorie, and Dr. Hubble. Grace Harcourt, she was sitting with me. I don't remember if Bo Williams was there or not. And I'm sure Jean Margaux wasn't. She wouldn't be, the snob."

"So who said what? What'd you hear?"

"It was just a snatch of conversation, a man's voice, I'm pretty sure. Somebody said something about money piling up at a bank in Liechtenstein. . . ."

"Liechtenstein?"

"That's right. He's getting a monthly stipend from Rockledge International and it's gathering compound interest all the time we're away on this trip!"

She looked pleased that she remembered that much. But that was all she could remember. Or so she said. Somebody was on Rockledge's payroll, in secret. And it was probably a man.

[Computer]: Why does that bother you so?

Why? Why? Because Rockledge'll try to steal the profits of this mission out from under me, that's why! It's just like those sleazy bastards—let the little guy do all the work and then they come in and snatch the money. Rape and pillage, that's the way they work.

[Computer]: I assume those are metaphors again.

Listen, you stupid hunk of germanium, I want you to get me a Dunn & Bradstreet on each one of my partners. One of them's a—

[Computer]: You will have to call up the financial program.

Okay! Gimme the financial program!

[Computer]: Financial.

I want a complete rundown on each one of my partners.

[Computer]: Displaying.

No, no, no! Not the data already in your memory! That's months old, for chrissakes. I want the up-to-the-minute stuff. And check the banks in Liechtenstein.

[Computer]: That will take several hours. Transmission time to Earth is currently—

Just do it! Fast as you can. Do it.

Jeez, I feel like a kid in a confessional booth. It's been three months since my last entry in this log. A pretty quiet three months.

Things have gone along okay, really smoother than I expected. One of the plasma thrusters crapped out last week, but Will Bassinio and I went EVA and replaced it with a spare. Will's my electronics specialist; a real whiz at chips and circuits and stuff like that. Lonz—Alonzo Ali, my first mate—monitored us from the command center while Erik did what he does best: charmed the passengers.

Erik's a good kid. Not a deep thinker, but he smiles pretty and the passengers seem to like him, especially the female passengers. On the official manifest he's my logistics specialist. Not much of a technician, but he does his job okay.

I think of them as passengers now, rather than partners. In this phase of the flight we're running sorta like a cruise liner. There won't be any real work to do until we get past the orbit of Mars and start actively prospecting for an asteroid to mine. In the meantime it's six meals a day and all the entertainment I can dream up for my magnificent seven.

They're not as much trouble right now as I thought they'd be. Darling's happy as a mugger in an old lady's home. He's always in the galley or the dining salon, stuffing himself on all the gourmet food I stored aboard. He's gaining weight fast; his clothes look like they're gonna start popping seams any minute.

Sheena has calmed down a lot. Maybe what I told her about being a celebrity when she comes back to Earth has helped. But I think it's Lowell Hubble who's made the real difference. He's the oldest man on board, lean gray-haired fatherly type. Neat little mustache that's still almost dark. Dresses in rumpled slacks and baggy cardigan sweaters. Even smokes a pipe. Sheena's taken up with him and they both seem delighted about it. He's even teaching her astronomy.

Is Hubble the Rockledge agent? I've been wondering about that. He's an astronomer, for chrissake. They don't make much money. There's no Dunn & Bradstreet report on him, although he comes from a pretty wealthy family. But was the ten million he ponied up his own money, or Rockledge's?

I asked Grace Harcourt to snoop around for me and see what she could find out.

"Me? Spy for you?" She laughed out loud.

I had invited her up to the command center, what would be called the bridge on a ship at sea, I guess. I like Grace. She's tough and feisty; has to be, to make it as an entertainment industry gossip columnist. There's a lot of competition in that business. And a lot of lawsuits.

I had met her years ago, when I was a NASA astronaut-in-training and she was still a local TV news reporter in Houston. We had gotten along really well right from the start, but my so-called career took me to Florida and she aimed for Hollywood. And hit it big.

Grace is tiny, a good two inches shorter than me. But she's smart, sharp. Not bad looking, either. A little more on her hips than there ought to be, but otherwise she's got a nicely curved figure that looks good in frilly blouses and pleated skirts. She also has a pleasant, heart-shaped face that knows how to smile.

But now she was laughing. "I'm a gossip columnist, Sam," she said, "not a secret agent."

"Snooping is snooping," I told her. "Just keep your pretty eyes and ears open for me, will you?"

She gave me a funny look. "How do you know I'm not working for Rockledge?"

That made me grin. "You're a gossip columnist, right? You never kept a secret in your life."

She laughed and admitted I was right. I've got no worries about Grace. She records her column every day and we transmit it to Earth. She bases her stuff on the same reports from her spies and finks that she'd be getting if she was at home in Beverly Hills. She also throws in a couple tidbits about our voyage now and then and shows her viewers some of the ship. No other daily column has ever been recorded from deep space before.

Then I had the run-in with Marjorie Dupray. She had been my zero-gee companion, along with Sheena, that first night. A very successful fashion designer, Marj had started out as a model and she's kept that lean, long-legged, model's figure. But she's got a mean look to her, if you ask me. Maybe it's that buzz cut of hers, with her hair dyed like a neon flamingo. Or the biker's leathers she likes to wear. She doesn't give off much of a female aura.

Why would a fashion designer agree to come on this voyage? And put up ten mil, to boot? I decided to question her, subtly, so she wouldn't know I was suspicious.

I invited her up to the command center one evening when I had the watch alone. She seemed moderately bored as I showed her the navigational computer and the Christmas Tree lights of the life support systems monitor board. But she perked up a bit when we got to the comm console.

"How long does it take a message to get back to Earth now?" she asked.

"Nearly half an hour," I said. "And longer every day. We are going where no man has gone before, you know."

"And no woman."

I made a little bow to acknowledge her feminist point of view, which surprised me. Then I asked:

"Are you getting any work done? Is our voyage into deep space inspiring you to create new clothing designs?"

She shook her head. It was a finely sculptured head, with a haughty nose and strong chin, high cheekbones that threw shifting shadows across her face. Marj is damned near a foot taller than me. I have nothing against tall women; in fact, I consider them a challenge. But that butch haircut of hers bothered me. And now the color was burnt orange.

But I was after information, not challenges.

"Don't you have contracts to fulfill? I thought this voyage was going to be a working session for you. How can you afford to take two years off?"

She gave me a pitying look. "I don't have to push it, Sam. When I get back from this trip I'll be the first and only designer to have been in deep space. I'll be able to throw rags together and the fashion industry will gobble them up and call them works of inspired genius."

"Oh." Maybe she was telling the truth. The fashion industry has always seemed kind of weird to me. "I thought maybe you were independently wealthy. Or you had another source of income."

"I have a few investments here and there," she said, with a slight smile.

"Like in Liechtenstein?" I blurted.

Her sculptured face turned cold as ice. "Is that what this is all about, Sam? You think I'm spying on you?"

I gave her my innocent-little-boy look. "What makes you think . . ."

"Sheena told me how upset you got. How you think one of us is working for Rockledge Industries."

"Well, yeah, I am upset about that. Wouldn't you be?"

"Me? Upset about something Sheena thinks she might have heard while she was guzzling booze and frying what little brains she's got on Rick's junk?" Marj smirked at me.

"Whoever made that slip about Liechtenstein must've also been high," I said.

"Well it wasn't me."

"I'm glad to hear it," I said. But either my expression or my tone told her I didn't altogether believe her profession of innocence.

Marj patted my cheek with one long, slender-fingered hand. "Sam, dear, there are times when I would gladly kick you in the balls."

If there's one thing I hate, it's condescension. "You'd hurt your delicate little foot, tall lady. I wear a lead jockstrap."

She laughed out loud. "I'll bet you do, at that."

I assured her that I did.

Anyway, that was almost a month ago. Since then nobody's said or done anything suspicious, and the cruise is going along without a hitch.

Which worries me. Maybe Grace really is the Rockledge agent. Maybe she's kept lots of secrets, especially about herself. How would I know? Or Marj. Or any one of them.

Jeez, I'm getting paranoid!

Anyway, we pass the point of no return in another six days. The ship is under a constant acceleration from the plasma thrusters. It's a very low acceleration; in the hub of the ship you still feel like you're in zero-gee, that's how low the acceleration is. But although those little thrusters don't give you much push, they're very fuel-efficient and can run for years at a time (when they don't crap out) and keep building up more and more velocity for you.

As an emergency backup, we're also carrying three pods of chemical rockets with enough delta-v among 'em to change our course, swing past Mars, and head back to the Earth-Moon system. So we can cut this ride short and go back home if there's any major trouble—up to the point of no return. Then, if we have a problem, no matter what the hell it may be, we've still got to coast all the way out to the Asteroid Belt and swing back to Earth on a trajectory that'll take us at least eleven months.

So, six days from now we become hostages to Newton's laws of motion and momentum. The point of no return. I hate to admit it, but I'm nervous about it.

THOSE MOTHER-HUMPING, SLIME-SUCKING, illegitimate sons of snakes from Rockledge! Now I know what they're up to, and why they've got an agent on board!

We passed the point of no return two days ago.

Today the main food freezers crapped out. All three of 'em, at the same time. Bang! Gone. Sabotage, pure and simple. Nineteen months more to go, and all our food is thawing out!

I wish I was an Arab, or even a Spaniard. Those people know how to curse!

It makes perfect sense. We die of starvation. That's all. Those bastards from Rockledge murder us—all except their own agent, who waits until we're all dead, then sends a distress call back to Earth where Rockledge has a high-energy booster all set and ready to zoom out to rescue their man. Or woman.

Or maybe they let the poor sucker die too. Dead spies tell no tales. And you don't have to pay them.

Oh hell, I know that doesn't make any sense! I'm starting to babble, I'm so pissed off.

All three food freezers shut down. We don't know exactly when because there was no indication on the Christmas Tree of the main control console. All the goddamned lights stayed clean green while our food supply started to thaw out.

It was Erik who noticed the problem. Bright-smiling, genial, slow-witted Erik.

I was showing off the command center to Jean Margaux, our high-society lady from Boston's North Shore. (She pronounces it Nawth Showah.) She's the one who got jealous the first night about my zero-gee antics with Sheena and Marj. What the hell, if I'm naming names I might as well name all of them.

Jean is the tall, stately type. Handsome face; good bones. Really beautiful chestnut-colored hair, and I think it's her natural shade. Not much bosom, but nice long legs and a cute backside. She likes to wear long slim skirts with slits in them that show off those legs when she moves.

Cool and aloof, looks down her nose at you. It's not as if she gives the impression that her shit don't stink; she gives the impression that she doesn't ever shit. But touch her in the right place and she dissolves like a pat of butter in a rocket exhaust. She turns into a real tigress. All it takes is a touch, so help me—and then afterward she's the Ice Queen again. Weird.

So I'm showing her the Christmas Tree, with all its red and green lights, only there wasn't a single red one showing. The ship was humming along in perfect condition, if you could believe the monitor systems. Alonzo Ali was on duty at the command console; Lonz is not only my first mate, he's a Phi Beta Kappa astronautical engineer and navigator from the International Space University.

So Erik comes into the command center with a puzzled frown on his normally open, wide-eyed face.

"There are no windows," Jean was saying. Coming from her, it sounded more like a complaint than a comment.

"Nope," I said. "With the ship swinging through a complete revolution every two minutes, you'd get kind of dizzy looking out a window."

"But we have windows in the lounge," she said. "And in our suites."

"Those are video screens," I corrected as gently as I could. "They show views from the cameras at the ship's hub, where they don't rotate."

"Oh," she said, as if I'd stuck a dead skunk in front of her.

Erik was kind of hanging around behind her, in my line of vision, not interrupting but sort of jiggling around nervously, like a kid who has to pee.

"Excuse me," I said to Jean. Her high-society airs sort of made me act like a butler in a bad video.

I stepped past her to ask Erik, "Is something wrong?"

"I think so," he said, furrowing his brow even deeper.

"What is it?" I asked softly.

"I'm not really sure," said Erik.

Jean was watching us intently. I restrained my urge to grab Erik by the throat and pull his tongue out of his head.

"What seems to be the trouble?" I asked, as diffidently as possible. No roughneck, I.

"Funny smell."

"Ah. A strange odor. And where might this odd scent be coming from?"

"The food freezers."

All this polite badinage had lulled me into a sense of unreality.

"The food freezers? Plural?"

"Yeah."

"The food freezers," I repeated, smiling and turning toward the blue-blooded Ms. Margaux. Then it hit me. *The food freezers!*

I lunged past Erik to the command console. The goddamned Christmas Tree was as green as Clancy's Bar on St. Patrick's Day.

"No malfunctions indicated," Lonz said, in that deep rich basso of his. He's from Kenya, and any time he gets tired of space he can take up a career in the opera.

My heart rate went back to normal, almost, but I decided to go down to the freezers and check them out anyway. Jean asked if she could accompany me. There was a strange light in her eyes, something that told me she anticipated a lesson in arctic survival.

I nodded and headed for the hatch.

"Isn't Erik coming, too?" Jean asked.

Oh-ho, I thought. She wants the cram course in arctic survival.

"Yeah, right. Come on Erik. Show me where you smelled this funny odor."

The logistics section is almost exactly on the opposite side of the wheel from the command center. We could have gone down one of the connecting tubes and through the hub, but I decided with Jean along it'd be better if we just walked around the wheel and stayed at a full one gee.

It's always a little strange, walking along inside the wheel. Your feet and your inner ear tell you that you're strutting along on a flat surface, while your eyes see that the floor is curving up in front of you, right out of sight. Anyway, we walked down the central corridor, past the lounge, the galley and dining salon, the passengers' living quarters, and the gym before we got to the logistics section. The workshops and maintenance facilities are all on the other half of the wheel. Our factory and processing smelter are down near the hub, of course, in microgravity.

Erik opens the big door to the first of the walk-in food freezers. It smells like a camel caravan had died in there several days ago. The second one smelled worse. By the time we got to the third one I guess our noses were suffering from sensory overload: it only smelled as bad as rancid milk poured over horse manure.

Jean kept her oh-so-proper attitude, but her face looked like she had stopped breathing. Erik was giving me a sort of hangdog grin, like he expected me to blame him for the catastrophe.

I kept my cool. I did not puke or even gag. I just raised my clenched fists over my head and uttered a heartfelt, "Son of a *BITCH!*"

Jean couldn't control her ladylike instincts any further; she yanked a facial tissue from a pocket in her blouse, pressed it to her face, and fled back toward her quarters.

I left Erik there and zipped back to the lounge to call the passengers together to ask for volunteers to help with the cleanup.

It's a very nice lounge, if I say so myself. Plush chairs, deep carpeting, big video screens that can serve as windows to the splendors of the universe outside. At the moment they were showing a video of some tropical beach: gentle waves lapping in, palm trees swaying against a clean blue sky, no people in sight. Must have been a clip from some travel agency's come-on. There hasn't been a beach that clean and empty of tourists since the first commercial flights of the hypersonic airliners.

"Wait just a moment, Sam," said Lowell Hubble, our pipe-smoking astronomer. No tobacco, of course, that stuff had been outlawed way back in '08 or '09. Whatever he had in the blackened, long-stemmed pipe he always held clamped in his teeth was smokeless and sweet-smelling. I think it was a bubblegum derivative.

"Are you telling us," he said from around the pipe, "that our food supply is ruined?"

"Most of the frozen food, yes," I admitted. "Looks that way. I need some help checking out the situation."

"We'll starve!" Rick Darling yelped.

"You'll starve last," quipped Grace Harcourt. Good old Grace: she could be tough or tender, and she knew when to be which.

Darling stuck out his lower lip at her. The others were staring at me apprehensively. They had been sitting in the recliner chairs scattered about the room; now they were hunching forward tensely on the front two inches of each chair. I was standing in front of the bar, trying to look cool and competent.

"Nobody's going to starve," I told them. "It's only the frozen food that's affected and I think we can save a good deal of it, if we move quickly enough."

"Isn't all the food frozen?" asked Bo Williams, our Pulitzer Prize author, the man who had already signed a megabuck contract to write the book about this voyage. Bo looked more like a professional wrestler than an author: shaved bullet head, no neck, heavy shoulders and torso, bulging gut.

"Most of it. But we have a backup supply of packaged food. And the reprocessors, of course."

"Canned food." Darling shuddered.

"Some of it's canned. Most of it's been preserved by irradiation. Food's been stored for half a century and more that way."

"Radiation?" Sheena Chang's big eyes went wider than usual. She was wearing violet contacts to go with the color of her outfit, a Frederick's of Hollywood version of a flight suit, real tight, with lots of zippers.

"It's all right," Hubble said, leaning over from his chair to pat her hand reassuringly. "Nothing to worry about."

"What was that about reprocessors?" Grace asked.

This was not a subject I wanted to discuss in any detail. "We can recycle the food, to a certain extent."

"Recycle?" For once I was not happy that Grace was a newshound.

"It's been done on space stations and long-duration missions." I tried to pass the whole thing off. "The Mars expedition has a recycling system."

"The food we eat will be recycled?" Damn Grace and her goddamned tenacity!

"Right," I snapped. "Now, I need . . ."

Rick Darling was catching on. "You mean our *garbage* will be recycled into fresh food?"

"Not just our garbage, sweetheart," Grace told him.

Jean Margaux, she who gave the impression she did not do that sort of thing, stared at me as if I had insulted her entire family tree.

Marjorie Dupray said grimly, "I'll starve first."

Marj wouldn't have far to go before she starved. She was all skin and bones already. As usual, she was wearing the crummiest clothes of the group: a shapeless sweater of dingy gray and baggy oversized slacks decorated with fake machine oil stains. But I knew that underneath that camouflage was a body as sleek and responsive as a racing yacht.

"Nobody needs to starve," I said, getting irritated with the bunch of them. Maybe this was the Ship of Fools, after all.

"Sure," Darling groused. "We can spend the next year and a half eating recycled . . ."

"Don't say it!" Jean snapped. "I can't bear even to think of it."

"Let's see how much of the frozen food we can rescue," I urged. "Who's gonna help us clean up the freezers?"

Not a hand was raised. None of my partners would volunteer to help.

"That's the crew's responsibility; not ours," said the always gracious Jean Margaux.

The others agreed.

It was grisly work.

We had to go in there and see what was spoiled beyond recovery, what could be saved if we cooked it immediately, and what was still reasonably okay. At the same time I wanted to figure out how all three freezers could fail without any warning lights showing up on the command console.

Erik and I did the dirty work with the food. Will checked out the freezers' electrical systems. He wore an oxygen mask with a little supply bottle on the belt of his flight suit. Sensitive kid.

"Where I grew up in South Philadelphia used to smell like this," he grumbled through the clear plastic mask as he entered the first of the freezers. "I never thought I'd get a whiff of home out here in space."

"Don't get homesick on me," I told him. "Just find out what went wrong."

About half of the food had turned to green slime, really putrid. The stench didn't seem to affect Erik at all; he just cleaned away with the same obtuse smile on his chiselled features as ever.

"Doesn't the smell bother you?" I asked him.

"What smell?"

"For chrissakes, you're the one who reported it in the first place!"

"Oh that. Yeah, it is rather annoying, isn't it?"

I just shook my head and Erik went back to work in blond, blue-eyed innocence.

So we shoveled several tons of spoiled food into the reprocessor, which chugged and burped and buzzed for hours on end, turning out neat little bricks of stuff, some colored reddish gray, others colored greenish gray. They were supposed to be synthetic meat and synthetic vegetables. I nibbled on one each, then wished we had brought a cargo bay filled with Worcester sauce, ketchup, soy sauce, and Texas three-alarm salsa.

WILL BASSINIO JUST showed me what went wrong with the freezers.

He looked really worn out when he reported to me this morning in the command center. Eyes red from lack of sleep, a black ring around his nose and mouth from the oxygen mask he'd been wearing for nearly twelve hours straight. He didn't smell so good, either. The rotting food had impregnated his coveralls.

"You been at it all night?" I asked him.

He nodded wearily. "Whoever did the job on the freezers was pretty fuckin' smart."

Will pulled three tiny chips from the chest pocket of his smelly, stained coveralls. They were so small I couldn't make out what they were.

"Timers," he explained before I could ask. "Somebody spliced 'em into the control unit of each freezer. Really neat job; took me all fuckin' night to find 'em. Interrupted the current flow and shut the freezers down, while at the same time sending an okay reading to the monitors up here on the bridge. Pretty fuckin' ingenious."

"Can you fix the freezers before all the food thaws out?" I asked.

Will gave me a sad shake of his head. "Whoever did this job knew what he was doing. I'd have to rebuild the whole control unit in each freezer. Take two-three weeks, maybe more."

"We don't have spares?"

"We were supposed to. They're listed in the logistics computer but the bin where they ought to be stored is dead-empty."

I felt my blood seething. Sabotage.

"Were they put into the control units before we launched, or during the flight?" I asked.

Will gave me a shrug. "Can't tell."

"There aren't any locks on the freezer doors," I muttered.

"Never saw anybody goin' in there," he muttered back. "Except that Darling guy, once. He said he was looking for a key lime pie."

Darling. The art critic. The guy who'd been stuffing himself ever since we had left Earth orbit.

The file I had on Darling claimed that he had inherited a modest fortune from his mother, a real estate broker in Florida. It would've been a larger fortune if his father hadn't kept frittering money away on half-baked schemes like opening a fundamentalist Christian theme park in Beirut. The old man died, eventually: gunned down by a crazed ecologist on the Ross Ice Shelf where he was trying to build a hotel and penguin-hunting lodge.

Darling claimed his ten million investment in the *Argo* expedition came from his inheritance. Said it was all the money he had in the world.

I called a lady in Anaheim that I knew, Kay Taranto. She specialized in tracking down deadbeats for the Disney financial empire. I asked her to find out if any money from Rockledge had suddenly appeared in Darling's chubby hands. Told her to check Liechtenstein. Kay was as persistent and dogged as a heat-seeking missile. If there was anything to find out about Darling, she was the one to do it.

Meanwhile, I told Will to go through the entire ship millimeter by millimeter to see if there were any other nasty little surprises planted here or there.

"Don't sleep, don't eat, don't even waste time breathing," I told him. "From now on you're my bug inspector. Look everywhere."

He gave me a sly grin. "Even under the beds?"

"And in them, if you have to," I said. "For every bug you find I'll give you a bonus—say, a week's salary?"

"How about a month's?"

I nodded an okay. It'd be worth it, easy.

I DON'T KNOW whose idea it was to have a continuous banquet until all the food that was about to spoil was eaten up. Probably Darling's. Kind of thing his perverted brain would think up.

For the past three days and nights the seven of them have been stuffing themselves like ancient Romans during Saturnalia. Ship of Bulemics. They must know that everything they upchuck is going into the reprocessor, but it looks like they just don't care. Not right now.

Of course, they're drinking all the wine on board, too. My only joy is that they're going to be so sick when they get to the end of the food that they'll just lay in their sacks for a *long* time and let me get on with the real job of this mission.

I'm staying up here at the command center for the duration of their orgy. I've got some old synthesized Dixieland playing on the intercom so

I can't hear their laughing and shouting from down in the dining room. Or their puking. I've ordered the crew to stay out of the passengers' area.

"Let 'em bust their guts," I told my men. "We've got work to do."

When you read that there's millions of asteroids out in the Belt you get the mental picture of a kind of forest of chunks of rock and metal, you know, clustered so thick that you can't sail a ship through without getting dinged.

No such luck.

Sure, there's millions of asteroids in the Belt. Some as big as mountains; a few of 'em are a couple of hundred kilometers wide. But most of 'em are the size of pebbles, even grains of sand. And they've got a tremendously wide volume of space to wander around in, out there between the orbits of Mars and Jupiter. You could put all the planets and moons of the solar system in that region and it'd still be almost entirely empty space.

The first thing I'm looking for is a nice little nickel-iron asteroid, maybe a couple hundred meters across. Nothing spectacular; a piece as small as a Little League baseball field will do fine. She'll contain more high-grade iron ore than the whole Earth's steel industry uses in ten years. Maybe fifty to seventy-five tons of platinum, an impurity that'd set a man up for life. To say nothing of the gold and silver that's sprinkled around in her.

Such an asteroid is worth trillions of dollars. Maybe hundreds of trillions.

Then there's the carbonaceous-type rocky asteroids. They contain something more valuable than gold, a lot more valuable. They contain water.

There's a new frontier being built in cislunar space, the region between low Earth orbit and the Moon's surface. We've got zero-gee factories in orbit and mining operations on the Moon. We've got big condominium habitats being built in the L-4 and L-5 libration points. More than fifty thousand people live and work in space now.

They get most of their raw materials from the Moon. Lunar ores give our frontier workers aluminum and titanium, even some iron, although it's low-grade stuff and expensive as hell to mine and smelt. There's plenty of silicon on the Moon; they've got a thriving electronics industry growing there.

But the people on the space frontier have got to import their heavy metals from Earth. And their water. They buy high-grade steels from outfits like Rockledge International, and pay enormous prices for lifting the tonnage up from Earth. Same thing for water, except the corporate bastards charge even more for that than they do for steel or even platinum.

Which is why Rockledge and the other corporate giants don't want to see me succeed on this venture. If I come coasting back to the Earth-Moon system with several thousand tons of high-grade steel and enough water to start building swimming pools in Moonbase—and undercutting the corporations' Earth-based prices—I'll have broken the stranglehold those fat-cat bastards have on the space settlements.

They don't like that. Which is why they're out to stop me. I've got to be on the lookout for their next attempt. They can't launch anything to intercept us or attack us outright; the IAA would know that they'd done it and there'd be criminal charges filed against them.

No, Rockledge and any partners-in-crime they may have are working from within. They've got an agent on board my ship and they've got a plan for wrecking this expedition. This sabotage of the food freezers is just their first shot. Will hasn't found any more time bombs yet, but that doesn't mean the ship's clean. Not by a long shot. They could hide a ton of surprises aboard the *Argo*; I just hope Will digs 'em up before they go off.

I know it sounds paranoid, but even paranoids have enemies.

KAY TARANTO FINALLY answered me today. We're so far beyond the orbit of Mars by now that messages take nearly an hour to travel from Earth, even at the speed of light. So two-way conversations are out of the question.

I took her call in my personal quarters, just off the command center. The transmission was scrambled, of course, and it took a little coaxing of the computer before I got a clear picture on my screen. Kay had never been a great beauty: she's got a lean, scruffy, lantern-jawed look to her. The only time I've ever seen her smile was when she nailed a victim who was trying to escape Disney's clutches. Now her face in my screen was un-smiling, dead serious.

"No joy, Sam," she said. "Far as I can tell, Darling is virginally pure, money-wise. No large sums deposited in any of his accounts. No deposits at all in the past four years. He's been living off the income from several nice chunks of blue-chip stocks. No accounts in Liechtenstein that I could find. No Rockledge stock in his portfolio, either. He just about cleaned out his piggy bank to raise the ten mill for your wacky venture. And that's all there is to it."

Then she let a faint glimmer of a smile break her iron-hard facade. "That'll be seventy-five thou, pal. And dinner's on you when you get back."

Thanks a friggin' lot, I said silently to her image on the screen. *Por nada.*

OKAY, SO WE found a carbonaceous chondrite first.

From everything the astrogeologists had told me, metallic asteroids are much more plentiful than the carbonaceous stones. But it's just happened that our sensors picked up a carbonaceous rock, *bang!* right off the bat. I fired two automated probes at it as soon as we got close enough. This morning Lonz initiated the course change we need to match orbit with the rock and rendezvous with it. We'll catch up to it in ten days.

The passengers—partners—have finally recovered from their food orgy. For a week or so they were pretty hung over, and pretty shamefaced. It's a pity I didn't think to make a video of their antics. I could blackmail them for the rest of their lives if I had it all on disk.

Anyway, I called a meeting in the lounge. They all looked pretty dreary, worn out, like they were recuperating from some tropical disease. All except Darling, who seemed pink and healthy. And a lot heavier than he was before. He's ditched his normal clothing and he's now wearing some kind of robe that looks like he stitched it together himself. It took me a couple of minutes of staring at it before I recognized what it was: two tablecloths from the dining lounge, with some designs hand-painted on them.

Shades of the Emperor Nero! Was he wearing eye makeup, too?

"We've located a carbonaceous asteroid," I announced, turning away from Darling. "We'll make rendezvous with it in ten days."

Hubble's ears perked up. "I'd like to see the data, if I may." His voice was still hoarse from all the Roman feather-throating he'd gone through. You'd think that his being an older man, a scientist and all that, he would've set a better example for the other bubbleheads. But no, he'd been just as wild as the rest of them.

I noticed, though, that Sheena was no longer sitting next to him. His father image had apparently gone down the toilet along with everything else.

"Sure," I said to him. "Come on up to the command center afterward. Right now, though, I thought it'd be a good idea if we came up with a proper name for the rock."

"You can't claim it, can you?" Grace asked.

Bo Williams shook his bald head. "No one can claim any natural object in space. That's international law."

"You can use it, though," Hubble said. "There's no law against mining or otherwise utilizing an astronomical body, even if you can't claim ownership."

"First come, first served," said Rick Darling. With a smirk.

"You're all well-versed on interplanetary law," I said, making myself smile at them. "But I still think we ought to give this rock a name. It's going to make us rich; the least we can do is name it."

"What will we get from it?" Sheena asked.

"Water," responded five or six voices simultaneously, including mine.

"Is that all?"

"Tons of water," I said. "Water sells for about one million U.S. dollars per ton at Lagrange One. Considering the size of this asteroid and its possible water content, we ought to clear a hundred million, easy."

"That would pay back our investment!" Marj Dupray piped.

"With a profit," added Jean Margaux, the first time I had seen her say something spontaneous.

"There'll be other valuables on a carbonaceous chondrite, as well," Hubble said, taking out his pipe for the first time. "Carbon, of course. A fair amount of nitrogen, I would suppose. . . . It could be quite profitable."

Not bothering to explain to them the difference between gross income and net profit, I said, "So let's pick a name for the rock and register it with the IAA."

They fell silent.

"I was sort of thinking we might name it Gunn One," I suggested modestly.

They booed and hooted. Each and every one of them.

"Aphrodite," said Sheena, once the razzing had quieted down.

Everybody turned to stare at her. Aphrodite?

She blinked those gorgeous eyes of hers; they were emerald green this morning. "I remember some painting by some old Italian of the birth of Venus, coming out of the sea. You know, like she's the gift of the sea."

"But what's that got to do with . . ."

"And that's Venus. There's already a planet named Venus."

"I know," Sheena said. "That's why I thought we could use her Greek name, Aphrodite."

I had never realized she knew anything at all about anything at all. But she knew about the goddess of love's different names. I went behind the bar to the computer terminal and checked on the names already registered for asteroids. There was a Juno and a Hera, a Helena and even a Cleopatra. But no Aphrodite.

"Aphrodite looks good," I said.

"I still fail to see what it has to do with a lump of rock floating around in space," Jean complained.

But we voted her down and sent a message to the IAA headquarters in Geneva: a new asteroid has been discovered and its name is Aphrodite.

A HUNDRED AND twenty-seven tons of water. Boy, do I feel good about that! A hundred and twenty-seven million bucks safely stowed in our inflatable tanks!

We've been working hard for a solid month, chewing up Aphrodite and baking the volatiles out of her rocks. The grinding equipment worked fine; so did the ovens. No sabotage there, thank God.

There isn't much of old Aphrodite left. Sheena got kind of upset when she realized we were tearing up the rock and grinding it and baking the pieces. We left a small chunk so the name's still valid, although we've perturbed its orbit so much that Hubble claims she'll fall in toward the Sun and cross the orbit of Mars and maybe even Earth's orbit.

Thirty-one thousand, seven hundred and fifty gallons of water, according to the volume of tankage we've filled. That masses out to one hundred and twenty-seven tons. Plus an almost equal amount of ammonia and methane. We've got an even dozen of our inflatable storage tanks hanging outside the ship's hub. I've already made a contract with Moonbase Corporation to buy the whole kit and kaboodle at ten percent below Rockledge's price. They'll process the ammonia and methane for the nitrogen and carbon, then mix the leftover hydrogen with oxygen from lunar ores to make still more water.

We're gonna drown Rockledge!

My partners have been happy and pretty well-behaved this past month. The news media back home have been interviewing them almost constantly; they're all becoming famous. This isn't the Ship of Fools anymore. The media's describing us now as "the grandest entrepreneurial venture in history."

I love the publicity, because the more attention the media pays us the harder it'll be for Rockledge or one of those other big corporate monsters to attack us.

And Lonz has found a *bee-yoo-tiful* nickel-iron asteroid hanging out there just two weeks from where we are. Laser measurements show she's a little over a hundred meters by thirty by twenty or so. Enough high-grade iron ore in her to give us a corner on the steel market for all the Lagrange construction jobs!

We're gonna be rich!

I NEED THE guidance counselor.

[Computer]: How may I help you?

I've got a problem.

[Computer]: Yes?

About a woman. Two women, really.

[Computer]: Go on.

It's Grace Harcourt and Sheena Chang. They're snarling and spitting at each other like a pair of cats.

[Computer]: Why do you think they're behaving that way?

It's over me, stupid! Why else?

[Computer]: Tell me what happened.

We're cruising toward this nickel-iron asteroid, going to make rendezvous in a few days. So I call the partners together in the lounge again to decide on a name for the rock.

And Sheena pipes up, "I don't think it's right for us to be destroying these asteroids."

That surprised me. But coming from her, I tried to explain things gently.

"Look, Sheena," I said. "The whole reason we're out here, the reason you and everybody else joined this expedition, is to get the natural resources that these asteroids contain and bring them back home, where people need them."

"You smashed up Aphrodite until there's practically nothing left of her, and now she's going to crash into Mars or the Earth or maybe even fall into the Sun and burn to death!"

"Sheena, it's just a hunk of rock."

"It's part of nature. It's part of the natural environment. We shouldn't be tampering with the environment. That's wrong."

"Oh good Christ!" said Grace, with a huff like a disgusted steam engine. She was sitting on one side of Sheena; Hubble was sitting on the other, sucking on his smokeless pipe.

"There's nothing alive on these asteroids," Hubble told her, back to his patient fatherly voice once more. "It doesn't hurt anyone to mine them."

"I still think it's wrong," Sheena insisted. I saw tears in her eyes.

"How long are we going to put up with this drivel?" Grace snarled.

Sheena went almost rigid in her chair, like somebody had wired it with a couple thousand volts.

Grace said, "I've spent most of my working days listening to airheaded actors and actresses attach themselves to 'causes.' Sheena, what the hell's the matter with your brain? We're talking about a dead chunk of rock. There's millions of them out here. Get real!"

Sheena just sat there for a minute or so, looking shocked. Jean Margaux was sitting right behind Grace; she had a funny kind of eager grin on her face, like she was waiting to see the gladiators rip each other's guts open. And Rick Darling was right beside Jean, with a cynical smirk on his bloated puss.

[Computer]: His cat was smirking?

Puss! Face! It's slang, you dumb pile of germanium.

[Computer]: You are expressing your suppressed hostilities; good.

I've never suppressed a goddamned hostility in my whole god-damned life!

[Computer]: Go on.

Where was I—oh, yeah. I was just as surprised at Grace's outburst as any of the others. Marj and Bo Williams were sitting in the back of the lounge. Bo started to say something but Sheena got there first.

"Listen, Miss High-and-Mighty Columnist," she said to Grace, "I had to kiss your backside when I was in the acting business, but now I'm going to be independently wealthy, thanks to Sam, and you can go scribble yourself!"

"You plasticized bitch," Grace shot back, "I'll bet my backside is the only one in southern California you haven't kissed."

"Jealous?"

"Of you? Take away the implants and what've you got?"

"A dumpy broad with celulite on her hips, like you."

"At least I've got a brain in my head!"

"So does a rat!"

They were nose-to-nose now, yelling, starting to get out of their chairs.

I jumped between them. "Hey, hey! Calm down, both of you!"

"Get this airhead out of here, Sam," Grace said. "There's nothing going on above her neck anyway."

Sheena's eyes were blazing fury. "She's jealous, jealous, jealous! Look at her, she's turning green all over!"

Hubble got up and coaxed Sheena back toward her quarters. I held Grace by the shoulders until they left. She was trembling with rage.

"This meeting's over," I told the others. "We'll pick a name for the as-teroid later."

I walked Grace forward, toward the command center, away from the other passengers' quarters where Sheena and Hubble had gone.

I kept some good cognac in my quarters. Hardly ever touched it myself, but it looked good in its cut crystal decanter and I thought it might help calm Grace down. Me, I prefer beer.

"What the hell happened in there?" I asked Grace.

She sat in the couch, still quivering so much there were almost white-caps on her cognac. I pulled up the powered recliner chair to face her, with the coffee table between us. My quarters aren't luxurious, but there's a little more space to them than the passengers' suites. Rank hath its privileges, after all.

Grace knocked back half her cognac, then said, "I can't take any more of her, Sam. She's driving me nuts."

"Sheena?"

"Who else? The way she flaunts herself. Makes eyes at all the men."

"I thought she had settled onto Hubble."

"She's after you, Sam. Can't you see that?"

"Me? I haven't laid a glove on her since the first month out."

"And she resents it."

"That's crazy."

Grace put her snifter down on the coffee table. It was plastic, of course, but painted to look like ebony.

"Sam, she's looking for a father figure. That's you."

"That's Hubble," I corrected her.

Grace shook her head. "It was Hubble until the food orgy. Then she saw that Lowell was just as human and silly as the rest of us. But, you, *mon capitaine,* were aloof and noble and doing your duty on the bridge while the rest of us were stuffing ourselves—in more ways than one, I might add."

"I don't want to hear about it," I said.

"You've got to listen to me, Sam! You asked me to find out who the Rockledge agent is. . . ."

"Sheena?"

"No, of course not. But if she's sore at you, if she feels you've rejected her, she could become a very willing tool for whoever among us is working for Rockledge."

That stopped me. "Sheena, helping Rockledge. Hmp. With an enemy like that, who needs friends?"

"This isn't funny, Sam."

But it made me laugh anyway.

Suddenly Grace got up from the couch, came around the coffee table, and plopped herself in my lap.

"You big dummy," she said. "I'm trying to protect you. Can't you see that?"

Then she said the words that strike terror into the heart of any man.

"Sam—I think I've fallen in love with you."

Well, what could I do? I mean with her sitting in my lap and all? One thing led to another and we wound up in bed. Grace is very tender, very sweet, underneath that facade of the tough Hollywood columnist that she wears most of the time.

But now she wants to hang around my neck. And this ship isn't big enough for me to hide! Besides, if she's right about Sheena I ought to be working on her, getting on her good side, so to speak.

[Computer]: In bed, you mean?

That's her best side, pal.

[Computer]: Is that necessary? It will complicate the interpersonal relationships. . . .

Everything's already so goddamned complicated that I feel like I'm a pretzel trapped in a spaghetti factory. What should I do?

[Computer]: What do you want to do?

I want to get them both off my back!

[Computer]: And what would be the best way to do that, do you think?

That's what I'm asking you!

[Computer]: How do you feel about this situation?

Oh Christ! I know this program. Whenever you're stuck you ask me how I feel. Get lost! Turn off!

[Computer]: Are you certain you want to do this?

End the program, dammit! When I want to jerk off I'll do it in the bathroom.

WELL, THOSE SNEAKING, slithering, slimy bastards at Rockledge have struck again.

This morning we got an order from the International Astronautical Authority—bless 'em—that forbids us from mining any more asteroids until further notice.

A moratorium on asteroid mining! Only temporary, they say. But "temporary" to those lard-bottomed bureaucrats could mean years! I could be old and senile before they lift the moratorium.

Those fatheaded drones claim that we've perturbed the orbit of Aphrodite so much that there's a chance it might strike the Earth. There's not much left of Aphrodite, but she's still big enough to cause damage wherever she lands. The media are already talking about the "killer aster-oid" and running stories about how an asteroid hit wiped out the di-nosaurs sixty-five million years ago.

Absolute bullshit!

What's happened is that Rockledge and the other big boys are putting pressure on the IAA to stop me—uh, us, that is. Now that they know we can undercut their price for water, they're using Aphrodite as an excuse. If the asteroid's orbit poses a threat, the IAA can send a team out with enough rocket thrusters to nudge it away from the Earth, for chrissakes. I'll pay the friggin' cost of the mission, if I have to. Take it off as a business expense; lower my goddamned taxes.

But what the IAA's done is put a moratorium on all operations that might change an asteroid's natural orbit. Hell, we're the only operation out here in the Belt. They're trying to stop us.

Well, fuck them!

I ordered Lonz to ignore the message. I'm not even going to acknowl-edge receiving it. We're going ahead and mining that big chunk of nickel-iron, and then we'll head back home with enough high-grade metal to make all the off-Earth settlements drool. They'll want to do business with us, and there's nothing the friggin' IAA can do to stop them from buying what I'm selling.

Then we'll let the lawyers fight it out. I'll have all the space settlements on my side, and the media will love a story that pits us little guys against the big, bad corporate monsters.

Moratorium, my ass!

YESTERDAY WE NAMED the asteroid Pittsburgh. I called the partners together again and told them, not asked them, what the name would be. I was born in Pittsburgh, and back in its heyday it was a big steel-making town. So will this asteroid be. Our sensors show she's practically solid metal.

This morning I sent my claim in to the IAA. I haven't acknowledged their moratorium order, and I haven't told the partners about it. Filing a claim for the asteroid doesn't violate their moratorium, of course, but it'll sure make them suspicious. What the hell! There's nothing they can do about it. It'd take them a year to get a ship out here to try to stop us.

You're not allowed to claim possession of an astronomical body, but once you've informed the IAA that you've established a working facility someplace you've got the right to use its natural resources there without anybody else coming in to compete with you. The facility can be scientific, industrial, or a permanent habitat. It could even be commercial, like a tourist hotel. That's how the various settlements on the Moon were established; no nation owns them, but once a group lays claim to a territory, the IAA prevents any other group from muscling in on the same territory.

With a chunk of metal like Pittsburgh the IAA ought to give S. Gunn Enterprises, Unlimited, exclusive rights to mine its resources—moratorium or no fucking moratorium. The asteroid's too small to allow another company to start whittling away at it. At least, that's the legal position that the IAA agreed to before the *Argo* left Earth orbit. Now we'll have to see if they stick to it.

In the meantime, there's work to do.

PITTSBURGH'S A BEAUTY! We're hovering about five hundred meters from her. At this distance she's huge, immense, like a black pitted mountain hanging over our heads. I've spent most of the day taking the partners out for EVAs. To say they were impressed would be the understatement of the decade.

Imagine an enormous lump of coal-black metal, its surface roughened and pitted, its ridges and crater rims gleaming where the Sun strikes them. It's so big it dwarfs you when you go outside, makes you feel like it's going to crush you, almost.

I brought the partners out in twos. Each time a pair of them floated free of the airlock and looked up through their bubble helmets I heard the same sound out of them: a gasp—surprise, awe, fear, grandeur, all that and more.

Hubble asked for permission to chip some samples for himself, to study in the little lab he's set up in his quarters. Bo Williams started reciting poetry, right there in his space suit. Even Jean Margaux, the Ice Queen, was audibly impressed.

Everybody except Darling came out to look.

"There's our fortune," I told each one of them over the suit-to-suit comm link. "Considering the mass of this beauty and the prices on today's metals market, you're looking at ten billion dollars, on the hoof. At least."

That made them happy. Which was a good thing, because we're getting down to the last of the preserved food. In a day or two we're going to have to start eating the recycled stuff.

The IAA is still sending their moratorium to us, every hour on the hour. I've instructed the crew to ignore it and not to tell the partners about it. I've ordered them not to acknowledge any incoming messages from anybody. Then I sent out a message to my own office in Florida that we were experiencing some kind of communications difficulty, and all the incoming transmissions were so garbled we couldn't make them out.

Lonz gave me a funny look when I sent that out. A guilty look.

"Nobody's gonna hold you responsible," I told him. "Don't worry about it."

"Right, boss," he said. But he still looked uneasy. And he's never called me boss before.

I SPENT MOST of the night watching the videos of Darling's movements during the time I was taking the other partners outside to see Pittsburgh close-up.

It bothered me that he refused to go EVA like the rest of them. So I activated the ship's internal monitoring system, the cameras that are set unobtrusively into the overhead panels of every section of the ship. I suppose I could have been watching everything that everybody does since the moment we left Earth orbit. Maybe that would've told me who the Rockledge fink is. Certainly it would have been as good as watching porno flicks.

But there are seven of them and only one of me. I'd have to spend seven times the hours I actually have in the hopes of catching somebody performing an act of sabotage—or doing something in bed I haven't done myself, and better.

Anyway, I discovered Darling's secret. Trouble is, it's got nothing to do with Rockledge or possible sabotage. The sneaky lard-ass has been hoarding food! While the rest of the partners were up in the command center or suiting up at the main airlock, he was tiptoeing down to the food lockers and hauling armfuls of goodies back to his own suite. He's got packaged food stored in his bureau drawers, canned food stuffed under his bed, whole cases of food hidden in his closets.

God knows how long he's been stealing the stuff. His personal wine cooler is filled with frozen food, which the bastard must have been stealing since before the freezers went on the fritz.

Did he know the freezers were going to commit hara-kiri?

THE WORK ON Pittsburgh is going slower than I had planned. The metal's so good that it's tougher than we had expected. So it takes longer for the laser torches to cut through it. Once we've got a slice carved off, the smelting and refining equipment works fine. We're building up a nice payload of high-quality steel for the Lagrange habitats and the steel-hungry factories in Earth orbit.

To say nothing of the lovely ingots of twenty-four carat gold and pure silver that we're cooking out of the ore. And the sheets of platinum!

Argo is starting to look like a little toy doughnut sitting alongside a cluster of shiny steel grapes. See, in zero gravity, when we melt down a slab of ore it forms itself into a very neat sphere of molten metal. Like a teeny little sun, glowing outside the ship. After we remove the impurities (the gold and silver and platinum, that is) we inject gas into the sphere to hollow it out while it's solidifying. A hollow sphere is easier for our customers to work with than a solid ball of steel. The gas comes right from the asteroid itself, of course; a byproduct of our mining operation.

All this is done remotely, without any people outside. Lonz and Will control the operation from the command center. They only go EVA if something goes wrong, some piece of equipment breaks down. Even then, the little maintenance robots can take care of the routine repairs. They've only had to go EVA twice in all the weeks we've been working on Pittsburgh.

We'll have to leave the asteroid soon if we want to get back to Earth on a reasonable schedule. The partners are grumbling about the recycled food—Darling's bitching the loudest, the lying thief. He's feasting on the real food he's cached in his suite while the rest of us are nibbling on shit-burgers. All the other partners are marveling that he's gaining weight while the rest of us are slimming down.

Finally I couldn't stand it any more. This evening when I came into the dining lounge there was fat-ass Darling in his homemade toga, holding a green briquette of recycled crap in one hand with his chubby pinky up in the air.

"I will *never* come out on a fly-by-night operation like this again," he was saying.

Jean Margaux sniffed at the red briquette she had in front of her. They were odorless, but her face looked as if she was getting a whiff of a pigsty on a blazing afternoon in August. Marj Dupray and Bo Williams were off at a table by themselves, whispering to each other with their heads nearly touching over their table.

"I'm sorry you don't like the food," I said to Darling. I could feel the tightness in my face.

"It's inedible," he complained.

"Then you'll just have to go back to your suite and gorge yourself on the food you've got hidden there," I said.

His fleshy face turned absolute white.

Jean looked amused. "Don't tell me you've got a candy bar hidden under your bed," she said to Darling.

"I resent your implication," the fat bastard said to me.

"Resent it all you like," I shot back. "After you've taken us to your suite and opened up your wine cooler."

He heaved himself to his dainty little feet. "I won't stay here and be insulted."

Jean looked kind of curious now. Bo and Marj had stopped their tete-a-tete and were staring at us.

With as much dignity as a small dirigible, Darling headed for the hatch.

I called after him, "Come on, Rick, invite us to your suite. Share the food you've hoarded, you puffed-up sonofabitch."

He spun around to face me, making the fringes of his toga flap and swirl. "You retract that statement or, so help me, when we get back to Earth I'll sue you for every penny you've got!"

"Sure, I'll retract it. After you've invited us to your suite."

"That's an invasion of my privacy!" he said.

Jean drew herself up to her full height. "Richard, dear, are you actually hiding food from us?"

Bo Williams got off his chair, too. "Yeah—what's the story, Rick? How come you're getting fatter while we're all getting thinner?"

Darling's eyes swung from one of them to the other. Even Marjorie was on her feet now, scowling at him.

"Can't you see what he's doing?" Darling spluttered and pointed a fat finger at me. "He's trying to make a scapegoat out of me! He's trying to get you all to hate me and forget that *he's* the one who's gotten us into this mess!"

"There's an easy way to prove you're innocent," Williams said. "Invite us in to your suite."

Bo can look menacing in his sleep, with that burly build of his and the shaved scalp. He's really a gentle guy, a frustrated poet who makes his living writing documentaries. But he looks like a Turkish assassin.

"I don't have to prove anything," Darling answered, edging back toward the hatch. "A man's innocent until proven guilty. That's the law."

What little patience I have snapped right then and there. "I'm the law aboard this vessel," I said. "And I order you to open up your suite for in-spection. Now."

He hemmed and hawed. He blubbered and spluttered. But with Bo and me pushing him, he backed all the way down the corridor to his suite. Sure enough, there was enough food cached away in there to cater a party.

Which is exactly what we had. I called Grace, Sheena, and Lowell Hub-ble. Even invited the crew while I went up to the command center and kept an eye on the automated equipment. They ate and drank everything Darling had squirreled away. He just sat on his own bed and cried until there was nothing left but crumbs and empty bottles.

Served him right. But I couldn't help feeling sort of sorry for the poor jerk when they all left him in his own suite, surrounded by the mess.

I KIND OF hate to leave Pittsburgh. This asteroid has made me filthy rich. We can't stay long enough to mine everything she's got to give us; even if we did the *Argo* would be toting so much mass that our thrusters would never be able to get us back to Earth.

No, we'll leave Pittsburgh with our smelting equipment and a beacon on her, to verify our claim. If the IAA works the way they should, nobody else will be able to touch her. In a few years the lawyers ought to have wrangled out this moratorium business, and I'll be able to send out a fleet of ships to finish carving her up and carting the refined metals back Earthward.

I'll be a billionaire!

MAROONED.

Those bastards at Rockledge have shown their hand at last. They're go-ing to kill me and my partners and steal my claim to Pittsburgh and the metals we've mined. As well as the water and volatiles we got from Aphrodite.

I'm beyond anger. A kind of a cold freeze has gripped me. I can't even work up the satisfaction of screaming and swearing. They've marooned us on the asteroid; me and all my partners. We'll die on Pittsburgh. I'm talking into the recording system built into my space suit. Maybe some-day after we're all dead somebody will find us and listen to this chip. If you do, take our bodies—and this chip—straight to the IAA's law-enforcement people. Murder, piracy, grand larceny, conspiracy, kidnapping—and it all goes right to the top of Rockledge. And God knows who else.

I don't even feel scared. I'm just kind of numb. Dumbstruck. Like being paralyzed.

Erik is the one. Smiling, blond, slow-witted Erik is the mastermind that Rockledge planted on the *Argo*. It's like one of those damned mystery novels where the murderer turns out to be the stupid butler. Who would have suspected Erik? Not me, that's for sure.

Lonz, Will and I had put in a long, tough day finishing up our operations on Pittsburgh. All the mining and smelting equipment we had put onto the asteroid was finally shut down. That cluster of steel grapes bulked very nicely on one side of the ship. The sheets of platinum and the ingots of gold and silver were all neatly tucked into our cargo bays. Our identification beacon was on the asteroid, beeping satisfactorily.

I scrolled through the checklist on the main console's screen one final time. We had done everything we had to do. The partners were all asleep—at least they were all in their beds. Or somebody's beds.

"Okay," I said to Lonz. "That's it. Let's see the nav program and set up the trajectory for home."

"Um, there's been a change in the mission plan, Sam," Erik said.

I turned around from the console to look at him. I hadn't even realized he'd entered the control center. His usual station was down by the galley, next to the lounge. He stood in the middle of the floor, smiling that slow, genial smile of his, like always.

"Whattaya mean?" I asked.

"We can't start the homeward trip just yet," he said.

"Why not?"

His smile didn't change one iota as he explained, "We've got to put you and your partners off the ship first."

"Put me and . . . ?"

"You're staying on Pittsburgh, Sam," Erik told me. "You're not coming back." And he pulled a slim little automatic pistol from his belt. It looked big enough to me, probably because he pointed it straight at my eyes.

"What the hell are you talking about?" But the sinking sensation in the pit of my stomach told me that I knew the answer to my own question.

I spun around toward Lonz and Will. They both looked unhappy, but neither one of them made a move to help me.

"You guys, too?" All of a sudden I felt like Julius Caesar.

"You wouldn't believe how much money we'll be getting," Will muttered.

"For chrissakes, didn't I treat you guys fair and square?" I yelped.

"You didn't make us partners, Sam," said Lonz.

"Holy shit. Why didn't you *tell* me you were unhappy? I could've . . ."

"Never mind," Erik said, suddenly forceful, in charge. "Sam, you'll have to stay in your quarters until we get everything arranged. Don't try anything. I don't want to make this messy."

Three against one would have made a mess all right, and the mess would be me. So I huffed and puffed and slinked to my quarters like a good, obedient prisoner. My mind was spinning, looking for an out, but I didn't know what they planned to do. That made it tough to figure out my next move. I heard them attach some kind of a lock to the outside of the door as soon as I closed it after me. And then all my lights went off; not even the emergency lamps lit. They had cut off all electrical power to my quarters. No lights, no computer access, no communications with anybody, nothing but darkness.

And waiting.

After a few hours they bundled us all into space suits and—one by one—had each of us jet from the *Argo*'s main airlock to the surface of Pittsburgh, where we had left the mining and smelting equipment. I was the last one to be pushed out.

"We've set up an inflated dome for the eight of you," Erik said, with that maddening slow grin of his, "and stocked with enough food to last a few months."

"Thanks a bunch!" I snapped.

"We could have killed you all outright," he said. "I thought I was going to have to after I made that slip about Liechtenstein in the lounge one of the first nights out."

I felt like a complete idiot. It never occurred to me that one of the guys I hired might be the Rockwell plant.

The sonofabitch knew what he was doing; I have to hand him that. If he had tried anything violent all eight of us would have fought for our lives. As far as I could tell the only weapon they had was Erik's one pistol. He might have killed several of us, but we might have swarmed him under. Lonz and Will, too. Eight against three. We might have carried it off.

But Erik worked it like an expert. He isolated us into individuals and, instead of killing us outright, merely forced us to go from the ship to the asteroid. Merely. It was a slow way of killing us. Food and shelter notwithstanding, nobody will return to Pittsburgh in less than a couple of years. Nobody can, even if Erik would leave us a radio and we screamed our lungs out for help.

"This is piracy," I said as the three of them nudged me toward the airlock. "To say nothing of murder."

"It's business, Sam," Erik said. "Nothing personal."

I turned to Lonz. "Do you think he's going to let you live?" Then to Will. "Or you? Neither one of you is going to make it back to Earth."

Lonz looked grim. "They're giving us enough money to set us up for life. There's no reason for us to talk, and no reason for Erik to worry about us."

I huffed at him from inside my helmet. "Dead men tell no tales, pals." Then I snapped the visor shut and stepped into the airlock.

"I'm sorry, Sam." I heard Will's voice say, muffled by my helmet.

"Sorry don't get the job done," I answered in my bravest John Wayne imitation.

Then the hatch closed and the pumps started sucking the air out of the lock.

The outer hatch slid open. There was Pittsburgh, hanging big and black and ugly against the even blacker background of space. Through the heavy tinting of my visor I could only see a few of the brighter stars. They looked awfully cold, awfully far away.

"Get going Sam," Erik's voice sounded genially in my earphones, "or we'll have to open your suit with a laser torch."

Like walking the goddamned plank. I jetted over to the asteroid. Sure enough, there was an inflated dome next to the equipment we had left. And seven space-suited figures standing outside it. Even in the bulky suits they looked scared shitless, huddled together, clinging to one another.

I planted my feet on the asteroid and turned back toward the *Argo*, spinning lazily against the backdrop of stars.

Raising one clenched fist over my head I yelled into my suit radio's microphone, "I'll see you—all of you—hanging from the highest yardarm in the British fleet!"

It was the only damned thing I could think of. About five minutes later a blazing flare of light bellowed from the *Argo*'s rocket nozzles and the ship—*my* ship—suddenly leaped away and dwindled in the dark sky until I couldn't see it any more.

TO SAY THAT my partners are upset is putting it so mildly that it's like saying that Custer's Seventh Cavalry was not terribly friendly with the Sioux Nation.

They're terrified. They're weeping. They're cursing and swearing and calling down the wrath of the gods. Who (as usual) remain totally aloof and unconcerned about our plight. It took me nearly half an hour to get them to stop babbling, and by that time I finally got it through my thick skull that they're mad at *me*!

"This is all your fault!" Rick Darling screamed at me. "I *begged* them to let me stay on the ship. I promised them I'd never inform on them. I even told them that I was *glad* they wanted to get rid of you! But they wouldn't listen! Now I'm going to die and it's all your fault!"

Funny thing is, each and every one of them is yelling some variation of the same story. Each one of them begged Erik to let them stay aboard, promised to go along with killing me—and all the others—providing they were allowed to get home safely.

Erik didn't take any of them up on their offers. Not even Sheena, who had a helluva lot to offer. The sonofabitch must be made of very strong stuff. Either that or he's gay, which I doubt, because Darling would've probably bent over backwards for him if that's what he wanted.

They're being so goddamned rotten that they've almost made me forget who our real enemy is. I let them babble and gabble and just clumped across the rough, pitted surface of Pittsburgh and went inside the dome Erik had so thoughtfully left for us. I ought to mention that the asteroid's too small to have any noticeable gravity. We're all outfitted with small magnets on our boots, which work very nicely on a body made predominantly of iron. But even though walking is as easy as stepping across a newly painted floor that's still slightly tacky, my body's feeling all the old sensations of nearly zero gravity.

I'm smiling to myself. As soon as my partners calm down enough to take stock of their situation, they're going to get good and sick. I'm certain that Erik hasn't included space-sickness medications in the pile of supplies he's left us.

Good! Serves the whining little pricks right.

SURE ENOUGH, THEY'VE all been sick as dogs for the past two days. I felt kind of queasy myself for the first few hours, but I got over it quickly enough.

I've spent the time checking out just how much Erik left us, in his less-then-infinite kindness. It's not much. Eight crates of food briquettes; about enough to last six months. No medical supplies, not even aspirin.

The dome's got air and water recyclers, offloaded from *Argo*'s spares. But no backup equipment and no spare parts. If anything goes wrong with the machinery, we die pretty quickly.

So our prospects are: (1) we starve to death in six months; (2) we die from lack of water or air if either of the recyclers craps out on us; or (3) we start murdering each other because there's nothing else for us to do but get on each other's nerves.

At least inside the dome we can get out of the space suits. There's no furniture in here; nothing to sit on but the crates of food briquettes, eight inflatable sleeping rolls, and a zero-gee bathroom facility. The toilet seems to work okay, although there's only the one of them. The women bitch about that constantly. Me, I worry about how much radiation we're absorbing; the metallized plastic of this dome doesn't stop cosmic ray primaries, and if there's a solar flare we'll probably get cooked inside of an hour or two.

There's also the possibility that a smaller asteroid might puncture our dome. That would be absolutely poetic: killed by an asteroid striking another asteroid.

REALITY IS SETTING in.

My seven keen-minded partners are mostly recovering from their zero-gee puking and starting to realize that we are well and truly marooned on this chunk of nickel-iron. With only six months worth of food.

They've even stopped hollering at me. They're getting morose, just sitting around this cramped little dome like a bunch of prisoners waiting for dawn and the firing squad.

"Would've been kinder of Erik to kill us outright and get it over with," said Bo Williams.

The others are sad-faced as basset hounds with toothaches. Trying to sleep on a three-centimeter-thick inflatable bag laid over a rough floor of solid nickel-iron does nothing to improve anybody's disposition.

"If that's the way you feel about," Lowell Hubble said to Bo, from behind his inevitable pipe, "why don't you just commit suicide and save us the self-pity? That would leave an extra ration of food to the survivors."

Williams' shoulder muscles bunched underneath his grimy shirt. "And why don't you try sucking on something else than that damned pacifier?"

"Why don't you both shut up?" Marj snapped.

"I think this entire line of conversation is disgraceful," said Jean. "If we can't behave like polite adults we should leave the dome until we've learned how to act properly."

We all stared at her. I started to laugh. In her own prissy way, Jean was right. We need some discipline. Something to keep our minds off our predicament.

"Maybe we ought to draw lots," Grace suggested with mock cheerfulness. "Short straw goes outside without a suit. Maybe we could stretch the food long enough . . ."

"And even add to our food supply," Williams said, eying Darling grimly. "Like the Donner party."

Sheena's eyes went like saucers. "Eat . . . ? Oh, I could never do that!"

"People do strange things when they're starving," Hubble said. He looked over at our overfed Mr. Darling, too.

If Rick understood what was going through their minds, he didn't show it. "If only there was some hope of rescue," he mewled. "Some slightest shred of hope."

It hit me right then.

"Rescue, my ass!" I said. And before Jean could even frown at me, I added, "We're gonna save ourselves, by damn!"

THEY LAUGHED AT Columbus. They laughed at Edison and the Wright brothers and Marconi.

None of my beloved partners laughed at me when I said we'd save ourselves. They just kind of gaped for a moment, and then ignored me, as if I had farted or done something else stupid or vulgar.

But what the hell, there isn't anything else we can do. And we need some discipline, some goal, some objective to keep our brains busy and our minds off starvation and death. Instead of breaking down into an octet of would-be murderers and cannibals, I dangled the prospect of salvation in front of their unbelieving eyes.

"We can do it!" I insisted. "We can save ourselves. We can turn this little worldlet of ours into a lifeboat."

"And pigs can fly," Bo Williams growled.

"They can if they build wings for themselves," I shot back.

Darling started, "How on earth do you propose . . ."

"We're not on Earth, oh corpulent critic of the arts. Erik thinks he's got us marooned here on Pittsburgh. But we're gonna ride this rock back to the Earth/Moon system."

Jean Margaux: "That's impossible!"

Marj Dupray: "It beats sitting around and watching the food supplies dwindle."

Grace Harcourt: "Can you really do it, Sam?"

Sheena Chang: "What do you think, Lowell?"

Hubble, our resident astronomer, took the pipe out of his mouth and squinted at me as if he had never seen me before. His mustache was getting ragged and grayer than usual. He needed a shave. All us men looked pretty shaggy, except for Darling, whose cheeks were still as smooth as a baby's backside. Is he permanently depilated, or doesn't he have enough testosterone in him to raise a beard?

Hubble said, "To move this asteroid out of its present orbit we'd need a propulsion system and navigational equipment."

"We've got 'em," I said. "Or at least, we can make 'em."

I know the mining and smelting facilities inside out. We had left the equipment here on Pittsburgh. My idea had been, why drag them all the way back home when you'll want them at the asteroid on the next trip out? The equipment's nuclear powered, of course: you'd need solar-cell panels as big as cities to generate enough electricity at this distance from the Sun.

When Sheena found out we had two (count 'em, two) nukes on Pittsburgh, she gasped with alarm. "But nuclear power is bad, Sam. It's got radiation."

"Don't worry about it, kiddo," I told her. "They're shielded real well." I didn't bother to inform her that her gorgeous body was getting more radiation from cosmic primaries than all the nuclear power plants on Earth gave off.

My idea was to use the mining lasers to slice off chunks of the asteroid, then use the smelting facility to vaporize the metal instead of just melting it down. If we could direct the vapor properly it'd push us like a rocket exhaust. I figured we could scoop out a pit in the asteroid's surface and use it as a rough-and-ready rocket nozzle. Or maybe one of the existing craters that've put the *pit* in ol' Pittsburgh would do.

We would't need pinpoint navigation. All I'd need was to get us moving at a good clip toward the Earth-Moon system. Once we crossed the orbit of Mars the automated meteor-watch radars'd' pick us up. Hell, Pittsburgh's big enough to scare the bejeezuz out of the IAA. An asteroid this big, heading for the Earth-Moon system? They'd at least send a robot probe to check us out; maybe a manned spacecraft with enough extra propulsion aboard to nudge us away from the inhabited region. Either way, there'd be a radio aboard and we could yell for help.

DAMN! HUBBLE'S DONE some calculations on his wrist computer and given me the bad news. Oh, my scheme will work all right, but it'll take seventy or eighty years before Pittsburgh gets past the orbit of Mars.

"She's just too massive," Hubble said. "If we want to accelerate this asteroid that quickly we need a lot more energy than we can get by burning off mass at the rate the smelting facility can produce."

Gloom. All seven of them became even more morose than ever. I felt down, too. For a while. Then Sheena saved the day.

(Not that we can tell day from night on Pittsburgh. The only way we can keep track of time is by the clocks built into our wrist computers. Even though the asteroid's slowly tumbling as it swings through space, inside the dome we get no sensation of daylight or nighttime. The sky's always dark, even when the Sun is visible outside. Our mood matched our environment: cold, dark, dreary.)

Sheena came up to me while I was trying to decide whether I'd make dinner out of a green briquette or a red one. They both looked kind of brown to me, but that may have been just the lighting inside the dome, which was pretty low and murky.

"Sam," she said. "Can I ask you a favor?"

We were all so glum and melancholy that I had forgotten how beautiful Sheena was. Whether it was natural or surgically enhanced, even in the shabby unwashed blouse and slacks she'd been wearing for days on end she looked incredibly lovely. I forgot about food, temporarily.

"A favor?" I said. "Sure. What is it?"

"Well . . ." she hesitated, as if she had to put her thoughts together. "Since we won't be using the mining equipment and all that other stuff, can't we toss those ugly old nuclear generators out? I mean, they can't be doing us any good sitting out there making radiation. . . ."

I jumped to my feet so hard that my magnetic soles couldn't hold me and I went skyrocketing straight up to the top of the dome.

"YAHOO!" I yelled. My seven partners gaped up at me. To say they were startled would be a very large understatement.

I turned in midair and glided down onto Lowell Hubble's shoulders. "The nukes!" I yelled, tapping out a jazz rhythm on his head. "Instead of using them to generate electricity we can *explode* the mothers!"

It took a while for me to calm down enough to explain it to them. There was enough energy in the nuclear piles of our two generators to blast out a sizeable portion of Pittsburgh—enough to propel us back toward the inner solar system.

"Like atomic bombs?" Bo Williams actually shuddered. "You've got to be crazy, Sam."

But Hubble was pecking away at his wrist computer. I could tell he was almost as excited as I was: he had even dropped his pipe.

"You can't set off nuclear explosions here," Grace said, looking kind of scared. "You'll get us all killed."

I gave her a grin and a shrug. "Might as well go down fighting. You want to wait until we put long pig on the menu?"

She didn't answer.

But Jean did. "Interplanetary law forbids using nuclear explosives in space unless specifically permitted by the IAA and under the supervision of their inspectors."

"So sue me," I told her. "Better yet, *call* the friggin' IAA and have them come out here and arrest me!"

Hubble had a different kind of objection. "Sam, I don't know if you can get those power piles to explode. They have all sorts of safeguards built into them. They're designed to fail-safe, you know."

"Then we'll have to pull 'em out of the generators and disengage all their safety systems."

"But the radiation!"

"That's what robots are for," I said grandly.

I SHOULD'VE KNOWN that those friggin' simpleminded robots we have for working the mining and smelting equipment couldn't handle the task of disassembling the nuclear reactors. Three of our five stupid tin cans can't even move across the goddamned surface of Pittsburgh; it's too rough for their delicate goddamned wheels. They're stranded where they sit. The two that can move aren't strong enough to pry the power piles out of the generators. Sure, everything here is in micro-g, but those piles are imbedded inside deep shielding, and friction makes it tough to slide them out.

I won't bore you with all the details. I had to ask for volunteers. I knew I'd have to go out there myself, but I'd need more than my two hands to get the job done.

I didn't expect any of my brave little partners to volunteer. They never had before, and what I was asking them to do now was really risky, maybe fatal.

To my surprise, Lowell Hubble raised his hand. "I'm too old to start a family," he said quietly, glancing at Sheena sideways.

We were standing in a little circle inside the dome. I had outlined what needed to be done and what the dangers were. I had also told them very firmly that I would accept only male volunteers.

"Nonsense!" Jean snapped. "That's male chauvinist twaddle."

As soon as Hubble put his hand up, Jean raised hers. "I'm too old to *want* to start a family," she said firmly.

The others glanced around at one another uneasily. Slowly, very slowly, each of them raised their hands. Even Sheena, although her hand was trembling. I felt kind of proud of them.

We did it by lottery. Almost. I wouldn't let Hubble out of the dome. I needed him for all the calculations we had to do, and maybe later for navigation, if all went well. Bo Williams hated that, I could tell, but he didn't complain. He could see that there's no use risking the one guy who can handle the scientific end of this madness. It's not just the radiation. What'll we do if Hubble trips out there and one end of the power pile mashes his head?

Chauvinist or not, I just took Bo and Darling out with me. Darling looked so scared I thought he was going to crap in his space suit, but he didn't dare complain a peep. We got the first pile out from behind its shielding okay, and then skeedaddled back inside the dome and let the robots finish the work. The dosimeters built into our suits screeched a little and flashed their yellow warning lights. Once we got back into the dome they went back to green, though.

A good day's work. Maybe we'll make it after all.

ACCORDING TO HUBBLE'S calculation, if we can make just one of the power piles explode it'll provide enough impetus to push Pittsburgh out of its orbit and send it zooming toward the inner solar system.

"You're sure?" I asked him.

He nodded like a college professor, the pipe back between his teeth. "If you can get it to explode."

"It'll explode, don't worry. Even if I have to beat it with a baseball bat."

He gave me a slightly amused look. "And where are you going to find a baseball bat?"

"Never mind that," I said. "Will we be safe? I don't really want to kill us if I can avoid it."

"Oh, safe enough, if you place the pile on the far end of Pittsburgh and set it off there. I've worked out the precise location for you."

"We won't get a fatal dose of radiation or anything?"

"No, the mass of the asteroid will protect us from radiation. Since there's no air outside the dome there will be no aerodynamic shock wave. No heat pulse or fallout, either, if the pile is properly sited in a crater."

"Then we'll be okay."

"We should be. The only thing to worry about is the seismic shock. The explosion will send quite a jolt through the body of the asteroid, of course."

"I was wondering about that? How many gs?"

He frowned slightly. "That's right, you astronauts think in terms of g-forces."

"Don't you?"

"No. I was more concerned with Pittsburgh's modulus of elasticity."

"Its what?"

He gave me a faraway look. "The explosion will send a shock wave through the solid body of the asteroid."

"You already said that."

"Yes. The question is: will that shock wave break up the asteroid?"

"Break it up? Break up Pittsburgh?"

"Yes."

"Well, will it? Will it?"

"I don't think so. But I simply don't have enough data to be certain."

"Thanks," I said.

So our choice is to sit on this rock until we starve to death or maybe blow it to smithereens with a jury-rigged atomic bomb.

I'm going with the bomb. And keeping my fingers crossed.

OKAY, WE'RE ALL in our pressure suits, inside the dome, lying flat inside our pitiful little inflated sleeping bags. When I press the button on the remote control unit in my hand the feebleminded robot out there on the other end of Pittsburgh will pull the control rods out of the power pile and it'll go critical in a matter of seconds.

Here we go.

Soon's I work up the nerve.

GOOD NEWS AND bad news.

The pile exploded all right, and jolted Pittsburgh out of its orbit. The asteroid didn't break up. None of us got killed. No significant radiation here in the dome, either.

That's the good news.

There's plenty of bad. First off, the explosion slammed us pretty damned hard. Like being kicked in the ribs by a big bruiser in army boots. We all slid and tumbled in our air bags and went sailing splat into the wall of the dome. Damned near tore it open before we untangled ourselves. Arms, legs, yelling, bitching. Good thing we were in the space suits; they cushioned some of the shock. The sleeping bags just added to the confusion.

Even so, Bo Williams snapped a shin bone when he slammed into a food crate. The rest of us are banged up, bruised, but Bo is crippled and in a lot of pain. Jean, of all people, pulled the leg straight and set the bone as well as anybody could without x-ray equipment.

"The last time I had to do anything like this was on a walking tour of Antarctica," she calmly told us.

We tore the offending food crate apart to make a splint for Bo's leg. A walking tour of Antarctica?

But the really bad news came from Lowell Hubble. He took a few observations of the stars, made a couple of calculations on his wrist computer, and told me—privately, very quietly—that the blast didn't do enough.

"Whaddaya mean, not enough?" I wanted to yell, but I whispered, just like he did. The rest of the gang was clustered around Bo, who was manfully trying to bear his pain without flinching. The undivided attention of the four women helped.

"The explosion just didn't have enough energy in it to push our orbit toward the Earth," Hubble whispered. Drawing circles in the air with the stem of his pipe, he explained, "We're moving inward, toward the Sun, all right. We'll cross the orbit of Mars, eventually. But we won't get much closer to Earth than that."

"Eventually? How soon's that?"

He stuck the pipe back in his mouth. "Three and a half years."

I let out a weak little whistle. "That won't do us a helluva lot of good, will it?"

"None at all," he said, scratching at his scruffy chin.

I felt itchy, too. In another week or two my beard will be long enough to be silky. Right now it just irritates the hell out of me.

"We've got the other nuke," I said.

"We're going to need it."

"I hate to have to go through the whole damned exercise again—pulling the pile out of its shielding, dismantling the control systems. We're down to one usable robot."

"I'll volunteer, Sam."

I turned and there was Rick Darling standing two meters away, a kind of little-boy look of mixed fear and anticipation on his fuzzless face.

"You'll volunteer?" My voice squeaked with surprise.

"To work with you on the nuclear pile," he said. "You tell me what to do and I'll do it."

"You're sure you want to?"

His lower lip was trembling. "Sam, I've been completely wrong about you. You are the bravest and strongest man I've ever met. I realize now that everything you've done has been for our own good. I'm willing to follow you wherever you choose to lead."

I was too shocked to do much more than mumble, "Okay. Good." Darling smiled happily at me and went back to his food crate.

Saints in heaven! I think Rick Darling is in love with me.

WELL, WE BOTH took enough radiation out there to make our suit dosimeters screech. They went all the way into the red. Lethal dose, unless we get medical attention pretty damned quick. Fat chance.

We got the pile out of the generator, ripped out most of the safety rods, and put it where Hubble told us it has to be in order to push us closer to Earth. It took hours. The goddamned tin shit-can of a robot broke down on us halfway through the job and Darling and I had to manhandle the load by ourselves.

We didn't do much talking out there, just a lot of grunting and swearing. Don't let anybody tell you that working in microgravity is easy. Sure, things have no weight, but they still have mass and inertia. You try traipsing across the surface of an asteroid with the core of a nuclear reactor practically on your back, see how much fun you get out of it.

Anyway, we're back in the dome. Hubble's gone outside to check the position of the pile and to rig a line so we can yank out the last of the control rods manually. Marj and Grace are out there helping him. Sheena and Jean are here in the dome, hovering over Bo Williams. He's got a fever and he doesn't look too damned good.

While we were taking off our space suits Darling said to me, "You don't have to be afraid of me, Sam. I know you don't like me."

"I never saw anything to like," the words popped out of my mouth before I knew it, "until today."

"I just want your respect," he said.

"You've got it."

"Would—would you stop calling me names, then? Please? They really hurt."

There were tears in his eyes. "I'm sorry . . . Rick. I did it without thinking."

He said, "I know you're hetero. I'm not trying to seduce you, Sam. I just want to be your friend."

I felt about an inch tall. "Yeah. That's fine. You've earned it."

He put out his fleshy hand. I took it in mine. We didn't really shake; we just grasped each other's hand for a long moment until I was too embarrassed to look at him any longer. I had to pull away.

IT'S BOOM TIME again.

We're all back in our suits, lying on the floor, wedged against the food cartons which are now up against the dome wall. Hubble's calculated which way the blast will push us, and I've tried to arrange us so we won't go sliding and slamming the way we did last time.

It took hours to get Bo Williams into his space suit, with his leg in Jean's makeshift cast. He's hot as a microwaved burger, face red, half unconscious and muttering deliriously. Doesn't look good.

I've got the control box in my hand again. If this blast doesn't do the job we're finished. Probably finished anyway. I've picked up enough radiation to light a small city. No symptoms yet, but that'll come, sure enough.

Okay. Time to press the button. Wonder if this rock'll stand up to another blast?

WHAT A RIDE!

The seismic shock lifted us all off our backs and bounced us around a bit, but no real damage. Bo Williams must've been unconscious when the bomb went off, or else the belt knocked him out.

A few new bruises, that's all. Otherwise we're okay. Hubble went outside and took some sightings. We're definitely going to cross Mars's orbit, but it's still going to take a couple-three months. Then it's just a matter of time before the IAA notices us.

If we don't starve first.

DISK'S MEMORY SPACE is running low.

Bo Williams died today, probably from infection that we didn't have the medicine to deal with. We sealed him inside his space suit. Erik's legally a murderer now. I guess Lonz and Will are, too. Or accessories, at least.

Been fourteen days since we lit off the second nuke. Hubble says we'll cross Mars's orbit in ten weeks. Definitely. He thinks.

Dome's starting to smell bad. I think the air recycler's breaking down. Food's holding out okay; nobody has much of an appetite.

THE AIR RECYCLER'S definitely on the fritz. All of us are dopey, sluggish. And irritable! Even sweet-tempered me is—am?—snapping at the others.

There's nothing to do. Terminal boredom. We just lay around and try to avoid each other. Munch on a crapburger now and then.

And wait.

Disk's almost full. I won't say anything else until it's the end.

THE AIR IN here's as bad as Los Angeles before they went to electric cars. Grace is coughing all the time. My eyes burn and I feel as slow and stupid as a brain-damaged cow on downers.

Most of the others sleep almost all the time. Like babies. They only get up to eat and use the toilet. And snarl at each other.

Hubble's looking grim. We're nowhere near the orbit of Mars yet and he knows as well as I do that the air's giving out.

DARLING POPPED THE question. Said it was his dying wish. I gave him a backhand smack across the chops and told him to get lost. He burst into tears and skittered away. Should've been kinder to him, I guess. We *are* dying. Not much farther to go.

THE LORD HELPS those who help themselves!

I am sitting in a private cubicle aboard the bridge ship *Bosporus*. A friggin' luxury yacht, compared even to the good old *Argo*.

You know the IAA intends to place five bridge ships in constant transit between Earth and Mars. Like trains running on a regular schedule. They'll be loaded up in the Earth-Moon region and then ply their way out to Mars with all the supplies and personnel that the scientists need for their ongoing exploration of the Red Planet.

And the bridge ships will make it safer and a lot cheaper for settlers to move out past the Earth-Moon system. I had thought that they'd help a lot with the eventual spread of the frontier into the Asteroid Belt and even beyond.

Well, anyway, *Bosporus* is the first of the bridge ships, and she's on her shakedown cruise. The IAA diverted her to come out and take a look at Pittsburgh.

Why? Because the old automated surveillance satellites still orbiting the Earth detected our two nuclear blasts, that's why! Three cheers for bureaucracy!

Way back in the middle of the last century, when there was something called a Cold War simmering between the U.S. of A. and what used to be the Soviet Union, both sides were worried sick about the other guy testing nuclear weapons. So they each put satellites into orbit to spot nuke tests anywhere on Earth—or even in space.

Well, the Cold War ended but the surveillance satellites kept being replaced and even upgraded. The bureaucracy just kept rolling along, building new and better satellites and putting them on station regular as clockwork. Oh, they gave a lot of excuses for doing it: making sure that small nations didn't develop nuclear weapons, using the satellites to make astronomical observations, that kind of garbage. I think the satellites are now tied into the IAA's overall surveillance net: you know, the sensors that look for meteoroids that might hit the Earth or endanger habitats in the Earth-Moon region.

Whatever—our two nuclear blasts rang alarm bells all over the IAA's sensor net. Then they saw good old Pittsburgh all of a sudden trucking toward the inner solar system. The *Argo* was on its preplanned trajectory, cruising back toward lunar orbit with its cargo of metals, water, and volatiles. Erik, bless him, had already reported a fatal accident that had killed the eight of us.

Somebody pretty high up in the IAA decided to send the *Bosporus* out for a look at Pittsburgh. We got saved. It wasn't just in the nick of time; we could have probably lasted another few days, maybe a week.

But good enough for government work.

YOU NEVER SAW such a commotion. I'm not only rich, I'm a friggin' hero!

The media swarmed all over us. They didn't wait for the *Bosporus* to make its way back to the Earth-Moon area. They bombarded us electronically; interviews, book contracts, video deals. And right behind them came the lawyers: IAA red-tape types wanting to know how dare I set off unauthorized nuclear explosions in space. Litigation sharpies trying to get their slice of the profits that both Rockledge and S. Gunn Enterprises, Unlimited, are now claiming. Criminal prosecutors, too, once they learned about Bo Williams's death and heard me screaming about piracy.

Sheena's a star again. She's already shooting footage for a docudrama about the flight. Grace is negotiating a book contract. Marj has seventeen design salons from around the world begging for her talents.

Hubble—well, he's an academic, really. He'll go back to his university and try to live down the notoriety. Rick Darling. I just don't know what he's going to do. He's independently wealthy now; or he will be, once we sort out the legalities and split the profits. He hasn't made another pass at me. In fact, he's been staying as far away from me as he can.

Which suits me okay. I took Jean to dinner in the *Bosporus*'s one and only wardroom last night, fed her a bottle of their best wine, and relocated that vulnerable spot of hers. We spent the night making the stars dance.

They're treating us for radiation disease, of course. When the *Bosporus*'s medical officer found out how much radiation I had absorbed, he put on a long face and tried to break it to me gently that I would never be able to father any children. I grinned at that, which I guess puzzled him. Until he asked me to strip and he saw the neat lead-lined jockstrap I wear.

THIS IS JUST to put a finish on these recordings. I'm going to lock them away with orders that they're not to be touched by anybody until ten years after my death.

Erik was sentenced to life imprisonment, which means he'll be frozen in a vat of liquid nitrogen and kept like a corpsicle until social scientists prove they can rehabilitate murderers. Maybe they'll thaw him out in a century or two. I hope not. I would've preferred it if they'd stuck him on an asteroid and sent him sailing out beyond the orbit of Mars. See how he'd like it.

I feel bad about Lonz and Will. They were both sentenced to twenty years at the penal colony on Farside. I had to testify at the trial, and even though I put all the blame on Erik, I had to admit that Will and Lonz went along with him in the whole nasty deal.

The one thing that frosts me is that Erik absolutely refused to implicate Rockledge. Took all the blame himself. They must have threatened his family or something, those fat-cat bastards.

Okay. That's it. Funny sitting here listening to my own voice for hours on end. There's a lot more I could put onto these disks, more details and stuff, but what the hell, enough's enough.

They'll be sore as hell at me if any of this leaks out. Every one of my erstwhile partners is telling his or her version of the story. Selling, I should say, not just telling. Sheena's got a video series going, "Queen of the Asteroids." She's fun to watch, but the stories are *yecchh*.

Oh, yeah. One thing that I shouldn't forget. The IAA scientists propositioned each of the women partners. I guess "propositioned" isn't the right word.

Once we were landed at the Moonbase medical facility for further antiradiation therapy and the inevitable psychological counseling, a group of scientists asked each of the women if they would consider having a baby. In the interests of science. To see what effect the radiation exposure would have. Maybe they'd be sterile. Maybe they'd have two-headed triplets.

It would all be clinically clean and scientifically pure. Artificial insemination and all that. Two with sperm from the males who were also on the asteroid, two with donor sperm from strangers. Maybe they even wanted to throw in a placebo, I don't know.

Each of the women turned them down flat. I think. Jean is staying at Moonbase for the time being, which is not like her at all. Marj set herself up in Bermuda, where she's franchising various Dupray space-inspired fashion lines to the highest bidders. Good old Grace gave me a kiss goodbye and high-tailed it to California as soon as the medics would let her go. Her book's going to be a best-seller, I guess, even though what I've managed to see of it looks more like fiction to me than fact. But what the hell!

They've all gone their separate ways. Rick Darling's bought himself a villa in the big new bridge ship, *Golden Gate*.

Me, I'm heading back for Pittsburgh. The asteroid's swung around the Sun and she's heading back toward the Belt. She's still got billions and billions of dollars worth of valuable metals, and I intend to get them, now that the courts have given me clear title.

But this time I'm going alone, except for some really top-notch robots.

It'll be lonely, out there all by myself.

Thank God!

Bridge Ship *Golden Gate*

JADE SAT IN DEEP SILENCE FOR A LONG WHILE BEFORE SHE noticed that the robot had returned, bearing her clothing in its spindly metal arms.

She dressed absently, her thoughts literally millions of kilometers away. The robot gathered up the scattered recording disks and left her alone in the big luxurious room.

It can't be, she told herself over and over. It just can't be. If it's true it means . . .

"Now you've heard Sam's disks."

Turning from her pale reflection in the blank screen above the disk player, she asked Darling, "How did you get them?"

He shrugged, a seismic movement of flesh beneath his robes. He had changed into a pure white costume decorated with gold and silver star bursts.

"I stole them," Darling said. "How else?"

"From Sam?"

Laboriously, Darling lowered himself onto the same pile of pillows he had been sitting on when she had first entered his chamber. He took a deep breath, like an exhausted athlete, as he sank into the cushions.

"Oh no, not from Sam. He was far too clever to allow anyone to steal them from him. But once Sam's will was probated, we discovered that he had left the disks to Grace Harcourt. Ever since she won the Pulitzer for her expose of Rockledge's industrial hanky-panky, she's been living—"

"On Pitcairn Island, I know. I tried to interview her but she wouldn't see me." Jade sat on the other set of cushions, facing Darling, her mind seething in growing turmoil.

"Yes, of course. I had the disks purloined from the plane that was taking them out to her."

"Why?"

Darling's fleshy face set almost into hardness. "You heard what he said about me. Do you think I want Grace—or anyone else in the world—to hear all that?"

"You fell in love with Sam?"

The hardness melted immediately. "I thought I did. It must have been the radiation. Or the excitement. He certainly did nothing to deserve love. Mine, or anyone else's."

"No one else has heard these disks?"

"No one."

There were more questions Jade knew she would have to ask. But she dreaded them, put them off, while the enormity of what she had just learned from the disks boiled over her like a tidal wave, smothering her, drowning her. She fought to maintain her composure, her life. She did not want Darling to see what was tearing away at her innards.

Darling seemed to sense her apprehension the way a snake senses the terror it instills in a small bird. He thinks it's because of him, Jade realized. He doesn't know, doesn't realize.

"Sheena married Lowell Hubble, after her Queen of the Asteroids series went into syndication," Darling ticked off on his beringed fingers, his eyes watching her intently. "Marjorie finally retired on Bermuda. Jean Margaux died recently in a traffic accident in Maine, not far from her summer home, I understand. There was some talk about foul play, even suicide."

Jade's heart nearly stopped.

"I checked that out," she said through gritted teeth. "No foul play. Suicide is possible, of course, but all that can be said for certain is that she lost control of her car and went over a cliff into the sea."

"Strange that she'd be driving her own car, though, don't you think? I would imagine a woman such as Jean would have a chauffeur on hand at all times. A young handsome chauffeur, undoubtedly." He smiled wickedly.

Jade barely managed to say, "Maybe."

"That leaves just me." Darling heaved a titanic sigh. "Living alone here in the midst of all this splendor."

Get him talking about himself, Jade thought desperately. Get away from Jean Margaux's death.

"Why alone?" she asked, trying to sound inquisitive. "You're wealthy. Your columns about art are world-famous. You could be surrounded by friends, associates, admirers."

He made a laugh that sounded forced and self-deprecating. "It would take quite a few of them to surround me, wouldn't it?"

"I didn't mean . . ."

"Dear lady, I live the way I live because I choose to. I know my limitations. My columns are frauds; how can *anyone* write valid art criticism without going to see the artwork in its actual setting? I write about holograms that are sent to me. People read my pieces for the personal nasties I throw in about the artists and dealers and other critics. I'm a worse gossip columnist than Grace Harcourt ever was, on her most vicious day."

"I see."

"Do you? Do you know what that radiation did to me? I can never father children! That's not bad enough. It also unbalanced my entire endocrine system so completely that I've blown up to this monstrous size you see!" He spread his arms and the robe billowed out like a silken cloud.

"I didn't know that," Jade said softly.

"Sam accused me of gluttony and called me terrible names," Darling said, his voice shaking, "but the truth is I was a slim and handsome man when I started out on that voyage of his. You saw the pictures! Did I look anything like *this*?"

"No," she admitted. "You certainly didn't."

"Thanks to that unkind bastard Sam I've become a balloon, a blimp, a mountain of fat—and it's all his fault! I've got to hide myself from the rest of the human race, because of that little unloving snot of a man!"

Tears were rolling down Darling's cheeks. "I loved him. I truly did. And he treated me worse than dirt. He turned me into *this*."

"He may be my father," Jade blurted.

Darling coughed and sputtered, cleared his throat, wiped at his eyes. "What did you say?"

Shocked at her own admission, Jade sat there in stunned silence. She had not intended to tell Darling what she had learned, what she now feared was true. She had intended to remain silent, to keep her secret to herself and share it with no one.

Instead, her voice trembling, Jade said, "Sam and Jean Margaux had a fling aboard the *Bosporus*. Jean stayed on the Moon for nearly a year. I was born at Moonbase. An orphan."

"But that doesn't mean . . ."

"How could someone be orphaned at birth in a place like Moonbase?" Jade demanded, painful urgency in her question. "It was a small town in those days, only a few hundred people, and most of them were retirees. The medical staff didn't allow pregnancies to come to term there; as soon as they found that a woman was pregnant they shipped her back to her home on Earth."

"But you were born there," Darling whispered, the truth slowly dawning on him.

"You'd have to have a lot of money to get away with it," said Jade. "Money to keep the medics quiet. Money to erase the computer records. Money to pay off the woman who . . . who adopted the abandoned baby."

"Jean Margaux . . . ?" Darling seemed stunned.

Jade nodded bitterly. "Twenty years later, when she heard there was a reporter looking into the time she'd spent at Moonbase, when she found out who the reporter was, where she'd been born, how old she was—she told her chauffeur to take the day off, and then drove her car off a cliff."

"My God."

"I'm really an orphan now," said Jade. "Sam died off at the end of the solar system, and I killed my own mother."

Suddenly she was crying uncontrollably. Her world dissolved and she was bawling like a baby. She found herself in Darling's arms, wrapped and held and protected by this strange man who was no longer a stranger.

"It's all right," Darling was crooning to her, rocking her gently back and forth. "It's all right. Cry all you want to. We'll both cry. For all the love that we never had. For all the love that we've lost."

She had no idea how long they cried together. Finally, though, she disengaged herself gently from his arms. Darling pointed to a door in the opulent room and suggested she freshen up. She saw that tears had runneled streaks down the makeup on his face.

By the time she returned to the main room a small meal sat steaming on the low table in front of her host and Darling's makeup had been newly applied. Although she felt anything but hungry, Jade sat on the cushions set up opposite Darling. He poured her a cup of tea.

"Are you all right now?" he asked softly.

Jade nodded. I'll never be all right, she knew. I made my own mother kill herself. She killed herself rather than face her own daughter. Killed herself rather than admit she had a daughter—me.

"There's the matter of your promise," Darling said as he uncovered a bowl of diced meat chunks. She saw that the bowl next to it was filled with bubbling melted cheese.

"Yes. My promise." She almost laughed. Nothing he could do to her could bother her now.

"I had intended," he said, spearing a square of meat deftly on a little skewer, "to demand that you never reveal anything you heard on Sam's disks."

She looked up at him. "That was going to be it?"

"Yes." He smiled at her. "What did you think?"

Glancing at the erotic scenes on the tapestries, she smiled back. "Something more physical."

"Dear me, no! Not at all!"

"I can understand why you're sensitive about Sam's disks."

"Yes. Of course you can."

"But I'm a reporter. . . ."

"You don't have to convince me. You can have the disks."

For a moment she was not sure she had heard him correctly. "I can have them?"

Darling nodded, and a tide of ripples ran across his cheeks and chins to disappear beneath the open collar of his robe.

"It's strange," he said wistfully. "You nurse your own pain until there's virtually nothing left in your life but the pain."

"That's a terrible way to live," she said. But a pang of loss and sadness and guilt pulsed through her.

"When I realized how much you've suffered, it made me see how I've been flagellating myself, blaming Sam for what's become of me."

"I've got my work," Jade said, as much to herself as Darling. "I've got a life."

"And I don't. I've become a hermit. I've withdrawn from the human race."

"It's not too late to come back."

"Like this?" He looked down at himself, layer upon layer of bulging fat.

"Endocrine imbalances can be corrected," Jade said tenderly.

"Yes, I know," he confessed. "It's nothing but an excuse to keep myself hidden away from the rest of the world."

She smiled at him. "You'd need some discipline. Or a thick hide."

"You still owe me a promise. You said you'd do whatever I asked."

She felt no fear now. "I remember. What do you want?"

Darling took in a deep breath. His eyes studied her face, as if searching for the courage to make his request.

"Will you be my friend?" he asked at last. "You're going to be on the *Golden Gate* for months. Will you come and visit me and . . . and help me to come out and meet other people?"

"I . . ." She had other commitments, a career, a longing for love and fulfillment, a gnawing guilt that burned sullenly within her like a hot coal. But in that instant of time she realized that love takes many forms, and that saving a man's life bears an obligation for a lifetime.

She saw an automobile tumbling off a cliff into the angry sea below. She saw Sam Gunn's round, slightly lopsided face grinning at her. She saw Raki's darkly handsome scowl and Spence Johansen's heart-fluttering smile and the tearful last memory of her adoptive mother as she left the Moonbase hospital forever. She saw Rick Darling staring at her with his entire life in his eyes.

"I'd be happy to be your friend," she said. "I need a friend, too."

The two of them—enormous overweight man and tiny elfin woman—leaned across the low table and embraced each other in new-found charity.

Asteroid Ceres

JADE CELEBRATED, IF THAT IS THE CORRECT WORD, HER twenty-first birthday alone.

Rick Darling had thrown an immense party for her the day before she left the *Golden Gate* at the farthest point in its orbit and took the bulbous shuttle craft to the surface of Ceres. Nearly half the population of the huge bridge ship had poured into Darling's posh villa, eating, laughing, drinking, narcotizing themselves into either frenzied gaiety or withdrawn moroseness.

Through it all, Darling had remained close to Jade's side, his new figure almost trim compared to his former obesity. At first Jade thought he stayed near her because he was afraid of the crowd. Slowly, as the party proceeded and Darling played the genial, witty, gracious host, Jade began to realize that *he* wanted to protect *her*.

Jade tried to relax at the party and have a good time, but she was still haunted by the thoughts of her newly discovered and newly lost mother. Despite the happy oblivious crowd swirling around her, she still saw the automobile plunging over the rocky cliff and into the unforgiving sea.

Now, more than a week after Darling's party, it was her birthday. Twenty-one years old. An entire lifetime ahead of her. An entire lifetime already behind her.

She stood at the window of her room in the habitat *Chrysalis*, in orbit around Ceres, and gazed out at the empty sky. There were no moons to be seen, no Earth hanging huge and tantalizingly close. Here in the Asteroid Belt, beyond the orbit of Mars, even giant Jupiter was merely another star in the sky, brighter than the rest but still little more than a distant speck of light against the engulfing dark.

Slightly wider than a thousand kilometers, Ceres was the largest of the asteroids. Still, its gravity was so minuscule that its underground caverns and tunnels were always thick with dust; the slightest movement stirred the choking black soot, and it hung in the air for hours before finally settling—only to be stirred up again by the next person's movements.

The rock rats who tried to live in that perpetual haze of lungrotting dust eventually assembled this makeshift habitat out of abandoned or secondhand spacecraft linked end-to-end in a rough Tinkertoy circle.

Chrysalis had a spin-induced gravity, just like the larger man-made habitats in the Earth-Moon system. But its induced gravity was very light, even lighter than the Moon's. The hotel manager who had personally shown Jade to her room had smilingly demonstrated that you could drop a fragile crystal vase from your hand, then go fill a glass of water and drink it, and still have time to retrieve the vase before it hit the carpeted floor.

Twenty-one years old, Jade mused to herself as she stared out at the dark sky. Time to make something of yourself. Time to leave the past behind; there's nothing you can do to change it. Only the future can be shaped, altered. Everything else is over and done with.

She lost track of how long she stood at the window, sensing the cold of the airless eternity on the other side of the glassteel. Perhaps time passes differently here, with no worlds or moons in the sky. Nothing but stars endlessly spinning through the sky. Never any real daylight, always the darkness of infinity. This little habitat is like the ancient Greek idea of the afterlife: gray twilight, emptiness, a shadow existence.

It took a real effort of will for Jade to pull herself from the window. You've got a job to do, she told herself sternly. You've got a life to lead. Then she added, Once you've figured out what you want to do with it.

The message light on the phone was on. She walked past the bed carefully in the light gravity; everyone in the hotel wore Velcro slippers and walked across the carpeting in a hesitant low-g shuffle.

Jade smiled when she saw Jim Gradowsky's beefy face fill the phone screen. He was munching on something, as usual.

"Just a note to tell you that Raki got promoted to vice president in charge of special projects. Thanks mostly to the Sam Gunn stuff you beamed us, and the interview with Rick Darling. You're on full salary, kid. Plus expenses. Raki is *very* happy with you. Looks like he'll be getting a seat on the board of directors next."

But Raki himself did not call, Jade said to herself. Then she thought, Perhaps it's best that way.

"Oh, yeah," Gradowsky went on. "Monica says hello and happy birthday. From me, too. You're doin' great work, Jade. We're proud of you."

The screen blanked but the message light stayed on. Jade touched it again.

Spencer Johansen smiled at her. Jade's breath caught in her throat.

"Hey there, Jade. I'm sending this message to your office, 'cause I haven't a clue as to where in the solar system you might be. How about giving a fella a call now and then? I mean, I'd like to see you, talk to you. Maybe I could even come out to wherever you are and visit. You know, this old habitat feels kinda lonesome without you. Send me a message, will you? I'd like to see you again."

Jade sank down slowly onto the edge of the bed, surprised that her knees suddenly felt so weak. Would Spence come all the way out here just to see me? No, it wouldn't be fair to ask him. I'll be leaving as soon as my interview comes through, anyway. And then out to Titan. It could be another two years before I see him again.

And why would he want to leave *Jefferson* and come out to see me? Jade asked herself. Is he a romantic fool or—suddenly she remembered Raki's cruel words: "The thrill is in the chase. Now that I've bagged her, what is there to getting her again?"

She shook her head. No, Spence isn't like that. He's not. I know he's not. But what if he is? an inner voice demanded. What if he is? Good thing there's several million kilometers between you.

Still, that did not mean she could not send him the message he asked for. Jade leaned forward and touched the phone's keyboard. She was stunned to find that two hours had elapsed before she ran out of things to say to Spence Johansen.

Space University

REGAL WAS THE ONLY POSSIBLE WORD FOR HER.

Jade stared in unabashed awe. Elverda Apacheta was lean, long-legged, stately, splendid, dignified, intelligent—regal. The word kept bobbing to the surface of Jade's mind.

Not that the sculptress was magnificently clad: she wore only a frayed jumpsuit of faded gray. It was her bearing, her demeanor, and above all her face that proclaimed her nobility. It was an aristocratic face, the face of an Incan queen, copper red, a study in sculptured planes of cheek and brow and strong Andean nose. Her almond-shaped deeply dark eyes missed nothing. They seemed to penetrate to the soul even while they sparkled with what appeared to be a delight in the world. The sculptress' thick black hair was speckled with gray, as much the result of exposure to cosmic radiation as age, thought Jade. It was tied back and neatly bound in a silver mesh. Her only other adornment was a heavy silver bracelet that probably concealed a communicator.

"Yes, I knew Sam well," she replied to Jade's lame opening question, in a throaty low voice. She spoke English, in deference to Jade, but there was the unmistakable memory of the high Andes in her accent. "Very well indeed."

Jade was wearing coral-colored parasilk coveralls with the stylized sunburst of the Solar Network logo emblazoned above her left breast pocket and the miniature recorder on her belt. She was surprised at her worshipful reaction to Elverda Apacheta. The woman was renowned as not only the first space sculptress, but the best. Yet Jade had interviewed other personalities who were very famous, or powerful, or notorious, or talented. None of them had been this breathtaking. Did this Incan queen affect everyone this way? Had she affected Sam Gunn this way?

The two women were sitting in the faculty lounge of the minuscule Ceres branch of the Interplanetary Space University. Little more than an extended suite of rooms in one of the interlinked spacecraft that made up the orbiting habitat *Chrysalis*, the university was mainly a communications center where Cerean workers and their children could attend classes through interactive computer programs.

The lounge itself was a small, windowless, quiet room tastefully decorated with carpeting of warm earth colors that covered not only the floor but the walls as well. The ideal place for recording an interview. Must have cost a moderate-sized fortune to bring this stuff all the way out here, Jade thought.

The sculptress reclined regally on a high-backed armchair of soft nubby pseudowool, looking every inch a monarch who could dispense justice or mercy with the slightest arch of an eyebrow. Jade felt drab sitting on the sofa at her right, despite the fact that her coveralls were crisply new while Apacheta's were worn almost to holes.

"I appreciate your agreeing to let me interview you," Jade said.

Elverda Apacheta made a small nod of acknowledgement.

"Many other of Sam's . . . associates, well, they either tried to avoid me or they refused to talk at all."

"Why should I refuse? I have nothing to hide."

No, you didn't have an illicit pregnancy, Jade thought. You didn't abandon your infant daughter.

Forcing herself to focus on the task at hand, Jade said, "There are rumors that you and Sam were . . ." she hesitated half a heartbeat, ". . . well, lovers."

The sculptress smiled sadly. "I loved Sam madly. For a while I thought perhaps he loved me too. But now, after all these years," strangely, the smile grew more tender, "I am not so sure."

A Can of Worms

WE WERE ALL MUCH YOUNGER THEN—SAID ELVERDA
Apacheta—and our passions were much closer to the surface. I could become enraged at the slightest excuse; the smallest problem could infuriate me.

You must remember, of course, that I had packed off to the asteroid where I had been living alone for almost three years. Even my supply shipments came in unmanned spacecraft. So it was a big surprise when a transfer ship showed up and settled into a rendezvous orbit a few hundred meters off my asteroid.

I thought of it as *my* asteroid. Nobody could own it, according to international law. But there were no restrictions against carving on it. Aten 2004 EA was the name the astronomers had given it, which meant that it was the one hundred and thirty-first asteroid discovered in the year 2004 among the Aten group. The astronomers are very efficient in their naming, of course, but not romantic at all.

I called my asteroid "Quipu-Camayoc," which means "The Rememberer." And I was determined to carve the history of my people upon it. The idea was not merely romantic, it was absolutely poetic. After all, we have lived in the mountains since before time was reckoned. Even the name of my people, my very own name—Apacheta—means a group of magical stones. Now my people were leaving their ancient mountain villages, scattering down to the cities, losing their tribal identities in the new world of factory jobs and electronic pleasures. Someone had to mark their story in a way that could be remembered forever.

When I first heard of the asteroid, back at the university at La Paz, I knew it was my destiny. The very name the astronomers had given it signified my own name: Aten 2004 EA—Elverda Apacheta. It was a sign. I am not superstitious, of course, and ordinarily I do not believe in signs and omens. But I knew I was destined to carve the history of my people on Aten 2004 EA and turn it into the memory of a vanishing race.

Quipu-Camayoc was a large stone streaked with metals, a mountain floating in space, nearly one full kilometer long. It was not in the Belt, of course; in those days no one had gone as far as the Belt. Its orbit was slightly closer to the Sun than Earth's orbit, so nearly once a year it came near enough to Earth for a reasonably easy flight to reach it in something like a week; that is when I usually got my supplies. This was many years ago, of course, before the first bridge ships were even started. The frontier had not expanded much beyond the Earth-Moon system; the first human expedition to Mars had barely gotten under way.

As I said, I was surprised when a transfer ship came into view instead of the usual unmanned spacecraft. I was even more surprised when someone jetted over to my quarters without even asking permission to come aboard.

I lived in my workshop, a small pod that contained all my sculpting equipment and the life support systems, as well as my personal gear—clothing, sleeping hammock, things like that.

"Who is approaching?" I called on the communicator. In its screen I centered a magnified picture of the approaching stranger. I could see nothing, of course, except a white space suit topped with a bubble helmet. The figure was enwrapped by the jet unit, somewhat like a man sitting in a chair that had no legs.

"Sam Gunn is my name. I've got your supplies aboard my ship."

Suddenly I realized I was naked. Living alone, I seldom bothered with clothing. My first reaction was anger.

"Then send the supplies across and go on your way. I have no time for visitors."

He laughed. That surprised me. He said, "This isn't just a social call, lady. I'm supposed to hand you a legal document. It's got to be done in person. You know how lawyers are."

"No, I don't know. And I don't want to." But I hurriedly pushed over to my clothes locker and rummaged in it for a decent set of coveralls.

I realize now that what I should have done was to lock the access hatch and not allow him to enter. That would have delayed the legal action against me. But it would only have delayed it, not prevented it altogether. Perhaps allowing Sam to enter my quarters, to enter my life, was the best course after all.

By the time I heard the pumps cycling in the airlock I was pulling a pair of old blue denim coveralls over my shoulders. The inner hatch cracked open as I zipped them up to the collar.

Sam coasted through the hatch, his helmet already removed and floating inside the airlock. He was small, not much more than 160 centimeters, although to his last breath he claimed to be 165. Which is nonsense. I myself was a good ten or twelve centimeters taller than he.

It would be difficult to capture his face in a sculpture. His features were too mobile for stone or even clay to do him justice. There was something slightly irregular about Sam's face: one side did not quite match the other. It made him look just the tiniest bit off-center, askew. It fitted his personality very well.

His eyes could be blue or gray or even green, depending on the lighting. His mouth was extremely mobile: he had a thousand different smiles, and he was almost always talking, never silent. Short-cropped light brown hair, with a tinge of red in it. A round face, a touch unbalanced toward the left. A slightly crooked snub nose; it looked as if it had been broken, perhaps more than once. A sprinkling of freckles. I thought of the *Norte Americano* character from literature, Huckleberry Finn, grown into boyish manhood.

He hung there, framed in the open hatch, his booted feet dangling several centimeters from the grillwork of the floor. He was staring at me.

Suddenly I felt enormously embarrassed. My quarters were a shambles. Nothing but a cramped compartment filled with junk. Equipment and computer consoles scattered everywhere, connecting wires looping in the microgravity like jungle vines. My hammock was a twisted disaster area; the entire little cabin was filled with the flotsam of a hermit who had not seen another human being in three years. I was bone-thin, I knew. Like a skeleton. I could not even begin to remember where I had left my last lipstick. And my hair must have looked wild, floating uncombed.

"God, you're *beautiful!*" said Sam, in an awed whisper. "A goddess made of copper."

Immediately I distrusted him.

"You have a legal paper for me?" I asked, as coldly as I could. I had no idea of what it was; perhaps something from the university in La Paz about the new grant I had applied for.

"Uh, yeah . . ." Sam seemed to be half dazed, unfocused. "I, uh, didn't bring it with me. It's back aboard my ship."

"You told me you had it with you."

"No," he said, recovering slightly. "I said I was supposed to hand it to you personally. It's back on the ship."

I glared at him. How dare he invade my privacy like this? Interrupt my work? My art?

He did not wilt. In fact, Sam brightened. "Why don't you come over and have a meal with me? With us, I mean. Me and my crew."

I absolutely refused. Yet somehow, several hours later, I was on my way to his transfer ship, riding on the rear saddle of a two-person jet scooter. I had bathed and dressed while Sam had returned to his ship for the scooter. I had even found a bright golden yellow scarf to tie around the waist of my best green coveralls, and a matching scarf to tie down my hair. Inside my space suit I could smell the perfume I had doused myself with. It is surprising how you can find things you thought you had lost, when the motivation is right.

What was my motivation? Not to accept some legal document, certainly. Sam's sudden presence made it painfully clear to me that I had been terribly alone for such a long time. I had not minded the loneliness at all—not until he punctuated it as he did. My first reaction had been anger, of course. But how could I remain angry with a man who was so obviously taken with my so-called beauty?

My asteroid was in shadow as we sailed toward his ship, so we could not see the figures I had already carved upon it. It bulked over us, blotting out the Sun, like some huge black pitted mountain, looming dark and somehow menacing. Sam kept up a steady chatter on the suit-to-suit radio. He was asking me questions about what I was doing and how my work was going, but somehow he did all the talking.

His ship was called *Adam Smith,* a name that meant nothing to me. It looked like an ordinary transfer vehicle, squat and ungainly, with spidery legs sticking out and bulbous glassy projections that housed the command and living modules. But as we approached it I saw that Sam's ship was large. Very large. I had never seen one so big.

"The only one like it in the solar system, so far," he acknowledged cheerfully. "I'm having three more built. Gonna corner the cargo business."

He rattled on, casually informing me that he was the major owner of the orbital tourist facility, the Earth View Hotel.

"Every room has a view of Earth. It's gorgeous."

"Yes, I imagine it is."

"Great place for a honeymoon," Sam proclaimed. "Or even just a weekend. You haven't lived until you've made love in zero-gee."

I went silent and remained so the rest of the short journey to his ship. I had no intention of responding to sexual overtures, no matter how subtle. Or blatant.

Dinner was rather pleasant. Five of us crowded into the narrow wardroom that doubled as the mess. Cooking in zero gravity is no great trick, but presenting the food in a way that is appetizing to the eye without running the risk of its floating off the plate at the first touch of a fork—that calls for art. Sam managed the trick by using plates with clear plastic covers that hinged back neatly. Veal piccata with spaghetti, no less. The wine, of course, was served in squeezsbulbs.

There were three crew persons on *Adam Smith*. The only woman, the communications engineer, was married to the propulsion engineer. She was a heavyset blonde of about thirty who had allowed herself to gain much too much weight. Michelangelo would have loved her, with her thick torso and powerful limbs, but by present standards she was no great beauty. But then her husband, equally fair-haired, was also of ponderous dimensions.

It is a proven fact that people who spend a great deal of time in low gravity either allow themselves to become tremendously fat, or thin down to little more than skin and bones, as I had. The physiologists have scientific terms for this: I am an *agravitic ectomorph,* so I am told. The two oversized engineers were *agravitic endomorphs.* Sam, of course, was neither. He was Sam—irrepressibly unique.

I found myself instinctively disliking both of the bloated engineers until I thought of the globulous little Venus figures that prehistoric peoples had carved out of hand-sized round rocks. Then they did not seem so bad.

The third crewman was the payload specialist, a lanky dark taciturn biologist. Young and rather handsome, in a smoldering sullen way. Although he was slim, he had some meat on his bones. I found that this was his first space mission, and he was determined to make it his last.

"What is your cargo?" I asked.

Before the biologist could reply, Sam answered, "Worms."

I nearly dropped my fork. Suddenly the spaghetti I had laboriously wound around it seemed to be squirming, alive.

"Worms?" I echoed.

Nodding brightly, Sam said, "You know the Moralist Sect that's building an O'Neill habitat?"

I shook my head, realizing I had been badly out of touch with the rest of the human race for three years.

"Religious group," Sam explained. "They decided Earth is too sinful for them, so they're building their own paradise, a self-contained, self-sufficient artificial world in a Sun-circling orbit, just like your asteroid."

"And they want worms?" I asked.

"For the soil," said the biologist.

Before I could ask another question Sam said, "They're bringing in megatons of soil from the Moon, mostly for radiation shielding. Don't want to be conceiving two-head Moralists, y'know. So they figured that as long as they've got so much dirt they might as well use it for farming, too."

"But lunar soil is sterile," the biologist said.

"Right. It's got plenty of nutrients in it, all those chemicals that crops need. But no earthworms, no beetles, none of the bugs and slugs and other slimy little things that make the soil *alive*."

"And they need that?"

"Yep. Sure do, if they're gonna farm that lunar soil. Otherwise they've gotta go to hydroponics, and that's against their religion."

I turned from Sam to the biologist. He nodded to confirm what Sam had said. The two engineers were ignoring our conversation, busily shoveling food into their mouths.

"Not many cargo haulers capable of taking ten tons of worms and their friends halfway around the Earth's orbit," Sam said proudly. "I got the contract from the Moralists with hardly any competition at all. Damned profitable, too, as long as the worms stay healthy."

"They are," the biologist assured him.

"This is the first of six flights for them," said Sam, returning his attention to his veal and pasta. "All worms."

I felt myself smiling. "Do you always make deliveries in person?"

"Oh no." Twirling the spaghetti on his fork beneath the plastic cover of his dish. "I just figured that since this is the first flight, I ought to come along and see it through. I'm a qualified astronaut, you know."

"I didn't know."

"Yeah. Besides, it lets me get away from the hotel and the office. My buddy Omar can run the hotel while I'm gone. Hell, he runs it while I'm there!"

"Then what do you do?"

He grinned at me. "I look for new business opportunities. I seek out new worlds, new civilizations. I boldly go where no man has gone before."

The biologist muttered from behind a forkful of veal, "He chases women." From his dead-serious face I could not tell if he was making a joke or not.

"And you deliver ten tons of worms," I said.

"Right. And the mail."

"Ah. My letter."

Sam smiled broadly. "It's in my cabin, up by the bridge."

I refused to smile back at him. If he thought he was going to get me into his cabin, and his zero-gee hammock, he was terribly mistaken. So I told myself. I had only taken a couple of sips of the wine; after three years of living like a hermit, I was careful not to make a fool of myself. I wanted to be invulnerable, untouchable.

Actually, Sam was an almost perfect gentleman. After dinner we coasted from the wardroom along a low-ceilinged corridor that opened into the command module. I had to bend over slightly to get through the corridor, but Sam sailed along blithely, talking every millimeter of the way about worms, Moralists and their artificial heaven, habitats expanding throughout the inner solar system and how he was going to make billions from hauling specialized cargos.

His cabin was nothing more than a tiny booth with a sleeping hammock fastened to one wall, actually just an alcove built into the command module. Through the windows of the bridge I could see my asteroid, hovering out there with the Sun starting to rise above it. Sam ducked into his cubbyhole without making any suggestive remarks at all, and came out a moment later with a heavy, stiff, expensive-looking white envelope.

It bore my name and several smudged stamps that I presume had been affixed to it by various post offices on its way to me. In the corner was the name and address of a legal firm: Skinner, Flaymen, Killum and Score, of Des Moines, Iowa, USA, Earth.

Wondering why they couldn't have sent their message electronically, like everyone else, I struggled to open the envelope.

"Let me," Sam said, taking one corner of it in two fingers and deftly slitting it with the minuscule blade of the tiniest pocket knife I had ever seen.

I pulled out a single sheet of heavy white parchment, so stiff that its edges could slice flesh.

It was a letter for me. It began, "Please be advised . . ."

For several minutes I puzzled over the legal wordings while Sam went over to the control console and busied himself checking out the instruments. Slowly the letter's meaning became clear to me. My breath gagged in my throat. A searing, blazing knot of pain sprang up in my chest.

"What's wrong?" Sam was at my side in a shot. "Cripes, you look like you're gonna explode! You're red as a fire engine."

I was so furious I could hardly see. I handed the letter to Sam and managed to choke out, "Does this mean what I think it means?"

He scanned the letter quickly, then read it more slowly, his eyes going wider with each word of it.

"Jesus Christ on a crutch!" he shouted. "They're throwing you off the asteroid!"

I could not believe what the letter said. We both read it half a dozen times more. The words did not change their meaning. I wanted to scream. I wanted to kill. The vision came to my mind of lawyers stripped naked and staked out over a slow fire, screaming for mercy while I laughed and burned their letter in the fire that was roasting their flesh. I looked around the command module wildly, looking for something to throw, something to break, anything to release the terrible, terrible fury that was building inside me.

"Those sons of bitches!" Sam raged. "Those slimy do-gooder bastards!"

The lawyers represented the Moralist Sect of The One True God, Inc. The letter was to inform me that the Moralists had notified the International Astronautical Authority that they intended to capture asteroid Aten 2004 EA and use it as structural material for the habitat they were building.

"They can't do that!" Sam bellowed, bouncing around the bridge like a weightless Ping-Pong ball. "You were there first. They can't throw you out like a landlord evicting a tenant!"

"The white man has taken the Indian's lands whenever he chose to," I said, seething.

He mistook my deathly quiet tone for acquiescence. "Not anymore! Not today. This is one white man who's on the side of the redskins."

He was so upset, so outraged, so vociferous that I felt my own fury cooling, calming. It was as if Sam was doing all my screaming for me.

"This letter," I hissed, "says I have no choice."

"Hell no, you won't go," Sam snapped. "I've got lawyers too, lady. Nobody's going to push you around."

"Why should you want to involve yourself?"

He shot me an unfathomable glance. "I'm involved. I'm involved. You think I can sit back and watch those Moralist bastards steal your rock? I *hate* it when some big outfit tries to muscle us little guys."

It occurred to me that at least part of Sam's motivation might have been to worm his way into my affection. And my pants. He would act the brave protector of the weak, and I would act the grateful weakling who would reward him with my somewhat emaciated body. From the few words that the taciturn biologist had said at dinner, and from my observation of Sam's own behavior, it seemed to me that he had a Casanova complex: he wanted every woman he saw.

And yet—his outrage seemed genuine enough. And yet—the instant he saw me he said I was beautiful, even though clearly I was not.

"Don't you worry," Sam said, his round little face grim and determined. "I'm on your side and we'll figure out some way to stick this letter up those lawyers' large intestines."

"But the Moralist Sect is very powerful."

"So what? You've got me, kiddo. All those poor praying sonsofbitches have on their side is God."

I was still angry and confused as Sam and I climbed back into our space suits and he returned me to my pod on my—no, *the* asteroid. I felt a burning fury blazing within me, bitter rage at the idea of stealing my asteroid away from me. They were going to break it up and use it as raw material for their habitat!

Normally I would have been screaming and throwing things, but I sat quietly on the two-person scooter as we left the airlock of Sam's ship. He was babbling away with a mixture of bravado, jokes, obscene descriptions of lawyers in general and Moralists in particular. He made me laugh. Despite my fears and my fury, Sam made me laugh and realize that there was nothing I could do about the Moralists and their lawyers at the moment, so why should I tie myself into knots over them? Besides, I had a more immediate problem to deal with.

Sam. Was he going to attempt to seduce me once we were back at my quarters? And if he did, what would my reaction be? I was shocked at my uncertainty. Three years is a long time, but to even think of allowing this man . . .

"You got a lawyer?" His voice came through the earphones of my helmet.

"No. I suppose the university will represent me. Legally, I'm their employee."

"Maybe, but you . . ." His voice choked off. I heard him take in his breath, like a man who has just seen something that overpowered him.

"Is that *it*?" Sam asked in an awed voice.

The Sun was shining obliquely on The Rememberer, so that the figures I had carved were shown in high relief.

"It's not finished," I said. "It's hardly even begun."

Sam swerved the little scooter so that we moved slowly along the length of the carvings. I saw all the problems, the places that had to be fixed, improved. The feathered serpent needed more work. The Mama Kilya, the Moon Mother, was especially rough. But I had to place her there because the vein of silver in the asteroid came up to the surface only at that point and I needed to use the silver as the tears of the Moon.

Even while I picked out the weak places in my figures I could hear Sam's breathing over the suit radio. I feared he would hyperventilate. For nearly half an hour we cruised slowly back and forth across the face of the asteroid, then spiraled around to the other side.

The one enormous advantage of space sculpture, of course, is the absence of gravity. There is no need for a base, a stand, a vertical line. Sculpture can be truly three-dimensional in space, as it was meant to be. I had intended to carve the entire surface of the asteroid.

"It's fantastic," Sam said at last, his voice strangely muted. "It's the most beautiful thing I've ever seen. I'll be hung by the cojones before I'll let those double-talking bastards steal this away from you!"

At that moment I began to love Sam Gunn.

TRUE TO HIS word, Sam got his own lawyers to represent me. A few days after *Adam Smith* disappeared from my view, on its way to the Moralists' construction site, I was contacted by the firm of Whalen and Krill, of Port Canaveral, Florida, USA, Earth.

The woman who appeared on my comm screen was a junior partner in the firm. I was not important enough for either of the two senior men. Still, that was better than my university had done: their legal counsel had told me bleakly that I had no recourse at all and I should abandon my asteroid forthwith.

"We've gotten the IAA arbitration board to agree to take up the dispute," said Ms. Mindy Rourke, Esq. She seemed very young to me to be a lawyer. I was especially fascinated by her long hair falling luxuriantly past her shoulders. She could only wear it like that on Earth. In a low-gee environment it would have spread out like a chestnut-colored explosion.

"I'll have my day in court, then."

"You won't have to be physically present," Ms. Rourke said. Then she added, with a doubtful little frown, "But I'm afraid the board usually bases its decisions on the maximum good for the maximum number of people. The Moralists will house ten thousand people in their habitat. All you've got is you."

What she meant was that Art counted for nothing compared to the utilitarian purpose of grinding up my asteroid, smelting it, and using its metals as structural materials for an artificial world to house ten thousand religious zealots who want to leave Earth forever.

Sam stayed in touch with me electronically, and hardly a day passed that he did not call and spend an hour or more chatting with me. Our talk was never romantic, but each call made me love him more. He spoke endlessly about his childhood in Nebraska, or was it Baltimore? Sometimes his childhood tales were based in the rainy hillsides of the Pacific Northwest. Either he moved around ceaselessly as a child or he was amalgamating tales from many other people and adopting them as his own. I never tried to find out. If Sam thought of the stories as his own childhood, what did it matter?

Gradually, as the weeks slipped into months, I found myself speaking about my own younger years. The half-deserted mountain village where I had been born. The struggle to get my father to allow me to go to the university instead of marrying, "as a decent girl should." The professor who broke my heart. The pain that sent me fleeing to this asteroid and the life of a hermit.

Sam cheered me up. He made me smile, even laugh. He provided me with a blow-by-blow description of his own activities as an entrepreneur. Not content with owning and operating the Earth View Hotel *and* running a freight-hauling business that ranged from low Earth orbit to the Moon and out as far as the new habitats being built in Sun-circling orbits, Sam was also getting involved in building tourist facilities at Moonbase as well.

"And then there's this advertising scheme that these two guys have come up with. It's kinda crazy, but it might work."

The "scheme" was to paint enormous advertisement pictures in the ionosphere, some fifty miles or so above the Earth's surface, using electron guns to make the gases up at that altitude glow like the aurora borealis. The men that Sam was speaking with claimed that they could make actual pictures that could be seen across whole continents.

"When the conditions are right," Sam added. "Like, it's gotta be either at dusk or at dawn, when the sky looks dark from the ground but there's still sunlight up at the right altitude."

"Not many people are up at dawn," I said.

It took almost a full minute between my statement and his answer, I was so distant from his base in Earth orbit.

"Yeah," he responded at last. "So it's gotta be around dusk." Sam grinned lopsidedly. "Can you imagine the reaction from the environmentalists if we start painting advertisements across the sky?"

"They'll fade away within a few minutes, won't they?"

The seconds stretched, and then he answered, "Yeah, sure. But can you picture the look on their faces? They'll *hate* it! Might be worth doing just to give 'em ulcers!"

All during those long weeks and months I could hardly work up the energy to continue my carving. What good would it be? The whole asteroid was going to be taken away from me, ground into powder, destroyed forever. I knew what the International Astronautical Authority's arbitrators would say: Moralists, ten thousand; Art, one.

For days on end I would stand at my console, idly fingering the keyboard, sketching in the next set of figures that the lasers would etch into the stone. In the display screen the figures would look weak, misshapen, distorted. Sometimes they glared at me accusingly, as if *I* was the one killing them.

Time and again I ended up sketching Sam's funny, freckled, dear face.

I found reasons to pull on my space suit and go outside. Check the lasers. Adjust the power settings. Recalibrate the feedback sensors. Anything but actual work. I ran my gloved fingers across the faces of the *hauqui,* the guardian spirits I had carved into this metallic stone. It was a bitter joke. The *hauqui* needed someone to guard them from evil.

Instead of working, I cried. All my anger and hate was leaching away in the acid of frustration and waiting, waiting, endless months of waiting for the inevitable doom.

And then Sam showed up again, just as unexpectedly as the first time.

My asteroid, with me attached to it, had moved far along on its yearly orbit. I could see Earth only through the low-power telescope that I had brought with me, back in those first days when I had fooled myself into believing I would spend my free time in space studying the stars. Even in the telescope the world of my birth was nothing more than a blurry fat crescent, shining royal-blue.

My first inkling that Sam was approaching was a message I found typed on my comm screen. I had been outside, uselessly fingering my carvings. When I came in and took off my helmet I saw on the screen:

HAVE NO FEAR, SAM IS HERE.
WILL RENDEZVOUS WITH YOU IN ONE HOUR.

My eyes flicked to the digital clock reading. He would be here in a matter of minutes! At least this time I was wearing clothes, but still I looked a mess.

By the time his transport was hovering in a matching orbit and the pumps in my airlock were chugging, I was decently dressed in a set of beige coveralls he had not seen before, my hair was combed and neatly netted, and I had applied a bit of makeup to my face. My expression in the mirror had surprised me: smiling, nearly simpering, almost as giddy as a schoolgirl. Even my heart was skipping along merrily.

Sam came in, his helmet already off. I propelled myself over to him and kissed him warmly on the lips. He reacted in a typical Sam Gunn way. He gave a whoop and made three weightless cartwheels, literally heels over head, with me gripped tightly in his arms.

For all his exuberance and energy, Sam was a gentle, thoughtful lover. Hours later, as we floated side-by-side in my darkened quarters, the sweat glistening on our bare skins, he murmured:

"I never thought I could feel so . . . so . . ."

Trying to supply the missing word, I suggested, "So much in love?"

He made a little nod. In our weightlessness, the action made him drift slightly away from me. I caught him in my arms, though, and pulled us back together.

"I love you, Sam," I whispered, as though it were a secret. "I love you."

He gave a long sigh. I thought it was contentment, happiness even.

"Listen," he said, "you've got to come over to the ship. Those two nutcases who want to paint the ionosphere are on their way to the Moralists' habitat."

"What does that have to do with . . ."

"You gotta meet them," he insisted. Untangling from me, he began to round up his clothes, floating like weightless ghosts in the shadows. "You know what those Moralist hypocrites are going to call their habitat, once it's finished? Eden! How's that for chutzpah?"

He had to explain the Yiddish word to me. Eden. The Moralists wanted to create their own paradise in space. Well, maybe they would, although I doubted that it would be paradise for anyone who deviated in the slightest from their stern views of right and wrong.

We showered, which in zero-gee is an intricate, intimate procedure. Sam washed me thoroughly, lovingly, using the washcloth to tenderly push the soapy water that clung to my skin over every inch of my body.

"The perfect woman," he muttered. "A dirty mind in a clean body."

Finally we dried off, dressed and headed out to Sam's ship. But first he maneuvered the little scooter along the length of my asteroid.

"Doesn't seem to be much more done than the last time I was here," he said, almost accusingly.

I was glad we were in the space suits and he could not see me blush. I remained silent.

As we moved away from The Rememberer, Sam told me, "The lawyers aren't having much luck with the arbitration board." In the earphones of my helmet his voice sounded suddenly tired, almost defeated.

"I didn't think they would."

"The board's gonna hand down its decision in two weeks. If they decide against you, there's no appeal."

"And they will decide against me, won't they?"

He tried to make his voice brighter. "Well, the lawyers are doing their damnedest. But if trickery and deceit won't work, maybe I can bribe a couple of board members."

"Don't you dare! You'll go to jail."

He laughed.

As we came up to Sam's transport ship, I saw its name stenciled in huge letters beneath the insect-eye canopy of the command module: *Klaus Heiss.*

"Important economist," Sam answered my question. "Back fifty years or so. The first man to suggest free enterprise in space."

"I thought that writers had suggested that long before space flight even began," I said as we approached the ship's airlock.

Sam's voice sounded mildly impatient in my earphones. "Writers are one thing. Heiss went out and raised money, got things started. For real."

KLAUS HEISS WAS fitted out more handsomely than *Adam Smith*, even though it seemed no larger. The dining lounge was more luxurious, and apparently the crew ate elsewhere. There were four of us for dinner: Sam and myself, and the two "nutcases," as he had called them.

Morton McGuire and T. Kagashima did not seem insane to me. Perhaps naive. Certainly enthusiastic.

"It's the greatest idea since the invention of writing!" McGuire blurted as we sat around the dining lounge table.

He was speaking about their idea of painting the ionosphere with advertisements.

McGuire was a huge mass of flesh, bulging in every direction, straining the metal snaps of his bilious green coveralls. He looked like a balloon that had been overfilled to the point of bursting. He proudly told me that he was known as "Mountain McGuire," from his days as a college football player. He had gone from college into advertising, gaining poundage every passing day. Living on Earth, he could not be classified as an agravitic endomorph. He was simply fat. Extremely so.

"I'm just a growing boy," he said happily as he jammed fistfuls of food into his mouth.

The other one, Kagashima, was almost as lean as I myself. Quiet too, although his oriental eyes frequently flashed with suppressed mirth. No one seemed to know what Kagashima's first name was. When I asked what the "T" stood for he merely smiled enigmatically and said, "Just call me Kagashima; it will be easier for you." He spoke English very well: no great surprise since he was born and raised in Denver, USA.

Kagashima was an electronics wizard. McGuire an advertising executive. Between them they had cooked up the idea of using electron guns to create glowing pictures in the ionosphere.

"Just imagine it," McGuire beamed, his chubby hands held up as if framing a camera shot. "It's twilight. The first stars are coming out. You look up and—POW!—there's a huge red and white sign covering the sky from horizon to horizon: *Drink Coke!*"

I wanted to vomit.

But Sam encouraged him. "Like skywriting, when planes used to spell out words with smoke."

"Real skywriting!" McGuire enthused.

Kagashima smiled and nodded.

"Is it legal," I asked, "to write advertising slogans across the sky?"

McGuire snapped a ferocious look at me. "There's no laws against it! The lawyers can't take the damned *sky* away from us, for god's sake! The sky belongs to everyone."

I glanced at Sam. "The lawyers seem to be taking my asteroid away from me."

His smile was odd, like the smile a hunter would have on his face as he saw his prey coming into range of his gun.

"Possession is nine-tenths of the law," Sam muttered.

"Who possesses the sky?" Kagashima asked, with that oriental ambiguity that passes for wisdom.

"We do!" snapped McGuire.

Sam merely smiled like a cat eying a fat canary.

AT SAM'S INSISTENCE I spent the night hours aboard his ship. His quarters were much more luxurious than mine, and since practically all space operations kept Greenwich Mean Time, there was no problem of differing clocks.

His cabin was much more than an alcove off the command module. It was small, but a real compartment, with a zipper hammock for sleeping and a completely enclosed shower stall that jetted water from all directions. We used the shower, but not the hammock. We finally fell asleep locked weightlessly in each other's embrace and woke up when we gently bumped into the compartment's bulkhead, many hours later.

"We've got to talk," Sam said as we were dressing.

I smiled at him. "That means you talk and I listen, no?"

"No. Well, maybe I do most of the talking. But you've got to make some decisions, kiddo."

"Decisions? About what?"

"About your asteroid. And the next few years of your life."

He did not say that I had to make a decision about us. I barely noticed that fact at the time. I should have paid more attention.

Glancing at the digital clock set into the bulkhead next to his hammock, Sam told me, "In about half an hour I'm going to be conversing with the Right Reverend Virtue T. Dabney, spiritual leader of the Moralist Sect. Their chief, their head honcho, sitteth at the right hand of You-Know-Who. The Boss."

"The head of the Moralists?"

"Right."

"He's calling you? About my asteroid?"

Sam's grin was full of teeth. "Nope. About his worms. We're carrying another load of 'em out to his Eden on this trip."

"Why would the head of the Moralists call you about worms?"

"Seems that the worms have become afflicted by a rare and strange disease," Sam said, the grin turning delightfully evil, "and the hauling contract the Moralists signed with me now contains a clause that says I'm not responsible for their health."

I was hanging in midair, literally and mentally. "What's that got to do with me?"

Drifting over so close that our noses were practically touching, Sam asked in a whisper, "Would you be willing to paint the world's first advertisement on the ionosphere? An advertisement for the Moralists?"

"Never!"

"Even if it means that they'll let you keep the asteroid?"

Ah, the emotions that surged through my heart! I felt anger, and hope, and disgust, even fear. But mostly anger.

"Sam, that's despicable! It's a desecration! To turn the sky into an advertising poster . . ."

Sam was grinning, but he was serious about this. "Now don't climb up on a high horse, kid. . . ."

"And do it for the Moralists?" My temper was boiling over now. "The people who want to take my asteroid away from me and destroy the memory of my own people? You want me to help *them*?"

"Okay, okay! Don't pop your cork over it." Sam said, taking me gently by the wrist. "I'm just asking you to think about it. You don't have to do it if you don't want to."

Completely bewildered, I allowed Sam to lead me up to the ship's command module. The same two husband-and-wife engineers were there at their consoles, just as blond and even more bloated than they had been the last time I had seen them, it seemed to me. They greeted me with smiles of recognition.

Sam asked them to leave and they wafted out through the main hatch like a pair of hot-air balloons. On their way to the galley, no doubt.

We drifted over to the comm console. No one needs chairs in zero gravity. We simply hung there, my arms floating up to about chest height, as they would in a swimming pool, while Sam worked the console to make contact with the Moralist Sect headquarters back on Earth.

It took more than a half hour for Sam to get Rev. Dabney on his screen. A small army of neatly scrubbed, earnest, glittering-eyed young men and women appeared, one after the other, and tried to deal with Sam. Instead, Sam dealt with them.

"Okay, if you want the worms to die, it's your seventy million dollars, not mine," said Sam to the young lawyer.

To the lawyer's superior, Sam spoke sweetly, "Your boss signed the contract. All I'm doing is informing you of the problem, as specified in clause 22.1, section C."

To *his* boss, "All right! I'll dump the whole load right here in the middle of nowhere and cut my losses. Is that what you want?"

To Rev. Dabney's astonished assistant administrator, "The lawsuit will tie you up for *years*, wiseass! You'll *never* finish your Eden! The creditors will take it over and make a Disney World out of it!"

To the special assistant to the High Pastor of the Moralist Sect, "This has gone beyond lawyers. It's even beyond the biologists' abilities! The damned worms are dying! They're withering away! What we need is a miracle!"

That, finally, brought the Right Rev. Virtue T. Dabney to the screen.

I instantly disliked the man. His face was largely hidden behind a dark beard and mustache. I suppose he thought it made him look like an Old Testament patriarch. To me he looked like a conquistador; all he needed was a shining steel breastplate and helmet. He seemed to me perfectly capable of burning my people at the stake.

"Mr. Gunn," he said, smiling amiably. "How may I help you?"

Sam said lightly, "I've got another ten tons of worms for you, as per contract, but they're dying. I don't think any of 'em are gonna survive long enough to make it to your habitat."

It took more than a minute for the messages to get back and forth from Earth to the *Klaus Heiss*. Dabney spent the time with hands folded and head bowed prayerfully. Sam hung onto the handgrips of the comm console to keep himself from bobbing around weightlessly. I stayed out of range of the video and fidgeted with seething, smoldering nervous fury.

"The worms are dying, you say? What seems to be the matter? Your first shipment made it to Eden with no trouble at all, I believe."

"Right. But something's gone wrong with this load. Maybe we got bad worms to start with. Maybe there's a fault in the cargo containers' radiation shielding. The worms are dying." Sam reached into his hip pocket and pulled out a blackened, twisted, dried out string of what must have once been an earthworm. "They're all going like this."

I watched intently for all the long seconds it took the transmission to reach Dabney's screen. When it did, his eyes went wide and his mouth dropped open.

"All of them? But how can this be?"

Sam shrugged elaborately. "Beats the hell out of me. My biologist is stymied, too. Maybe it's a sign from God that he doesn't want you to leave the Earth. I dunno."

Dabney's bearded face, when *that* line of Sam's finally hit him, went into even greater shock.

"I cannot believe the Lord would smite his faithful so. This is the work of evil."

"So what do we do about it?" Sam asked cheerfully. "My contract guarantees full payment for delivery. I'm not responsible for the condition of the cargo after your people inspected my cargo bay and okayed the shipment."

Sam blanked out the screen and turned to me. "Have you made up your mind, kiddo?"

"Made up my mind?"

"About the ads in the ionosphere."

"What do his dying worms have to do with me? Or with painting an advertisement on the ionosphere?"

"You'll see!" he promised. "Will you do it?"

"No! Never!"

"Even if it means saving your asteroid?"

I was too angry even to consider it. I turned my back to Sam and gritted my teeth with fury.

Sam sighed deeply, but when I whirled around to face him once more, he was grinning at me in that lopsided cunning way of his. Before I could say anything, he flicked on the screen again. Dabney's expression was crafty now. His eyes were narrowed, his lips pressed tight.

"What do you suggest as a solution to this problem, Mr. Gunn?"

"Damned if I know," said Sam. "Seems to me you need a miracle, Reverend."

He took special delight in Dabney's wince when that "damned" reached him.

"A miracle, you say," replied the Moralist leader. "And how do you think we might arrange a miracle?"

Sam chuckled. "Well—I don't know much about the way religions work, but I've heard that if somebody is willing to make a sacrifice, give up something that he really wants or even needs, then God rewards him. Something about casting bread upon the waters, I think."

I began to realize that there was nothing at all wrong with the Moralists' worms. Sam was merely holding them hostage. For me. He was risking lawsuits that could cost him everything he owned. For me.

Dabney's expression became even more squint-eyed than before. "You wouldn't be Jewish by any chance, would you, Mr. Gunn?"

Sam's grin widened to show lots of teeth. "You wouldn't be anti-Semitic, would you, Reverend?"

Their negotiation went on for the better part of three hours, with those agonizing long pauses in between each and every statement they made. After an hour of jockeying back and forth, Dabney finally suggested that he—and his sect—might give up their claim to an asteroid that they wanted to use for building material.

"That might be just the sacrifice that will save the worms," Sam allowed.

More offers and counteroffers, more tiptoeing and verbal sparring. It was all very polite. And vicious. Dabney knew that there was nothing wrong with the worms. He also knew that Sam could open his cargo bay to vacuum for the rest of the trip to Eden, and the Moralists would receive ten tons of very dead and desiccated garbage.

Finally, "If my people make this enormous sacrifice, if we give up our claim to this asteroid that we so desperately need, what will you be willing to do for me . . . er, us, in return?"

Sam rubbed his chin. "There's hundreds of asteroids in the Aten group, and more in the Apollos. They all cut across Earth's orbit. You can pick out a different one. It's no great sacrifice to give up this one little bitty piece of rock that you're claiming."

Dabney was looking down, as if at his desktop. Perhaps an aide was showing him lists of the asteroids available to help build his Eden.

"We picked that particular asteroid because its orbit brings it the closest to Eden and therefore it is the easiest—and least expensive—for us to capture and use."

He held up a hand before Sam could reply, an indication of very fast reflexes on his part. "However, in the interests of charity and self-sacrifice, I am willing to give up that particular asteroid. I know that some Latin American woman has been carving figures on it. If I—that is, if we allow her to remain and give up our claim to the rock, what will you do for the Moralist Sect in return?"

Now Sam's smile returned like a cat slinking in through a door open merely the barest crack. I realized that he had known all along that Dabney would not give in unless he got something more out of the deal than merely the delivery of the worms he had already paid for. He wanted icing on his cake.

"Well now," Sam said slowly, "how about an advertisement for the Moralist Sect that glows in the sky and can be seen from New England to the Mississippi valley?"

No! I screamed silently. Sam couldn't help them do that! It would be sacrilegious.

But when the transmission finally reached Dabney, his shrewd eyes grew even craftier. "What are you talking about, Mr. Gunn?"

Sam described the concept of painting the ionosphere with electron guns. Dabney's eyes grew wider and greedier with each word.

Finally his bearded face broke into a benign smile. "Mr. Gunn, you were right. The Bible describes our situation perfectly. 'Cast thy bread upon the waters and it shall be returned unto you a thousandfold.' "

"Does that mean we've got a deal?" Sam asked flatly.

I pushed over toward him and banged the blank key hard enough to send me recoiling toward the overhead. Sam looked up at me. There was no surprise on his face. He looked as if he had expected me to fight him.

"You can't do this!" I said. "You're playing into his hands! You can't . . ."

"You want to stay on the asteroid or not?"

I stopped in mid-sentence and stared at him. Sam's eyes were flat gray, boring into me.

"This is the way business is done, kid," he said. "You want the asteroid. They want the asteroid. I make a threat they know is phony, but they pretend to consider it—as long as they get something they don't have now. What it boils down to is, you can stay on the asteroid if Holier-Than-Thou gets to paint his advertisements across the ionosphere. That's the deal. Will you go for it or not?"

I couldn't speak. I was too furious, too confused, torn both ways and angry at Sam for putting me in this agony of indecision. I wanted to stay on the asteroid, yes, but not at the price of allowing the Moralists to deface the sky!

The message light on the screen began blinking. Sam touched the blank key again, and Dabney's face filled the screen once more, smiling an oily smile, the kind of unctuous happiness that a salesman shows when he's finally palmed off some shoddy goods at a shameful price.

"We have a deal, Mr. Gunn. We will rethink our options on acquiring that particular asteroid. Your, ah . . . friend," he made a nasty smirk, "can stay and chip away at the rock to her heart's content. In return, you will help us to produce our ads in the ionosphere."

Sam glanced at me. I could negate the whole thing with merely a shake of my head. Instead, I nodded. And bit my lip so hard I tasted blood in my mouth.

Sam grinned at the display screen. "We've got a deal, Bishop."

"Reverend," corrected Dabney. Then he added, "And I presume our cargo of worms will arrive at Eden in a healthy condition?"

"That's up to you," said Sam, straight-faced. "And the power of prayer."

They chatted amiably for a few minutes more, a pair of con men congratulating each other. Each of them had what he wanted. I began to realize that Sam would make a considerable amount of money from producing the Moralists' ionospheric advertisements. My anger took a new turn. I could feel my face turning red, my cheeks burning with rage.

Sam finally ended his conversation with Rev. Dabney and turned off the comm console. It seemed to me that Dabney's bearded image remained on the screen even after it went dark and dead. It burned in my vision like the afterimage of an explosion.

Sam turned to me with a wide grin splitting his face. "Congratulations! You can stay on the asteroid."

"Congratulations yourself," I said, my voice trembling, barely under control. "You have put yourself into the advertising business. You should make a great deal of profit out of defacing the sky. I hope that makes you happy."

I stormed out of the bridge and headed for the locker where I had left my space suit. Yes, I could stay on my asteroid and finish my work. But my love affair with Sam Gunn was shattered completely.

He let the fat engineer fly me back to my quarters. Sam knew I was furious and it would be best for him to leave me alone.

But not for long. After four or five sleepless hours, bobbing around my darkened quarters like a cork tossed on a stormy sea, I saw the message light of my comm console flick bright red. I reached out and turned it on.

Sam's face appeared on the screen, a half-guilty boyish grin on his face. "Still mad at me?"

"No, not really." And I realized it was true even as I spoke the words. I was angry at Dabney and his smug Moralist power; angry at myself, mostly, for wanting to carve The Rememberer so much that I was willing to let them do whatever they wanted, so long as they left me alone.

"Good," said Sam. "Want me to bring some breakfast over to you?"

I shook my head. "I think not."

"Got to make a course change in another couple hours," he said. "So I can bring this can of worms to Eden."

"I know." He would be leaving me, and I could not blame him if he never returned. Still, it was impossible for me to allow him to come close to me. Not now. Not this soon after the deal he had struck. I knew he had done it for me, although I also knew he had his own reasons, as well.

"Listen—I can get somebody else do design the pictures for the Moralists. You don't have to do it."

He was trying to be kind to me, I knew. But my anger did not abate. "Who draws the pictures doesn't matter, Sam. It's the fact that the advertisements will be spread across the sky. For *them*. That disgusts me."

"I'm doing this for you, kid."

"And for the profits," I snapped. "Tell the whole truth."

"Yep, there's a pot full of money in it," Sam admitted. "You wouldn't have to depend on your university grant anymore."

"Never!" I spat.

He grinned at me. "That's my girl. I would've been disappointed if you agreed to it. But I had to ask, had to give you the first shot at the money."

Money. Art and money are always bound together, no matter what you do. The artist must eat. Must breathe. And that requires money.

But I stubbornly refused to give in to the temptation. I would *not* help that slithering Dabney to spread his advertising filth across the world's sky. Never.

Or so I thought.

THINGS HAPPENED SO fast over the next few weeks that, to this day, I am not entirely certain how the chain of events began. Who did what to whom. I am only certain of one thing: Dabney had no intention of carrying out his part of the bargain he had struck with Sam, and he never did.

I was alone again, and missing Sam terribly. For three years I had lived in isolation without a tear or a regret. I had even relished the solitude, the freedom from the need to adjust my behavior to the expectations of others. Sam had burst into my life like a joyful energetic skyrocket, showering pretty sparks everywhere. And now that he was gone, I missed him. I feared I would never see him again, and I knew if he forgot me it would be my own fault.

Suddenly my sorrowing loneliness was shattered by the arrival of a team of two dozen propulsion engineers, with legal documents that stated they were empowered to move my asteroid to Eden, where it was to be broken up and used as structural material for the Moralists' habitat.

Without thinking twice I put in a frantic call for Sam. It turned out he was halfway around the Earth's orbit. He had delivered his worms to Eden and was now on his way back to the Moon to pick up electronics components for a new construction site at the L-4 libration point.

There were no relay stations around Earth's orbit in those days. My call had to fight past the Sun's coronal interference. Sam's image, when he came onto my comm screen, was shimmering and flecked with pinpoint bursts of light, like an old hologram.

As soon as he said hello I unloaded my tale of woe in a single burst of unrelieved fury and fear.

"They're taking possession of the asteroid!" I finished. "I told you they couldn't be trusted!"

For once in his life Sam was silent and thoughtful. I watched his expression change from mild curiosity to shocked surprise and then to a jaw-clenched anger as my words reached him.

At last he said, "Don't go off the deep end. Give me a few hours to look into this. I'll call you back."

It took almost forty-eight hours. I was frantic, my emotions swinging like a pendulum between the desire to hide myself or run away altogether and the growing urge to take one of the high-powered lasers I used for rock carving and slice the propulsion team into bite-sized chunks of bloody dead meat.

I tried to reach Sam a thousand times during those maddening horrible hours of waiting. Always I got one of the crew members from his ship, or a staff person from his headquarters at the Earth View Hotel. Always they gave me the same message: "Sam's looking into the problem for you. He said he'll call you as soon as he gets everything straightened out."

When he finally did call me, I was exhausted and ready for a straitjacket.

"It doesn't look good," said his wavering, tight-lipped image. Without waiting for me to respond, Sam outlined the situation.

The Right Reverend Virtue T. Dabney (his T stood for Truthful, it turned out!) had screwed us both. The Moralists never withdrew their claim from the IAA's arbitration board, and the board had decided in their favor, as Dabney had expected. The Moralists had the right to take my asteroid and use it as construction material.

Worse still, Sam's cargo of worms had arrived at Eden in fine, slimy, wriggling earthwormy health. And even worse than that, Sam had signed the contract to produce the ionospheric advertisements for the Moralist Sect. The deal was set, as legal and legitimate as an act of the world congress.

"If I don't go through with the ads," Sam said, strangely morose, "the bastards can sue me for everything I've got. They'll wind up owning my hotel, my ships, even the clothes on my back."

"Isn't there *anything* we can do?" I pleaded to his image on my screen.

For long minutes he gave no response, as my words struggled across nearly three hundred million kilometers to reach him. I hung weightless before the screen, suspended in the middle of my shabby little compartment while outside I could *feel* the thumps and clangs of the propulsion team attaching their obscene rocket thrusters and nuclear engines to my asteroid. I felt like a woman surrounded by rapists, helpless and alone.

I stared so hard at Sam's image in my screen that my eyes began to water. And then I realized that I was crying.

At last, after a lifetime of agony, Sam's face broke into a sly grin. "Y'-know, I saw a cartoon once, when I was a kid. It was in a girlie magazine."

I wanted to scream at him. What does this have to do with my problem? But he went on calmly, smiling crookedly at his reminiscence, knowing that any objections from me could not reach him for a quarter of an hour.

"It showed these two guys chained to the wall of a dungeon, ten feet off the floor. Chained hand and foot. Beards on them down to their kneecaps. Totally hopeless situation. And one of the guys—" Sam actually laughed! "—one of the guys has this big stupid grin on his face and he's saying, 'Now here's my plan.'"

I felt my lungs filling themselves with air, getting ready to shriek at his nonsense.

"Now, before you blow your top," Sam warned, "let me tell you two things: First, we're both in this together. Second—well . . . here's my plan."

He kept on speaking for the next hour and a half. I never got the chance to object or even get a word in.

THAT IS HOW I came to paint the first picture in Earth's ionosphere.

Sam had expected me all along to draw the advertisements for him. He never planned to use another artist. "Why should some stranger make all that money?" was his attitude.

While the propulsion engineers fitted out my asteroid with their nuclear rocket systems and supply ships from the Moon towed huge spherical tanks of gaseous propellants, Sam relayed the Rev. Dabney's rough sketches of what the ionospheric advertisements should look like.

They were all photographs of Dabney himself, wrapped in pure white robes with heavenly clouds of gold behind him and just the hint of a halo adorning his saintly head.

I would have trashed them immediately if I had not been aware of Sam's plan.

The timing had to be perfect. The first ad was scheduled to be placed over the midwestern section of the United States, where it could be seen from roughly Ohio to Iowa. If everything went the way Mountain McGuire and T. Kagashima claimed it would, the picture would drift slowly westward as the day/night terminator crawled across the Earth's surface.

Sam himself came to visit me on the day that the first ad was to be produced. He was in the latest and largest of his cargo carriers, the *Laissez Faire,* which he jokingly referred to as "The Lazy Fairy."

My asteroid was already on its way to Eden. The propulsion engineers had connected the last of their propellant tanks, turned on their systems, and left me alone to glide slowly, under the low but steady thrust of the nuclear rockets, to a rendezvous with Eden. They would return in a few days to make final course corrections and take me off the asteroid forever.

Sam looked absolutely impish when he stepped into my compartment. His grin was almost diabolic. My place was an even bigger mess than usual, what with the sketches for the advertisements floating here and there and all my other sketches and computer wafers hanging weightlessly in midair.

"How can you ever find anything in here?" Sam asked, glancing around.

I had remained at my drawing board, behind it actually. It formed something of a defensive shield for me. I did not want to fling myself into Sam's arms, no matter how much I really did want to do it. I couldn't let him think that I was willing to be his lover again in return for the help he was giving me. I couldn't let myself think that, especially because it was very close to being true.

He gave no indication of expecting such a reward. He merely eyed me mischievously and asked, "You really want to go through with this?"

I did not hesitate an instant. "Yes!"

He took a deep breath. "Okay. I'm game if you are. The lawyers have checked everything out. Let's do it."

I slid out from behind my drawing board and went to the computer. Sam came up beside me and activated my communications console. For the next half-hour we were all business, me checking my drawing and Sam connecting with McGuire and Kagashima.

"I'm glad they attached the rockets and that other junk to the end of the asteroid you haven't carved yet," Sam muttered as we worked. "Would've been a crime if they had messed up the work you've already done."

I nodded curtly, not trusting myself to look into his eyes. He was close enough to brush against my shoulder. I could feel the warmth of his body next to me, even while I sweated with cold apprehension.

Working together as a team linked across hundreds of millions of kilometers, Sam, McGuire, Kagashima and I painted the first picture high in the ionosphere of Earth. From my computer my design went forth to a set of electron guns on board the same orbiting station that housed Sam's hotel. In the comm screen I saw the picture forming across the flat midsection of North America.

The Virgin of the Andes.

I had no intention of spreading the pompous Dabney's unctuous features across the sky. Not even the *Norte Americanos* deserved that. Instead I had drawn a picture from my heart, from my childhood memories of the crude paintings that adorned the whitewashed walls of my village church.

You must understand that it was years before I myself saw my creation in the way it was meant to be seen, from the ground. All I had to go on that day was the little screen of my comm system, and even there I was seeing the Virgin backwards, like looking at a stained glass window from outside the cathedral.

Everyone was caught by surprise. A few startled gringos tried to photograph the picture that suddenly appeared over their heads at sunset, but none of the photos showed the true size or scope or even the actual colors of my Virgin. The colors especially were impossible to capture, they were so pale and shimmering and subtly shifting each moment. By the time television stations realized what was happening and dispatched their mobile news units, the Virgin had disappeared into the darkness of night.

All of North America went into startled, shocked turmoil. Then the word spread all across the world.

Ionosphere paintings last only for those precious few minutes of twilight, of course. Once the Sun dips below the horizon, the delicate electrical effects that create the subtle colors quickly disappear, and the picture fades into nothingness.

Except that the *information* which created the picture is stored in a computer, *gracias a Dios*. Many years later, when it was safe for me to return to Earth, I allowed the university to paint my Virgin over the skies of my native land. I saw it at last the way it was meant to be seen. It was beautiful, more beautiful than anything I have ever done since.

But that was not to happen for many years. As Sam and I watched my Virgin fade into darkness he turned to me with a happy grin.

"Now," he said cheerfully, "the shit hits the fan."

And indeed it did. Virtually every lawyer in the solar system became involved in the suits, countersuits, and counter-countersuits. Dabney and his Moralists claimed that Sam had violated their contract. Sam claimed that the contract specifically gave him artistic license, and indeed those words were buried in one of the sub-sub-clauses on the next-to-last page of that thick legal document. The advertising industry was thunderstruck. Environmentalists from pole to pole screamed and went to court, which prompted art critics and the entire apparatus of "fine art"—the museums, magazines, charitable associations, social clubs, wealthy patrons and even government agencies—to come to the defense of a lonely young artist that none of them had ever heard of before: Elverda Apacheta. Me!

Sam and I paid scant attention to the legal squabbles. We were sailing on my asteroid past the Moralists' half-finished Eden and out far beyond Earth's orbit. Sam's "Lazy Fairy" was crammed to its sizable capacity with propellants for the nuclear rockets attached to The Rememberer. He jiggered the propulsion engineers' computer program so that my asteroid headed for deep space, out past even the orbit of Mars, out to the Belt where its brother and sister asteroids orbited by the millions.

When the Moralists' engineers tried to come out and intercept "their" runaway, Sam gleefully informed them:

"This object is a derelict, under the definition stated in the IAA's regulations of space commerce. It is heading for deep space, and any attempt to intercept it or change its course will be regarded by the IAA and the world government as an act of piracy!"

By the time the Moralists' lawyers came to the conclusion that Sam was bluffing, we were moving fast enough and far enough so that Dabney decided it would not be worthwhile trying to recover my asteroid. The Rememberer sailed out to the Asteroid Belt, half a dozen propulsion engineers were fired by the Moralists (and immediately hired by S. Gunn Enterprises, Unlimited) and Sam and I spent more than a year together.

"AND THAT IS how I became famous." Elverda Apacheta smiled slightly, as if someone had paid her a compliment she did not deserve. "Even though I am a sculptress, I am known to the public for that one painting. Like Michelangelo and the Sistine ceiling."

Jade asked, "And Sam? You say he spent more than a year with you on your asteroid?"

Now the sculptress laughed, a rich throaty sound. "Yes, I know it sounds strange to imagine Sam staying in one place for two days on end, let alone three hundred and eighty. But he did. He stayed with me that long."

"That's . . . unusual."

"You must realize that half the solar system's lawyers were looking for Sam. It was a good time for him to be unavailable. Besides, he wanted to see the Asteroid Belt for himself. You may recall that he made and lost several fortunes out there."

"Yes, I know," said Jade.

Elverda Apacheta nodded slowly, remembering. "It was a stormy time, cooped up in my little workshop. We both had other demons driving us: Sam wanted to be the first entrepreneur to set up operations in the Asteroid Belt. . . ."

"And he was," Jade murmured.

"Yes, he was. And I had my own work. My art."

"Which is admired and adored everywhere."

"Perhaps so," admitted the sculptress, "but still I receive requests to produce the Virgin of the Andes. No matter what I do, that painting will haunt me forever."

"The Rememberer is the most popular work of art off-Earth. Every year thousands of people make the pilgrimage. Your people will never be forgotten."

"Perhaps more tourists would go to see it if it were in a lower orbit," the sculptress mused. "Sam worked it out so that it swung through the Asteroid Belt, returned to Earth's vicinity, and was captured into a high orbit, about twelve thousand kilometers up. He was afraid of bringing it closer; he said his calculations were not so exact and he feared bringing it so close that it would hit the Earth."

"Still, it's regarded as a holy shrine and one of the greatest works of art anywhere," Jade said.

"But it's rather difficult for people to get to." Elverda Apacheta's smooth brow knitted slightly in an anxious little frown. "I have asked the IAA to bring it closer, down to where the tourist hotels orbit, but they have not acted on my request as yet."

"You know how slow bureaucracies are," said Jade.

The sculptress sighed. "I only hope I live long enough for them to make their decision."

"Did the Moralists try to recapture your asteroid?"

"Oh no. That was the beauty of Sam's scheme. By pushing The Rememberer into such a high-velocity orbit, he made it too expensive for the Moralists to go chasing after us. They screamed and sued, but finally they settled on another one of the Aten group. More than one, I believe."

"And Sam left you while you were still coasting out in the Belt?"

She smiled sadly. "Yes. We quarreled a lot, of course. It was not entirely a honeymoon trip. Finally, he detached his ship to investigate some of the smaller asteroids that we had discovered. He said he wanted to register a priority in their discovery. 'It's the only way I'll ever get my name in the history books,' he told me. That was the last I saw of him."

"No further contact at all?"

"Oh, we called each other. We spent hours talking. But he never came back to me." Elverda Apacheta looked away from Jade, toward the view of Earth in the lounge's lone window. "In a way I was almost glad of it. Sam was very intense, and so was I. We were not meant to stay together for very long."

Jade said nothing. For long moments the only sound in the lounge was the faint whisper of air coming through the ventilating ducts.

"The last time I spoke with him," Elverda Apacheta said, "he had a premonition of death."

Jade felt her entire body tense. "Really?"

"Oh, it was nothing dark and brooding. That was not Sam's nature. He merely asked me someday to do a statue of him exactly as I remembered him, without using a photograph or anything else for a model. Strictly from memory. He said he would like to have that as his monument once he is gone."

"His statue on the Moon."

The sculptress nodded. "Yes. I did it in glass. Lunar glass. Have you seen it?"

"It's beautiful!"

Elverda Apacheta laughed. "It does not look like Sam at all. He was not a tall, dauntless explorer with a jutting jaw and steely eyes. But it's the way he wanted to be, and in a strange sort of way, inside that funny little body of his, that is the way he really was. So that is the way I made his statue."

And she laughed. But the tears in her eyes were not from joy.

Jade found her own vision blurring. For the first time since she had found out the truth about her birth, she realized that Sam Gunn, her own father, would have loved her if he had only known she existed.

Titan

STANDING IN AN ARMORED PRESSURE SUIT ON THE SHORE OF the methane sea, Jade aimed her rented camcorder at the huge fat crescent of Saturn peeking through a rare break in the clouds that filled the hazy orange sky. The planet was striped like a faded beach ball, its colors pale, almost delicate tones of yellow and pink with whitish splotches here and there. The ring system looked like a scimitar-thin line crossing its bulging middle, though the rings cast a wide solid shadow on Saturn's oblate disk.

"Dear Spence," Jade said into her helmet microphone. "As you can see, I've made it to Titan. And I truly do wish you were here. It's eerie, strange and beautiful and kind of scary."

The clouds scudded across the face of Saturn, blotting it from view. The sky darkened, and the perpetual gloom of Titan deepened. Jade turned slightly and focused the camera on the methane sea. It looked thick, almost oily. Near the horizon a geyser pushed slowly skyward, a slow-motion fountain of utterly cold liquid nitrogen.

"It only took two months to get here from Ceres on the high-boost ship. It was expensive, but the university runs a regularly scheduled service to the campus here. Titan's become *the* hub for studies of the outer solar system, although there are actually more people living and working in the Jupiter system. Which is natural, I suppose, since they discovered those giant whale things living in the Jovian ocean."

Waves were lapping sluggishly against the ice rocks on which Jade stood. The whole methane sea seemed to be heaving itself slowly, reluctantly toward her.

"Tidal shift," whispered a small voice in her helmet earphones. "Please return to base." She was being monitored by the Titan base's automated safety cameras, of course.

"The tide's starting to come in," Jade said. "Time for me to get back to the base," she swung the camera around, "up on those cliffs. I don't know how much of it you can see in this murk, but it's pretty comfortable—for a short visit. Like a college dormitory, I guess."

She started walking toward the powered stairs that climbed up to the cliff top.

"I do wish you were here, Spence. Or I was there. I miss you. This will be the last interview for the Sam Gunn biography. I'll be coming back to Selene after this. It'll take six months, even at constant boost, but I'm looking forward to getting back home. Please video me back as soon as you can."

Two months of enforced inactivity aboard the plasma torch ship that had brought her to Titan had given Jade plenty of time to think about Spence Johansen.

She wanted to end her video message with "I love you," but found that she could not. I'm not sure of myself, she realized. I'm not sure of him. There'll be time enough for that when I get back, she told herself. Then she added ruefully, if Spence hasn't married again by then.

SOLOMON GOODMAN LOOKED very young to be a famous professor and Noble laureate. He's not much more than thirty, she told herself.

Unlike most of the other people she had interviewed, Professor Goodman had no qualms about talking to her. He had immediately acceded to her request for an interview even before Jade had reached Ceres, and had personally set her up with a reservation aboard the plasma torch ship that had brought her out to Titan.

Now she sat in his office. What looked like a large picture window was actually a smart screen, she realized. A beautifully clear image of Saturn showed on it, obviously taken from a satellite camera above Titan's perpetual cloud cover. Jade could see the mysterious spokes in Saturn's rings and the streaks of pale colors banding the planet's oblate body.

Goodman sat slouched in a pseudo-leather couch, his long legs stretched out, almost touching Jade's booted feet. She pictured him as a skinny, gangling student even though he was now getting pudgy, potbellied. His hair was still quite dark and thickly curled; his slightly puffy face could look quite pleasant when he smiled.

A robot had brought a tray of tea things and deposited them on the low table between the couch and the padded chair on which Jade was sitting.

"One of the perks of university life," Goodman said, almost defensively. "Real old English tea in the afternoon. I got into the habit when I was at Oxford. Really gives you a lift for the later part of the day."

Jade let him pour a cup of steaming tea for her, then added a bit of milk herself. The tea service was real china, brought in all the way from Earth. The Nobel prize brought its privileges, she thought.

"So what do you want to know about Sam?" Goodman asked, smiling at her. Jade noticed that he had large hands; they dwarfed the delicate cup and saucer he was holding.

"Well," Jade said, turning on the recorder in her belt, "you were the last person to see him alive, weren't you?"

His smile faded. He put the cup and saucer down on the tray in front of him.

Looking up at Jade with an almost guilty expression on his face, Goodman said, "I guess you could say that I killed Sam Gunn."

Einstein

GOODMAN LEANED EVEN DEEPER INTO THE COUCH, HEAD tilted back, eyes focused on something, someplace far beyond the ceiling of his office.

You can't pace the floor in zero gravity—he said, almost to himself. So Sam was flitting around the cramped circular control center of our ship like a crazed chipmunk, darting along madly, propelling himself by grabbing at handgrips, console knobs, viewport edges, anything that could give him a moment's purchase as he whirled by.

I was sweating over my instruments, but every nine seconds Sam whizzed past me like a demented monkey, jabbering, "It's gotta be there. It's *gotta* be there!"

"There's *something* out there," I yelled over my shoulder, annoyed with him. Angry at myself, really. It was my calculations that had put us into this fix.

The instruments were showing a definite gravitational flux, damned close to what I had calculated when I was still back on campus. But out here, well past the orbit of Pluto—farther than anybody had gone before—what I needed to see was a planet, a fat little world orbiting out in that darkness more than seven billion miles from Earth.

Planet X. The tenth planet. Not a cometary body, an icy dirtball like so many of the objects out there in the Kuiper Belt. A planet, a real solid body with a gravitational flux considerably stronger than Earth's.

I mean, they can argue about whether Pluto or those other icy bodies should be considered planets. But from the gravitational flux I'd detected, this one had to be a real, sizeable planet. Bigger than Earth, most likely.

Astronomers had been searching for Planet X since before Percival Lowell's time, but I had worked out *exactly* where it should be, me and the CalTech/MIT/Osaka linked computers. And Sam Gunn had furnished the money and the ship to go out and find it.

Only, it wasn't there.

"It's gotta be there." Sam orbited past me again. "*Gotta* be."

The first time I met Sam, I thought he was nuts. Chunky little guy. Hair like a nest of rusted wire. Darting, probing eyes. Kind of shifty. The eyes of a politician, maybe, or a confidence man.

"Fly out there?" I had asked him. "Why not just rent time on an orbital telescope, or use the lunar observa—"

"To claim it, egghead!" Sam had snapped. "A whole planet. I want it."

He couldn't have been that dumb, I thought. He'd amassed several fortunes, and lost all but the latest one. To fly out beyond Pluto would cost every penny he had, and more.

"You can't claim a planet," I explained patiently. "International agreements from back in . . ."

"Puke on international agreements!" he shouted. "I'm not a national government. I'm S. Gunn Enterprises, Unlimited. And a whole planet's *gotta* be worth a fortune."

Sam had a reputation for shady schemes, but I couldn't for the life of me see how he planned to profit from claiming Planet X. Nor any reason for me to leave my home and job at the university to go out to the end of the solar system with him.

I didn't reckon on Sam's persuasiveness. He didn't have a silver tongue. Far from it. His language was more often crude, even obscene, rather than eloquent. But he was a nonstop needler, wheedler, pleader, seducer. In the language of my forefathers, he was a *nudge*. His tongue didn't have to be silver; it was heavy-duty, long-wearing, blister-proof, diamond-coated solid muscle.

So I found myself ducking through the hatch of the special ship he had commissioned. Only the two of us as crew; I was to do the navigating, while Sam did everything else, including the cooking. Before I could ask myself why I was doing this, I was being flattened into the acceleration couch as we roared out into the wild black yonder.

But Planet X wasn't there.

Sam slowed down, puffing, until he was dangling right behind me, his feet half a meter off the floor. My softboots were locked in the foot restraints and still he barely came up to my height. He was wheezing, and I realized there was a lot of gray in his reddish hair. His face looked tired, old, eyes baggy and sad.

"Of all the eggheads in all the universities in all the solar system," he groaned, "you've . . ."

Suddenly I realized what the instruments were telling me. I shouted, "It's a black hole!"

"And I'm the tooth fairy."

"No, really! It's not a planet at all. It's a black hole. Look!"

Sam snarled, "How in hell can I see something that's invisible by definition?"

With trembling fingers I pointed to the gravitational flux meters and the high-energy detectors. We even went over to the optical telescope and bumped our heads together like Laurel and Hardy, trying to squint through the eyepiece together.

Nothing to see. Except a faint violet glow, the last visible remains of the thin interplanetary gas that was being sucked into the black hole on a one-way trip to oblivion.

It really was a black hole! The final grave of a star that had collapsed, God knows how many eons ago. A black hole! Practically in our backyard! And I had discovered it! Visions of the Nobel Prize made me giddy.

Sam sprang straight to the communications console and started tapping frantically at its keyboard, muttering about how he could rent time to astronomers to study the only black hole close enough to Earth to see firsthand.

"It's worth a freakin' fortune," he chortled, his fingers racing along the keys like a concert pianist trying to do Chopin's *Minute Waltz* in thirty seconds. "A dozen fortunes!"

He filed his claim and even gave the black hole a name: Einstein. I grinned and nodded agreement with his choice.

It took nearly eleven hours for Sam's message to get to Earth, and another eleven for their reply to reach us. I spent the time studying Einstein while Sam proclaimed to the universe how he was going to build an orbiting hotel just outside Einstein's event horizon and invent a new pastime for the danger nuts.

"Space surfing! A jetpack on your back and good old Einstein in front of you. See how close you can skim to the event horizon without getting sucked in! It'll make billions!"

"Until somebody gets stretched into a bloody string of spaghetti," I said. "That grav field out there is *powerful,* Sam, and I think it fluctuates. . . ."

"All the better," said Sam, clapping his hands like a kid in front of a Christmas tree. "Let a couple of the risk freaks kill themselves and all the others will come boiling out here like lemmings on migration."

I shook my head in wonder.

When the comm signal finally chimed I was still trying to dope out the basic parameters of our black hole. Yes, I was thinking of Einstein as ours; that's what being near Sam does to you.

His round little face went pugnacious the instant he saw the woman on the screen. I felt an entirely different reaction. She was beautiful, with thick platinum blonde hair and the kind of eyes that promised paradise.

But her voice was as cold as a robot's. "Mr. Gunn, we meet again. Your claim has been noted and filed with the Interplanetary Astronautical Authority. In the meantime, I represent the creditors from your most recent bankruptcy. To date . . ."

She droned on while Sam's face went from angry red to ashy grey. This far from Earth, all messages were one-way. You can't hold a conversation with an eleven-hour wait between each transmission. The blonde went into infinite detail about how much money Sam owed, and to whom. Even though I was only half listening, I learned that our ship was not paid for, and my own university was suing Sam for taking my instrumentation without authorization!

Finally she smiled slightly and delivered the knockout. "Now Mr. Gunn—aside from all the above unpleasantness, it may interest you to realize that your claim to this alleged black hole is without merit or substance."

Sam made a growl from deep in his throat.

"International law dating back to 1967 prohibits claiming sovereignty to any body found in space. . . ."

"I'm not claiming sovereignty," Sam snapped to the unhearing screen. "And this ain't a body, it's a black hole."

She serenely continued, ". . . although it is allowed to claim the *use* of a body found in space, I'm afraid that the law clearly states that you must establish an operational facility on the body in question before such a claim will be recognized by the Interplanetary Astronautical Council."

Sam snorted like a bull about to charge. Me, I thought about establishing an operational facility on the body attached to that incredibly beautiful face.

"So I'm afraid, my dear Mr. Gunn," her smile widened to show dazzlingly perfect teeth, "that unless you establish an operational facility on your so-called black hole, your claim is worthless. And, oh yes! one more thing—an automated ship is on its way to you, filled with robot lawyers who will have authorization to take possession of your ship and all its equipment, in the name of your creditors. Good-bye. Have a nice day."

The screen went blank.

Sam gave a screech that would make an ax-murderer shudder and flung himself at the dead screen. He bounced off and scooted weightlessly around the control center again, gibbering, jabbering, screaming insults and obscenities at the blonde, the IAA, the whole solar system in general, and all the lawyers on Earth in particular.

"I'll show 'em!" he raged. "I'll show 'em all!"

I stayed close to my instruments—actually, they were still the university's instruments, I guess.

After God knows how many orbits around the control center, screaming and raging, Sam propelled himself toward the hatch in the floor that led down to the equipment bay.

"They want an operational facility, they'll get an operational facility!"

I wrenched my feet free so fast I twisted an ankle, and went diving after him.

"Sam, what the hell are you thinking of?"

He was already unlocking the hatch of our EVA scooter, a little one-man utility craft with a big bubble canopy and so many extensible arms it looked like a metal spider.

"I'm gonna pop an instrument pod down Einstein's throat. That's gonna be our operational facility."

"But it'll just disappear into the black hole!"

"So what?"

"It won't be an operational facility."

"How do you know what it'll be doing inside the event horizon? The gravity field will stretch out its signals, won't it?"

"Theoretically," I answered.

"Then we'll be getting signals from the probe for years, right? Even after it goes past the event horizon."

"I guess so. But that doesn't prove the probe will be operating inside the black hole, Sam."

"If the mother-humping lawyers want to prove that it's not working, let 'em jump into the black hole after it. And kiss my ass on the way down!"

I argued with him for more than an hour while he got the instrument pod together and revved up the EVA craft. What he wanted to do was *dangerous*. Maybe adventure freaks would like to skim around the event horizon of a black hole. Me, I don't feel really safe unless there's good California soil shaking beneath my feet.

But Sam would not be denied. Maybe he was a danger freak himself. Maybe he was desperate for the money he thought he could make. Maybe he just wanted to screw all the lawyers on Earth, especially that blonde.

He didn't even put on a pressure suit. He just clambered up into the cockpit of the EVA craft, slammed its hatch, and worked one of its spidery arms to pick up the instrument pod.

Reluctantly I went back to the control center to monitor Sam's mission.

"Stay well clear of the event horizon," I warned him over the radio. "I don't know enough about Einstein to give you firm parameters. . . ."

Sam was no fool. He listened to my instructions. He released the instruments well clear of the event horizon. But the pod just orbited around the faint violet haze that marked Einstein's position. It didn't go spiraling into it.

"Goddam mother-humping no-good son of a lawyer!"

Sam jockeyed the EVA craft into a matching orbit and gave the pod a push inward. Not enough. Then another, swearing a blue streak every instant.

"That's close enough," I yelled into the microphone, sweating bullets. "The event horizon fluctuates, Sam. You mustn't . . ."

I swear the black hole reached out and grabbed him. The event horizon sort of burped and engulfed Sam's craft. I know it's impossible, but that's what happened.

"Hey!" he yelled. "Heyyyyyy!"

According to everything we knew about black holes up to that moment, Sam was being squeezed by Einstein's immense gravitational forces, torn apart, crushed, mashed, squashed, pulverized.

"What's going onnnn?" Sam's radio voice stretched out eerily, like in an echo chamber.

"What's going on?" I asked back.

"It's like sliding down a chuuute!"

"You're not being pulled apart?"

"Hell nooo! But I can't see anything. Like falling down an elevator shaaaft!"

Sam should have been crushed. But he wasn't. His radio messages were being stretched out, but apparently he himself was not. He was falling into the black hole on a one-way trip, swallowed alive.

I started to laugh. We had named the black hole exactly right. Inside the event horizon space-time was being warped, all right. But Sam was now part of *that* continuum and to him, everything seemed normal. Our universe, the one we're in, would have seemed weirdly distorted to him if he could see it.

It had all been there in old Albert's equations all along, if we had only had the sense enough to realize it.

Sam Gunn, feisty, foulmouthed, womanizing, fast-talking Sam Gunn had discovered a shortcut to the stars, a space-time warp that one day would allow us to get around the limits of speed-of-light travel. That black hole was not a dead-end route to oblivion; it was a space-time warp that opened somewhere/somewhen else in the universe. Or maybe in another universe altogether.

But it was a *one-way* route.

Sam gave his life to his discovery. He was on a one-way trip to God knows where. Maybe there'd be kindly aliens at the other end of the warp to greet him and give him their version of the Nobel Prize.

I got the terrestrial Nobel, of course. And now I'm heading up an enormous team of scientists who're studying Einstein and trying to figure out how to put black hole warps to practical use.

And Sam? Who knows where he is?

But you can still hear him. Thanks to Einstein's time-stretching effects, you can hear Sam swearing and cussing every moment, all the way down that long, long slide to whatever's on the other side of the warp.

And according to Einstein (Albert), we'll be able to hear Sam yelling forever. Forever.

Surprise, Surprise

JADE LEANED BACK IN THE YIELDING WARMTH OF THE FORM-shaping chair, suddenly weary and drained. She turned off the computer on her lap. The interview with Professor Goodman was on its way to Selene. The final interview. Her long trek after Sam Gunn's story was at last finished.

She felt as if she had been struggling all her life to reach the top of a mountain, and now that she had done it, there was nothing to see, nothing more to do. The challenge had been met, and now she was surrounded by emptiness. There was no feeling of triumph, or even accomplishment. She was merely tired and empty and alone on a pinnacle with nowhere else to go.

She leaned her head back into the chair's comforting warmth. The dormitory room that the university had given her was more luxurious than most of the hotels she had slept in. The chair adjusted itself to her body shape and temperature, enfolding her like a gently pulsating womb. How pleasant it would be, Jade thought, to just close my eyes and sleep—forever.

But the smart screen on the wall of the small room showed a view of Titan's spaceport out on the murky surface, and the sleek torch ship that had landed there only minutes earlier. The retractable dome was rising silently over it. Soon the ship would be disgorging its payload of passengers and cargo. In another two days it would start back toward the big scientific base in Mars orbit. And Jade would be on it, heading back toward Selene, toward the habitats crowding the Earth-Moon system, toward the world of her birth.

And what then? she asked herself. What then?

She drifted into an exhausted dreamless sleep. When the phone buzzed it startled her; her nerves jumped as if an emergency klaxon were hooting.

Her laptop had slipped to the thickly carpeted floor. Thinking idly that the university life had all sorts of unwritten perquisites, Jade picked up the tiny box and pressed its ON switch.

Spence Johansen's grinning face filled the little screen.

"Hello there," he said.

Jade waited for him to go on, knowing that this was either a recorded message or a call from the Earth-Moon area, hours distant even at the lightspeed of video communications.

"Hey, Jade, say something! I'm here. On Titan. Up in the flight lounge. Surprised?"

She nearly dropped the computer again.

"Spence? You're here? It's really you?"

"Sure, I just arrived."

"I'll be right up!"

Jade tossed the computer onto her bed and dashed for the door, all fatigue forgotten, all the weariness melted away. By the time she tore through the corridors and rode the power stairs up to the flight lounge, Spence already had a pair of tall frosted drinks sitting on the bar, waiting for her.

She threw herself into his arms. Their long passionate kiss drew admiring stares and a few low whistles from the other new arrivals and regulars in the lounge.

"Whatever . . . how did you . . . why . . . ?" Jade had a million questions bubbling within her.

Johansen smiled, almost sheepishly. "Ol' *Jefferson* got kind of boring after you went away. I missed you, Jade. Missed you a lot."

"So much that you came all the way out here?"

He shrugged.

She perched on the bar-stool next to his, ignoring the drink standing before her, all her attention on this man who had traveled across half the solar system. To be with her.

"I missed you, too, Spence."

"Did you?"

"Enormously." She suddenly grinned maliciously. "Considering where we are, I might say *titanically*."

Spence Johansen threw his head back and laughed a genuine, hearty, full-throated laugh. And Jade knew that she loved him.

She took his big hand in her little one and tugged him off the bar-stool. "Come on," she said. "There's so much I've got to tell you. Come on to my room where we can be alone together."

Without another word, Spence allowed the elfin little woman to lead him away.

THERE IS NO natural day/night cycle on Titan. Ten times farther from the Sun than Earth is, Saturn's major moon is always in gloomy twilight, at best. Usually its murky, clouded atmosphere even blots out the pale light from Saturn itself.

The university base kept Greenwich Mean Time. The lights in the windowless base's corridors and public areas dimmed at 2000 hours and went down to a "night" equivalent at 2200, then came up to "morning" at 0700.

Jade and Spence had no way of knowing the time. He had purposely put his shaving kit in front of the dorm room's digital clock, so that from the bed they could not see it. The only light in the room was from the video window, which they had set on views of the methane sea up on the surface: shadowy, muted, almost formless.

Jade told Spence about all her discoveries, and the pain that they brought. He seemed utterly surprised when she explained that she was probably Sam Gunn's daughter.

"Talk about kismet," he whispered low. "For both of us."

"If Sam were alive he could give the bride away," Jade said.

"And then be my best man." Spence chuckled softly in the shadows. "Just like him to turn the ordinary rules upside down."

They made love again, languidly, unhurriedly. They slept and then made love once more. And talked. Talked of the past, of the wondrous ways that lives can intertwine, of the surprises and sheer luck—good or bad—that can determine a person's fate. Talked of the pain one person can inflict on another without even knowing it. Talked of the happiness that can be had when two people click just right, as they had done.

Suddenly a new question popped into Jade's mind. "How many children do you have?" she asked. "Am I going to be a stepmother?"

In the darkened room she could barely see him shake his head. "Never stayed married long enough to have kids. But now . . ." His voice drifted into silence.

"I want babies. Lots of them."

"Me too," he said. "At least two."

"A boy and a girl."

"Right."

"And then maybe two more."

He laughed softly. "Maybe we ought to have twins."

"That would be more efficient, wouldn't it?"

"Want a big wedding? The main chapel at Selene and all the trimmings?"

Jade shook her head. "I never even thought about it. No, I don't think I know enough people to invite."

"My parents are gone, but we could ask your adoptive mother to come up."

"No!" Jade snapped. "She abandoned me. I haven't seen her for seventeen years. Let it stay that way."

"But she's the only kin you have."

She peered at the video window, the murky gloom of the methane sea. "I have family. Lots of family. Monica Bianco and Zach Bonner and Felix Sanchez. Frederick Mohammed Malone. Rick Darling. Elverda Apacheta. The owner of the Pelican Bar. They're my family. They'd come to Selene for my wedding, if I asked them to."

Spence said, "And here I thought you were an orphan."

"Not anymore," Jade answered, surprised at the reality of it. I'm not alone, she told herself. I have friends all across the solar system now. And a man who loves me.

"I'm pretty old for you," Spence said in the darkness. "Hell, if Sam really is your father, I'm a year or two older than he is."

"Would you be embarrassed to have a wife young enough to be your daughter?" she asked, half teasing, half fearful of his answer.

"Embarrassed? Hell no! Every guy my age will eat his heart out with envy the minute he meets you."

Jade laughed, relieved.

"But there's you to think about," he said, turning toward her in the bed. "How're you going to feel, tied to an old fart like me when you're so young? There's plenty of stories about old men with young wives. . . ."

"Old stories," Jade quickly said. "Stories from ancient times. You're as young and vigorous as Sir Lancelot was, and you'll stay that way for another thirty or forty years, at least, thanks to modern medicine."

He propped himself on one elbow and, with his other hand, traced a finger from her lips to her chin, down her throat and the length of her body. Jade felt her skin tingle at his touch.

"Well," he said, quite seriously, "I'm sure going to keep abreast of all the research going on in the field of aging and rejuvenation."

Jade burst out laughing and grabbed for him. They made love again and then drifted back to sleep.

It was the phone buzzer that awoke Jade. She blinked once, twice, coming out of the fog, suddenly panicked that she had been dreaming. Then she felt the warmth of Spence's body next to hers and heard him snoring softly, almost like the purr of a contented cat.

Smiling, she groped in the dark for the oblong box that controlled the wall screen. Without turning on any lights she pecked at the keys until the scene of the methane sea was replaced by bold yellow lettering:

URGENT CALL FROM PROF. GOODMAN.

Jade had to turn on her bedside lamp to see the control wand well enough to tap out the command that put Goodman on the video window without activating the wall camera that would let him see her.

Spence stirred groggily. "Whassamatter?"

"I don't know," she said.

Goodman was apparently in the communications center, hunched over a technician who was sitting at one of the consoles. Display screens covered the wall behind him, no two of them showing the same picture.

The professor was scowling fiercely. Or was his expression one of fear? Or even utter surprise, shock? Jade could not tell.

"Professor Goodman? This is Jade."

"Oh!" He jumped back slightly, as if pricked by a hot needle. "There's no video."

"I know. You have an urgent message for me?"

He bobbed his head up and down so hard that a lock of his curly hair flopped in front of his eyes. Brushing it back, he broke into a strange, toothy smile that just might have been a grimace of pain.

"It just came in . . . from the automated station at Einstein. . . ."

"Einstein? The black hole?"

"Yes. No video, of course. But—well, listen for yourself."

A long, low bass note, throbbing slightly, like the last distant echo of faraway thunder or the rumble of a torch ship's engines.

Spence sat up in the bed beside Jade. "What the hell is that?" he whispered.

"What is it?" Jade asked Goodman's image on the video screen.

The professor looked startled all over again. "Oh! Excuse me. In my haste I activated the raw data chip. Here—here's the same message, but time-compressed and computer-enhanced."

". . . you wouldn't believe what these guys can do! It's fantastic!"

Sam Gunn's voice!

Jade felt her heart clutch in her chest. "What is that?" she blurted.

"It's Sam!" Goodman almost yelled. "Sam! He's on his way back! He's coming out of the black hole!"

"That's impossible," Spence said, his voice hollow.

"I know! But he's doing it," Professor Goodman answered, oblivious to the fact that he was now speaking to a man's voice.

"He's alive?" Jade asked.

"Yes! Yes!" Goodman seemed ecstatic. "He found aliens on the other side of the black hole. An intelligent extraterrestrial species! They've provided him with the means to come back through the space-time warp!"

"*Sacre dieu,*" Jade breathed.

"He's alive and coming back to us!" Goodman was almost capering around the comm center now. "He's discovered intelligent extraterrestrial life. It's a miracle. Two miracles! Miraculous, the whole thing is miraculous!"

"The time distortion," Jade asked. "How long will it take before Sam is back with us?"

Goodman sobered, but only slightly. "We're working on that. Trying to get a Doppler fix on the raw data. It's only a rough estimate, but from what we've got now I'd say that Sam will pop out of the event horizon in another twenty to twenty-five years."

"Years?" Spence gasped.

"He's been gone for more than fifteen," Goodman said. Then he fell to musing. "Maybe there's a symmetry here. Maybe it'll take him exactly as long to return as it did to go through the other way. Still, it'll be fifteen years, at least. Unless . . ."

Jade turned to Spence and clutched him by the shoulders. "He's alive! Sam's alive!"

"And on his way back. The little SOB is coming back to us."

"And he's met intelligent aliens."

"Holy cow," said Spence, fervently.

TWO DAYS LATER Jade and Spence stood at the observation bay of the torch ship as it sped away from Titan, heading back toward civilization and the Earth-Moon system.

Holding one arm protectively around the tiny young woman he loved, Johansen pointed with his free hand: "There's Jupiter, the big bright one. And Mars, the smaller red star, down to your left."

Jade nestled into the crook of his arm, rested her head against his chest. "And Earth? Can we see Earth?"

"Yep. Kind of faint at this distance, but it still looks distinctly blue. See it, out there to the left of Jupiter."

Jade saw the distant blue speck and knew that her mother lay buried there. And there was another woman on Earth, Jade realized, still alive. But for how long? The one thing she had learned in the past year or so was that life surges along, always changing, whether you want it to or not. Nothing remains the same.

"Spence?" she asked, turning to look up into his face. "Would you mind if we went down to Earth? Just for a few days."

"Earth? I thought you couldn't. . . ."

"I can wear an exoskeleton for a few days. And attach myself to a heart pump."

"But why?"

"My adoptive mother lives in Quebec. I want to see her. I want to tell her that I understand why she had to leave me."

"I thought you hated her."

"I thought so, too. Maybe I did. But I don't anymore. I can't. Not anymore."

He gazed down into her lovely green eyes, knowing that he could not deny her anything.

"Couldn't you speak with her on a video link? It's just as good, almost."

Jade shook her head gently. "No. This has to be in person. For real. Flesh to flesh."

He shrugged. "I might need an exoskeleton myself. Been a long time since I faced a full g."

The ship was accelerating at just under one-sixth gravity. They had weeks of leisure ahead of them. Solar News was planning an elaborate special series on Sam Gunn, now that the news of his return had broken. Raki had promised Jade that she would narrate the entire series and be the on-camera star. Her career was assured, even though she had carefully withheld the information that she was probably Sam Gunn's daughter.

"Will you go out to the black hole for the show?" Spence asked.

"No," said Jade. "We can record that with the remote cameras already on station at Einstein and patch me into the scene. There's not much to see, really. No point going out there until Sam's about to emerge, and he won't be coming out for another fifteen or twenty years."

"But he's on his way back."

"I wonder if he's aged? Maybe I'll be his age when he comes out."

Spence let a little grin show on his face.

"It's so like Sam," Jade went on. "He has the whole solar system in a commotion. Intelligent alien life! All these years the astronomers have been searching and Sam's the one to find them."

Spence made a sound that might have been a barely suppressed laugh.

Jade took no notice of it. "The scientists, the politicians, the *military*—they're all in an uproar. To say nothing of the world's religious leaders."

Spence made no reply.

"Well," Jade said, with a sigh, "at least we have fifteen or twenty years to get ready for it."

"Maybe," Spence said at last.

She looked sharply at him. "What do you mean?"

"I don't know for sure," he replied. "But there's a strange flavor to all this."

Jade knit her brows.

"I mean," said Spence, "Sam disappears while a shipload of lawyers are on their way to strip him naked. Then fifteen years later he pops up again claiming he's met intelligent extraterrestrial creatures."

"You don't think. . . . !"

"Before we left Titan I used the university library access system to look up the status of all the lawsuits filed against Sam. The statute of limitations runs out on the last one next year."

"But the signals from the black hole!"

"He's Sam Gunn, honey. He's been hiding out *someplace* for the past fifteen years. Maybe he really did fall into a black hole." Spence pulled her tighter and gazed out at the wide starry universe. "I wouldn't put any money on it, though."

She smiled up at him. "And you claim to be his friend."

"I knew Sam pretty well. I wouldn't put *anything* past him."

"He couldn't have! It just isn't possible."

Spence grinned and looked out at the stars again. "He's Sam Gunn, honey. Unlimited."

Reviews

SAM GUNN BIO
IS SMASH HIT

Amid rumors that he's not dead after all, Solar News's biographical series about Sam Gunn has swept the ratings across the solar system.

Produced by neophyte Jane Inconnu, of Selene, the biography is told through the voices of men and women who knew Sam Gunn over the many years of his exploits on Earth and in space.

Widely regarded as an adventurer who operated on the ragged edge of the law, Sam Gunn . . .

—*HOLLYWOOD INTERPLANETARY*

THE LITTLE GIANT:
THE *SAM GUNN* SAGA

The public loves success stories, and none more than the saga of an ordinary person who struggles against giant corporations and government bureaucracies—and wins. This accounts, no doubt, for the wild success of Solar News's biographical series on space entrepreneur Sam Gunn.

Widely reviled during his lifetime as a con man, a womanizer, and an out-and-out crook, the Sam Gunn depicted in Solar's biopic series comes across as daring, sharp-witted and, yes, lovable. His adventures span the solar system, from Earth out beyond Pluto. . . .

—*NEW YORK TIMES–DAILY NEWS*

SAM GUNN SERIES "A FRAUD"
SAYS CORPORATE MAGNATE

"Sam Gunn was not the daring Robin Hood he's depicted to be on Solar News's series," claims Pierre D'Argent, CEO of Rockledge Industries, Inc.

"He was a conniving little schemer who wouldn't stop at anything, including blackmail, to get what he wanted."

Mr. D'Argent, who had tangled with Mr. Gunn several times in the past, hinted that Rockledge may take legal action against Solar News for defamation, libel and fraud.

Asked what he thought of the rumors that Mr. Gunn is returning to Earth, Mr. D'Argent said only, "God help us!"

—*WALL STREET JOURNAL*

NOVICE PRODUCER
WINS EMMY

Jane Avril Inconnu, producer of the smash-hit series *Sam Gunn,* won the Emmy Award for Best Producer of a Nonfiction Series at last night's awards ceremony in Beijing.

Wearing a cermet exoskeleton because she is unaccustomed to the full gravity of Earth, Ms. Inconnu, who recently married former astronaut Spencer Johansen, was overcome with emotion as she accepted the award. . . .

—*ALL CHINA NEWS SERVICE*

IS SAM GUNN DEAD?
WAS HE EVER?

With all the hype raised by the Solar News biography of Sam Gunn, the question of his alleged death has come to the forefront of the public's attention.

According to reports, Gunn was sucked into a mini–black hole in the Kuiper Belt, beyond the orbit of Pluto. It was widely regarded as a one-way journey: either Gunn was crushed by the immense gravitational tidal forces of the black hole, or he was propelled into a different space-time dimension, forever separated from our own continuum.

But rumors are flying that Gunn is on his way back! Either he has found a way to return through the black hole, or he never fell into it in the first place. Physicists, astronomers—and lawyers—are debating the possibilities hotly.

Former U.S. Senator and Associate Justice of the International Court Jill Meyers, who was once an astronaut and worked with Gunn, has outfitted a fusion torch ship to go to the Kuiper Belt and meet Sam as he returns.

—*SELENE GAZETTE*

Torch Ship *Hermes*

THE TWO WOMEN WERE SITTING ALONE IN THE COMFORT-
able lounge aboard the fusion torch ship as it accelerated at a half-*g* toward the outer reaches of the solar system.

Jade felt mildly uncomfortable at the gravity load, three times what she
was accustomed to on the Moon, but the medics had assured her that her
bones could stand the strain—although not much more.

Jill Meyers looked startlingly like Sam Gunn, Jade thought: short, almost elfin in stature, with a plain round face and a snub nose sprinkled
with freckles. But her eyes were a clear and steady tawny gold, and she
wore her straight mousy-brown hair shoulder length.

"I really appreciate your inviting me to make this trip with you," Jade
began.

Meyers shrugged lightly. "You've earned it. I watched your entire series,
beginning to end. I don't remember when I've laughed so much—and
cried, too."

"I'm glad you liked it."

"You really captured Sam, Ms. Inconnu."

"Please call me Jade."

"Good. And I'm Jill."

Jade had been stunned by Meyers's invitation to accompany her on
this flight to the Kuiper Belt. It had come as she was leaving the Emmy
ceremonies in Beijing and starting back to Selene. Does she know that
Sam might be my father? Jade asked herself immediately. She reasoned
that Jill Meyers didn't know, couldn't know. Sam himself didn't know it.
Still, she wondered.

"Your quarters are satisfactory?" Meyers asked her.

"Completely! Spence says it's the best honeymoon suite he's ever seen."

Meyers laughed graciously and Jade figured she had no idea how many
honeymoon suites Spence had actually used.

"So what can I tell you about Sam that you don't already know?"

Jade clicked her belt recorder and pretended to think about the question for a few moments. Then she answered, "You were involved when Sam tried to sue the Pope, weren't you?"

"More than that, Jade. Much more than that. After all, I knew Sam back in the days when we were both astronauts working for the old NASA."

"Just how old is Sam?"

"His age? Well, Sam must be just about my own age. Never mind what that is. Suffice to say we've both been around a long time. And neither of us is anywhere near finished yet. I never did believe that he died out at that mini–black hole beyond Pluto's orbit. Not Sam.

"That's why I'm riding out there. He promised to marry me, even though I haven't seen the little sonofagun in almost twenty years."

Jade looked down at her wrist computer.

"What're you doing, trying to calculate his age? Or my age? If you want me to tell you about Sam you'd better pay attention and stop the figuring. All right, Sam must be nearly a hundred, maybe more. It's hard to tell. He acts like he's twelve or thirteen, most of the time. I'm younger, of course.

"Yes, he's a womanizer. And yes, he's made and lost more fortunes than I've got freckles on my nose. So what? He's Sam Gunn, the one and only.

"You want to know about the time he tried to sue the Vatican?"

Jade nodded vigorously.

"All right. But stop trying to calculate my age!"

Acts of God

WHO ELSE BUT SAM GUNN WOULD SUE THE POPE?

I'd known Sam since we were both astronauts with NASA, riding the old shuttle to the original Mac Dac Shack—but sue the *Pope*? That's Sam.

At first I thought it was a joke, or at least a grandstand stunt. Then I began to figure that it was just the latest of Sam's ploys to avoid marrying me. I'd been chasing him for years, subtly at first but once I'd retired from the Senate, quite openly.

It got to be a game that we both enjoyed. At least, I did. It was fun to see the panicky look on Sam's Huck Finn face when I would bring up the subject of marriage.

"Aw, come on, Jill," he would say. "I'd make a lousy husband. I like women too much to marry one of 'em."

I would smile my most Sphinxlike smile and softly reply, "You're not getting any younger, Sam. You need a good woman to look after you."

And he'd arrange to disappear. I swear, his first expedition out to the Asteroid Belt was as much to get away from me as to find asteroids for mining. He came close to getting himself killed then, but he created the new industry of asteroid mining—and just about wiped out the metals and minerals markets in most of the resource-exporting nations on Earth. That didn't win him any friends, especially among the governments of those nations and the multinational corporations that fed off them.

I still had connections into the Senate's intelligence committee in those days, and I knew that at least three southern hemisphere nations had put out contracts on Sam's life. To say nothing of the big multinationals. It was my warnings that saved his scrawny little neck.

Sam lost the fortune he made on asteroid mining, of course. He'd made and lost fortunes before that; it was nothing new to him. He just went into other business lines; you couldn't keep him down for long.

He was running a space freight operation when he sued the Pope. And the little sonofagun *knew* that I'd be on the International Court of Justice panel that heard his suit.

"Senator Meyers, may I have a word with you?" My Swedish secretary looked very upset. He was always very formal, always addressed me by my old honorific, the way a governor of a state would be called "Governor" even if he's long retired or in jail or whatever.

"What's the matter, Hendrick?" I asked him.

Hendrick was in his office in The Hague, where the World Court is headquartered. I was alone in my house in Nashua, sipping at a cup of hot chocolate and watching the winter's first snow sifting through the big old maples on my front lawn, thinking that we were going to have a white Christmas despite the greenhouse warming. Until Hendrick's call came through, that is. Then I had to look at his distressed face on my wall display screen.

"We have a very unusual . . . situation here," said Hendrick, struggling to keep himself calm. "The chief magistrate has asked me to call you."

From the look on Hendrick's face, I thought somebody must be threatening to unleash nuclear war, at least.

"A certain . . . person," Hendrick said, with conspicuous distaste, "has entered a suit against the Vatican."

"The Vatican!" I nearly dropped my hot chocolate. "What's the basis of the suit? Who's entering it?"

"The basis is apparently over some insurance claims. The litigant is an American citizen acting on behalf of the nation of Ecuador. His name is," Hendrick looked down to read from a document that I could not see on the screen, "Samuel S. Gunn, Esquire."

"Sam Gunn?" I did drop the cup; hot chocolate spilled all over my white corduroy slacks and the hooked rug my great grandmother had made with her very own arthritic fingers.

SAM WAS OPERATING out of Ecuador in those days. Had himself a handsome suite of offices in the presidential palace, no less. I drove through the slippery snow to Boston and took the first Clipper out; had to use my ex-Senatorial *and* World Court leverage to get a seat amidst all the jovial holiday travelers.

I arrived in Quito half an hour later. Getting through customs with my one hastily packed travel bag took longer than the flight. At least Boston and Quito are in the same time zone; I didn't have to battle jet lag.

"Jill!" Sam smiled when I swept into his office, but the smile looked artificial to me. "What brings you down here?"

People say Sam and I look enough alike to be siblings. Neither Sam nor I believe it. He's short, getting pudgy, keeps his rusty-red hair cropped short. Shifty eyes, if you ask me. Mine are a steady brown. I'm just about his height and the shape of my face is sort of round, more or less like his. We both have a sprinkle of freckles across our noses. But there all resemblance—physical and otherwise—definitely ends.

"You know damned well what brings me down here," I snapped, tossing my travel bag on one chair and plopping myself in the other, right in front of his desk.

Sam had gotten to his feet and started around the desk, but one look at the blood in my eye and he retreated back to his own swivel chair. He had built a kind of platform behind the desk to make himself seem taller than he really was.

He put on his innocent little boy face. "Honest, Jill, I haven't the foggiest idea of why you're here. Christmas vacation?"

"Don't be absurd."

"You didn't bring a justice of the peace with you, did you?"

I had to laugh. Every time I asked myself why in the ever-loving blue-eyed world I wanted to marry Sam Gunn, the answer always came down to that. Sam made me laugh. After a life of grueling work as an astronaut and then the tensions and power trips of Washington politics, Sam was the one man in the world who could make me see the funny side of everything. Even when he was driving me to distraction, we both had grins on our faces.

"I should have brought a shotgun," I said, trying to get serious.

"You wouldn't do that," he said, with that impish grin of his. Then he added a worried, "Would you?"

"Where did you get the bright idea of suing the Vatican?"

"Oh, that!" Sam visibly relaxed, eased back in his chair and swiveled around from side to side a little.

"Yes, that," I snapped. "What kind of a brain-dead nincompoop idea is that?"

"Nincompoop?" He looked almost insulted. "Been a long time since I heard that one."

"What's going on, Sam? You know a private citizen can't sue a sovereign state."

"Sure I know that. *I'm* not suing the Vatican. The sovereign nation of Ecuador is suing. I'm merely acting as their representative, in my position as CEO of Ecuador National Space Systems."

I sank back in my chair, thinking fast. "The Vatican isn't a party to the International Court of Justice's protocols. Your suit is null and void, no matter who the plaintiff may be."

"Christ, Jill, you sound like a lawyer."

"You can't sue the Vatican."

Sam sighed and reached out one hand toward the keyboard on his desk. He tapped at it with one finger, then pointed to the display screen on the wall.

The screen filled with print, all legalese of the densest kind. But I recognized it. The Treaty of Katmandu, the one that ended the three-way biowar between India, China and Pakistan. The treaty that established the International Peacekeeping Force and gave it global mandatory powers.

" 'All nations are required to submit grievances to the International Court of Justice,' " Sam quoted from the treaty, " 'whether they are signatories to this instrument or not.' "

I knew it as well as he did. "That clause is in there to prevent nations from using military force," I said.

Sam gave a careless shrug. "Regardless of why it's in there, it's there. The World Court has jurisdiction over every nation in the world. Even the Vatican."

"The Vatican didn't sign the treaty."

"Doesn't matter. The treaty went into effect when two-thirds of the membership of the UN signed it," Sam said. "And any nation that doesn't obey it gets the Peacekeepers in their face."

"Sam, you *can't* sue the Pope!"

He just gave me his salesman's grin. "The nation of Ecuador has filed suit against the Vatican State. The World Court has to hear the case. It's not just my idea, Jill—it's the law."

The little sonofabitch was right.

I EXPECTED SAM would invite me to dinner. He did, and then some. Sam wouldn't hear of my staying at a hotel; he had already arranged for a guest suite for me in the presidential palace. Which gave the lie to his supposed surprise when I had arrived at his office, of course. He knew I was coming. It sort of surprised me, though. I wouldn't have thought that he'd want me so close to him. He had always managed to slip away when I'd pursued him before. This time he ensconced me in presidential splendor in the same building where he was sleeping.

I should have been suspicious. I've got to admit that, instead, I sort of half thought that maybe Sam was getting tired of running away from me. Maybe he wanted me to be near him.

He did. But for his own reasons, of course.

When we ate dinner that evening it was with the President of Ecuador himself: Carlos Pablo Francisco Esperanza de Rivera. He was handsome, haughty and kind of pompous. Wore a military uniform with enough braid to buckle the knees of a Ukrainian weightlifter. Very elegant silver hair. A noble profile with a distinguished Castilian nose.

"It is an extremely serious matter," he told me, in Harvard-accented English. "We do not sue the head of Holy Mother Church for trivial reasons."

The fourth person at the table was a younger man, Gregory Molina. He was dark and intense, the smoldering Latino rebel type. Sam introduced him as the lawyer who was handling the case for him.

We sat at a sumptuous table in a small but elegant dining room. Crystal chandelier, heavy brocade napkins, damask tablecloth, gold-rimmed dishes and tableware of solid silver. Lavish Christmas trimmings on the windows; big holiday bows and red-leafed poinsettias decorating the dining table.

Ecuador was still considered a poor nation, although as the Earth-bound anchor of Sam's space operations there was a lot of money flowing in. Most of it must be staying in the presidential palace, I thought.

Once the servants had discreetly taken away our fish course and deposited racks of roast lamb before us, I said, "The reason I came here is to see if this matter can be arbitrated without actually going to court."

"Of course!" said *El Presidente*. "We would like nothing better."

Sam cocked a brow. "If we can settle this out of court, fine. I don't really want to sock the Pope if we can avoid it."

Molina nodded, but his burning eyes told me he'd like nothing better than to get the Pope on the witness stand.

"I glanced through your petition papers on the flight down here," I said. "I don't see what your insurance claims have to do with the Vatican."

Sam put his fork down. "Over the past year and a half, Ecuador National Space Systems has suffered three major accidents: a booster was struck by lightning during launch operations and forced to ditch in the ocean; we were lucky that none of the crew was killed."

"Why were you launching into stormy weather?" I asked.

"We weren't!" Sam placed a hand over his heart, like a little kid swearing he was telling the truth. "Launch pad weather was clear as a bell. The lightning strike came at altitude, over the Andes, out of an empty sky."

"A rare phenomenon," said Molina. "The scientists said it was a freak of nature."

Sam resumed, "Then four months later one of our unmanned freight carriers was hit by a micrometeor and exploded while it was halfway to our lunar mining base. We lost the vehicle and its entire cargo."

"Seventy million dollars, U.S.," Molina said.

President de Rivera's eyes filled with tears.

"And just six months ago a lunar quake collapsed our mine in the ring-wall of Aristarchus."

I hadn't known that. "Was anyone killed?"

"The operation was pretty much automated. A couple technicians were injured," Sam said. "But we lost three mining robots."

"At sixteen million dollars apiece," Molina added.

The president dabbed at his eyes with his napkin.

"I don't see what any of this has to do with the Vatican," I said.

The corners of Sam's mouth turned down. "Our mother-loving insurance carrier refused to cover any of those losses. Claimed they were all acts of God, not covered by our accident policy."

I hadn't drunk any of the wine in the crystal goblet before me, so there was no reason for me to be slow on the uptake. Yet I didn't see the association with the Vatican.

"Insurance policies always have an Acts of God clause," I said.

"Okay," Sam said, dead serious. "So if our losses were God's fault, how do we get Him to pay what He owes us?"

"Him?" I challenged.

"Her," Sam snapped back. "It. Them. I don't care."

President de Rivera steepled his long, lean fingers before his lips and said, "For the purposes of our discussion, and in keeping with ancient tradition, let us agree to refer to God as Him." And he smiled his handsome smile at me.

"Okay," I said, wondering how much he meant by that smile. "We'll call Her Him."

Molina snickered and Sam grinned. *El Presidente* looked puzzled; either he didn't appreciate my humor or he didn't understand it.

Sam got back to his point. "If God's responsible for our losses, then we want to get God to pay for them. That's only fair."

"It's silly," I said. "How are you—"

Sam's sudden grin cut me off. "The Pope is considered to be God's personal representative on Earth, isn't he?"

"Only by the Roman Catholics."

"Of which there are more than one billion in the world," Molina said.

"The largest religion on Earth," said the president.

"It's more than that," Sam maintained. "Nobody else claims to be the personal representative of God. Only the Pope, among the major religious leaders. One of his titles is 'the vicar of Christ,' isn't it?"

The two men nodded in unison.

"The Catholics believe that Christ is God, don't they?" Sam asked.

They nodded again.

"And Christ—God Herself—personally made St. Peter His representative here on Earth."

More nods.

"And the Pope is Peter's descendent, with all the powers and responsibilities that Peter had. Right?"

"Exactly so," murmured *El Presidente*.

"So if we want to sue God, we go to his personal representative, the Pope." Sam gave a self-satisfied nod.

Only Sam Gunn would think of such a devious, convoluted scheme.

"We cannot sue the Pope personally," Molina pointed out, as earnest as a missionary, "because he is technically and legally the head of a state: the Vatican. A sovereign cannot be sued except by his own consent; that is ancient legal tradition."

"So you want to sue the state he heads," I said.

"The Vatican. Yes."

"And since an individual or corporation can't sue a state, the nation of Ecuador is entering the suit."

Sam smiled like a Jack-o'-lantern. "Now you've got it."

I PICKED MY way through the rest of the dinner in stunned silence. I couldn't believe that Sam would go through with something so ridiculous, yet there he was sitting next to the president of Ecuador and a fervent young lawyer who seemed totally intent on hauling the Pope before the World Court.

I wondered if the fact that the present Pope was an American—the first U.S. cardinal to be elected Pope—had anything to do with the plot hatching inside Sam's shifty, twisted, Machiavellian brain.

After the servants had cleared off all the dishes and brought a tray of liqueur bottles, I finally gathered enough of my wits to say, "There's got to be a way to settle this out of court."

"Half a billion would do it," Sam said.

He hadn't touched any of the after-dinner drinks and had only sipped at his wine during dinner. So he wasn't drunk.

"Half a billion?"

"A quarter billion in actual losses," Molina interjected, "and a quarter billion in punitive damages."

I almost laughed in his face. "You want to punish God?"

"Why not?" The look on his face made me wonder what God had ever done to him to make him so angry.

President de Rivera took a silver cigarette case from his heavily braided jacket.

"Please don't smoke," I said.

He looked utterly shocked.

"It's bad for your lungs and ours," I added.

Sighing, he slipped the case back into his pocket. "You sound like my daughter."

"Thank you," I said, and made a polite smile for him.

"Do you think we can settle out of court?" Sam asked.

"Where's the Pope going to get half a billion?" I snapped.

Sam shrugged good-naturedly. "Sell some artwork, maybe?"

I pushed my chair from the table. Molina and the president shot to their feet. De Rivera was closer to me; he held my chair while I stood up.

"Allow me to escort you to your room," he said.

"Thank you so much," I replied.

Sam, still seated, gave me a suspicious look. But he didn't move from his chair. The president gave me his arm and I placed my hand on it, just like we were Cinderella and the Prince at the ball. As we walked regally out of the dining room I glanced back at Sam. He was positively glowering at me.

We took an intimately small elevator up two flights. There was barely room enough in it for the two of us. De Rivera wasn't much taller than I, but he kept bobbing up on his toes as the elevator inched its way up. I wondered if it was some sort of exercises for his legs, until I realized that he was peeking down the front of my blouse! I had dressed casually. Modestly. And there wasn't much for him to see there anyway. But he kept peeking.

I took his proffered arm once again as he walked me to my door. The wide upstairs corridor was lined with portraits, all men, and furniture that looked antique and probably very valuable.

He opened the door to my suite, but before he could step inside I maneuvered myself into the doorway to block him.

"Thank you so much for the excellent dinner," I said, smiling my kiss-off smile.

"I believe you will find an excellent champagne already chilled in your sitting room," said the president.

I gave him the regretful head shake. "It's much too late at night for me to start drinking champagne."

"Ah, but the night is young, my lovely one."

Lovely? Me? I was as plain as a pie pan and I knew it. But *El Presidente* was acting as if I was a ravishing beauty. Did he think he could win me over to his side by taking me to bed? I've heard of tampering with a judge but this was ridiculous.

"I'm really very tired, Mr. President."

"Carlos," he whispered.

"I'm *really* very tired, Carlos."

"Then it would be best for you to go directly to bed, would it not?"

I was wondering if I'd have to knee him in the groin when Sam's voice bounced cheerfully down the corridor. "Hey Jill, I just remembered that there was another so-called act of God that cost us ten-twenty mill or so."

The president stiffened and stepped back from me. Sam came strolling down the corridor with that imp's grin spread across his round face.

"Lemme tell you about it," he said.

"I'm very tired and I'm going to sleep," I said firmly. "Goodnight, Sam. And goodnight, Carlos."

As I shut the door I saw Carlos glaring angrily at Sam. Maybe I've broken up their alliance, I thought.

Then I realized that Sam had come upstairs to rescue me from Carlos. He was jealous! And he cared enough about me to risk his scheme against the Pope.

Maybe he did love me after all. At least a little.

WE TRIED TO settle the mess out of court. And we might have done it, too, if it hadn't been for the other side's lawyer. And the assassins.

All parties concerned wanted to keep the suit as quiet as possible. Dignity. Good manners. We were talking about the Pope, for goodness' sake. Maintain a decent self-control and don't go blabbing to the media.

All the parties agreed to that approach. Except Sam. The instant the World Court put his suit on its arbitration calendar, Sam went roaring off to the news people. All of them, from BBC and CNN to the sleaziest tabloids and paparazzi.

Sam was on global television more than the hourly weather reports.

He pushed Santa Claus out of the headlines. You couldn't punch up a news report on your screen without seeing Sam's Jack-o'-lantern face grinning at you.

"I think that if God gets blamed for accidents and natural disasters, the people who claim to represent God ought to be willing to pay the damages," Sam said gleefully, over and again. "It's only fair."

The media went into an orgy of excitement. Interviewers doggedly tracked down priests, ministers, nuns, lamas, imams, mullahs, gurus of every stripe and sect. Christmas was all but forgotten; seven "holiday specials" were unceremoniously bumped from the entertainment networks so they could put on panel discussions of Sam's suit against the Pope instead.

Philosophers became as commonplace on the news as athletes. Professors of religion and ethics got to be regulars on talk shows all over the world. The Dalai Lama started his own TV series.

It was a bonanza for lawyers. People everywhere started suing God—or the nearest religious establishment. An unemployed mechanic in Minnesota sued his local Lutheran Church after he slipped on the ice while fishing on a frozen lake. An English woman sued the Archbishop of Canterbury when her cat got itself run over by a delivery truck. Ford Motor Company sued the Southern Baptists because a ship carrying electronic parts from Korea sank in a typhoon and stopped Ford's assembly operation in Alabama.

Courts either refused to hear the suits, on the grounds that they lacked jurisdiction over You-Know-Who, or held them up pending the World Court's decision. One way or another, Sam was going to set a global precedent.

The Pope remained stonily silent. He virtually disappeared from the public eye, except for a few ceremonial masses at St. Peter's and his regular Sunday blessing of the crowds that he gave from his usual balcony. There were even rumors that he wouldn't say the traditional Christmas Eve mass at St. Peter's.

He even stopped giving audiences to visitors—after the paparazzi and seventeen network reporters infiltrated an audience that was supposed to be for victims of a flood in the Philippines. Eleven photographers and seven Filipinos were arrested after the Swiss Guard broke up the scuffle that the news people started.

The Vatican spokesman was Cardinal Hagerty, a dour-faced Irishman with the gift of gab, a veteran of the Curia's political infighting who stonewalled the media quite effectively by sticking to three points:

One: Sam's suit was frivolous. He never mentioned Ecuador at all; he always pinpointed the notorious Sam Gunn as the culprit.

Two: This attempt to denigrate God was sacrilegious and doomed to failure. Cardinal Hagerty never said it in so many words, but he gave the clear impression that in the good old days the Church would have taken Sam by the scruff of his atheistic little neck and burned him at the stake.

Three: The Vatican simply did not have any money to spend on malicious lawsuits. Every penny in the Vatican treasury went to running the Church and helping the poor.

The uproar was global. All across the world people were being treated to "experts" debating the central question of whether or not God should be—or could be—held responsible for the disasters that are constantly assailing us.

There were bloody riots in Calcutta after an earthquake killed several hundred people, with the Hindus blaming Allah and the Moslems blaming Kali or Rama or any of the other hundreds of Hindu gods and goddesses. The Japanese parliament solemnly declared that the Emperor, even though revered as divine, was not to be held responsible for natural disasters. Dozens of evangelist ministers in the U.S. damned Sam publicly in their TV broadcasts and as much as said that anyone who could stop the little bugger would be a hero in the eyes of God.

"What we need," yowled one TV evangelist, "is a new Michael the Archangel, who will smite this son of Satan with a fiery sword!"

In Jerusalem, the chief rabbi and grand mufti stunned the world by appearing in public side-by-side to castigate Sam and call upon all good Jews and Moslems to accept whatever God or Allah sends their way.

"Humility and acceptance are the hallmarks of the true believers," they jointly told their flocks.

My sources on the Senate intelligence committee told me that the chief rabbi added privately, "May He Who Is Nameless remove this evil man from our sight."

The Grand Mufti apparently went further. He promised eternal paradise for anyone who martyred himself assassinating Sam. In a burst of modernism he added, "Even if the assassin is a woman, paradise awaits her." I thought he must have been either pretty damned furious at Sam or pretty damned desperate.

Officially, the Vatican refused to defend itself. The Pope would not even recognize the suit, and the Curia—which had been at odds with the new American Pope—backed him on this issue one hundred percent.

Even though they knew that the World Court could hear the suit in their absence and then send in the Peacekeepers to enforce its decision, they felt certain that the Court would never send armed troops against the Vatican. It would make a pretty picture, our tanks and jet bombers against their Swiss Guardsmen. Heat-seeking missiles against medieval pikes. In St. Peter's, yet.

But the insurance conglomerate that carried the policy for Ecuador National Space Systems decided that it would step forward and represent the Vatican in the pretrial hearing.

"We've got to put a cork in this bottle right away," said their president to me. "It's a disgrace, a shameful disgrace."

His name was Frank Banner, and he normally looked cheerful and friendly, probably from the days when he was a salesman who made his living from sweet-talking corporate officials into multimillion-dollar insurance policies. We had known each other for years; Frank had often testified to Senate committees—and donated generously to campaign funds, including mine.

But now he looked worried. He had flown up to Nashua to see me shortly after I returned from Quito. His usual broad smile and easygoing manner were gone; he was grim, almost angry.

"He's ruining the Christmas season," Frank grumbled.

I had to admit that it was hard to work up the usual holiday cheer with this lawsuit hanging over us.

"Look," he said, as we sipped hot toddies in my living room, "I've had my run-ins with Sam Gunn in the past, Lord knows, but this time the little pisser's gone too goddamned far. He's not just attacking the Pope, although that in itself is bad enough. He's attacking the very foundation of western civilization! That wiseassed little bastard is spitting in the eye of every God-fearing man, woman and child in the world!"

I had never seen Frank so wound up. He sounded like an old-time politician yelling from a soapbox. His face got purple and I was afraid he'd hyperventilate. I didn't argue with him; I merely snuggled deeper into my armchair and let him rant until he ran out of steam.

Finally he said, "Well, somebody's got to stand up for what's right and decent."

"I suppose so," I murmured.

"I'm assigning one of our young lawyers to act as an *amicus curiae* in your pretrial hearing."

"I'm not sure that's the proper legal term," I said.

"Well, whatever!" His face reddened again. "*Somebody's* got to protect the Pope's ass. Might as well be us."

I nodded, thinking that if Sam somehow did win his suit against the Pope it would turn the entire insurance industry upside down. *Amicus curiae* indeed.

The moment I laid eyes on the lawyer that Frank sent I knew we'd have nothing but trouble.

Her name was Josella Ecks, and she was a tall, slim, gorgeous black woman with a mind as sharp as a laser beam. Skin the color of milk chocolate. Almond-shaped eyes that I would have killed for. Long silky legs, and she didn't mind wearing slitted skirts that showed them off cunningly.

I knew Sam would go ape over her; the little juvenile delinquent always let his hormones overpower his brain.

Sure enough, Sam took one look at her and his eyes started spinning like the wheels in a slot machine. I felt myself turning seventeen shades of green. If Sam had seemed a little jealous of Carlos de Rivera, I was positively bilious with envy over Josella Ecks.

The four of us met ten days before Christmas in my formal office in the World Court building in The Hague: Sam, his lawyer Greg Molina, the delectable Ms. Ecks, and my plain old self. I settled into my desk chair, feeling shabby and miserable in a nubby tweed suit. Josella sat between the two men; when she crossed her long legs her slitted skirt fell away, revealing ankle, calf and a lot of thigh. I thought I saw steam spout out of Sam's ears.

She didn't seem to affect Greg that way, but then Gregory Molina was a married man; married to President de Rivera's daughter, no less.

"This pretrial hearing," I said, trying to put my emotions under some semblance of control, "is mandated by the International Court of Justice for the purpose of trying to come to an amicable agreement on the matter of *Ecuador v. Vatican* without the expense and publicity of an actual trial."

"Fine by me," Sam said breezily, his eyes still on the young woman sitting beside him. "As long as we can get it over with by eleven. I've gotta catch the midnight Clipper. Gotta be back at Selene City for the Christmas festivities."

I glowered at Sam. Here the future of Christianity was hanging in the balance and he was worried about a Christmas party.

Greg was more formal. His brows knitting very earnestly, he said, "The nation of Ecuador would be very much in favor of settling this case out of court." He was looking at me, not Josella. "Providing, of course, that we can arrive at a reasonable settlement."

Josella smiled as if she knew more than he did. "Our position is that a reasonable settlement would be to throw this case in the trash bin, where it belongs."

Sam sighed as if someone had told them there is no Santa Claus. "A reasonable settlement would be a half billion dollars, U.S."

Josella waggled a finger at him. I saw that her nails were done in warm pink. "Your suit is without legal basis, Mr. Gunn."

"Then why are we here, oh beauteous one?"

I resisted the urge to crown Sam with the meteoric iron paperweight on my desk. He had given it to me years earlier, and at that particular moment I really wanted to give it back to him—smack between his leering eyes.

Josella was unimpressed. Quite coolly she answered, "We are here, Mr. Gunn, because you have entered a frivolous suit against the Vatican."

Greg spoke up. "I assure you, Ms. Ecks, the nation of Ecuador is not frivolous."

"Perhaps not," she granted. "But I'm afraid that you're being led down the garden path by this unscrupulous little man."

"Little?" A vein in Sam's forehead started to throb. "Was Napoleon little? Was Steinmetz little? Did Neil Armstrong play basketball in college?"

Laughing, Josella said, "I apologize for the personal reference, Mr. Gunn. It was unprofessional of me."

"Sam."

"Mr. Gunn," she repeated.

"I still want half a bill," Sam growled.

"There isn't that much money in the entire Vatican," she said.

"Baloney. They take in a mint and a half." Sam ticked off on his fingers, "Tourists come by the millions. The Vatican prints its own stamps and currency. They're into banking and money exchange, with no internal taxes and no restrictions on importing and exporting foreign currencies. Nobody knows how much cash flows through the Vatican, but they must have the highest per capita income in the solar system."

"And it all goes to funding the Church and helping the poor."

"The hell it does! They live like kings in there," Sam growled.

"Wait," I said. "This is getting us nowhere."

Ignoring me, Sam went on, "And the Pope has *absolute* authority over all of it. He's got all the executive, legislative and judicial powers in his own hands. He's an absolute monarch, responsible to nobody!"

"Except God," Greg added.

"Right," Sam said. "The same God who owes me half a billion dollars."

I repeated, "This is getting us nowhere."

"Perhaps I can set us on a useful course," Greg said. I nodded hopefully at him.

Greg laid out Sam's case, chapter and verse. He spent nearly an hour tracing the history of the Petrine theory that is the basis for the Pope's claim to be "the vicar of Christ." Then he droned on even longer about the logic behind holding the Pope responsible for so-called acts of God.

"If we truly believe in a God who is the cause of these acts," he said, with implacable logic, "and we accept the Pope's claim to be the representative of God on Earth, then we have a firm legal, moral, and ethical basis for this suit."

"God owes me," Sam muttered.

"The contract between God and man implied by the Ten Commandments and the Scriptures," said Greg, solemnly, "must be regarded as a true contract, binding on both parties, and holding both parties responsible for their misdeeds."

"How do you know they're misdeeds?" Josella instantly rebutted. "We can't know as much as God does. Perhaps these acts of God are part of His plan for our salvation."

With an absolutely straight face, Greg said, "Then He must reveal his purposes to us. Or be held responsible for His acts in a court of law."

Josella shook her head slowly. I saw that Sam's eyes were riveted on her.

She looked at me, though, and asked, "May I present the defendant's argument, Your Honor?"

"Yes, of course."

Josella started a careful and very detailed review of the legal situation, with emphasis on the absurdity of trying to hold a person or a state responsible for acts of God.

"Mr. Gunn is attempting to interpret literally a phrase that was never so meant," she said firmly, with a faint smile playing on her lips.

Sam fidgeted in his chair, huffed and snorted as she went on and on, cool and logical, marshaling every point or precedent that would help her demolish Sam's case.

She was nowhere near finished when Sam looked at his wristwatch and said, "Look, I've got to get to Selene. Big doings there, and I'm obligated to be present for them."

"What's happening?" I asked.

"Christmas stuff. Parties. We've brought in a ballet troupe from Vancouver to do 'The Nutcracker.' Nothing that has anything to do with this legal crapola." He turned to Greg. "Why don't you two lawyers fight it out and lemme know what you decide, okay?"

Sam had to lean toward Josella to speak to Greg, but he looked right past her, as if she weren't there. And he was leaving Greg to make the decision? That wasn't like Sam at all. Was he bored by all these legal technicalities?

He got to his feet. Then a slow grin crept across his face and he said, "Unless the three of you would like to come up to Selene with me, as my guests. We could continue the hearing there."

So that was it. He wanted Josella to fly with him to the Moon. Greg and I would be excess baggage that he would dump the first chance he got.

And Josella actually smiled at him and replied, "I've never been to the Moon."

Sam's grin went ear-to-ear. "Well, come on up! This is your big chance."

"This is a pretrial hearing," I snapped, "not a tourist agency."

Just then the door burst open and four women in janitorial coveralls pushed into my office. Instead of brooms they were carrying machine pistols.

"On your feet, all of you, godless humanists!" shouted their leader, a heavyset blonde. "You are the prisoners of the Daughters of the Mother!" She spoke in English, with some sort of accent I couldn't identify. Not Dutch, and certainly not American.

I stabbed at the panic button on my phone console. Direct line to security. The blonde ignored it and hustled the four of us out into the corridor to the bank of elevators. The corridor was empty; I realized it was well past quitting time and the court's bureaucrats had cleared out precisely at four-thirty.

But security should be here, I thought. No sign of them. They must have been out Christmas shopping, too. The Daughters of the Mother pushed us into an elevator and rode up to the roof. It was dark and cold up there; the wind felt as if it came straight from the North Pole.

A tilt-rotor plane sat on the roof, its engines swiveled to their vertical position, their big propellers swinging slowly like giant scythes, making a whooshing sound that gave the keening sea wind a basso counterpoint.

"Get in, all of you." The hefty blonde prodded me with the snout of her pistol.

We marched toward the plane's hatch.

"Hey, wait a minute," Sam said, pulling his sports jacket tight across his shivering body. "I'm the guy you want; leave these others out of it. Hell, they'd just as soon shoot me as you would."

"I said all of you!" the blonde shouted.

Where was security? They couldn't be so lax as to allow a plane to land on our roof and kidnap us. They *had* to be coming to our rescue. But when?

I decided to slow us down a bit. As we approached the plane's hatch, I stumbled and went down.

"Ow!" I yelled. "My ankle!"

The big blonde wrapped an arm around my waist, hauled me off the concrete and tossed me like a sack of potatoes through the open hatch of the plane. I landed on the floor plates with a painful thump.

Sam jumped up the two-step ladder and knelt beside me. "You okay? Are you hurt?"

I sat up and rubbed my backside. "Just my dignity," I said.

Suddenly the whole roof was bathed in brilliant light and we heard the powerful throbbing of helicopter engines.

"YOU ARE SURROUNDED!" roared a bullhorn voice. "THIS IS THE POLICE. DROP YOUR WEAPONS AND SURRENDER."

I scrambled to the nearest window, Sam pressing close behind me. I could see two helicopters hovering near the edge of the roof, armored SWAT policemen pointing assault rifles at us.

"What fun," Sam muttered. "With just a little luck, we could be in the middle of a firefight."

The blonde came stumping past us, heading for the cockpit. Greg and Josella were pushed into the plane by the other three Daughters. The last one slammed the hatch shut and dogged it down.

"YOU HAVE THIRTY SECONDS TO THROW DOWN YOUR WEAPONS AND SURRENDER!" roared the police bullhorn.

"WE HAVE FOUR HOSTAGES ABOARD, INCLUDING JUSTICE MEYERS." The blonde had a bullhorn, too. "IF YOU TRY TO STOP US WE WILL SHOOT HER FIRST."

Sam patted my head. "Lucky lady."

They bellowed threats back and forth for what seemed like an eternity, but finally the police allowed the plane to take off. With us in it. There were four police helicopters, and they trailed after us as our plane lifted off the roof, swiveled its engines to their horizontal position, and then began climbing into the dark night sky. The plane was much faster than the choppers; their lights dwindled behind us and then got lost altogether in the clouds.

"The Peacekeepers must be tracking us by radar," Sam assured me. "Probably got satellite sensors watching us, too. Jet fighters out there someplace, I bet."

And then I realized he was speaking to Josella, not me.

We rode for hours in that plane, Sam jabbering across the aisle to Josella while I sat beside him, staring out the window and fuming. Greg sat on the window seat beside Josella, but as I could see from their reflections in the glass, Sam and Josella had eyes only for each other. I went beyond fuming; I would have slugged Sam if we weren't in so much trouble already.

Two of the Daughters sat at the rear of the cabin, guns in their laps. Their leader and the other one sat up front. Who was in the cockpit I never knew.

Beneath my anger at Sam I was pretty scared. These Daughters of the Mother looked like religious fanatics to me, the kind who were willing to die for their cause—and therefore perfectly willing to kill anybody else for their cause. They were out to get Sam, and they had grabbed me and the other two as well. We were hostages. Bargaining chips for the inevitable moment when the Peacekeepers came at them with everything in their arsenal.

And Sam was spending his time talking to Josella, trying to ease her fears, trying to impress her with his own courage.

"Don't worry," he told her. "It's me they want. They'll let you and the others loose as soon as they turn me over to their leader, whoever that might be."

And the others. I seethed. As far as Sam was concerned, I was just one of the others. Josella was the one he was interested in, tall and willowy and elegant. I was just a sawed-off runt with as much glamour as a fire hydrant, and pretty much the same figure.

Dawn was just starting to tinge the sky when we started to descend. I had been watching out the window during the flight, trying to puzzle out where we were heading from the position of the moon and the few stars I could see. Eastward, I was pretty certain. East and south. That was the best I could determine.

As the plane slowed down for its vertical landing, I mentally checked out the possibilities. East and south for six hours or so could put us somewhere in the Mediterranean. Italy, Spain—or North Africa.

"Where in the world have they taken us?" I half-whispered, more to myself than anyone who might answer me.

"Transylvania," Sam answered.

I gave him a killer stare. "This is no time to be funny."

"Look at my wristwatch," he whispered back at me, totally serious.

Its face showed latitude and longitude coordinates in digital readout. Sam pressed one of the studs on the watch's outer rim, and the readout spelled RUMANIA. Another touch of the stud: TRANSYLVANIA. Another: NEAREST MAJOR CITY, VARSAG.

I showed him my wristwatch. "It's got an ultrahigh-frequency transponder in it. The Peacekeepers have been tracking us ever since we left The Hague. I hope."

Sam nodded glumly. "These Mother-lovers aren't afraid of the Peacekeepers as long as they've got you for a hostage."

"There's going to be a showdown, sooner or later," I said.

Just then the plane touched down with a thump.

"Welcome," said Sam, in a Hollywood vampire accent, "to Castle Dracula."

It wasn't a castle that they took us to. It was a mine shaft.

Lord knows how long it had been abandoned. The elevator didn't work; we had to climb down, single file, on rickety wooden steps that creaked and shook with every step we took. And it was *dark* down there. And cold, the kind of damp cold that chills you to the bone. I kept glancing up at the dwindling little slice of blue sky as the Daughters coaxed us with their gun muzzles down those groaning, shuddering stairs all the way to the very bottom.

There were some dim lanterns hanging from the rough stone ceiling of the bottom gallery. We walked along in gloomy silence until we came to a steel door. It took two of the Daughters to swing it open.

The bright light made my eyes water. They pushed us into a chamber that had been turned into a rough-hewn office of sorts. At least it was warm. A big, beefy redheaded woman sat scowling at us from behind a steel desk.

"You can take their wristwatches from then now," she said to the blonde. Then she smiled at the surprise on my face. "Yes, Justice Meyers, we know all about your transponders and positioning indicators. We're not fools."

Sam stepped forward. "All right, you're a bunch of geniuses. You've captured the most-wanted man on Earth—me. Now you can let the others go and the Peacekeepers won't bother you."

"You think not?" the redhead asked, suspiciously.

"Of course not!" Sam smiled his sincerest smile. "Their job is to protect Senator Meyers, who's a judge on the World Court. They don't give a damn about me."

"You're the blasphemer, Sam Gunn?"

"I've done a lot of things in a long and eventful life," Sam said, still smiling, "but blasphemy isn't one of them."

"You don't think that what you've done is blasphemy?" The redhead's voice rose ominously. I realized that her temper was just as fiery as her hair.

"I've always treated God with respect," Sam insisted. "I respect Her so much that I expect Her to honor her debts. Unfortunately, the man in the Vatican who claims to be Her special representative doesn't think She has any sense of responsibility."

"The man in the Vatican." The redhead's lips curled into a sneer. "What does he know of the Mother?"

"That's what I say," Sam agreed fervently. "That's why I'm suing him, really."

For a moment the redhead almost bought it. She looked at Sam with eyes that were almost admiring. Then her expression hardened. "You *are* a conniving little sneak, aren't you?"

Sam frowned at her. "Little. Is everybody in the world worried about my height?"

"And fast with your tongue, too," the redhead went on. "I think that's the first part of you that we'll cut off." Then she smiled viciously. "But only the first part."

Sam swallowed hard, but recovered his wits almost immediately. "Okay, okay. But let the others go. They can't hurt you and if you let them go the Peacekeepers will get out of your hair."

"Liar."

"Me?" Sam protested.

The redhead got to her feet. She was huge, built like a football player. She started to say something but the words froze in her throat. Her gaze shifted from Sam to the door behind us.

I turned my head and saw half a dozen men in khaki uniforms, laser rifles in their hands. The Peacekeepers, I thought, then instantly realized that their uniforms weren't right.

"Thank you so much for bringing this devil's spawn to our hands," said one of the men. He was tall and slim, with a trim mustache and an olive complexion.

"Who in hell are you?" the redhead demanded.

"We are the Warriors of the Faith, and we have come to take this son of a dog to his just reward."

"Gee, I'm so popular," Sam said.

"He's ours!" bellowed the redhead. "We snatched him from The Hague."

"And we are taking him from you. It is our holy mission to attend to this pig."

"You can't!" the redhead insisted. "I won't let you!"

"We'll send you a videotape of his execution," said the leader of the Warriors.

"No, no! *We've* got to kill him!"

"I am so sorry to disagree, but it is our sacred duty to execute him. If we must kill you also, that is the will of God."

They argued for half an hour or more, but the Warriors outnumbered and outgunned the Daughters. So we were marched out of that underground office, down the mine gallery and through another set of steel doors that looked an awful lot like the hatches of airlocks.

The underground corridors we walked through didn't look like parts of a mine anymore. The walls were smoothly finished and lined with modern doors that had numbers on them, like a hotel's rooms.

Sam nodded knowingly as we tramped along under the watchful eyes of the six Warriors.

"This is the old shelter complex for the top Rumanian government officials," he told me as we walked. "From back in the Cold War days, when they were afraid of nuclear attack."

"But that was almost a century ago," Josella said.

Sam answered, "Yeah, but the president of Rumania and his cronies kept the complex going for years afterward. Sort of an underground pleasure dome for the big shots in the government. Wasn't discovered by their taxpayers until one of the bureaucrats fell in love with one of the call girls and spilled the beans to the media so he could run off with her."

"How do you know?" I asked him.

"The happy couple works for me up in Selene City. He's my chief bookkeeper now and she supervises guest services at the hotel."

"What kind of hotel are you running up there in Selene?" Greg asked.

Sam answered his question with a grin. Then he turned back to me and said, "This complex has several exits, all connected to old mine shafts."

Lowering my voice, I asked, "Can we get away from these Warriors and get out of here?"

Sam made a small shrug. "There's six of them and they've all got guns. All we've got is trickery and deceit."

"So what—"

"When I say 'beans,'" Sam whispered, "shut your eyes tight, stop walking, and count to ten slowly."

"Why . . . ?"

"Tell Greg," he said. Then he edged away from me to whisper in Josella's ear. I felt my face burning.

"What are you saying?" one of the Warriors demanded.

Sam put on a leering grin. "I'm asking her if she's willing to grant the condemned man his last request."

The Warrior laughed. "We have requests to make also."

"Fool!" their leader snapped. "We are consecrated to the Faith. We have foresworn the comforts of women."

"Only until we have executed the dog."

"Yes," chimed another Warrior. "Once the pig is slain, we are free of our vows."

A third added, "Then we can have the prisoners." He smiled at Greg.

"Now wait," Sam said. He stopped walking. "Let me get one thing straight. Am I supposed to be a pig or a dog?"

The leader stepped up to him. "You are a pig, a dog, and a piece of camel shit."

The man loomed a good foot over Sam's stubby form. Sam shrugged good-naturedly and said, "I guess you're entitled to your opinion."

"Now walk," said the leader.

"Why should I?" Sam stuffed his hands into the pockets of his slacks.

A slow smile wormed across the leader's lean face. "Because if you don't walk I will break every bone in your face."

They were all gathered around us now, all grinning, all waiting for the chance to start beating up on Sam. I realized we were only a few feet away from another airlock hatch.

"You just don't know beans about me, do you?" Sam asked sweetly.

I squeezed my eyes shut but the glare still burned through my closed lids so brightly that I thought I'd go blind. I remembered to count . . . six, seven . . .

"Come on!" Sam grabbed at my arm. "Let's get going!"

I opened my eyes and still saw a burning afterimage, as if I had stared directly into the sun. The six Warriors were down on their knees, whimpering, pawing madly at their eyes, their rifles strewn across the floor.

Sam had Josella by the wrist with one hand. With the other he was pulling me along.

"Let's *move*!" he commanded. "They won't be down for more than a few minutes."

Greg stooped down and took one of the laser rifles.

"Do you know how to use that?" Sam asked.

Greg shook his head. "I feel better with it, though."

We raced to the hatch, pushed it open, squeezed through it, and then swung it shut again. Sam spun the control wheel as tightly as he could.

"That won't hold them for more than a minute," he muttered.

We ran. Of the four of us I was the slowest. Josella sprinted ahead on her long legs, with Greg not far behind. Sam stayed back with me, puffing almost as badly as I was.

"We're both out of shape," he panted.

"We're both too old for this kind of thing," I said.

He looked surprised, as if the idea of getting old had never occurred to him.

"What did you do back there?" I asked, as we staggered down the corridor.

"Miniaturized high-intensity flash lamp," Sam said, puffing. "For priming mini-lasers."

"You just happened . . ." I was gasping. ". . . to have one . . . on you?"

"Been carrying a few," he wheezed, "ever since the fanatics started making threats."

"Good thinking."

We found a shaft and climbed up into the sweet clean air of a pine forest. It was cold; there was a dusting of snow on the ground. Our feet got thoroughly soaked and we were shivering as Sam pushed us through the woods.

"Clearing," he kept telling us. "We gotta get to a clearing."

We found a clearing at last, and the thin sunshine filtering through the gray clouds felt good after the chill shadows of the forest. Sam made us close our eyes again and he set off another of his flash bulbs.

"Surveillance satellites oughtta see that," he said. "Now it's just a matter of time to see who gets us first, the Peacekeepers or the dog-pig guys."

It was the Peacekeepers, thank goodness. Two of their helicopters came clattering and whooshing down on that little clearing while a pair of jump-jets flew cover high overhead. I was never so happy to see that big blue and white symbol in my life.

The Peacekeepers had mounted a full search-and-rescue operation. Their helicopter was spacious, comfortable, and even soundproofed a little. They thought of everything. While Sam filled in one of their officers on the layout of the Rumanian shelter complex, two enlisted personnel brought us steaming hot coffee and sandwiches. It made me realize that we hadn't eaten or slept in close to twenty-four hours.

I was starting to drowse when I heard Sam ask, over the muted roar of the 'coptor's turbines, "Who were those guys?"

The Peacekeeper officer, in her sky-blue uniform, shook her head. "Neither the Daughters of the Mother nor the Warriors of God are listed in our computer files."

"Terrorists," Greg Molina said. "Religious fanatics."

"Amateurs," said Josella Ecks, with a disdainful curl of her lip.

That startled me. The way she said it. But the need for sleep was overpowering my critical faculties. I cranked my seat back and closed my eyes. The last thing I saw was Sam holding Josella's hand and staring longingly into her deep, dark, beautifully lashed eyes.

I wanted to murder her but I was too tired.

SAM WENT TO Selene the next day and, sure enough, Josella went with him. Greg Molina returned to Quito, dropping in to my office just before he left.

"Will the trial be held in The Hague or at Selene?" he asked.

"Wherever," I groused, seething at the thought of Sam and Josella together a quarter-million miles away.

"I assume there will be a trial, since there was no agreement at the pretrial hearing," he said.

Grimly, I answered, "It certainly looks that way."

Looking slightly worried, "If it's on the Moon, will I have to go there? Or can I participate electronically?"

"It would be better if you were there in person."

"I've never been in space," he admitted.

"There's nothing to it," I said. "It's like flying in an airplane."

"But the lack of gravity . . ."

"You'll get used to it in a day or so. You'll enjoy it," I assured him.

He looked unconvinced.

It took me a whole day of fussing and fuming before I bit the bullet and rocketed to the Moon after Sam. And Josella. Pride is one thing, but I just couldn't stand the thought of Sam chasing that willowy young thing—and catching her. Josella Ecks might think she was smart and cool enough to avoid Sam's clutches, but she didn't know our sawed-off Lothario as well as I did.

And it would be just like Sam to try to get the other side's lawyer to fall for him. Even if he wasn't bonkers about Josella, he'd want to sabotage her ability to represent his adversary in court.

So I told myself I was doing my job as a judge of the International Court of Justice as I flew to Selene.

I hadn't been to the Moon in nearly five years, and I was impressed with how much bigger and more luxurious the underground city had grown. Selene's main plaza had been mostly empty the last time I'd seen it, an immense domed structure of bare lunar concrete rumbling with the echoes of bulldozers and construction crews. Now the plaza—big enough to hold half a dozen football fields—was filled with green trees and flowering shrubbery. On one side stood the gracefully curved acoustical shell of an open-air theater. Small shops and restaurants were spotted along the pleasant winding walk that led through the plaza, all of them decked out with Christmas ornaments. The trees along the walk twinkled with lights.

There were hundreds of people strolling about, tourists walking awkwardly, carefully, in their weighted boots to keep them from stumbling in the one-sixth gravity. A handful of fliers soared high up near the curving dome, using colorful rented plastic wings and their own muscle power to fly like birds. For years Sam had said that tourism would become a major industry in space and at last his prediction was coming true. Christmas on the Moon: the ultimate holiday trip.

The lobby of the Selene Hotel was marvelous, floored with basalt from Mare Nubium polished to a mirror finish. The living quarters were deeper underground than the lobby level, of course. There were no stairs, though; too easy for newcomers unaccustomed to the low gravity to trip and fall. I walked down a wide rampway, admiring the sheets of water cascading noiselessly down tilted panes of lunar glass on either side of the central rampway into spacious fish ponds at the bottom level. Freely flowing water was still a rare sight on the Moon, even though aquaculture provided more of the protein for lunar meals than agriculture did.

Soft music wafted through hidden speakers, and tourists tossed chunks of bread to the fish in the pools, not realizing that sooner or later the fish would be feeding them. I saw that others had thrown coins into the water and laughed to myself, picturing Sam wading in there every night to collect the loose change.

I hadn't told Sam I was coming, but he must have found out when I booked a suite at the hotel. There were real flowers and Swiss chocolates waiting for me when I checked in. I admired the flowers and gave the chocolates to the concierge to distribute to the hotel's staff. Let them have the calories.

Even before I unpacked my meager travel bag I put in a call to Sam's office. Surprisingly, he answered it himself.

"Hi, there!" Sam said brightly, his larger-than-life face grinning at me from the electronic window that covered one whole wall of my sitting room. "What brings you to Selene?"

I smiled for him. "I got lonesome, Sam."

"Really?"

"And I thought that I'd better make certain you're not suborning an officer of the court."

"Oh, you mean Josella?"

"Don't put on your innocent face for me, Sam Gunn," I said. "You know damned well I mean Josella."

His expression went serious. "You don't have to worry about her. She's got more defenses than a porcupine. Her arms are a lot longer than mine, I found out."

He actually looked sad. I felt sorry for him, but I didn't want him to know it. Not yet. Sam had a way of using your emotions to get what he wanted.

So I said, "I presume you're free for dinner."

He sighed. "Dinner, lunch, breakfast, you call it."

"Dinner. Seven o'clock in the hotel's restaurant." All the lunar facilities kept Greenwich Mean Time, which was only an hour off from The Hague.

I had expected Sam to be downcast. I'd seen him that way before, moping like a teenaged Romeo when the object of his desire wouldn't go along with him. Usually his pining and sighing only lasted until he found a new object of desire; I think twenty-four hours was the longest he'd ever gone in the past. Like a minor viral infection.

But when I got to the restaurant Sam was practically bouncing with excitement. As the maitre d' led me to the table, Sam jumped to his feet so hard that he rose clear above the table and soared over it, landing on his toes right in front of me like a star ballet dancer. People stared from their tables.

Gracefully, Sam took my hand and bent his lips to it. His lips were curved into a tremendously self-satisfied smile.

Alarm bells went off in my head. Either he's finally scored with Josella or he's found a new love. I knew he couldn't possibly be this happy just to see me again.

Sam shooed the maitre d' away and helped me into my chair. Then he chugged around the table and sat down, folded his hands and rested his chin on them, and grinned at me as if he was a cat who'd just cornered the canary market.

I saw that there was a chilled bottle of French champagne in a silver bucket next to the table. A waiter immediately brought a dish of caviar and placed it in the center of the table.

"What's going on?" I asked.

Sam cocked an eyebrow at me. "Going on? What do you mean?"

"The champagne and caviar. The grin on your face."

"Couldn't that be just because I'm so happy to see you?"

"No it couldn't," I said. "Come on, Sam, we've known each other too long for this kind of runaround."

He laughed softly and leaned closer toward me. "He's coming here."

"Who's coming here?"

"*Il Papa* himself," Sam whispered.

"The Pope?" My voice squeaked like a surprised mouse.

His head bobbing up and down, Sam said, "William I. The bishop of Rome. Vicar of Christ. Successor to the prince of the Apostles. Supreme pontiff of the universal church. Patriarch of the west, primate of Italy, archbishop and metropolitan of the Roman province, sovereign of the state of Vatican City, servant of the servants of God." He took a breath. "That one."

"The Pope is coming here? To the Moon? To Selene?"

"Just got the word from Cardinal Hagerty himself. Pope Bill is coming here to deal with me personally."

I felt as if I was in free fall, everything inside me sinking. "Oh my God," I said.

"Nope," said Sam. "Just His representative."

IT WAS SUPPOSED to be very hush-hush. No news reporters. No leaks. The Pope came incognito, slipping out of Rome in plain clothes and riding to the Moon in a private rocket furnished by Rockledge Industries and paid for by Frank Banner's insurance consortium.

For once in his life Sam kept a secret that wasn't his own. He bubbled and jittered through the two days it took for the Pope to arrive at Selene. Instead of putting him up in the hotel, where he might be recognized, Sam ensconced Pope William, Cardinal Hagerty and their retinue of guards and servants—all male—in a new wing of Selene's living quarters that hadn't been opened yet for occupancy.

Their quarters were a little rough, a little unfinished. Walls nothing but bare stone. Some of the electrical fixtures hadn't been installed yet. But there was comfortable furniture and plenty of room for them.

Suddenly I was a World Court judge in charge of a pretrial hearing again. I set up the meeting in the Pope's suite, after a half-day of phone discussions with Sam and Cardinal Hagerty. Greg Molina reluctantly came up from Quito; Sam provided him with a special high-energy boost so he could get to us within twenty-four hours.

So there we were: Sam, the Pope, Cardinal Hagerty, Greg, Josella and me, sitting around a circular table made of lunar plastic. Of the six of us, only Sam and I seemed truly at ease. The others looked slightly queasy from the low gravity. Cardinal Hagerty, in particular, gripped the arms of his chair as if he was afraid he'd be sucked up to the bare stone ceiling if he let go.

I was surprised at Josella's uneasiness. She was seated next to me—I made certain to place myself between her and Sam. She had always seemed so cool and self-possessed that I felt almost pained for her.

While Greg went through the formality of reading the précis of Sam's suit against the Vatican, I leaned over and whispered to Josella, "Are you having trouble adjusting to the gravity?"

She looked surprised, almost shocked. Then she tried to smile. "It's . . . not that. It's this room. I feel . . . it must be something like claustrophobia."

I wondered that she hadn't been bothered before, but then I figured that the other rooms of the hotel had big electronic window walls and green plants and decorations that tricked the eye into forgetting that you were buried deep underground. This conference room's walls were bare, which made its ceiling seem low. Like a monk's cell, I thought.

Halfway through Greg's reading of the précis, Cardinal Hagerty cleared his throat noisily and asked, "If there's nothing new in this travesty, could we be dispensing with the rest of this reading?"

Hagerty was by far the oldest person in the group. His face was lined and leathery; his hair thin and white. He looked frail and cranky, and his voice was as creaky as a rusted door hinge.

Sam nodded agreement, as did Josella. Greg tapped his hand-sized computer and looked up from its screen.

"Now then," said the Pope, folding his hands on the tabletop, "let's get down to the nitty-gritty."

He was smiling at us. Pope William looked even younger in person than on TV. And even more dynamic and handsome. A rugged and vigorous man with steel-gray hair and steel-gray eyes. He looked more like a successful corporate executive or a lawyer than a man of God. Even in his white Papal robes, it was hard for me to think of him as a priest. And a celibate.

He had the knack of making you feel that he was concentrating all his attention on you, even when he wasn't looking directly at you. And when his eyes did catch mine, I got goose bumps, so help me. Dynamic? He was *dynamite.*

Of course, he didn't affect Sam the way he hit me.

"You want the nitty-gritty?" Sam replied, with no hint of awe at speaking face-to-face with the Pope. "Okay. God owes me half a billion dollars."

"Ridiculous," Cardinal Hagerty croaked.

"Not according to the insurance industry," Sam countered. He jabbed a finger toward Josella. "Tell 'em, kid."

Josella looked startled. "Tell them what?"

"Your employers claim that the accidents that've almost wrecked Ecuador National Space Systems were acts of God. Right?"

"Yes," Josella answered warily.

Sam spread his hands. "See? *They're* the ones who put the blame on God, not me. All I'm trying to do is collect what's owed me."

Pope William turned his megawatt smile on Sam. "Surely you don't expect the Church to pay you for industrial accidents."

"Don't call me Shirley," Sam mumbled.

"What?"

Barely suppressing his glee, Sam said, "We've been through all this. The insurance industry says God's responsible. You claim to be God's representative on Earth. So you owe Ecuador National Space Systems half a billion dollars."

Pope William's smile darkened just a bit. "And what will you do if we refuse to pay—assuming, that is, that the World Court should decide in your favor."

"Which is ridiculous," said Hagerty.

Sam was unperturbed. "If the World Court really is an International Court of Justice, as it claims to be," he gave me the eye, "then it has to decide in my favor."

"I doubt that," said the Pope.

"Ridiculous," uttered Cardinal Hagerty. It seemed to be his favorite word.

"Think about it," Sam went on, sitting up straighter in his chair. "Think of the reaction in the Moslem nations if the World Court seems to treat the Vatican differently from other nations. Or India or China."

Pope William's brows knit slightly. Hagerty's expression could have soured milk.

"Another thing," Sam added. "You guys have been working for a century or so to heal the rifts among other Christians. Imagine how the Protestants will feel if they see the Vatican getting special treatment from the World Court."

"Finding the Vatican innocent of responsibility for your industrial accidents is hardly special treatment," said Pope William.

"Maybe you think so, but how will the Swedes feel about it? Or the Orthodox Catholics in Greece and Russia and so on? Or the Southern Baptists?"

The Pope said nothing.

"Think about the publicity," Sam said, leaning back easily in his chair. "Remember what an American writer once said: 'There is no character, howsoever good and fine, but can be destroyed by ridicule.'"

"'By ridicule, howsoever poor and witless,'" the Pope finished the citation. "Mark Twain."

"That's right," said Sam.

Cardinal Hagerty burst out, "You can't hold the Vatican responsible for acts of the Lord! You can't expect the Church to pay every time some daft golfer gets struck by lightning because he didn't have sense enough to come in out of the rain!"

"Hey, *you're* the guys who claim you're God's middleman. You spent several centuries establishing that point, too, from what I hear."

"All right," said Pope William, smiling again, "let's grant for the sake of argument that the World Court decides against the Vatican. We, of course, will refuse to pay. It would be impossible for us to pay such a sum, in fact. Even if we could, we'd have to take the money away from the poor and the starving in order to give it to you."

"To the nation of Ecuador," Sam corrected.

"To Ecuador National Space Systems," grumbled Cardinal Hagerty.

"Which is you," said the Pope.

Sam shrugged.

Pope William turned to me. "What would happen if we refused to pay?"

I felt flustered. My face got hot. "I . . . uh—the only legal alternative would be for the Court to ask the Peacekeepers to enforce its decision."

"So the Peacekeepers will invade the Vatican?" Cardinal Hagerty sneered. "What will they do, cart away the *Piéta*? Hack off the roof of the Sistine Chapel and sell it at auction?"

"No," I admitted. "I don't see anything like that happening."

"Lemme tell you what'll happen," Sam said. "The world will see that your claim to be God's special spokesman is phony. The world will see that you hold yourselves above the law. Your position as a moral leader will go down the toilet. The next time you ask the nations to work for peace and unity the whole world will laugh in your face."

Cardinal Hagerty went white with anger. He sputtered, but no words came past his lips. I thought he was going to have a stroke, right there at our conference table.

But the Pope touched him on the shoulder and the Cardinal took a deep, shuddering breath and seemed to relax somewhat.

Pope William's smile was gone. He focused those steel-gray eyes on Sam and said, "You are a dangerous man, Mr. Gunn."

Sam stared right back at him. "I've been called lots of things in my time, but never dangerous."

"You would extort half a billion dollars out of the mouths of the world's neediest people?"

"And use it to create jobs so that they wouldn't be needy anymore. So they won't have to depend on you or anybody else. So they can stand on their own feet and live in dignity."

Sam was getting worked up. For the first time in my life, I saw Sam becoming really angry.

"You go around the world telling people to accept what God sends them. You'll help them. Sure you will. You'll help them to stay poor, to stay miserable, to be dependent on Big Daddy from Rome."

"Sam!" I admonished.

"I've read the Gospels. Christ went among the poor and shared what he had with them. He told a rich guy to sell everything he had and give it to the poor if he wanted to make it into heaven. I don't see anybody selling off the papal jewels. I see Cardinals jet-setting around the world. I see the Pope telling the poor that they're God's chosen people—from the balconies of posh hotels."

Greg Molina smiled grimly. He must be a Catholic who's turned against the Church, I thought.

Sam kept on, "All my life I've seen the same old story: big government or big religion or big corporations telling the little guys to stay in their places and be grateful for whatever miserable crumbs they get. And they stay in their places and take what you deign to give them. And their children grow up poor and hungry and miserable and listen to the same sad song and make more children who grow up just as poor and hungry and miserable."

"That's not his fault," I said.

"Isn't it?" Sam was trembling with rage. "They're all the same, whether it's government or corporate or religion. As long as you *stay* poor and miserable they'll help you. And all they do is help you to stay dependent on them."

Pope William's expression was grim. But he said, "You're entirely right."

Sam's mouth opened, then clicked shut. Then he managed to utter, "Huh?"

"You are entirely right," the Pope repeated. He smiled again, but now it was almost sad, from the heart. "Oh, maybe not *entirely*, but right enough. Holy Mother Church has struggled to help the world's poor for centuries, but today we have more poor people than ever before. It is clear that our methods are not successful."

Sam's eyes narrowed warily, sensing a trap ahead. Cardinal Hagerty grumbled something too low for me to hear.

"For centuries we have ridden on the horns of a dilemma; a paradox, if you will," the Pope continued. "The goal of Holy Mother Church—the task given to Peter by Christ—was to save souls, not bodies. The Church's eyes have always been turned toward Heaven. Everything we have done has been done to bring souls to salvation, regardless of the suffering those souls must endure on Earth."

Before Sam could object, the Pope added, "Or so we have told ourselves."

Cardinal Hagerty let out his breath in what might have been a sigh. Or a hiss.

Pope William smiled at the old man, then continued, "The news media have hinted at . . . frictions between myself and the Curia—the bureaucracy that actually runs the Vatican."

"I've heard such rumors," I said.

Clasping his hands together, the Pope said, "The differences between myself and the Curia are based on the assessment that you have just made, Mr. Gunn. The Church has indeed told its faithful to ignore the needs of this world in order to prepare for the next. I believe that such an attitude has served us poorly. I believe the Church must change its position on many things. We can't save souls who have given themselves to despair, to crime and drugs and all kinds of immorality. We must give our people *hope*."

"Amen to that," Sam muttered.

"Hope for a better life here on Earth."

Ordinarily Sam would have quipped that we weren't on Earth at the moment. But he remained quiet.

"So you see," Pope William said, "we are not so far apart as you thought."

Sam shook himself, like a man trying to break loose from a hypnotic spell. "I still want my half bill," he said.

Pope William smiled at him. "We don't have it, and even if we did, we wouldn't give it to you."

"Then you're going to go down the tubes, just like I said."

"And the changes I am trying to make within the Vatican will go down the tubes with me," Pope William replied.

Sam thought a moment, then said, "Yeah, I guess they will."

Leaning toward Sam, Pope William pleaded, "But don't you understand? If you press your case, all the reforms that the Church needs will never be made. Even if you don't win, the case will be so infamous that I'll be blocked at every turn by the Curia."

"That's your problem," Sam replied, so low I could barely hear him.

"Why do you think I came up here?" the Pope continued. "I wanted to make a personal appeal to you to be reasonable. I need your help!"

Sam said nothing.

Cardinal Hagerty recovered his voice. "I thought from the beginning that this trip was a waste of precious time."

Pope William pushed his chair back from the table. "I'm afraid you were right all along," he said to the Cardinal.

"So we'll have a trial," Sam said, getting to his feet.

"We will," said the Pope. He was nearly six feet tall; he towered over Sam.

"You'll lose," Sam warned.

The Pope's smile returned, but it was only a pale imitation of the earlier version. "You're forgetting one thing, Mr. Gunn. God is on our side."

Sam gave him a rueful grin. "That's okay. I'm used to working against the big guys."

SAM AND I walked slowly along the corridor that led from the Pope's quarters to the main living section of Selene. Josella trudged along on Sam's other side; Greg was a few steps ahead of us.

"Sam," I said, "I'm going to recommend against a trial."

He didn't look surprised.

"You can't do this," I said. "It's not right."

Sam seemed subdued, but he still replied, "You can recommend all you want to, Jill. The Court will still have to hear the case. The law's on my side."

"Then the law is an ass!"

He grinned at me. "Old gray-eyes got to you, didn't he? Sexy guy, for a Pope."

I glared at him. There's nothing so infuriating as a man who thinks he knows what's going on inside your head. Especially when he's right.

Josella said, "I'll have to report this meeting to my superiors back in Hartford."

"How about having supper with me?" Sam asked her. Right in front of me.

Josella glanced at me. "I don't think so, Sam. It might be seen as a conflict of interest."

Sam laughed. "We'll bring the judge along. We'll discuss the case. Hey Greg," he called up the corridor, "you wanna have dinner with the rest of us?"

So the four of us met at the hotel's restaurant after freshening up in our individual rooms. I made certain to follow Sam to his suite, down the corridor from Josella's, before going to my own.

"Bodyguarding me?" he asked mischievously.

"Protecting my interest," I said. Then I added loftily, "In the integrity of the World Court and the international legal system."

Sam gave me a wry smile.

"I don't want you tampering with the opposition's lawyer," I said.

"Tamper? Me? The thought never entered my mind."

"I know what's in your mind, Sam. You can't fool me."

"Have I ever tried to?" he asked.

And I had to admit to myself that he never had. To the rest of the world Sam might be a devious womanizing rogue, a sly underhanded con man, even an extortionist, but he'd always been up-front with me. Damn him!

The restaurant was crowded, but Sam got us a quiet table in a corner. He and Greg were already there when I arrived. Shortly after me, Josella swept in, looking like an African princess in a long, clinging gold-mesh sheath. Sam's eyes went wide. He had barely flickered at my Parisian original, but I didn't have Josella's figure or long legs.

Sam sat Josella on one side of him, me on the other. Greg was across the table from him. I think he was enjoying having two women next to him. I only hoped he couldn't see how jealous I was of Josella.

Trying to hide that jealousy, I turned to Greg. I was curious about him. Over predinner cocktails, I asked him, "You're a Catholic, aren't you? How do you feel about all this?"

Greg looked down into his drink as he stirred it with his straw. "I am a Catholic, but not the kind you may think. There are many of us in Latin America who recognized ages ago that the bishops and cardinals and all the 'official' Church hierarchy were in the service of the big landlords, the government, the tyrants."

"Greg was a revolutionary," Sam said, with a smirk.

"I still am," he told us. "But now I work from inside the system. I learned that from Sam. Now I help to create jobs for the poor, to educate them and help them break free of poverty."

"And free of the Church?" Josella asked.

Greg said, "Most of us remain Catholics, but we do not support the hierarchy. We have worker priests among us, men of the people."

"Isn't that what Pope William wants to encourage?" I asked.

"Perhaps so," Greg said. "His words sound good. But words are not deeds."

"You're really going to insist on a trial?" I asked Sam.

He didn't look happy about it, but he said softly, "Got to. Ecuador National is close to bankruptcy. We need that money."

Greg nodded. I believed him, not Sam.

Dinner was uncomfortable, to say the least. Pope William had gotten to all of us, even Sam.

But by the time dessert was being served, at least Sam had brightened up a bit. He turned his attention to Josella.

"Is your last name Dutch?" he asked her.

She smiled a little. "Actually, its derivation is Greek, I believe."

"You don't look Greek."

"Looks can be deceiving, Mr. Gunn."

"Call me Sam."

Josella seemed to consider the proposition for a few moments, then decided. "All right—Sam."

"Did you call your bosses in Hartford, Josie?" he asked her.

"Did I! Old man Banner himself got on the screen. Is he pissed with you!"

Sam laughed. "Good. He's the sonofabitch who shifted the blame to God."

"That's a standard clause in every policy, Sam."

"Yeah, but I asked him personally to reconsider in my case and he laughed in my face."

"He said if you took this case to trial he'd personally break your neck," Josella said, very seriously. "He used a lot of adjectives to describe you, your neck, and how much he'd enjoy doing it."

"Great!" Sam grinned. "Did you make a copy of the conversation?"

Josella gave him a slow, delicious smile. "I did not. I even erased the core memory of it in my computer. You won't be subpoenaing *my* boss's heated words, Mr. Gunn."

Sam feigned crushing disappointment.

"This Mr. Banner hates Sam so much?" Greg asked.

"I think he truly does," said Josella.

"Perhaps he is the one who sent the assassins after Sam," Greg suggested. "At least one set of them."

"Mr. Banner?" she looked shocked.

A thought struck me. "You said the assassins were amateurs, Josella. Have you had much experience with terrorists?"

"Only what I read in the news media," she answered smoothly. "It seems to me that *real* terrorists blow you away as soon as they get the chance. They don't drag you across the landscape and gloat at you."

"Then let's be glad they were amateurs," Sam said.

"Professionals would have killed us all, right there in your office," Josella said to me. Flatly. As if she knew exactly how it was done.

"Without worrying about getting caught?" Greg asked.

"Considering the response time of the Dutch security people," Josella said, "they could have iced the four of us and made it out of the building with no trouble. If they had been professionals."

"Pleasant thought," Sam said.

THERE WAS PLENTY of night life in Selene, but as we left the restaurant Sam told us that he was tired and going to his quarters. It sounded completely phony to me.

Then Josella said she was retiring for the night, too. Greg looked a little surprised.

"I understand there's a gaming casino in the hotel," he said. "I think I'll try my luck."

We said good-night to Greg and headed for the elevator to take us down to the level where our rooms were. On Earth, the higher your floor, the more prestigious and expensive. On the Moon, where the surface is pelted with micrometeors and bathed in hard radiation, prestige and expense increase with your distance downward.

Sam made a great show of saying good-night to Josella. She even let him kiss her hand before she closed her door. I walked with him as far as the door to my own suite.

"Want to come in for a nightcap?" I asked.

Sam shook his head. "I'm really pretty pooped, kid. This business with the Pope's hit me harder than I thought it would."

But his eyes kept sliding toward Josella's door, down the corridor.

"Okay, Sam," I said, trying to make it sound sweet and unsuspecting. "Good-night."

He pecked me on the cheek. A brotherly kiss. I hadn't expected more, but I still wanted something romantic or at least warm.

I closed my door and leaned against it. Suddenly I felt really weary, tired of the whole mess. Tired of chasing Sam, who was interested in every female in the solar system except me. Tired of this legal tangle with the Vatican. And scared of the effect that Pope William had on me. I wondered if one of the changes he wanted to make in the Church was to allow priests to marry. Wow!

I honestly tried to sleep. But I just tossed and fussed until I finally admitted that I was wide awake. I told the phone beside the bed to get Sam for me.

It got his answering routine. "I'm either sleeping or doing something else important. Leave your name and I'll get back to you, promise."

Sleeping or doing something else important. I knew what "something else" was. I pulled on a set of coveralls and tramped down the corridor to Sam's door. I knocked. No answer. Knocked harder. Still no answer. Pounded on it. He wasn't there.

I knew where he was. Steaming with rage, I stomped down the corridor to Josella's door and banged on it with both fists. I even kicked it.

"I know you're in there, Sam!" I shouted, not giving a damn who in the hotel could hear me. "Open up this goddamned door!"

Josella opened it. She was wearing nothing but the sheerest of night-gowns. And she had a pistol in her hand.

"Senator Meyers," she said, with a sad kind of resignation in her voice. "I had hoped to avoid this."

Puzzled, I pushed past her and into her room. Sam was sitting on the bed, buck naked, a sheet wrapped around his middle.

"Aw, shit, Jill," he said, frowning. "Now she's got you, too."

It hit me at last. Turning to Josella, I said, "*You're* an assassin!"

She nodded, her face very serious.

"She wants to waste me," Sam said gloomily, not moving from the bed.

"But why?" I blurted.

Josella kept the pistol rock-steady in her hand. "Because the ayatollahs are unanimous in their decision that this unbeliever must die."

"You're a Moslem?"

She smiled tightly. "Not all Moslem women wear veils and chadors, Senator Meyers."

"But why would the Moslems want to kill Sam? He's suing the Pope, not Islam."

"He is making a travesty of all religions. He is mocking God. The Church of Rome has yet to see the light of true revelation, but we slaves of Allah can't allow this blasphemy to continue."

"It's Islam's contribution to global religious solidarity," Sam said, disgust dripping from his words.

"I had wanted to do it cleanly, professionally," Josella said, "without any complications."

"That's why you let Sam into your room," I said.

"Yes," she said. "To give the condemned man his last wish. Although Sam didn't know he was condemned when I granted his wish."

"So you made it with her, after all," I said to Sam, angrily.

He made a sour face. "She screwed me, all right."

"And now what?" I asked Josella. "You kill us both?"

"I'm afraid so."

"And how do you get away?"

She shrugged. Inside that sheer nightgown it looked delicious, even to me. "There's a shuttle leaving for Earth orbit at midnight. Passage on it has already been booked for a young man named Shankar. By the time your bodies are discovered I will be Mr. Shankar, complete with mustache and beard."

"It'll have to be a damned good disguise," Sam groused.

Almost smiling, Josella said, "It will be. Even my fingerprints will be different."

"You said you're a professional," I stalled for time. "You mean you've done this kind of thing before?"

Josella nodded slowly. "For six years. My job has been to assassinate policy-holders whose estates would go to Islamic causes."

"You've worked for insurance companies and they never knew?"

"Of course not."

"She's a lawyer, for chrissake," Sam snapped. "She's trained to lie."

The phone rang. We heard Josella's taped voice say sweetly, "I am not able to answer your call right now. Please leave your name and I'll call you back as soon as I possibly can."

"Josella?" I recognized that bombastic voice. It was Frank Banner. "This is Banner. Haven't been able to sleep for the past two nights. This damned business with Sam Gunn is driving me nuts. He's actually going ahead with his suit in the World Court, is he? Damned little pissant jerk! We can't let him drag the Pope through the mud the way he wants to. We just can't! Tell him we'll settle with him. Not his damned half-billion, that's outrageous. But tell him we'll work out something reasonable if he'll drop this damned lawsuit."

I felt my mouth drop open. I looked at Sam and he was grinning as if he'd been expecting this all along.

"And tell him that if I ever see him in the same room with me I'll break every bone in his scrawny goddamned neck! Tell him that, too!"

The phone connection clicked dead. Sam flopped back on the bed and whooped triumphantly.

"I knew it!" he yelled. "I knew that Francis Xavier Banner couldn't let the Pope come to trial. I knew the tightfisted sonofabitch would finally break down and offer to settle my insurance claims!" He laughed wildly, kicking his bare hairy legs in the air and pounding the mattress with his fists.

I just stood there, dumbfounded. Had this whole complex procedure been nothing more than an elaborate scheme by Sam to get his insurance carrier to accept his accident claims? Yes, I realized. That was Sam Gunn at his wiliest: threaten the Pope to get what he considered he was owed.

The gun in Josella's hand wavered, then she let her arm drop to her side.

"You don't have to kill Sam now," I said. "There's not going to be a court case after all."

"No," she said. "The blasphemer must still die."

Sam got to his bare feet, clutching the bedsheet around his middle like a Roman senator who didn't quite know how to drape his toga properly.

"You're a fraud," Sam said.

Josella's dark eyes snapped at him. "Fraud?"

"You're about as professional a killer as that fat blonde Daughter."

"You think so?" Josella's voice went hard and cold, like an icepick. She still had the gun in her hand.

"You said professionals do the job without hesitation," Sam said. "No talk, just boom, you're dead."

Josella nodded.

"So you're an amateur," Sam said, grinning at her. "You did a lot more than talk before you hauled out your gun."

"I did that with all the others, too," Josella said. It was a flat statement, neither a boast nor an excuse. "It's my trademark. Two of the older men I didn't even have to kill; they died of natural causes."

"Bullshit all the others. You've never killed anybody and we both know it."

"You're wrong—"

"Yeah, sure. I'm going to start believing what a lawyer tells me, at my advanced age."

Josella looked confused. I know I was.

But Sam knew exactly what he was doing. "Put your gun back wherever the hell you were hiding it and get out of here," he told her. "Get on the midnight shuttle and don't come back."

"I can't do that," said Josella. "My mission is to kill you—or die. If I let you go, they'll kill me."

"Oh shit," Sam muttered.

"You mean that your own people will murder you if you don't kill Sam?"

Josella nodded. "I must succeed or die. That is what I promised them."

With a disgusted frown, Sam clutched his bedsheet a little tighter and reached for the phone with his free hand.

"Don't!" Josella warned, raising her gun.

"I'm not calling security."

"Then who . . . ?"

Sam called Pope William. The Pope looked shocked, even on the tiny screen of the Picturephone, and even more surprised when Sam told him what his call was about.

"Sanctuary," he said. "This lady here needs your protection."

Blinking sleep from his steely eyes, Pope William said, "Maybe you'd better come over here to explain this to me."

It was almost comical watching Sam and Josella get dressed while she still tried to keep her pistol on us. Then the three of us trotted down the nearly empty corridors, back to the Pope's quarters. Two of his own security men, Swiss guards in plain coveralls, were waiting for us.

They brought us to a kind of sitting room, a bare little cell with four chairs grouped around a coffee table. Nothing else in the room: not a decoration or any refreshments or even a carpet on the stone floor. Josella sat down warily, put her pistol on her lap.

Pope William entered the room a few moments after we did. He was wearing a white sweatshirt and an old pair of Levis and he still filled the room with a warm brilliance.

It was long past midnight before Sam got the whole thing explained to the Pope. Josella didn't help, insisting that she wanted no help from unbelievers.

"I won't try to convert you," William said, smiling at her. "But I can offer you protection and help you create a new persona for yourself."

"A kind of witness protection plan," Sam said, trying to encourage her. "See, we're bringing the Vatican into the twenty-first century."

Me? I was stewing. The two of them were falling all over themselves trying to help Josella and ignoring me altogether.

Josella was starting to nod, seeing that maybe there was a way out of the blind corner she'd trapped herself in. She took the gun from her lap, popped open its magazine, and laid the pieces on the coffeetable.

"All right," she said. "I'll go along with you."

"But what about those other killings?" I heard myself blurt out. "She's admitted to murdering God knows how many men!"

Sam glowered at me.

Pope William smiled. "How do we know, Senator Meyers, that this entire episode—Sam's lawsuit, my coming to the Moon, the various assassination attempts—how do we know that all of this hasn't been God's way of bringing this one woman to repentance and salvation?"

"I won't convert," Josella snapped. "I'm a Moslem."

"Of course," said the Pope. "I only want you to change your life, not your religion."

"All this," I heard the disbelief in my own voice, "just for her?"

"There is more joy in heaven over one sinner who's redeemed than there is over one of the faithful," Pope William said.

Even God was concentrating on Josella, I thought, ashamed of my jeal-ousy but feeling it seething inside me nonetheless.

Sam grinned at him. "So you think this whole thing has been an act of God, huh?"

"Everything is an act of God," said Pope William. "Isn't that right, Josella?"

She nodded silently.

Sam and I left Josella with the Pope. As we walked back along the cor-ridors I tried to stop feeling so damned jealous. But the thought of her with Pope William just plain boiled me. All of a sudden it struck me that Josella might be more of a threat to William than she was to Sam. His soul, that is; not his body.

I started to laugh.

"What's so funny?" Sam asked.

"Nothing," I said. "It's just—everything's turned upside down and in-side out."

"Nope," Sam said. "Everything worked out just the way I thought it would. Ol' Francis X. was an altar boy, y'know. Went to Notre Dame and almost became a priest, before he found out how much he enjoyed mak-ing money."

"You knew that all along?"

"I was counting on it," Sam answered cheerfully.

We were at my door. I realized I was very weary, drained physically and emotionally. Sam looked as chipper as a sparrow, despite the hour.

"Tomorrow's Christmas Eve," he said.

I tapped my wristwatch. "You mean today; it's well past midnight."

"Right. I gotta get a high-g boost direct to Rome set up for Billy Boy if he's gonna say Christmas Eve mass in St. Peter's. Even then it's gonna be awful close. See ya!"

He hustled down the corridor to his own suite, whistling shrilly off-key. And that's the last I saw of Sam until Christmas.

POPE WILLIAM WAS overjoyed, of course. He invited me to breakfast that morning, just before his high-boost shuttle was set to take off. Even Cardinal Hagerty managed to smile, although it looked as if the effort might shatter his stony face. Josella was nowhere in sight, though.

"My prayers have been answered," the Pope told me.

"The Lord certainly moves in mysterious ways," I said.

"Indeed She does," said the Pope, with a mischievous wink.

More mysterious than either of us realized at the time. Sam set up a direct high-g flight to Rome for the papal visitors, so that Pope William could get back in time for his Christmas Eve mass in St. Peter's. But all of a sudden an intense solar flare erupted and raised radiation levels in cislunar space so high that all flights between the Earth and the Moon had to be canceled. All work on the lunar surface stopped and everybody had to stay underground for forty-eight hours. It was as if God was forcing all of Selene's residents and visitors to observe the Christmas holiday.

Which is how William I became the first Pope to celebrate a public mass on the Moon. On Christmas Eve, in Selene's main plaza. The whole population turned out, even Sam.

"I figure about five percent of this crowd is Roman Catholic," Sam said, looking over the throng. We were seated up on the stage of the theater shell, behind the makeshift altar. Several thousand people jammed the theater's tiers of seats and spilled out onto the grass of the plaza's greenway.

"That doesn't matter," I said. "For one hour, we're all united."

Sam grinned. The Pope didn't have his best ceremonial robes with him; he offered the mass in a plain white outfit. "They're doing 'The Nutcracker' this evening," Sam whispered to me. "Wanna see it?"

Low-gravity ballet. Once I had dreams of becoming a dancer on the Moon. "I wouldn't miss it."

"Good," said Sam.

We watched the elaborate ritual of the mass, and the thousands of transfixed men and women and children standing out on the plaza, their eyes on the Pope. I spotted a slim, dark-skinned young man in a trim mustache and beard who looked awfully familiar.

"Y'know," Sam whispered, "maybe I've been wrong about this all along."

I nodded.

"I mean," he went on, "if a guy really wants to make a fortune, he ought to start a religion."

I turned and stared at him. "You wouldn't!"

"Maybe that's what I ought to do."

"Oh Sam, you devil! Start a religion? You?"

"Who knows."

I tried to glare at him but couldn't.

"And another thing," he whispered. "If we ever do get married, you'll have to live here on the Moon with me. I'm not going back to Earth; it's too dangerous down there."

My heart skipped a couple of beats. That was the first time Sam had ever admitted there was any kind of chance he'd marry me.

He shrugged good-naturedly. "Merry Christmas, Jill."

"Merry Christmas," I replied, thinking that it might turn out to be a very interesting new year indeed.

Torch Ship *Hermes*

"SO DID YOU AND SAM EVER GET MARRIED?" JADE ASKED.

Sitting in one of the comfortable armchairs in the torch ship's lounge, Jill Meyers smiled enigmatically. "Not yet. I got the little SOB to within an eyelash of saying 'I do' a couple of times, but both times he scampered out on me before we could make it official."

"And now . . . ?"

"Why do you think I've hired this ship? I'll get him this time. I want to see the look on his face when he sees me—with a minister at my side."

Despite herself Jade laughed.

"You know, there's somebody else on this ship you should talk to," Meyers said. "He was working with Sam when Sam got accused of genocide."

"Genocide!"

"You haven't heard about that one? Well, I guess they did hush it up afterward. But still—"

"He's on this ship? I've got to interview him!"

Meyers nodded. "I'll introduce you to him. His name's Steve Wright."

Steven Achernar Wright

WITHOUT HESITATION, JILL MEYERS PHONED STEVE WRIGHT and invited him to the ship's lounge for a drink. He turned out to be a pleasant enough fellow, somewhere near fifty, Jade judged. He had a shy, almost boyish manner, and unruly sandy hair that tended to flop over his forehead at the slightest excuse.

Once Jade started asking questions about Sam Gunn, his shyness turned to a reluctant, almost hostile series of monosyllabic grunts.

Until Jill Meyers told him, "Jade produced the video biography about Sam."

A new light dawned in Wright's eyes. "I haven't seen it, but I heard it treated Sam pretty well."

A little more conversation and a couple of drinks from the robot-tended bar, and Wright began to relax and talk nonstop.

"Look, I was the closest thing to a lawyer that Sam ever had. I mean, he *hated* lawyers. Probably that's because he was always getting himself into legal troubles, you know, operating out at the edge of the law the way he always did.

"I don't know if he really fell into that black hole or not. And I guess I don't really care. Maybe he found real aliens out there and maybe not. We'll see if he brings any back with him."

Jade made a sympathetic smile, then asked, "Why are you running all the way out to the Kuiper Belt to meet Sam?"

"Why? Because I feel responsible for the little guy, that's why. He went tootling off to find Planet X with that university geek and left behind, like, a ton and three-quarters of lawsuits."

"But he's been away so long the statute of limitations on all the suits has run out," Jill Myers pointed out.

"Maybe not. That Beryllium Blonde that he's tangled with has come up with the idea that since Sam claims he was in a space-time warp, time hasn't passed for him the way it has for the rest of us and therefore the statutes of limitations should be considered suspended for all the time Sam was allegedly in the warp!"

"What?" Meyers snapped. "That's ridiculous!"

"Is it? She's claiming that if time hasn't elapsed for him then it shouldn't elapse for the lawsuits. And the courts are taking it very seriously."

"No!"

"So I'm going out there to warn the little bugger that his legal troubles aren't over. Not by a long shot."

"The Beryllium Blonde?" asked Jade. "Is her name Jennifer something?"

"Marlow," Wright said. "You don't know about her?"

"A little," said Jade.

"Or about the Toad, either? Cheez, what kind of a producer are you? Didn't you do any research before you came aboard this torch ship?"

The Prudent Jurist

YOU MIGHT HAVE KNOWN—SAID STEVE WRIGHT—THAT THE
very first person to be hauled in to trial by the spanking-new Interplanetary Tribunal would be Sam Gunn. And on trial for his life, at that.

Things might not have been too bad, even so, if it weren't for Sam's old nemesis, the Beryllium Blonde. She wanted Sam's hide tacked onto her office wall. Sam, of course, wanted her body. Anyplace.

And then there was the Toad, as well.

Sam's voice had been the loudest one in the whole solar system against letting lawyers get established off-Earth.

"When it comes to interplanetary jurisprudence," he often said—at the top of his leathery lungs—"what we need is less juris and more prudence!"

But it was inevitable that the Interplanetary Astronautical Authority would set up a court to enforce its rulings and carry Earth-style legalities out to the edge of the frontier. After all, the Asteroid Belt was being mined by little guys like Sam and big corporations like Rockledge Industries.

And major consortiums like Diversified Universities & Laboratories, Ltd. (which Sam called DULL) were already pushing the exploration of Jupiter and its many moons.

When the scientists announced the discovery of life on the Jovian moon Europa, of course, the environmentalists and theologians and even the Right To Lifers *demanded* that laws—and lawyers—be established in space to protect it.

And Sam wound up on trial. Not just for murder. Genocide.

Me, I was the closest thing to a lawyer in Sam's then-current company, Asteroidal Resources, Inc. Sam had started up and dissolved more corporations than Jupiter has moons, usually making a quick fortune on some audacious scheme and then blowing it on something even wilder. Asteroidal Resources, Inc. was devoted to mining heavy metals from the Asteroid Belt, out beyond Mars, and smelting them down to refined alloys as his factory ships sailed back to the Earth-Moon system.

The company was based on solid economics, provided needed resources to the Earth-Moon system's manufacturers, and was turning a tidy—if not spectacular—profit. For Sam, this was decidedly unusual. Even respectable.

Sam ran a tight company. His ships were highly automated, with bare-bones skeleton crews. There were only six of us in ARI's headquarters in Ceres, the largest of the asteroids. None of us was a real lawyer; Sam wouldn't allow any of them into his firm. My paralegal certificate was as far as Sam was willing to go. He snarled with contempt when other companies began bringing their lawyers into the belt.

And when I said that the office was *in* Ceres, that's exactly what I mean. Even though it's the biggest chunk of rock in the belt, Ceres is only a little over nine hundred kilometers across; barely big enough to be round, instead of an irregular lump, like the other asteroids. No air, hardly any gravity. Mining outfits like Sam's and big-bad Rockledge and others had honeycombed the rock to set up their local headquarters inside it.

My official title was Director, Human Resources. That meant that I was the guy who handled personnel problems, payroll, insurance, health claims, and lawsuits. Sam always had three or four lawsuits pending; he constantly skirted the fringes of legality—which was why he didn't want lawyers in space, of course. He had enough trouble with the Earthbound variety.

The Beryllium Blonde, by the way, was a corporate lawyer, one of the best, with a mind as sharp and vindictive as her body was lithe and curvaceous. A deadly combination, as far as Sam was concerned.

The entire Human Resources Department in ARI consisted of me and a computer. I had very sophisticated programs to work with, you know, but there was no other human in Human Resources.

Still, I thought things were humming along smoothly enough in our underground offices until the day Sam came streaking back home on a high-g burn, raced straight from the landing pad to my office without even taking off his flight suit, and announced: "Orville, you're gonna be my legal counsel at the trial. Start boning up on interplanetary law."

My actual name is Steven. Steven Achernar Wright. But for some reason Sam called me Orville. Sometimes Wilbur, but mostly Orville.

"Legal counsel?" I echoed, bounding out of my chair so quickly that I sailed completely over my desk in the low gravity. "Trial? For what? What're you charged with?"

He shook his head. "Murder, I think. Maybe worse."

And he scooted into his office. All I really saw of the little guy was a sawed-off blur of motion topped with rusty-red hair. Huckleberry Finn at Mach 5.

I learned about the charges against Sam almost immediately. My phone screen chimed and the impressive black and silver seal of the International Astronautical Authority appeared on its screen, followed an eye-blink later by a very legal-looking summons and an arrest warrant.

The charges were attempted murder, grand larceny, violation of sixteen—count 'em, sixteen—different IAA environmental regulations and assault and battery with willful intent to cause grievous bodily harm.

Oh yes, and the aforementioned charge of genocide.

All that happened before lunch.

I TAPPED INTO the best legal programs on the sys and, after half a day's reading, arranged to surrender Sam to the IAA authorities at Selene City, on the Moon. He yowled and complained every centimeter of the way. Even when we landed on the Moon Sam screeched loud enough to set up echoes through Selene City's underground corridors, right up to the headquarters of the IAA.

The IAA chief administrator cheerfully released Sam on his own recognizance. He and Sam were old virtual billiards buddies, and besides Sam couldn't get away; his name, photo, fingerprints, retinal patterns, and neutron scattering index were posted at every rocket port on the Moon. Sam was stuck on the Moon, at least until his trial.

Maybe longer. The World Government's penal colony was at Farside, where convicts couldn't even see Earth in their sky and spent their time trying to scrounge helium-three from the regolith, competing with nanomachines that did the job for practically nothing for the big corporations like Masterson and Wankle.

THE TRIAL STARTED promptly enough. I begged for more time to prepare a defense, interview witnesses, check the prosecution's published statement of the facts of the case ("And scatter a few bribes around," Sam suggested). No go. The IAA refused any and all requests for a delay in the proceedings. Even their cheerful chief administrator gave me a doleful look and said, "No can do. The trial starts tomorrow, as scheduled."

That worried me. Nobody wanted to appear on Sam's behalf; there were no witnesses to the alleged crimes that weren't already lined up to testify for the prosecution. I couldn't even dig up any character witnesses.

"Testify to Sam's character?" asked one of his oldest friends. "You want them to throw the key away on the little SOB? Or maybe you expect me to commit perjury?"

That was the *kindest* response I got.

What worried me even more was the fact that several hundred "neutral observers" had booked passage to the Moon to attend the trial; half of them were environmentalists who thirsted for Sam's blood; the other half were various enemies the little guy had made over his many years of blithely going his own way and telling anybody who didn't like it to stuff his head someplace where the sun doesn't shine.

The media sensed blood—and *Sam's* blood, at that. He had been great material for them for a long time: the little guy who always thumbed his nose at authority and got away with it. But now Sam had gone too far, and the kindest thing being said about him in the media was that he was "the accused mass-murderer of an entire alien species, the man who wiped out the harmless green lichenoids of Europa."

If all this bothered Sam he gave no indication of it. "The media," he groused. "They love you when you win and they'll use you for toilet paper when you don't."

I studied his round, impish, Jack-o'-lantern face for a sign of concern. Or remorse. Or even anger at being haled into court on such serious charges. Nothing. He just grinned his usual toothy grin and whistled while he worked, maddeningly off-key.

Sam was more worried about the impending collapse of Asteroidal Resources, Inc. than his impending trial. The IAA had frozen all his assets and embargoed all his vehicles. The two factory ships on their way in from the belt were ordered to enter lunar orbit when they arrived at the Earth-Moon system and to stay there; their cargoes were impounded by the IAA, pending the outcome of the trial.

"They want to break me," Sam grumbled. "Whether I win the trial or lose, they want to make sure I'm flat busted by the time it's over."

And then the Toad showed up, closely followed by Beryllium Blonde.

WE WERE SITTING at the defendant's table in the courtroom, a very modernistic chamber with severe, angular banc and witness stand of lunar stone, utterly bare smoothed stone walls and long benches of lunar aluminum for the spectators. The tables and chairs for the defendant and prosecution were also burnished aluminum, cold and hard. No decorations of any kind; the courtroom was functional, efficient, and gave me the feeling of inhuman relentlessness.

"Kangaroo court," Sam muttered as we took our chairs.

The crowd filed in, murmuring and whispering, and filled the rows behind us. Various clerks appeared. No media reporters or photographers were allowed in the courtroom but there had been plenty of them out in the corridor, asking simple questions like, "Why did you wipe out those harmless little green lichenoids, Sam?"

Sam grinned at the them and replied, "Who says I did?"

"The IAA, DULL, just about everybody in the solar system," came their shouted response.

Sam shrugged good-naturedly. "Nobody's heard my side of it yet."

"You mean you didn't kill them?"

"You claim you're innocent?"

"You're denying the charges against you?"

For once in his life, Sam refused to be baited. All he said was, "That's what this trial is for; to find out who did what to whom. And why."

They were so stunned at Sam's refusal to say anything more that they stopped pestering him and allowed us to go into the courtroom. I was sort of stunned, too. I was used to Sam's nonstop blather on any and every subject under the Sun. Sphinxlike silence was something new, from him.

The courtroom was settling down to a buzzing hum of whispered conversations when the three black-robed judges trooped in to take their seats at the banc. No jury. Sam's fate would be decided by the three of them.

As everybody rose to their feet, Sam looked at the three judges and groaned. "Buddha on iceskates, it's the Toad."

His name was J. Everest Weatherwax, and he was so famous that even I recognized him. Multitrillionaire, captain of industry, statesman, public servant, philanthropist, Weatherwax was a legend in his own time. He had helped to found DULL and funded unstintingly the universities that joined the consortium. He was on the board of directors of so many corporations nobody knew the exact number. He was also one the board of governors of the IAA. His power was truly interplanetary in reach, but he had never been known to use that power except for other people's good.

Yet Sam clearly loathed him.

"The Toad?" I whispered to Sam as we sat down and the chief judge— a comely gray-haired woman with steely eyes—began to read the charges against Sam.

"He's a snake," Sam hissed under his breath. "An octopus. He controls people. He *owns* them."

"Mr. Weatherwax?" I was stunned. I had never heard a harsh word said against him before. His good deeds and public unselfishness were known throughout the solar system.

"Just look at him," Sam whispered back, his voice dripping disgust.

I had to admit that Weatherwax did look rather toad-like, sitting up there, looming over us. He was very old, of course, well past the century mark. His face was fleshy, flabby, his skin was gray and splotchy, his shoulders slumped bonelessly beneath his black robe. His eyes bulged and kept blinking slowly; his mouth was a wide almost lipless slash that hung slightly open.

"God help any fly that comes near him," Sam muttered. "Zap! with his tongue."

Weatherwax's money had founded DULL. He had saved the ongoing Martian exploration company when that nonprofit gaggle of scientists had run out of funding. He had made his money originally in biotechnology, almost a century ago, then diversified into agrobusiness and medicine before getting into space exploration and scientific research in a major way. He had received the Nobel Peace Prize for settling the war between India and China. Rumor had it that if he would only convert to Catholicism, the Pope would make him a saint.

As soon as the chief judge finished reading the charges, Sam shot to his feet.

"I protest," he said. "One of the judges is prejudiced against me."

"Mr. Gunn," said the chief judge, glaring at Sam, "you are represented by legal counsel. If you have any protests to make, they must be made by him."

Sam turned to me and made a nudging move with both hands.

I got to my feet slowly, thinking as fast as I could. "Your honor, my client feels that the panel might be less than unbiased, since one of the judges is a founder of the organization that has brought these charges against the defendant."

Weatherwax just smiled down at us, drooling ever so slightly from the corner of his toadish mouth.

The chief judge closed her eyes briefly, then replied to me, "Justice Weatherwax has been duly appointed by the International Astronautical Authority to serve on this panel. His credentials as a jurist are impeccable."

"Since when is he a judge?" Sam stage-whispered at me.

"The defense was not aware that Mr. Weatherwax had received an appointment to the bench, your honor," I said as diplomatically as I could.

"*Justice* Weatherwax received his appointment last week," she answered frostily, "on the basis of his long and distinguished record of service in international disputes."

"I see," I said meekly. "Thank you, your honor." There was nothing else I could do.

"Settling international disputes," Sam grumbled. "Like the China-India War. Once he stopped selling bioweapons to both sides they *had* to stop fighting."

"However," the chief judge said, turning to Weatherwax, "if the justice would prefer to withdraw in the face of the defendant's concern . . ."

Weatherwax stirred and seemed to come to life like a large mound of protoplasm touched by a spark of electricity.

"I assure you, Justice Ostero, that I can judge this case with perfect equanimity." His voice was a deep groan, like the rumble of a distant bullfrog.

The chief justice nodded once, curtly. "So be it," she said. "Let's get on with these proceedings."

It was exactly at the point that the Beryllium Blonde entered the courtroom.

IT WAS AS if the entire courtroom stopped breathing; like the castle in Sleeping Beauty, everything and everybody seemed to stop in their tracks, just to look at her.

Lunar cities were pretty austere in those days; the big, racy casinos over at Hell Crater hadn't even been started yet. Selene City was the largest of the Moon's communities, but even so it wasn't much more than a few kilometers of rock-walled tunnels. Even the so-called Grand Plaza was just a big open space with a dome sealing it in. Okay, so most of the ground inside the plaza was green with grass and shrubs. After two days, who cared? You could rent wings and go flying on your own muscle power, but there wasn't much in the way of scenery.

The Beryllium Blonde was *scenery*. She stepped into the courtroom and lit up the place, like her golden hair was casting reflections off the bare stone walls. The panel of three judges—two women and the Toad—just stared at her as she walked demurely down the courtroom's central aisle and stopped at the railing that separated the lawyers and their clients from the spectators.

We were all spectators, of course. She was absolutely gorgeous: tall and shapely beyond the dreams of a teenaged cartoonist. A face that could launch a thousand rockets—among other things.

She looked so sweet, with those wide blue eyes and that perfect face. Her glittery silver suit was actually quite modest, with a high buttoned Chinese collar and trousers that looped beneath her delicate little feet. Of course, the suit was form-fitting: it clung to her as if it'd been sprayed onto her body, and there wasn't a man in the courtroom who didn't envy the fabric.

Even Sam could do nothing more than stare at her, dumbfounded. It wasn't until much later that I learned why he called her the Beryllium Blonde: beryllium, a steel-gray metal, quite brittle at room temperature, with a very high melting point; used mostly as a hardening agent.

How true.

"Am I interrupting?" she asked, in a breathy innocent voice.

The chief judge had to swallow visibly before she found her voice. "No, we were just getting started. What can I do for you?" This from the woman who was known, back in Australia, as the Scourge of Queensland.

"I am here to help represent the prosecution, on a pro bono basis."

All four of the prosecution's expensive lawyers shot to their feet and welcomed her to their midst.

Sam just moaned.

"It goes back a long way," Sam told me after the preliminaries had ended and the court had adjourned for lunch. We had scooted back to the hotel suite we were renting, the two of us desperately trying to hold the company together despite the trial and embargo and everything else.

"She tried to screw me out of my zero-gee hotel, way back when," he said.

I wondered how literally Sam meant his words. He had the solar system's worst reputation as an insensitive womanizing chauvinist boor. Yet somehow Sam never lacked for female companionship. I've seen ardent feminists succumb to Sam's charm. Once in a while.

"Hell hath no fury like a woman scorned," Sam said, sighing mightily at his memories. "Of course, we spent a pretty intense time together before the doo-doo hit the fan." He sighed again. "All she was after was the rights to my hotel."

"While you were truly and deeply in love," I wisecracked.

Sam looked shocked. "I think I was," he said, sounding hurt. "At least, while it lasted."

"So she has a personal bias against you. Maybe I can get her thrown off the case—"

"Don't you dare!" Sam shrieked, nearly jumping over the coffee table.

"But—"

He gave me his Huck Finn grin. "If I've got to be raped, pillaged and burnt at the stake," he said happily, "I couldn't think of anybody I'd prefer to have holding the matches."

Had Sam given up?

I DON'T KNOW about Sam, but after the first two days of testimony I was ready to give up.

Fourteen witnesses—a baker's dozen plus one—all solemnly testified that Sam had deliberately, with malice aforethought and all that stuff, wiped out the harmless lichenoid colony that dwelled under Europa's ice mantle. And had even bashed one of the DULL scientists on the head with an oxygen tank when the man had tried to stop him.

The spectators on the other side of the courtroom rail sobbed and sighed through the testimony, hissed at Sam and groaned piteously when the last of the witnesses showed a series of computer graphics picturing the little green lichenoids before Sam and the empty cavity under the ice where the lichenoids had been but were no longer—because of Sam.

"What need have we of further witnesses?" bellowed a heavyset woman from the back of the courtroom.

I turned and saw that she was on her feet, brandishing an old-fashioned rope already knotted into a hangman's noose.

The chief judge frowned at her, rather mildly, and asked her to sit down.

For the first time since his profession of impartiality Weatherwax spoke up. "We want to give the accused a fair trial," he rumbled, again sounding rather like a bullfrog. "Then we'll hang him."

He made a crooked smile to show that he was only joking. Maybe.

The chief judge smiled, too. "Although we haven't yet decided how a sentence of capital punishment would be carried out," she said, looking straight-faced at Sam, "I'm sure it won't be by hanging. In this low-gravity environment that might constitute cruel and unusual punishment."

"Thanks a lot," Sam muttered.

THEN THE CHIEF judge turned to me. "Cross-examination?"

The scientist who had shown the computer graphics was still sitting in the witness chair, to one side of the judges' banc. I didn't have any questions for him. In fact, I wanted him and his cute little pictures off the witness stand as quickly as possible.

But just as I started to shake my head I heard Sam, beside me, speak up.

"I have a few questions for this witness, your honors."

The three judges looked as startled as I felt.

"Mr. Gunn," said the chief judge, with a grim little smile, "I told you before that you are represented by counsel and should avail yourself of his expertise."

Sam glanced at me. We both knew my expertise consisted of a gaggle of computer programs and not much else.

"There are aspects of this case that my, uh . . . counsel hasn't had time to study. I was on the scene and I know the details better than he possibly could."

The three judges conferred briefly, whispering and nodding. At last the chief judge said, "Very well, Mr. Gunn, you may proceed." Then she smiled coldly and added, "There is an old tradition in the legal profession that a man who represents himself in court has a fool for a client."

Sam got to his feet, grinning that naughty-little-boy grin of his. "And a fool for a lawyer, too, I guess."

All three judges nodded in unison.

"Anyway," Sam said, jamming his hands into the pockets of his baby-blue coveralls, "there are a couple of things I think the court should know in deeper detail."

I glanced over at the Beryllium Blonde while Sam sauntered up to the witness box. She was sitting back, smiling and relaxed, as if she was enjoying the show. Her four colleagues were watching her, not Sam.

The witness was one of the DULL scientists who'd been on Europa, Dr. Clyde Erskine. He was a youngish fellow, with thinning sandy hair and the beginnings of a pot belly.

Sam gave him his best disarming smile. "Dr. Erskine. Are you a biologist?"

"Uh . . . no, I'm not."

"A geologist?"

"No." Rather sullenly, I thought.

"What is your professional specialty, then?" Sam asked, as amiably as he might ask a bartender for a drink on the house.

Erskine replied warily. "I'm a professor of communications at the University of Texas. In Austin."

"Not a biologist?"

"No, I am not a biologist."

"Not a geologist or a botanist or zoologist or even a chemist, are you?"

"I am a doctor of communications," Erskine said testily.

"Communications? Like, communicating with alien life forms? SETI, stuff like that?"

"No," Erskine said. "Communications between humans. My specialty is mass media."

Sam put on a look of shocked surprise. "Mass media? You mean you're a public relations flack?"

"I am a doctor of communications!"

"But what you were doing on Europa was generating PR material for DULL, wasn't it?"

"Yes," he admitted. "That was my job."

Sam nodded and took a few steps away from the witness, as if he were trying to digest Erskine's admission.

Turning back to the witness chair, Sam asked, "We've heard fourteen witnesses so far. Were any of them biologists?"

Erskine frowned in thought for a moment. "No, I don't believe any of them were."

"Were any of them scientists of any stripe?"

"Most of them were communications specialists," Erskine answered.

"PR flacks, like yourself."

"I am not a flack!" Erskine snapped.

"Yeah, sure," said Sam. He hesitated a moment, then asked, "How many people were on Europa?"

"Uh . . . let me see," Erskine muttered, screwing up his eyes to peer at the stone ceiling. "Must have been upwards of three dozen. . . . No, more like forty, forty-five."

"How many of 'em were scientists?" Sam asked.

"We all were!"

"I mean biologists, geologists—not PR flacks."

Erskine's face was getting red. "Communications is a valid scientific field—"

"Sure it is," Sam cut him off. "How many biologists among the forty-five men and women stationed on Europa?"

Erskine frowned in thought for a moment, then mumbled, "I'm not quite certain. . . ."

"Ten?" Sam prompted.

"No."

"More than ten?"

"Uh . . . no."

"Five?"

Silence.

"More or less?" Sam insisted.

"I think there were three biologists," Erskine muttered, his voice so low that I could hardly hear him.

"Yet none of them have testified at this trial," Sam said, a hint of wonder in his voice. "Why is that, do you think?"

"I don't know," Erskine replied sullenly. "I guess none of them was available."

"Not available." Sam seemed to mull that over for a moment. "Then who prepared all the slides and graphs you and your cohorts have shown at this trial?"

Erskine glanced up at the judges, then answered, "The communications department of the University of Texas."

"At Austin."

"Yes."

"Not the handful of scientists who were on Europa and are now mysteriously not available?"

"The scientists gave us the input for the computer graphics."

"Oh? They were available to help you prepare your presentations but they're not available for this trial? Why is that?"

"I don't know."

Sam turned away from the witness. I thought he was coming back to our table, but suddenly Sam wheeled back to face Erskine again. "Do you have any samples of the Europa lichenoids?"

"Samples? Me? No."

"Do any of the biologists have samples of them? Actual physical samples?"

"No," Erskine said, brows knitting. "They were living under more than seven kilometers of ice. We were—"

"Thank you, Dr. Erskine," Sam snapped. Looking up at the judges he said grandly, "No further questions."

Erskine looked slightly confused, then started to get to his feet.

"Redirect, please," said the Beryllium Blonde.

All three judges smiled down at her. I smiled too as she walked from behind the prosecution's table toward the witness box. Just watching her move was a pleasure. Even Sam gawked at her. Beads of perspiration broke out on his upper lip as he sat down beside me.

"Dr. Erskine," the Blonde asked sweetly, "which scientists helped you to prepare the graphics you showed us?"

Erskine blinked at her as if he were looking at a mirage that was too good to be true. "They were prepared by Dr. Heinrich Fossbinder, of the University of Zurich."

"Dr. Fossbinder is a biologist?"

"Dr. Fossbinder is a Nobel laureate in biology. He was head of the biology team at Europa."

"All three of 'em," Sam stage-whispered loud enough to draw a warning frown from the judges.

The Blonde proceeded, undeterred. "But if you have no samples of the Europa life-forms, how were these computer images produced?"

Erskine nodded, as if to compliment her on asking an astute question. "As I said, the lichenoids were living beneath some seven kilometers of ice. We very carefully sank a fiber-optic line down to within a few dozen meters of their level and took the photographs you saw through that fiber-optic link."

With an encouraging smile that dazzled the entire courtroom, the Blonde asked, "Was your team drilling a larger bore hole, in an effort to extract samples of the life-forms?"

"Yes we were."

"And what happened?"

Erskine shot an angry look at Sam. "He ruined it! He came in with his ore-crushing machinery and chewed up so much of the ice that the entire mantle collapsed. Our bore hole was shattered and the lichenoids were exposed to vacuum."

"What effect did that have on the native life-forms of Europa?" she asked in a near-whisper.

"It killed them all!" Erskine answered hotly. "Wiped them out!" He pointed a trembling finger at Sam. "He killed a whole world's biosphere!"

The courtroom erupted in angry shouts. I thought the audience was going to lynch Sam then and there.

The Beryllium Blonde smiled at the raging spectators and said, barely loud enough to be heard over their yelling, "The prosecution rests."

The chief judge banged her gavel and recessed for the day, but hardly any of the audience paid her any attention. They wanted Sam's blood. A cordon of security guards formed around us, looking worried. But as we headed for the door, I saw that Sam was unperturbed by any of the riotous goings-on; his eyes were locked on the Blonde. It was as if no one else existed for him.

THE OUTLOOK WASN'T brilliant that evening. The prosecution had presented what looked like an airtight case. I had no witnesses except Sam, and in our discussions of the case he hadn't once refuted the prosecution's testimony.

"You really wiped out the colony of lichenoids?" I asked him repeatedly.

His only answer was a shrug and an enigmatic, "They're not there, are they?"

"And you actually banged that scientist on the head with an oxy bottle?"

He grinned at the memory of it. "I sure did," he admitted, impishly.

We were having dinner in our hotel suite. Sam couldn't show his face in a restaurant, that's how much public opinion had turned against him. We had needed six security guards just to walk us from the courtroom to the hotel.

"But he wasn't a scientist," Sam added, heaping broiled scungilli on his plate. Selene's aquaculture produced the best shellfish off-Earth, and the hotel's chef was a Neapolitan master artist.

"He was a science writer for DULL," Sam went on. "Most of the so-called scientists on Europa were public-relations flacks and administrators."

"Like Erskine?"

He nodded. "They weren't doing research. They were busy pumping out media hype about their great green discovery."

"That's neither here nor there, Sam," I said, picking at my own clams *posilipo*.

"Isn't it?" He made a know-it-all smile.

"Sam, are you keeping something from me?" I asked.

"Me?"

"If you've got some information that will help win this case, some facts, witnesses—anything! We need it now, Sam. I'm supposed to open your defense tomorrow morning and I don't have a thing to go on."

"Except my testimony," he said.

That's what I was afraid of.

YET THE NEXT morning I put Sam on the witness chair and asked him one single question: "Mr. Gunn, can you tell us in your own words what took place on Europa during the time you were there?"

"Soitinly!" Sam said, grinning.

The judges were not amused. Neither was the Beryllium Blonde, sitting at the prosecution's table, watching Sam intently, her blue eyes focused on him like twin lasers.

THE WHOLE THING started—Sam said—with the Porno Twins. Cindy and Mindy.

You gotta understand that working those mining ships out there in the Asteroid Belt is hard, lonely work. Sure, there are women among the crews, but there's always eight or nine more guys than gals on those factory ships, and the guys get—well, the polite word for it is horny.

(The chief judge huffed at that but didn't interrupt. The Toad snorted. The Beryllium Blonde smiled.)

The Porno Twins supplied a needed service for the miners. Virtual sex, on demand. Oh sure, there were VR services from Earth-Moon, but the time lag meant that you couldn't do real-time simulations: you had to buy a VR program that was prepackaged. It might have a few variables, but you more or less got a regular routine, take it or leave it.

The Porno Twins had come out to the belt and established themselves in a spacecraft that could swing around the area and maneuver close enough to the factory ships to do real-time simulations. You know, positive feedback and all that. You could *talk* with 'em, and they'd respond to you. It was great!

Well, anyway, the guys told me it was great. Some of the women used them, too, but that's their business. I never did. Virtual reality is terrific and all that, but I prefer the real thing. I want to feel some warmth instead of grappling with an electronic fantasy.

I saw the twins' advertisements, of course. They were really attractive: two very good-looking dolls who were identical down to their belly buttons, except that one was right-handed and the other was a lefty. Mindy and Cindy. Geniuses at what they did. They were natural redheads, but with VR they could be any color or shade you wanted.

It was the idea of their being twins that made them so popular. Every guy's got a fantasy about that and they were happy to fulfill your wildest dreams, anything you asked for. And it was all perfectly safe, of course: they were usually a million kilometers away, feeding your fantasy at the speed of light with a real-time virtual reality link.

I had thought about dropping in on them for a real visit, you know, in the flesh. Me and every other guy in the belt. But they stayed buttoned up inside their own spacecraft; no visitors. None of us knew what kind of defenses they might have on their craft, but I guess we all realized that their best defense was the threat of leaving the belt.

So nobody molested them. If anybody gave even a hint that he might try to sneak out to their ship, his fellow miners dissuaded him—as they say—forcefully. Nobody wanted the Twins to leave us alone out in the dark and cold between Mars and Jupiter.

It was sheer coincidence that I happened to be the closest ship to theirs when their life-support system malfunctioned. I guess I'm lucky that way, if you can call it lucky when lightning strikes you.

I was trying to repair the mining boat *Clementine* when I heard their distress call. Most mining boats have minimal crews; *Clementine* was the first to be designed to run with no crew at all. Except it didn't work right.

Mining boats attach themselves to an asteroid and grind up the rock or metal, sort it by chemical composition, and store it in their holds until they make rendezvous with a factory boat and unload the ores. *Clementine* was chewing up its target asteroid all right, but there was a glitch in the mass spectrometer and the idiot computer running the boat couldn't figure out which stream of ore should go into which hold, so it stopped all operations halfway into the program and just clung to the asteroid like a scared spider, doing absolutely nothing except costing me money.

So I jetted out to *Clementine* from Ceres in my personal torch ship, leaving the company's important business in the capable and well-trained hands of my crackerjack staff. I figured they could run things for maybe four-five days before driving me into bankruptcy.

So I'm in a battered old hard suit hanging weightless with my head stuck in the computer bay and my feet dangling up near the navigation sensors when the radio bleeps.

"This is *SEX069*," said a sultry female voice. "We have an emergency situation. Our life support system has suffered a malfunction. Our computer indicates we have only eleven point four days until the air recycling scrubbers fail completely. We need help immediately."

I didn't have to look up the IAA registry to find out who *SEX069* was. That was the Porno Twins' spacecraft! I pulled my head out of the computer bay, cracking my helmet on the edge of the hatch hard enough to make me see stars, and jackknifed myself into an upright position by the set of navigation sensors. Not easy to do in a hard suit, by the way.

Being designed to operate uncrewed, *Clementine* didn't have an observation port or even cameras outside its dumb hull. But it had a radio, so I squirted off a message to the Twins as fast as my gloved fingers could hit the keypad.

"This is Sam Gunn," I said, in my deepest, manliest voice. "Received your distress call and am on my way to you." Then I couldn't resist adding, "Have no fear, Sam is here!"

I got out of *Clementine* fast as I could and into my personal torch ship, *Joker*. While I was taking off my hard suit I had the Twins squirt me their location and their computer's diagnostic readings.

Their craft was several million kilometers away, coasting in a Sun-centered orbit not far from the asteroid Vesta.

Now, *Joker's* built for my comfort—and for speed. Her fusion-MHD drive could accelerate at a full g continuously, as long as she had reaction mass to fire out her nozzles. Any other rock jockey in the belt would have had to coast along for weeks on end to reach the Twins. I could zip out to Vesta in a matter of hours, accelerating like a bat out of sheol.

"SPARE US THE profanity, Mr. Gunn," said the Toad.

"And kindly stick to the facts of the case," the chief judge added, frowning. "We don't need a sales pitch for your personal yacht."

Sam shrugged and glanced at me. I realized that if he was trying to drum up interest in *Joker,* he must be feeling pretty desperate, financially.

THE POINT IS—Sam blithely continued—that *Joker* was the only craft in the belt that had a chance in . . . in the solar system, of helping the Twins. Nobody else could get to them in eleven days or less.

But as I sat in the bridge, in my form-accommodating, reclinable swiveling command chair, which has built-in massage and heat units (the chief judge glowered at Sam), and looked into the details of the Twins' diagnostics, I realized they were in even deeper trouble than I had thought. The graphs on the screens showed that not only had their recycler failed, they were also losing air; must've been punctured by a centimeter-sized asteroid, punched right through their armor and sprung a leak in their main air tank. Maybe it knocked out their recycling system, too.

Their real problem was with their automated maintenance equipment. How could their system allow the air recycling equipment to go down? And their damned outside robot was supposed to fix punctures as soon as they happened. Theirs didn't. It was just sitting on the outer skin of the hull, frozen into immobility. Maybe an asteroid had dinged it, too. Their diagnostics didn't show why the robot wasn't working.

They needed air, or at least oxygen. And they needed it in a hurry. Even if I got to them in a day or so and fixed the leak and repaired their recycling system they wouldn't have enough air to survive.

I spent the next few hours chewing on their problem. Or really, getting the best computers I could reach to chew on it. *Joker* has some really sophisticated programs in its access (the chief judge scowled again) but I also contacted my headquarters on Ceres and even requested time on the IAA system. I had to come up with a solution that would work. And fast.

By the time I had showered, put on a fresh set of coveralls, and taken a bite of food, the various analyses started showing up on the multiple display screens in *Joker*'s very comfortable yet efficiently laid-out bridge. ("Mr. Gunn!" all three judges yelped.)

Okay, so here's the situation. The Twins' air is leaking out through the puncture. I can fix the puncture in ten minutes, while their dumb robot sits on its transistors and does nothing, but they'll still run out of air in a couple of days. I can give them oxygen from *Joker*'s water tanks— electrolyze the water, that's simple enough. But then I won't have enough reaction mass to get away and we'll both be in trouble.

Now, I've got to admit, the thought of being marooned off Vesta with the Porno Twins had a certain appeal to it. But when I thought it over, I figured that although being with them could be great fun, *dying* with them wasn't what I wanted to do.

Besides, they flatly refused to even consider letting me inside their leaking craft.

"Oh, no, Mr. Gunn!" they said, in unison. "We could never allow you to board our ship."

Cindy and Mindy were on my main display screen, two lovely redheads with sculpted cheekbones and emerald-green eyes and lips just trembling with emotion.

"That wouldn't be right," said Cindy. Or maybe it was Mindy.

"We've never let anyone into our ship," said the other one.

"If we let you, then all the other miners would want to visit us, too."

"In person!"

"In the flesh."

"But this would be a mission of mercy," I pleaded.

They blushed and lowered their eyes. Beautiful long silky lashes, I noticed.

"Mr. Gunn," said Mindy. Or maybe Cindy. "How would you feel if we allowed one of your miners to board our vessel?"

"You'd want the same privilege, wouldn't you?" the other one asked.

"I sure would," I admitted, feeling deflated and erect at the same time.

"For your information," said Cindy (Mindy?), "we've received calls from seventeen other mining ships, responding to our distress message."

"They're all on their way to us."

"And they all will want to come aboard once they reach us."

"Which we won't allow, of course."

"Of course," I said, downcast. "How soon can they reach you?"

"Not for several weeks, at least."

"We've informed them all that there's no sense in their coming to us, since they can't reach us in time."

"But they've all replied that they'll come anyway."

I wondered who the hell was doing any mining. The Twins could cause a financial collapse of the metals and minerals market at this rate.

"MR. GUNN," SAID the chief judge sharply, "will you please stick to the facts pertaining to this case? We have no prurient interest in your sexual fantasies."

"Or your financial problems," added the Toad.

"But you've gotta understand the situation," Sam insisted. "Unless you can see how the distances and timing were, you won't be able to grasp the reasons for my actions."

The chief judge heaved a long, impatient sigh. "Get on with it, Mr. Gunn," she groused.

OKAY, OKAY. WHERE was I . . . oh, yeah.

I didn't believe the computer analyses when I first saw them. But each system came up with the same set of alternatives and the only one that had any chance of helping the Twins was the one I took.

It looked crazy to me, at first. But the computers had taken into account *Joker*'s high-thrust capability; that was they key to their solution.

All I had to do was zip out to Jupiter at three g's acceleration, grab some oxygen from one of the ice-covered Galilean moons, refuel *Joker*'s fusion generator by scooping hydrogen and helium isotopes from Jupiter's upper atmosphere, and then roar back to the belt at another three g's and deliver the oxygen to the Twins.

Simple.

Also impossible.

So that's what I did.

"MAY I INTERRUPT?" asked the Beryllium Blonde, rising to her feet behind the prosecution's table.

All three judges looked happy to accommodate her. Or maybe they were just getting tired of listening to Sam. His voice had a kind of nervous edge to it; after a while it was like listening to a mosquito whining in your ear.

"Mr. Gunn," she said, smiling ingenuously at Sam, in the witness box, "you told this court that you consulted several computer analyses before deciding on your course of action?"

"That's right," Sam replied, grinning goofily at her. He seemed over-joyed that she was talking to him.

"And did each of these computer analyses specifically direct you to the Jovian moon Europa?"

Sam shifted a little on the chair. "No, they didn't. They all showed that Ganymede would be my best bet."

"Then why did you go to Europa?"

"I was coming to that when you interrupted me."

"Isn't it true, Mr. Gunn, that your entire so-called 'mission of mercy' was actually a clever plot to break the embargo on commercial exploita-tion of the Jupiter system?"

That's where Sam should have said a simple and emphatic *no!* and let it go at that. But not Sam.

Apparently some things were more important to Sam even than women. He lost his goofy expression and stared straight into her china-blue eyes.

"The IAA's embargo on the commercial development of the Jupiter system is a shuck," Sam said evenly.

A general gasp arose. Even the judges—especially the judges—seemed shocked. For the first time since the trial had begun, the Toad looked angry.

Undeterred, Sam went on, "Why embargo commercial enterprises from the entire Jupiter system? What's the sense of it? Even if you want to protect those little green things on Europa, just putting Europa off-limits would be good enough. Why close off the whole system?"

"Why indeed," the Blonde countered, "now that you've killed off those poor little green creatures."

"Would you rather let two human women die?" Sam demanded.

"Two prostitutes?"

"Look who's talking."

The chief judge whacked her gavel so hard its head flew off, nearly beaning the clerk sitting at the foot of the banc.

But before the judge could say anything, Sam exclaimed, "One of the is-sues at stake here is the moral question of human life versus animal rights."

A rail-thin, bald and bleary-eyed man shot to his feet from the middle of the spectators. "Animals have legal rights! A dog or a cat has just as much right to life and dignity as a human being!"

"Yeah," Sam retorted, "unless the human being's life is in danger. If I'm a fireman rushing into a burning building, who am I gonna grab first, a human baby or a puppy dog?"

"Stop this!" the chief judge bellowed, slapping the top of the banc with the flat of her hand. "I will have order in this courtroom or I'll clear the chamber!"

The gaunt animal-rights man sat down, muttering to himself.

"And you, Mr. Gunn," said the chief judge, scowling down at Sam, "will not turn this trial into a circus. Stick to the facts of the case!"

"One of the 'facts' of this case," Sam replied evenly, "is the accusation that I wiped out an entire alien life-form. Even if that's true—and I'm not admitting it is—I did what I did to save the lives of two human woman."

He turned back to the Blonde. "And they're not prostitutes; they're producers of virtual reality simulations. Which is more than I can say for some of the broads in this courtroom!"

"Your honors!" the Blonde cried, her hands flying to her face. But I was close enough to see that her cheeks weren't blushing and there was pure murder in those deep blue eyes.

The chief judge threw her hands in the air. "Mr. Gunn, if you cannot or will not restrict your testimony to the facts of this case, we will hold you in contempt of court."

For just an instant the expression on Sam's face told me that he was considering a term in the penal colony as better than certain bankruptcy. But the moment passed.

"Okay," he said, putting on his most contrite little-boy face. "I'll stick to the facts—if I'm not interrupted."

The Blonde huffed and stamped back to the prosecution table.

AS I SAID, the computer analyses showed that I had to zoom out to the Jupiter system at three g's, grab some oxygen from Ganymede, restock my fusion fuel and reaction mass by scooping Jupiter's atmosphere, and then race back to the Twins—again at three g's. Three point oh two, to be exact.

It was trickier than walking a tightrope over Niagara Falls on your hands, blindfolded; more convoluted than a team of Chinese acrobats auditioning for the Beijing Follies; as dangerous as—

("Mr. Gunn, please!" wailed the chief judge.)

Well, anyway, it was going to be a female dog and a half. Riding for several days at a time in three g's is no fun; you can't really move when every part of your body weighs three times normal. A hiccup can give you a hernia. If you're not *extremely* careful you could end up with your scrotum hanging down to your ankles. I always wear a lead jockstrap, of course, but even so . . .

(I thought the judges were about to have apoplexy, but Sam kept going without even taking a breath, so by the time they were ready to yell at him he was already miles away, subject-wise.)

I cranked my reclining command chair all the way down so it could work as an acceleration couch. I couldn't take the chance of trying to raise my head and chew solid food and swallow while under three gee's, so while the acceleration was building up I set up an intravenous feeding system for myself from *Joker*'s medical systems. The ship has the best medical equipment this side of Lunar University, by the way. That was pretty easy. The tough part was sticking the needle into my own arm and inserting the intravenous feed.

(Half the courtroom groaned at the thought.)

And then there was the waste elimination tubing, but I won't go into that.

(More groans and a couple of gargling, retching sounds.)

I welded the computer keyboard to the end of my command chair's right armrest even though the computer was fully equipped with voice recognition circuitry. Didn't want to take any chances on the system—as ultrasophisticated as it is—failing to recognize my voice because I was strangling in three gee's.

By the time *Joker*'s acceleration passed two gee's I was flat on my back in the couch, all the necessary tubes in place, display screens showing me the ongoing analyses of this crazy mission. I had to get everything right, down to the last detail, or end up burning myself to a crisp in Jupiter's atmosphere or nose-diving into Ganymede and making a new crater in the ice.

"YOU KEEP SAYING Ganymede," the Toad demanded. "How did you end up at Europa?"

"I'm coming to that, oh saintly one," Sam replied.

I HAD TO drag *Clementine* along with me, because I was going to need the ores she'd managed to store in her holds before her super-duper computer fritzed. Those chunks of metal were going to be my heat shield when I skimmed Jupiter's upper atmosphere. I just hoped there was enough of 'em to make a workable heat shield.

The way the numbers worked out, I would accelerate almost all the way to the Jupiter system, then flip around and start decelerating. I'd still be doing better than two gee's when I hit Jupiter's upper atmosphere. Even though the gases are pretty thin at that high altitude, I needed a heat shield if I didn't want *Joker* to get barbecued, with me inside her.

So even though I was flat on my back and not able to move much more than my fingers and toes, I had plenty of work to do. I couldn't trust *Clementine*'s smartass computer to handle the heat shield job; her computer was too glottle-stop sophisticated for such a menial job. I had to manually direct the manipulators to pull chunks of ore from her holds and place them up ahead of *Joker* by a few meters, all the time lying on the flat of my back, spending most of my energy just trying to breath.

Believe me, breathing in three gee's is not fun, even when you're on a padded couch. The g force is running from your breastbone to your spine, so every time you try to expand your lungs to take in some air, you've got to push your ribs against three times their normal weight. It's like having an asthma attack that never goes away. I was exhausted before the first day was over.

It would've been better if I could've just pumped some sedatives through the IV in my arm and slept my way to Jupiter. But I had to build up the heat shield or I'd be fricasseed when I hit Jupiter's atmosphere. I tapped into the best reentry programs on Earth as I put together those chunks of metal. They had to be close enough to one another so that the shock waves from the heated gases would cancel one another out before they got through the spaces between chunks and heated up *Joker*.

"YOU DID THIS while on the way to Jupiter?" asked the other woman judge. "While accelerating at three gravities?"

Sam put his right hand over his heart. "I did indeed," he said.

The woman shook her head, whether in admiration or disbelief I couldn't figure out.

"A question, please?" asked the Beryllium Blonde from her seat at the prosecution table.

For the first time, the chief judge looked just a trifle annoyed. "There will be ample time for cross-examination, counselor."

"I merely wanted to ask if Mr. Gunn was aware of the embargo on unauthorized flights into the Jovian system imposed by the Interplanetary Astronautical Authority."

AWARE OF IT?—Sam replied—I sure was. I sent out a message to the research station on Europa to tell 'em I was entering the Jupiter system on a mission of mercy. I set my comm unit to continue sending the message until it was acknowledged. They ignored it for a day and a half, and then finally sent a shi—an excrement-load of legalese garbage that took my computer twenty minutes to translate into understandable English.

("And what was the message from Europa?" the chief judge asked.)

Boiled down to, "Keep out! We don't care who you are or why you're heading this way; just turn around and go back to where you came from."

I got on the horn and tried to explain to them that I was trying to save the lives of two women and I wouldn't disturb them on Europa, but they just kept beaming their legal kaka. Either they didn't believe me or they didn't give a hoot about human lives.

Well, I couldn't turn around even if I'd wanted to. My flight profile depended on using Jupiter's atmosphere to aerobrake *Joker,* swing around the planet, and make a slowed approach to Ganymede. So I programmed my comm unit to keep repeating my message to Europa. It was really pretty: we're both hollering at each other and paying no attention to what the other guy's hollering back. Like two drivers in Boston yelling at each other over a fender-bender.

But while I'm roaring down toward Jupiter I start wondering: why does DULL need the whole Jupiter system roped off, when all they're supposed to be studying is Europa? I mean, they looked at Jupiter's other Galilean moons and didn't find diddly-poo. And if there's any life on Jupiter it's buried so deep inside those clouds that we haven't been able to find it.

Why embargo the whole Jupiter system when all they're supposed to be studying is Europa?

The question nagged at me like a toothache. Even while I was putting my makeshift heat shield together, I kept wondering about it in the back of my mind. I kept mulling it over, using the question to keep me from thinking about how much my chest hurt and wondering about how many breaths I had left before my ribs collapsed.

Once the heat shield was in place—or as good as a ramshackle collection of rocks can be—I could devote my full attention to the question. Mine, and the computer's.

One thing I've learned over the years of being in business: when you're trying to scope out another company's moves, follow the money trail. So I started sniffing out the financial details of Diversified Universities & Laboratories, Ltd. It wasn't all that easy; DULL is a tax-exempt, nonprofit organization; it isn't publicly owned and its finances are not on public record.

But even scientists like to see their names in the media, and corporate bigwigs like it even more. So I started scrolling through the media stories about the discovery of life-forms on Europa and DULL's organization of a research station on the Jovian moon.

I learned two very interesting things.

The cost of setting up the research operation on Europa was funded by Wankle Enterprises, Incorporated, of New York, London and Shanghai.

It was Wankle's lawyers—including a certain gorgeous blonde—who talked the IAA into placing the whole Jupiter system, planet, moons, all of it, under embargo. No commercial development allowed. No unauthorized missions permitted.

Make that three things that I learned: The IAA's embargo order has some fine print in it. DULL is allowed to permit "limited resource extraction" from the Jupiter system as a means of funding its ongoing research activities on Europa. And guess who got permission from DULL to start "limited resource extraction" from Jupiter and its moons? Wankle Enterprises, Inc.

Who else?

THE SPECTATORS STIRRED and muttered. The judges were staring at Sam with real interest now, as if he'd suddenly turned into a different species of witness. All five of the prosecution attorneys—including the Beryllium Blonde—were on their feet, making objections.

"Irrelevant and immaterial," said the first attorney.

"Rumor and hearsay," said number two.

"Wankle Enterprises is not on trial here," said number three, "Sam Gunn is."

"He's trying to smear Diversified Universities and Laboratories, Limited," number four bleated.

The Blonde said, "I object, your honors."

The chief judge raised an eyebrow half a millimeter. "On what grounds, counselor?"

"Mr. Gunn's statements are irrelevant, immaterial, based on rumor and hearsay, an attempt to shift the focus of this trial away from himself and onto Wankle Enterprises, and a despicable attempt to smear the good name of an organization dedicated to the finest and noblest scientific research."

The chief judge nodded, then glanced briefly at her colleagues on either side of her. They both nodded, much more vigorously.

"Very well," she said. "Objection sustained. Mr. Gunn's last statement will be stricken from the record."

Sam shrugged philosophically. "None of those three facts can stay on the record?"

"None."

"I found out something else, too," Sam said to the judges. "A fourth fact about DULL."

"Unless it is strictly and necessarily relevant to this case," said the chief judge sternly, "it will not be allowed as testimony."

Sam thought it over for a moment, an enigmatic smile on his Jack-o'-lantern face. Then, with a shake of his head that seemed to indicate disappointment but not defeat, Sam returned to his testimony.

OKAY, I'LL SAVE the fourth fact for a while and then we'll see if it's relevant or not.

Where was I—oh, yeah, I'm dropping into Jupiter's gas clouds at a little under three g's, the insides of my chest feeling like somebody's been sandpapering them for the past few days.

I put in a call to the Twins, telling them to hang in there, I'd be back with all the oxygen they needed in less than a week. I didn't tell them how awful I felt, but they must have seen it in my face.

It took about eleven minutes for my comm signal to reach them, and another eleven for their answer to get back to me. So I gave them a brave "Don't give up the ship" spiel and then went about my business checking out my heat shield—and DULL's finances.

Cindy and Mindy both appeared on my comm screen, wearing less than Samoan nudists at the springtime fertility rites. If my eyeballs hadn't weighed a little more than three times normal they would've popped right out of their sockets.

"We truly appreciate what you're doing for us, Sam," they said in unison, as if they'd rehearsed it. "And we want you to know that we'll be *especially* appreciative when you come back to us."

"Extremely appreciative," breathed Cindy. Mindy?

"Extraordinarily appreciative," the other one added, batting her long lashes at me.

I was ready to jump off my couch and fly to them like Superman. Except that the damned gee-load kept me pinned flat. All of me.

Everything would've worked out fine—or at least okay—if my swing through Jupiter's upper atmosphere had gone as planned. But it didn't.

Ever see an egg dropped from the top of a ninety-storey tower hit the pavement? That's what *Joker* was doing, just about: dropping into Jupiter's atmosphere like a kamikaze bullet. I had to use the planet's atmosphere to slow down my ship while at the same time I scooped enough Jovian hydrogen and helium isotopes to fill my propellant tanks. With that makeshift heat shield of rocks flying formation in front of *Joker* all the while.

Things started going wrong right away. The heat shield heated up too much and too soon. *Joker*'s skin temperature started rising really fast. One by one my outside cameras started to conk out; their circuitry was being fricasseed by white-hot shock-heated gases. Felt like I was melting, too, inside the ship despite the bridge's absolutely first-rate climate control system.

The damned heat shield started breaking up, which was something my hotshot computer programs didn't foresee. I should've thought of it myself, I guess. Stands to reason. Each individual rock in that jury-rigged wall in front of me was blazing like a meteor, ablating away, melting like the Wicked Witch of the West when you throw water on her.

(The chief judge frowned, puzzled, at Sam's reference but Weatherwax gave a toad-like smile and even nodded.)

I would've peeled down to my skivvies if I'd been able to, but I was still plastered into my reclined command chair like a prisoner chained to a torture rack. Must've lost twenty pounds sweating. Came as close to praying as I ever did, right there, zooming through Jupiter's upper atmosphere.

The camera on *Joker*'s ass end was still working, and while I sweated and almost prayed I watched Jupiter's swirling clouds whizzing by, far, far below me. Beautiful, really, all those bands of colors and the way they curled and eddied along their edges, kinda like the way—

("Spare us the travelogue," said the Toad, his bulging eyes blinking with displeasure. The chief judge added, "Yes, Mr. Gunn. Get on with it.")

Well, okay. So I finally pull out of Jupiter's atmosphere with my propellant tanks full and *Joker*'s skin still intact—barely. But the aerobraking hadn't followed the computer's predicted flight path as closely as I'd thought it would. Wasn't off by much, but as I checked out my velocity and position I saw pretty damned quickly that I wasn't going to be able to reach Ganymede.

Joker had slowed to less than one g, all right, and other than the failed cameras and a few strained seams in the skin the ship was okay. I could sit up and even walk around the bridge, if I wanted to. I even disconnected all the tubing that was hooked into me. Felt great to be free and able to take a leak on my own again.

But Ganymede was out of reach.

Now the whole reason for this crazy excursion was to grab oxygen to replenish the Porno Twins' evaporating supply. I checked through the computer and saw that the only ice-bearing body I could reasonably get to was—you guessed it—good ol' Europa.

"MR. GUNN," THE Toad interrupted, his voice a melancholy croak, "do you honestly expect this court to believe that after all your derring-do, Europa was the only possible body that you could reach?"

Sam gave him his most innocent look. "I'm under oath, right? How can I lie to you?"

The chief judge opened her mouth as if she were going to zing Sam, then she seemed to think better of it and said nothing.

"Besides," Sam added impishly, "you can check *Joker*'s computer logs, if you haven't already done that."

The Beryllium Blonde called from the prosecution table, "A point of information, please?"

All three judges smiled and nodded.

Without rising, the Blonde asked, "There are twenty-seven moons in the Jupiter system, are there not?"

"Twenty-nine," Sam snapped, "including the two little sheepdog rocks that keep Jupiter's ring in place."

"Aren't most of these moons composed of ices that contain a goodly amount of oxygen?"

"Yes they are," Sam replied before anyone else could, as politely as if he were speaking to a stranger.

"Then why couldn't you have obtained the oxygen you claim you needed from one of those other satellites?"

"Because, oh fairest of the sadly mush-brained profession of hired truth-twisters, my poor battered little ship couldn't reach any of those other moons."

"Truly?"

Sam put his right hand over his heart. "Absolutely. *Joker* was like a dart thrown at a dartboard. I had aimed for a bull's-eye, but the aerobraking flight had jiggled my aim and now I was headed for Europa. Scout's honor. It wasn't my idea. Blame Isaac Newton, or maybe Einstein."

The Blonde said nothing more, but it was perfectly clear from the expression on her gorgeous face that she didn't believe a word Sam was saying. I looked up at the judges—it took an effort to turn my eyes away from the Blonde—and saw that none of the three of them believed Sam either. Mentally I added the possibility of perjury charges to the list Sam already faced.

IT WASN'T MY idea to hit Europa—Sam insisted—but there wasn't much else I could do. Sure, I had my tanks full of propellant for the fusion torch, but I was gonna need that hydrogen and helium for the high-g burn back to Vesta and the Twins. I couldn't afford to spend any of it juking around the Jupiter system. I was pointed at Europa when I came out of Jupiter's atmosphere. Act of God, you could call it.

(I couldn't fail to notice the grin that crept across Sam's face as he spoke. Neither could the judges. Either he was not telling it exactly the way it had happened or he was downright pleased that this "act of God" had pointed him squarely at Europa.)

I called the DULLards on Europa again and gave them a complete run-down of the situation. Recorded my message and had the comm system keep replaying it to 'em. They didn't respond. Not a peep.

I had nothing to do for several hours except feel good that I didn't have all those damned tubes poking into me. But even though I could get up and walk around my luxuriously appointed bridge and take solid food from my highly automated and well-stocked galley, my brain kept nibbling at a question that'd been nagging at me since before I hit Jupiter.

Why did DULL insist on keeping the whole Jupiter system off-limits to outside developers?

And why did the IAA agree to let them do that?

All of a sudden my comm system erupted with noise from Europa. They started screaming at me that I wasn't allowed in the Jupiter system, I can't land on Europa, I'd better haul ass out of there, yaddida, yaddida, and so on. Threatened me with lawsuits and public flogging and whatnot.

I told them I was on a mission of mercy and two human lives depended on my grabbing some of their ice. Three lives, come to think of it. My butt was on the line, too.

But even if they heard me they didn't listen. They just kept screaming that I wasn't allowed to land on Europa or be anywhere in the Jupiter system. Different faces appeared on my comm screen every fifteen seconds, seemed like, all of them getting more and more frantic as I came hurtling closer to Europa's ice-covered surface.

"I hear what you're saying," I told them. "I'm not going to disturb your little green lichenoids. I just need to grab some ice and, believe me, I'll be out of your way as fast as a jackrabbit in mating season."

I might as well have been talking to myself. In fact, I think I was. They paid no attention to what I was saying.

A really nasty-looking lug come on my comm screen. "This is Captain Majerkurth. I'm in charge of security here on Europa. If you try to land here I will personally break your balls."

"Security?" I blurted. "What do you need security for? And what army are you a captain in?"

"I am a captain in the security department of Wankle Enterprises, on loan to Diversified Universities and Laboratories, Limited," he replied evenly—an even snarl, that is.

"Well, if I were you, *mon capitain*," I said, "I'd start getting my people under shelter. My spacecraft is accompanied by about a hundred or so rocks that're going to hit Europa like a meteor shower."

That was the remains of my heat shield, of course. Most of the rocks had ablated down to pebble size, but at the velocity we were traveling they could still do some damage. Europa's icy surface was going to get peppered and there wasn't anything I could do about it except warn them to get under shelter.

Well, to make a long story short (the judges all sighed at that) I landed on Europa nice and smooth, a real gentle touchdown. With *Clementine* still dragging along beside me, of course. The meteor shower I promised Captain Majerkurth didn't harm anything, near as I can tell: just a few hundred new little craterlets in Europa's surface of ice.

So I've got *Clementine* chewing up ice and storing it in her holds. Bypassed her dumbass mass spectrometer, otherwise her computer would've stopped everything because it couldn't figure out what elements were going into which bins. Didn't matter. It was all ice, which added up to hydrogen for *Joker*'s fusion torch and oxygen for the Twins.

I expected Majerkurth to show up, and sure enough, I hadn't been sitting on Europa for more than an hour before this flimsy little hopper pops up over my horizon, heading my way on a ballistic trajectory. For half a second I thought the hardass had fired a missile at me, but my computer analyzed the radar data in picoseconds and announced that it was a personnel hopper, not a missile, and it was gonna land beside *Joker*.

I buttoned up *Joker* good and tight. I had no intention of letting Majerkurth come aboard. But the space-suited figure that climbed down from the hopper wasn't the security captain.

"Mr. Gunn, this is Anitra O'Toole. Permission to come aboard?"

I stared at the image in my display screen. You can't tell much about a person when she's zipped into a space suit, but Anitra O'Toole looked small—maybe my own height or even a little less—and her voice was kind of . . . well, she sounded almost scared.

"Are you one of Majerkurth's security people?" I asked.

"Security? Goodness no! If Captain Majerkurth knew I was here he'd . . ." She hesitated, then pleaded, "Please let me come aboard, Mr. Gunn. Please!"

What could I do? I could never refuse a woman asking for help, and she seemed to need my help pretty desperately. It was like the time I—

("Please stick to the facts of this case!" the chief judge demanded.)

Yeah, okay. So I let her in. Anitra O'Toole turned out to be young, kinda pretty in a cheerleader way, and very worried. Oh, and she was one of the three biologists among the DULL team on Europa.

And she was scared, too. She wouldn't say why, at first, or why she wanted to come aboard *Joker*. She just fidgeted and blathered about her husband waiting for her back on Earth and how she was afraid that her marriage was coming apart because they'd been separated so long and her career might be going down the tubes as well.

I only had a few hours to be on Europa, but while my brain-dead *Clementine* was ingesting ice I tried to be as hospitable as possible. I sat Anitra down in my quarters, just off the bridge, and programmed the galley to produce a gourmet dinner of roast squab, sweet potatoes, string beans—

("Mr. Gunn!" growled the Toad.)

All right, all right. I popped a bottle of champagne for her. *Joker* has the best wine cellar in space, bar none.

Now, don't get me wrong. I don't try to seduce married women, even when they tell me their marriage is in trouble. Especially then, as a matter of fact. Too complicated; too many chances for lawsuits or grievous bodily harm.

I was more interested in her saying that her career might be going down the tubes. One of three biologists on Europa, working on a newly discovered form of extraterrestrial life, and her career was in trouble?

"Why?" I asked her.

Anitra had these big violet eyes and the kind of golden blonde hair that most women get out of a bottle. Sitting there beside me in a one-piece zipsuit, she looked young and unhappy and vulnerable, like a runaway waif. I stayed an arm's length away; it wasn't easy, but I kept thinking about the Twins as much as I could.

"The adaptation isn't working," Anitra said, miserable. "All this planning and genetic engineering and they still won't reproduce."

"What won't reproduce?" I asked.

She sipped at the champagne. I refilled her glass.

"Could you take me back to Earth?" she blurted.

I started to say no, which was the truth. But long, long ago I had learned that the truth doesn't always get the job done.

"I'm heading back to the belt. My company headquarters is in Ceres," I said. "I could arrange transportation from there."

She clutched at my wrist, nearly spilling my champagne. "Would you?"

"Why do you want to leave Europa so badly?"

Those violet eyes looked away from me. "My husband," she said vaguely.

"Won't DULL set you up with transportation? They have regular resupply flights, don't they? You could hook a ride back Earthside with them."

"No," she said, barely a whisper. "I've got to go now, while I've got the chance. And the nerve."

"But your work here on the lichenoids . . ."

"That's the whole point!" she burst. "It isn't working and everybody's going to find out and I'm going to be ruined professionally and nobody will want me, not even Brandon."

I figured Brandon was her husband.

("Is there a point to all this?" asked the chief judge, frowning.)

The point is this. Anitra O'Toole told me that the lichenoids DULL was studying are not native to Europa. They were engineered in a biology lab in Zurich and planted on Europa by the DULL team.

THE COURTROOM ERUPTED. As if a bomb had gone off. Half the spectators jumped to their feet, shouting. The Beryllium Blonde and her four cohorts were screaming objections. The chief judge was banging the stump of her gavel on the banc, demanding order.

But what caught my eye was the look on the splotchy face of the Toad.

Weatherwax was staring at Sam as if he would have gladly strangled him if he'd had the chance.

It took a while and a lot of whacking of the stump of her gavel, but once order was restored to the courtroom, the chief judge fixed Sam with a beady eye and asked, "Are you maintaining, Mr. Gunn, that there never were indigenous life-forms on Europa?"

Sitting in the witness chair with his hands folded childlike on his lap, Sam replied courteously, "Yes, ma'am, that's exactly what I'm saying. The whole story was a subterfuge, engineered by the people who run DULL."

"This is outrageous!" Weatherwax roared. Everyone in the courtroom realized that he was *the* man who ran DULL.

The chief judge was a little more professional. She turned to the prosecution's lawyers, who were still standing and fuming.

"Cross-examination?"

The Beryllium Blonde stalked out from behind the table like a battle cruiser maneuvering into range for a lethal broadside.

She stood before Sam for a long, silent moment while the entire court held its breath. He stared up at her; maybe he was trying to look defiant. To me, he looked like a kid facing the school principal.

"Mr. Gunn," she started, utterly serious, no smile, her eyes cold and calculating, "the allegation you have just made is extremely serious. What evidence do you have to support it?"

"The testimony of Dr. Anitra O'Toole, of Johns Hopkins University's biology department."

"And where is Dr. O'Toole? Why isn't she here at this trial?"

Sam took a breath. "As far as I know, she is still on Europa. They won't let her leave."

"Won't let her leave?" the Blonde registered disbelief raised to the nth power.

"She's being held prisoner, more or less," Sam said. "That's why Wankle put a security team on Europa: to see that the scientists don't talk and can't get away."

"Really, Mr. Gunn! And why isn't her husband demanding her return to Earth?"

"Because, as far as he knows, she's on Europa voluntarily, placing her career before their marriage. Besides, my sources tell me the guy's shacked up with a certain blonde lawyer."

Her eyes went wide and she smacked Sam right in the mouth. Hauled off and whacked him with the flat of her hand. The crack echoed off the courtroom's stone walls.

A couple of spectators cheered. The judges were so stunned none of them moved.

Sam ran a thumb across his jaw. I could see the white imprint of her fingers on his skin.

With a crooked grin, Sam went on, "He's here in Selene City. I could have him subpoenaed to appear here, if you like."

The Blonde visibly pulled herself together, regained her self-control by sheer force of will. She put on a contrite expression and looked up at the judges.

"I apologize for my behavior, your honors," she said, in a hushed little-girl voice. "It was inexcusable of me to allow the witness's slanderous statement to affect me so violently."

"Apology accepted," said the Toad. The chief judge's brows knit, but she said nothing.

So the Blonde got away with slugging Sam and even made it look as if it was his own fault. Neat work, I thought.

She turned back to Sam. "Do you have any *evidence* of your allegation about the lichenoids, Mr. Gunn?"

"I have Dr. O'Toole's statement on video. I activated *Joker*'s internal camera system once I allowed her on board my ship."

"Video evidence can be edited, doctored, manufactured out of computer graphics—"

"Like the slides of the Europa lichenoids we saw earlier," Sam countered.

"You are defaming scientists whose reputations are beyond reproach!" the Blonde exclaimed.

"Nobody's reputation is beyond reproach," Sam said hotly. "You oughtta know that."

Turning to the judges, he went on without taking a breath, "Your honors, none of these scientists were trying to hoodwink the public. They were drawn into a plot by the people who run Wankle Enterprises, a plot to stake out a monopoly on the resources of the whole Jupiter system!"

The chief judge answered sternly, "How can you make such an allegation, Mr. Gunn, without proof?" But I noticed she was eying the Toad as she spoke.

"Look, this is the way it worked," Sam said, ignoring her question. "DULL's operation on Europa is funded by Wankle Enterprises, right? Wankle's people went to DULL more than five years ago and suggested an experiment: they wanted DULL's scientists to engineer terrestrial lichen to survive in the conditions of Europa, living in the watery slush at the bottom of Europa's mantle of ice. The idea was to see how life-forms would behave under extraterrestrial conditions."

"Which is a valid scientific project," the Blonde said.

"Yeah, that's what they told the scientists. So the biologists engineer the critters and they send a team out to Europa to see if they can actually survive there."

The chief judge interrupted. "You are contending, Mr. Gunn, that there were no native life-forms on Europa?"

"No native life-forms on or in or any way connected with Europa. If they'd found native life forms they wouldn't have had to engineer this experiment, would they?"

"But DULL announced the discovery of native life-forms."

"Right!" Sam exulted. "That's when our slimy friend here sprung his trap. They announced that the scientists had discovered native life-forms on Europa, instead of telling the media that the lichenoids had been engineered in a bio lab in Zurich."

"That is utterly ridiculous," said the Blonde. I noticed that the Toad was slumping more than usual in his chair.

"The hell it is," Sam snapped. "The poor suckers on Europa were caught in a mousetrap. They were stuck on Europa, dependant on DULL and Wankle for transportation home. Dependant on them for air to breathe! They couldn't get to the media; they were surrounded by three dozen DULL public-relations flacks and a Wankle security team. Even if they could blow the whistle, it'd look as if they were in on the fraud from the beginning. One way or another their careers would be finished. DULL would never let them sweep the floor of a laboratory again, let alone practice scientific research."

"Monstrous," muttered the chief judge. Whether she meant Sam's allegations were monstrous or DULL's actions, I couldn't figure out.

"Meanwhile, DULL's communications experts are putting the pressure on the scientists to go along with the deception. After all, once the lichenoids adapt to the conditions under the ice on Europa they'll really be extraterrestrial organisms, right? The scientists could announce their true origins in the scientific journals in a year or two or three. Who's going to notice, by then, except other scientists?"

The Blonde stamped her lovely foot for attention. "But why go through this subterfuge? It's all so pointless and ridiculous. Why would reputable scientists, why would the directors and governors of

DULL, go through such an elaborate and foolish subterfuge? Mr. Gunn's wild theory falls apart on the question of motivation, your honors."

"Not so, oh temptress of the heavenly spheres," Sam replied. "Motivation is exactly where my theory is strongest."

He paused dramatically. Two of the judges leaned forward to hear his next words. Weatherwax looked as if he wanted to be someplace else. Anyplace else.

"Once DULL's public-relations program announced that native organisms had been found on Europa, what did the IAA do?" Before anyone could reply, Sam went on, "They roped off the whole Jupiter system—the whole damned system! Jupiter itself and all its moons, sealed off, embargoed. No commercial development allowed. Forbidden territory. No go there, bwana, IAA make big taboo."

"Mr. Gunn, please!" said the third judge.

"No commercial development allowed in the entire Jupiter system," Sam repeated. "Except for the company that was funding the Europa research station. They were allowed 'limited resource extraction' to repay for their funding the Europa team. Right?"

The chief judge murmured, "Right."

"Who was funding the Europa station? Wankle Enterprises. Who was allowed to develop 'limited resource extraction'—which means scooping Jupiter's clouds and mining its moons? Wankle Enterprises. Who has a monopoly on the thousands of trillions of dollars worth of resources in the Jupiter system? Wankle Enterprises. Surprise!"

"Limited resource extraction," snapped the Blonde, "means just that. Limited."

"Yeah, sure. What does 'limited' mean? How much? There's no definition. A billion dollars? A trillion? And what happens if the environmentalists or some other corporation or the Dalai Lama complains that Wankle's taking too much out of the Jupiter system? Wankle simply announces that the lichenoids on Europa weren't native life-forms after all. Ta-daaa! The scientists get a black eye and Wankle has established operations running all over the Jupiter system. That gives them the edge on any competition, thanks to the monopoly the IAA mistakenly granted them."

Weatherwax stirred himself. "We've listened long enough to these paranoid ramblings," he rumbled. "I haven't heard a single iota of evidence to support Mr. Gunn's ravings."

"Call Dr. O'Toole back from Europa," Sam said. "Or watch the video I made of her in my quarters aboard *Joker*. Call Professor Fossbinder in from Zurich. Call Brandon O'Toole, for Pete's sake; he's right here in Selene City. He knows that his wife was engineering lichen before she shipped out to Europa. He'll tell you all about it, if he isn't besotted by our Beryllium Blonde here."

And he quickly raised his fists into a boxer's defensive posture.

The Blonde just stood there, her lovely mouth hanging open, her eyes wide and darting from Sam to the Toad and back again.

Weatherwax heaved an enormous sigh, then croaked, "I move that we adjourn this hearing for half an hour while we discuss this new . . . allegation, in chambers."

The chief judge nodded, tight-lipped. We all rose and the judges swept out; the courtroom was so quiet I could hear their black robes rustling. The audience filed out, muttering, whispering; but Sam and I sat tensely at the defendants' table, he drumming his fingers on the tabletop incessantly, his head turned toward the prosecution's table and the Blonde. She was staring straight ahead, sitting rigid as an I-beam—a gorgeously curved I-beam. Her four cohorts sat flanking her, whispering among themselves.

After about ten minutes, a clerk came out and told us that we were wanted in the judges' chambers. I felt surprised, but Sam grinned as if he had expected it. The clerk went over and conferred briefly with the prosecution lawyers. They all got up and filed out of the courtroom, looking defeated. Even the Blonde seemed down, tired, lost. I felt an urge to go over and try to comfort her, but Sam grabbed me by the collar of my tunic and pointed me toward the slightly open door to the judges' chambers.

Weatherwax was sitting alone on an imitation leather couch big enough for four; the other two judges were nowhere in sight. He had taken off his judicial robe, revealing a rumpled pale green business suit that made him look more amphibious than ever.

"What do you want, Gunn?" he growled as we sat on upholstered armchairs, facing him.

"I want my ships released and my business reopened," Sam said immediately.

Weatherwax slowly blinked his bulging eyes. "Once this case is dismissed, that will be automatic."

Dismissed? I was startled. Was it all over?

"And," Sam went on, "I want full disclosure about the lichenoids. I want the scientists cleared of any attempt to hoodwink the public."

Again the Toad blinked. "We can always blame the PR people; say they got the story slightly askew."

Sam gave a short, barking laugh. "Blame the media, right."

"Is that all?" Weatherwax asked, his brows rising.

Sam shrugged. "I'm not out to punish anybody. Live and let live has always been my motto."

"I see."

"Of course," Sam went on, grinning impishly, "once you admit publicly that the lichenoids on Europa are a genetic experiment and not native life-forms, then the embargo on commercial development in the Jupiter system ends. Right?"

This time Weatherwax kept his froggy eyes closed for several moments before he conceded, "Right."

Sam jumped to his feet. "Good! That oughtta do it."

The Toad remained seated. There was no attempt on the part of either of them to shake hands. Sam scuttled toward the door and I got up and went after him.

But Sam stopped at the door and turned back to the Toad. "Oh, yeah, one other thing. Now that we've come to this agreement, there's no further need for you to keep the scientists bottled up on Europa. Let Dr. O'Toole come back here."

Weatherwax tried to glare at Sam but it was pathetically weak.

"And tell your sexy lawyer underling to take her claws off O'Toole's husband," Sam added, with real iron in his voice. "Give those two kids a chance to patch up their marriage."

Without even waiting for a response from the Toad, he yanked the door open and stepped outside. With me right behind him.

BY DINNERTIME THAT evening the media were running stories about how Wankle's chief public-relations consultant, Dr. Clyde Erskine of the University of Texas at Austin, had made a slight misinterpretation about the lichenoids on Europa. Sam whooped gleefully as we watched the report in our hotel suite.

He switched to the business news, which was also about the Europa "misinterpretation," but which included the fact that the IAA had decided to lift the embargo on commercial development of the Jupiter system.

Sam howled and yelped and danced across our dinner table.

"Weatherwax moved fast," I said, still sitting on the hardbacked chair while Sam did a soft-shoe around our dinner plates.

We had already been notified by the IAA that Sam's ore carriers were no longer embargoed and Asteroidal Resources, Inc. was back in business.

Sam deftly jumped down to the floor and sat on the edge of the table, facing me.

"He's got the power to move fast, Orville. The Toad has a reputation for good-deed-doing, but he's really a power-clutching sonofabitch who's spent the past ninety years or so worming his way into the top levels of a dozen of the solar system's biggest corporations."

"And the IAA," I added.

"And he founded DULL to serve as a cloak for his plan to grab the whole Jupiter system for himself," Sam went on, a little more soberly. "This plot of his has been years in the making. Decades."

"And now it's unraveled, thanks to you."

Sam pretended to blush. "I am quietly proud," he said softly.

I leaned back in my chair. "To think that none of this would have happened if it hadn't been for the Porno Twins. . . ."

Sam's face went quizzical. "Oh, it would have happened, one way or the other," he said, with a puckish grin. "The Twins just provided the opportunity."

I gaped at him. "You mean you were after Weatherwax all along? From before . . ." His grin told me more than any words. "Then your testimony was a fabrication?"

"No, no, no," Sam insisted, jumping to his feet so he could loom over me. That's hard to do, at his height, so I stayed seated and let him loom. "The Twins' emergency was real and the only way I could save them was to make that dash out to Jupiter, just like I testified."

"Really?"

He shrugged. "More or less."

"You had this all scoped out from the beginning, didn't you? You *knew* the whole business and . . ." I stopped talking, lost in stunned admiration for Sam's long-range planning. And guts.

He was making like a Jack-o'-lantern again. "Why do you think Weatherwax got himself appointed a judge?"

"So he could make sure you were found guilty," I said.

"Yeah, maybe, if things worked out the way he wanted them to. But he also wanted to be on the judge's panel so that if things didn't work out his way, he could stop the trial and cut a deal with me."

"Which is what he did."

"You betcha!"

"But why didn't you take Dr. O'Toole back with you? You left her on Europa."

"Had to," Sam said. "Majerkurth showed up with his team and threatened to blow holes in *Joker* if I didn't let her go. I tried to drop an empty oxygen bottle on him, but it missed him and hit one of the PR flacks he had brought along with him."

I laughed. "So that was the basis of the assault charge."

"And the attempted murder, too. I would've offed Majerkurth if I'd thought it would've helped Anitra. As it was, I was outgunned. So I had to let her go—after promising her that I'd fix everything toot sweet."

"Well, you did that, all right. I'll bet she's on her way home to her husband right now."

"I hope so."

I reached for my glass of celebratory champagne and took a sip. Then I remembered:

"The Twins! What happened to them?"

THAT WAS KINDA sad—Sam told me.

I zoomed back to Vesta at three-plus gs with *Clementine* full of European ice that *Joker*'s electrolysis system was converting into oxygen for them and hydrogen for her own fusion torch.

(I noticed that Sam didn't slip in a sales pitch for *Joker*. He was feeling much better now.)

Once I got there, I could've patched their leaky air tank and booted up their recycling system and even fixed their stupid maintenance robot—all from the comfort of my bridge in *Joker*. But I wanted to see them! In the flesh! I was so doggone close to them that I fibbed a little and told them I had to come aboard to make the necessary repairs.

Mindy and Cindy stared at me from my display screen for a long time, not moving, not even blinking. All I could see of them was their beautiful identical faces with their cascading red hair and their bare suggestive shoulders. It was enough to start me perspiring.

"We never let *anyone* come aboard our ship, Mr. Gunn," said the one on the left. The one on the right shook her head, as if to reinforce her twin's statement.

"Call me Sam," I said. "And if I can't come aboard, I can't fix your life-support system."

Well, we yakked back and forth for hours. They really wanted to stick to their guns, but we all knew that the clock was ticking and they were going to run out of air. Of course, I wouldn't have let them die. I would've done the repairs remotely, from *Joker*'s bridge, if I had to.

But I didn't let them know that.

"All right," Mindy said at long last. Maybe it was Cindy. Who could tell. "You can come aboard, Mr.—"

"Sam," breathed Cindy. I think.

"You can come aboard, but only if you agree to certain conditions."

The deal was, I could come aboard their ship but I couldn't have any contact with them. They were going to lock themselves in their compartments and I was forbidden to even tap at their doors.

I was disappointed, but hoped that they'd relent once I'd finished repairing their ship. They offered me virtual reality sex, of course, but I was looking forward to the real thing. The only man in the solar system to make it with the Porno Twins in person! That was a goal worthy of Sam Gunn.

So even though I was bone-weary from being squashed by three-plus gs for several days, and still sore from the tubes that I had to insert into various parts of my anatomy, I was as eager and energetic as a teenager when I finally docked *Joker* to *SEX069*. Great stuff, testosterone.

I went straight to their bridge like a good little boy and got their maintenance robot working again. Just a little glitch in its programming; I fixed that and within minutes the dim-witted collection of junk was welding a patch onto the puncture hole in the air tank that the meteoroid had made. There really wasn't anything much wrong with the ship's air recycling system, but I took my time starting it up again, thinking all the while about getting together with Cindy and Mindy for a bit of horizontal celebration.

Once I started pumping oxygen from *Clementine* into their air tanks, I began wondering how I could coax the Twins out of their boudoirs. I checked out their internal communications setup and—voila!—there were the controls for the security cameras that looked into every compartment in the ship.

The first step toward getting them to come out and meet me, I thought, would be to peek into their chambers and see what they were up to.

Wrong! Bad mistake.

They were both in one little compartment, huddled together on the bed, clutching each other like a pair of frightened little kids. And they were *old*! Must've been in their second century, at least: white hair, pale skin that looked like parchment, skinny and bony and—well, old.

The teeth nearly fell out of my mouth, that's how far my jaw dropped. Yet, as I stared at them hugging each other like Hansel and Gretel lost in the forest, I began to see how beautiful they really were. Not sexy beautiful, not anymore, but the bone structure of their faces, the straight backs, the long legs. The irresistible Cindy and Mindy that we'd all seen on our comm screens were what they had really looked like a century ago.

I should have felt disappointed, but I just felt kind of sad. And yet, even that passed pretty quickly. Here were two former knockouts who were still really quite beautiful in an elderly way. I know a sculptress who would've made a wonderful statue portrait of the two of them.

They were living by themselves, doing their own thing in their own way, bringing joy and comfort to a lot of guys who might have gone berserk without them and their services. And now they were huddled together, terrified that I was gonna break in on them and find out who and what they really were.

So I swallowed hard and tapped the intercom key and said, "I'm finished. Your ship is in fine shape now, although you ought to buy some nitrogen to mix with the oxygen I've left for you."

"Thank you, Sam," they said in unison. Now that I could see them, I heard the quaver in their voices.

"I'm leaving now. It's been a pleasure to be able to help you."

They were enormously grateful. Grateful not only that I had saved their lives, but that I hadn't intruded on their privacy. Grateful that they could keep up the fantasy of Mindy and Cindy, the sexy Porno Twins.

"WOW," I SAID, once Sam finished. "You were downright noble, Sam."

"Yeah," he answered softly. "I was, wasn't I?"

"And that was the last you saw of the Twins?"

"Not exactly."

I felt my brows rise.

With a self-deprecating shrug, Sam admitted, "They were so super-duper grateful that they insisted on giving me a blank check: I can have a virtual reality session with the two of 'em whenever I want to."

"So?"

Sam's grin went from ear to ear. "So I gave in and tried it. I've never been a fan of VR sex; I prefer the real thing."

"So?" I repeated.

His grin got even wider. "So I'm heading back to Ceres tomorrow. I mean, a blank check is just too good to ignore!"

And that's how Sam Gunn beat the rap on the charge of genocide and opened the Jupiter system for development. He went out to Ganymede and set up a new corporation to scoop helium-three from the clouds of Jupiter and sell it for fuel to fusion power plants all over the solar system.

Then he dumped every penny he had, and a lot he didn't legally have, into zipping out past Pluto to find Planet X. You know the rest: he found a mini–black hole out there and fell into it and found aliens and all that.

Now he's on his way back. You know, despite everything, it's going to be great to see him again. Life was pretty dull without Sam around! Productive, of course, and safe and comfortable. But dull.

Me, I never left Selene City. I'm still running Sam's old company, Asteroidal Resources, Inc., from our new corporate headquarters here on the Moon.

Of course, Sam wanted me to return to Ceres after the trial, but I happened to run into the Beryllium Blonde in Selene City and she seemed so dejected and lonely—but that's another story.

Pierre D'Argent

"I'M GETTING ENOUGH MATERIAL FOR A FOLLOW-ON SE-ries," Jade said to Jim Gradowsky's image on the wall screen of her compartment. She wasn't actually having a dialog with her boss; the distance between Selene and the torch ship *Hermes* made that impossible. Instead she was giving Jumbo Jim a report on what she had come up with since the Sam Gunn bio had been aired.

Spence Johansen sat on the king-sized bed, studiously reading a manual on *Hermes*'s fusion propulsion system. A former astronaut, Spence had buddied up with several of the ship's officers and was learning all he could about the massive torch ship.

Jade was telling Gradowsky about her newfound friendship with Jill Meyers when she noticed the yellow light at the bottom of the wall screen blinking. She cut her report short and called out to the screen, "Show incoming message, please."

To her surprise, Jumbo Jim's face filled the screen, grinning lopsidedly. "Hi, Jade. Hope everything's okay with you on your honeymoon trip." Before Jade could reply that she was working (not that Gradowsky would have received her reply for an hour or more), Jumbo Jim added, "Hey, Monica sends love and kisses. Says she misses you."

Jade realized that Gradowsky didn't send a call across the solar system just for social chitchat.

Sure enough, her boss's face grew serious. "Uh, Jade, you know that Rockledge's lawyers have been threatening to sue us for libel or something, 'cause of the series. Well, Raki got our own lawyers to threaten 'em right back, infringing freedom of the press or something like that.

"So yesterday we get a long message from Pierre D'Argent, you know, Rockledge Industries's CEO. He's waving an olive branch. Says he'll drop the suit if we'll run his story in a follow-on series. Says he can show the world what a rotten no-good crook Sam was."

Jade felt her cheeks flaming with anger.

"Well, anyway, here's D'Argent's story. I've listened to it and it's damned interesting, even if he hates Sam's guts. I think we could go with it. And it would make the lawyers on both sides very happy.

"Lemme know what you think."

Controlling her anger, Jade glanced at Spence, his nose still buried in the propulsion manual. She leaned back in the compartment's padded little desk chair and waited for D'Argent's story to begin.

Piker's Peek

I KNOW SAM GUNN'S SUPPOSED TO BE SOME SORT OF FOLK hero, a space-age Robin Hood or something, but let me tell you, he's nothing more than a cheating, womanizing, loudmouthed little scoundrel. And those are his good points!

Take the business about Hell Crater, for example.

I was perfectly happy running Rockledge Industries's space operations despite the fact that Sam Gunn was always causing us trouble. True, we had euchered him out of that orbital honeymoon hotel he had started, but we knew how to make a profit out of it and Sam didn't. And we paid him a decent price for it; not as much as he had expected, but more than he deserved, certainly.

Of course, we had withheld the space-sickness cure that our Rockledge research labs had come up with. Without it, people coming to enjoy a romantic tryst in weightlessness spent their honeymoons upchucking. With it, Rockledge could buy out Sam on the cheap when he was on the verge of bankruptcy and make a first-class orbital tourist facility out of his vomit palace.

Well, perhaps we did take slightly unfair advantage of Sam, but that's the way the world turns. Business is business. Sentiment has no part in it. Still, Sam took it personally, and he took it hard. My spies in his operation—which he called S. Gunn Enterprises, Unlimited, no less— told me had vowed vengeance.

"I'll get that silver-plated SOB," was one of his milder remarks, I was told. He snarled that choice little bon mot after he had Rockledge's check in his bank account, I might add.

Frankly, I thought Sam was finished. I thought we had heard the last of him. How wrong I was!

Imagine my surprise when, some months later, my phone told me that Sam Gunn wanted to have a meeting with me. Surprise quickly turned to suspicion when I played back Sam's call.

"Pierre, you old silver fox," Sam said, grinning malevolently, "I know we've had our differences in the past. . . ."

He had a nerve, addressing me by my first name. For people of Sam's ilk I expected to be called Mr. D'Argent. But Sam never paid any attention to the finer points of politesse.

On and on he went. If there's one thing that Sam can do, it's talk. His tongue must be made of triple-laminated heat shield cermet. I sat back in my desk chair and studied his sly, shifty-eyed face while he chattered nonstop. Sam looks like a grown-up Huckleberry Finn, although he hasn't grown up all that much. He claims he's one hundred sixty-five centimeters tall, which is an obvious lie. If he's one sixty-five, Napoleon must have been two meters and then some.

Sam's face is round, topped with a thatch of wiry rust-red hair. His snub nose is sprinkled with freckles, and his eyes seem never to be the same color twice. Hazel eyes, he says. The eyes of a born con artist, I say. For the life of me I can't understand what women see in him, but Sam is never without a beautiful woman hanging on him. Or two. Or three.

I was just considering fast-forwarding his message when at last he got to the point.

"Pierre, I have an idea that'll knock your jockstrap out from under you. But it's going to take a big chunk of capital to put it into operation. So I figured, with Rockledge's money and my brains we could make an indecent profit. Wanna talk about it?"

And that was it. His message was over. The phone screen froze on Sam's grinning image and a string of callback numbers.

I didn't call him back. Not at first. Let him stew in his own juices for a while, I thought, and I waited for an onslaught of messages from Sam. As a matter of fact, I was looking forward to seeing the detestable little snot get down on his knees and beg me to listen to him.

But Sam didn't beg. He didn't even try to call me again. I waited for days, going about my business as normal, without hearing a peep from Sam. I began to wonder what he'd wanted. Why did he call? He said he needed a large amount of capital to finance his latest scheme. What was he up to? Had he gone to someone else to raise the money? To BLM Aerospace, perhaps?

In those days, incidentally, my office was on Earth. In beautiful Montreal, actually. Rockledge Industries was a truly diversified and multinational corporation, with fingers in literally thousands of operations all over the Earth and, of course, in orbital space. We were even beginning to build O'Neill type habitats at the L-4 and L-5 libration points along the Moon's orbit. We were so fully committed financially that I didn't know where I'd come up with funding for whatever harebrained scheme Sam had in mind, even if I were foolish enough to invest Rockledge money in it.

So it was something of a surprise when, one fine crisp winter morning as I took my usual walking commute from my condominium home to my office through the glassteel tube that connects the two towers at their twentieth floors, I saw Sam walking along with me.

Outside the tube!

My eyes must have popped wide. Sam was out there in the mid-February cold, apparently walking on air. He just plodded along, step by step, with nothing visible between him and the city streets, twenty storeys below. He paid no attention to me, nor to the other men and women in the tube who stopped to gape in amazement at him.

The temperature out there was below zero and I could see from the clouds scudding overhead and the way that the bare tree branches were swaying far below that a considerable wind was blowing. Sam was wearing nothing heavier than a suit jacket as he leaned into the wind and trudged along, his shifty eyes squeezed almost shut, but a crooked grin on his freckled, snub-nosed face, doggedly slogging toward the Rockledge corporate office tower.

I found myself slowing down to keep pace with him, slack-jawed. A crowd of other commuters was gathering, watching Sam with equal astonishment. A woman tapped at the curving glassteel wall to get his attention. Sam paid her no heed.

An older man rapped hard on the glassteel with his walking stick, looking annoyed.

"Get down from there, you damned fool!" he shouted.

Sam abruptly stopped his forward motion and turned to stare at us. For an instant he seemed frozen in midair. Then he looked down. His eyes went wide as he realized there was nothing below him but thin air. He dropped as if an invisible trapdoor had opened beneath him, plummeting downward like a dead weight.

I banged my nose painfully against the transparent wall of the tube, trying to follow his figure as it hurtled down toward the streets. I heard a dozen other thumps and grunts as others in the crowd did the same. Sam dropped like a stone and disappeared from our view.

My God! I thought. He's committed suicide! For a moment I felt horrified, but then (I must confess) I said to myself, That's the last I'll see of the exasperating little bastard.

I was, of course, quite wrong.

I raced to my office, sprinting past several assistants who tried to catch my attention. I had to call the police, turn on the local news, find out what had happened to Sam.

Imagine my stupefied shock, then, when I saw Sam sitting behind my desk, grinning from ear to ear like a poorly carved Jack-o'-lantern.

"You!" I gasped, out of breath from surprise, astonishment and exertion. "I saw you—"

"You saw a hologram, Pierre old buddy-pal. Looked realistic, didn't it?"

I sank into the bottle-green leather armchair in front of my desk. "Hologram?"

"The old geezer with the cane was stooging for me. Caught your attention, didn't it?"

Astonishment quickly gave way to pique. Sam had tricked me, and wormed his way into my private office in the bargain.

"Get out from behind my desk," I snapped.

"Certainly, oh gracious captain of industry," said Sam. He got up from my swivel chair, pretended to dust off its seat, and bowed as I came around the desk. He scampered around the other end of the desk and took the leather armchair. It was too big for him: his feet dangled several centimeters off the floor and he looked like a child in a man's chair.

I scowled at him as I sat down. Sam grinned back at me. For several moments neither of us said anything, something of a record for silence on Sam's part.

"All right," I said at last, "you've finagled your way into my office. Now what's this latest castle in the sky of yours all about?"

"For a corporate bigshot, you're damned perceptive, Pierre. But the castle I want to build isn't in the sky. It's on the Moon. Hell Crater, to be exact."

I didn't have to say another word, not for the better part of the next hour. Sam spun out his grandiose plan to build what he called a resort facility at Hell Crater: hotels, restaurants, gambling casinos, legalized prostitution (which Sam called "sexual therapy"), electronic games and virtual reality simulations based on the completely realistic holographic system he had used to stun me and the other commuters.

Hell Crater, it turns out, was named after a nineteenth-century Jesuit astronomer, Maximilian J. Hell; an Austrian, I believe. Sam loved the idea of turning the thirty-kilometer-wide crater into a lunar Sin City, a couple of hundred kilometers south of Alphonsus, where the lunar nation of Selene stood.

"We can string up a cable car transportation system from Selene to Hell," Sam enthused, "and show the tourists some terrific scenery on the way: Mare Nubium, the Straight Wall, Mt. Yeager—lots to see."

He finally took a breath.

I countered, "Sam, you can't expect me to recommend to Rockledge's senior management that we invest in a den of vice. Prostitution? Gambling? Impossible."

"It's all completely legal," he pointed out. "The nation of Selene doesn't have jurisdiction, and even if they did we wouldn't be breaking any of their laws. This isn't the Vatican, for cryin' out loud."

"Rockledge's board of directors—"

"Would go to Hell as fast as they could," Sam said, grinning. Then he admitted, "As long as they could go incognito."

"It's impossible, Sam. Forget about it."

He shrugged. "I'll have to go elsewhere, then."

I wasn't frightened by that. "And just who do you think would be foolish enough to finance your crazy scheme?"

"I dunno. Maybe the D'Argent Trust."

I laughed in his face. "My wife controls the Trust. If you think for one nanosecond that she'd invest in a glorified whorehouse—"

"She might," Sam said, "in exchange for some information about the activities of certain Rockledge employees."

I felt my brows knit. "Which Rockledge employees?"

"A certain knockout blonde named Marlowe."

"She's in the comptroller's office."

"But she spends a lot of time with the head of the space operations department."

"That's not true! And besides, it's strictly business!"

Sam chuckled. "Pierre, your face is as red as a Chinese pomegranate."

"You're the one who had an affair with that woman!" I remembered. "You and she—"

"It was a lot of fun," Sam said, with a sly smile. "Until I found out she was working for you and trying to slick me out of my share of the orbital hotel. She was screwing me, all right."

"Industrial espionage," I said, with as much dignity as I could manage.

"Yeah, sure." He sighed. "Well, I've got my memories. And some damned good pictures of her."

"I don't care what you have. My relationship with Ms. Marlowe has always been strictly professional. I mean, business."

"You think your wife would believe that?"

"You're making totally unfounded accusations," I snapped. "Ms. Marlowe and I—"

"Make a beautiful couple. Wanna see the pictures?"

"They're fakes! They've got to be! I never—"

"You never," Sam said. "But would Mrs. D'Argent believe you? One look at your blonde bosom buddy and you're in deep sheep dip, Pierre, *mon vieux*."

"It's a filthy lie!" I screamed. I hollered. I lost my cool. I ranted and threatened to have Sam assassinated or at least take him to court. He simply sat there and grinned that maddening gap-toothed grin of his at me while I fussed and fizzed and finally gave in to him.

That's how Rockledge Industries and S. Gunn Enterprises, Unlimited, went into partnership.

I squeezed the funding from various Rockledge projects and kept it as quiet as I could. Half a billion dollars might seem like small change to a hundred-billion-dollar corporation such as Rockledge, but still, one should be careful. For nearly two years I didn't see Sam at all (much to my relief), except for monthly progress reports that he sent through my private laser link from the Rockledge office in Selene. I lived in fear that I'd be discovered, and in dread of the next annual meeting of the board of directors.

The corporate comptroller assigned Ms. Marlowe, of all people, to the Hell Crater project. I spoke to her only by phone or e-link. I was very careful not to have any face-to-face meetings with her, which Sam could turn into more material for his blackmail.

I must confess that Sam ran the project efficiently and energetically. Major construction projects always run into snags, but the Hell Crater complex was built smoothly and swiftly.

"We'll be ready to open by the time your next annual board meeting convenes," Sam told me, by laser link from the Moon.

I confessed, "I can't understand how you managed to get it built so quickly."

He grinned that lopsided pumpkin grin of his. "I paid off the right people, Pierre."

"I know the wages you've paid are above industry standards, but I still don't see how you've done so well."

There's a lag of almost three seconds in conversations from the Moon; it takes that long for a signal to get there and back again. I sat at my desk watching Sam's self-satisfied smirk, waiting for his response.

"It's not the wages," Sam said at last. "It's the bribes."

"Bribes!" I yelped.

Again the wait. Then, "Oh come on, now, Mr. Straight Arrow. You don't think that Rockledge people have paid off a building inspector here and there, or bought protection from the local union goons? You're not that naïve, are you, Pierre, *mon infant?*"

Bribes. All I could think of was the corporate CEO and the board of directors. Bad enough to be building a Sin City, but spending Rockledge money on bribery! I began to wonder if they'd give me a golden parachute when they pushed me out the window.

"Don't be so uptight about it," Sam advised me. "Your CEO's a sporting type, from what I hear. He's gonna love the idea, wait and see."

I decided not to wait. Better to make a clean breast of it before it was too late. So the next time the CEO came to Montreal I asked for a private meeting with him, away from the office. We met in a dinner-theater restaurant. The food was mediocre and the musical revue they were playing featured more nudity than talent. But the CEO seemed to enjoy himself, while I wondered if the other patrons thought we might be a gay couple, sitting off in a shadowy corner at a table for two.

He looked every inch the successful modern business executive: handsome, lean and youthful (thanks to his unabashed patronage of rejuvenation clinics). I felt almost shabby next to him; my hair had turned silver before I was thirty.

I had to wait until the intermission before I could get his undivided attention. To my surprise, when I told him that I had invested in a resort facility on the Moon, he smiled at me. "I was wondering when you'd bring up the subject. Hell Crater, isn't it?"

I expressed a modicum of astonishment at his knowledge of the project.

"You don't stay at the top of the heap, D'Argent, unless you have excellent information conduits. One of the comptroller's people has been keeping me informed about the Hell Crater project."

It was Ms. Marlowe, I realized. She was climbing up the corporate ladder in her own inimitable style.

"There's something about the project that you don't know yet," I said, dreading the confession I was about to make. "About the firm that's actually building the complex—"

"It's Sam Gunn," he replied easily.

"You know?"

"As I said, I have my sources of information."

Sweat broke out on my upper lip. "I didn't mention it until now because—"

"I understand completely. You've been very clever about this entire operation. If it flops, it's Sam Gunn's failure."

"And if it succeeds?"

"We'll squeeze him out, of course."

I felt immensely relieved. "That's exactly what I had planned to do all along," I said, stretching the truth a little.

"We're making money on the orbital hotel," said the CEO. "A resort facility on the Moon makes sense. Especially if it's beyond the legal strictures of terrestrial moralists."

He had no qualms about the den of vice Sam was building!

"Besides," the CEO added, "it will be a great place to meet agreeable young women."

Just at that moment the three-piece orchestra blared a fanfare and the entire cast of the revue came capering out onto the stage once again, without a stitch of clothing in sight.

Despite the CEO's smiling approval of the Hell Crater resort, I was understandably edgy when the board meeting came around. Twenty-two men and women sat around the long polished table in our Amsterdam office: most of them gray-haired and grumpy-looking. I doubted they would look so favorably on our being a partner in a lunar Sin City.

The youthful-looking CEO was also the board chairman. He sat at the head of the long conference table, impeccable in a form-fitted dark blue suit and butter-yellow turtleneck shirt. I envied him. I wanted his job. I wanted his power. But I feared that once the board of directors found out about Hell Crater I could kiss my ambitions goodbye.

Like a dozen other division chiefs, I sat along the side wall of the rectangular conference room, squarely between the comptroller himself and the head of human resources, widely known as Sally the Sob Sister. Sally was a "three-fer" in our corporate diversity program: she was female, black Hispanic, and handicapped (as far as the government was concerned) by her obesity. She was munching something, as usual, slyly reaching down into the capacious tote bag she had deposited at her feet. On the comptroller's other side sat Ms. Marlowe, golden blonde, radiantly beautiful, her china-blue eyes fastened on the CEO's chiseled features.

The meeting went along well enough; only a few points of disagreement and the usual grumbles from directors who felt that a nine percent increase in the corporation's net income wasn't good enough to suit them.

They droned on all morning. We broke for lunch and adjourned to the next room, where a sumptuous buffet table had been laid out. Sally the Sob Sister made a virtual Mt. Everest on her plate and gobbled it all down fast enough to come back for more. I couldn't eat a thing, although I took a few leafs of salad and pretended to nibble on them, standing in a corner by the windows that looked out on the canal that runs through the heart of Amsterdam.

"I say, Pierre, I want to ask you about something."

I turned to see one of the women directors, Mrs. Haverstraw. She was British, an elegant lady with snow-white hair beautifully coiffed and a long, horselike face complete with huge projecting teeth. She could barely keep her lips closed over them. She wore a light blue skirted suit, touched off with massive sapphires at her wrists, throat, and earlobes.

"Mrs. Haverstraw," I said, in my best fawning manner. "And how is Mr. Haverstraw?"

"He's dead. Kicked off last month. Skydiving accident."

"I'm so sorry."

"I'm not. He always was a pompous twit. Rich as Croesus, though, I'm happy to say."

"I'm so glad."

"Yes, rather. I wanted to ask you, though, about this invitation to go to the Moon."

I felt the blood drain out of my face.

"Does Rockledge have a tourist center on the Moon now?" Mrs. Haverstraw asked. "And if we do, why hasn't the board been informed of it?"

I swallowed hard and asked her, in a very small voice, "Um, may I see the invitation, please?"

"I haven't it with me. It came electronically, just this morning, as I was leaving for this meeting." She smiled toothily. "I remember the first line of it, though. It said, 'Go to Hell.' "

I wanted to throw up.

If Mrs. Haverstraw had received an invitation to visit Hell Crater, then every member of the board must have as well. So that was Sam's plan all along. He conned me into this scheme to destroy me, to humiliate me in front of the board of directors, to get me fired, ruined, disgraced. I could hear his mocking laughter in my mind.

"I say, Mr. D'Argent, are you quite all right?"

I focused on Mrs. Haverstraw, who was staring at me quizzically.

"I'm . . . I'm a little surprised, that's all," I said, thinking faster than I ever had before in my life. "We had . . . planned to announce the, eh, tourist facility at the meeting today. Under new business."

"Oh, goodie," said Mrs. Haverstraw, suddenly almost girlish in her enthusiasm. "I love surprises."

I went back into the conference room, my mind spinning. The meeting resumed, dragging along. Next to me, the comptroller sat staring blankly into space, stupefied into quiescence by the boring proceedings. On my other side, Sally continued to sneak food into her mouth. Crumbs littered the carpeting around her. Ms. Marlowe breathed deeply and continued to focus on the CEO.

At last, the CEO looked around the long conference table and smiled handsomely. "That completes our agenda, ladies and gentlemen. Except for one item of new business."

Mrs. Haverstraw looked my way.

I got to my feet, brushed a few of Sally's errant crumbs from my trousers, and cleared my throat uneasily. If the board didn't like the idea of Rockledge's building a Sin City on the Moon, my career was finished. Clever of the CEO to make me the messenger.

Half a dozen of the directors had already pushed their chairs back from the table, ready to leave. They glared and grumbled.

"As you know," I began, trying to put the best face on the situation, "the space operations division has always been at the frontier of innovation and . . ." I struggled for a word ". . . and, uh, progress."

Several gray heads nodded, although I saw a few impatient stares as well.

"Today I'd like to announce that we have nearly completed a tourist facility on the Moon, at Hell Crater."

That stirred them. The CEO kept his expression neutral, although I thought he snuck a quick glance in Ms. Marlowe's direction.

I took a deep breath and began to explain what we were building at Hell Crater, all the while thinking of how Sam would have done it. I'm no spellbinder, but I managed to spin out a vision of a tourist facility that would rival anything on Earth, while skirting the matter of gambling and prostitution.

"And on the Moon," I went on, "with its one-sixth gravity, there's no problem of people becoming space sick, yet they still weigh only one-sixth of what they do on Earth."

"What about our space sickness cure?"

"We'll still sell it to people going into orbit. That's a firm market. And tourists heading for the Moon will be in weightlessness for a day or so. They'll buy our pills too."

"But will people go all the way to the Moon for a vacation?"

"Of course they will," I enthused, crossing my fingers behind my back. "And they'll book their passages aboard Rockledge spacecraft."

"This is a *family* resort?" one of the younger men asked. "Not for adults?"

"There will be plenty of entertainment for adults as well as families," I said.

They grilled me for the better part of an hour. By the end of it, the board was satisfied that the Hell Crater project would be a moneymaker. I even began to believe it myself.

"That explains the invitation I received this morning," said the oldest member of the board, a crooked smile snaking across his withered face. "I was going to ask you about it, after the meeting."

"'Go to Hell,'" quoted a balding director seated halfway down the long table. "Catches your attention, doesn't it?"

Everyone laughed, rather guardedly, I thought.

Swallowing hard again, I apologized weakly. "Publicity people sometimes lack a sense of decorum."

"Well, I'm ready to go," said the younger director who had asked about adult entertainment. "How about the rest of you?"

Thus the entire Rockledge board of directors decided to attend the grand opening of the Hell Crater resort.

You've got to understand that up until this moment none of the directors knew that Rockledge was in partnership with Sam Gunn. I wanted to keep it that way as I met with the CEO after the board meeting, in the privacy of his airport-sized office.

"Although we're a full partner with, um, the builders of the facility," I said, "I thought it best to keep Rockledge's name out of the limelight on this. After all, we're not really in the resort business."

He pursed his sculpted lips. "Perhaps we should be, Pierre. There's a lot of money in entertainment."

It was the first time he'd ever called me by my first name! I didn't even realize that he knew my first name !

I managed to hide my elation and warn, "There is also a lot of risk in the entertainment business, sir. I believe we should enter this area very carefully."

"Good thinking," he said. Then, with a sly smile spreading across his sculpted features he added, "I believe the comptroller should have a representative go to Hell with the board and a few chosen members of senior management."

"Yes," I agreed immediately. "Of course."

So the entire board of directors, their spouses or significant others, and a select few employees (including Ms. Marlowe) packed into a Rockledge rocket vehicle that took us to the Moon. The CEO ordained a high-thrust flight, so we were in zero gravity for only twenty hours, enough to prove the efficacy of the corporation's space sickness pills.

Despite her nervousness at flying into space, my wife thoroughly enjoyed our first day at Hell Crater. Sam was nowhere in sight, of course, one of the few times he displayed enough common sense to remain behind the scene. Not a mention of his name anywhere in the complex.

The complex was built inside a huge dome of lunar concrete that was covered with rubble from the Moon's dusty surface soil for protection against radiation and the day/night temperature swings. From outside it looked like a large perfectly symmetrical hill. Inside, the dome was studded with amusement arcades; fine restaurants and fast-food cafeterias; Dante's Inferno Casino; an office where you could rent wings and fly on your own muscle power through the dome; The Imaginarium, which featured the very latest in virtual reality simulations (including sex fantasies); and a garishly lit "entertainment center" blatantly named Hell's Belles.

There were lights and raucous music everywhere, and plenty of smiling attendants in colorful uniforms to guide us and answer our questions. The Rockledge contingent were the only guests in the complex, a total of about fifty of us. The resort wasn't open to the general public yet, so we had the run of the place, no waiting in lines, no being told, "I'm sorry, we're fully booked." And no news media to snoop on us.

Burrowed belowground there was a five-star hotel, a medical complex that specialized in cosmetic and rejuvenation therapies, a tastefully decorated mall of boutique shoppes, and living quarters for the surprisingly large staff.

We wandered from one spectacular site to another, goggle-eyed. I was shocked to see that my wife was passionate about gambling; I couldn't tear her away from the slot machines. We were each given a thousand credits on the house, and she was running it up into a respectable fortune. I realized that Sam was letting her win; it would simply be added to Rockledge's payments to S. Gunn Enterprises, sooner or later. It was just as well that she was so fascinated with the slots, I told myself. Let her stay in the casino; then she won't get curious about Hell's Belles or the sex simulations at the virtual reality center.

Even the CEO seemed to enjoy himself immensely. I'd never before seen him smile so broadly, nor heard him laugh out loud.

"This place is going to be a great success," he said to me, actually clapping me on the back as we stood at the blackjack table. "Congratulations, Pierre."

His wife was nowhere in sight, even though she herself was a member of the board of directors. Ms. Marlowe was standing close to the CEO, in a spectacularly low cut sequined gown.

Then he leaned closer and whispered in my ear, "Now to pry it away from Sam Gunn."

The hotel suite my wife and I shared was sumptuous, to say the least. But as I lay in the darkness of our bedroom that first night, an uneasiness began to assail me. I wasn't worried about booting Sam out of Hell; the little sneak would do the same to me if he could. No, what worried me was the splendor of it all. This is all too good, I thought. Sam must have spent huge amounts of money to build this complex, far more than the Rockledge funding I had funneled to him.

We were scheduled for an excursion to Selene the next morning, although about half the board members said they wanted to remain in Hell; lunar scenery and a tour of the oldest human settlement on the Moon didn't interest them as much as the attractions of the resort complex. A few of the younger men wanted to try their hands at flying like birds (and then, once their wives were gone, enjoying either virtual or actual sex). I told the CEO I wasn't going to Selene either because I had to stay and confer with Sam. He nodded understandingly and gave me a knowing wink. My wife was less sympathetic. She absolutely refused to go outside the complex's dome without me.

"But I have business to conduct, darling," I told her.

She arched an eyebrow at me. "At that virtual reality place, no doubt. I understand you can program sexual fantasies there."

I was aghast that she could think that of me. "Heavens no!" I said. "I have to meet with Sam Gunn."

"Sam Gunn? That reprehensible little brat? I'd rather you visited Hell's Belles."

I assured her that I was meeting with Sam, and she finally decided to believe me. "I believe I'll take a look at the cosmetic clinics down on the lower level. They have some lovely shops down there, too," she said.

I knew she intended to spend every credit she'd made at the slot machines the night before, and then some. Ah well, I thought. Peace at any price. Then I remembered an old bit of wisdom from Monte Carlo: money won by a gambler is merely loaned.

Sam's private office was rather modest, compared to the ego palaces of men like my CEO. It was part of a small suite nestled into the office complex between Dante's Inferno and The Imaginarium. His private office held a small desk and a couple of chairs, nothing more, although the walls were smart screens. When I walked in, one wall displayed a view of Mare Nubium: empty, desolate, yet strangely beautiful, especially with a nearly full Earth hanging in the black sky.

Sam was leaning back in his swivel chair and grinning like the proverbial Cheshire Cat. The wall behind his desk was a collage of photos of Sam with the movers and shakers of the world, as well as Sam with various scantily clad women, each one a knockout.

"So how do you like the place, Oh Silver-Haired Partner of Mine?"

I felt a frown knit my face. Sam was being altogether too familiar, just like the irreverent rogue. I said nothing as I sat in front of his desk, but my frown turned to surprise. The chair was much lower than I had expected; even in the soft lunar gravity I thumped onto its seat. Sam was actually sitting higher than I was.

"It's a trick Josef Stalin used," he told me before I could say a word. "Put your chair on a platform and saw the legs down on your visitors' chairs."

"I should have expected as much," I growled, "from you."

"Don't be touchy, Silver One. Isn't the complex terrific? Your boss seemed to have a great time. I see he brought *la Marlowe* with him."

"It's terrific all right," I growled. "Too terrific."

Sam's pie plate of a face took on a look of hurt innocence. "Whaddaya mean?"

"Sam, you couldn't possibly have built all this and staffed it so handsomely on the funding Rockledge has provided you."

He steepled his fingers in front of his face for a moment, then nodded. "No fooling you, eh?"

"What's going on?"

"Well, I knew the half-bill you ponied up wouldn't cover everything I wanted to do, so I took in another partner."

"Another partner? You can't do that! The terms of our agreement—"

"Not really a partner, not legally," Sam interjected, looking like a mischievous imp. "I used your funding as leverage for a loan that really paid for building the complex. And staffing it."

"A loan? Who in his right mind would loan you a penny, unless you held the threat of blackmail over him?"

"There are people," Sam said slowly, "who specialize in high-risk loans."

"People? Who?"

"They also have a lot of experience in running gambling casinos and, uh, other entertaining diversions."

"Experience in—" Suddenly it hit me. "Oh my God! The Mafia! You're in with the Mafia!"

Sam tut-tutted. "They haven't called themselves that in half a century. And they're international now, not just Sicilian: there's Russians, Japanese, Colombians; they've gone global, just like all the other major industries."

"The Mafia," I groaned. "You're in league with—"

"Call them the Syndicate. That's the name they prefer."

"They're the bloody Mafia!" I snapped.

"Be polite to them," Sam warned. "Call them the Syndicate when you talk to them."

"Me? Talk to the likes of them? Never!"

Sam shook his head sadly. "Never say never, pal." And he pointed with a stubby finger past my shoulder.

Turning, I saw a slinky, sultry, sallow-cheeked young woman with lustrous long black hair and smoldering dark almond-shaped eyes set in high cheekbones. How long she had been standing in the doorway of Sam's office I had no way of knowing. I distinctly remembered having closed the door when I came into the office. She must have opened it without making a sound.

Sam got to his feet. "Pierre, *mon confrere,* may I introduce Ilyana Campanella Chang. Ilyana, Pierre D'Argent, head of space operations for—"

"For Rockledge Industries, I know," she said in a smoky voice. Ms. Chang was wearing a skintight black dress that showed a tantalizing amount of bosom and shimmered as she walked to the chair next to mine. "Walked" is only an approximation of the way she moved. She reminded me of a jungle beast, a sleek black leopard or maybe a slithering boa constrictor. I couldn't take my eyes off her. She sat down and crossed her long, beautiful legs.

Sam was staring at her, too. He had always been partial to sultry brunettes. And bubbly blondes. And tempestuous redheads. Sam was an equal-opportunity chaser, making no discrimination against anyone female who was even mildly attractive. Ms. Chang was much more than mild. Much.

"Ilyana is the Syndicate's local representative," Sam said, in a voice choked with testosterone. Or perhaps it was fear.

She smiled silkily at me. "What you call the Mafia. As Sam told you, we have become a global enterprise. My own family heritage is part Russian, part Italian, and part Chinese."

"The Ma—" I cut the word short. "I mean, the Syndicate. You?"

"Does that surprise you?" she asked.

I glanced at Sam. He was still walleyed, obviously enraptured by this vision of dangerous loveliness.

"Frankly, it does," I replied. "I wouldn't think that a young woman such as yourself would be involved in criminal activities."

Her smile widened enough to show teeth. "I was born to it. I'm a Family person, on both sides of my family."

"I'll be damned," I muttered.

"Well, you are in Hell," Sam said, regaining some of his composure.

"And you will remain here," said Ilyana, with a hint of steel in her voice, "until our business is brought to a satisfactory conclusion."

"Our business? What business?"

"Our global operation is expanding," said Ms. Chang. "We're going interplanetary."

I understood her immediately. "You want to get your hooks into this facility, here on the Moon."

She smiled approvingly at me. "Mr. Gunn, here—our darling Sam—has borrowed a rather large sum of money from the Syndicate. It is time to repay."

I drew myself up straighter. "That's got nothing to do with me."

"I'm afraid it does," she said.

Before I could reply, Sam jumped in. "I told you, I used your money as collateral on a bigger loan. None of the regular banks would handle it, so the Syndicate loaned me enough to get this complex built."

"And staffed," said Ilyana. "Those are mostly our people out there, dealing at the gaming tables, working in the restaurants and shops and, uh . . . therapy centers."

"She means Hell's Belles," Sam explained.

"I knew I shouldn't have let you talk me into this!" I shouted.

"Too late, old pal. Now it's time to pay the piper."

I started to answer, but hesitated. All right, Sam had snookered me into this, true enough. But the complex was built. Everything was working fine. It could become a major tourist attraction and a big moneymaker for Rockledge. I reasoned that if I bailed Sam out on this stupid loan, it would be only on the condition that he relinquish all his interest in the resort. Rockledge would have the complex free and clear, which was exactly what the CEO and I wanted.

"How much money are we talking about?" I asked.

"Fifteen billion," Sam said.

Before I could faint, Ilyana said, "Eighteen billion. You forgot this afternoon's interest."

"Oh, yeah, that's right."

"Eighteen *billion*?" I screeched.

"Tomorrow morning it will be twenty point six," Ilyana said sweetly. "The interest mounts rather steeply."

"How steeply?"

"Forty percent," Sam answered.

"Compounded semi-daily," Ilyana added.

"That's usury!"

Her smile turned pitying. "Rockledge owns a credit service that charges almost as much."

"It's still usury," I insisted.

"Nevertheless," she said, "that is what is owed. Sam doesn't have the wherewithal to pay it, so you must."

"Me? When elephants fly! Why don't you just kill the little sonofabitch and be done with it?"

Ilyana made a little pout. "What good would killing Sam do? We want the money you owe us, not a corpse."

"Besides," Sam chimed in, "Ilyana and I are thinking about getting married, settling down. Right, hon?"

She blew him a kiss. The little rat! He's romancing this Mafia princess to save his own skin while he's putting my neck on the guillotine!

Ilyana turned back to me. "I'm afraid you must pay, Mr. D'Argent. You are Sam's partner, after all, and responsible for his debts. Surely a giant corporation such as Rockledge can afford a few billions."

"Over my dead—" Again I stopped myself short. Maybe she didn't want to kill Sam, but I didn't know how she felt about murder in general.

"Mr. D'Argent," Ilyana said, almost pleadingly, "don't make this diffi-

cult for us and for yourself. You must pay. Otherwise your board of directors will never return to Earth. Alive, that is."

"You . . . you're threatening the entire board?"

"And their spouses, I'm afraid," Ilyana said, nearly managing to look sad.

"My wife . . ."

"Your spaceship will have a terrible accident when it leaves the Moon.
There will be no survivors."

"And no witnesses," Sam added, almost cheerfully.

I glowered at him. "You'll be a witness."

"Ah, but I'm going to be married into the Family," Sam said. "Right,
Ilyana, my precious angel?"

She blew him another kiss.

Then she got up from her chair like a beautiful python gliding up a
tree and said, "You two gentlemen will want to talk this over, I know. Sam,
darling, please call me when you've decided what you're going to do."

Sam nodded vigorously. Ilyana went to the door while we both
watched her, half hypnotized by her graceful beauty.

She opened the door, then turned back toward us. "Oh, by the way, the
chairman of *our* board is staying at the hotel here and would like to meet
you both this evening."

"The chairman of your board?" I echoed.

"Yes. In bygone years he'd be called the *capo di tutti capi*. Or perhaps
the Godfather."

She smiled sweetly and left the office, closing the door behind her
without making a sound.

For several moments Sam and I were absolutely silent. At last I said,
"She must be marvelous in bed."

"How would I know?" Sam replied, spreading his hands in a gesture of
innocence. "For all I know, she's still a virgin."

"You mean you haven't—"

"Not one finger. If I even tried to, a dozen goons would drag me off to
her Godfather, who would hang me by my cojones and use my head for
batting practice."

I groaned. "Sam, Sam . . . how did I ever let you talk me into this?"

"That's not important now. The problem now is, how are we going to
get out of this?"

He had a point.

I couldn't go to my CEO and ask for twenty billion dollars. The half-billion I had funneled to Sam had been a major strain. And I couldn't face their Godfather without having the twenty billion to hand over to him. As I sat there sweating, Sam drummed his fingers on his desk.

"I'm pretty sure they won't kill you," he said at last.

"Pretty sure?"

"What good would it do them?"

"It certainly wouldn't do *me* much good," I groused. "Nor my wife. Nor the board of directors."

"Let me think about this," Sam said, scratching at his red thatch of hair. "There's gotta be a way out."

I thought of the line from Marlowe's *Doctor Faustus*: "Why this is hell, nor am I out of it."

My wife and I were scheduled to have dinner with the CEO, his wife, and several key board members at Hell Crater's finest restaurant, The Fallen Angel. Ordinarily an invitation like this would have been a step toward promotion, perhaps even an opportunity to join the board. I should have been overjoyed and eager with anticipation. Instead, as I put on my tuxedo that evening and struggled with the shirt studs, what I felt was anxiety bordering on dread.

I explained to my wife that I had to have cocktails with Sam Gunn and a few of his associates before dinner. She frowned with distaste, but accepted the situation.

"Business before pleasure," she said grandly. Then added, "So long as it's not monkey business with that little womanizer."

Sam's reputation was known everywhere, even among corporate wives. Especially among corporate wives.

The Godfather's suite was only a few doors down the corridor from our own. I gave my wife a peck on the cheek while she was deciding which of the necklaces laid out on the dressing table before her would be best to wear with the gown she had bought earlier that afternoon. She barely nodded as I took my leave of her. Good thing, too, because Ms. Chang opened the door to her Godfather's suite when I pressed the buzzer. She was wearing an ankle-length sheath of glittering metallic black, its skirt slit up to her shapely hip. If my wife had seen her, real hell would have broken loose over my head.

Ms. Chang gestured me into the suite's thickly carpeted sitting room. Four rather lumpy-looking men in dark suits looked me over as if they had X-ray eyes. No one spoke a word. I stood uneasily by the door for a moment. Then in came Sam from the adjoining room, with the Godfather at his side, both of them in tuxedos.

He didn't look Sicilian. I mean, he wasn't a heavy, swarthy, sour-faced man. Not at all. Don Guido Alexandreivich Popov was as slim as a saber blade. His thickly luxuriant hair was a light sandy blond; his eyes a piercing light gray. He wasn't much taller than Sam, and several centimeters shorter than I. Yet he radiated power, a self-assurance that comes from having enormous resources at your command.

Ms. Chang performed the introductions. Popov's handshake was firm without being blatantly muscular. His eyes searched mine as he smiled and said, "So where's my twenty bill?"

I must have blanched, because he laughed and added, "I don't expect it this evening. Relax. Have a drink." His voice was slightly scratchy, rough, as if his vocal cords had been damaged.

As he directed me toward the bar, Ms. Chang said, "Actually, it's twenty point six billion. As of the opening of business tomorrow morning."

Popov shrugged. "Twenty, twenty point six, let's not quibble."

One of the dark-suited thugs slipped behind the bar and poured him what appeared to be a tumbler of spring water. Sam asked for a pinot grigio and Ms. Chang ordered vodka, neat. I needed a whisky, badly, but I decided that I should keep my head clear.

"I'll have the same as Mr. Popov," I said to the man behind the bar.

He glanced at Popov, who smiled and tapped me on the shoulder. "I'm used to drinking grappa," he said. "Are you?"

"Grappa?" I asked. "What's that?"

"It's the Italian version of acetylene," Sam piped up. "You can use it to burn through bank safes."

Popov laughed, a grating, painful sound. "Maybe you'd prefer something else, Mr. D'Argent."

I settled for sparkling water.

Popov gestured me to a chair by the window. He took the one opposite me while Sam and Ms. Chang nestled in the love seat between us.

He took a sip of his drink. "I need it for my throat. Soothes the vocal cords."

Or burns them out, I thought. But I kept my thoughts to myself. Sam sat by Ms. Chang's side, grinning like a schoolboy on a date with the prom queen. The musclemen in their dark suits stayed back by the bar, silent as ponderous wraiths. An uncomfortable silence enveloped the room.

"So," Popov said at last, "how are we going to resolve this situation?"

"I don't see how you can expect Rockledge Corporation to pay a debt that Sam's run up," I said, as firmly as I could.

"He's your partner," said Popov. "You're legally responsible."

"We never approved the loan he took from you."

"Makes no difference."

"It does, legally."

"I guess it's a little unusual for you," Popov granted, "but it happens all the time in my business."

"It's not that unusual in the legitimate world," Sam said. "It's the 'deep pockets' ploy. Go after the guy with the deepest pocket of money."

Popov nodded and beamed at Sam like a prospective Godfather-in-law.

"But Rockledge didn't incur this debt."

Popov shrugged.

"It would ruin my career if I so much as asked my CEO to pay it."

He shrugged more elaborately.

"I can't do it," I said.

"That's too bad," Popov replied. "I had hoped to avoid making a mess."

"You can't murder the entire board of directors!" I said. "You'd never get away with it. And what good would it do you, anyway?"

Popov sighed patiently, then ticked off on his fingers, "One: We'll get away with it. We make a business out of getting away with things like this. Rockets blow up sometimes. It'll be a tragic accident. Two: Rockledge will have to find a new CEO and a whole new board of directors. Guess who owns enough Rockledge stock to take control, once the old board is out of the way?"

I felt stunned. "You? You wouldn't! You couldn't!"

"He would and he could," Sam said. "Trust me on that."

"I wouldn't trust you as far as I could throw a . . . a . . . a herd of buffalos!"

"Now, now," Popov said placatingly, "let's not get emotional here. We're talking business."

"You're talking murder."

"But it's business, not personal. I've got nothing against you, personally. This is strictly business."

Sam's face suddenly lit up. "But suppose that, instead of business, we made it a sporting proposition."

"What do you mean, Sam?" Ms. Chang asked, shifting slightly on the love seat to rub against Sam like a purring cat. It was enough to raise my already high blood pressure an extra few points.

"Uncle Guido," Sam asked, "have you ever played cards for a twenty-billion-dollar stake?"

"Twenty point six," Ms. Chang murmured.

Popov stared at Sam as if he didn't understand what the little devil was talking about. Then a slow smile of recognition crept across his craggy face.

"Double or nothing?" he asked.

Sam grinned. "Why not? What've we got to lose?"

Before I could object, the two men shook hands on it.

Popov got to his feet, and the rest of us did, too. "I understand you have a dinner engagement, Mr. D'Argent."

"Yes, I do, but—"

"Enjoy your dinner." He turned to Sam. "What do you say to meeting me in Dante's Inferno at midnight, Sam?"

"Okay by me."

"Double or nothing," Popov reminded us.

"Okay by me," Sam repeated.

Of course it was okay by him! He'd be playing with Rockledge's money!

Dinner that evening was the longest, dreariest, most nerve-racking meal I've ever had. I couldn't eat a bite, but nobody seemed to notice or care. My wife and Mrs. CEO were seated next to one another and chattered away happily. The CEO himself sat at my other side and made broad hints about how I was about to take a big step up the corporate ladder. Even his wife allowed that if I made it to the board of directors I could sit beside her. I thought to myself that getting higher in the corporation merely gave me more leg room when I hanged myself.

I couldn't let the board of directors get on that rocket that Popov was going to blow up. It would be easy enough to keep my wife and myself off it; I could always claim that I had some details about the resort to take care of. But how I could keep the CEO and the rest of the board off the rocket without telling them of the fix that Sam had gotten me into? It would be bad enough to confess that I'd put the corporation into this mess, but to admit that it was Sam Gunn who'd led me by the nose into it—that would be unbearable.

And there was Sam, the miserable little rat, with the exquisite Ms. Chang at an intimate candlelit table for two, far on the other side of the restaurant. They seemed totally absorbed in each other.

Desperate times call for desperate measures, I told myself. Excusing myself from the table while the dessert course was being served, I made a beeline for the men's room. It was positively opulent, but I had no time to admire the faux marble paneling and asteroidal gold plumbing fixtures. Locking myself into a booth, I slipped my phone off my wrist and called Popov.

He was apparently still in his suite, and still in his tuxedo. In the wrist phone's minuscule screen I couldn't see if anyone else was in the room with him.

Popov smiled when he recognized my face. "Mr. D'Argent."

"I have a proposition for you, sir," I said, without preamble.

"A proposition?"

I took a deep breath and plunged in. Popov listened in silence. Finally, when I was finished, he nodded solemnly.

"I'm wary of Sam Gunn, also," he said, in his harsh, painful rasp. "I don't believe his intentions toward my niece are entirely honorable."

"He's about as honorable as Jack the Ripper," I said.

Popov pursed his lips. "This will break my Ilyana's heart."

"Better now than later, when Sam betrays her."

"Yes, I suppose so," he said slowly.

It took several more minutes, but at last he agreed to my proposition. Then I placed a quick call to Rockledge's legal department, back at corporate headquarters on Earth. The chief counsel didn't like being disturbed during her dinner hour, but once she heard what I wanted her to do she willingly agreed to do it.

"We're partnered to S. Gunn Enterprises?" she yelped. "You'd damned will better get out of *that* deal!"

By the time I got back to the dinner table, everyone was having coffee and liqueurs. It was past eleven PM when my wife and I finally got back to our hotel suite. The phone's message light was blinking, and before I could get to it my wife called out to the phone to play the message.

Sam's impish face came up on the screen, looking dead serious for a change. "Pierre, *mon jouer aux cartes,* can you come up to my office right away? It's important. Any time before eleven-thirty. Please." And his face took on such an expression of distress that my wife looked troubled.

"The poor man looks as if his heart is going to break," she said.

More likely his gall bladder, I thought, but I kept it to myself. Has he found out about my deal with Popov? I wondered.

"I'm not going to Sam's office," I grumbled. "Not at this time of night."

"But he said it's important." My wife has her faults, and one of them is a soft heart. Show her a picture of a puppy or a kitten and she'll buy whatever's being pushed. Sam was playing the puppy, of course. I realized that he must know more about me and my wife than I had ever suspected.

Grumbling, I went through the motions of phoning him back; no answer. Not even a video mail system where I could leave a message.

"You'd better go to his office," my wife said. "And quickly, it's nearly eleven-thirty."

I got as far as the elevator at the end of the corridor. Sam was waiting for me there, his woebegone look replaced by an expression of impish glee.

"I didn't think you'd want to miss the big card game," he said, waving his hand in front of the elevator's heat-sensitive call button. He didn't know a thing about my Popov deal; he was grinning like a kid playing hooky from school.

"My wife—"

"I've sent her a bottle of champagne with a note apologizing for taking you away from her," Sam said cheerfully. "She'll be asleep in twenty minutes, half an hour at most."

Before I could say another word the elevator doors slid open. Two of Popov's grim-faced thugs were already in it.

"Come to escort me to the game?" Sam said to them. "How thoughtful the Godfather is!"

I had no option except to go with Sam up to the main floor, with all its garish lights and arcades, and into Dante's Inferno.

The casino was strangely empty. Popov's people had closed the gaming center to the general public—meaning Rockledge personnel. Sam and I, followed by the two silent, stone-faced goons, threaded our way through tables for roulette, craps, blackjack, all covered by gray plastic sheets. The slot machines and video games were dark and still. Most of the overhead lights were off: the casino was draped in shadows, mysterious and somehow threatening.

Except for one green-topped card table, sharply lit by halogen lamps, in the middle of the vast floor. Popov sat there, still in his tux, Ms. Chang at his side and a half-dozen more gorillas on their feet behind him. One empty chair waited across the table from Popov. An unopened pack of cards rested on the table, with two piles of chips, one in front of Popov, the other at the empty chair that was waiting for Sam.

"You're late, Sam," said Popov as we stepped into the pool of glaringly bright light.

"I had to stop on the way and pick up my partner," Sam said carelessly, gesturing toward me. Just like the lying little sneak, blaming me.

Sam plopped in the empty chair and noisily cracked his knuckles. I shuddered. Popov smiled in such a sinister way that it made me shudder even more. Ms. Chang smiled too, but much more alluringly.

"We each have a hundred thousand dollars worth of chips," Popov said, his grating voice sounding ominous. "We play until one of us goes broke. Okay by you?"

"Okay by me," said Sam.

I stood behind Sam. There was no other chair for me to sit in. Popov called the first round: five-card draw poker.

I have never seen such cheating in my entire life! As I stood behind Sam, I saw treys turn into aces before my astounded eyes; cards changed their suits, going from spades to hearts or whatever Sam needed. It was all I could do to keep my eyes from popping out of my skull.

Popov must have been cheating too. He had to be, or else Sam would have blown him out of the water in the first ten minutes. He'd win a hand, and Sam would fiddle with one of his shirt studs and take the next pot. I realized that both men were loaded with every electronic and optical sensor known to humankind.

Sam began to pull ahead. The pile of chips in front of him grew while Popov's diminished. Ms. Chang played hostess, getting up from time to time to bring drinks to the two players. The goons behind Popov never moved; they stood there like menacing statues.

After a while I realized that whenever Ms. Chang refreshed Sam's drink Popov started winning. Sam didn't seem to mind: soon enough he'd pull ahead again with full houses and straight flushes, no matter which cards he was dealt.

"Let's take a kidney break," Popov said at last. His chips were down to a perilously low level.

"Okay by me," said Sam cheerfully from behind a small mountain of chips. He got up and headed for one of the restrooms; Popov went in the opposite direction, convoyed by his gorillas, leaving Ms. Chang alone.

I was getting frantic. If Sam won, I'd be ruined—and Popov would take it out on me. I glanced at my wristwatch. It was almost two AM I hadn't counted on Sam's cheating. I could have kicked myself for being so stupid. Of course the despicable little scoundrel would cheat!

I followed Sam into the restroom. "Sam, you're cheating," I accused.

"No kidding," he answered lightly. "What do you think the Godfather is doing, playing tiddlywinks?"

"I can't allow cheating. It's wrong, Sam."

"Tell Popov. Those goons standing behind him are reading my cards with infrared sensors for him."

"The cards are marked?"

"Does Santa Claus live at the North Pole?"

"But—"

"I've been using nanomachines kind of creatively, myself," Sam admitted. "It's one helluva game."

A duel of double-dealing, swindling con artists. I had the terrible feeling that in a competition like this against Sam, the Mafia was like a gang of schoolyard bullies trying to beat up on Superman.

Sam started back to the table with me following glumly behind him. Sam's got to lose, I kept repeating to myself. Everything depends on Popov beating him.

For the next couple of hours the game seesawed back and forth while I stood there sweating. Gradually, Popov's pile of chips was growing, Sam's shrinking. Both men were still cheating with every device known to modern technology.

One of Popov's goons moved Ms. Chang's chair to Sam's side of the table, and she sat demurely beside him. I still had to stand. Sam covered his cards so carefully that I could no longer see them. Ahah! I thought. He doesn't trust his inamorata.

For the next hour Popov won steadily. Sam fiddled with his shirt studs, scratched behind his ears, adjusted his cufflinks, all to no avail. He even took off one of his shoes and shook it as if it were filled with pebbles. It did no good. The chips were flowing across the table to Popov's pile, hand after hand. Sam looked grimmer and grimmer; he pulled his bow tie loose and ran his hands through his bristly hair. Popov just smiled wider and wider. Even the thugs standing behind his chair began to relax and nudge each other knowingly.

At last Sam looked across the table at Popov and his massive pile of chips and said, "Okay, Godfather. Let's put an end to this. High card takes it all."

Popov looked at Sam for a long, silent moment. "One trick for the whole pot?"

Sam nodded slowly. I saw sweat trickling down his cheek.

Popov nodded back and called for a fresh pack of cards. "High card wins it all," he said as one of the goons unwrapped the new deck.

Sam shuffled the cards. Popov cut the deck, then pushed it across the green-topped table to Sam.

"Draw," he said.

Sam pushed the deck back toward him. "You go first, Godfather."

Popov looked from Sam to Ms. Chang to me and then back at Sam again. He reached out one hand and took the top card from the deck.

An eight of clubs.

No one spoke. No one even breathed. My mind was spinning. My legs went weak. An eight! Sam can top an eight easily. I'm ruined!

Sam shook his head slightly, then pulled the next card.

Four of diamonds.

"Oh, Sam," breathed Ms. Chang.

"Shit," said Sam.

The goons behind Popov chuckled. Popov himself allowed a satisfied smile to creep across his craggy face.

"Well, that's it, Mr. D'Argent," he said to me, playing his role to the end. "You owe me forty billion dollars."

With a relieved smile I replied, "No, I don't. Sam owes you, not me."

"You're my partner!" Sam yelped. "You've got to—"

"As of midnight Rockledge Industries dissolved its partnership with S. Gunn Enterprises," I announced. "You're on your own, Sam."

He shot out of his chair. "You can't break our partnership unilaterally!"

"I can and I did," I told him, perhaps a trifle smugly. "You should have read our agreement more carefully, Sam. The contract clearly states in clause thirty-seven, subparagraph sixteen, that either party can dissolve the partnership on moral grounds."

"Moral grounds!" Sam yipped. "What moral grounds?"

I drew myself up to my full height. "Rockledge Industries will not be party to an operation that promotes gambling and prostitution, even though it might be legal in the locality in which it is situated."

"But you knew about it from the git-go!"

I shook my head. "That makes no difference. The partnership is dissolved. Rockledge has no further responsibilities to you, Mr. Gunn."

He stood there gaping at me, his collar open and bow tie hanging loosely down the wrinkled, sweaty front of his shirt.

"You can't do this to me!" Sam whined.

"It's done," I said. Then I turned on my heel and headed for the casino's exit, grinning happily. This was going to cost Rockledge twenty billion, I knew, but it'd be worth it to get rid of Sam Gunn—and my CEO, in the bargain.

From behind me I heard Popov's voice: "Sam, you owe me forty bill."

I quickened my pace and practically ran out of the casino, thinking, This is the end of Sam Gunn.

By the time I got my hotel suite I was almost feeling sorry for Sam. But then I told myself that he'd brought this on himself. It's not my fault. He's the one who went to the Mafia, or the Syndicate, or whatever they called themselves. Sam should have known better. Play with fire and you get burned.

I took a dose of tranquilizers and crawled into bed beside my sleeping wife, knocking over the ice bucket and what was left of the champagne in the process. They fell to the luxurious carpet in dreamy lunar slow motion. She barely stirred. I thought I'd have bad dreams but actually I slept quite soundly. Perhaps knowing that I'd never again be troubled by Sam Gunn helped.

The next morning as my wife and I waited in our hotel-furnished dressing gowns for room service to deliver our breakfast, Ms. Chang phoned. She was pale and had dark circles beneath her eyes; she looked much less slinky and sultry than the night before, for which I was thankful, since my wife was in the room.

"I just want you to know, Mr. D'Argent, that the little problem we discussed earlier about your return flight to Earth has been resolved. There will be no difficulties about it, none at all."

I felt a wave of relief surge through me. Despite my better instincts, though, I asked, "And what about Mr. Gunn?"

Her face became somber. "Don't ask about Sam, Mr. D'Argent. It's too gruesome to talk about."

And she broke off the connection.

So we rode back to Earth in comfort and safety.

Once I was safely back in my office in Montreal, I phoned my CEO to tell him that I'd dissolved Rockledge's partnership with Sam.

"Dissolved it? You mean he owns the Hell Crater complex without us?"

"Yes," I said, trying to hide my elation. "And we're paying Sam's company—or what's left of it—twenty billion dollars to get out of the deal."

"Twenty billion?" I'd never seen the CEO turn purple before.

It all went exactly as I planned it. The CEO wanted to fire me, of course, but I used the corporation's intricate dismissal procedures to delay that process until Rockledge's next quarterly board meeting. Once the board members—including Mrs. CEO—heard that we had incurred a debt of twenty billion, ostensibly to S. Gunn Enterprises, they scowled mightily at the CEO. He tried to pin the fiasco on me, of course, but I pointed out that despite my warnings he had enthusiastically supported the idea of Rockledge getting into the euphemistically named entertainment industry.

"Once I learned that entertainment, in this case," I said sternly, "meant gambling and prostitution—and the Mafia—I wanted to pull out of the deal immediately. But I was overruled by the CEO."

The board members gasped at the mention of the Mafia. They grumbled among themselves. They groused at the CEO. By the end of the meeting, just as I had planned, they voted to remove the CEO as board chairman. They wanted to fire him altogether, but he narrowly averted that fate, by a single vote: his wife's.

He glowered at me as the meeting broke up and the board members filed out of the conference room.

"I'll get you for this," he growled at me.

"No you won't. You're going to resign from the corporation; you and Ms. Marlowe, both."

His eyes went wide. "You . . . that's blackmail!"

"A little trick I learned from Sam Gunn," I gloated.

That was how I became Chief Executive Officer of Rockledge Industries. I owe it all to Sam. I almost felt sorry for the contemptible runt, leaving him to his fate with the Godfather.

Until, that is, I saw a videodrama featuring a craggy-faced, raspy-voiced actor named Gus Popov.

An actor! The whole business of the Mafia had been an act, a ploy, a swindle by that little sonofabitch to bilk me out of the twenty billion Sam needed to build the Hell Crater complex. I wanted to kill him. I wanted to—

I hesitated in mid-fury. I had actually come out of this deal rather well. I was now CEO of Rockledge Industries and all the problems with Hell Crater had been pinned on my predecessor. Sam had actually done me a favor: unknowingly, I was sure, but I was far better off now than I'd been a year earlier.

I never found out who Ms. Chang really was: probably another actor; maybe one of Hell's Belles, for all I knew. A pity. She was certainly beautiful. As for Sam's whereabouts, who knew? The solar system's a big place, with plenty of room for a scoundrel like Sam to hide. I had the feeling, though, that he had never left Hell Crater. Why should he? He owned the place!

I started thinking about how Rockledge might take it away from him. After all, he had squeezed Rockledge out of Hell Crater; there must be a way for us to squeeze him back.

It was about six months after I had moved into the old CEO's office when I got a call from—guess who?

"Hi, Pierre, you double-dealing SOB," Sam said cheerfully. "Hell Crater's a big moneymaker. Thanks for financing it."

I was so furious I couldn't do anything but splutter at Sam's image on my wall screen.

"Calm down, calm down!" Sam said, grinning like an evil elf. "How'd you like to get your money back? I've got this deal cooking for a transit system out to the Asteroid Belt. . . ."

Zoilo Hashimoto

JADE TERMINATED THE D'ARGENT NARRATIVE AND CALLED back her unfinished message to Jim Gradowsky.

"Jim," she said, "I just listened to D'Argent's story. It's good material. He's so obviously biased against Sam that he makes Sam look almost like an angel. Let's go with it."

Spence called from the bed, "You getting hungry, Jade? It's almost dinner hour."

She smiled at her husband. "Just let me finish this and then we can dress for dinner."

"I've got to take a shower," Spence said.

"Me too. You go first while I finish this message to Jim."

Spence gave her a wolfish grin. "I'll wait. Then we can shower together."

"In that teeny little stall?"

"We'll have to stay very close to each other."

Jade smiled back at him. "Okay. Give me a minute."

Turning back to the wall screen, she went on, "Jim, I got this story out of the blue. A guy named Hashimoto sent it to me at the office and Monica forwarded it to me. Apparently he saw the bio and figured he'd put in what he knows about Sam. It's a good story. I think we should include it in the follow-on."

The Mark of Zorro

"NOBODY CAN CONSISTENTLY MAKE MONEY IN THE COM-
modities market," she said, puffing hard. "The little bastard is cheating,
some'ow."

"How?" I asked.

Wiping a rivulet of sweat from her brow, she answered, "That's what I
want you to find out."

We were dangling on the sidelines of the volleyball court. The game is
rather different in zero gravity. The net is circular, held in the middle of
the court by hair-thin monofilament wires. Hit one of those wires and it
will slice you like a loaf of salami in a delicatessen. The court itself is
spherical, the curving walls hard and unpadded glassteel. The ball can
take strange bounces off those walls. So can the players.

There were hardly any spectators watching from the other side of the
glassteel. This was a private game, something of a grudge match, as a matter of fact.

Carole C. Chatsworth was a big, blonde, blowsy Cockney who looked
and sounded as if she belonged in some cheap burlesque show. Actually,
she was a brilliant, hard-driving, absolutely ruthless bureaucrat who had
worked her way to the top of the Interplanetary Security Commission's
enforcement division.

And she was a cutthroat volleyball player, the kind who would slam
you off the wall or push you into the wire if you got in her way.

She was also my boss, and she was convinced that Sam Gunn was ille-
gally reaping a fortune on the commodities futures market.

"No one can be as lucky as that little sod," she told me, her eyes following the flying, sweating players. " 'E's rigging the market some'ow."

When C.C. gets an idea in her head, forget about trying to argue her
out of it. The only two questions she'll put up with are: What do you want
me to do? and, How soon?

She had allowed herself to bloat up enormously in zero-gee. The rumor
was that she'd originally come up to this orbiting hotel when Sam Gunn
owned it and Sam had bedded her. Or maybe the other way around. After

all, it was supposed to be a "honeymoon hotel" in those days. Sam's motto for the place was, "If you like waterbeds, you'll love zero-gee."

C.C. never went back Earthside. She moved the ISC headquarters to the hotel, and actually got the Commission to buy half the orbital habitat to provide room for her staff's offices and living quarters. She was ready to bed down with Sam for life. But Sam pulled one of his disappearing acts on her, leaving her humiliated, furious, and certain that his only interest in her had been to get her to buy out his share of the hotel and run off to the Asteroid Belt with her money.

Maybe hell hath no fury like a woman jilted, but C.C. assuaged her anguish with food. She grew larger and larger, gobbling everything in sight, especially chocolate. Whenever a friend, or a fellow bureaucrat or even a physician commented on her size, she laughed bitterly and said, "But I weigh exactly the same as when I first came up 'ere: zero!"

Now she looked like a lumpy dirigible in a soggy, stained sweat suit as she waited for her next turn in the volleyball competition.

"I thought we'd fixed the little bastard's wagon when 'e tried to sue the Pope," she muttered, watching the volleyball action with narrowed, piggy eyes. "But some'ow 'e's making 'imself rich in the futures market. 'E's cheating. I know 'e is."

I did not demur. It would have done no good, especially to my career.

"You're going to Selene City with the team that's auditing Sam's books," she told me. "Officially, you're one of the auditors. That'll be your cover."

My real job, she told me *very* firmly, was "to find out how that little cheating, womanizing, swindling scumbag of a deviant 'umper is rigging the commodities market."

So off I went to the Moon to find Sam Gunn.

I SUPPOSE I should introduce myself. My name is Zoilo Hashimoto, the only son of a Japanese-American construction engineer and a Cuban baseball player whose career was cut short by her pregnancy with me. Dad was killed before I was born in the great tsunami that wiped out the hotel complex he was building on Tarawa. Mom returned to baseball as an umpire after her second marriage broke up, which was after my four sisters were born. She was known as a strict enforcer of the rules on the field. Believe me, she was just as strict at home.

Somewhere in my genetic heritage there must have been a basketball player, for despite the diminutive size of both my parents I am nearly two meters tall—six feet, five inches in old-fashioned English units.

I have been told I am handsome, with deep brown eyes and high cheek bones that make me look decidedly oriental. Yet I have never been very successful with women. Perhaps I am too shy, too uncertain of myself. I once tried to grow a beard, but it looked terrible, and the unwritten dress code of the ISC demands clean-shaven men. The unwritten rules are always the important ones, of course.

I had started my career in law enforcement, figuring that I could safely retire after twenty years of police work with enough of a pension to follow my one true passion: archeology. I longed to help search for the ancient cities that were being unearthed on Mars (pardon the unintentional pun). I was never a street officer; the robots had taken over such dangerous duties by the time I graduated college with my degree in criminology. Instead, I specialized in tracking down financial crooks. I worked with computers and electronic ferrets rather than guns and stun wands.

But enough about me. Let me tell you how I met Sam Gunn.

I DUTIFULLY WENT to the Moon, to Sam's corporate headquarters at Selene City, foolishly expecting Sam to be there, especially with a team of ISC auditors combing through his records. But Sam wasn't, of course.

He was out at a new solar power satellite that was just going online to provide fifteen gigawatts of electrical power to the growing industrial cities of central Asia.

Years earlier Sam had been one of the first to go out to the asteroids to mine their metals and minerals. He had amassed a considerable fortune and a fleet of ore-processing factory ships. But then disaster struck and he lost it all. In desperation he had tried to sue the Pope, and although he got what he wanted without going to trial, he quickly lost it all. C.C. Chatsworth had been a major force in seeing to it that Sam was broken and humiliated.

But now he was getting rich again. In the commodities market, of all places.

Sam's present company was in business to service and maintain several solar power satellites and other facilities in Earth orbit and on the Moon. And he was out at the newest of the sunsats, rather than in his offices in Selene City.

I was reluctant to go the satellite to meet him. Those huge sunsats ride in geosynchronous orbit, nearly thirty-six thousand kilometers above the equator, on the fringes of the outer Van Allen Belt. There's a lot of ionizing radiation out there, and I didn't like the idea of living in it, even inside a shielded space suit.

But that's where Sam was and that's where I had to go. Or face the sizeable wrath of the sizeable C.C. Chatsworth.

So I rode an OTV (orbital transfer vehicle, to landlubbers) from Selene to Sunsat Seventeen. An OTV is the most utilitarian of utility vehicles, nothing more than a collection of tankage, cargo containers, crew pod and engines.

I sat crammed behind the two pilots during the whole nine-hour trip, staring out the curving port of the crew pod, watching the graceful blue and white sphere of Earth grow and grow until it was a massive, dazzling presence of overwhelming beauty, deep blue oceans and resplendent white clouds, wrinkled old mountains with bony fingers of snow clutching their crests. Even the sprawling cities looked almost pretty from this vantage point.

Then the sunsat swung into view, blocking out everything else, huge and square and so close that my heart clutched in my chest; I thought we were going to plunge right into it.

It was ten kilometers long and six klicks across, a huge flat expanse of solar cells that drank in sunlight and converted it silently to electricity. Off at one end were the magnetrons that transformed the electricity into microwave energy, and the big steerable antennas that beamed the microwaves to receiving antenna farms on Earth.

I had expected the sunsat to glitter and gleam, like a jewel or a huge light in the sky. Instead it was dark and silent, greedily soaking up sunlight, not reflecting it.

Except down at the end where the magnetrons were. They were sparking and flashing spectacularly, blue electrical snakes writhing all across them, shooting off brilliant lightning flashes into the dead black emptiness of space. It was all in eerie silence, naturally, but in my mind I could imagine the crackling and hissing of gigawatts of electricity straining to get loose.

"Nothing to be alarmed about," said the OTV pilot over his shoulder to me, shoehorned in behind him. The man's voice was decidedly quavering. "Besides, we'll be docking several klicks away from that mess."

He docked us at the port on the shaded underside of the sunsat, where the so-called living quarters were. There were only three people there, two Asian women and a frowning, bearded, bald, portly European man. They all looked nervous, worried. Much to my consternation, the OTV pulled away and headed back for the Moon as soon as it detached its cargo pods. Its crew never waited to find out if I wanted to return with them.

I was informed by the worried-looking trio that Sam was "up topside," working with the technicians who were trying to fix the "transient" that was afflicting the magnetrons.

They pulled a space suit out of a locker and before I realized what was happening they were stuffing me into it. The suit was brand new and stiff; it smelled of freshly cured plastic and cleaning oils, like a new car. Believe it or not, in those days it was difficult to find a suit that would fit someone as tall as I. This one barely did; my fingers were cramped in the gloves, and my toes crunched uncomfortably into the boots. I felt as if I had to stoop to keep the suit from popping open on me.

Once I was suited up they hustled me to the access tube that led up and out to the sunlit side of the satellite.

I had been in space suits before; they saw that on my dossier, so they felt no qualms about sending me outside alone with only the barest briefing on how to attach the suit's tether to one of the guard rails that ran the length of the satellite, between the rows of solar panels.

They told me which radio frequencies were which, and left me at the hatch of the access tube. I nodded to them from inside my helmet, went through the hatch, and started to pull myself weightlessly along the rungs set into the curving inner wall of the tube.

I am one of those fortunate few who have never been bothered by weightlessness. Practically everyone gets queasy at first, a fact that ruined Sam's original plan for his honeymoon hotel. Yes, there are patches and pills you can take. Biofeedback training, too. Still, most people want to barf when they first experience zero-gee. Not me. I found it exhilarating, right from the first moment.

So I swam weightlessly the length of the access tube and opened the hatch at its other end. Stepping out onto the broad, flat surface of the sunsat was something like stepping from a cool darkened room into the full brilliance of a blazing Arizona summer afternoon.

My suit creaked and groaned from the sudden heat load of the Sun's unfiltered fury. I heard the fans whir up and the pumps gurgle. But none of that mattered. The scenery was too breathtaking to care about anything else.

I was standing on a wide, flat expanse of dark, glassy solar panels. Actually, I was standing in an aisle between rows of panels. The sunsat was a world of its own, a world that stretched for kilometers in every direction, row upon row of panels so dark they looked almost like emptiness, like the void of space itself. Between the rows, however, metal strips of aisles glinted in the brilliant sunlight.

I could not see the Earth; it was on the satellite's other, shaded side. For all I could see, I was alone in the universe on this giant raft of solar panels, just me and the distant stars and the blazing Sun with its pulsing, glowing corona and a halo of zodiacal light extending on either side of it.

For the first time in my life I felt a dizzying surge of vertigo. It took me several moments to catch my breath. Then I remembered what I was here for, and tapped the keypad at my wrist to turn on the suit-to-suit radio frequency.

". . . never seen such a collection of misbegotten, ham-handed, under-brained, overpaid jerkoffs in my whole *life*! Don't you guys know *any-thing*? Where'd you get your degrees, Genghis Dumb University?"

Those were the first words I heard Sam Gunn speak.

I attached my tether to the guard rail and started slowly toward the end of the sunsat where six space-suited figures were hovering off to one side of the sparking, sputtering magnetrons like a half-dozen toy balloons tethered to various guard rails. In their midst was one stumpy little figure, bobbing up and down like a Mexican jumping bean on amphetamines, literally at the end of his tether.

"Eleven billion dollars to build this pile of junk," Sam was yelling, "and all of it's going down the toilet because nobody here knows how to shut down a stupid, frigging power bus!"

"Ah . . . Mr Gunn?" I said into my helmet microphone.

He paid no attention. He kept up his tirade, describing in considerable detail the physical, mental and moral shortcomings of the technicians surrounding him, their families, their friends, their entire gene pool, even their herds of goats and sheep.

"Mr. Gunn!" I bellowed.

". . . never been smart enough to wipe your own—WHAT?" he snarled, turning in my direction.

"I am Zoilo Hashimoto, from—"

"Leapin' lizards, Sandy!" Sam exclaimed. "It's Zorro, come to right wrongs and carve a zee into my chest!"

"Zoilo," I corrected. I might as well have saved my breath.

"That's what we need around here. The masked avenger. The mark of Zorro. You can start by transplanting some brains into these zombies."

The six space-suited technicians simply hung on their tethers, silent as corpses, unmoving and apparently unmoved by Sam's insults.

"Would you believe," Sam said to me, "that they sent me the only six techs in all of Asia that can't speak English? They expect me to talk to them in Sanskrit or whatever."

"That must be frustrating," I said.

"Not all that bad." I detected a grin in his voice. "I can call them anything that pops into my head and they don't take offense. . . . as long as I stick to English."

Then he whirled back toward them and unleashed a blast of heavily accented Japanese that galvanized the technicians into frenzied action. I understood a little of what he said and I have no intention of repeating it.

It took the better part of two hours, but Sam finally got the electrical sparking stopped. He had to do the toughest part of the job by himself; the technicians either could not or would not go within fifty meters of the crackling blue fireworks. I had to hang there like a lanky sausage, with nothing to do but watch Sam work while I worried about how much radiation I was absorbing.

When the sparking finally stopped, however, the six technicians began dismantling the magnetron with the intense purposiveness of a team of ants tearing into a jelly doughnut that someone had carelessly dropped.

"C'mon," Sam said, pulling himself along the guide rail toward me, "let's go back inside, Zorro."

"Zoilo," I corrected.

"Yeah, sure."

As we headed for the tube hatch I tried to make some conversation. "How much time do you spend outside like this?"

"Too damned much," Sam snapped.

"I mean, the radiation levels out here are—"

"That's why I wear a lead jockstrap, pal."

I thought he was joking. Years later I found out that he wasn't.

I followed him back to the access tube and down to the office/habitat area. The worried trio I had met earlier was nowhere in sight, although where they could hide in the narrow confines of the office/habitat area was beyond me.

We stopped in front of the space suit lockers and began to work our way out of our suits. Once Sam lifted off his helmet I took a good look at him. I had seen videos and stills of him, naturally. I knew that round, snub-nosed face with its bristling rust-red hair almost as well as I knew my own. Yet seeing him live and close-up was different: he looked more animated, livelier. And his eyes seemed to twinkle with the awareness that he knew things I didn't.

Sam's space suit looked grimy, hard-used. Its torso and helmet were covered with corporate logos and mission patches, everything from *Vacuum Cleaners Inc.* to an ancient, faded *Space Station Freedom.* Several emblems puzzled me: one that said *Keep the baby, Faith,* and another that looked like the gaudily striped flattened sphere of the planet Jupiter with four little stars beside it and the word *Roemer* beneath.

"C'mon," Sam said. "Lemme show you where you'll be sleeping tonight."

"Don't you want to know why I'm here?" I asked.

He gave me an exaggerated frown. "I know why you're here. C.C. wants to pin my balls to her office wall, right?"

It was clear that he understood exactly why I had come; no cover story was necessary with Sam. So I nodded, then realized that Sam was at eye level with me, despite the fact that I was almost a foot taller than he. I had unconsciously slipped my feet into the floor loops, to anchor myself down. Sam, on the other hand, floated free and bobbed weightlessly beside me.

"Why is it," he asked the empty air, "that when a little guy makes some money, everybody in the goddamned government wants to investigate him?"

"Mr. Gunn," I started to explain, "you have had an extremely—"

"Call me Sam," he snapped.

"Very well. You may call me Zoilo."

"I already do, Zorro."

"Zoilo."

"I still can't figure out why the double-dipped ISC is worried about my good luck on the commodities market."

"Ms. Chatsworth is concerned that more than good luck may be involved," I replied.

He grinned at me, a gap-toothed grin of pure boyish glee.

"She thinks I'm cheating?"

He said it with such wide-eyed innocence that I was left speechless.

Sam laughed and said, "C'mon, let's get some shut-eye. The next OTV won't be here until tomorrow afternoon."

He floated down the corridor, propelling himself with deft touches of his fingers against the metal walls. I pulled my stockinged feet out of the floor loops and clambered hand-over-hand after him, using the grips that studded the walls.

To say that the personnel quarters aboard Sunsat Seventeen were spartan would be an understatement. They consisted of a row of lockers, nothing more. A mesh sleeping cocoon was fastened to one side, a fold-down sink on the other. There was an electrical outlet and a data port for connecting a computer. The locker was barely tall enough for me to squeeze into it; I had to keep my chin pressed down on my chest.

The next morning I groaned as I unfolded myself out in the corridor. Sam, on the other hand, was chipper and as bright as a new-minted penny.

"Whatsamatter, Zorro," he asked, almost solicitously, "you in pain or something?"

Stretching in an effort to ease the crick in my neck, I explained that the privacy booths were too cramped for comfort.

"Gee," Sam said, bouncing lightly off the floor to rise to eye level with me, "I always thought they were really spacious."

Over breakfast in the minuscule galley I asked, "Why are you here, Sam, instead of in your office in Selene City? Surely you can hire engineers to supervise the work here."

He gave me a sour look as he spooned up oatmeal. "Yeah, sure. I can hire the entire graduating class of MIT if I want to."

"Then why are you here?"

"Because every engineer I hire costs me money, and money is something I don't have much of, that's why."

"But the High Asia Sunsat Combine must be paying at least minimum rates for your maintenance contract."

He chewed thoughtfully for a moment; the oatmeal was that lumpy. Then he swallowed and said, "Nobody would sign a contract with S. Gunn Enterprises unless our bid was considerable *under* standard rates. Your sweetheart Ms. Chatsworth has seen to that."

"But that's illegal. It's restraint of . . ." My voice trailed off as I realized the import of what he was telling me.

"C.C. and her connections in the government saw to it that I got screwed out of my old corporation. She's got a vendetta going against me. The only work I can find is these crappy maintenance contracts, and even then I've got to do it at a helluva lot less than standard pay."

I heard myself ask weakly, "Well, how many contracts do you have?"

"Six, right now. Three sunsats, a couple of orbiting astronomical tele-scopes, and the laundry facility at the new retirement center in Selene City."

"Laundry?"

He laughed bitterly. "Great job for a pioneer, isn't it? Washing old folks' dirty sheets."

Sam had truly been a pioneering entrepreneur, I knew. The zero-gee hotel, the first asteroid mining expedition, even the early work of cleaning debris out of the low-orbit region around Earth—he had been the trailblazer. Now he was reduced to maintenance contracts, and hiring fourth-rate technicians because he couldn't afford better.

Yet . . . somehow he was getting rich on the commodities futures market.

"Well," I said, "at least maintenance contracts provide a steady income."

"Oh yeah, sure." A frown puckered his brows. "They're usually safe and easy, all right. But this bunch of clowns trying to operate Sunsat Seventeen are making this particular job a pain in the butt."

"The magnetrons?"

"The everything!" Sam exclaimed. "The hardware's crappy. The technicians don't know what they're doing. And I'm supposed to make it all come out peachy-keen."

"In the meantime, though," I pointed out, "you're piling up quite a fortune in the commodities market."

He toyed with the oatmeal remaining in his bowl. "Am I?" he asked softly.

"According to our records, you certainly are."

Sam sighed mightily, like a man weary of being dragged down by lesser mortals. "I've been pretty lucky, I guess. In the market, I mean."

From the gleam in Sam's eye, I knew he was enjoying the fact that C.C. was annoyed enough to send me to investigate him. He certainly did not appear to be worried about my presence. Not in the slightest.

After breakfast I retired to my locker and plugged in my pocket computer, scrunching myself up close to its tiny microphone so that my lips almost touched it. I didn't want Sam to hear me.

All that morning and right through lunch I searched through Sam's records. Not that I hadn't before, but now I was looking specifically into his transactions in the commodities market. There was a pattern to be found; there always is, in any crooked scheme. Find the pattern and you find the crook.

It quickly became clear that Sam was buying and selling almost exclusively in the metals market: meteoric iron and precious metals, mostly. He speculated on the cargoes bound inward from the Asteroid Belt on the factory ships, guessing which ships would return laden with profitable cargoes and which would not. He was right ninety-three percent of the time, an impossible score for pure luck.

The commodities futures market was a crapshoot, and like all gambles, the odds were stacked against the gambler. Yet Sam was beating those odds a staggering ninety-three percent of the time. Impossible, unless he was cheating somehow.

You see, there were a huge number of variables in each mission out to the asteroids, too many for anyone to guess right ninety-three percent of the time. Or even fifty-three percent of the time, for that matter.

There were thousands of independent miners out there in the Asteroid Belt hunting down usable asteroids, chunks of metals and minerals that could be mined profitably. The factory ships went out on Hohmann transfer orbits, using the minimum amount of energy, spending the least amount of money to reach a destination in the belt.

Picking the right destination was crucial. No sense spending a year in space to arrive at a spot where no miners and no ore were waiting for you. Rendezvous points and times were selected beforehand, but a thousand unforeseen factors could ruin your plans. Usually the small mining teams auctioned off their ores to the highest bidder. But often enough they decided not to wait for you because somebody else showed up with ready credits for the ores.

All these factors were heavily influenced by timing and distance. The Asteroid Belt is mostly empty space, even though there are millions of asteroids floating out there between Mars and Jupiter. Think of megatrillions of cubic kilometers of nothingness, with a few grains of dust drifting through the void: that's what the so-called "belt" is like.

It takes propulsion energy—which means money—to maneuver in space, to move the millions of kilometers between usable asteroids. The miners were mostly small-time independent operators who were always short on funds; they were always willing to take immediate credits instead of waiting for your particular factory ship to reach the rendezvous point you were aiming for.

There were more pending lawsuits over broken contracts for ore deliveries than there were divorce cases on Earth. The miners evaded the law, by and large, because it cost a corporation more to catch and fine them than the fines could possibly return. Besides, fining a miner was a study in frustration anyway. Most of them simply declared bankruptcy and started up again under a new name.

All this made the commodities market an arena fraught with uncertainties. How do you know which factory ship will come back with a rich cargo of metals or minerals? How can you guess what such cargoes will be worth on the market, when it takes a year or more for the factory ship to make the return journey to Earth?

The answer is, you wait as long as you possibly can before you invest your money (or, more accurately, make your bet). The safest thing to do is to wait until a factory ship has actually taken on a specific cargo of metals, check with the price of such metals on the futures market, and only then sink your money into that particular ship.

So investors waited eagerly for communications from the various factory ships. It takes more than half an hour for a message to travel from the belt to the Earth-Moon system. There's no way around that time lag. Even moving at the speed of light as they do, electronic or optical laser messages average about thirty minutes to cover the distance between the belt and the Earth-Moon region.

As soon as a favorable message is received, investors start bidding up the price of that ship's cargo.

But some investors, the ones with more guts than brains, put their money into a ship's cargo *before* the good word comes from the Asteroid Belt. They bet that the news will be good before the news is received. Most of those investors quickly go broke.

Sam Gunn invested that way. And he was not going broke. Far from it. He was getting rich.

There was no way for him to do that legally. Of that, C.C. Chatsworth was convinced. So was I. But I had to find out how he was cheating the system. Or face the wrath of C.C. She was determined to put *somebody's* testicles on her office wall. If she couldn't get Sam's, she'd take mine.

The OTV duly arrived and carried Sam and me back to Selene. The city was almost entirely underground, as all lunar cities were in those days. Even the imposing grand plaza, as long as six football fields with a dome of seventy-five meters' height, was totally enclosed, except for the huge curved glassteel windows at its far end.

The plaza was grassed and landscaped and dotted with flowering shrubbery, however, so it looked very Earthlike even though the light lunar gravity allowed tourists to soar like birds on big, colorful plastic wings they rented.

The ISC was paying for a minimum-sized studio apartment at the government-rented set of rooms on Level One, barely large enough for a bed, mini-kitchen and phonebooth-sized bathroom. I had to hunch over to squeeze into the shower.

Sam, on the other hand, ensconced me in a spacious office next to his own, in the imposing headquarters tower of Moonbase Inc., where he had rented space for his own S. Gunn Enterprises. I was surprised that his offices were so spacious, until I realized that he slept in his own office and saved himself the cost of an apartment. It was strictly against the building's regulations, of course, but somehow Sam managed to get away with it.

I spent days digging into the personnel files of each and every individual who might be tipping Sam off about ore shipments from the Asteroid Belt. Using the ISC's powers of subpoena I investigated their personal financial records. I could find nothing that hinted at bribery or collusion.

Besides, how could anyone tip Sam before the rest of the market? The news from the factory ships traveled at the speed of light from the Asteroid Belt to the Earth-Moon system. There was no way around that.

Evenings I spent with Sam. He wined and dined me as if I were a long-lost brother or a wealthy potential customer. He even found dates for me, lovely young women who seemed more interested in Sam than in me. But nevertheless, Sam saw to it that I was not lonely at Selene. I knew he was trying to bribe me, or at least make me feel that he was a fine person and incapable of chicanery. Yet I began to realize how lonely, how empty, my life had been up to that point. Being with Sam was fun!

On the other hand, each day I received a phone call from C.C., her quivering, jowled face grimacing at me angrily. "'Ave you nailed 'im yet?" she would demand. Each day she grew angrier, her fleshy face redder. It got so bad that I stopped taking all incoming calls. But she called anyway and left messages of rage that escalated daily.

I became so desperate that I asked him point-blank, "How do you do it, Sam?"

"Do what?"

"Cheat the market."

We were in Selene's finest restaurant, Earthview, waiting for our evening's companions to show up. The restaurant was deep underground, rather than in the plaza. On the Moon, where the airless surface is bathed in deadly radiation and peppered by meteoric infall, the deeper belowground you are, the more your prestige. Earthview was on Selene's bottom level, where the executives kept their own plush quarters.

The restaurant was several storeys high, however. The volume had originally been an actual cave; now it was occupied by tiers of dining tables covered with the finest napery and silverware made from asteroidal metal. No two tables were on the same level. Each one stood on a pedestal atop an impossibly slim column of shining stainless steel while curving ramps twined between them. On Earth the human waiters and bussers would have been exhausted after an hour's work. Here in the low gravity of the Moon they could work four-hour shifts with comparative ease. Still, one tipped generously at Earthview.

"Cheat the market?" Sam put on such a look of hurt innocence that I had to laugh.

"Come on, Sam," I said. "You know that you're cheating and I know that you know."

He blinked his eyes several times. They were green now. I could have sworn they'd been blue. But Sam was wearing a trim leisure suit of forest green, and his eyes almost matched his attire. Contact lenses? I wondered.

"How could I possibly cheat the market?" he asked.

"That's what I'd like to know," I said.

Sam broke into a boyish grin. "Look, Zorro old pal, your ISC auditors have been plowing through my company's files for more than a week now. They've even snooped into my personal accounts. What have they found?"

"Nothing," I admitted.

"You know why?" he asked, with a devilish cock of one eyebrow.

"Why?"

"Because there's nothing to find. I'm as pure as the driven snow. Clean as a whistle. Spotless. Unblemished. Unsullied. Right up there with the Virgin Mary—well, maybe not *that* unsullied. But you'll have to find another chest to carve your zee into."

I had given up long ago on getting him to pronounce my name correctly. To him I was Zorro and there was no use wasting energy trying to change him.

In truth, I was getting to like Sam. He was enjoying this fencing, I saw. He liked to talk; he even seemed to enjoy listening to me talk. I found myself telling him about my boyhood in Cuba and my longing to explore the buried cities of Mars.

"Archeology, hey?" he mused. "Lots of good-looking women students. Lonely outposts far from civilization." He nodded happily. "Could be a good life, Zorro."

Sam was especially enjoying the fact that I was living on an ISC expense account, running up a huge dent in C.C.'s budget. That's why he insisted that we dine at the Earthview. There was no more expensive restaurant in the solar system.

After that fruitless (although thoroughly enjoyable) dinner, I decided to *cherchez les femmes*. Sam was wooing half a dozen women simultaneously, and avoiding several others—including a judge of the World Court, a former United States Senator, Jill Meyers.

I found that although several of Sam's "dates" loathed most of the other women he was pursuing, none of them had a harsh word to say about Sam himself.

"I know he plays around," said a lean, lanky young redhead from Colorado who was working at Selene as a tour guide. She shrugged it off. "I guess that's part of what makes him so interesting—you never know what he's going to do next."

An older, wiser Chinese women who operated excavating equipment up on the surface told me, "Sam is like lightning: he never hits the same place twice." Then she smiled sagely and added, "Unless you put out something that attracts him."

The typical reaction was that of a grinning, curly-haired Dutch blonde, "At least he's not a bore! Sam's always a lot of fun, even if he does exasperate you sometimes."

I would not get any useful information from his lovers. They had no useful information to give me.

It was frustrating, to say the least. Somehow Sam knew what the factory ships were bringing back toward Earth before the information was received on Earth. But that was impossible. The ships broadcast their information in the clear; no coded messages were allowed. The messages were received by the ISC's own communications satellite and immediately relayed to every receiving antenna in the Earth-Moon system at the same time. All right, when the Moon was in the right part of its orbit, receivers on the Moon might catch the incoming messages a second and a half sooner than receivers on Earth. So what? That made no real difference. The Moon lagged a second and a half behind when it was on the other side of its orbit. I repeat, So what?

Yet, just to make certain, I ran a correlation of Sam's right "guesses" with the position of the Moon in its orbit. Nothing. It made no difference whether the Moon was a second and a half ahead or behind.

Sam was enjoying my frustration. We became buddies, of a sort. He pulled me away from my desk time and again to show me around Selene, take me for walks up on the surface, even escort me to the gambling casino at Hell Crater and treat me to a pile of chips—which I promptly lost. Dice, roulette, baccarat, even the slot machines; it made no difference, I lost at them all, much to Sam's glee.

I began to clutch at straws. Somehow, I knew—I *knew*—Sam was getting the incoming messages from the factory ships before the rest of the Earth-Moon system. He could make his buying decisions based on advance knowledge; of that I was certain. That meant that he was receiving those messages sooner than everyone else. In turn, that meant that the speed of light was not the same for Sam as it was for everyone else.

I was challenging Einstein; that's how crazy Sam was making me.

He had somehow rigged the speed with which those messages traveled from the Asteroid Belt to Earth. But that was impossible! The speed of light is the one immutable factor in all of Einstein's relativity. It can't be changed. It travels at one speed in vacuum and one speed only. Sam couldn't slow it down or speed it up.

Or—if he could—why would he be wasting his time playing the commodities market? He could be opening up the path to interstellar travel!

In desperation I asked my computer to search for any correlations it could discern in all of Sam's market transactions. Anything at all.

The list that scrolled across my screen was even more frustrating than my other failed ideas. There were plenty of correlations, but none of them made any sense. For example, Sam's buys of metals futures seemed to follow some astrological pattern: the computer actually worked out a pattern in which Sam's investments correlated with the astrological signs for the days in which he made his buys.

Sam sold his futures, of course. That's how he made money. He bought when the price was low, before most other investors dared to risk their money. Then he waited until the price for that particular cargo rose, and sold it off at a handsome profit. While his buys had that weird astrological correlation, his sales did not; they were strictly related to the market price for the metals.

I was losing weight worrying over this problem. And I started to have bad dreams, nightmares in which C.C. Chatsworth was fiendishly slicing me into thin sections on those volleyball wires, cackling insanely while my blood floated all around me in zero-gravity bubbles.

Sam, strangely enough, was very solicitous, fussing over me like a distraught uncle.

"You gotta eat better, Zorro," he told me as I picked at my dinner.

We were back at the Earthview. Sam had just returned from another quick trip to Sunsat Seventeen. The magnetrons were still giving trouble. Sam grumbled about the Asian consortium's insistence that seventy-five percent of the satellite's hardware had to be manufactured in Asia.

"And not the Pacific Rim countries, where they know how to build major hardware," he groused. "Not Japan or even China."

Despite my growing despair, I went for his bait. "Then where is the hardware being built?" I asked.

Sam frowned from across the circular dining table. "Upper Clucksville, from the looks of it. Afghanistan, Tzadikistan, Dumbbellistan—guys who had trouble making oxcarts are now building klystrons and power busses and I'm stuck with a contract that says I've gotta make it all work right or it comes outta *my* profits!"

"Why did you ever agree to such a contract?" I wondered out loud.

"Outta the goodness of my heart," said Sam, placing a hand on his chest. "Why else?"

A bell rang in my mind.

Sam was gone the next morning, back to the same Sunsat Seventeen. I went up to my roomy office and immediately got to work. Ignoring the pretty view of the plaza's greenery and the Olympic-sized swimming pool where young tourists were doing quintuple flips in lunar slow-motion from the thirty-meter diving platform, I booted up my computer and started checking out the hunch that had popped into my mind the night before.

In the back of my mind it occurred to me that Sam had generously given me this office next to his own so that he could keep an eye on me. He probably had the desktop computer bugged, too, so he could see what I was looking into. So I used my trusty old palm-sized machine instead. It was slower, because it had to access files stored back on Earth and that meant a second-and-a-half lag. But using Sam's computer would have been foolish, I thought.

Yes! I was right. Every time Sam made a successful buy on the futures market he was in orbit, not on the Moon. Almost. He made a few buys from his office here in Selene City as well, but they were sometimes winners, more often losers. When he called in his buys from orbit they were winners, every time except once, and that once happened when a factory ship broke down months after Sam's purchase of its cargo of industrial steel; the cargo was almost a year late in reaching the market. Everyone lost money on that one.

His sell orders came from Selene, from orbit, from wherever he happened to be. But his successful buys, the ones that were making him rich, *always* came from orbit.

I was so excited by this discovery that it wasn't until late that afternoon that the reaction hit me. So what? So Sam makes his buy decisions while he's working in orbit, instead of when he's on the Moon. What does that prove?

It didn't prove anything, I realized. It certainly reinforced the idea that Sam was cheating the system, somehow. But how he was doing it remained a mystery.

I felt terribly let down. As if I had spent every bit of my energy trying to break down a solidly locked door, only to find that the room beyond that door was totally empty.

I sat at the desk Sam had loaned me, staring out at the scantily clad tourists performing athletic feats that were impossible on Earth, feeling completely drained and exhausted. In my mind's eye I saw C.C. roasting me over the coals of bureaucratic wrath. And Sam grinning at me like a gap-toothed Jack-o'-lantern, knowing that he had outsmarted me.

I should have been angry with Sam. Furious. The little trickster was ruining my career, my life. Yet I just couldn't work up the rage. Sam had been kind to me. I knew it had all been in his own self-interest, but the little wise guy had actually behaved as if we were real friends.

Nevertheless, I had to get to the bottom of this. Sam was cheating and it was my job to nail him. Or I would be nailed myself.

I hauled myself up from the desk chair and headed for Selene's spaceport, checking my palm computer for the departure time of the next OTV heading for Sunsat Seventeen.

I'm going to catch him in the act, I told myself. He's not going to outsmart me any longer.

When I finally arrived at the sunsat, he was outside again, working with the same team of technicians while the same trio of engineers gave me worried frowns and mumbles as I pulled on the same slightly-too-small space suit.

"Sam told us we should stay inside," said one of the women engineers.

"He said it's going to be real hairy topside," the other one added.

The bald, bearded man said, "He said he had to test the escape pod again."

"Again?" The word caught my attention.

The man nodded solemnly while the two women checked out my backpack.

"How often does he check out the escape pod?" I asked.

He shrugged. "Every time he comes here, just about."

One of the women said, from behind me, "Sam's worried that this sunsat might be unsafe."

My mind was clicking fast. I couldn't imagine any disaster that could make this sixty-square kilometer slab of metal so unsafe that they would have to abandon it. The so-called escape pod was a modified OTV; it could fly all the way back to the Moon, if necessary.

And Sam took out the escape pod almost every time he came to this sunsat.

Click. Click. Click. Those facts meshed together. They added up to something—but I didn't know the full answer. Not yet.

"Tell Sam that I'm coming out to the escape pod," I commanded. "Tell him not to leave until I get to him."

I flew up the access tube as fast as I could and pulled myself hand-over-hand along the guard rail that led out to the escape pod. All the while, I was thinking that the pod ought to be stationed close to the habitat module, not out at the end of the structure.

I got there almost in time. Just as I reached the docking module, the pod detached and floated away into the emptiness.

"Sam!" I yelled into my helmet microphone. "Come back here! I'm going with you."

"Sorry, Zorro, no can do," Sam's voice chirped cheerfully in my earphones. "Go on back inside and have a cup of coffee. I'll only be out for a couple hours or so. Gotta check the emergency systems."

The pod was drifting slowly away; he hadn't fired its main engine yet.

"Sam, you're full of bullshit and we both know it!"

"Such harsh language," he replied. "That's not like you, Zorro."

I had to do something. I couldn't just hover there and watch him get away with it. I don't remember thinking over my options. I simply acted without rational thought.

I unclipped my tether and jumped off the satellite, trying to reach the slowly drifting escape pod.

Just as I did, I heard Sam warning, "Counting down to main engine ignition: ten, nine, eight . . ."

I desperately needed to reach the pod before its rocket engine lit up. Reaching awkwardly behind me, I tried to find the bleed valve for my air tank. If I could squirt a little air out, it would act as a rocket thrust and zip me out to the pod before Sam could light up its main engine.

My gloved fingers found the valve while I mentally tried to picture how it worked. I pushed down on the knob, then turned it just a hair.

Too much. I was snapped into a crazy spin, my arms and legs flailing wildly, pulled away from my body by centrifugal force. The escape pod, the sunsat, the stars whirled madly around me.

I could still hear Sam counting, ". . . three, two . . ."

A noiseless flash of light made me blink even while my head was whacking from side to side inside my helmet. I thought I heard Sam's voice yelling something, but then everything went blurry. I thought I was unconscious or maybe dead, but my head was still thumping painfully and every part of my body was screaming with pain and I was getting terribly dizzy.

Finally I did black out. My last thought was that this was a thoroughly idiotic way to die, spinning like a rag doll while Sam rocketed off to do whatever it was he did to cheat the commodities market.

When I came to, the first thing I saw was Sam's round, freckled face staring down at me. He was smiling, sort of, even though the expression on his face was far from pleased.

"You just cost me a couple hundred million bucks, Zorro," he said. Softly.

I blinked. My head was throbbing, thundering with pain. My back and shoulders and arms and legs—all of me ached agonizingly.

But what cut through the haze of hurt was the sight of Sam. He was in his beat-up old space suit, helmet off. Something new had been added to his collection of patches and insignias. He had painted a slashing red zigzag across the suit's chest. A letter zee. The mark of Zorro.

"Wh . . ." My throat was dry and raw. It took a real effort to work up enough saliva to swallow. "What happened?" I asked weakly.

Sam tried to frown at me but his face just wasn't cut out for it.

"Just as I lit up the pod's engine you went pinwheeling past me like a bowling ball with legs."

We were in the escape pod, I realized. A padded bulkhead curved above me, and beyond Sam's back I could see the control panel and the small circular viewport above it. I was lying on one of the acceleration couches.

"You rescued me," I said.

Sam hunched his shoulders. "It was either that or watch you zip all the way out to Mars. I figured you'd run out of air in about ten minutes, the way you were squirting it out of your backpack."

I tried to sit up, but my head pounded like a thunderburst and I got woozy.

"Take it easy, babe," Sam said. "Just lay there and relax. We're on our way back to the sunsat, but it'll take an hour or so."

"An hour . . . ?"

"I had to burn a helluva lot of propellant to catch you, Zorro. And then burn off that velocity and head back. Lotta delta-vee, pal. So we're on a minimum energy trajectory, headin' back to the ol' corral." Those last few words he pronounced with a fake western twang.

"You saved my life," I said, realizing that it was true. I felt an enormous sense of gratitude welling up inside me.

Sam brushed it off with a wave of his hand. "It was either that or have C.C. come after me for murder."

"She couldn't—"

"Couldn't she? Once she figured out that you knew how I was getting a jump on the market, she'd automatically assume I killed you to keep you quiet."

I blinked with shock. "But I didn't—"

"Pretty smart cookie, Zorro, ol' pal." Sam was smiling, but it seemed a little on the bitter side. "That's why I painted your zee on my chest. You got me, fair and square."

There are times when a man should keep his big mouth shut and accept praise, whether he deserves it or not. This was certainly one of those times. Unfortunately, my brain was too addled from the beating I had just undergone to pay attention to my own advice.

"What do you mean, I got you?" I asked, befuddled. "What does the zee on your chest have to do with it?"

Sam's grin turned more impish. He touched one end of the zee and said, "A factory ship." Then, sliding his finger along the zigzag red line, he added, "The Baade Orbital Telescope," the finger slid across the other leg of the zee, "the reflector I hung out at the Mars L-5 position," finally the finger came to rest at the other end of the zee, "and the ISC's main receiving telescope in Earth orbit."

Then he pointed to the patch on his chest, just above the zee, the one that said *Roemer*. "He figured out the speed of light."

I got it! Like a flash of lightning, I suddenly understood what Sam had been doing all along.

Everybody knew approximately when a factory ship was due to send its message back toward Earth, telling what kind of an ore load it was going to be carrying home. The messages are sent by tight laser beam to the ISC's receiving facility in Earth orbit. Once the satellite gets the word, it broadcasts the news to all the market centers in the Earth-Moon system.

Sam intercepted the signal. It was that simple. He positioned one of the orbiting astronomical telescopes his company maintained to intercept the laser signal, bounce it to a reflector he had prepositioned along the orbit of Mars, and then finally send it Earthward. The signal was received at the Earth satellite station ten or twenty minutes later than it normally would have been and nobody was the wiser because nobody bothered to check the exact moment that the factory ship sent its signal.

Meanwhile, Sam used that ten or twenty minutes to buy metals futures before anyone else knew what the factory ship was carrying.

It was so simple! Once you understood what he was doing it seemed absolutely obvious.

And totally illegal.

"Sam," I said, still somewhat breathless with the astonishment of discovery, "you could go to jail for twenty years."

He shrugged. "Yeah, I suppose so."

A dead silence fell between us. Sam got up from the couch and floated weightlessly to the control panel. I cranked the couch up to a sitting position, grateful that my head only felt as if it was being split open by a bandsaw.

"You've been cheating the market, Sam."

He glanced back at me, over his shoulder, an elfin grin on his round face. "I don't think there's anything in the ISC rules about intercepting laser signals. I checked those rules pretty thoroughly, you know."

"Insider knowledge," I said firmly, "is a crime."

"What insider knowledge?" he asked, trying to look innocent. "I just happened to learn about the factory ships' cargos before anybody else did."

"By rigging their communications."

"Nothing illegal about that."

"Yes there is."

"Prove it!"

"C.C. will prove it," I said. "She'll haul you up before the interplanetary tribunal and they'll send you to the penal colony on Farside."

"Maybe," Sam said. I could see from the way his brow furrowed that he was actually worried.

Well, Sam knew me better than I knew myself, of course. He had already decided to stop tinkering with the market; C.C. and her minions (including me) were getting too close for comfort.

"I only did it to put together enough money to buy a couple of factory ships and go out to the Asteroid Belt again," he told me.

"You mean this whole scheme was just your way of raising capital?" I was incredulous.

"What else?" he asked, wide-eyed. "None of the sheep-dip banks would lend me a dime. C.C blackballed me. The big-shot investors stick with the big-time operators, like Rockledge and Pogorny. Nobody'd loan me enough money to build an outhouse, let alone a few factory ships."

I thought it over for a few moments. "So . . . if I didn't turn you in, you'd stop this market rigging on your own?"

"Yep," he answered immediately. "Honest injun. Cross my heart. Scout's honor." And he held up one hand in a three-fingered Boy Scout salute.

The man *had* saved my life. I had done something foolishly stupid and he had saved me from certain death. I owed him that.

Besides, the thought of Sam in jail, or toiling away at the Farside penal colony . . . I couldn't bear that.

But then the image of C.C. rose in my mind, like a volcano of blubber about to erupt and spew over me. The best I could hope for was to admit I hadn't been able to find Sam's scam and let her demote me to third-rank sewer inspector or something even worse. If she ever got a hint that I *had* discovered Sam's trick and let him go—I'd be breaking rocks on Farside myself.

There was only one honorable thing for me to do. After getting Sam's solemn pledge that he would never, *never* tamper with the market again, I returned alone to Selene City and called in my resignation from the ISC.

C.C. called me back in ten seconds. I was in my spartan studio apartment, packing for my return to Earth, when the wall screen lit up. There she was, Mt. Vesuvius in the flesh, steaming and glowering at me.

" 'E got to you, did 'e?" she said, without preamble.

"No," I replied, trying to shield myself as much as I could behind my garment bag. "On the contrary, I think I scared him enough so that he'll stay out of the market from now on."

"Oh, really?" she said, dripping sarcasm.

"Really," I said, with as much dignity as a man can muster while he's holding a half-dozen pairs of underdrawers in his hands.

"Then it might interest you to know that one Samuel Gunn 'as just bought an entire factory ship's cargo of 'eavy metals, ten minutes before the news of the ship's successful rendezvous with nine different ore miners reached the bloody market."

Sam had broken his promise! I was stunned. Not angry, just sad that he really couldn't be trusted.

"Well," I said, "you'll have to send someone else to snoop out how he does it. I failed, and I've quit. I'm out of the game."

"You'll be out more than that, you bleedin' traitor!" For the next several minutes C.C. described at the top of her voice how she was going to blackball me and see to it that I never worked anywhere on Earth again. "Or on the Moon, for that matter!" she added, with extra venom.

I was ruined and I knew it. But actually, what made me feel even worse was the knowledge that Sam had gone back on his word. He'd continue to fiddle with the market until C.C. finally caught him. He couldn't get away with it forever; if I figured his scheme out (even with Sam's help) someone else could, too. Sam was heading for jail, sooner or later. The thought depressed me terribly.

That was before Sam's final message reached me.

I was heading glumly out to the rocket port for the ride back to Earth and my lonely, dusty, empty apartment in Florida's sprawling Tampa-Orlando-Jacksonville industrial belt. No job and no prospects. No friends, either. Just about everyone I knew worked at the ISC. They would all shun me, fearful of C.C.'s wrath.

There were two messages waiting for me at the port's check-in counter. The clerk there—a lissome young woman whom Sam had introduced me to scarcely a week earlier—showed me to a booth where I could take my messages in privacy.

The first was from someone I had never seen before. He was white-haired, with a trim beard and the tanned, leathery look of a man who had spent a good deal of his life outdoors. Yet he wore the rumpled tweeds of an academic.

"Mr. Hashimoto, this is rather a strange situation," he said into the camera. He was recording the message, not knowing where I was or when I would hear his words. "I am Hickory J. Gillett, dean of the University of New Mexico Archeology Department. We have just received a bequest of two hundred million dollars from an anonymous donor who wants us to create an endowed chair of archeology. His only requirement is that you accept the position as our first Professor of Martian Archeology."

I nearly fainted. Professor of Martian Archeology. Endowed chair. It was my dream come true.

Hardly conscious of what I was doing, I touched the keypad for my second message.

Sam Gunn's impish face grinned at me from the screen. "So I pulled off one final stunt," he said. "See you on Mars, Prof. Save one of the female students for me."

And he slashed one pointed finger through the air in the zigzag of a letter zee.

The Maitre D'

"IT'S A PLEASURE HAVING SOMEONE SO FAMOUS ON BOARD with us," said the maitre d' as he showed Jade and Spence to their table in *Hermes*'s small but luxuriously decorated dining salon.

"Me?" Jade felt surprised. "I'm not famous. Not like Senator Meyers."

The maitre d' smiled patiently. He was a portly man, his hair receding from his forehead but still dark, as was his trim mustache and pointed Vandyke. Aside from the cooks, he was the only human working in the dining salon. The waiters were all utilitarian robots, their flat tops exactly the same height as the tables. They rolled noiselessly across the carpeting on tiny trunions.

"You are the producer of the Sam Gunn biography, aren't you?" he asked in a deferential, sibilant near-whisper.

"Yes, that's true," Jade replied as she sat on the chair he was holding for her.

"I knew Sam," the maitre d' said. "And Senator Meyers, too, although she doesn't recognize me. I looked somewhat different back in those days."

Jade recognized a come-on. "You'll have to tell me about it," she said guardedly.

Glancing about at the salon's six tables, all of them filled with passengers, the maitre d' said, "Perhaps after dinner? You could linger over a cognac and after these other guests have left I could tell you about it."

Jade glanced at Spence, who was scowling suspiciously.

"All right," she said. "After dinner."

The maitre d' bowed politely and left their table.

"You trust him?" Spence asked, almost in a growl.

"You don't?"

"He's too oily for my taste."

Jade laughed softly. "We're not going to eat him, Spence. Just listen to what he has to say."

Spence nodded, but he still did not seem happy about it.

Their dinner was excellent. Jill Meyers stopped at their table on her way out and for a few moments Jade was afraid that the former Senator would invite herself for an after-dinner drink. But she left soon enough and Jade saw that she and Spence were the only guests remaining in the salon.

The maitre d' came to their table with a magnum of cognac in one hand and three snifters in the other. He had pulled his black tie loose and unbuttoned his collar.

"If I may?" he asked.

"Please do," said Jade, gesturing to the empty chair he was standing by.

As the man put the bottle and glasses down on the table and pulled out the chair, Spence asked, "So when did you know Sam?"

The Flying Dutchman

IT WAS A LONG TIME AGO—SAID THE MAITRE D' AS HE
poured cognac into the snifters. I was working for Sam at the L-5 habitat
Beethoven. Of course, there was a beautiful woman right in the middle of
everything.

I ushered her into Sam's office and helped her out of the bulky dark
coat she was wearing. Once she let the hood fall back I damned near
dropped the coat. I recognized her. Who could forget her? She was exquisite, so stunningly beautiful that even irrepressible Sam Gunn was struck
speechless. More beautiful than any woman I had ever seen.

But haunted.

It was more than her big, soulful eyes. More than the almost frightened way she had of glancing all around as she entered Sam's office, as if
expecting someone to leap out of hiding at her. She looked *tragic*, lovely
and doomed and tragic.

"Mr. Gunn, I need your help," she said to Sam. Those were the first
words she spoke, even before she took the chair that I was holding for her.
Her voice was like the sigh of a breeze in a midnight forest.

Sam was standing behind his desk, on the hidden little platform back
there that makes him look taller than his real 161 centimeters. As I said,
even Sam was speechless. Leather-tongued, clatter-mouthed Sam Gunn
simply stood and stared at her in stupefied awe.

Then he found his voice. "Anything," he said, in a choked whisper. "I'd
do anything for you."

Despite the fact that Sam was getting married in just three weeks' time,
it was obvious that he'd tumbled head over heels for Amanda Cunningham the minute he saw her. Instantly. Sam Gunn was always falling in love,
even more often than he made fortunes of money and lost them again. But
this time it looked as if he'd really been struck by the thunderbolt.

If she weren't so beautiful, so troubled, seeing the two of them together
would have been almost ludicrous. Amanda Cunningham looked like a
Greek goddess, except that her shoulder-length hair was radiant golden
blonde. She wore a modest knee-length sheath of delicate pink that

couldn't hide the curves of her ample body. And those eyes! They were bright china blue, but deeply, terribly troubled, unbearably sad.

And there was Sam: stubby as a worn old pencil, with a bristle of red hair and his gap-toothed mouth hanging open. Sam had the kind of electricity in him that made it almost impossible for him to stand still for more than thirty seconds at a time. Yet he stood gaping at Amanda Cunningham, as tongue-tied as a teenager on his first date.

And me. Compared to Sam I'm a rugged outdoorsy type of guy. Of course, I wear lifts in my boots and a tummy tingler that helps keep my gut flat. Women have told me that my face is kind of cute in a cherubic sort of way, and I believe them—until I look in the mirror and see the pouchy eyes and the trim black beard that covers my receding chin. What did it matter? Amanda Cunningham didn't even glance at me; her attention was focused completely on Sam.

It was really comical. Yet I wasn't laughing.

Sam just stared at her, transfixed. Bewitched. I was still holding one of the leather-covered chairs for her. She sat down without looking at it, as if she were accustomed to there being a chair wherever she chose to sit.

"You must understand, Mr. Gunn," she said softly. "What I ask is very dangerous. . . ."

Still standing in front of his high-backed swivel chair, his eyes never leaving hers, Sam waved one hand as if to scoff at the thought of danger.

"It involves flying out to the Belt," she continued.

"Anywhere," Sam said. "For you."

"To find my husband."

That broke the spell. Definitely.

Sam's company was S. Gunn Enterprises, Unlimited. He was involved in a lot of different operations, including hauling freight between the Earth and Moon, and transporting equipment out to the Asteroid Belt. He was also dickering to build a gambling casino and hotel on the Moon, but that's another story.

"To find your husband?" Sam asked her, his face sagging with disappointment.

"My ex-husband," said Amanda Cunningham. "We were divorced several years ago."

"Oh." Sam brightened.

"My current husband is Martin Humphries," she went on, her voice sinking lower.

"Oh," Sam repeated, plopping down into his chair like a man shot in the heart. "Amanda Cunningham Humphries."

"Yes," she said.

"*The* Martin Humphries?"

"Yes," she repeated, almost whispering it.

Mrs. Martin Humphries. I'd seen pictures of her, of course, and vids on the society nets. I'd even glimpsed her in person once, across a ballroom crowded with the very wealthiest of the wealthy. Even in the midst of all that glitter and opulence she had glowed like a beautiful princess in a cave full of trolls. Martin Humphries was towing her around the party like an Olympic trophy. I popped my monocle and almost forgot the phony German accent I'd been using all evening. That was a couple of years ago, when I'd been working the society circuit selling shares of nonexistent tritium mines. On Mars, yet. The richer they are, the easier they bite.

Martin Humphries was probably the richest person in the solar system, founder and chief of Humphries Space Systems, and well known to be a prime SOB. I'd never try to scam him. If he bit on my bait, it could be fatal. So that's why she looks so miserable, I thought. Married to him. I felt sorry for Amanda Cunningham Humphries.

But sorry or not, this could be the break I'd been waiting for. Amanda Cunningham Humphries was the wife of the richest sumbitch in the solar system. She could buy anything she wanted, including Sam's whole ramshackle company, which was teetering on the brink of bankruptcy. As usual. Yet she was asking Sam for help, like a lady in distress. She was scared.

"Martin Humphries," Sam repeated.

She nodded wordlessly. She certainly did not look happy about being married to Martin Humphries.

Sam swallowed visibly, his Adam's apple bobbing up and down twice. Then he got to his feet again and said, as brightly as he could manage, "Why don't we discuss this over lunch?"

Sam's office in those days was on Beethoven. Funny name for a space structure that housed some fifty thousand people, I know. It was built by a consortium of American, European, Russian and Japanese corporations. The only name they could agree on was Beethoven's, thanks to the fact that the head of Yamagata Corp. had always wanted to be a symphony orchestra conductor.

To his credit, Sam's office was not grand or imposing. He said he didn't want to waste his money on furniture or real estate. Not that he had any money to waste, at the time. The suite was compact, tastefully decorated, with wall screens that showed idyllic scenes of woods and waterfalls. Sam had a sort of picture gallery on the wall behind his desk, S. Gunn with the great and powerful figures of the day—most of whom were out to sue him, if not have him murdered—plus several photos of Sam with various beauties in revealing attire.

I, as his "special consultant and advisor," sat off to one side of his teak and chrome desk, where I could swivel from Sam to his visitor and back again.

Amanda Humphries shook her lovely head. "I can't go out to lunch with you, Mr. Gunn. I shouldn't be seen in public with you."

Before Sam could react to that, she added, "It's nothing personal. It's just . . . I don't want my husband to know that I've turned to you."

Undeterred, Sam put on a lopsided grin and said, "Well, we could have lunch sent in here." He turned to me. "Gar, why don't you rustle us up some grub?"

I made a smile at his sudden Western folksiness. Sam was a con man, and everybody knew it. That made it all the easier for me to con him. I'm a scam artist, myself, par excellence, and it ain't bragging if you can do it. Still, I'd been very roundabout in approaching Sam. Conning a con man takes some finesse, let me tell you.

About a year ago I talked myself into a job with the Honorable Jill Meyers, former U.S. Senator and American representative on the International Court of Justice. Judge Meyers was an old, old friend of Sam's, dating back to the early days when they'd both been astronauts working for the old NASA.

I had passed myself off to Meyers's people as Garret G. Garrison III, the penniless son of one of the oldest families in Texas. I had doctored up a biography and a dozen or so phony news media reports. With just a bit of money in the right hands, when Meyers's people checked me out in the various web nets, there was enough in place to convince them that I was poor but bright, talented and honest.

Three out of four ain't bad. I was certainly poor, bright and talented.

Jill Meyers wanted to marry Sam. Why, I'll never figure out. Sam was—is!—a philandering, womanizing, skirt-chasing bundle of testosterone who falls in love the way Pavlov's dogs salivated when they heard a bell ring. But Jill Meyers wanted to marry the little scoundrel, and Sam had even proposed to her—once he ran out of all the other sources of funding that he could think of. Did I mention that Judge Meyers comes from Old Money? She does: the kind of New England family that still has the first shilling they made in the molasses-for-rum-for-slaves trade back in colonial days.

Anyway, I had sweet-talked my way into Judge Meyers's confidence (and worked damned hard for her, too, I might add). So when they set a date for the wedding, she asked me to join Sam's staff and keep an eye on him. She didn't want him to disappear and leave her standing at the altar.

Sam took me in without a qualm, gave me the title of "special consultant and advisor to the CEO," and put me in the office next to his. He knew I was Justice Meyers's enforcer, but it didn't seem to bother him a bit.

Sam and I got along beautifully, like kindred souls, really. Once I told him the long, sad (and totally false) story of my life, he took to me like a big brother.

"Gar," he told me more than once, "we're two of a kind. Always trying to get out from under the big guys."

I agreed fervently.

I've been a grifter all my life, ever since I sweet-talked Sister Agonista into overlooking the fact that she caught me cheating on the year-end exams in sixth grade. It was a neat scam for an eleven-year-old: I let her catch me, I let her think she had scared me onto the path of righteousness, and she was so happy about it that she never tumbled to the fact that I had sold answer sheets to half the kids in the school.

Anyway, life was always kind of rough-and-tumble for me. You hit it big here, and the next time you barely get out with the hide on your back. I had been at it long enough so that by now I was slowing down, getting a little tired, looking for the one big score that would let me wrap it all up and live the rest of my life in ill-gotten ease. I knew Sam Gunn was the con man's con man: the little rogue had made more fortunes than the New York Stock Exchange—and lost them just as quickly as he could go chasing after some new rainbow. I figured that if I cozied up real close to Sam I could snatch his next pot of gold before he had a chance to piss it away.

So when Judge Meyers asked me to keep an eye on Sam I went out to the Beethoven habitat that same day, alert and ready for my big chance to nail the last and best score.

Amanda Cunningham Humphries might just be that opportunity, I realized.

So now I'm bringing a tray of lunch in for Sam and Mrs. Humphries, setting it all out on Sam's desk while they chat, and then retreating to my own little office so they can talk in privacy.

Privacy, hah! I slipped the acoustic amplifier out of my desk drawer and stuck it on the wall that my office shared with Sam's. Once I had wormed the earplug in, I could hear everything they said.

Which wasn't all that much. Mrs. Humphries was very guarded about it all.

"I have a coded video chip that I want you to deliver to my ex-husband," she told Sam.

"Okay," he said, "but you could have a courier service make the delivery, even out to the Belt. I don't see why—"

"My ex-husband is Lars Fuchs."

Bingo! I don't know how Sam reacted to that news but I nearly jumped out of my chair to turn a somersault. Her first husband was Lars Fuchs! Fuchs the pirate. Fuchs the renegade. Fuchs and Humphries had fought a minor war out there in the Belt a few years earlier. It had ended when Humphries's mercenaries had finally captured Fuchs and the people of Ceres had exiled him for life.

For years now Fuchs had wandered through the Belt, an exile eking out a living as a miner, a rock rat. Making a legend of himself. The Flying Dutchman of the Asteroid Belt.

It must have been right after he was exiled, I guessed, that Amanda Cunningham had divorced Fuchs and married his bitter rival, Humphries. I later found out that I was right. That's exactly what had happened. But with a twist. She divorced Fuchs and married Humphries on the condition that Humphries would stop trying to track Fuchs down and have him killed. Exile was punishment enough, she convinced Humphries. But the price for that tender mercy was her body. From the haunted look of her, maybe the price included her soul.

Now she wanted to send a message to her ex. Why? What was in the message? Humphries would pay a small fortune to find out. No, I decided; he'd pay a *large* fortune. To me.

MRS. HUMPHRIES DIDN'T have all that much more to say and she left the office immediately after they finished their lunch, bundled once more into that shapeless black coat with its hood pulled up to hide her face.

I bounced back into Sam's office. He was sitting back in his chair, the expression on his face somewhere between exalted and terrified.

"She needs my help," Sam murmured, as if talking in his sleep.

"Our help," I corrected.

Sam blinked, shook himself, and sat up erect. He nodded and grinned at me. "I knew I could count on you, Gar."

Then I remembered that I was supposed to be working for Judge Meyers.

"HE'S GOING OUT to the Belt?" Judge Meyers's chestnut-brown eyes snapped at me. "And you're letting him do it?"

Some people called Jill Meyers plain, or even unattractive (behind her back, of course), but I always thought of her as kind of cute. In a way, she looked almost like Sam's sister might: her face was round as a pie, with a stubby little nose and a sprinkling of freckles. Her hair was light brown and straight as can be; she kept it in a short, no-nonsense bob and refused to let stylists fancy it up for her.

Her image in my desk screen clearly showed, though, that she was angry. Not at Sam. At me.

"Garrison, I sent you to keep that little so-and-so on track for our wedding, and now you're going out to the Belt with him?"

"It'll only be for a few days," I said. Truthfully, that's all I expected at that point.

Her anger abated a skosh; suspicion replaced it.

"What's this all about, Gar?"

If I told her that Sam had gone bonkers over Amanda Humphries she'd be up at Beethoven on the next shuttle, so I temporized a little.

"He's looking into a new business opportunity at Ceres. It should only take a few days."

Fusion torch ships could zip out to the Belt at a constant acceleration. They cost an arm and two legs, but Sam was in his "spare no expenses" mode, and I agreed with him. We could zip out to the Belt in four days, deliver the message and be home again in time for the wedding. We'd even have a day or so to spare, I thought.

One thing about Judge Meyers: she couldn't stay angry for more than a few minutes at a time. But from the expression on her face, she remained highly suspicious.

"I want a call from you every day, Gar," she said. "I know you can't keep Sam on a leash; nobody can. But I want to know where you are and what you're doing."

"Yes, ma'am. Of course."

"Every day."

"Right."
Easier said than done.

SAM RENTED A torch ship, the smallest he could find, just a set of fusion engines and propellant tanks with a crew pod attached. It was called *Achernar,* and its accommodations were really spartan. Sam piloted it himself.

"That's why I keep my astronaut's qualifications up to date with the chickenshit IAA," he told me, with a mischievous wink. "No sense spending money on a pilot when I can fly these birds myself."

For four days we raced out to Ceres, accelerating at a half-g most of the time, then decelerating at a g-and-a-half. Sam wanted to go even faster, but the IAA wouldn't approve his original plan, and he had no choice. If he didn't follow their flight plan the IAA controllers at Ceres would impound *Achernar* and send us back to Earth for a disciplinary hearing.

So Sam stuck to their rules, fussing and fidgeting every centimeter of the way. He hated bureaucracies and bureaucrats. He especially loathed being forced to do things their way instead of his own.

The trip out was less than luxurious, let me tell you. But the deceleration was absolute agony for me; I felt as if I weighed about a ton and I was scared even to try to stand up.

Sam took the strain cheerfully. "Double strength jockstrap, Gar," he told me, grinning. "That's the secret of my success."

I stayed seated as much as possible. I even slept in the copilot's reclinable chair, wishing that the ship had been primitive enough to include a relief tube among its equipment fixtures.

PEOPLE WHO DON'T know any better think that the rock rats out in the Belt are a bunch of rough-and-tumble, crusty, hard-fisted prospectors and miners. Well, sure, there are some like that, but most of the rock rats are university-educated engineers and technicians. After all, they work with spacecraft and teleoperated machinery out at the frontier of human civilization. They're out there in the dark, cold, mostly empty Asteroid Belt, on their own, the nearest help usually so far away that it's useless to them. They don't use mules and shovels, and they don't have barroom brawls or shootouts.

Most nights, that is.

Sam's first stop after we docked at the habitat Chrysalis was the bar.

The Chrysalis habitat, by the way, was something like a circular, rotating junkyard. The rock rats had built it over the years by putting used or abandoned spacecraft together, hooking them up like a Tinkertoy merry-go-round and spinning the whole contraption to produce an artificial gravity inside. It was better than living in Ceres itself, with its minuscule gravity and the constant haze of dust that you stirred up with every move you made. The earliest rock rats actually did live inside Ceres. That's why they built the ramshackle Chrysalis as quickly as they could.

I worried about hard radiation, but Sam told me the habitat had a superconducting shield, the same as spacecraft use.

"You're as safe as you'd be on Earth," Sam assured me. "Just about."

It was the *just about* that scared me.

"Why are we going to the bar?" I asked, striding along beside him down the habitat's central corridor. Well, maybe "central corridor" is an overstatement. We were walking down the main passageway of one of the spacecraft that made up Chrysalis. Up ahead was a hatch that connected to the next spacecraft component. And so on. We could walk a complete circle and come back to the airlock where *Achernar* was docked, if we'd wanted to.

"Gonna meet the mayor," said Sam.

The mayor?

Well, anyway, we went straight to the bar. I had expected a kind of rough place, maybe like a biker joint. Instead the place looked like a sophisticated cocktail lounge.

It was called the Crystal Palace, and it was as quiet and subdued as one of those high-class watering holes in Old Manhattan. Soft lighting, plush faux-leather wall coverings, muted Mozart coming through the speakers set in the overhead. It was mid-afternoon and there were only about a dozen people in the place, a few at the bar, the rest in high-backed booths that gave them plenty of privacy.

Sam sauntered up to the bar and perched on one of the swiveling stools. He spun around a few times, taking in the local scenery. The only woman in the place was the human bartender, and she wasn't much better looking than the robots that trundled drinks out to the guys in the booths.

"What's fer yew?" she asked. She looked like she was into weightlifting. The gray sweatshirt she was wearing had the sleeves cut off; plenty of muscle in her arms. The expression on her squarish face was no-nonsense, unsmiling.

"West Tennessee," said Sam. "Right?"

The bartender looked surprised. "Huntsville, 'Bama."

"Heart of the Tennessee Valley," Sam said. "I come from the blue grass country, myself."

Which was a complete lie. Sam was born in either Nevada or Pennsylvania, according to which of his dossiers you read. Or maybe Luzon, in the Philippines.

Well, in less than six minutes Sam's got the bartender laughing and trading redneck jokes with him. Her name was Belinda. I just sat beside him and watched the master at work. He could charm the devil out of hell, Sam could.

Sam ordered Tennessee corn mash for both of us. While he chatted up the bartender, though, I noticed that the place was emptying out. The three guys at the bar got up and left first, one by one. Then, out of the corner of my eye, I saw the guys in the booths heading for the door. No big rush, but within a few minutes they had all walked out. On tiptoes.

I said nothing, but soon enough Sam realized we were alone.

"What happened?" he asked Belinda. "We chased everybody out?"

She shook her head. "Rock rats worry about strangers. They prob'ly think you're maybe a tax assessor or a safety inspector from the IAA."

Sam laughed. "Me? From the IAA? Hell, no. I'm Sam Gunn. Maybe you've heard of me?"

"No! Sam Gunn? You couldn't be!"

"That's me," Sam said, with his Huckleberry Finn grin.

"You were the first guy out here in the Belt," said Belinda, real admiration glowing in her eyes.

"Yep. Captured a nickel-iron asteroid and towed her back to Earth orbit."

"Pittsburgh. I heard about it. Took you a couple of years, didn't it?"

Sam nodded. He was enjoying the adulation.

"That was a long time ago," Belinda said. "I thought you'd be a lot older."

"I am."

She laughed, a hearty roar that made the glasses on the back bar rattle. "Rejuve therapy, right?"

"Why not?"

Just then a red-haired mountain strode into the bar. One of the biggest men I've ever seen. He didn't look fat, either: just *big*, with a shaggy mane of brick-red hair and a shaggier beard to match.

He walked right up to us.

"You're Sam Gunn." It wasn't a question.

"Right," said Sam. Swiveling toward me, he added, "And this young fellow here is Garret G. Garrison III."

"The third, huh?" the redhead huffed at me. "What happened to the first two?"

"Hung for stealin' horses," I lied, putting on my thickest Wild West accent.

Belinda laughed at that. The redhead simply huffed.

"You're George Ambrose, right?" Sam asked.

"Big George, that's me."

"The mayor of this fair community," Sam added.

"They elected me th' fookin' chief," Big George said, almost belligerently. "Now, whattaya want to see me about?"

"About Lars Fuchs."

George's eyes went cold and narrow. Belinda backed away from us and went down the bar, suddenly busy with the glassware.

"What about Lars Fuchs?" George asked.

"I want to meet him. I've got a business proposition for him."

George folded his beefy arms across his massive chest. "Fuchs is an exile. Hasn't been anywhere near Ceres for dog's years. Hell, this fookin' habitat wasn't even finished when we tossed him out. We were still livin' down inside th' rock."

Sam rested his elbows on the bar and smiled disarmingly at Big George. "Well, I've got a business proposition for Fuchs and I need to talk to him."

"What kind of a business proposition?"

With a perfectly straight face Sam answered, "I'm thinking of starting a tourist service here in the Belt. You know, visit Ceres, see a mining operation at work on one of the asteroids, go out in a suit and chip some gold or diamonds to bring back home. That kind of thing."

George said nothing, but I could see the wheels turning behind that wild red mane of his.

"It could mean an influx of money for your people," Sam went on, in his best snake-oil spiel. "A hotel here in orbit around Ceres, rich tourists flooding in. Lots of money."

George unbent his arms, but he still remained standing. "What's all this got to do with Fuchs?"

"Shiploads full of rich tourists might make a tempting target for a pirate."

"Bullshit."

"You don't think he'd attack tour ships?"

"Lars wouldn't do that. He's not a fookin' pirate. Not in that sense, anyway."

"I'd rather hear that from him," Sam said. "In fact, I've got to have his personal assurance before my backers will invest in the scheme."

George stared at Sam for a long moment, deep suspicion written clearly on his face. "Nobody knows where Lars is," he said at last. "You might as well go back home. Nobody here's gonna give you any help."

WE LEFT THE bar with Big George glowering at our backs so hard I could feel the heat. Following the maps on the wall screens in the passageways, we found the adjoining rooms that I had booked for us.

"Now what?" I asked Sam as I unpacked my travel bag.

"Now we wait."

Sam had simply tossed his bag on the bed of his room and barged through the connecting door into mine. We had packed for only a three-day stay at Ceres, although we had more gear stowed in *Achernar*. Something had to happen pretty quick, I thought.

"Wait for what?" I asked.

"Developments."

I put my carefully folded clothes in a drawer, hung my extra pair of wrinkle-proof slacks in the closet, and set up my toiletries in the lavatory. Sam made himself comfortable in the room's only chair, a recliner designed to look like an astronaut's couch. He cranked it down so far I thought he was going to take a nap.

Sitting on the bed, I told him, "Sam I've got to call Judge Meyers."

"Go right ahead," he said.

"What should I tell her?"

"Tell her we'll be back in time for the wedding."

I doubted that.

TWO DAYS PASSED without a word from anyone. Sam even tried to date Belinda, he was getting so desperate, but she wouldn't have anything to do with him.

"They all know Fuchs," Sam said to me. "They like him and they're protecting him."

It was common knowledge that Humphries had sworn to kill Fuchs, but Amanda had married Humphries on the condition that he left Fuchs alone. Everybody in Ceres, from Belinda the barmaid to the last rock rat, thought that we were working for Humphries, trying to find Fuchs and murder him. Or at least locate him, so one of Humphries's hired killers could knock him off. Fuchs was out there in the Belt somewhere, cruising through that dark emptiness like some Flying Dutchman, alone, taking a strangely measured kind of vengeance on unmanned Humphries ships.

I had other fish to fry, though. I wanted to find out what was on the chip that Amanda had given Sam. Her message to her ex-husband. What did she want to tell him? Fuchs was a thorn in Humphries's side; maybe only a small thorn, but he drew blood, nonetheless. Humphries would pay a fortune for that message, and I intended to sell it to him.

But I had to get it away from Sam first.

JUDGE MEYERS WAS not happy with my equivocating reports to her. Definitely not happy.

There's no way to have a conversation in real time between Ceres and Earth; the distance makes it impossible. It takes nearly half an hour for a message to cross one way, even when the two bodies are at their closest. So I sent reports to Judge Meyers and—usually within an hour—I'd get a response from her.

After my first report she had a wry grin on her face when she called back. "Garrison, I know it's about as easy to keep Sam in line as nailing tapioca to a wall in zero-gee. But all the plans for the wedding are set; it's going to be the biggest social event of the year. You've got to make sure that he's here. I'm depending on you, Garrison."

A day later, her smile had disappeared. "The wedding's only a week from now, Garrison," she said after my second call to her. "I want that little scoundrel at the altar!"

Third call, the next day: "I don't care what he's doing! Get him back here! Now!"

That's when Sam came up with his bright idea.

"Pack up your duds, Gar," he announced brightly. "We're going to take a little spin around the Belt."

I was too surprised to ask questions. In less than an hour we were back in *Achernar* and heading out from Ceres. Sam had already filed a flight plan with the IAA controllers. As far as they were concerned, Sam was going to visit three specific asteroids, which might be used as tourist stops if and when he started his operation in the Belt. Of course, I knew that once we cleared Ceres there was no one and nothing that could hold him to that plan.

"What are we doing?" I asked, sitting in the right-hand seat of the cockpit. "Where are we going?"

"To meet Fuchs," said Sam.

"You've made contact with him?"

"Nope," Sam replied, grinning as if he knew something nobody else knew. "But I'm willing to bet *somebody* has. Maybe Big George. Fuchs saved his life once, did you know that?"

"But how——?"

"It's simple," Sam answered before I could finish the question. "We let it be known that we want to see Fuchs. Everybody says they don't know where he is. We go out into the Belt, away from everything, including snoops who might rat out Fuchs to Martin Humphries. Somebody from Chrysalis calls Fuchs and tells him about us. Fuchs intercepts our ship to see what I want. I give him Amanda's message chip. QED."

It made a certain amount of sense. But I had my doubts.

"What if Fuchs just blasts us?"

"Not his style. He's only attacked unmanned ships."

"He wiped out an HSS base on Vesta, didn't he? Killed dozens."

"That was during the war between him and Humphries. Ancient history. He hasn't attacked a crewed ship since he's been exiled."

"But suppose——"

The communications console pinged.

"Hah!" Sam gloated. "There he is now."

But the image that took form on the comm screen wasn't Lars Fuchs's face. It was Jill Meyers's.

She was beaming a smile that could've lit up Selene City for a month. "Sam, I've got a marvelous idea. I know you're wrapped up in some kind of mysterious mission out there in the Belt, and the wedding's only a few days off so . . ."

She hesitated, like somebody about to spring a big surprise. "So instead of you coming back Earthside for the wedding, I'm bringing the wedding out to you! All the guests and everything. In fact, I'm on the torch ship *Statendaam* right now! We break Earth orbit in about an hour. I'll see you in five days, Sam, and we can be married just as we planned!"

To say Sam was surprised would be like saying Napoleon was disturbed by Waterloo. Or McKenzie was inconvenienced when his spacecraft crashed into the Lunar Apennines. Or—well, you get the idea.

Sam looked stunned, as if he'd been poleaxed between the eyes. He just slumped in the pilot's chair, dazed, his eyes unfocused for several minutes.

"She can't come out here," he muttered at last.

"She's already on her way," I said.

"But she'll ruin everything. If she comes barging out here Fuchs'll never come within a light-year and a half of us."

"How're you going to stop her?"

Sam thought about that for all of a half-second. "I can't stop her. But I don't have to make it easy for her to find me."

"What do you mean?"

"Run silent, run deep." With a deft finger, Sam turned off the ship's tracking beacon and telemetry transmitter.

"Sam! The controllers at Ceres will think we've been destroyed!"

He grinned wickedly. "Let 'em. If they don't know where we are, they can't point Jill at us."

"But Fuchs won't know where we are."

"Oh yes he will," Sam insisted. "Somebody at Ceres has already given him our flight plan. Big George, probably."

"Sam," I said patiently, "you filed that flight plan with the IAA. They'll tell Judge Meyers. She'll come out looking for you."

"Yeah, but she'll be several days behind. By that time the IAA controllers'll tell her we've disappeared. She'll go home and weep for me."

"Or start searching for your remains."

He shot me an annoyed glance. "Anyway, we'll meet with Fuchs before she gets here, most likely."

"You hope."

His grin wobbled a little.

I thought the most likely scenario was that Fuchs would ignore us and Judge Meyers would search for us, hoping that Sam's disappearance didn't mean he was dead. Once she found us, I figured, she'd kill Sam herself.

IT WAS EERIE out there in the Belt. Flatlanders back on Earth think that the Asteroid Belt is a dangerous region, a-chock with boulders, so crowded that you have to maneuver like a kid in a computer game to avoid getting smashed.

Actually, it's empty. Dark and cold and four times farther from the Sun than the Earth is. Most of the asteroids are the size of dust flakes. The valuable ones, maybe a few meters to a kilometer or so across, are so few and far between that you have to hunt for them. You can cruise through the Belt blindfolded and your chances of getting hit even by a pebble-sized 'roid are pretty close to nil.

Of course, a pebble could shatter your ship if it hit you with enough velocity.

So we were running silent, but following the flight plan Sam had registered with the IAA. We got to the first rock Sam had scheduled and loitered around it for half a day. No sign of Fuchs. If he was anywhere nearby, he was running as silently as we were.

"He's gotta be somewhere around here," Sam said as we broke orbit and headed for the next asteroid on his list. "He's gotta be."

I could tell that Sam was feeling Judge Meyers's eager breath on the back of his neck.

Me, I had a different problem. I wanted to get that message chip away from him long enough to send a copy of it to Martin Humphries. With a suitable request for compensation, of course. Fifty million would do nicely, I thought. A hundred mill would be even better.

But how to get the chip out of Sam's pocket? He kept it on his person all the time; even slept with it.

So it floored me when, as we were eating breakfast in *Achernar*'s cramped little galley on our third day out, Sam fished the fingernail-sized chip out of his breast pocket and handed it to me.

"Gar," he said solemnly, "I want you to hide this someplace where *nobody* can find it, not even me."

I was staggered. "Why . . . ?"

"Just a precaution," he said, his face more serious than I'd ever seen it before. "When Fuchs shows up things might get rough. I don't want to know where the chip is."

"But the whole point of this flight is to deliver it to him."

He nodded warily. "Yeah, Humphries must know we're looking for Fuchs. He's got IAA people on his payroll. Hell, half the people in Ceres might be willing to rat on us. Money talks, pal. Humphries might not know why we're looking for Fuchs, but he knows we're trying to find him."

"Humphries wants to find Fuchs, too," I said. "And kill him, no matter what he promised his wife."

"Damned right. I wouldn't be surprised if he has a ship tailing us."

"I haven't seen anything on the radar plot."

"So what? A stealth ship could avoid radar. But not the hair on the back of my neck."

"You think we're being followed?"

"I'm sure of it."

By the seven sinners of Cincinnati, I thought. This is starting to look like a class reunion! We're jinking around in the Belt, looking for Fuchs. Judge Meyers is on her way, with a complete wedding party. And now Sam thinks there's an HSS stealth ship lurking out there somewhere, waiting for us to find Fuchs so they can pounce on him.

But all that paled into insignificance for me as I stared down at the tiny chip Sam had placed in the palm of my hand.

I had it in my grasp! Now the trick was to contact Humphries without letting Sam know of it.

I couldn't sleep that night. We were approaching the second asteroid on Sam's intinerary on a dead-reckoning trajectory. No active signals going out from the ship except for the short-range collision avoidance radar. We'd take up a parking orbit around the unnamed rock mid-morning tomorrow.

I waited until my eyes were adapted to the darkness of the sleeping compartment, then peeked down over the edge of my bunk to see if Sam was really asleep. He was on his side, face to the bulkhead, his legs pulled up slightly in a sort of fetal position. Breathing deep and regular.

He's asleep, I told myself. As quietly as a wraith I slipped out of my bunk and tiptoed in my bare feet to the cockpit, carefully shutting the hatches of the sleeping compartment and the galley, so there'd be no noise to waken Sam.

I'm pretty good at decrypting messages. It's a useful talent for a con man, and I had spent long hours at computers during my one and only jail stretch to learn the tricks of the trade.

Of course, I could just offer the chip for sale to Humphries without knowing what was on it. He'd pay handsomely for a message that his wife wanted to give to Lars Fuchs.

But if I knew the contents of the message, I reasoned, I could most likely double or triple the price. So I started to work on decrypting it. How hard could it be? I asked myself as I slipped the chip into the ship's main computer. She probably did the encoding herself, not trusting anybody around her. She'd been an astronaut in her earlier years, I knew, but not particularly a computer freak. Should be easy.

It wasn't. It took all night and I still didn't get all the way through the trapdoors and blind alleys she'd built into her message. Smart woman, I realized, my respect for Amanda Cunningham Humphries notching up with every bead of sweat I oozed.

At last the hash that had been filling the central screen on the cockpit control panel cleared away, replaced by an image of her face.

That face. I just stared at her. She was so beautiful, so sad and vulnerable. It brought a lump to my throat. I've seen beautiful women, plenty of them, and bedded more than my share. But gazing at Amanda's face, there in the quiet hum of the dimmed cockpit, I felt something more than desire, more than animal hunger.

Could it be love? I shook my head like a man who's just been knocked down by a punch. Don't be an idiot! I snarled at myself. You've been hanging around Sam too long; you're becoming a romantic jackass just like he is.

Love has nothing to do with this. That beautiful face is going to earn you millions, I told myself, as soon as you decrypt this message of hers.

And then I smelled the fragrance of coffee brewing. Sam was in the galley, right behind the closed hatch of the cockpit, clattering dishes and silverware. In a weird way I felt almost relieved. Quickly I popped the chip out of the computer and slipped it into the waistband of the undershorts I was wearing.

Just in time. Sam pushed the hatch open and handed me a steaming mug of coffee.

"You're up early," he said, with a groggy smile.

"Couldn't sleep," I answered truthfully. That's where the truth ended. "I've been trying to think of where I could stash the chip."

He nodded and scratched at his wiry, tousled red hair. "Find a good spot, Gar. I think we're going to have plenty of fireworks before this job is finished."

Truer words, as they say, were never spoken.

The three asteroids Sam had chosen were samples of the three different types of 'roids in the Belt. The first one had been a rocky type. It looked like a lumpy potato, pockmarked with craterlets from the impacts of smaller rocks. The one we were approaching was a chondritic type, a loose collection of primeval pebbles that barely held itself together. Sam called it a beanbag.

He was saving the best one for last. The third and last asteroid on Sam's list was a metallic beauty, the one that some Latin American sculptress had carved into a monumental history of her Native American people;

she called it The Rememberer. Sam had been involved in that, years ago, I knew. He had shacked up with the sculptress for a while. Just like Sam.

As we approached the beanbag, our collision-avoidance radar started going crazy.

"It's surrounded by smaller chunks of rock," Sam muttered, studying the screen.

From the copilot's chair I could see the main body of the asteroid through the cockpit window. It looked hazy, indistinct, more like a puff of smoke than a solid object.

"If we're going to orbit that cloud of pebbles," I said, "it'd better be at a good distance from it. Otherwise we'll get dinged up pretty heavily."

Sam nodded and tapped in the commands for an orbit that looped a respectful distance from the beanbag.

"How long are we going to hang around here?" I asked him.

He made a small shrug. "Give it a day or two. Then we'll head off for The Rememberer."

"Sam, your wedding is in two days." Speaking of remembering, I thought.

He gave me a lopsided grin. "Jill's smart enough to figure it out. We'll get married at The Rememberer. Outside, in suits, with the sculpture for a background. It'll make terrific publicity for my tour service."

I felt my eyebrows go up. "You're really thinking of starting tourist runs out here to the Belt?"

"Sure. Why not?"

"I thought that was just your cover story."

"It was," he admitted. "But the more I think about it, the more sense it makes."

"Who's going to pay the fare for coming all the way out here, just to see a few rocks?"

"Gar, you just don't understand how business works, do you?"

"But—"

"How did space tourism start, in the first place?" Before I could even start thinking about an answer, he went on. "With a few bored rich guys paying millions for a few days in orbit."

"Not much of a market," I said.

He waggled a finger at me. "Not at first, but it got people interested. The publicity was important. Within a few years there was enough of a demand that a real tourist industry took off. Small, at first, but it grew."

I recalled, "You started a honeymoon hotel in Earth orbit back then, didn't you?"

His face clouded. "It went under. Most of the honeymooners got space sick their first day in weightlessness. Horrible publicity. I went broke."

"And sold it to Rockledge Industries, right?"

He got even more somber. "Yeah, right."

Rockledge made a success of the orbital hotel after buying Sam out, mainly because they'd developed a medication for space sickness. The facility is still there in low Earth orbit, part hotel, part museum. Sam was a pioneer, all right. An ornament to his profession, as far as I was concerned. But that's another story.

"And now you think you can make a tourist line to the Belt pay off?"

Before he could answer, three things happened virtually simultaneously. The navigation computer chimed and announced, "Parking orbit established." At that instant we felt a slight lurch. Spacecraft don't lurch, not unless something bad has happened to them, like hitting a rock or getting your airtight hull punctured.

Sure enough, the maintenance program sang out, "Main thruster disabled. Repair facilities urgently required."

Before we could do more than look at each other, our mouths hanging open, a fourth thing happened.

The comm speaker rumbled with a deep, snarling voice. "Who are you and what are you doing here?"

The screen showed a dark, scowling face: jowly, almost pudgy, dark hair pulled straight back from a broad forehead, tiny deepset eyes that burned into you. A vicious slash of a mouth turned down angrily. Irritation and suspicion written across every line of that face. He radiated power, strength, and the cold-blooded ruthlessness of a killer. Lars Fuchs.

"Answer me or my next shot will blow away your crew pod."

I felt an urgent need to go to the bathroom. But Sam stayed cool as a polar bear.

"This is Sam Gunn. I've been trying to find you, Fuchs."

"Why?"

"I have a message for you."

"From Humphries? I'm not interested in hearing what he has to say."

Sam glanced at me, then said, "The message is from Mrs. Humphries."

I didn't think it was possible, but Fuchs's face went harder still. Then, in an even meaner tone, he said, "I'm not interested in anything she has to say, either."

"She seemed very anxious to get this message to you, sir," Sam wheedled. "She hired us to come all the way out to the Belt to deliver it to you personally."

He fell silent. I could feel my heart thumping against my ribs. Then Fuchs snarled, "It seems more likely to me that you're bait for a trap Humphries wants to spring on me. My former wife hasn't anything to say to me."

"But—"

"No buts! I'm not going to let you set me up for an ambush." I could practically *feel* the suspicion in his voice, his scowling face. And something more. Something really ugly. Hatred. Hatred for Humphries and everything associated with Humphries. Including his wife.

"I'm no Judas goat," Sam snarled back. I was surprised at how incensed he seemed to be. You can never tell, with Sam, but he seemed really teed off.

"I'm Sam Gunn, goddammit, not some sneaking decoy. I don't take orders from Martin Humphries or anybody else in the whole twirling solar system and if you think . . ."

While Sam was talking, I glanced at the search radar, to see if it had locked onto Fuchs's ship. Either his ship was super-stealthy or it was much farther away than I had thought. He must be a damned good shot with that laser, I realized.

Sam was jabbering, cajoling, talking a mile a minute, trying to get Fuchs to trust him enough to let us deliver the chip to him.

Fuchs answered, "Don't you think I know that the chip you're carrying has a homing beacon built into it? I take the chip and a dozen Humphries ships come after me, following the signal the chip emits."

"No, it's not like that at all," Sam pleaded. "She wants you to see this message. She wouldn't try to harm you."

"She already has," he snapped.

I began to wonder if maybe he wasn't right. Was she working for her present husband to trap her ex-husband? Had she turned against the man whose life she had saved?

It couldn't be, I thought, remembering how haunted, how frightened she had looked. She couldn't be a Judas to him; she had married Humphries to save Fuchs's life, from all that I'd heard.

Then a worse thought popped into my head. If Sam gives the chip to Fuchs I'll have nothing to offer Humphries! All that money would fly out of my grasp!

I had tried to copy the chip but it wouldn't allow the ship's computer to make a copy. Suddenly I was on Fuchs's side of the argument: Don't take the chip! Don't come anywhere near it!

Fate, as they say, intervened.

The comm system pinged again and suddenly the screen split. The other half showed Judge Meyers, all smiles, obviously in a compartment aboard a spacecraft.

"Sam, we're here!" she said brightly. "At The Rememberer. It was so brilliant of you to pick the sculpture for our wedding ceremony!"

"Who the hell is that?" Fuchs roared.

For once in his life, Sam actually looked embarrassed. "Um . . . my, uh, fiancée," he stumbled. "I'm supposed to be getting married in two days."

The expression on Fuchs's face was almost comical. Here he's threatening to blow us into a cloud of ionized gas and all of a sudden he's got an impatient bride-to-be on the same communications frequency.

"Married?" he bellowed.

"It's a long story," said Sam, red-cheeked.

Fuchs glared and glowered while Judge Meyers's round freckled face looked puzzled. "Sam? Why don't you answer? I know where you are. If you don't come out to The Rememberer I'm going to bring the whole wedding party to you, minister and boys' choir and all."

"I'm busy, Jill," Sam said.

"Boys' choir?" Fuchs ranted. "Minister?"

Not even Sam could carry on two conversations at the same time, I thought. But I was wrong.

"Jill, I'm in the middle of something," he said, then immediately switched to Fuchs: "I can't hang around here; I've got to get to my wedding."

"Who are you talking to?" Judge Meyers asked.

"What wedding?" Fuchs demanded. "Do you mean to tell me you're getting married out here in the Belt?"

"That's exactly what I mean to tell you," Sam replied to him.

"Tell who?" Judge Meyers asked. "What's going on, Sam?"

"Bah!" Fuchs snapped. "You're crazy! All of you!"

I saw a flash of light out of the corner of my eye. Through the cockpit's forward window I watched a small, stiletto-slim spacecraft slowly emerge from the cloud of pebbles surrounding the asteroid, plasma exhaust pulsing from its thruster and a blood-red pencil-beam of laser light probing out ahead of it.

Fuchs bellowed, "I knew it!" and let loose a string of curses that would make an angel vomit.

Sam was swearing too. "Those sonsofbitches! They knew we'd be here and they were just laying in wait in case Fuchs showed up."

"I'll get you for this, Gunn!" Fuchs howled.

"I didn't know!" Sam yelled back.

Judge Meyers looked somewhere between puzzled and alarmed. "Sam, what's happening? What's going on?"

The ambush craft was rising out of the rubble cloud that surrounded the asteroid. I could see Fuchs's ship through the window now because he was shooting back at the ambusher, his own red pencil-beam from a spotting laser lighting up the cloud of pebbles like a Christmas ornament.

"We'd better get out of here, Sam," I suggested at the top of my lungs.

"How?" he snapped. "Fuchs took out the thruster."

"You mean we're stuck here?"

"Smack in the middle of their battle," he answered, nodding. "And our orbit's taking us between the two of them."

"Do something!" I screamed. "They're both shooting at us!"

Sam dove for the hatch. "Get into your suit, Gar. Quick."

I never suited up quicker. But it seemed to take hours. With our main thruster shot away, dear old *Achernar* was locked into its orbit around the asteroid. Fuchs and the ambusher were slugging it out, maneuvering and firing at each other with us in the middle. I don't think they were deliberately trying to hit us, but they weren't going out of their way to avoid us, either. While I wriggled into my spacesuit and fumbled through the checkout procedure *Achernar* lurched and quivered again and again.

"They're slicing us to ribbons," I said, trying to keep from babbling.

Sam was fully suited up; just the visor of his helmet was open. "You got the chip on you?"

For an instant I thought I'd left it in the cockpit. I nearly panicked. Then I remembered it was still in the waistband of my shorts. At least I hoped it was still there.

"Yeah," I said. "I've got it."

Sam snapped his visor closed, then reached over to me and slammed mine shut. With a gloved hand he motioned for me to follow him to the airlock.

"We're going outside?" I squeaked. I was really scared. A guy could get killed!

"You want to stay here while they take potshots at us?" Sam's voice crackled in my helmet earphones.

"But why are they shooting at us?" I asked. Actually, I was talking, babbling really, because if I didn't I probably would've started screeching like a demented baboon.

"Fuchs thinks we led him into a trap," Sam said, pushing me into the airlock, "and the bastard who's trying to bushwhack him doesn't want any living witnesses."

He squeezed into the airlock with me, cycled it, and pushed me through the outer hatch when it opened.

All of a sudden I was hanging in emptiness. My stomach heaved, my eyes blurred. I mean there was nothing out there except a zillion stars but they were so far away and I was falling, I could feel it, falling all the way to infinity. I think I screamed. Or at least gasped like a drowning man.

"It's okay, Gar," Sam said, "I've got you."

He grasped me by the wrist and, using the jetpack on his suit's back, towed me away from the riddled hulk of *Achernar*. We glided into the cloud of pebbles surrounding the asteroid. I could feel them pinging off my suit's hard shell; one of them banged into my visor, but it was a fairly gentle collision, no damage—except to the back of my head: I flinched so sharply that I whacked my head against the helmet hard enough to give me a concussion, almost, despite the helmet's padded interior.

Sam hunkered us down into the loose pile of rubble that was the main body of the asteroid. "Safer here than in the ship," he told me.

I burrowed into that beanbag as deeply as I could, scooping out pebbles with both hands, digging like a terrified gopher on speed. I would've dug all the way back to Earth if I could have.

Fuchs and the ambusher were still duking it out, with a spare laser blast now and then hitting *Achernar* as it swung slowly around the 'roid. The ship looked like a shambles, big gouges torn through its hull, chunks torn off and spinning lazily alongside its main structure.

They hadn't destroyed the radio, though. In my helmet earphones I could hear Judge Meyers's voice, harsh with static:

"Sam, if this is another scheme of yours . . ."

Sam tried to explain to her what was happening, but I don't think he got through. She kept asking what was going on and then, after a while, her voice cut off altogether.

Sam said to me, "Either she's sore at me and she's leaving the Belt, or she's worried about me and she's coming here to see what's happening."

I hoped for the latter, of course. Our suits had air regenerators, I knew, but they weren't reliable for more than twenty-four hours, at best. From the looks of poor old *Achernar,* we were going to need rescuing and damned soon, too.

We still couldn't really see Fuchs's ship; it was either too far away in that dark emptiness or he was jinking around too much for us to get a visual fix on him. I saw flashes of light that might have been puffs from maneuvering thrusters, or they might have been hits from the other guy's laser. The ambusher's craft was close enough for us to make out, most of the time. He was viffing and slewing this way and that, bobbing and weaving like a prizefighter trying to avoid his opponent's punches.

But then the stiletto flared into sudden brilliance, a flash so bright it hurt my eyes. I squeezed my eyes shut and saw the afterimage burning against my closed lids.

"Got a propellant tank," Sam said, matter-of-factly. "Fuchs'll close in for the kill now."

I opened my eyes again. The stiletto was deeply gashed along its rear half, tumbling and spinning out of control. Gradually it pulled itself onto an even keel, then turned slowly and began to head away from the asteroid. I could see hot plasma streaming from one thruster nozzle; the other was dark and cold.

"He's letting him get away," Sam said, sounding surprised. "Fuchs is letting him limp back to Ceres or wherever he came from."

"Maybe Fuchs is too badly damaged himself to chase him down," I said.

"Maybe." Sam didn't sound at all sure of that.

We waited for another hour, huddled inside our suits in the beanbag of an asteroid. Finally Sam said, "Let's get back to the ship and see what's left of her."

There wasn't much. The hull had been punctured in half a dozen places. Propulsion was gone. Life support shot. Communications marginal.

We clumped to the cockpit. It was in tatters; the main window was shot out, a long ugly scar from a laser burn right across the control panel. The pilot's chair was ripped, too. It was tough to sit in the bulky space suits, and we were in zero gravity to boot. Sam just hovered a few centimeters above his chair. I realized that my stomach had calmed down. I had adjusted to zero-gee. After what we had just been through, zero-gee seemed downright comfortable.

"We'll have to live in the suits," Sam told me.

"How long can we last?"

"There are four extra air regenerators in stores," Sam said. "If they're not damaged we can hold out for another forty-eight, maybe sixty hours."

"Time enough for somebody to come and get us," I said hopefully.

I could see his freckled face bobbing up and down inside his helmet. "Yep . . . provided anybody's heard our distress call."

The emergency radio beacon seemed to be functioning. I kept telling myself we'd be all right. Sam seemed to feel that way; he was positively cheerful.

"You really think we'll be okay?" I asked him. "You're not just trying to keep my hopes up?"

"We'll be fine, Gar," he answered. "We'll probably smell pretty ripe by the time we can get out of these suits, but except for that I don't see anything to worry about."

Then he added, "Except . . ."

"Except?" I yelped. "Except what?"

He grinned wickedly. "Except that I'll miss the wedding." He made an exaggerated sigh. "Too bad."

So we lived inside the suits for the next day and a half. It wasn't all that bad, except we couldn't eat any solid food. Water and fruit juices, that was all we could get through the feeder tube. I started to feel like a Hindu ascetic on a hunger strike.

We tried the comm system, but it was intermittent at best. The emergency beacon was faithfully sending out our distress call, of course, with our position. It could be heard all the way back to Ceres, I was sure. Somebody would come for us. Nothing to worry about. We'll get out of this okay. Someday we'll look back on this and laugh. Or maybe shudder. Good thing we had to stay in the suits; otherwise I would have gnawed all my fingernails down to the wrist.

And then the earphones in my helmet suddenly blurted to life.

"Sam! Do you read me? We can see your craft!" It was Judge Meyers. I was so overjoyed that I would have married her myself.

Her ship was close enough so that our suit radios could pick up her transmission.

"We'll be there in less than an hour, Sam," she said.

"Great!" he called back. "But hold your nose when we start peeling out of these suits."

Judge Meyers laughed and she and Sam chatted away like a pair of teenagers. But then Sam looked up at me and winked.

"Jill, I'm sorry this has messed up the wedding," he said, making his voice husky, sad. "I know you were looking forward to—"

"You haven't messed up a thing, Sam," she replied brightly. "After we've picked you up—and cleaned you up—we're going back to The Rememberer and have the ceremony as planned."

Sam's forehead wrinkled. "But haven't your guests gone back home? What about the boys' choir? And the caterers?"

She laughed. "The guests are all still here. As for the entertainment and the caterers, so I'll have to pay them for a few extra days. Hang the expense, Sam. This is our wedding we're talking about! Money is no object."

Sam groaned.

In a matter of hours we were aboard Judge Meyers's ship, *Parthia,* showered, shaved, clothed and fed, heading to The Rememberer and Sam's wedding. Sam was like Jekyll and Hyde: while he and I were alone together he was morose and mumbling, like a guy about to face a firing squad in the morning. When Judge Myers joined us for dinner, though, Sam was chipper and charming, telling jokes and spinning tall tales about old exploits. It was quite a performance; if Sam ever goes into acting he'll win awards, I'm sure.

After dinner Sam and Judge Meyers strolled off together to her quarters. I went back to the compartment they had given me, locked the door, and took out the chip.

It was easier this time, since I remembered the keys to the encryption. In less than an hour I had Amanda's hauntingly beautiful face on the display of my compartment's computer. I wormed a plug into my ear, taking no chances that somebody might eavesdrop on me.

The video was focused tightly on her face. For I don't know how long I just gazed at her, hardly breathing. Then I shook myself out of the trance and touched the key that would run her message.

"Lars," she said softly, almost whispering, as if she were afraid somebody would overhear her, "I'm going to have a baby."

Holy mother in heaven! It's a good thing we didn't deliver this message to Fuchs. He would've probably cut us into little pieces and roasted them on a spit.

Amanda Cunningham Humphries went on, "Martin wants another son, he already has a five-year-old boy by a previous wife."

She hesitated, looked over her shoulder. Then, in an even lower voice, "I want you to know, Lars, that it will be your son that I bear, not his. I've had myself implanted with one of the embryos we froze at Selene, back before all these troubles started."

I felt my jaw drop down to my knees.

"I love you, Lars," Amanda said. "I've always loved you. I married Martin because he promised he'd stop trying to kill you if I did. I'll have a son, and Martin will think it's his, but it will be your son, Lars. Yours and mine. I want you to know that, dearest. Your son."

Humphries would pay a billion for that, I figured.

And he'd have the baby Amanda was carrying aborted. Maybe he'd kill her, too.

"So what are you going to do about it, Gar?"

I whirled around in my chair. Sam was standing in the doorway.

"I thought I locked—"

"You did. I unlocked it." He stepped into my compartment and carefully slid the door shut again. "So, Gar, what are you going to do?"

I popped the chip out of the computer and handed it to Sam.

He refused to take it. "I read her message the first night on our way to the Belt," Sam said, sitting on the edge of my bed. "I figured you'd try to get it off me, one way or another."

"So you gave it to me."

Sam nodded gravely. "So now you know what her message is. The question is, what are you going to do about it?"

I offered him the chip again. "Take it, Sam. I don't want it."

"It's worth a lot of money, Gar."

"I don't want it!" I repeated, a little stronger.

Sam reached out and took the chip from me. Then, "But you know what she's doing. You could tell Humphries about it. He'd pay a lot to know."

I started to reply, but to my surprise I found that I had to swallow hard before I could get any words out. "I couldn't do that to her," I said.

Sam looked square into my eyes. "You certain of that?"

I almost laughed. "What's a few hundred million bucks? I don't need that kind of money."

"You're certain?"

"Yes, dammit, I'm certain!" I snapped. It wasn't easy to toss away all that money, and Sam was starting to irritate me.

"Okay," he said, breaking into that lopsided smile of his. "I believe you."

Sam got to his feet, his right fist closed around the chip.

"What will you do with it?" I asked.

"Pop it out an airlock. A few days in hard UV should degrade it so badly that even if somebody found it in all this emptiness they'd never be able to read it."

I got up from my desk chair. "I'll go with you," I said.

So the two of us marched down to the nearest airlock and got rid of the chip. I had a slight pang when I realized how much money we had just tossed out into space, but then I realized I had saved Amanda's life, most likely, and certainly the life of her baby. Hers and Fuchs's.

"Fuchs will never know," Sam said. "I feel kind of sorry for him."

"I feel sorry for her," I said.

"Yeah. Me too."

As we walked down the passageway back toward my compartment, curiosity got the better of me.

"Sam," I asked, "what if you weren't sure that I'd keep her message to myself? What if you thought I'd sneak off to Humphries and tell him what was on that chip?"

He glanced up at me. "I've never killed a man," he said quietly, "but I'd sure stuff you into a lifeboat and set you adrift. With no radio."

I blinked at him. He was dead serious.

"I wouldn't last long," I said.

"Probably not. Your ship would drift through the Belt for a long time, though. Eons. You'd be a real Flying Dutchman."

"I'm glad you trust me."

"I'm glad I can trust you, Gar." He gave me a funny look, then added, "You're in love with her, too, aren't you?"

It took me a few moments to reply, "Who wouldn't be?"

SO WE FLEW to The Rememberer with Judge Meyers and all the wedding guests and the minister and boys' choir, the caterers and all the food and drink for a huge celebration. Six different news nets were waiting for us: the wedding was going to be a major story.

Sam snuck away, of course. He didn't marry Jill Meyers after all. That's why she's on this ship, the *Hermes,* to meet him all the way out in the Kuiper Belt at that black hole he supposedly discovered.

She still wants to marry Sam. Don't ask me why. All I know is that she'll have to be pretty damned clever to get him to hold still for it.

Disappearing Act

IT WAS NEARLY MIDNIGHT WHEN THE MAITRE D' FINISHED his tale.

"So Lars Fuchs never knew that Amanda's baby was his own son?" Jade asked, her voice slightly hollow with thoughts of her own birth, her own parents.

"Neither did Martin Humphries," the maitre d' replied somberly.

Spence asked, "Fuchs died on that Venus expedition, didn't he?"

"Yes," said Jade. "And Amanda died in childbirth, according to the nets. But Humphries is still alive."

"He hasn't been seen in public in years," the maitre d' pointed out. "The rumor is that he had some sort of mental breakdown."

"Still, I don't know if we can use your story. I'll have to check with our legal department."

The maitre d' nodded. "I understand. Frankly, I wouldn't want Martin Humphries's people coming after me."

"Then why'd you tell us?" Spence asked.

The portly man shrugged. "It seemed like the thing to do. For Sam, I guess. To set the record straight. He wasn't the bastard everybody thinks he was."

Jade smiled at him, but then she said, "I can't pay you for the story unless our lawyers say we can use it."

The maitre d' smiled back. "That's okay. I'm doing well enough here. When we get back to Selene I'll have enough to open my own business."

"Oh?"

"Selling Martian artifacts."

"You can't do that! It's forbidden by the IAA!"

The maitre d's smile widened, showed teeth. "I've hired a squad of students who spend their summers with the Mars exploration teams. They make cups and bowls and stuff out of native Martian rock. Voila! Martian artifacts."

Spence gaped at him. "That . . . that's fraud."

"No, it clearly states on every bill of sale that the artifact was made on Mars. I give no guarantee of age, or of—"

The ship's captain came bustling into the salon, looking tense, upset. He hurried straight to the table where Jade, Spence and the maitre d' were sitting.

Spence got to his feet.

To Jade, the captain said, "We just received a message."

"Oh?"

"From Sam Gunn."

"From Sam?" all three of them asked in unison.

"The little scoundrel is flying back to Earth! He's popped out of that black hole and he's heading Earthward at a full g acceleration!"

"That's impossible!" Spence snapped.

Instead of replying the captain aimed a palm-sized remote at the smart wall.

Sam Gunn's round, freckled face appeared on the screen. "To whom it may concern," he said cheerfully. "I'm back from the mini–black hole and on my way toward Earth. See ya there!"

The image winked off.

"That's all?" Spence demanded.

"We tracked the source of the message. It's a torch ship heading inbound at one full g."

"Where'd he get a torch ship?"

"*Sacre dieu,*" said Jade. "Every lawyer in the solar system's going to be waiting for Sam when he gets to Earth."

"Including the Beryllium Blonde," Spence muttered.

"Have you told Senator Meyers?"

The captain nodded. "Before anyone else."

"She must be furious," said the maitre d'.

A puzzled, disbelieving expression on his face, the captain replied, "She laughed! She laughed out loud. I thought she'd snapped."

"Not Jill Meyers," Jade said.

"She's given orders to turn around and get back to Earth," the captain said. "As fast as we can."

TORCH SHIP *HERMES* orbited the Moon exactly once, just long enough for Jade and Spence to be picked up by a shuttle from Selene. Then the ship—with Jill Meyers and her entourage still aboard—returned to Earth.

But Sam Gunn was nowhere to be found. His ship had arrived in Earth orbit, but when customs inspectors boarded it the ship was empty. They impounded it, sealed it, and told the authorities—and the news media— that Sam Gunn had disappeared.

That started a feeding frenzy in the media. Jumbo Jim Gradowsky conferred with Solar News's corporate bigwigs and released Jade's hurriedly edited follow-on series about Sam. It was a smash hit, top of the audience ratings. Solar rereleased Jade's original biography, then packaged the two shows together and scored still another smashing success.

Yet there was no sign of Sam Gunn. He had disappeared. There were rumors that he was in Selene, but no one admitted to seeing him. Then, after weeks of such rumors, the news flashed through Selene that Sam Gunn had been working with a professor at the university. And he'd been arrested by Selene's security police.

Jade looked up the professor, Daniel C. Townes IV. A physicist. She called him several times, but always got his answering machine.

Then he walked into her office, tall, lanky, looking slightly bemused.

"I understand you're looking for me," he said, folding his long-legged figure into the little plastic chair in front of Jade's desk.

She almost leaped across the desk. "Do you know where Sam Gunn is?"

He frowned slightly. "I know where one of them is," said Townes.

Takes Two to Tangle

ONE SAM GUNN IS BAD ENOUGH—SAID PROFESSOR TOWNES. But now there's at least two of them, maybe more, and it's all my fault.

Well, mostly my fault. Sam had something to do with it, of course. More than a little, as you might suspect if you know anything about Sam.

And, if you know anything about Sam, you know that of course there was a woman involved. A beautiful, statuesque, golden-haired Bishop of the New Lunar Church, no less.

I didn't know anything about Sam except the usual stuff that the general public knew: Sam Gunn was a freewheeling space entrepreneur, a little stubby loudmouthed redheaded guy who always found himself battling the big boys of huge interplanetary corporations and labyrinthine government bureaucracies. Sam was widely known as a womanizer, a wiseass, a stubby Tasmanian Devil with a mind as sharp as a laser beam and a heart as big as a spiral galaxy.

He had disappeared years earlier out on some wild-ass trek to the Kuiper Belt. Everybody thought he had died out in that frozen darkness beyond Pluto. There was rejoicing in the paneled chambers of corporate and government power, tears shed among Sam's legion of friends.

And then after his long absence he showed up again, spinning a wild tale about having fallen into a black hole. He was heading back to Earth, coming in from the cold, claiming that friendly aliens on the other side of the black hole had showed him how to get back to our space-time, back to home. Sam's enemies nodded knowingly: of *course* the aliens would want to get rid of him, they said to each other.

And they sent just about every lawyer on Earth after Sam. He owed megabucks to dozens of creditors, including some pretty shady characters. He was so deeply in debt that there was no place on Earth he could land his spacecraft without having umpteen dozen eager lawyers slam him with liens and lawsuits.

Which is why Sam landed not on Earth, but on the Moon. At Selene, which was now an independent nation and apparently the only human community in the solar system that didn't have Sam at the head of its "most wanted" list.

He came straight to the underground halls of Selene University. To my office!

Imagine my surprise when Sam Gunn showed up at my doorway, all one hundred sixty–some centimeters of him.

And asked me to invent a matter transmitter for him.

"A matter transmitter?" I must have sputtered, I was so shocked. "But that's nonsense. It's kiddie fantasy. It's nothing but—"

"It's physics," Sam said. "And you're a physicist. Right?"

He had me there.

I am Daniel C. Townes IV, PhD. I am a particle physicist. I was on the short list last year for the Nobel Prize in physics. But that was before I met Sam Gunn.

Sam had popped into my office unannounced, sneaking past the department secretary during her lunch break. (Which, I must confess, often takes a couple of hours.) He just waltzed through my open doorway, walked up to my desk, stuck out his hand and introduced himself. Then he told me he needed a matter transmitter. Right away.

I sagged back in my desk chair while Sam perched himself on the only bare corner of my desk, grinning like a gap-toothed Jack-o'-lantern. His face was round, with a snub nose and a sprinkling of freckles. Wiry reddish hair; I think they call that color auburn. His eyes were light, twinkling.

"Physics is one thing," I said, trying to regain my dignity. "A matter transmitter is something else."

"Come on," Sam said, wheedling, "you guys have transmitted photons, haven't you? You yourself just published a paper about transmitting atomic particles from one end of your lab to the other."

He had read the literature. That impressed me.

You have to understand that I was naïve enough to think that I might be the youngest person ever to receive the physics Nobel. I had to be careful, though. More than one young genius had been cut down by the knives that whirl through academia's hallowed halls in the dark of night.

Sam aged me, though.

I think he had roosted on my desk because that made him taller than I was, as long as I remained sitting in my swivel chair. I have to confess, though, that there wasn't anyplace else he could have sat. My office was littered with reports, journals, books, even popular magazines. The visitor's chair was piled high with memos that the secretary had printed out from the department's unending file of meaningless trivia. There might be no paper on the Moon, but we sure do pile up the monofilament plastic sheets that we use in its place.

"So how about it, Dan-o?" Sam asked. "Can you make me a matter transmitter? It's worth a considerable fortune and I'll cut you in on it, fifty-fifty."

"What makes you think—"

"You're the expert on entanglement, aren't you?"

I was impressed even more. Entanglement is not a subject your average businessman either knows or cares about.

Curiosity is a funny thing. It not only kills cats, it makes physicists forget Newton's Third Law, the one about action and reaction.

I heard myself ask him, "Did you really survive going through a black hole?"

Grinning even wider, Sam nodded. "Yep. Twice."

"What's it like? What did you experience? How did it feel?"

Sam shrugged. "Nothing to it, really. I didn't see or feel anything all that unusual."

"That's impossible."

Sam just sat there on the corner of my desk, grinning knowingly.

"Unless," I mused, "the laws of physics change under the intense gravitational field . . ."

"Or I'm telling you a big, fat lie," Sam said.

"A lie?" That stunned me. "You wouldn't—"

"Look," Sam said, bending closer toward me, "I need a matter transmitter. You whip one up for me and I'll give you all the data in my ship's computer."

I could feel my eyes go wide. "Your ship? The one that went through the black hole?"

"Twice," said Sam.

Thus began my partnership with Sam Gunn.

INGRID MACTAVISH WAS something else. A missionary from the New Morality back Earthside, she had come to Selene to be installed as a Bishop in the New Lunar Church. She was nearly two meters tall, with bright golden hair that *glowed* and cascaded down past her shoulders, and eyes the color of perfect sapphires. A Junoesque goddess. A Valkyrie in a virginal white pants suit that fit her snugly enough to send my blood pressure soaring.

I'll never forget my first encounter with her. She just stormed into my office and, without preamble, demanded, "Is it true?"

It's hard to keep a secret in a community as small and intense as Selene. Rumors fly along those underground corridors faster than kids on jetblades. Sam wanted me to keep my work on the matter transmitter absolutely, utterly, cosmically top-secret. But the word leaked out, of course, after only a couple of weeks. I was surprised that nobody blabbed about it before then.

That's what brought Bishop MacTavish into my office, all one hundred and eighty-two centimeters of her.

"Is it true?" she repeated.

She was practically radiating righteous wrath, those sapphire eyes blazing at me.

I swallowed as I got politely to my feet from my desk chair. I'm accustomed to being the tallest person in any crowd. I'm just a tad over two meters; I'd been a fairly successful basketball player back at Cal-Tech, but here on the Moon even Sam could jump so high in the light gravity that my height wasn't all that much of an advantage.

Bishop MacTavish was not accustomed to looking up at anyone, I saw.

"Is what true?" I asked mildly. A soft answer turneth away wrath, I reasoned.

I think it was my height that softened her attitude. "That you're working on a device to transmit people through space instantaneously," she replied, her voice lower, gentler.

"No, that is not true," I replied. Honestly.

She sank down into the chair in front of my desk, which I had cleaned off since Sam's first visit. There were hardly more than three or four slim reports resting on it.

Bishop MacTavish looked startled for a moment; then she slipped the reports out from beneath her curvaceous rump and let them fall to the floor in the languid low gravity of the Moon.

"Thank God," she murmured. "That's one blasphemy we won't have to deal with."

"Blasphemy?" I asked, my curiosity piqued.

She blinked those gorgeous eyes at me. "A matter transmitter, if it could be made successfully, could also be used as a matter duplicator, couldn't it?"

It took me a moment to understand what she was saying; I was rather hypnotized by her eyes.

"Couldn't it?" she repeated.

"Duplicator? Yes, I suppose it might be feasible. . . ."

"And every time you use it you'd be murdering a human being."

"What?" That truly stunned me. "What are you talking about?"

"When someone goes into your transporter his body is broken down into individual atoms, isn't it? The pattern is sent to the receiver, where the body is reconstituted out of other atoms. The original person has been destroyed. Just because a copy comes out of the receiver—"

"No, no, no!" I interrupted. "That's fantasy from the kiddie shows. Entanglement doesn't work that way. Nothing gets destroyed."

"It doesn't?"

I shook my head. "It's rather complicated, but essentially the process matches the pattern of the thing to be transported and reproduces that pattern at the other end of the transmission. The original is not destroyed; it isn't harmed in any way."

She cocked a suspicious brow at me.

"It takes a lot of energy, though," I went on. "I doubt that it will ever be practical."

"But such a machine would be creating living human beings, wouldn't it? Only God can create people. A matter duplicator would be an outright blasphemy, clearly."

"Maybe so," I muttered. But then I came back to my senses. "Uh . . . although, that is, well, I thought that people create people. You know . . . uh, sexually."

"Of course." She smiled and lowered her lashes self-consciously. "That's doing God's work."

"It is?"

She nodded, then took a deep breath. I nearly started hyperventilating.

"But if you're not working on a matter transmitter," she said, breaking into a happy smile as she started to get up from the chair, "then there's no cause for alarm."

The trouble with being a scientist is that it tends to make you honest. Oh, sure, there've been cheats and outright frauds in science. But the field has a way of winnowing them out, sooner or later. Honesty is the bedrock of scientific research. Besides, I didn't want her to leave my office.

So I confessed, "I am working on a matter transmitter, I'm afraid."

She looked shocked. "But you said you weren't."

"I'm not working on a device to transport people. That would be too dangerous. My device is intended merely to transmit documents and other lightweight, nonorganic materials."

She thumped back into the chair. "And you're doing this for Sam Gunn?"

"Yes, that's true."

She took an even deeper breath. "That little devil. Blasphemy means nothing to him."

"But the transmitter won't be used for people."

"You think not?" she said sharply. "Once Sam Gunn has a matter transmitter in his hands he'll use it for whatever evil purposes he wants."

"But the risks—"

"Risks? Do you think for one microsecond that Sam Gunn cares about risks? To his body or his soul?"

"I . . . suppose not," I replied weakly.

"This has got to be stopped," she muttered.

I finally came to my senses. "Why? Who wants to stop this work? Who are you, anyway?"

"Oh!" She looked suddenly embarrassed. "I never introduced myself, did I?"

I tried to smile at her. "Other than the fact that you're worried about blasphemy and you're the most incredibly beautiful woman I've ever seen, I know nothing at all about you."

Which wasn't entirely true. I knew that she believed the act of procreation was doing God's work.

"I am Bishop Ingrid MacTavish," she said, extending her hand across my desk, "of the New Lunar Church."

"You must be a newcomer to Selene," I said as I took her hand in mine. Her grip was firm, warm. "I'd have noticed you before this."

"I arrived yesterday," she said. Neither one of us had released our hands. "Actually, I'm an ethicist."

"Ethicist?"

"Yes," she said. "There are certain ethical inconsistencies between accepted moral practice on Earth and here in Selene."

That puzzled me, but only for a moment. "Oh, you mean nanotechnology."

"Which is banned on Earth."

"And common practice here on the Moon. We couldn't survive without nanomachines."

"That's one of the reasons why I decided to set up my ministry here on the Moon."

Interesting, I thought. "And the other reason?"

She hesitated, then answered, "I've been hired temporarily by a consortium of law firms to find Sam Gunn and serve him with papers for a large number of major lawsuits."

At that moment, with impeccable timing, Sam bounced into my office. "Hey, Dan-o, I've been thinking—"

Ingrid jumped to her feet, stumbling clumsily because she was unaccustomed to the light lunar gravity.

Sam rushed over to help her and she lurched right into his arms. With her height, and Sam's lack of same, Sam's face got buried in Ingrid's commodious bosom momentarily while I stood behind my desk, too stunned to do anything more than gape at the sight.

Sam jerked away from her, his face flame-red. The little guy was actually embarrassed! Ingrid's face was red, too, with anger. She swung a haymaker at Sam. He ducked; she staggered off-balance. I came around my desk like a shot and grabbed Ingrid by her shoulders, steadying her.

Sam backed away from us, stuttering, "I didn't mean to . . . that is, it was an accident. . . . I was only trying . . ." Then he seemed to see Ingrid for the first time, *really* see her in all her statuesque beauty. His eyes turned into saucers.

"Who . . . who are you?" Sam asked, his voice hollow with awe.

Ingrid pulled free of me, but I noticed that she placed one hand lightly on my desktop. "I'm your worst nightmare," she hissed.

"No nightmare," Sam said. "A dream."

She wormed a hand into the hip pocket of her snug-fitting trousers and pulled out a wafer-thin data chip. "Sam Gunn, I hereby serve you legal notification of—"

Sam immediately clasped his hands behind his back. "You're not serving me with anything, lady. You've got no jurisdiction here in Selene. You have to go through the international court and even then you can only serve me if I'm on Earth, in a nation that's got an extradition treaty with the North American Alliance. Which Selene hasn't."

Ingrid smiled thinly at him. "Well, you know your law, I must admit."

Sam made a little bow, his hands still locked behind his back. "How'd you get in here, anyway? Selene doesn't allow Earthside lawyers to come here. Legal issues with Earth are handled electronically."

"Which is why you're hiding here in Selene," Ingrid replied.

With a Huck Finn grin, Sam acknowledged, "Until I can recoup my fortune and deal with all those malicious lawsuits."

"Malicious?" Ingrid laughed. "You owe Masterson Aerospace seven hundred million for the spacecraft you leased. Forty-three million—and counting—to Rockledge Industries for expenses on the orbital hotel that you haven't paid for in more than two years. Nine million—"

"Okay, okay," Sam conceded. "But how can I settle with them when they've got all my assets frozen?"

"That's your problem," said Ingrid.

"Why don't we discuss it over dinner?" Sam suggested, his grin turning sly.

"Dinner? With you? Don't be ridiculous."

"Scared?"

She hesitated, then glanced at me. I caught her meaning. She didn't want to be alone with Sam.

"Sam," I said, "we have a lot to talk about. I've got a working model just about finished, but to build a real machine I'm going to need some major funding and—"

Sam's no dummy. He caught on immediately. "Okay, okay. You come to dinner, too."

Turning back toward Ingrid, he asked, "Is that all right with you? Now you'll have a chaperone."

Ingrid smiled brightly. "That's perfectly fine with me, Mr. Gunn."

THE EARTHVIEW IS the oldest and, to my mind, still the best restaurant in Selene. On Earth, the higher you are in a building the more prestigious and expensive; that's why penthouses cost more than basement apartments—on Earth. On the Moon, though, the surface is dangerous: big temperature swings between sunlight and shadow, ionizing radiation constantly sleeting in from the Sun and stars, micrometeoroids peppering the ground and sandpapering everything exposed to them.

So in Selene, prestige and cost increase as you go down, away from the surface. The Earthview took in four full levels: its main entrance was on the third level below the Grand Plaza, and an actual human maitre d' guided you to tables set along the winding descending rampway that led all the way down to the seventh level.

The place got its name from the oversized screens that studded the walls, showing camera views of the surface with the Earth hanging big and blue and majestic in the dark lunar sky. I never got tired of gazing at Earth and its ever-changing pattern of dazzling white clouds shifting across those glittering blue oceans.

Sam had reserved the best table in the place, down at the very lowest level. While we waited for Ingrid to arrive, Sam and I had a drink: lunar "rocket fuel" with carbonated water for me and plain South Pole water for Sam. He pumped me for everything I knew about her.

"I didn't realize she's working for lawyers at first," I said. "She told me she's an ethicist, and a Bishop in the New Lunar Church."

"A Bishop? That's enough to give a man religion, almost," Sam mused.

"I never heard of the New Lunar Church before. Must be something new."

"Fundamentalist," Sam said knowingly. "Connected to the New Morality back Earthside."

"She did say something about blasphemy."

"Blasphemy?"

"In connection with the matter transmitter."

"Blasphemy," Sam muttered.

I took a sip of my drink. "Sam, there's something I've got to ask you."

"Ask away," he said blithely.

"Why do you want a matter transmitter? I mean, what in the world do you plan to do with it? You can't use it for people—"

"Why not?"

"It's too dangerous. We don't know enough about entanglement to risk people. Not even volunteers."

"Maybe there are some pets in Selene we can test it with," Sam muttered.

"Pets?" I shuddered at the idea of sending a dog or cat into the device I was building. Even a goldfish. Maybe the bio labs have some mice, I thought.

"Relax," Sam said, smiling easily. "I don't want to send people through space. Or pets. Just certain kinds of paperwork."

"Paperwork?"

"Legal tender. Money." He screwed up his face in a thoughtful frown for a moment. Then, "Legal documents too, I guess."

"Why?"

"Tax haven." Sam smiled his happiest, sunniest smile. "I'm going to turn Selene into a tax haven for all those poor souls down on Earth who're trying to hide their assets from their money-grabbing governments."

"A tax shelter? Selene?"

"Sure. Earthside governments won't let you carry your money off-planet. They won't even allow you to bring letters of credit or any other papers that can be transformed into money."

"It's all done electronically," I murmured, reaching for my drink again.

"Right. And taxed electronically. Every goddamned financial transaction between Earth and the Moon is monitored by those snake-eyed tax collectors and their computers."

"That's Earthside law, Sam."

"Yeah, sure. But if a person could send money or its equivalent from Earth to the Moon through a matter transmitter, privately, instantaneously, with nobody else knowing about it . . ." He leaned back in his chair and gave me that sly smile of his.

"Money would stream into Selene," I realized. "Money that people want to hide from their tax collectors."

"Selene could get very wealthy, very fast."

"The governments on Earth would be furious," I said.

"Right again. But what can they do about it? They tried to muscle Selene once with Peacekeeper troops and got their backsides whipped."

"But . . ."

"Besides, the richer Selene gets, the more Earthside politicians we can buy."

"Bribery?"

"Lubrication," Sam corrected. "Money is the oil that smoothes the machinery of government."

"Bribery," I said, firmly.

Sam shrugged.

A tax haven. A shelter for the fortunes that wealthy Earthsiders wanted to hide from their governments. It was wrong. Insidious. Definitely evil. But it could work!

And it could even result in more funding being available for Selene University. More funding for my research.

If I could make a matter transmitter.

"So how's the zapper coming along?" Sam asked, reaching for his South Pole water.

For the next fifteen minutes or so I nattered on about entanglement and the bench model I was almost ready to test. Sam appeared to listen closely; he asked questions that showed he understood most of what I was telling him.

Then all of a sudden he looked past my shoulder and his eyes went wide as pie plates. I turned in my chair. Ingrid MacTavish was coming down the rampway toward our table.

Even in the modest pure white floor-length outfit she was wearing she looked spectacular. Radiant. Heads turned as she followed the maitre d' past the other tables. And not just men's heads, either. Ingrid looked like a glowing golden-haired empress proceeding regally toward her throne. She was even followed by a quartet of acolytes, all of them women, all of them dressed in unadorned white suits. Compared to Ingrid they looked like four dumpy troglodytes.

Sam bounded to his feet and held her chair for her, making the normally impassive maitre d' frown at him. The acolytes seated themselves at the next table.

"Bishop MacTavish," Sam murmured as she sat down.

"Mr. Gunn," she replied. Then, with a nod toward me, "Dr. Townes."

I swallowed hard and tried to say something but no words came out. All I could do was smile and hope I didn't look like a complete idiot.

Sam was at his charming best all through dinner. Not a word about his legal troubles. Or about the matter transmitter. He regaled us both with improbable tales of his past misadventures.

Despite myself, I felt intrigued. "Tell us about the black hole, Sam," I begged. "What really happened to you?"

Ingrid seemed equally curious. "Did you actually meet truly intelligent alien creatures?"

"*Very* intelligent aliens," Sam said.

"What were they like? Did they have souls? Were they able to—"

"We didn't talk religion," Sam replied. "They were little guys. Smaller than me. Smart, though. High level of technology. I want to go back and learn how they operate that black hole."

"Do you?" Ingrid asked. "Wouldn't that be dangerous?"

Sam gave her his what-the-hell grin. "Lady, danger's my middle name."

"You're not worried about the danger to your soul?"

Sam blinked at her. "My soul's in decent shape. It's my finances that I'm worried about."

Ingrid scoffed, "What does it profit a man if he gains the whole world . . ."

"I don't want the whole world," Sam replied. "I just want my assets unfrozen and all you lawyers off my back."

"What would you give in return for that?"

That stopped Sam. But only for a moment. "You could make all these lawsuits go away?"

"I think a settlement could be arranged," she said.

"A settlement?"

"A settlement."

"Forgive me my debts," Sam mused, "as I forgive my debtors."

"Even the Devil can quote scripture," Ingrid retorted.

They were talking as if I wasn't there. I felt like a spectator at a tennis match; my eyes shifted back and forth from one to the other.

"Mr. Gunn, the New Morality—"

"Sam," he said. "Call me Sam."

Ingrid smiled. "Very well. Sam."

"May I call you Ingrid?" he asked her.

Her smile widened slightly. "Bishop MacTavish, Sam."

"No," Sam replied, not taken aback at all. "I'll call you Aphrodite: the goddess of beauty."

I saw anger flare in her deeply blue eyes, but only for the flash of a second. She controlled it immediately.

"That's the name of a pagan goddess."

"It's the only name I can think of that fits you," Sam said, looking totally sincere.

And then I heard myself blab, "Galileo said, 'Names and attributes must be accommodated to the essence of things, and not the essence to the names, for things come first and names afterward.'"

They both stared at me. "Whaat?"

"Well, I mean . . . that is . . ." I was back in the conversation, but floundering like a particle in Brownian motion.

"Galileo was a notorious heretic," Ingrid said.

"The Church apologized for that, er . . . misunderstanding," I said. Then I added, "Three hundred and fifty-nine years afterward."

"What's Galileo got to do with anything?" Sam demanded.

"Well, he said names should be given based on the observable attributes of the thing being named." Turning to Ingrid, I said, "I think naming you Aphrodite is completely appropriate."

She looked thoughtfully at me. Then, her face totally serious, "You mean that as a compliment, Dr. Townes. And I accept it as such. Thank you."

"Dan," I said. "Please call me Dan."

She nodded, then turned back to Sam. "But you, Sam, you're trying to seduce me, aren't you?"

"Me?" The innocence on Sam's face was about as obvious as a flying elephant. And as phony.

"You," Ingrid said sternly.

Gesturing toward the next table, Sam asked, "Is that why you brought the Four Horsewomen of the Apocalypse? For protection?"

"I don't need protection from you, Sam. I can take care of myself."

Sam hmmfed. "I bet you're still a virgin."

"That's none of your business."

He shrugged. "Now what was this about forgiving me my debts?"

It took her a moment to get her mind back on business. At last she folded her hands on the tabletop and said slowly, carefully, "The New Morality is willing to intervene on your behalf in the various lawsuits against you."

"The New Morality, huh?" If this surprised Sam he certainly didn't show it. "They own a lot of stock in Masterson, and Rockledge too, don't they?"

"That's neither here nor there."

"And what do I have to do to get the New Morality to save my ass?"

Her eyes flared again at Sam's crudity. I figured he had chosen his words precisely to rattle her.

"You will give up this effort of yours to create a matter transmitter."

"Wait a minute!" I yelped. "That's *my* work you're talking about!"

"It is blasphemous presumption," said Bishop MacTavish. "You are both placing your souls in grave danger."

"Bullsnorts!" Sam snapped. "The New Morality doesn't want a matter transmitter because it would loosen their control over people."

"This is a matter of religion, Sam," Ingrid said. "The state of your soul—"

"Stow it, Aphrodite. This is a matter of politics. Power. The New Morality isn't worried about my soul, but they're scared that a matter transmitter might let people do things they don't want them to do."

Ingrid turned to me. She actually reached across the table and took my hands in hers. "Daniel, you understand, don't you? You can see that I'm trying to save your soul."

I was thinking more about my body. And hers.

"Ingrid," I said, my voice nothing more than a husky whisper, "we're talking about my work. My life."

"No," she replied softly. "We're talking about your soul."

Up to that moment I hadn't even considered that I might possess a soul. But gazing into those incredible eyes, with her hands in mine, I started thinking about how wonderful it would be to please her, to make her smile at me, to be with her for all eternity.

"Hey! Break it up!" Sam said sharply. "I'm supposed to be the seducer here."

At that, all four of the women at the next table got to their feet. I saw that they were all pretty hefty; they looked like professional athletes.

"Bishop MacTavish," one of them said in a sanctimonious whisper, "it's time to leave."

Ingrid looked up at her quartet of bodyguards as if breaking free of a trance. She pulled her hands away from me and nodded. "Yes. I must go."

And she left me there, staring after her.

I THOUGHT I knew as much about entanglement as any person living. More, in fact. But all I knew was about subatomic particles and quantum physics. Not about people. And I got myself entangled with Bishop Ingrid MacTavish so completely that I couldn't even see straight half the time.

We had dinners together. She visited my lab several times and we had lunch with my grad student assistants. She and I took long walks up in the Main Plaza, strolling along the bricked lanes that curved through the greenery so lovingly tended up there beneath the massive concrete dome of the Plaza. I kissed her and she kissed me back. I fell in love.

But she didn't.

"I can't let myself love you, Daniel," she told me one evening, as we sat on a park bench near the curving shell of the auditorium. We had attended a symphonic concert: all Tchaikovsky, lushly romantic music.

"Why not?" I asked. "I love you, Ingrid. I truly do."

"We live in different worlds," she said.

"You're here on the Moon now. We're in the same world."

"No, it's your work. Your soul."

She meant the matter transmitter, of course. I spread my hands in a halfhearted gesture and said, "My soul isn't in any danger. The damned experiment isn't working. Not at all."

She looked hopefully at me. "It *is* damned! It's that devil Sam Gunn. He's leading you down the road to perdition."

"Sam? He's no devil. An imp, maybe."

"He's evil, Daniel. And this matter transmitter he wants you to make for him—it's the Devil's work."

"Come on, Ingrid. That's what they said about the telescope, for God's sake."

"Yes, for God's sake," she murmured.

"Do you really think what I'm doing is evil?"

"Why do you think your experiment won't work? God won't allow you to succeed."

"But—"

"And if you do succeed, if you should somehow manage to make the device work the way Sam Gunn wants it to, it will only be because the Devil has helped you."

"You mean it'll be witchcraft?" My voice must have gone up two octaves.

Ingrid nodded, her lips pressed into a tight line. "Don't you see, Daniel? I'm struggling to save your very soul."

And there it was. She was attracted to me, I knew she was. But my work stood in the way. And her medieval outlook on life.

"Ingrid, I can't give up my work. It's my career. My life."

She bowed her head. Her voice so low I could barely hear her, she said, "I know, Daniel. I know. I can't even ask you to give it up. I do love you, dearest. I love you so much that I can't ask you to make this sacrifice. I won't ruin your life. I should do everything in my power to get you away from this devilish task you've set yourself. But I can't bring myself to do it. I can't hurt you that way. Even if it means both our souls."

She loved me! She admitted that she loved me! But nothing would come of it as long as I worked on Sam's matter transmitter.

I told Sam about it the following morning. Actually, he ferreted the information out of me.

Sam was already in my lab when I came in that morning. He was always bouncing into the lab, urging me to make the damned benchtop model work so we could go ahead and build a full-scale transmitter.

"Why isn't it working yet?" he would ask, about twenty thousand times a day.

"Sam, if I knew why it isn't working I'd know how to make it work," I would always reply.

And he would buzz around the lab like a redheaded bumblebee, getting in everybody's way. My three technicians—graduate student slave labor—were getting so edgy about Sam's presence that they had threatened to go to the dean and complain about their working conditions.

This particular morning, after that park bench confession from Ingrid the evening before, I had to drag myself to the lab. Sam, as I said, was already there.

He peered up at me. "What bulldozer ran over you?"

I blinked at him.

"You look as if you haven't slept in a week."

"I haven't," I muttered, heading for the coffee urn the techs had perking away on one of the lab benches.

"The good Bishop MacTavish?" Sam asked, trailing after me.

"Yep."

"She still trying to save your soul?"

I whirled around, my anger flaring. "Sam, I love her and she loves me. Stay out of it."

He put up his hands in mock surrender. "Hey, I'm just an innocent by-stander. But take it from me, pal, what she really wants from you is to give up on the transmitter."

"You want her yourself, don't you? That's why—"

"Me?" Sam seemed genuinely astounded by the idea. "Me and that religious fanatic? You've gotta be kidding!"

"You're not attracted to her?"

"Well, she's gorgeous, true enough. But there are too many other women in the world for me to worry about a psalm-singing bishop who's working for lawyers that're trying to skin me alive." He took a breath. "Besides," he added, "she's too tall for me."

"She loves me. She told me so."

Sam hoisted himself up onto the lab bench beside the coffee urn and let his stubby legs swing freely. "Let me give you a piece of priceless wisdom, pal. Hard-earned on the field of battle."

I grabbed the cleanest-looking mug and poured some steaming coffee into it. Sam watched me, his expression somewhere between knowing and caring.

"What wisdom might that be?" I asked.

"It's about love. Guys fall in love because they want to get laid. Women fall in love because they want something: it might be security, it might be their own sense of self-worth, it might even be because they pity the guy who's coming on to them. But to women, sex is a means to an end, not an end in itself."

I felt like throwing the coffee in his face. "That's the most cynical crap I've ever heard, Sam."

"But it's true. Believe me, pal. I know. I've got the scars to prove it."

"Bullshit," I snapped, heading for the nonworking model on the bench across the lab. I noticed that one of the grad students had hung a set of prayer beads from the ceiling light over the equipment. A cruel joke, I thought.

"Okay," Sam said brightly, hopping down from his perch. "Prove that I'm wrong."

"Prove it? How?"

"Make the dingus work. Then see if she really loves you, or if she's just trying to make you give up on the experiment."

Talk about challenges! I stared at the clutter of equipment on the lab bench. Wires and heavy insulated cables snaked all over the place, hung in festoons from the ceiling (along with the prayer beads) and coiled across the floor. They say a neat, orderly laboratory is a sign that no creative work's being done. Well, my lab was obviously a beehive of intense creativity.

Except that the damned experiment refused to work.

Make the transmitter work, and then see if Ingrid still says she loves me. What was that old Special Forces motto? Who dares, wins. Yeah. But I thought there was a damned good chance of my daring and losing.

Yet I had to do it. To prove to Ingrid that the transmitter wouldn't destroy my soul, if for no other reason.

So I fiddled around with the power feeds and the connections between the plasma chamber and the thin mesh grid in the middle of the platform that served for the beam's focus. The same damned flimsy sheet of monofilament that I wanted to transmit to the other side of the lab sat on the grid just as it had for the past two weeks, like a permanent symbol of frustration.

Entanglement. All the equipment had to do was to match the quantum states of the monofilament's atoms and transmit that information to the receiver across the lab. That's a lot of information to juggle, but I had six oversized quantum computers lined up against the lab's wall, more than enough qubits to handle the job. In theory.

I checked the computers; they were connected in parallel, humming nicely, awaiting the command to go to work.

Everything checked, just as it had for the past two weeks. I went to the master control on the other side of the bench. I noticed my three grad students edging toward the door. They weren't worried about the equipment exploding; they knew from experience that I was the one who blew up when the system failed to work.

Sam was standing by the door, arms folded across his chest, a curious expression on his face: kind of crafty, devious.

"Ready," I called out. Then, "Stand clear."

The latter call was strictly routine. The nearest human body to the equipment was several meters away, by the door. Except for me, and I made sure I was on the other side of the apparatus from the focus grid, shielded by the bulk of the plasma chamber.

As if I needed protection. I pushed the keypad that activated the equipment. It buzzed loudly. The plasma chamber glowed for a moment, then went dark. The sheet of monofilament stayed right there on the focus grid, just as it had since the first time I tried to make the godforsaken junkpile perform.

I took a deep breath and started counting to one hundred.

Then I heard a scuffle behind me. Turning, I saw Sam had a hammer-lock on one of my grad students; he was dragging the kid toward me.

"He had this in his pocket," Sam said, tossing me a slim plastic oblong from his free hand. The grad student was grimacing; Sam had his arm screwed up pretty tight behind his back.

"It's a remote of some kind," I muttered, turning the device over in my hand.

"He clicked it on just before you pressed the start button," Sam said.

I turned to the student, W. W. Wilson. He was the beefy kind; I was surprised Sam could hold an armlock on him.

"Woody," I asked, dumbfounded, "what the hell is this?"

Woody just glared at me, his chunky face red with either anger or pain. Maybe some of both. He was a biology graduate who had volunteered to work in my lab for a little extra spending money.

Sam hiked the Woody's arm up a little higher and said, "You either tell us or I'll personally pump you so full of babble juice your brain'll shrink to the size of a walnut."

"Go ahead and torture me!" Woody cried. "I'm prepared to suffer for my faith!"

"Let him go, Sam," I said. "We're not the Gestapo."

Sam shot me a disapproving frown, but released Woody's arm. I clicked the cover off the remote and studied its interior. It seemed simple enough. It looked somewhat like an old-fashioned cell phone. But it had no keypad, no display screen.

I looked up at Woody. "What frequency band does this work on?"

Woody just scowled at me as he rubbed his arm.

"I can find out for myself easily enough." I started for the array of test equipment stored in the lab's lockers.

"Microwave," Woody muttered. "Just enough power to scramble the recognition circuitry."

"Sabotage," Sam growled. "A goddam saboteur planted here by the New Lunar Church."

My heart sank.

"Not that bunch of pansies," Woody snarled. "I was sent here by the New Morality, straight from Earthside headquarters in Atlanta."

Sam jabbed a finger at him. "You must be doing real well in your bio classes."

"I lead the class discussions in Intelligent Design," Woody said, with some pride. "I can tie those Darwinians into pretzel knots."

"And you screwed up Dan-o's experiment."

"I'll do more than that!" Woody suddenly leaped past Sam and me and grabbed the cover of the plasma chamber. He ripped it off and threw it to the floor.

"I'll wreck this Devil's tool once and for all!" he yelled, reaching for the focal grid. The grid was oversized, much bigger than I needed it to be; I had scavenged it from a colleague's experiment with a PET full-body scanner. Yet Woody was wrenching it out of its hold-down screws; the screech of the screws ripping out of the benchtop was enough to freeze my blood.

I was paralyzed with shock, but Sam sprang onto the kid's back like a monkey jumping onto a racing horse, knocking him on top of the lab bench. They wrestled around on the half bent focal grid, arms and legs thrashing, grunting and swearing. Woody was much bigger, of course; he got atop Sam and started punching him with both fists.

It seemed like hours, but it was really only a few seconds. I finally came out of my surprised funk and grasped Woody by the shoulders and pulled him off Sam. I threw him to the floor; he hit with a heavy thud.

Sam sat up, a little groggily, on the focus grid. His nose was leaking a thin stream of blood; otherwise he looked okay.

"Sam, are you all right?"

He shook his head slightly. "Nothing rattles. That kid can't punch worth shit. Hey, *look out!*"

I turned. Woody was on his feet. He slammed a fist onto the control panel keyboard. "Die, spawn of Satan!" he screamed.

The power thrummed, the plasma chamber pulsed, the overhead lights dimmed and then went dark. The emergency backup lights came on. But nothing else happened. Sam still sat on the focus grid, with that damned sheet of monofilament beneath his butt.

I swung around on Woody and socked him in the jaw as hard as I could. His head snapped back, his knees folded, and he collapsed to the floor, unconscious.

Sam whistled appreciatively. "That's a helluva punch you've got there, Dan-o." He jumped down from the bench and bent over Woody. "He's out like a light."

And from across the lab, where the receiving grid was, Sam Gunn said, "What'm I doing over here?"

I stared at Sam, clear on the other side of the lab. Then I turned back to Sam, who was still standing by the bench, right beside me.

Two of them!

I think I fainted.

When I came to, both Sams were standing over me. I was sitting on the floor next to Woody's still-unconscious body, my back propped against the lab bench.

"Are you okay?" one of the Sams asked me.

"You need a doctor?" asked the other one.

I looked from one to the other. Identical, down to the number and location of his freckles.

"It worked," I said. "The experiment. It worked!"

"Of course it worked," said Sam I.

"Once this bozo stopped sabotaging it," Sam II said, casting a frown at Woody.

My erstwhile lab assistant was groaning now, his legs shuffling back and forth. His eyes fluttered open.

Both Sams grabbed his arms and helped him up to a sitting position.

Woody looked at each of them in turn, his eyes widening with horror, his face going pasty white. He screeched like a giant fingernail scraping across a chalkboard, scrambled to his feet, and bolted for the door. My two other grad students were right behind him. They all looked terrified.

"Unclean!" Woody yelled as he tore out of the lab. "Unclean!"

Both Sams shook their heads. "He should've said 'Eureka.'"

I struggled to my feet unassisted. I felt a little woozy, my legs rubbery, but my mind was whirling madly. I did it! I proved that entanglement can be used not merely to transmit macroscopic objects but to duplicate them: a human being, no less!

Visions of the Nobel danced through my head.

But then I thought of Ingrid. What would her reaction be?

A little unsteadily, I headed for my desk and the phone. Both Sams trailed along behind me.

Time for the moment of truth.

I PHONED INGRID right then and there, and asked her to come to my lab. In the phone's smallish screen, her exquisite face looked more curious than anything else.

"To your lab?" she asked. "Right now?"

I nodded. "Big news. I want you to see it before anyone else does."

Her expression changed immediately. To dread. "I'll be there in a few moments."

I paced the lab from one end to the other while the Sams got themselves into an argument.

"First thing we do is set up the tax shelter."

"Better secure the spacecraft first. That Bishop MacTavish is going to try to seize it."

"Let her! Once the tax shelter's in operation we'll have money pouring in."

"Never let the enemy cut off your line of retreat."

"We don't need the ship anymore! We can just about print money, for God's sake."

"Print money?" Whichever Sam it was suddenly got a thoughtful, crafty look on his snub-nosed face. "Print money."

The other Sam grinned at his twin. "Duplicate financial instruments. Ought to be a pile of money there."

"Duplicate women!"

"Wow! Twins!"

"Made to order."

"Now wait a minute," I said. "The duplicator is mine, not yours."

They both turned to me, their faces identically disappointed, stunned with betrayal.

"You wouldn't refuse me the use of your contraption, would you, Dan-o?"

"After all, I'm the one who got you started on this experiment. Without me, you'd still be doodling with theory and equations."

Before I could reply the lab door swung open and Ingrid strode in, looking like an avenging angel in a gold sweater and hip-hugging jeans. I nearly fainted again.

She said not a word, but stared at the two Sams for what seemed like an hour and a half. Both Sams grinned impishly at her and then bowed, simultaneously.

"You did it," she said to me in a near-whisper.

"It was sort of an accident," I began. "I had no intention of duplicating Sam."

Ingrid sank to the nearest stool. I thought I saw tears in her eyes.

"Oh, Daniel," she said, in a sorrowful moan. "Now all hell is going to break loose over you."

TO SAY THAT all hell broke loose would be an exaggeration, but not much of one. News of my success spread throughout Selene in a microsecond, it seemed. My grad students must have shouted it out to everyone they passed in the corridors, like Paul Revere warning of the redcoats.

Ingrid looked truly heartbroken, but when the Sams told her about Woody her chin snapped up and her eyes suddenly turned fiery.

"The New Morality?" she asked. "He said he was sent here directly by the New Morality?"

"Straight from their headquarters," Sam I replied. Or was he Sam II?

"In Atlanta," the other Sam added.

"They bypassed me to plant a spy in your laboratory?" Ingrid asked.

"That's what he told us," I said.

"They never told me about it," she murmured. "They knew I'd be opposed to such a low trick."

"They didn't trust you," said a Sam.

"No, they didn't, did they?" Ingrid looked crestfallen, heartbroken. "They merely used me as a distraction while their spy did his best to ruin your experiment."

"But they failed," I said. "And I succeeded."

She nodded, her expression turning even bleaker. "And what happens now, Daniel? What happens to you, my love? What happens to us?"

Before I could even begin to think of an answer, a quartet of Selene security police strode into the lab.

"By order of the council," their leader pronounced, "these premises are to be evacuated and sealed until further notice."

The Sams started to object, but the officer went on, "And Sam Gunn is hereby placed under protective custody."

"You mean I'm going to jail?" both Sams yelped.

All four policemen fixed the two Sams with beady gazes. "Which of you is Sam Gunn?" their leader asked.

"I am," said both Sams in unison.

The officer looked from one Sam to the other, obviously trying to decide what to do. Then he turned to his cohorts and commanded, "Bring 'em both in."

THE FOLLOWING MORNING I was awakened by a phone message inviting me to a meeting of Selene's governing council, which would convene at eleven AM precisely. "Invite" is a relative term: when the governing council invites you, you show up, on time and ready to cooperate.

It wasn't a trial, exactly. More of an executive hearing. It took place in a windowless conference room up in the executive office tower that rises from the middle of the Grand Plaza to the roof of the dome. The room's walls were paneled with smart screens, much like the screens down at the Earthview restaurant, but when I entered, shortly before eleven, the walls were dead blank gray. Not a good sign, I thought.

The entire governing council of Selene was already seated at the oblong conference table, all six of them. Douglas Stavenger himself sat on one of the chairs lined along the wall. He hadn't been on the council for years, but as the de facto leader of Selene, the man who had led the battle that resulted in Selene's independence, he had obviously taken an interest in our case. He looked much younger than his calendar years: as everyone knew, Stavenger's body was filled with nanomachines.

The council chairman was a prune-faced man with thinning gray hair. Obviously he didn't take rejuvenation therapies, which led me to the conclusion that he was a religious Believer of one sort or another. He directed me to the empty chair at the foot of the table.

As I sat down I heard a raucous hullabaloo from the corridor outside. All heads turned toward the door, which burst open. Both Sams stalked in, escorted by a squad of uniformed security guards. Both Sams were yammering away like trip-hammers.

"What's the idea of putting me in jail?"

"Who's in charge here?"

"What's this bull droppings about protective custody?"

"I want a lawyer!"

"I want two lawyers!"

"You can't do this to me!"

One Sam Gunn jabbering nonstop is bad enough; here were two of them.

Pruneface, up at the head of the table, raised both his clawlike hands over his gray head. "Mr. Gunn!" he shouted, in a much more powerful voice than I'd have thought him capable of, "please shut up and sit down! There!" And he pointed to the two empty chairs flanking me.

"Why am I here?"

"What's going on?"

"This is an emergency meeting of the governing council," the chairman explained, in a slightly lower tone. "An informal hearing, if you will."

Both Sams trudged grudgingly to the foot of the table and sat on either side of me.

"Now then," the chairman said, from the head of the table, "Dr. Townes, could you kindly explain how in the world you produced a duplicate of Sam Gunn?"

I blinked at him. "You want me to explain how entanglement works?"

"In layman's language, if you please."

I glanced around at the other council members. Three women, two men. In their forties or older, I guessed from their appearances. Probably at least two of them were scientists or engineers: Selene's population leans toward the technical professions.

I took a deep breath and began, "Basically, my device assesses the quantum states of the atoms in the subject and reproduces those quantum states in the atoms at the receiving end of the equipment."

"It is a matter duplicator, then?"

"It was intended to be a transmitter, but, yes sir, it has functioned as a duplicator. There are still some details that are not quite clear, but—"

The door behind the chairman slid open and Ingrid entered the conference room, wearing a gold-trimmed white uniform with a choker collar and full-length trousers.

"I'm sorry to be late," she said, her face deadly serious. "I wasn't informed of this hearing until a few minutes ago."

Everyone stood up.

"Bishop MacTavish," murmured the chairman, indicating an empty chair halfway down the table.

Once we seated ourselves again, the chairman explained, "Bishop MacTavish is here as a qualified ethicist."

"And a representative of the New Lunar Church," said the councilman on the chairman's right.

The Sam on my left squawked, "What's the New Lunar Church got to do with this?"

"Excuse me, Mr. Chairman," Ingrid said, "but I'm afraid you're working under a misapprehension. I am here in my capacity as legal counsel."

"For Rockledge Industries, et al," muttered the Sam on my right.

"No," Ingrid replied. "I am representing Dr. Townes." And she smiled so sweetly at me that my heart nearly melted.

Both Sams leaned in to me and whispered, "Watch out. This could be a trap."

Was Ingrid a Judas goat? I refused to believe it. But the possibility gnawed at me.

When the council members started asking me questions about my experiment Ingrid rose to her feet and said sternly, "This council has no legal right to question Dr. Townes, except as to how his work might affect the safety of Selene and its citizens."

"But he's duplicated a human being!" one of the councilwomen sputtered.

"Sam Gunn, no less," grumbled the councilman beside her.

"I am morally opposed to such a duplication as much as any of you," Ingrid said, still on her feet. "I regard it as little short of blasphemy. As a Believer and a Bishop of the New Lunar Church, I am appalled."

Here it comes, I thought. She'll recommend burning me at the stake.

But Ingrid went on, "Yet, as a woman who has lived in the freedom of a democratic civilization—and as an applicant for citizenship in your nation of Selene—I cannot support the imposition of limitations on Dr. Townes's research, or on the intellectual freedom of any person."

My eyebrows popped up almost to my scalp. Both Sams looked surprised; so did most of the council members. I saw Douglas Stavenger nodding his agreement, a slight smile of satisfaction on his face.

"The New Lunar Church has no objection to this work?" the council chairman asked.

"I shudder to think that a human being would aspire to usurping God's creative powers," Ingrid said. "But after having thought on the matter and prayed on it, I have concluded that Dr. Townes has not actually created a human being; he has merely duplicated one."

"So the council has no moral right to object to his work?" asked the chairman.

"Not in my view, nor in the view of the New Lunar Church."

"Very well," said the chairman, a grin spreading across his face. "Now let's get down to the real reason for this hearing. Dr. Townes, you caused a power outage through three-quarters of Selene. Is the university going to pay for that?"

"Power outage?" I gasped. "I thought it was only in my own lab."

"Surely you noticed that the emergency lights were on throughout several levels for four hours after your experiment."

"That contraption of yours drained the system," grumped one of the councilmen, "knocked out two inverters, and overheated the coolant in the cryogenic transmission lines from our main solar panel farm, up on the surface."

"It did?" Now that he mentioned it, I realized that after our little fracas in my lab the corridors had been lit by the emergency lamps. Even my quarters had been, when I got there after the police took Sam away.

"We can't have that kind of drain on our power system," said the chairman. "I think the council will agree that you must be prohibited from running your equipment again."

"Until you can provide your own electrical power for it," said the grumpy councilman.

Ingrid hadn't sat down yet. Raising her voice over the murmurs of conversation buzzing around the table, she said, "If I may, I would like to take this opportunity to serve Mr. Gunn with the subpoenas I've been carrying."

The chairman gestured grandly. "Go right ahead."

"You can't do that!" yelped one of the Sams.

The other, just as red-faced, added, "Selene's constitution specifically states—"

"Our constitution," said the chairman sternly, "allows specific exceptions to the extradition clause, Mr. Gunn."

Both Sams snapped their jaws shut with audible clicks.

Turning to the Sams, Ingrid asked, "Which of you is the original?"

"He is," said both Sams in unison, pointing at one another.

Ingrid frowned at them. "One of you is a copy. I have to serve these papers to the original."

"That's him," they both said.

Ingrid looked from one of them to the other. Then she turned back to the chairman. "As you can see, although no one has the right to curtail Dr. Townes's intellectual freedom, his experiment has created certain practical difficulties."

I REALIZED THAT I'd created a Pandora's Box. So I compromised. Actually, I caved in. I promised the council that I'd dismantle my equipment and scrap it. I would not publish anything about my experiment. I would forget about entanglement and study other aspects of quantum physics.

Which meant I could kiss the Nobel Prize goodbye.

The council was very relieved. Ingrid, though, seemed strangely unhappy.

That evening in the cafeteria, as we nibbled at a dinner neither one of us had any appetite for, I said to her, "I thought you wanted me to scrap the duplicator."

She gazed at me with those luminous azure eyes of hers. "I did, Daniel. But now I realize that I've ruined your life."

"It's not ruined, exactly."

"I'm dreadfully sorry."

I tried to put a good face on the situation. "It's a big universe, Ingrid. There are plenty of other questions for me to work on."

"But you—"

A hubbub over by the doorway distracted us. Both Sams were scurrying through the cafeteria like a pair of spaniels hunting for a bone.

"Hey! There they are!" said Sam I to Sam II. Or vice versa.

They rushed to our table and pulled up chairs. "Gotta hurry Dan-o. My ship's ready to leave."

"Leave? For where?"

The other Sam replied, "Back to that black hole in the Kuiper Belt. Wanna come with me?"

Ingrid was immediately suspicious. "How did you get the money to—"

"Rockledge!" both Sams crowed. "And Masterson Aerospace and all those other big buffoons who were suing me."

"They're financing your mission to the Kuiper Belt?"

"Yeah." The Sams' grins were ear-to-ear. It was eerie: they were *exactly* alike. "They're willing to pay mucho dinero to get rid of me."

I got their meaning. "They're hoping that this time you go away and stay away."

Nodding and laughing, one of the Sams said, "Yeah. But what they don't know is that only one of me is going."

"And the other?"

They both shrugged.

"I don't know," said one. "Maybe I'll go back into the zero-gee hotel business."

"Or go back to the resort at Hell Crater," said the other one.

"Or turn Selene into a tax shelter. How's the Church of Rightful Investments sound to you?" They both winked at Ingrid simultaneously.

"You've stolen my matter transmitter!" I snapped.

A Sam raised both his hands in a gesture of innocence. "Me? Steal? No way!"

Before I could let out a satisfied sigh, though, the other Sam added, "But now that we know a transmitter can work, there oughtta be some bright physicist who's willing to build me a new one."

"Sam, you can't!" Ingrid and I objected together.

They both grinned at us. "Maybe not. We'll see."

So I'm going out to the Kuiper Belt with one of the Sams. Much to my surprise and delight, Ingrid wants to go with me. She really does love me! We're going to be married over an electronic link to the Vatican, no less, while we're on our way out.

The Kuiper Belt. A mini–black hole. Maybe there really are aliens out there. Of course, that might be one of Sam's tall tales, but what the hell, Ingrid's with me and we're bound to find something worth a Nobel out there.

It's a big universe!

Solar News Headquarters, Selene

DANIEL C. TOWNES IV GOT TO HIS FEET LIKE A LONG, LANKY ladder unfolding.

"That's about it," he said. "Sam's already aboard his torch ship. Ingrid and I will shuttle out to it an hour from now."

Jade sputtered, "But . . . *two* Sams?"

The physicist nodded somberly. "I don't know if one solar system is enough to hold two Sam Gunns. Maybe one of them would be better off going through that black hole."

He turned toward the door to Jade's office.

"Wait!" she cried, getting up and starting around her desk. "I've got half a million questions I need answered!"

Townes shook his head. "Sorry. No time. I just thought you ought to know what Sam's been up to since he returned to Selene."

He dipped his chin in a brief nod, then ducked through the door and was gone.

Leaving Jade standing in her cubbyhole office, her thoughts in a whirl.

Two Sams? she asked herself. Can I believe that? Was Townes telling the truth?

She sank back into her swivel chair. For a long while she simply sat there while her mind spun out questions to which she had no answers.

But at last she muttered to herself, "Sam's here. In Selene. One of them is, at least. He's here. And I've got to find him."

But how? she wondered. I need help. And then it hit her: There's somebody else who wants to find Sam really badly. Turning to her desktop console, Jade said, "Phone, find Senator Jill Meyers. I need to speak with her."

Orchestra(ted) Sam

JADE WAS SURPRISED AT HOW NERVOUS SHE FELT AS SHE waited in the arrivals lounge at Selene's Armstrong Spaceport. In ten minutes the shuttle from Space Station Epsilon would arrive, and her plan to smoke Sam Gunn out of hiding would start to unfold. She hoped.

Rocket shuttles from the space stations orbiting Earth were never delayed by weather or traffic. Once they broke orbit they were essentially in a dead fall that ended at Armstrong's scoured and blasted concrete pads out on the floor of the giant crater Alphonsus.

Too nervous to remain seated, Jade paced along the curving glassteel window that looked out at the landing area. Two spindly-looking shuttles were standing on their pads. Beyond them the sky was as black as infinity but studded with brilliant hard pinpoints of stars and the streaming whiteness of the Milky Way. Out on the horizon she could see the low, slumped, tired-looking mountains that formed Alphonsus's ringwall.

Jane Avril Inconnu was a petite, slim young woman with jade-green eyes and flaming red hair that she had allowed to curl down to her shoulders. In her fitted tunic and slacks of grayish green she looked almost elfin. Several of the other people waiting in the lounge seemed to recognize her from the videos she had hosted, but none of them had the courage to come up and speak to her. For which she was grateful; she had enough on her mind without trying to make friendly chitchat.

Can we do it? she asked herself for the thousandth time. Can we get him to come out into the open? Despite having spent the past several years of her life producing biographical videos about Sam Gunn, she had never met the wily, devious little imp himself.

A glint of light caught her eye. Again, another sparkle against the starry black sky. As she watched, her nose almost pressed against the cold glassteel window, she saw the shuttle take shape, its ungainly silhouette glittering in the harsh light of the distant Sun.

The shuttle touched down, feather soft, on the hot jets of its retros, blowing dust and grit across the landing pad. An access tunnel wormed out like a wheeled caterpillar and connected to its main hatch.

Jade ran to the reception area, suddenly as impatient as a schoolgirl. Working her way to the front of the small crowd waiting for the arrivals to get through customs, she wondered yet again if she could carry her plan through to success.

At last Jill Meyers appeared in the doorway, a small travel bag clutched in one hand. She saw Jade and grinned maliciously. Meyers was short and stubby, her face round and snub-nosed, with a sprinkling of freckles. Her light brown hair was cut short, and she wore a nondescript beige travel suit.

The older woman hugged Jade with her free arm while several of the other debarking passengers stared. Jill Meyers, former U.S. Senator and a respected judge on the International Court of Justice, was immediately recognizable.

Before Jade could say hello or even take a breath, Meyers whispered into her ear, "Now we get that little SOB to marry me!"

IT WASN'T EASY to keep Jill Meyers's arrival in Selene a secret, but Jade figured that if Sam did find out that she was on the Moon it might help to smoke him out of hiding. She even half-expected Sam to show up in her office, sooner or later, brash and breezy, ready to embark on some twisty scheme or other.

Jade was not prepared, however, for the Beryllium Blonde.

She recognized Jennifer Marlowe immediately from the disks she had reviewed while producing her Sam Gunn bios. She was golden blonde, radiantly so, with long legs, wide innocent eyes of cornflower blue, and a figure that would drive any man to wild testosterone-soaked fantasies. Dressed in a glittering metallic sheath that hugged her curves deliciously, she swept unannounced into Jade's cubbyhole of an office.

"Good morning," she said, with a gleaming smile. "I'm Jennifer Marlowe, of the law firm of Raippe, Pillage and Burns."

Astonished, Jade slowly rose from her desk chair and said, "Yes, you are, aren't you?"

Marlowe sat on the spindly chair before Jade's desk, still smiling enough wattage to light a shopping mall. But there was something cold behind her smile, Jade thought. Something hard and hostile.

"What can I do for you?" Jade asked, settling back into her own swivel chair.

The smile dimmed somewhat. "I'm here on a rather delicate matter, Ms. Inconnu."

"Call me Jade; everybody does."

"Your eyes. Of course."

"Does this 'delicate matter' have anything to do with Sam Gunn?"

The Blonde sighed dramatically. "Of course. Who else?"

"I thought all those lawsuits against Sam had been settled," said Jade.

"All but one," the Blonde replied.

Jade raised her eyebrows a notch, waiting.

"A breach of promise suit," the Blonde explained. "Sam promised to marry me—"

"Marry you!" Jade blurted, shocked. "Marry you?"

"That's right," the Blonde replied gravely. "And I'm here to see that he makes good on his promise. Or else."

"Or else what?"

"Or else I'll take all his assets. Every penny. I'll leave him with nothing but the clothes on his back. Maybe not even that much."

"NO WONDER SAM'S in hiding," said Jill Meyers that evening. She had invited Jade to dinner in the suite she had rented under an assumed name: Minerva de Guerre.

"This is going to make him burrow even deeper, wherever he is," Jade said unhappily, picking at the salad before her.

Meyers shook her head, equally dismayed. "I had a talk with Doug Stavenger this afternoon. Strictly informal, of course. You'd think in a community as small and tight as Selene it'd be impossible for Sam to hide for long."

Jade said, "There've been people living in the equipment and storage levels for years, castoffs and hideaways existing on their wits. I've even heard that sometimes they break into the emergency shelters up on the surface and live there for as long as they dare."

"Stavenger didn't mention that."

"He wouldn't, not to a distinguished visitor. He wouldn't want you to know there's an underground subculture in Selene."

"Why does the governing council permit it?"

Jade shrugged. "It's small enough so that it would be more trouble to root out than it's worth. At least, that's the official line."

"This isn't going to help us find Sam."

"No," Jade agreed. "It isn't."

Meyers drummed her fingers on the table top. "There's *got* to be a way to find Sam."

"But if we do, La Marlowe will get him. One way or the other."

"What's she really after?" Meyers wondered aloud. "I mean, Sam doesn't have anything in the way of assets, does he? He must be pretty close to broke."

With a slight shake of her head, Jade answered, "He must have something that she's interested in."

"But what could it be?"

JUMBO JIM GRADOWSKY was a large man, terminally untidy in his clothing and personal habits, his desk a perpetual disaster area. And he was clearly unhappy.

"You're moping," he said to Jade. Despite the successes of Jade's series on Sam Gunn, Solar News's corporate headquarters on Earth had not deigned to enlarge the office space in Selene. Profits first, was the motto in Orlando.

Sitting in front of Jumbo Jim's messy, cluttered desk, Jade nodded despondently. "I guess I am moping," she admitted.

"You're going through your assignments like a sleepwalker," Jim added, pushing aside a small mountain of reports and memos to reach for the milkshake mug on the corner of his desk. Several of the monomolecular sheets slid languidly to the floor.

"I guess I am," Jade repeated. Then, pulling herself up straighter, she said, "It's this Sam Gunn thing. I can't get it out of my mind."

Gradowsky took a long pull on his milkshake. Wiping chocolate foam from his lips with the back of his hand, he said, "All right, here's what I'm going to do. You're off all assignments for the next three days. You spend the time tracking Sam down."

"Three days? Jim! Thanks!" Jade wanted to jump over the desk and kiss him.

"Three days," Gradowsky warned, holding up three fingers. "Then I want you here with all your brains working."

"Thanks, Jim," she repeated, bolting from the chair and heading for the door.

Monica Bianco was sympathetic but not terribly helpful. Her office, like Jade's, was nothing more than a cubicle with shoulder-high partitions, although she had adorned the wobbly walls with photos of her abundant family back Earthside. Every time Jade saw the pictures she thought about how much she wished she had a family. But she had no one—except, maybe, Sam Gunn.

"I don't see how you can flush him out," Monica was saying. "If he's squirreled away in the maintenance level or out in one of the emergency shelters it'd take a small army to find him."

Jade agreed gloomily. But she insisted, "There's got to be some way."

"Like what?"

"Like . . . I don't know."

Monica leaned back in her chair. "You've been following Sam's life for the past three years. Don't you have a feeling for how he thinks? How his mind works?"

"Well, sort of."

"So?"

Jade thought about it for several silent moments. Then it hit her. "That's it!" she shouted, and ran from Monica's office, leaving the older woman sitting open-mouthed behind her desk.

Sam wouldn't hide out in some ratty corner of a warehouse, she told herself as she slid behind the desk in her own cubicle. Not Sam!

She called up the guest list of the Selenite Hotel, the poshest hostelry on the Moon. He wouldn't use his own name, of course, Jade told herself as she scanned the list. Some of the names were blanked out and photo IDs missing, guests who wanted complete privacy.

Then she spotted a face that was obviously phony. A gold turban wrapped around the head of a man whose luxuriant black beard was so thick that all she could see of his face was a generous beak of a nose and tiny, squinty eyes of some indeterminate light color.

Who else? Jade asked herself.

The name beneath the image read "Sri Malabar Singh Satay." Jade laughed aloud. A phony if I ever saw one! she told herself. Just as phony as that snout and beard.

To make sure, she looked up his biography. It was impressive. If the data could be believed, Malabar Singh Satay was one of Earth's foremost musicians, a concert pianist, and scion of a fabulously wealthy Sikh family that had fled the biowar that had depopulated the Indian subcontinent and now made their principal residence on the island of Malabar in the East Indies.

Yeah, right! Jade said to herself. So what's he doing on the Moon?

She contacted the Selenite Hotel and was put through to Mr. Satay's suite with only a minimum of delay. A darkly beautiful woman with large, lustrous eyes answered her call and agreed, in a silky voice that carried an exotic slightly singsong lilt, to allow Jade to interview Mr. Satay that very afternoon.

Jade laughed to herself all the way to the hotel. He thinks he can fool me with that phony beard and schnozzola, she thought. Fingering the voice analyzer she was carrying in her purse, Jade told herself, I've got his voiceprint on the chip; no matter what kind of crazy accent he tries to use, the analyzer will pin him down. Once it chimes, Sam's game is up.

The same woman opened the door to Satay's suite and welcomed Jade in with a bow and a sweeping gesture. Despite the fact that she wearing a perfectly ordinary pants suit and hardly any jewelry at all, she looked exotic and terribly beautiful to Jade. Must be the perfume, Jade told herself as she followed the woman into a sumptuously furnished living room. A massive grand piano stood in one corner, beneath a smart screen that showed a view of the long-destroyed Taj Mahal.

"I am Indra," the young woman said. "Mr. Satay's daughter."

Daughter? Jade immediately felt her face flush with emotion. But before she could say a word, Malabar Singh Satay stepped into the room like a Mogul emperor entering his throne chamber.

He was much taller than Jade had expected, his skin a dark, almost coppery color. The turban adds to his height, she told herself. And the beard hides most of his face.

"Ms. Inconnu," said Satay in a low, gravely voice. He pressed his hands together before his face and dipped his chin slightly. The voice analyzer in Jade's purse remained silent.

She bowed back, self-consciously. "Mr. Satay," she murmured. She saw that he was wearing white silk gloves. To protect his pianist's hands, she thought. And not leave any fingerprints.

Satay was much taller than Sam would be, Jade realized. Tall and slim and somehow elegant-looking in a thigh-length brocaded jacket with a high, tight collar. He gestured Jade to the striped couch in the middle of the big room, then perched straight-backed on the facing armchair. Indra moved silently behind Jade; she couldn't tell if the woman had taken a chair or left the room altogether.

"I am so very glad you asked for this interview," Satay said. "It is always a pleasure to be interviewed by the news media, yes indeed. I am afraid that I am something of an egotist. It must very likely be an essential part of a concert pianist's personality."

Fumbling for an idea, Jade stammered, "It . . . it's not often that we . . . the people of Selene, that is . . . we don't get many distinguished musicians visiting us."

He seemed to smile. With the beard and luxuriant mustache, it was difficult to tell.

"Oh my goodness, not at all. On the contrary, Ms. Inconnu, Selene has a very illustrious symphony orchestra. Indeed, many of the finest musicians on Earth have come here to retire and then extended their careers in the low gravity and relaxed social atmosphere of your delightful community. I feel honored to be allowed to perform with them, certainly I do."

As they chatted on, Jade became more and more convinced that this elegant man actually was who he claimed to be, and not Sam Gunn in disguise. After nearly an hour of talking, he got up and went to the piano, stripped off the silk gloves, and began to play the languid opening bars of Beethoven's "Moonlight Sonata" for Jade.

"Rather appropriate, considering where we are," he said over the music, "don't you believe so?"

Jade had to agree. It wasn't until Satay had completed the piece with its stirring final movement that she realized she was no closer to finding Sam than she had been before meeting the pianist.

As the last notes faded away, Jade sat on the sofa, too awed by the music to applaud.

"That's . . . beautiful," she breathed, knowing that her words were terribly lame.

"Thank you so very much," Satay replied, without moving from the piano bench. He eyed her for a silent moment, then asked, "Are you not the woman who narrated those illuminating biographical shows about Sam Gunn?"

"Yes," Jade said. "I am."

"They were magnificent, truly," said Satay. "You captured such a complex personality so well, so faithfully. A magnificent achievement."

It was Jade's turn to say, "Thank you."

"You must know him very well, very well indeed."

"Actually, I've never met him."

"Never met him?" Satay's bushy brows rose almost to the edge of his turban.

"No. Never."

"Would you like to?"

Jade felt her pulse quicken. "Yes! Of course!"

"He's coming here this evening," Satay said. Then, his face darkening, he added, "He has been courting my daughter."

"Sam?"

"Sam."

Jade turned and saw that Indra was not in the room. She had left her father alone with her.

Slowly, she asked, "When you say 'courting,' do you mean that Sam has proposed marriage to your daughter?"

His face darkening even more, Satay replied, "Not a word about marriage, not one syllable."

Jade nodded.

"The man is notorious," Satay growled.

"Yes, he is."

"My daughter seems infatuated with him."

"Sam can be very . . . infatuating."

His bearded face broke into a fierce smile. "I have it! Why don't you join us for dinner? We will make a foursome of the evening."

Her heart thundering, Jade said, "I'd love to."

JADE SCOOTED TO her meager apartment and changed into her best evening wear: a simple sleeveless black frock adorned with a pearl necklace and earrings. Trying to calm the excited pounding of her pulse, she made her way back to the hotel and Satay's suite.

The pianist was wearing a splendid gold brocade jacket that made Jade feel shabby. Indra was dressed in a silk sari of deep rose interwoven with glittering silver threads.

Sam was not there.

"He is late," Satay murmured as his daughter poured iced tea for them.

"He'll be here," said Indra as she handed Jade a tall frosted glass. "He must be very careful, you know."

"Careful?" Jade asked.

Indra nodded. "Unscrupulous people are searching for him. They want to—"

The doorbell chimed. Indra fairly flew to the front door, her sari flapping. Jade saw that her father looked grim.

Indra opened the door and in he stepped. Sam Gunn.

He's an elf! she thought. Jade saw that Sam barely stood as tall as Satay's shoulder. Even Indra was a few centimeters taller than he. He was smiling widely at her, a gap-toothed grin that looked slightly lopsided. His face was round and freckled, his nose a button. His brick-red hair was neatly combed, except for a couple of cowlicks sprouting from the back of his head.

My hair's a little lighter in color than Sam's, Jade thought. And my face is very different. But we're almost exactly the same height.

Sam kissed Indra's hand as he entered the spacious room; she smiled beamingly at him. He clasped his hands in front of his face and bowed politely to Satay, who bowed back, stone-faced.

Then Sam turned and seemed to realize for the first time that there was one other person in the room.

He looked at Jade, blinked, then said, "Hey, I know you."

Jade said nothing. She couldn't. Her throat was so constricted that not a word could come out.

Walking toward her across the thickly luxuriant carpeting, Sam said, "You're the kid who hosted those bioshows about me. Jane something, isn't it?"

"Mr. Gunn," Satay intervened, "may I present Ms. Jane Avril Inconnu."

"She not only narrated your shows, Sam," Indra added, "she produced them."

Sam stepped up to Jade. We're *exactly* the same height, she told herself.

With a grin, Sam said, "You're a natural redhead, like me. Not many of us around."

"You have to have the right genes," Jade heard herself say.

Satay announced, "I have dinner laid on here. I know how much you want to avoid being seen in public."

It seemed to take an effort for Sam to take his eyes away from Jade. "Yeah, right," he said absently. "Too many prying eyes out there."

Indra hooked her arm around Sam's and guided him toward the dining room. Following them, Jade took Satay's proffered arm.

"Why are you afraid of prying eyes?" Jade asked as they took their seats around the square glass-topped dining table. A pair of squat, silvery robots stood along one wall, glasses and pitchers on their flat tops.

"Yes," said Indra. "You told me that all those lawsuits against you have been dropped." She was seated across the table from Jade, and the two men faced each other.

"I'm involved in a pretty delicate business," Sam said as one of the robots rolled up beside him. He took a water glass, then asked Indra what she wanted.

"A martini, please," Indra replied. Satay asked for a double.

"And you?" he asked Jade.

"Is there any wine?"

The robot's synthesized voice replied, "There is an excellent Sancerre in my cooler, ma'am."

Sam opened the insulated door in the robot's chest and pulled out a green-tinted bottle. "From France," he murmured appreciatively.

Once they had all sipped at their drinks, Jade asked again, "Why all the secrecy, Mr. Gunn?"

"Call me Sam."

"Why all the secrecy, Sam?"

He laughed; Jade thought it was a trifle forced. "You're a newshound, all right. A regular bloodhound."

"Well?" Jade insisted.

Sam glanced at Satay, then said, "I'm involved in negotiations to buy the Selene Philharmonic Orchestra."

"Buy the orchestra?" Jade asked, surprised. "But you can't! It's owned by the people of Selene."

"Not really," Sam said.

"That is what I thought, also," Satay interjected. "I was led to believe that the Philharmonic is a municipal organization, not privately owned."

"It's a little tricky," Sam started to explain. But when he looked at Jade he asked, "What do I call you, anyway? Ms. Inconnu? Jane? What?"

"Mrs. Johansen," Jade answered. "You know my husband."

"Spence?" Sam's voice jumped an octave. "You're married to Spence Johansen? He's here at Selene?"

"Yes, to both questions."

Sam thought that over for all of three seconds. Then, "Okay, but I can't call you Mrs. Johansen: too stuffy."

"My friends call me Jade."

"Jade," he repeated. Indra cast a less-than-friendly glance at Jade, then touched Sam's arm possessively.

"Perhaps we should begin our meal," Satay suggested. "Before the robots become impatient."

They all laughed politely.

Throughout the dinner Sam regaled them with tales of his adventures with Spencer Johansen, and Larry Karsh, Elverda Apacheta, even his double who—he claimed—had returned to the black hole out beyond the orbit of Pluto. On and on, Sam talked nonstop until they had finished dessert and were sipping cognac from oversized snifters.

"I still don't understand about this orchestra business," Jade said, trying to get back to the subject she was interested in. "Why should you want to buy the Philharmonic?"

"Sam is a philanthropist at heart," Indra said.

"Really?"

Sam gave her a wry grin. "It's like this. Legally, the orchestra is owned by a consortium of Selene's citizens. Its revenues come from private donations—which are never enough to cover its expenses. The difference is made up out of taxes and annual fund drives."

"So?"

"So I figured that if I owned the orchestra I could foot its expenses, whatever they are, and spare the citizens of Selene the annual begging campaign."

"And the taxes," Indra added.

Sam nodded.

"But where would the money come from?" Jade asked. "As I understand it you're broke."

Waggling a hand in the air, Sam said, "Well, not exactly broke. I still get a trickle of money from my share of the Hell Crater resort complex."

"I thought you signed all that away to Rockledge."

With a grin, Sam replied, "So did a certain silver-haired slimeball named Pierre D'Argent. But I kept one percent. He was so glad to get his hands on the complex that he overlooked that little piece of fine print."

"One percent of the gross," Indra said, with a tiny giggle.

"Is that true?" asked Jade.

He looked deeply into her eyes before answering. "More or less," he said at last.

Satay spoke up. "I must say that it will be quite an experience for the orchestra to be under your management."

"Yeah, I guess," Sam said absently, still staring at Jade. "You know, kid, you remind me of somebody . . . but I can't put a finger on who it is."

Jean Margaux, Jade replied silently, her insides trembling. But she said nothing.

A long awkward silence filled the sumptuous room. Sam kept staring at Jade, as if trying to fathom her innermost secrets.

At last Indra said sharply, "There are people here in Selene who would not want to allow Sam to gain control of the orchestra."

"The notorious Sam Gunn," Satay murmured.

"That's why I've got to be careful," Sam said, still unable to take his eyes off Jade.

At last she found her voice. "There's also the Beryllium Blonde, isn't there?"

Sam frowned. "La Marlowe? She came all the way here to nail me with a phony breach of promise suit."

"Breach of promise?" Indra's dark eyes flashed.

"I never promised her anything," Sam said, patting her hand. "She's just a lawyer trying to make an ill-gotten buck."

"What about Jill Meyers?" Jade blurted.

Sam's eyes snapped wide with genuine surprise. "Jill's here too?"

Realizing she had blundered, Jade tried to retreat. "She's got more claim to marriage than the Blonde."

With obvious irony, Satay asked, "Sam, are you perhaps a Moslem? How many wives can you have?"

"That is not funny, father," said Indra.

Sam looked from father to daughter and then back to Jade. "You can see why I have to be careful," he muttered.

THE DINNER ENDED on a definitely sour note. Jade excused herself at last and headed back toward her apartment, two levels above the hotel. As she walked disconsolately along the long, gray-walled corridor, she heard someone call her name.

Turning, she saw it was Sam pushing his way past a strolling elderly couple.

"Wait up a minute," he said, hurrying toward her. "You can't just walk away from me, can you?"

"Not from you," Jade admitted. "It's just . . ."

"Just what?" He seemed sincerely troubled that Jade was obviously so upset.

"You're in real danger, Sam," she temporized. "Marlowe and Jill Meyers both intend to get you to marry them. And Satay wants you to marry his daughter—or get out of her life."

"I've been in trouble before. I can handle it."

"But why—"

"Look," he said, waving his arms as they walked along the nearly deserted corridor, "I cuddled up to Indra so I could get to meet her father. I need Satay on my side to help impress the committee that's running the orchestra."

"Impress the committee?"

"Those stuffed shirts think I'll steal the orchestra and take it to the other end of the Milky Way or something. They don't trust me!"

Jade started to laugh, but then she saw that he seemed genuinely hurt.

She said, "Can you blame them? Your reputation doesn't put you on track for sainthood."

"Aw, Jade! From you? You've followed my life and you know what I've done: the good, the bad, and the so-so. You think I'm a bum too?"

That made her smile. "No, I don't think you're a bum, Sam."

"Half the things I've been blamed for I never did. Honest!" He clapped one hand to his heart and raised the other over his head.

"The other half is quite enough," Jade countered. "You're no saint, Sam."

Breaking into a grin, he replied, "Who wants to be?"

They were only a few meters from Jade's front door. As they walked up to it, Jade asked, "Sam, what's your real reason for wanting to buy the orchestra? And how can you handle it, financially?"

"You going to invite me in?" he asked, with a sly grin.

"No."

"Scared?"

"Yes, but not in the way you think."

He cocked his head to one side, his grin slowly vanishing. "Okay. I'll answer your questions, but not out here in the corridor."

Jade knew she had to outmaneuver him. Thinking swiftly, she said, "Let's do lunch tomorrow. There's somebody I want you to meet."

"Not the Blonde."

"No."

"Not Jill?"

Smiling, Jade said, "I want you to meet Minerva La Guerre."

"Never heard of her."

"She's heard of you," Jade said.

He shrugged. "Okay. Lunch tomorrow. Where?"

"In her hotel suite. I'll set it up."

"High noon," he said.

"You'll answer my questions then?"

Another shrug. "We'll see."

JADE GAVE SAM a swift peck on his cheek, surprising him so thoroughly that he stood there with his mouth hanging open while she ducked into her apartment and locked the door behind her. She leaned against the door, breathless. *He's my father!* Jade told herself. *I know it. I can feel it.*

With a glance at the security screen by the door she saw that Sam was slowly walking back up the corridor, in the direction they had come from.

Her insides trembling, Jade walked uncertainly to her desk. She sat tiredly on the spindly little wheeled chair and stared at the phone's blank display screen. Then she nodded, her mind made up, and phoned Jill Meyers. After that, she called the Beryllium Blonde.

JENNIFER MARLOWE WAS smiling with lots of brilliant white teeth, but Jade thought her eyes betrayed her true feelings: the Blonde was tense, wary, suspicious.

Jill Meyers was the epitome of graciousness as she led Marlowe and Jade across the sitting room of her suite and into the small dining area next to the kitchen and the waiting robots. Jade followed behind them.

"You know," Jill was saying, "I was asked to serve on the panel of judges when Sam was being tried for genocide."

"You were?" the Blonde said, her cornflower blue eyes taking in every stick of furniture, every sparkle of jewelry that Jill wore.

"I declined," Jill said, gesturing to one of the chairs. "I was too emotionally involved."

"You would have voted to acquit Sam."

Jill laughed. "I would have voted to have him hanged. Before the first witness was called."

Marlowe giggled appreciatively as she sat demurely on the chair Jill indicated. Even in zipped-up coveralls of baby blue, Jade thought, she couldn't help looking like a sexy centerfold model.

Once the three of them were seated and the serving robot had brought them glasses of fruit juice, Jill said, "This meeting is Jade's idea. Sam's going to be here in half an hour, so I suggest we get down to brass tacks."

La Marlowe turned to Jade. "And just what do you hope to accomplish, Ms. Inconnu?"

It's Mrs. Johansen, Jade corrected silently. But she let it go. Aloud, she replied, "Two things: I want you to drop your suit against Sam, and I want Sam to marry Jill."

If either point surprised the Blonde she didn't show it.

"How do you propose to do that?" she asked.

"I'll need your help."

Jill broke in, "Off the record, is there any real basis for your suit? I mean, I've known Sam longer than both of you combined and I've never heard him utter the word 'marriage.'"

Marlowe smiled enigmatically. "I have it all on disk. Sam promised to marry me."

"Disks can be faked," Jade said.

"This one has been authenticated," Marlowe said calmly.

"By whom?"

"By two separate and independent teams of analysts."

"Hired by your law firm?"

Smiling again, with even more teeth, Marlowe said, "Why, Ms. Inconnu, that would be unethical, wouldn't it?"

"How much?" asked Jill.

Jade was surprised by the question. Marlowe simply widened her smile slightly.

"How much do you want to drop your suit?" Jill asked. She looked slightly irritated, Jade thought.

"You're a very wealthy woman," said Marlowe. "Old money is the best kind."

"How much?"

"I'm sure a jury would award me ten million, at least."

Before Jill could reply, Jade said, "Wait a minute. There's something else involved here."

"Something else?"

"What?"

Jade said, "Sam's up to something. He—"

"He's *always* up to something," said Marlowe.

"So what else is new?" Jill quipped.

"Why is he trying to get control of the orchestra?" Jill asked. "I mean, Sam doesn't do things like that without some ulterior motive."

Both the women nodded agreement.

"I wonder what he's really up to," Jade murmured.

Jill grinned. "It must be something convoluted, knowing Sam."

Marlowe said, "Whatever it is, he still has to deal with my breach of promise suit before he does anything else."

A silence fell upon them. Jade realized that Jill hadn't pursued her offer of settling Marlowe's suit, not since the sum of ten million dollars had been mentioned. That's how old money keeps its money, Jade thought. Philanthropy goes only so far.

"Why does he want the orchestra?" Jade wondered again.

"Ask him when he gets here," said Jill Meyers.

"If he shows up," Marlowe said. "I wouldn't put it past him to pull another disappearing act."

"But he promised me!" Jade protested.

Both the other women stared at her. Marlowe said, "How can you be so naïve? You've done all this biographical research about Sam and you still think—"

The doorbell chimed.

For an instant none of them moved. Then Jill said to the suite's communications system, "Display entry hall, please."

A misty Japanese landscape on the far wall of the dining alcove dissolved into an image of Sam Gunn out in the entry hall. He was fidgeting nervously and whistling something too low for Jade to make out.

"Hey, is anybody home?" he shouted. "Have I got the right room number?"

Jade pushed away from the table and sprinted toward the door. He could be halfway down the corridor by the time I get there, she worried.

But when she slid the door open, Sam Gunn was standing there, in slightly faded coveralls, a lopsided gap-toothed grin on his round, freckled face.

"There you are," he said. "I was starting to worry."

"It's a big suite," Jade began to explain, "and we were back in—"

But Sam was looking past her. Turning, Jade saw that the Blonde was standing in the middle of the spacious living room.

"You!" Sam gasped.

"Hello, Sam," said the Blonde. Then she added, "Darling."

Turning back to Jade, Sam growled, "You've led me into a trap! How could you?"

"It's not a trap, Sam," Jade said, struggling to keep the tremor out of her voice.

"You can't hide from me forever," Marlowe said, moving toward Sam like a cobra slithering toward its prey and sliding an arm in his. For his part, Sam stood there openmouthed and wide-eyed like a paralyzed mongoose.

Jade cleared her throat. "Um, Sam, there's someone else I want you to meet."

Jill Meyers entered the room, smiling almost shyly. "Hello, Sam."

"My God!" Sam blurted. "I'm surrounded by assassins!"

But he disengaged from La Marlowe and went to Jill with open arms. "I thought so! I *knew* Minerva La Guerre had to be a phony name!"

"And you came anyway?"

"Sure," Sam said carelessly. "Why not?"

He gave Jill a hug; then, with Jill on one arm and Marlowe on the other, he grinned at Jade and asked, "So what's this all about?"

"You promised to marry me," said Marlowe.

"You've promised to marry me," Jill Meyers said, "several times."

"I never spoke the word 'marriage' to either of you and you both know it."

"I have you on disk, Sam," Marlowe said.

"Yeah, along with Godzilla, King Kong, and the Emperor Ming of Mongo."

"You agreed to marry me, Sam," Jill repeated.

The Blonde insisted, "I've got authenticated evidence—"

Jade wished she had a referee's whistle hanging around her neck. She raised both her hands and shouted, "Wait! Hang on for a minute. This is getting us nowhere."

Sam disengaged his arms and bowed politely to her. "And just where do want us to go, Oh most beautiful of producers?"

Jade pointed to the long, low-slung sofa against the wall. "You sit there, please." Turning to Marlowe, "And you there, on the armchair."

"And me?" Jill Meyers asked.

"This armchair, on the other side of the sofa."

Once they were seated, Sam looked up Jade with a pleasant smile. "Okay, we're all in our places with bright shining faces. Now what?"

Jade replied, "Sam, you promised me that you'd tell me why you're so interested in the Selene Philharmonic."

"I never promised."

"Yes you did."

"Did not."

Jade began to fire another retort, then she realized, No, the little scamp never did promise. He implied that he'd tell me, but he never promised.

"You're right, Sam. You didn't promise. I apologize."

"But he promised to marry me," Marlowe said, as firmly as a judge pronouncing sentence on a doomed prisoner.

"Okay," Sam said lightly. "I'll marry you."

"Oh no you don't!" Jill Meyers snapped. "If you marry anybody, Sam Gunn, it's going to be me. I've waited too long and been left at the altar too many times to let you go off with . . . with this . . . with anybody else."

Smiling as benignly as a saint painted by Raphael, Sam said, "Don't worry, Jill, I'll marry you. Honest."

"You can't marry both of us!" Marlowe said.

Sam raised two fingers. "You forget, people, that there are two of me. My duplicate is out at the black hole in the Kuiper Belt, but I can call him back. He'll be overjoyed to make you his wife, Jennifer. I know, believe me."

"Your duplicate! I don't want a duplicate. I want the original Sam Gunn."

Spreading his arms in a gesture that might, in another man, have indicated helplessness, Sam said, "But which of us is the original? We have the same physical makeup, down to the quantum vibrations of our atoms. We have the same memories, the same personality. Take your pick. For crying out loud, neither one of us knows who's the original and who's the copy."

Marlowe gaped at him, her startling blue eyes wide.

Jill laughed. "I'll take either one. Whichever I can get."

Laughing back at her, Sam said, "Atta girl! That's my Jill."

Marlowe sank back in her armchair, silent, looking confused.

"What's the matter, Jen?" Sam asked. "You can have your dream come true. You can marry me. We'll live happily ever after, more or less."

The Beryllium Blonde slowly shook her head. "I don't want either one of you!" She rose to her feet, her face a mask of frustrated anger.

"All right, Sam. You win. I'll drop the suit; fat lot of good it would do me if one of you is willing to go through with a wedding."

She turned and headed for the front door.

"Ms. Marlowe!" Jill called to her.

The Blonde stopped, but didn't turn around.

To her back, Jill Meyers said, "Ten million is way too much. But I'll send you one million. You've earned that much in aggravation, I imagine."

The Blonde turned and said, "Thank you," through gritted teeth. Then she marched to the door and left.

Once the door slid shut, Jill broke into delighted laughter. "Talk about chutzpa! Your twin would marry her! How could you say that, Sam?"

"Because he's exactly like me. He'd marry her and they'd have a terrific honeymoon. I wouldn't give you much of a chance for afterward, though."

Jade sank into the armchair that the Blonde had vacated.

Sam turned to her. "Okay. La Marlowe has left the field of battle and I've surrendered to my beloved Jill. Is there any other business?"

"Beloved Jill?" Meyers murmured, delighted.

"Yeah," said Sam. "After all these years, you still want me?"

Jade was surprised to see tears in Jill Meyers's eyes.

"Yes, I still want you, Sam. I love you."

"I can't imagine why," he bantered. "But, for what it's worth, I love you too, Jill."

She leaped out of her chair and onto Sam's lap. Jade felt her cheeks flush as they kissed passionately.

Sam at last came up for air. His face looked red, too. "Okay, kid," he said to Jade. "I guess that wraps up everything with a nice blue ribbon."

"Um, not quite," Jade said, almost in a whisper.

"What? You want to know about the orchestra?"

"That, and—"

Sam didn't give her a chance to finish. "Okay, I'll tell you. But it's strictly between us, right?"

Among us, Jade corrected silently.

With Jill still on his lap, Sam explained, "If that committee of bluenoses lets me take control of the orchestra, I'll appoint Satay as its musical director. Then he can apply for citizenship in Selene and get it."

"He wants citizenship here?" Jade asked.

"And Selene won't allow him in?" asked Jill Meyers.

"Selene's very strict about awarding citizenship," Sam answered. "Otherwise they'd have a horde of refugees streaming here."

"But Satay's a famous musician," said Jade.

"And you're a judge of the International Court," Sam countered. "Have you applied for citizenship?"

"No," Jill admitted.

"If you did, you'd find out how tough they can be." Stroking her back gently, Sam went on, "Fortunately, you're going to marry a Selenite. That'll make you a citizen automatically."

Jill kissed him on the cheek.

Sam cocked a brow at her. "Say, is that why you want to marry me? To get citizenship here?"

Before Jade could blink, Jill pulled both Sam's ears hard enough to make him yowl.

"Okay, okay," he yelped. "I was only kidding!"

"Wait a minute!" Jade interrupted. "Back up! Why is it important to you to appoint Satay the leader of the Philharmonic?"

"Like you said, kid, he's a famous musician."

"There's got to be more to it than that."

"He wants to get away from the Indonesian government," Sam said, "and their taxes."

Jade considered that for a moment, then asked, "And what do you get out of it, Sam?"

"Me?"

"Yes, you. There's something in this for you, isn't there?"

"Child, you cut me to the quick."

"Knock it off, Sam," Jill Meyers said. "What's cooking in that twisted mind of yours?"

"Gosh, you people are so suspicious!"

Jade suddenly understood. "Satay has a considerable fortune, doesn't he? Family money that he'll bring to Selene with him."

"I suppose," Sam replied, trying to look innocent.

"And if you help him gain citizenship, he'll be grateful to you, won't he?"

Sam nodded, then admitted, "He'll also be grateful to Jill."

"To me?"

"For marrying me. Then I won't be a danger to his daughter anymore."

"Ah-ha," Jill said.

"How will his daughter feel about that?" Jade asked.

Sam shrugged, not an easy thing to do with Jill still on his lap. "She's young. She'll find somebody. Besides, she doesn't have control of the money."

"And just what do you intend to do with Satay's money?" Jade demanded.

"The matter duplicator," said Jill. "I should have thought of it before this."

"Matter transmitter," Sam corrected. "I've sworn off duplicating things. Or people."

"Two Sam Gunns are enough to make an honest man of you?"

Sam waggled his free hand. "More or less."

"Matter transmitter," Jade murmured.

"You bet. If the Indonesian government tries to keep Satay's money in Indonesia," Sam explained, "I'll be able to zap most of it here to Selene."

"Once you get a matter transmitter working," said Jade.

"*If* you get a matter transmitter working," Jill corrected.

"It'll work," Sam assured them.

"But Professor Townes is out in the Kuiper Belt with the other Sam, isn't he?" Jade said.

"So what? He proved that a matter transmitter can work. Now any bright team of kids can duplicate his results."

"If they're real," Jill muttered.

Sam gave her a hurt look. "They're real, Oh love of my life. We'll produce a matter transmitter and turn Selene into the greatest tax haven in the solar system."

"Is that all you can imagine doing with a matter transmitter?" Jade asked.

His expression turned crafty. "Well, I've gotta admit that another thing or two has crossed my mind."

Jill giggled. "I'll bet."

"It ought to make transportation through the solar system a lot easier," Sam mused.

"And cheaper?" asked Jill.

Sam pursed his lips, then answered, "You've got to pay for the energy, honey. It takes a lot of energy to zap a mass even my size across a laboratory."

"You blacked out half of Selene doing it."

"So we'll build big fusion power plants," Jill said. "You could get rich, Sam."

"With my looks and your brains," he said to Jill, "the whole solar system is our oyster!"

Jill laughed and kissed him lightly.

"Okay," Sam said, turning to Jade. "Does that clear up everything for you?"

Suddenly Jade's throat felt dry, so tight she could hardly speak. "Almost," she choked out.

"What else?" Sam asked.

Jade had to swallow hard before she could say, "I . . . Sam, I think you're my father."

For long moments the room was absolutely silent. Jill, sitting on Sam's lap, stared at Jade. Sam, for once in his life, seemed dumbfounded. His hazel eyes were wide, his mouth hung open.

Jade stared at him. She couldn't speak. She could hardly breathe.

"Your . . ." Sam gulped before he could say, "Your father?"

Jade nodded.

"Jean Margaux," Sam said in a whisper. "That's who your face reminded me of."

Jill slid off Sam's lap. "Maybe you two ought to talk this through by yourselves."

Sam clutched at her. "No. Don't go."

Jade couldn't fathom the expression on Sam's face: Anger? Guilt? Fear?

"Jean and I had an affair after we came back from the Belt," Sam muttered, remembering.

Jade found her voice at last, although it was barely above a whisper. "Rick Darling told me."

"She tried to contact me after I left Selene," Sam went on. "I never called her back."

"She was my mother," said Jade.

The beginnings of a crooked little smile snaked across Sam's face. "You've got my red hair, all right."

Jill spoke up. "We could do a DNA comparison. That'd prove it, one way or the other."

Sam shook his head. "We don't need that." He slowly got to his feet. "Jade, I'm sorry it's taken all these years for us to meet each other. I'm sorry that I haven't been a real father to you."

Jade rushed to him and, as Sam folded his arms around her, she felt for the first time in her life that she'd found her place in the universe. Tears filled her eyes, and she heard Sam snuffling, as well.

"By God," Jill Meyers said, "you've got me crying, too."

THUS IT WAS that Sam Gunn and Senator/Justice Jill Meyers were married in Selene's nondenominational chapel. It was not a grand wedding, not the enormous bash that Jill had once planned, so long ago. A simple, brief ceremony.

But Douglas Stavenger, Selene's power behind the throne, gave the bride away. Spencer Johansen served as Best Man. Frederick Mohammed Malone came from his space habitat and stood beside Sam on legs newly made strong by stem cell therapy to serve as an usher. As did Larry Karsh, who flew to Selene from his mansion in Utah with his wife and son. Jane Avril Inconnu Johansen was Matron of Honor.

The small group gathered in the chapel's pews included gangling Russell Christopher from New Chicago, Zoilo Hashimoto, and a pair of elderly women, twins, who smiled and cried at the same time through the entire ceremony.

The reception, back at the Selenite Hotel, was hosted by Garrett G. Garrison III. Jim Gradowski ate almost all the roast beef, while Monica Bianco nibbled daintily on caviar canapés. Champagne flowed. A good time was had by all.

When the moment came for the bridegroom to offer a toast, Sam stood on a chair and raised his champagne flute.

"For once in my life, I don't know what to say," he admitted.

The crowd hooted.

"Well, in the past week I've found a daughter and married the one woman in the solar system who's willing to put up with me. I think I'm the luckiest guy on Earth."

"We're not on Earth, Sam!" shouted Spence Johansen, one arm tight around Jade's shoulders.

"That's right. I stand corrected."

"Where're you going on your honeymoon?" Melinda Karsh asked. Her teenaged T.J. stood between her and his father.

Jill looked surprised. "Honeymoon? We haven't even thought about that."

But Sam said, "You know, I've never been to Saturn. It's supposed to be spectacular, with those rings and all."

"There's a big habitat out there," said Professor Solomon Goodman, "with a scientific community of about ten thousand men and women."

Sam looked at Jill. "How about it? Would you like to spend a month or three at Saturn?"

Jill nodded enthusiastically. "Sounds like fun."

"Ten thousand men and women," Sam mused. "I wonder what they do for entertainment?"

"Now Sam," said Jill, "we'll be going out there for a honeymoon, not for business."

"Yeah, I know. But still . . ."